Beneath Southern Skies

BESTSELLING AUSTRALIAN AUTHORS

Amy Andrews · Marion Lennox
Ally Blake · Nikki Logan

MILLS & BOON

CONTENTS

Driving Her Crazy

Amy Andrews

ABOUT AMY ANDREWS

———

Amy Andrews has always loved writing, and still can't quite believe that she gets to do it for a living. Creating wonderful heroines and gorgeous heroes and telling their stories is an amazing way to pass the day. Sometimes they don't always act as she'd like them to—but then neither do her kids, so she's kind of used to it. Amy lives in the very beautiful Samford Valley, with her husband and aforementioned children, along with six brown chickens and two black dogs.

She loves to hear from her readers. Drop her a line at amyandrews.com.au.

This and other titles by Amy Andrews are available in ebook format—check out millsandboon.com.au.

DEAR READER,

What better way to kick off my story than with a road trip? Don'tcha just love a good road-trip story? The idea of being stuck in a moving vehicle with another person for hours on end with no chance of escape is somehow quite titillating—especially if there's some sexual chemistry happening.

And Sadie and Kent have some serious chemistry going on! Teaming a world-renowned photojournalist who has "loner" stamped all over him and refuses to fly with a chatty rookie reporter who suffers from travel sickness was always bound to cause friction, but a trip covering thousands of kilometers pushes them both to their limit!

I had a lot of fun writing *Driving Her Crazy* (seriously, what a *perfect* title!) and was lucky to have the dramatic beauty of the Australian outback as the setting for Sadie and Kent's growing attraction. From mobs of wild emus to the chandelier-like stars lighting the vast endless dome of an outback night, this book has plenty of action both inside and outside of Kent's sturdy four-wheel drive. But it is also a book with a serious side. It explores issues of women and their body images and how toxic relationships can seriously screw with a person's head long after they've ended. It touches on PTSD and recovering mentally and physically from crippling injuries. It's a book about finding love when you're not ready for it and in the last place you expect it.

I hope you enjoy!

Love,

Amy

This book is for all women out there
who have ever looked in the mirror
and headed straight for the chocolate/wine/Tim Tams.
And for men with rose-colored glasses.

PROLOGUE

SADIE BLISS'S BREATH caught at the emotive image. Wandering through the ritzy New York gallery surrounded by a crowd of A-listers who blinged and glittered so much it hurt her eyes, she was stopped in her tracks by its starkness.

The background murmur of voices and clinking of champagne glasses faded as the world shrank to just the photograph, the centrepiece of the exhibit.

Mortality.

She'd seen it already, of course, in *Time* magazine, but there was something so much more immediate about it this close. As if it had just been snapped. As if the tragedy were unfolding before her eyes.

She felt as if she were standing in the daunting arid landscape, weighed down by the heat perfectly captured as it shimmered like a mirage from the sand. Smelling the jet fuel from the twisted Black Hawk carcass that she'd seen in the other shots. Hearing the cries of the young soldier as he clutched one bloody hand to his abdomen and reached the other rosary-beaded one into the impossibly blue sky. Calling for someone. God maybe? Or his girlfriend?

Watching his tears turning the grime on his face to muddy tracks. Tasting his despair as life faded from his eyes.

The caption beneath said: *Corporal Dwayne Johnson, nineteen, died from fatal wounds before help could arrive.*

Goosebumps needling her skin, tears pricking at her eyes brought Sadie back to the here and now. She moved on wishing she'd never been given the coveted ticket to the much anticipated opening night of Kent Nelson's *A Decade of Division*. All the pieces snapped from the award-winning photojournalist's lens were disturbing, but this image, known throughout the world, was particularly harrowing.

A portrait of a young man facing death.

A private moment of anguish.

And although the artist in her appreciated the abstract prettiness of the rosary beads against the bright blue dome of a foreign sky, the image was too intimate—she felt as if she was intruding.

Sadie pushed through the crowd out of the gallery into the sultry June night. She needed a moment. Or two.

CHAPTER ONE

Four months later...

KENT NELSON STOOD staring across at the view of Darling Harbour, his gaze following the line of the iconic white sails of the Sydney Opera House. He stood with his back to the woman swinging idly in her chair, his good leg planted firmly in front of the other as he leaned into the hand resting high against the floor to ceiling tinted window.

'So, let me get this straight,' Tabitha Fox said, tapping her pen on her desk, her bangles jangling, as she too admired the view. Not the one she was used to seeing when she looked towards her windows but a mighty fine one nonetheless. 'You want to *drive* several thousand kilometres to take a few photos?'

Kent turned, his ankle twinging as he rested his butt against the glass, and folded his arms across his chest. 'Yes.'

Tabitha frowned. She'd known Kent a long time, they'd been to uni together about a thousand years ago, even shared a bed for a while, but since the accident in Afghanistan he'd been practically invisible.

Until he'd turned up today wanting to take pictures any staff photographer could take.

'Okay...why?'

Kent returned her curious gaze with a deliberately blank one of his own. 'I'm your freelance photographer—it's what you pay me for.'

Tabitha suppressed a snort. His official status might be freelance photographer for the glossy weekend magazine *Sunday On My Mind,* but they both knew he'd 'declined' every job offered and, she'd bet her significant yearly salary, probably hadn't taken a photo since the accident.

She narrowed her eyes at him as she tried to see behind the inscrutable expression on his angular face. 'There are these things called planes. They're big and metal and don't ask me how but they fly in the air and get you to where you want to go very quickly.'

A nerve kicked into fibrillation along his jaw line and Kent clenched down hard. 'I don't fly,' he pushed out through tight lips.

The words were quiet but Tabitha felt the full force of their icy blast. Cold enough to freeze vodka. She regarded him for a moment or two as her nimble brain tried to work the situation to her advantage. She drummed her beringed fingers against her desk.

An outback road trip. Local people. The solitude. The joys. The hardships. The copy laid out diary style.

And most importantly, breathtaking vistas capturing the beauty and the terror in full Technicolor shot by a world-renowned, award-winning photographer on his first job since returning from tragedy in Afghanistan.

For that reason alone the paper would sell like hot cakes.

'Okay.' Tabitha nodded, her mind made up. 'Two for the price of one. Journey to the Red Centre stuff—the most spectacular photos you can take.'

'As well as the Leonard Pinto feature?'

She nodded again. 'Might as well get my money's worth out of you. Lord knows when you'll grant us some more of your time.'

Kent grunted. Tabitha Fox was probably the most business-savvy woman he'd ever met. She'd built *Sunday On My Mind* from a fluffy six-page pull-out supplement to a dynamic, gritty, feature-driven eighteen-page phenomenon in five years.

He lounged against the glass for a moment. 'Tell me, I'm curious. How'd you get him? Pinto? He's pretty reclusive.'

'He came to me.'

Kent raised an eyebrow. 'A man who shuns the media and lives in outer whoop-whoop came to you?'

Tabitha smiled. 'Said he'd open up his life to us—nothing off limits.'

Kent fixed her with his best *'and pigs might fly'* look. 'What's the catch?'

'Kent, Kent, Kent,' she tutted. 'So cynical.'

He shrugged. After spending a decade in one war zone or other, cynical was his middle name. 'The catch?' he repeated.

'Sadie Bliss.'

Kent frowned. The journo on the story with the most spectacular byline in the history of the world? 'Sadie Bliss?'

Tabitha nodded. 'He wanted her.'

Kent blinked. 'And you agreed?' The Tabitha he knew didn't like being dictated to. She especially didn't like relinquishing her editorial control.

She shrugged. 'She's young and green. But she can write. And, I—' she smiled '—can edit.'

Kent rubbed a hand along his jaw. 'Why? Does she know him?'

'I'm not entirely sure. But he wanted her. So he got her. And so did you. She can...' Tabitha waved her hand in the air, her bangles tinkling '...navigate.'

Kent narrowed his gaze. 'Wait. You want her to travel with me?' Three thousand kilometres with a woman he didn't know in the confines of a car? He'd rather be garrotted with his own camera strap.

Not happening.

Tabitha nodded. 'How else am I going to get my road trip story?'

Kent shook his head. 'No.'

Tabitha folded her arms. 'Yes.'

'I'm not good company.'

Tabitha almost burst out laughing at the understatement. 'In that case it'll be good for you.'

'I go solo. I've always gone solo.'

'Fine,' Tabitha sighed, inspecting her fingernails. 'Sadie and her *staff* photographer can fly to Pinto and get the job done in a fraction of the time and at half the cost and you can go back to your man-cave and pretend you work for this magazine.'

Kent felt pressure at the angle of his jaw and realised he was grinding down hard. He'd already burned his bridges at a lot of places the last couple of years. He was lucky Tabitha was still taking his calls after the number of times she'd covered for him.

But days in a car with a woman whose name was Sadie Bliss? She sounded like a twenty year old cadet whose mother had named her after one too many fruity cocktails.

'I do believe,' Tabitha said, swinging in her chair as she prepared to play her ace, 'you owe me a couple.'

Kent shut his eyes as Tabitha called in his debts. 'Fine,' he huffed as he opened them again because he wanted—needed—to do this. To get back into it again.

And he did owe her.

Tabitha grinned at him like the cat that got the cream. 'Thank you.'

Kent grunted as he strode to her desk, barely noticing his limp, and sat down. 'Do you like his nudes?'

Tabitha nodded. 'I think he's sublime. You?'

Kent shook his head. 'They're all too skinny. Androgynous or something.'

Tabitha rolled her eyes. 'They're ballet dancers.'

Leonard's nude of Marianna Daly, Australian prima ballerina, had won international acclaim for his work and hung in the National Gallery in Canberra.

'Well, they're not Renaissance women, that's for sure.'

Tabitha raised an elegantly plucked eyebrow. 'You like Rubenesque?'

Kent grunted again. 'I like curves.'

Tabitha smiled. *Oh, goody.* She picked up the phone her gaze not leaving his. 'Is Sadie here yet?' She nodded twice still spearing Kent with her Mona Lisa smile. 'Can you send her in?' she asked, replacing the receiver before the receptionist had a chance to respond.

Kent narrowed his gaze. 'I don't trust that smile.'

Tabitha laughed. 'Suspicious as well as cynical.'

Kent had no intention of subjecting himself to her Cheshire grin. He rose from the chair and prowled to the window, resuming his perusal of the view as the door opened.

Sadie checked her wavy hair was still behaving itself constrained in its tight ponytail as she stepped into the plush corner office, determined not to be intimidated. So what if the legendary Tabitha Fox could make grown men weep? She'd given Sadie the job and, lowly cadet reporter or not, she knew her big break when she saw it.

Even if Leo's agenda was questionable.

'Ah Sadie, come in.' Tabitha smiled. 'I'd like you to meet someone.'

She nodded her head towards Kent. 'This is your photographer, Kent Nelson.'

Sadie turned automatically, her gaze falling on broad shoulders before her brain registered the name. She blinked.

'*The* Kent Nelson?' she asked his back, the image that had affected her a few months ago revisiting.

Kent shut his eyes briefly. Great. *A groupie.* He turned as Tabitha said, 'The one and only.'

Sadie was speechless. Multi-award-winning, world-acclaimed photojournalist Kent Nelson was coming with her to the back of beyond to take photos of a reclusive celebrity?

She almost asked him who he'd pissed off but checked her natural urge to be sarcastic.

Kent was pretty damn speechless himself as one look at Sadie Bliss blew his mind. And his was not a mind easily blown. Tabitha was smirking in his peripheral vision so he hoped he wasn't staring at her like a cartoon character whose eyes had just popped out on springs because, try as he might, he was powerless to pull his gaze away from all those curves.

Curves that started at her pouty mouth and *did not let up.*

Sure, she'd tried to contain them in her awful pin-striped suit but they looked as if they were going to bust out at any moment. They looked as if they had a mind of their own.

Bliss? *Very appropriate.* A man could starve to death whilst lost in those curves and not even care.

Great. Just what he needed. Three days in a car with a rookie reporter whose curves should come with a neon warning sign.

Sadie looked at Tabitha with a scrunched brow. 'I'm sorry, I don't understand... *Kent Nelson* is the photographer on my story?'

'We-e-ll-ll...' Tabitha wheedled. 'Plans have changed a little.'

Sadie could feel the pound of her pulse through every cell in her body as a sinking feeling settled into her bones.

They wanted to take her off the story.

Give it to someone else.

Sadie cleared her throat. 'Changed?'

She was determined to act brisk and professional. She might not have scored this story on merit, but she intended to show everyone she had the chops for feature writing. And if Ms Tabitha bloody Fox thought she wouldn't fight for her story, then she was mistaken.

Sunday On My Mind, the country's top weekend magazine supplement, was exactly where she wanted to be.

And if she had to write one more best-dog-in-show story she was going to scream.

'We want you to do two stories. The feature on Leonard. And another.' Tabitha flicked her gaze to Kent briefly before refocusing on the busty, ambitious brunette who had been bombarding her inbox with interview requests for the last three months. 'On an outback road trip.'

Sadie held herself tall even though inside everything was deflating at the confirmation that the story was still hers. She didn't even allow herself the tiniest little triumphant smile as Tabitha's words beyond '*two stories*' sank in.

'A road trip?'

She looked at Kent, who was watching her with an expression she couldn't fathom. She was used to men gawking at her. Being lumbered with an E cup from the age of thirteen had broken her in to the world of male objectification early. But this wasn't that. It was brooding. Intense.

He was intense.

She'd seen pictures of him before, of course. The night of the exhibition there'd been a framed one of him taken on location somewhere in a pair of cammo pants and a khaki T-shirt. His clothing had been by no means tight but the shirt had sat against his chest emphasising well-delineated pecs, firmly muscled biceps and a flat belly.

His light brown hair had been long and shaggy—pushed back behind his ears. His moustache and goatee straggly. He'd been laughing into the lens, his eyes scrunched against the glare, interesting indentations bracketing his mouth.

He'd held a camera with a massive lens in his hands as if it were an extension of him. As a soldier carried a gun.

The whole rugged, action-man thing had never been a turn-on for her—she preferred her men refined, arty, like Leo—but she'd sure as hell been in the female minority that night in New York.

Hell, had the man himself been there, she doubted he would have left alone.

But looking at him today she probably wouldn't have recognised him

if they'd passed in the street. Gone was the long hair and scraggy goatee that gave him a younger, more carefree look. Instead he was sporting a number-two buzz cut, which laid bare the shape of his perfectly
symmetrical skull and forehead. His facial hair had also been restricted
to stubble of a number-two consistency, emphasising the angularity of
his cheekbones and jaw, shadowing the fullness of what she had to admit
was a damn fine mouth, exposing the creases that would become indentations when he smiled.

If he smiled.

The man sure as hell wasn't smiling now. He had his arms folded beneath her scrutiny and Sadie became aware suddenly she was watching
his mouth a little too indecently. Quickly, she widened her gaze out.

Unfortunately it found a different focus. The way his folded arms
tightened the fabric of his form-fitting, grey turtle-neck skivvy across
the bulk of his chest. The bunch of muscles in his forearms, where the
long sleeves had been pushed up to the elbows.

'Yes,' Kent said smoothly, interrupting her inspection. 'A road trip.'

He watched as Sadie took that on board with eyes as remarkable as the
rest of her. Finally he understood what people meant when they talked
about doe-eyed. They were huge, an intense dark grey, framed with long
lashes. They didn't need artfully applied shadow or dark kohl to draw
attention—they just did.

His gaze drifted to the creamy pallet of her throat, also bare of any
adornment. In fact, running his gaze over her, he realised Sadie Bliss was
a bling-free zone. No earrings, no necklaces, no rings.

In stark contrast to Tabitha there was nothing on Sadie's person that
sparkled or drew the eye.

Not an ounce of make-up.

Not a whiff of perfume.

Even her mouth, all red and lush, appeared to be that way all on its
own merit.

Sadie cleared her throat as his gaze unnerved her. An odd little pull
deep down inside did funny things to her pulse and she glanced at Tabitha
to relieve it.

'From Darwin to Borroloola? That's like…a thousand kilometres.'

Sadie did not travel well in cars.

Tabitha shook her head but it was Kent who let loose the next bombshell. 'Actually, it's Sydney to Borroloola. You can fly from Borroloola to Darwin and then back to Sydney once the interview is done.'

Sadie forgot all about the funny pull, Kent's celebrity status and the good impression she was trying to make with Tabitha. 'Are you nuts?' she said, turning to face him. 'That would have to be at least...' she did a quick mental calculation '...three times the distance!'

Kent remained impassive at her outburst although it was refreshing to hear a knee-jerk, unfiltered opinion for once instead of one couched in the usual kiss-arse afforded to his level of celebrity. Tarnished as it was.

Did she honestly think he wanted to spend three days in a car with her? But he knew Tabitha well enough to know that she was an immovable force when her mind was made up.

'Three thousand, three hundred and thirteen kilometres to be precise.'

Sadie felt nauseated at the mere thought. 'And we're not flying because...?'

Kent didn't blink. 'I don't fly.'

'It'll be great,' Tabitha enthused, jumping in as Kent's voice became arctic again. 'You and Kent. A car. A travel diary. The Red Centre. The true outback. Journalism at its most organic.'

Sadie gave Tabitha a look that suggested she was probably also certifiable. 'But that will take days!'

'Let me guess,' Kent drawled, amused by her horrified demeanour. 'City girl, right?'

Sadie looked back at him. 'No,' she denied, despite the fact that she was an urban creature to her core. Fast lane, city lights, cocktail bars and foreign film festivals.

'I just get really, really car sick.' It sounded so lame when she said it out loud but she doubted the great Kent Nelson would tolerate stopping every two minutes so she could hurl up her stomach contents.

Kent's jaw tightened again. *Great.* Three days in a car with a city chick and her weak constitution.

It just kept getting better.

'I guess that's why they invented motion sickness medication,' he said woodenly.

Sadie shook her head vigorously. 'Oh, trust me, you do *not* want to be around me when I'm on that. I get totally trippy. It is not pretty.'

Kent raised an eyebrow. Vomiting or tripping. Sounded like a trip forged in hell.

Maybe another place, another time in his life he would have been more than happy to see Little-Miss-Curvy getting trippy. But now just the thought was plain annoying.

'Thanks for the heads up,' he said.

'This could be a great opportunity for you, Sadie,' Tabitha interjected. 'Two feature stories for the price of one. Of course, if you don't think you're up to it we can always find someone else…'

Sadie wanted to stamp her foot at the not-so-subtle ultimatum. But she didn't. Tabitha was right. It *was* a gift. How was her boss to know about Sadie's nervousness at facing her ex-lover again? Or that when she did, she wanted to look a million dollars, not like a wrung-out dish mop?

At least a gruelling car journey would help the crash diet she'd put herself on since finding out about this opportunity two days ago. The last time she'd seen Leo, she'd been thin, her curves straitjacketed by a strict eating regime.

Not naturally svelte, she had taken a while to slim down when they'd first started their relationship. But Leo's love and encouragement had been a fantastic incentive. Every time he'd raved about the symmetry of her prominent collar, wrist and hipbones, or the way the milkiness of her skin stretched sparingly over the hard surfaces beneath, she'd felt accomplished.

He used to stroke her hair as it fell in between the angles of her bony scapulas and tell her it looked like rippling satin flowing between a sculpted valley. That her creamy skin was the perfect foil.

The only thing curvy about her then had been her breasts. And, no matter how much Leo had lamented them, not even rigid dieting had had an effect on their size. He'd offered to pay for a reduction and she'd been thrilled at the suggestion. Thrilled that the brilliant artist had seen something special in her body. Seen it as a work of art, an empty canvas.

Thrilled that she'd become his muse, revelling in his almost obsessive need to paint her.

She was excruciatingly aware now she was not the woman he had sent away. That he had loved.

And she had a lot to prove.

So there was one upside to this proposed nightmare road trip. Between starvation and puking up constantly she could lose a stone or two before seeing him again.

'No. It's fine,' she said, briskly pulling herself out of the food-obsessing habits of a past life. 'I can do it. I just can't promise the upholstery of the hire car will ever be the same again.'

'No hire car,' Kent said. 'We'll be using my all-terrain vehicle.'

Sadie nodded at him. *Of course.* An all-terrain vehicle. Mr Intense-and-rugged probably also had the Batmobile tucked away somewhere.

'When do we leave?' She sighed.

'I'll pick you up in the morning. Pack light. No places serving drinks with umbrellas where we're going.'

'Gee,' she said sweetly, 'imagine my surprise.'

Sadie's fallback position had always been sarcasm—a defence mechanism against a world that constantly misjudged her because of the size of her chest. As an adult she tried her best to contain it but, sadly, it was too ingrained in her nature to be completely stifled.

And if Kent Nelson insisted on this ridiculous road trip, on spending days in a car alone together, then he could consider this a heads up.

Tabitha might have forced her hand, but she didn't have to like it.

Sadie was ready when Kent rang the doorbell the next morning. She was wearing loose denim cut-offs and a modest polo shirt, her hair fell freely around her shoulders and a pair of ballet flats completed the ensemble. Her medium-sized backpack and a small insulated bag were waiting at the door.

Kent blinked at the transformation from serious city career girl in a power suit to girl-next-door. Again, her clothes did nothing to emphasise the curves—if anything they were on the baggy side.

It was just that Sadie's curves were uncontainable.

Dressed like this, still absent of any bling, it was easy to believe she was only the twenty-four years Tabitha had informed him of yesterday.

Which made her precisely twelve years younger than him.

She was a baby, for crying out loud.

'What's in here?' Kent asked as he grabbed the fridge bag off her and lifted her pack. An hour ago he'd been whistling as he'd loaded the vehicle for the trip, a buzz he hadn't felt in a long time coursing through his veins.

The buzz was still there.

He just wasn't sure, in the presence of Sadie, if it was one hundred per cent related to the drive any more.

'Ginger ale,' she said, watching how the muscles in his tanned forearms bunched.

Before yesterday she would have admired the delineation, the symmetry, the beauty of the fluid movement. Today they just made her insides feel funny.

And that was the last thing she needed.

Her insides would feel funny enough the minute they hit the first bend in the road.

'I don't expect you to carry my stuff,' she said testily.

She wasn't some delicate elfin thing that would shatter if she picked up anything heavier than her handbag. One look would have told him that. But he was already striding away despite a rather intriguing limp.

From the crash, she assumed.

She followed at a more sedate pace, glancing at the sturdy-looking Land Rover parked on the road with trepidation. With its functional metal cab, sturdily constructed roof railings and massive bull bar it looked like something the Australian army had engineered for land and amphibious combat. And had been test driven in a pigsty if the sludge-and-muck-encrusted paint job was any indication.

Staring at the tank on wheels, Sadie absently wondered whether Kent Nelson was compensating for something.

'I didn't know you could get mud masks for cars,' she murmured as she joined him at the open back doors.

Kent grunted as he rearranged the supplies to accommodate her backpack. 'She's not young, she's not very pretty but she'll do the job.'

Sadie preferred pretty.

And men who didn't talk about cars as if they were female. Especially this car. *This car was one hundred per cent male.*

'Does *she* have air conditioning?'

Kent nodded. He held up the cool bag. 'You want this up front?' he asked.

'Thanks.'

She took it from him as he shut the doors and noticed a muddy sticker supporting a Sydney football team near the handle and another for an

Australian brewery. He looked like a man who knew his way around a ball. And a beer.

Leo had drunk gin.

Kent looked down on her. The morning sun fell on the pale skin of her throat and he noticed the pulse beating there. 'Got your pills?' he asked gruffly.

She patted her bag. 'At the ready.'

'Should you take one now? I'm not going to stop every two minutes for you to throw up.'

Sadie ignored his warning. Stopping every two minutes didn't exactly sound like a picnic to her either. 'I'll wait till we get out of the city. Save my performance for the windy bits.'

Kent narrowed his eyes as he took the opportunity to study her face some more. She had dark rings surrounding the deep grey of her irises, which seemed to lure him in even further. 'Just how trippy is trippy?'

Sadie realised his mouth was quite near and she had to wonder what it would look like kicked up a little, those creases becoming deep grooves, because it looked pretty damn perfect as it was. As if some old master with an eye for masculine perfection had sculpted it just for him, and the artist in her, never far from the surface, appreciated its flawlessness.

The woman, on the other hand, was just plain jealous.

Her own ridiculously plump mouth, devoid of collagen despite what every catty woman she'd ever met had implied, seemed garish by comparison. It was why she rarely wore lipstick or gloss.

Her mouth did not need any more attention.

Kent felt her gaze on his mouth and the pull of those incredible eyes as she studied him. 'Sadie?' he prompted.

Sadie blinked as she realised he was frowning and she was staring. Not only that, but she'd lost her place in the conversation. Her brain scrambled to catch up. She took a step back from him. What *had* they been talking about?

Pills. Right. 'I sing,' she said. 'Loudly. And not very well.'

Kent grimaced. Great. Stuck in a car with karaoke Barbie. 'Try to refrain.' He looked at his watch and said, 'Let's go.'

Sadie took a deep breath as she headed to the passenger seat. Her heart thudded in her chest on a surge of adrenaline. The call of the wild? The excitement of a new adventure? The beginnings of an illustrious career?

She hoped so because the alternatives weren't palatable. Dread at the oncoming nausea. Or, worse, being alone in a confined space with an unimpressed man whose mouth had her wishing she'd paid more attention in sculpting classes.

She'd climbed up into the high-clearance, all-wheel drive. At five eight, she wasn't exactly short, but Sadie still felt as if pole-vaulting lessons would have been handy. The sturdy cab felt like a cocoon of armour around her, even if the ground seemed a long way down.

As soon as she buckled up Kent thrust a folded up map at her. 'Here,' he said. 'I've marked the journey in red.'

Sadie looked at him as the mere thought of having to *read* and travel made her feel ill. 'You don't have a GPS?'

Kent shot her an impatient look. 'We're doing this the old-fashioned way,' he said and started the engine.

Fabulous. 'And what happens if we lose the map?' she enquired sweetly. 'Do we use the stars?'

Kent suppressed a smile at her derision. He held her gaze. 'Unfortunately I didn't bring my sextant.'

That look—intense, focused—fanned over her like a sticky web, doing strange things to her pulse and causing heat to bloom in her belly and other places further south.

Oh, he'd brought his sextant all right…

CHAPTER TWO

EVEN THOUGH SHE was looking out of the window, Sadie didn't notice the city streets of Sydney giving way to the red rooves of suburbia or to the greenery of semi-rural market gardens. She was too busy puzzling over her reaction to the man sitting an arm's length away.

On the surface, he was everything she didn't usually go for. Physically impressive. Outdoorsy. A beer and football kind of a guy.

But then there was his age.

Through some online investigation last night she'd discovered he was thirty-six and she *did* have a track record with older men.

Leo had been twenty years her senior.

She supposed a psychologist would say she had a Daddy Complex. Her father had left when she was twelve and got himself a new family, including a set of twins who'd turned into sports-mad little boys.

She'd always felt the fact that she was a girl and had been more arty than sporty had been a huge let-down for her father. And after years of trying to win his attention and affection she'd finally conceded defeat as she'd headed off to college.

So, maybe his abandonment *had* spread invisible tentacles into her life. *Whatever.*

It didn't change the facts. Nothing else about Kent Nelson should have appealed.

Yet somehow it did.

She studied his profile as he drove, his eyes fixed on the road. His buzz cut melded into the stubble of his sideburns, which flowed into that covering his jaw, hugging the spare planes of his face, emphasising cheekbones that stood out like railings. It made him look...severe. A far cry from the bearded guy who had been laughing at the camera in the snap from the gallery.

It made him look intense.

Guarded.

It made him look haunted.

As a journalist, and a huge fan of his work, it was exceedingly intriguing.

As a woman—it scared the hell out of her.

Kent gripped the steering wheel as Sadie's speculative gaze seemed to burn a hole at the angle of his jaw. After almost eighteen months in and out of hospitals and another six months of physical therapy, it had been a while since he'd had any kind of constant company—female or otherwise—and her concentration was unnerving.

He turned to look at her and almost rolled his eyes as she quickly pretended she hadn't been staring at him by feigning interest in the scenery outside her window.

Very mature.

His gaze fell to her legs, the denim riding well and truly up above her knees and pulling taut across thighs as lush and round as the rest of her. *Rubenesque* slipped into his brain and he flicked his gaze back to the road.

'I hope you brought something warmer—it's going to get cold out at night.'

Sadie blinked. They'd been in the car for over an hour and this was the first thing he said to her? She really, really hoped he wasn't one of those men who thought there was a direct correlation between her cup size and her IQ.

She slapped her forehead theatrically. 'And I only packed bikinis and a frilly negligee.'

Kent gripped the steering wheel as images of her in a bikini screwed with his concentration. 'A lot of people think of the outback as hot,' he quantified, still not looking at her. 'But it cools down really quickly at night.'

Sadie shot him an impatient look. 'Thank you. But how about we assume from now on I'm a reasonably intelligent person who wouldn't go on any trip without having thoroughly researched it first?'

Kent turned his head at the note in her voice. It was more than sarcasm. It was...touchy. As if she'd had to prove her intelligence one too many times. He guessed with her assets people didn't often see beyond them.

He looked back at the road. 'Fair enough.'

Sadie groaned as they passed a sign indicating their ascent through the Blue Mountains was about to begin. It came with a warning of sharp corners and hairpin bends.

The nausea kicked in at the thought of what lay ahead. '*Fabulous*,' she muttered as she searched through her bag for her pills. 'Dangerous curves.'

Kent wished there were a pill he could take for the ones inside the car, but her look of abject misery kept his brain off her treacherous curves. He could practically hear her teeth grinding as she pawed through the contents of a handbag big enough to fit an entire pharmacy full of motion sickness tablets.

For crying out loud! 'Do you get sick if you're the driver?' he asked.

Sadie shook her head absently, missing the exasperation in his tone as she read the back of the medication box. It was a new brand to her, one supposedly with reduced side effects. 'Nope.'

'Well, that's easy, then, isn't it?' he said as he indicated and pulled the car into one of the regular truck laybys that lined the route.

'What are you doing?' Sadie frowned as he unbuckled.

'Letting you drive.'

Sadie didn't move for a moment. 'You want me to drive your car?'

He nodded. 'You do have a licence, right?'

Sadie looked around at the behemoth in which she was sitting. She drove a second-hand Prius. 'Not a tank licence.'

Kent's mouth pressed into an impatient line. 'You'll be fine.' He stepped out and strode around to her side.

Sadie had the ridiculous urge to lock her door before he reached her, but then it was open and he was filling the space along with the whoosh of traffic and the acrid aroma of exhaust fumes.

She looked at Kent, surprised at her elevated height to find she was looking him straight in the eye. They were brown, she noticed, now she was focused on something other than his mouth. She was close enough to see flecks of copper and amber shimmering there too, throwing a hue into the darker brown. They reminded her of something—a memory—she couldn't quite recall.

Kent watched her watching him as if she was trying to figure something out. 'Don't they say an ounce of prevention is worth a pound of cure?' he prompted.

Sadie suddenly remembered. The tiger-eye marble she'd had in her collection as a kid. One of her father's many attempts to get her interested in something other than reading and drawing.

'Are you sure?' she asked, looking around the vehicle again, absently pulling her bottom lip between her teeth. If it had been a hire car she wouldn't have hesitated. 'I've never driven anything quite so…big. I'd hate to crash it.'

Kent did not drop his gaze to her mouth. The fact that he even noticed her lip being ravished by her teeth was irritating enough. He raised an eyebrow. 'Do you make a habit of crashing cars?'

She shook her head, releasing her lip. 'No, never.' She looked back at him and frowned. She'd have thought a he-man like Kent would never have relinquished the wheel.

'What?' he asked warily.

Sadie shook her head. 'I've never met a man yet who'd give up the driver's seat for a woman.' Her father had never let her mother drive when they were in the car together. 'Doesn't it emasculate you or something?'

Kent blinked. That hadn't been a question he'd expected. What kind of Neanderthals did she hang out with? 'I think I'm secure enough in my masculinity to not be threatened by a woman in the driver's seat.'

Sadie's gaze dropped from the spiky stubble of his angular jaw to the breadth of his shoulders. She had to admit if this man's masculinity could be threatened then no man's was safe!

'Look,' he said impatiently as she continued to sit. 'It's win-win. You don't get to throw up every two minutes and I get to spot photo opps. I also don't get to see you all trippy, which, given that we hardly know each other, is a good thing.'

Sadie couldn't dispute his logic. The last thing she needed was to lose her inhibitions around a man who looked as if he kept his well and truly in check.

If he had any.

'Fine.'

Sadie undid her belt and twisted in her seat to get out. She glanced at him, waiting for him to shift, her gaze snagging on his mouth. He didn't for a moment and there was a split second when neither of them moved. When his beautiful mouth filled her entire vision and she found herself wishing he would say something just so she could admire how it moved. Then he stepped back and she half slid, half jumped to the ground on legs that seemed suddenly wobbly.

After giving Sadie a quick tutorial on the various idiosyncrasies of his vehicle, Kent left her to it, making no comment as she lurched it out onto the highway. Her grip on the steering wheel was turning her knuckles white and he was afraid she might split all the skin there if she didn't ease up.

'Relax,' he ordered. 'You're doing fine.'

Strangely his command did not help Sadie relax. Her gaze flicked between the rear view and side mirrors as her heartbeat pelted along in time to the engine. She wasn't sure if it was from nervousness about driving a strange car/tank that belonged to someone else or the weird moment she and Kent had shared as she'd exited the vehicle.

'Relax,' he said again.

'Believe it or not,' Sadie said, gritting her teeth as she eyeballed the road, 'you telling me to relax is *not* helping.'

Kent held up his hands in surrender. 'Okay.'

'I just need to get used it,' she quantified. 'It's not normal to be so high up. I feel like I'm driving a truck.'

Kent grimaced. It was hardly a semi-trailer. 'I said okay.'

He turned then and dragged his camera case out of the back passenger floor well. Sadie was obviously stressed about driving the big, bad vehicle and he had little patience with princesses. Best to keep himself occupied and his lip zipped. And one more equipment check before they got too far away from civilisation wouldn't go astray.

About ten minutes later he noticed her grip slacken and her shoulders relax back into the seat. Ten minutes after that she even started multitasking.

'So. What's the plan?' Sadie asked, more comfortable now with how the car handled. 'Where are our scheduled stops?'

Kent looked up from his disassembled camera. 'Scheduled stops?'

Sadie nodded. 'You know? Of a night time? When we're tired?'

'I hadn't scheduled any stops. We're driving all the way through.'

Sadie looked briefly away from the road to blast him with a *you-have-to-be-kidding me* look. A non-stop journey would probably take two full days.

Without a single break?

'Don't we have to sleep some time?'

He speared her with a direct look. 'Do you really want to make this journey any longer than it has to be? We can pull over and catch some kip along the way. Either in the car or I have a couple of swags.'

Sadie supressed a shudder. *Oh, goody. Maybe they'd find a jolly jumbuck to stuff inside.* She flicked a quick glance towards him. 'I don't camp.'

Kent blinked at the way she said camp—as if she'd said prison. 'What do you mean, you don't camp?'

'It's simple,' she said, returning her eyes to the road. 'You don't fly. I don't camp.'

Great. Car sick. Didn't camp. Sadie Bliss was stacking up the black marks against her name and truly pushing his patience. 'What on earth have you got against sleeping under the stars?'

'Nothing,' Sadie assured him. 'Give me five of them and I'm happy as a pig in mud.'

Kent shook his head. 'You haven't lived, city girl.'

'I guess we're just going to have to agree to disagree on that one,' she said sweetly.

Kent's mouth took on a grim line. 'I have a feeling there may be a bit of that this trip.'

Sadie did too. 'So? Where should we stop tonight, do you think?' she prompted.

Kent pulled the map out of the glovebox, where Sadie had thrown it in disgust earlier, and did some calculations. 'It's about another ten hours to Cunnamulla,' he said, looking at the digital clock display on the dash. It was just gone nine-thirty. 'That'll put us there after seven tonight. It'll also put us over the Queensland border.'

'Okay.' Sadie nodded.

'Doubt there's any five-star accommodation there though,' he mused.

'We could go another couple hours on to Charleville. It's twice the size. Still don't think they run to five star.'

Sadie shot him a sarcastic smile. 'Thanks, I'll settle for a shower, a flushing toilet and a bed.'

'Cunnamulla it is.'

With that sorted, silence reigned as they wended their way through the beautiful Blue Mountains, and down the other side of the Great Dividing Range. Kent went back to his camera bag, soothed by the familiarity of the routine. It had been a while since he'd lugged this stuff around, lived with it every day, and it was comforting to know it still felt good.

He occasionally shot a glance Sadie's way. He had to admit, after her initial misgivings she was handling the vehicle with great competence. He'd been afraid she was going to whine about the heavy steering or the engine noise or the lack of a stereo system all the way to Borroloola, but she'd got on with the job with no complaints.

No chatter whatsoever.

His kind of travelling companion.

Until it all went to hell two minutes later.

'So are we going to sit in silence or are we going to get to know each other?' she asked.

Now she was out of the worst of the windy roads Sadie was free to concentrate on other things. And it had occurred to her that she was sitting next to a man who was pretty hot property, especially since he'd gone underground. How far would a feature on *the* Kent Nelson get her career? If she had to spend days on end in a car with his particular brand of he-man, she might as well get something for it.

And truly, the way he kept breaking down that camera and reassembling it, as if it were a gun, was slightly unnerving.

Kent sighed. He should have known it was too good to be true. 'Silence is golden.'

Sadie quirked an eyebrow at his terse reply. 'Silence is loud.'

He clicked a lens in place, then looked at her. 'Listen to me, Sadie Bliss. Let's not pretend that either of us is too thrilled by being stuck in this car together. I know women feel the need to chat and fill up all the empty spaces, but I'm okay with the empty spaces.' It sure as hell beat the crowding in his head. 'I like the empty spaces.'

'I don't feel the need,' she dismissed irritably. 'It's just, you know…
conversational. Polite.'

Kent shoved the camera back in its soft-sided bag. 'I can handle rude.'

That she could believe. But she doubted she could. 'So…we're just
going to…not talk? For three thousand kilometres?'

'Well, I'm sure we'll need to say the odd word or two. Like, *We need
petrol*," and, *"How about here for lunch?"* But let's try and keep it to a minimum, huh?'

Sadie blinked at his hard profile. His arrogance that she'd just fall in
with his imperious command irked. He might be used to women falling over themselves to do as he said, but she just wasn't built that way.

And his insistence on silence only piqued her curiosity. The shadows
in his eyes told her there was stuff he didn't want to talk about. And she
was pretty sure his refusal to fly was just scratching the surface. Just
looking at his guarded exterior made her want to know more.

She wanted to ask about the picture. She wanted to know about that
day.

Probably best not to start there though…

She waited a few minutes to lull him into a false sense of security.
They were heading for Mudgee on a relatively straight stretch of highway, the scenery fairly standard Australian bush fare. Lots of gums and
low, scrubby vegetation.

Fairly uninspiring really.

Especially compared to the story she knew he must be harbouring
deep down where the shadows lived.

He'd just opened the map when she said, 'It could be fun.' She waited
a beat. 'Getting to know each other.'

Kent didn't look up from the map. 'I doubt it.'

He already knew too much about her. Curves that wouldn't quit. A
mouth that was made to be kissed. A weak constitution and a penchant
for five-star living.

Trouble.

A real pain in his butt.

Sadie took his blunt rejection on the chin and was pleased she didn't
insult easily. Nor did she dissuade. 'Oh, come on,' Sadie goaded. 'It's
really easy when you try. See, I ask something about you. We discuss it.
Then you ask something about me.'

He kept his nose in the map and Sadie felt a peculiar desperation. Why, she wasn't sure.

'Easy,' she added as the silence built.

It built some more.

'Oh, come on, there must be something you want to know about me.'

Kent looked up at her, regarding her steadily. She'd obviously been to the terrier school of journalism.

Excellent. Chatty and dogged.

Two more black marks.

He suddenly remembered wondering yesterday why Leonard Pinto had requested a rookie journo for his feature.

'Why did Leonard Pinto want you?'

Sadie almost choked on her own spit as the question caught her unawares. She certainly hadn't been prepared for his first question to skip so much of the preliminary stuff that was the norm in these situations. Where were you born? How old are you? Where'd you go to school?

Or even the ruder ones that people tended to just come straight out and ask her no matter how inappropriate.

Is that your real name?

Are those your real boobs?

Do you have silicone in those lips?

'Jeez,' she said lightly, letting her sarcastic nature run free. 'Cutting straight to the chase. No name, rank and serial number? No opening pleasantries? I hope you're more subtle than this on dates.'

Kent raised his eyebrows at her deliberate sidestep, but he hadn't missed the whitening of her knuckles on the steering wheel.

'I'm rusty.'

Sadie snorted. The man looked utterly well oiled. In one hundred per cent working order. Even his limp didn't seem to impede him. 'You don't say?'

Kent watched her for a moment or two as she kept her gaze firmly on the road ahead. Her profile was as striking as the rest of her, from her wavy hair to her pouty lips to the thrust of her breasts.

And he really, really didn't want to be noticing her breasts. 'Why does Pinto want you?' he repeated.

Sadie flicked a quick glance his way. 'Why don't you fly?'

Kent blinked. He hadn't expected her to push back so quickly. Or for her salvo to hit its target quite so effectively. 'Is he a relative?' he persisted.

Sadie didn't even let a beat go by. 'Is it because of the chopper accident?' she replied.

Kent narrowed his gaze as he looked at her and she turned and shot him a *two-can-play-at-this-game* look before returning her attention to the road. 'Or maybe he saw your picture on the magazine website and just wants to get into your pants?' he parried.

It might only be a head shot, but a man who painted nudes for a living had to appreciate the perfect pout of that mouth.

The air in Sadie's lungs stuttered to a halt as she forgot to breathe in for a few seconds. Her fingers tightened on the steering wheel. She wasn't about to tell him that Leonard Pinto had been in her pants plenty.

And that there was no way he'd want to go there again. Not with her carrying so much weight.

'You're right,' she said, slamming the car into a lower gear as she slowed for some roadworks. 'Silence *is* golden.'

Kent shot her a sardonic smile. 'I knew you'd see it my way.'

Half an hour later Sadie was pretty bored with the scenery. Kent had the buds of his MP3 player in his ears and was intermittently flipping through a travel book or gazing out at the scenery flashing by. Occasionally she could see those fascinating lips moving—presumably to the music she couldn't hear.

Or he hadn't taken his meds today.

He sure hadn't taken his chatty pill.

He seemed to be having a little party for one in his seat—perfectly content—and it irritated her. If he seriously thought he could ignore her for three thousand kilometres, then he truly did need those meds.

It should have been refreshing to be ignored by a man for a change. But it was strangely off-putting. Attention she could deal with. She could deflect. But inattention, lack of interest even, that wasn't in her repertoire.

She was going to get him talking if it killed her.

She reached across and yanked on the closest ear bud. 'How about a game, instead?' she suggested as he fixed her with a steady glare.

Kent waited a beat of two before replying. *She wanted to play games?* He notched up another black mark as he held out his hand for the bud. 'No.'

'Come on,' she cajoled undeterred. 'This is supposed to be a road trip, right? You play games on road trips. It's in all the movies.'

Kent refused to think about the kind of games he could play with Sadie Bliss. He was not going to think about strip anything. He wasn't going there. 'I don't do games,' he said bluntly as he relieved her of his ear bud.

She quirked an eyebrow. 'What, not even I Spy?'

Kent regarded her for a moment, all perky and pushy. He needed to nip that in the bud or this trip was going to be interminable. 'How about truth or dare?'

Sadie's pulse spiked at the silky note in his voice and the way his gaze seemed to flick, ever so briefly, to her mouth. It was tempting but she doubted he'd go for truth. And she was damned if she was going to dare this man to do anything.

'Maybe once we've got to know each other a little better?' she retreated.

Kent pulled his gaze away from her, startled at the thought. He didn't want to know Sadie Bliss. A sign flashed by and he grabbed a mental hold. 'I spy with my little eye,' he said, 'something beginning with petrol station.'

Sadie kept her eyes firmly on the indicated services ahead. She scrunched her brow. 'You know you're only supposed to say the first letter, right?'

He ignored her sarcasm. 'Pull in, I'm starving. Breakfast seems a very long time ago.'

Sadie had been starving for the last three days. 'We've only been in the car for three hours,' she pointed out.

'I need snacks,' he said. 'And you can use the facilities.'

'Gee, thanks,' Sadie said rolling her eyes as she indicated left. 'But my days of enforced toileting ended a long, long time ago. You may have women in your life with weak bladders but, I can assure you, mine is made of cast iron.'

'So it's just your stomach that's weak?' he enquired drily.

Sadie shot him a look as she prepared to park. 'Really? You want to annoy me now? As I'm parking *your* tank in this itty-bitty car space?'

Kent assessed the one remaining, very narrow car space. She made a good point. 'Nope.'

Sadie turned back to the job at hand as she nervously pulled the car into the middle of three parking bays. The heavy steering was fine for wide open spaces but it felt as if she was trying to grapple a huge metallic beast into a matchbox as she centred the vehicle.

It was gratifying to get a grunt of respect from Kent.

He flung his door open as soon as she killed the engine. 'You coming?'

Sadie shook her head. 'I'm good.'

'You want something?'

She shook it again. 'I brought some snacks with me.'

Sadie watched him stride to the sliding doors of the service station, pleased to be released from his company for a few minutes. His jeans gently hugged his bottom and the backs of his thighs without being skin tight. His T-shirt was loose enough for the breeze to blow it against the broad contours of his back. And his limp, barely discernible, added an extra edge to his rugged appeal.

A blonde woman with a baby on her hip coming out of the sliding door as Kent went in actually stood for a moment admiring the view. She seemed perplexed for a second after the closing glass doors snatched him away. As if she couldn't remember why she was standing in the car park gawping at a closed door.

I hear ya, honey.

He was back in a few minutes loaded down with enough carbohydrates to exceed his recommended daily intake from now until the end of his days. She felt hyperglycaemic just looking at them.

'Here,' he said as he passed her a packet of Twisties. 'I got one for you, too.'

Twisties? Dear God, he was going to eat Twisties—her one weakness—right in front of her. She passed them back.

'Thanks, I've got these,' she said, waving a celery stick at him.

Kent grimaced as he opened his packet. 'You're going to eat *celery*? On a road trip.'

He had a way of emphasising celery as if it were suet or tripe. 'It's healthy,' she said defensively, and was about to launch into a spiel about the amazing properties of the wonder food when the aroma of carbohydrates wafted out to greet her like an old friend and she momentarily lost her train of thought.

How could that special blend of additives and preservatives smell so damn good? Her stomach growled.

Loudly.

Kent raised an eyebrow. 'I think your stomach wants a say.'

Sadie stuffed the celery into her mouth and started the car to stop her from reaching over and lifting a lurid orange piece out and devouring it like the Cookie Monster. 'It's because I listen to my stomach too damn often that I'm as big as I am,' she muttered testily as she reversed.

Kent eyed her critically as he buckled up, thinking she looked pretty damn good to him. He shook his head. Women in the western world amazed him. Their lives were so privileged they had nothing but trivialities to worry about. He really didn't have the patience for it.

'Please tell me you're not going to eat celery for three days.'

Sadie gave him an exasperated glare. 'What's it matter to you?'

He bugged his eyes at her. To think less than two years ago he had been in the thick of a combat zone and now he was talking to a madwoman with a weak constitution but an apparently strong bladder about *celery* of all things.

'I think it's making you cranky.'

Sadie flicked her gaze to the road, then back at him. He had orange Twistie dust on the tips of his fingers and his lips, which just went to show perfection could be improved upon. She wondered what he'd taste like beneath the flavours of salt and cheese.

Her stomach growled again and she started to salivate.

And not for celery.

Maybe not even for Twisties.

'No,' she denied, looking back to the road. 'You and your damn Twisties are making me cranky.'

'I guess that means you won't want any M&M's either?' he enquired.

Sadie almost groaned out loud. How on earth did he keep in such magnificent shape? She could feel the fat cells on her butt multiplying just by looking at the familiar chocolate snacks.

'Thank you,' she denied primly. 'I'll stick with my celery.'

Kent shrugged. 'Suit yourself,' he said as he threw a Twistie into the air near his face and caught it in his mouth.

The crunch thankfully drowned out another resounding growl from her belly.

* * *

By the time they'd crossed the state border and arrived in Cunnamulla, Sadie was definitely ready to call it a day. She was tired and over
her strong, silent travelling companion, who had snacked all day, read,
slept, listened to music and devoured two pies and a large carton of iced-
coffee for lunch, whilst disparaging her pumpkin and feta salad with a
Diet Coke.

All with only the barest minimum of conversation.

She wanted a shower. Then a bed.

The welcome glow of a vacancy sign cheered her enormously. 'This
okay?' she asked him.

Kent nodded. 'As good as any, I guess.'

Sadie parked the car in front of the reception and she and Kent went
inside, the night air already starting to cool.

'Two rooms, please,' Sadie said to the middle-aged woman behind
the desk.

'I'm sorry, we only have one left,' she apologised.

'Oh,' Sadie murmured, her shoulders sagging.

The woman looked from Sadie to Kent, then back to Sadie, and brightened. 'It has two doubles, though?'

Kent opened his mouth to tell the woman they'd go elsewhere but
Sadie, standing tall again, butted in. 'We'll take it.'

He blinked at her. 'I'm sure there are other hotels here that will have
two separate rooms,' he said to her.

'I'm sure there are,' Sadie agreed wearily. 'And if you want to go and
track them down I'll wish you luck. But I'm exhausted. My butt is numb.
The thought of getting back in the car again makes me want to cry. So
I'm going to stay right here, if it's all the same to you.'

Kent looked down at her doe eyes, the lashes fluttering against her
cheek. She did look pretty done in and she had driven all day without
complaint.

'Fine. I can sleep in the car.'

Sadie cocked an eyebrow. She doubted the confines of his back car
seat would be very accommodating for a man of his proportions. 'I'm
an adult. You're an adult. There are two beds. I promise not to wake up
in the middle of the night and try to seduce you.'

Kent gave her a grudging smile. His first for the day. 'Well, now you've just taken all the fun out of it. And you, going to the trouble of bringing your frilly negligee.'

Sadie blinked, surprised to discover that beneath all that guarded silence, a sense of humour lurked. 'Well, will you look at that,' she murmured. 'He does know how to smile.'

Kent suppressed another smile. 'Don't get used to it.'

Sadie absently massaged her neck, too tired for this conversation. 'Fine, tough guy, sleep in the car. Just don't moan tomorrow when you have a crick in your neck.'

He shrugged. 'I've slept far rougher.' Being embedded with active forces in the Middle East on several occasions had been far from luxurious.

Not that he'd slept much then.

Or now, for that matter.

Sadie sighed. 'Well, bully for you, He-man.'

Kent was so surprised by the nickname he actually laughed this time. He'd never been called that before, at least not to his face, and it was bemusing. 'Did you just call me a he-man?'

Sadie felt his laughter undulate through every muscle in her body right down to her toes. It might have taken her all day but it had been worth the wait. 'I call it as I see it.'

Kent opened his mouth to deny it but Sadie was looking up at him with long, sleepy blinks and he had the wildest urge to see what she'd look like between motel sheets.

He turned to the woman behind the desk, who'd been watching their exchange like an engrossed spectator at a tennis match. 'Where do I sign?' he asked.

CHAPTER THREE

THE ROOM WAS clean but basic. A bar fridge, a television, a bathroom. And two very hard-looking double beds. Still, they beckoned, more inviting than a Bedouin tent, and right now Sadie wouldn't have swapped it for the Waldorf Astoria.

'I bags the shower,' she said as she threw her backpack on the bed closest to the bathroom and delved through it for some clean clothes.

'Do you want something to eat?' Kent asked plonking himself on the other bed and flipping through the information folder placed next to the fluffy towel folded into a fan with a wrapped bar of soap strategically placed in the centre. 'They serve bar meals until eight.'

Sadie was starving. But not as much as she was sleepy. She was used to denying herself food. Sleep not so much. Sleep was as vital to her as air.

And woe betide anyone who deprived her.

'Nope,' she said, picking up her towel.

'Celery again?' Kent asked.

He wasn't sure how much she'd brought in that fridge bag but there seemed to be an endless supply of it today. Every time he opened a packet of something or rustled a wrapper more appeared.

Sadie was too exhausted to make a pithy comeback. 'Too tired. Need to sleep,' she muttered, closing the bathroom door even before the last word was out of her mouth.

Kent heard the shower turn on and fell back against the bed. It felt like a rock and he literally bounced a little. The back seat of his vehicle would have been softer. But then it wouldn't have had a hot, busty, naked woman just three metres and a wall away.

Getting wet. Getting soapy.

He felt heat bloom in his loins and placed the open information folder over his face.

Sadie Bliss was a bad idea. No matter what her body, her delectable smart mouth, her quick wit or her name might suggest.

He didn't need a psych consult to know he was still pretty messed up. He'd had nearly two years of being held ransom by his body and the surgeons and physios had pronounced him cured—or as cured as he was going to get. But it was pretty dark inside his head still. He'd put off tackling the psychological fallout from the accident, thinking and hoping that time would heal as it had his physical ailments.

But it hadn't.

So, he really didn't need a fling with Sadie Bliss. Or, more importantly, she didn't need a fling with him.

He wasn't in a good headspace.

And she was too chatty, too pushy.

Too young.

He didn't have a right to screw with that.

What he needed to do was get back to what he was good at—taking pictures. Use his art as therapy. As a way back to the rest of his life. Then he could worry about the Sadie Blisses of the world.

He heard the taps shut off.

Pictured her reaching for her towel...

He sat up and pulled his shirt off. The room was stuffy and he suddenly felt very hot. He wondered over to the air-con panel and flicked it on. Then he picked up the phone on his bedside table and placed an order with the woman at the desk. He prowled to the bar fridge, pulled out a bottle of beer, parked his butt against the cabinet, cracked the lid and took a fortifying gulp.

The harsh metallic rattle from the shower curtain being pulled back rang like chimes of doom around the room.

Lord. Just how thin were these walls?

And then came a blood-curdling scream.

* * *

Sadie had never seen a spider so huge in all her life. She saw the odd tiny creature scurrying around her flat but she was pretty adept at wielding a can of insect spray, and it seemed the local population of creepy crawlies had put the word out to avoid Sadie's abode at all costs.

But this thing, hanging on the back of the door as if it were the mother ship, was a monster. It was big, and hairy and very, very ugly.

There was a belting on the door followed by, 'Sadie!'

The spider didn't even move at the noise so near its epicentre—yes, it was big enough to have an epicentre—and nor did Sadie. 'Kent!'

'Are you okay?' he demanded through the door.

'Big, big, *big* spider,' she called.

Kent looked at the door in disbelief. A *spider*? Her horror-flick scream had scared ten years off his life. Did she have a clue how very trivial a spider was in the grand scheme of things?

Now, some of the things he'd seen—they were worth screaming about.

'Bloody hell Sadie, I thought you were being murdered.'

'If this thing gets hold of me, I'm sure it'll have a good go,' she yelled.

'It can't be that big.'

'It is,' she said, anchoring the towel more securely under her arm.

And it was between her and her clothes.

She eyed her pyjamas hanging on the back of the door. Had the spider crawled over them? She shuddered at the thought.

Just how long had it been in here watching her?

'I think it's one of those bird eating suckers,' she announced.

'The ones that are only found in South America?'

Sadie shook her head. 'Not any more.'

'Sadie…'

'Okay, I know, I'm sorry. I'm a horrible girly, city-chick cliché. But truly it's huge and spiders just plain creep me out.'

Kent leaned his forehead against the door. He'd been landed with a car-sick, celery-eating, arachnophobe.

Who'd have thought that would come in such a fine package?

'What do you want me to do?'

Even through the door Sadie could hear his exasperation. Could sense his impatience with her girly theatrics. But it was easy to judge when you were on the other side of the door—*the safe side*. 'I want you to come in here and kill it!'

Kent sighed. The fact that she was being held captive in the bathroom by a spider didn't bother him a bit—eventually she'd have to figure it out herself. And if he only had faith she'd do it silently he'd leave her to it.

But a day in a car with Sadie Bliss had told him she didn't really do quiet contemplation. 'Are you decent?'

Sadie rolled her eyes. 'Why? Do you think the spider cares?' she yelled.

He took a breath. 'I'm coming in.'

'Easy, very easy,' Sadie ordered. 'It's on the back of the door and I do not want to see how far that thing can jump.'

Kent opened the door slowly whilst Sadie watched his progress, her eyes peeking out over the edge of the shower curtain she'd pulled around herself for extra protection as if it were an invisibility cloak.

Kent glanced her way, two doe eyes and the top of her head the only things visible as she eyeballed the back of the door. 'You know it's more scared of you than you are of it, right?' he murmured as he slowly opened the door further.

Sadie didn't take her eyes off the terrifying arachnid. 'I doubt it.' It looked like something from an ancient Roman arena.

Once the door was almost all the way open and Sadie could no longer see the hairy critter she relaxed slightly. She looked at Kent, realising for the first time he was shirtless. His broad chest and flat abdomen, complete with a light smattering of hair that arrowed down behind the band of his low-slung jeans, filled her vision.

It was truly a sight to behold.

Why was it again she'd never been into buff men?

For a moment she almost forgot she was being terrorised by a mutant spider.

Almost.

'Right,' she whispered, dragging her gaze off his chest to the other terrifying object in the room. 'I'm going to climb out of the bath and walk very slowly towards you. Once I'm safely out of the room you can do your he-man thing.'

Kent wasn't entirely sure he was ready for Sadie to come out from behind the curtain. But he sure as hell wanted to see the creature that had Little-Miss-Curves all het up.

'Okay,' he whispered dramatically back, her dirty look bouncing easily off his shoulders.

Sadie quietly pushed back the curtain and gingerly stepped out of the bath. She could feel Kent's gaze on her and couldn't figure out which animal to keep her eye on the most.

She gripped the towel more firmly to her body.

Slowly she sidled along the wall furthest from the door, edged around the vanity basin where her toiletry bag sat. When she drew level with Kent she realised they were just one hotel towel and a pair of Levi's from being naked. His bare, broad shoulders and his spare stubbled face filled her vision. He smelled of Twisties and beer.

Who'd have ever thought *that* could be such a potent combination?

'Thank you,' she murmured as he fell back against the front of the door to allow her to squeeze past.

And it was a squeeze. Her body brushed his as she slipped from the room and Kent felt the caress of towelling against his chest all the way down to his groin. For a moment he stood still and did nothing; the impact of her eyes, her mouth, her bare creamy shoulders and the damp tendrils of hair framing it all was temporarily paralysing.

But he was aware of her watching him, her hands fidgeting while she waited for his *he-man* move, and his brain came back online.

He strode into the bathroom and slowly shut the door. Her clothes were hanging on the back. And, yes, he had to admit, it was one of the larger Huntsman spiders he'd seen. He shook his head and grabbed her clothes. The spider scuttled to the top of the door, then onto the ceiling. He walked over to the bath/shower unit, stepped into the tub to open the window on the wall opposite the shower head so the poor creature could make its escape.

He turned to step out, his gaze falling on a scrap of material hanging on the shower-curtain rail. A silky-looking pink thong with a little diamanté twinkling at the front.

For a heartbeat there was nothing in his head but elevator music. Then there was a whole lot more.

None of it conducive to his sanity.

None of it conducive to going out there and facing her again.

'Is it gone?'

Her voice sliced like a machete through the inappropriate images in his head and Kent dragged his transfixed gaze off Sadie's underwear to the back of the door. He stepped out of the tub and had the door open in two strides.

'Not yet,' he said, thrusting her clothes at her and shutting the door behind him. 'I opened the window. It'll crawl out soon enough.'

Sadie blinked. 'You did what?' She clutched her clothes to her chest. 'Are you nuts? You opened the window? So all his mates could join him?' She took a step back. 'What if it doesn't go?'

It was the second time she'd questioned his mental faculties and, even if they weren't already a little on the dicey side, her silky pink thong probably hadn't helped. He wished she'd get dressed already. Damp strands of dark hair brushed creamy shoulders offsetting the natural rouge of her mouth and, frankly, insane had never looked so damn good.

Kent smiled patiently. 'We'll keep the door shut.'

'What if it crawls back in here, under the door? What if it runs over my face in the middle of the night?' She shuddered. 'You do know human beings are supposed to swallow eight spiders in their lifetime, right?'

He clamped down on the urge to tell her there was no way she'd choke that sucker down and instead rolled his eyes. 'I'm sure it's looking for the fastest exit it can make, Sadie. It's probably just trying to recover from the stroke it suffered when you screamed fit to wake the dead. I'm surprised the cops haven't been called to investigate.'

Sadie shook her head mutinously. 'I need it dead. I won't be able to sleep knowing its alive and in here. And trust me, you *do not* want to be around me when I'm sleep deprived.'

'Because you're such a treat now?'

'Please,' she asked. 'Please get rid of it.'

Kent knew he was doomed. He would have done just about anything that mouth was asking. Hell, he would have slain a dragon for her had there been one of those in the bathroom.

'Fine.'

He stalked to his bed and unzipped a long side pocket of his backpack, pulling out a metal walking cane he'd brought along in case there was some serious hiking required to find the perfect shot. He adjusted its length, then returned to the bathroom, ignoring Sadie, who was watching the shut door with trepidation.

He kicked the door shut behind him to block out the view of her still-naked-beneath-the-towel stance, only to have her push it open again. 'Oh, no, you don't,' she said from behind him. 'I want to see it dead. I don't want you coming back out here telling me it's gone just to shut me up because you think I'm being neurotic.'

Kent turned. She was standing back a little from the doorway, her large grey eyes piercing him with a do-not-mess-with-me look.

Kent raised an eyebrow. 'I see we have trust issues.'

Sadie glared at him. 'My issues are none of your damn business. Just make it dead.'

Kent grinned at her prickliness as he turned back to locate the poor creature who'd had the supreme bad luck of choosing this particular room to explore. Although, seeing a naked Sadie Bliss had to have been some consolation.

It was crouched in the corner of the ceiling above the bath. 'Come on, itsy-bitsy,' he said as he approached the bath, the walking stick extended. 'Time to move along.'

Sadie inched a little closer. 'I said dead, damn it,' she snapped from the doorway

'Yeh, yeh, don't get your knickers in a twist,' he said as he positioned himself.

Bad. Word. Choice.

The diamanté from Sadie's thong glimmered in the light and tantalised his peripheral vision.

Sadie's gaze was drawn to it too. *Oh, no!* She hadn't meant to leave it hanging there. She'd just forgotten everything the second *itsy-bitsy* decided to show.

What the hell must he be thinking?

'Right,' Kent said, pushing the rounded knob of the stick towards the spider. 'Time to move along.'

'What are you doing?' she snapped again.

'I'm not killing the spider, Sadie,' he said as he gently swept it towards the open window.

Sadie gasped as the spider scuttled onto the end of the stick. She took a step back as she opened her mouth to warn Kent but in two seconds he'd dropped the stick from vertical to horizontal, the end with the spider poking out of the window. Once it hit the great outdoors the spider didn't need any encouragement, practically leaping to its freedom.

Kent pulled the stick inside and took two strides to the window, pulling it shut. 'There. Happy now?' he asked as he turned around.

Sadie felt a sudden release of tension from her neck muscles as relief buzzed through her system. She might even have smiled had not her thong been dangling from the curtain rail just behind his head. It made her aware of their state of undress. Of his ripped naked chest. Of his perfect mouth surrounded by fascinating stubble.

Of how it would feel to kiss him.

She nodded instead, focusing only on him. 'Thank you,' she said, one hand at her throat, the other still clutching her clothes. 'I'll be able to sleep easy now.'

Kent grunted. With a vision of her in that towel and a pink thong, he certainly wouldn't be.

He walked out of the bathroom, brushing past her on the way out. 'Just get dressed, Sadie Bliss,' he muttered and headed back to his beer.

When Sadie emerged from the bathroom a couple of minutes later the television was on and Kent was reclining against the bed head, still in just his jeans, his feet bare. Both his legs were out in front of him, his right ankle crossed over the left. He held his beer tucked close to his body, resting against his groin area. He was channel surfing.

He turned the volume down a little but deliberately didn't look at her as he said, 'I can turn it off if it's going to keep you awake.'

She shook her head, ignoring the nice delineation of abdominal muscles and the fascinating trail of hair bisecting them. 'No, it's fine. I sleep like a log.'

Sadie lifted her backpack to the ground and pulled back the sheets. Uncaring that her hair was wet and tomorrow it would be a wild tangle, she slipped between them, enjoying their fresh clean feel and smell. Not even the rock-hard mattress spoilt the moment.

She half moaned, half sighed. 'God, that feels good.'

Kent, still looking resolutely at the television screen didn't bother to reply. It was bad enough her low moan completely destroyed his concentration.

'Night,' she said, pulling the sheets up to her chin, rolling away from him as she obeyed the dictates of her brain to shut her eyes and sleep.

Kent took a swig of his beer. He couldn't believe that anyone could just fall instantly asleep. He turned his head to look at her, the steady rise and fall of the sheet seeming to indicate that Sadie Bliss could.

How he envied her that. He hadn't had a decent night's sleep since the accident. Before that even. Living in war zones was not conducive to the recommended eight hours. And these days he barely got by on four or five.

A knock heralded the arrival of his food and he was grateful for something to do to fill up the long hours ahead.

Kent was relieved when Sadie finally moved five hours later. He was beginning to wonder if she'd lapsed into a coma. If it weren't for her regular deep breathing and the occasional soft, snuffly snore, he'd have checked her pulse hours ago.

He, on the other hand, was still well and truly awake. He'd eaten his steak, drunk two more beers, ordered them some breakfast on a card he'd hung on the outside doorknob, gone through his camera gear again, fiddled with the air-conditioning thermostat several times trying to find a happy medium and consulted the map at least half a dozen times.

He'd watched some B-grade movie and reruns of eighties sit-coms for hours. And now he was flicking between channels, avoiding the twenty-four-hour news stations in favour of twenty-four-hour infomercials.

Sadie flopping onto her back was a welcome distraction. Her head had rolled his way, the light flickering from the television throwing her face into interesting relief. Her skin looked even paler in the glow and long shadows fell on her cheeks from her eyelashes. Her delectable full mouth also eerily pale in the ghostly television glow seemed pursed as if ready for action.

His gaze drifted down. The sheet had ridden low exposing her T-shirt. Her perfectly plain, high-necked, nothing remotely provocative T-shirt. Hell, she was even wearing a bra! But that didn't obscure the fascinating bloom of her breasts, large and round and perfect, tenting the shirt, stretching it across their expanse. His eyes followed the line of the shirt as it fell again towards the flat of her ribs and the slight rise of her belly and he could just make out a thin strip of creamy skin before the sheet covered the rest of her.

His gaze drifted up again as he contemplated what she'd look like without the shirt. And the sheet. Would her nipples be pale too, like the rest of her, or would they be darker, closer to the colour of her mouth?

What would they taste like?

His groin stirred.

Then she moved, murmured something unintelligible, flung an arm above her head.

Kent looked away hurriedly.

What the hell was the matter with him? Perving on a woman whilst she slept? Imagining her naked. Like some oversexed teenager? Like some perverted stalker.

The number of things that were wrong with this scenario bought him to his feet. He rummaged through his bag, found some shorts and a T-shirt, dragged his shoes back on, grabbed the room key and headed out of the door.

Unlike Sydney, which never seemed to sleep, Cunnamulla at one in the morning was deserted. Nothing was open, no lights were on, no traffic rattled by as Kent launched himself into the cool night air with vigour. He pounded the pavements of the sleepy little town for an hour with only the occasional bark from a dog for company.

The physio had recommended he started light jogging as soon as the orthopod had cleared him five months ago and, like everything he did in life, Kent adopted it with gusto. It had helped to strengthen his right ankle significantly but it had also been a useful tool to cope with his insomnia. The accompanying exhaustion usually resulted in good quality sleep, unlike the other alternatives—alcohol and pills.

Beer and sleeping tablets certainly got him off to sleep very effectively but it was fitful and haunted by the things he could keep at bay during the day. The cries of Dwayne Johnson begging for his mother. The smell of jet fuel. The searing heat of nearby flames.

He seemed to wake more exhausted than he went to bed. And hung over to boot.

Running was far, far preferable.

Sadie was still sleeping soundly when he let himself back into the room. He barely looked at her as he headed for the bathroom. He shut the door, stripped off his clothes, turned the taps on and stepped into the spray. He closed his eyes, braced his outstretched arms against the wall, dropped his head, letting the water run over his neck for a while.

When he finally lifted his head and opened his eyes, the pink thong hanging from the curtain rail was the first thing he saw.

He turned the cold on full blast.

Sadie woke to a knock at the door at seven o'clock. She opened her eyes. A tray with empty plates, used cutlery and three beer bottles greeted her and beyond that was Kent. He was curled up in his bed, sound asleep. His face was relaxed, his cheekbones not so pronounced, the creases around his mouth smoothed out, his lips slack and innocent rather than distinct and wicked.

He looked much, much younger.

He was still shirtless, the sheet pulled low on his abdomen and twisted around his legs. His right leg from the knee down was exposed and her gaze came to rest on his grossly deformed ankle.

The knock came again and he stirred.

Sadie jumped out of bed. 'Coming,' she called walking past the still flickering television on her way to the door. She opened it to the woman from last night bearing a smile and a tray.

'Good morning,' she chirped. 'Your breakfast.'

'Oh,' Sadie said, taking the laden tray. 'Er, thank you.'

Kent woke to the voices and rolled onto his back. His eyes felt gritty. It had taken another hour of infomercials before he'd finally fallen asleep after his shower, but he was used to having to wake and be instantly ready so he vaulted upright instead.

Sadie backed into the room, pushing the door shut with her foot, and turned around. She met Kent's bleary gaze. 'You ordered this, I assume?'

He nodded. 'Breakfast is the most important meal of the day.' He patted the bed. 'Put it here.'

Sadie plonked it where he indicated. She lifted the metallic covering on one of the plates. A full cooked breakfast greeted her—bacon, eggs, sausages, fried onions, tomatoes, and baked beans.

Her stomach growled at the waft of cooked meat and she started to salivate.

Her fat cells did too.

It looked so damn good. But she knew she couldn't indulge. In just a few shorts days her pants were already looser. And she'd be seeing Leo soon.

She replaced the lid and picked up one of the pieces of perfectly browned toast. 'Thanks,' she said, nibbling at the dry corner.

Kent scrunched his face as he looked up at her. She was wearing some baggy yoga-style pants to go with her baggy T-shirt. It was the unsexiest get-up he'd seen in his life. But even it didn't manage to keep the curvy figure beneath in check.

The curvy figure she was obviously trying to straighten out by depriving it of adequate nutrition. *That was it?* She was just going to eat one piece of dry toast?

'You don't want any more?'

'I never eat much breakfast,' Sadie lied as she bent over slightly and poured herself a cup of tea from the small metal teapot with a leaking lid. 'Usually just need a cuppa and I'm good.'

Her gaze flicked to his momentarily but she quickly looked away. She didn't expect or want him to know about the demons that drove her to this crash diet.

She doubted a he-man of his ilk would understand.

Their enforced proximity was bad enough without laying herself totally bare to him.

Kent watched as she pulled her gaze away and her hair swung back and forth across her shoulders at the activity. It was a tangle of waves this morning. As if she'd spent the night in a wind tunnel.

'And I suppose you're going to eat nothing but celery and salads again today?'

Sadie sat cross-legged on her bed, facing the television. A news show was on. 'Carrots, actually,' she said primly.

Kent stared at her for a moment, then shook his head. He was on a road trip with a rabbit. He'd never understood women who obsessed over what they perceived to be every figure flaw and every calorie they shoved in their mouths. He'd dated his share and they were, without exception, boring.

And Sadie not realising just how gorgeous she looked was nothing short of criminal. Was she anorexic?

Or just screwed up by one too many magazine covers?

Kent eyed the piece of toast that she was nibbling, contemplating his next words carefully because he wanted to say them, to get involved in this juvenile silliness, about as much as he wanted to saw off the top of his head. But maybe she was like this because no one in her life had ever sat her down and told her that she had a smoking-hot body.

Although God alone knew what was wrong with men of her age today—were they blind or just incredibly stupid?

'Look, this is nothing to do with me and you can eat…or not eat… whatever you want but—and I say this with absolutely no disrespect or sexual harassment or icky older-man creepiness in mind—your body is fine.'

Sadie blinked. If that was a compliment it could sure do with some work. And gave her an opportunity to steer the conversation away from what she was and wasn't eating.

'Wow. You really are rusty,' she murmured.

Kent shot her an impatient look. 'I'm not here to stroke your ego, Sadie Bliss.' Or land himself in the middle of a lawsuit.

Or something else entirely inappropriate.

'Well, that's just as well because you'd be failing, Kent Nelson. You do know when you tell a woman her body is *fine* she interprets that as *you're okay but you could look better*, right? Unless, of course, you prefix it. *Mighty* fine or *damn* fine work quite well.'

The sad truth was Sadie knew that none of those prefixes applied. A few years back, when she'd been with Leo, mighty fine had fitted the bill. Now she was just struggling to keep back the tide.

Kent stared at her. Did she really think he gave a rat's arse about the female interpretation of fine? He shook his head. 'I don't suppose you have a clue how very much I *don't* care about the word fine? You do know that there's a whole heap of bad things happening out there in the world, right?' he growled.

'Really?' she snapped, tired of his paternalistic carry-on. 'I hadn't noticed, being a *journalist* and all.'

Kent glared, feeling exasperation rising in his throat threatening to choke him. *Why couldn't women just take a compliment in the spirit it was intended?*

'All I'm trying to say,' he said, swallowing hard against the lump, trying to get the conversation back on track, 'is you really need to eat better. You could get sick.'

Sadie wasn't prepared for such a left-field comment. For a man who obviously thought her figure concerns didn't rate compared to bigger global issues—which of course they didn't—his apparent concern for her was unexpected.

And he did look concerned. It softened the beautiful harshness of his mouth and her mind went blank for a moment as she tried to remember why she was so het up.

She sighed as her brain came back on line. 'Look, I'm fine. I promise. It's just…complicated, okay? And it's really none of your business. So can we please drop it?'

She did not want to get into this with a man as accomplished as Kent. How could he possibly understand what was personally at stake for her over seeing Leo again? How much she had to prove.

Kent held her gaze, the appeal luminous in her large grey eyes. Her *back the hell off* polite considering their recent exchange.

Complicated he understood.

And she was right, it wasn't his business. And what did he care if some crazy chick in well-to-do Australia chose to forgo food that millions of women would lay down their lives for just so they could feed their children for a few more days?

'Sure,' he agreed, pulling the metal covering off his cooked breakfast as he inhaled the rich aroma of meat and onions. Sadie Bliss was a transient connection in his life. If she chose to starve, then so be it. He sure as hell wasn't.

He'd been in too many places where food was scarce to not appreciate the bounty in front of him.

He picked up his fork and tucked in.

Sadie resolutely tried to ignore Kent annihilating his coronary-bypass plate with gusto. But it smelled so damn good it was hard to concentrate on anything else. Add to that his naked chest and it was a regular double feature. She tried to follow the news programme but what was going on in her peripheral vision was much more interesting.

After a while, though, she became aware of something else. Kent, eating with one hand, gently massaging his injured ankle with the other. He seemed engrossed alternately in his meal and the television so she didn't think he was even aware he was doing it.

She slid surreptitious looks his way. The ankle looked pretty smashed up and the top of his foot had a chunk missing, a smooth shiny piece of bright pink skin lay over top as if it had been grafted. He looked her way and caught her watching.

She held his gaze. 'Does it hurt?' she asked.

Kent frowned for a moment, wondering what she was talking about, then realised he was rubbing his ankle. He'd overdone it slightly with the run and it was suffering a little this morning.

Normally he would have told her to mind *her* business but her simple enquiry caught him off guard. Too often people asked him what had happened, pried and pushed for all the gory details.

But not Sadie Bliss.

She'd simply asked him if it hurt.

He looked down at the foot he'd come so close to losing on several occasions, his fingers massaging the ridged scar tissue, the dips and planes of the deformed joint. 'It aches sometimes.' He shrugged. 'It's just habit really.'

Sadie nodded. Weren't they all just creatures of habit?

CHAPTER FOUR

'So, WHERE TO today?' Sadie asked as she vaulted up into the passenger seat an hour later.

The roads, now they were hitting the outback proper, tended to be long stretches of straight with very few curves or bends so she figured she was safe to take the passenger seat again.

'Mt Isa,' Kent said as he pulled out of the hotel car park. 'It's about thirteen hours. That'll leave only a nine-ish-hour drive tomorrow to Borroloola.'

Sadie nodded. 'I'll give Leo a ring from the hotel tonight and let him know to expect us.'

Kent quirked an eyebrow. 'Leo?'

Sadie mentally chastised herself for the slip. But she smiled at Kent calmly and said, 'Mr Pinto.'

Kent wasn't buying it. 'Leo's very...familiar,' he pushed. 'I hear he's only Leo to his friends.'

Sadie looked out of the window as they left the last of Cunnamulla behind. 'Is he?'

Kent considered her deliberate evasion, intrigued despite himself. Which was just as well. Seeing that thong last night had tripped some kind of switch in his head. And he didn't like where it was taking him. Maybe the Pinto/Bliss conundrum would give him something else to think about other than Sadie oozing curves and sex all over the passenger seat.

'Thirteen hours is a long time to stay silent, Sadie Bliss. I bet you can't even manage two.'

Sadie looked back at him, ignoring his deliberate baiting. 'Why do you say my name like that?' she diverted.

'What? Sadie Bliss?'

She listened as he said it again, rolling it around his tongue like a particularly delicious morsel. She imagined what that tongue could do to certain parts of her anatomy and muscles deep in her belly went into free fall.

He shrugged. 'Sensational byline. Very rockstar. Is it real?'

Sadie rolled her eyes at the familiarity of the question. 'Yes. Just like my boobs and my lips it's one hundred per cent real.'

Kent flicked a glance at her. She was glaring at him with exasperation. 'Okay, okay,' he said because, no matter what, there wasn't one iota of that conversation he was going anywhere near.

Sadie deliberately ticked down the minutes until two hours were up before turning to Kent and yanking on his ear bud.

'Let's make a deal,' she said.

Kent raised an eyebrow. 'Bet that was the longest two hours of your life.'

'Nope. Two minutes in a bathroom with a mutant spider was much longer.'

'Okay, so let's see if we can go another two, shall we?' he suggested as he located his swinging ear bud.

Sadie shook her head. 'We're not going to sit here all day and not talk to each other again.'

Kent flicked a glance at her, then back at the road. 'We're not?'

Sadie shook her head. 'It's ridiculous.'

Kent shrugged. 'It was working for me.'

She folded her arms. 'Have I mentioned how very annoying I can be when I set my mind to it?'

Kent didn't doubt it. He remembered how she'd harped on about the spider last night until he'd hunted the poor thing from the room. 'You mean you haven't set it already?'

She ignored him. 'We'll just agree on a subject and stick to the boundaries of it.'

He eyed her warily. 'Like what?'

She shrugged. 'How about starting at the beginning? Our childhoods?'

Kent considered it for a moment. It was a safe topic. No skeletons to hide. It could be a good trade for some peace and quiet. He reached for a packet of potato chips he had left over from yesterday. 'Okay,' he agreed, opening them as he drove along. 'But then I get silence for the rest of the day.'

Sadie shook her head, ignoring the aroma of carbohydrates, leaning forward to grab the carrot sticks she'd chopped earlier. 'For another two hours,' she bargained.

Kent tapped his fingers on the wheel. 'Mid-afternoon.'

'Lunchtime,' she returned without even taking a breath.

'After lunch,' he clarified.

Sadie considered it for a moment. It was better than nothing. She nodded at him and then launched straight into it. 'So, what's the Kent Nelson story?'

Kent kept his eyes trained on the road as he munched on chips. 'Not a lot to tell.'

She laughed at that and Kent blinked as he realised he hadn't heard it before. Her laughter was deep and throaty and he found himself utterly intrigued. It wasn't tittery or tinkly or musical like so many of the women he knew. It was full roar, like the rest of her. So few people, especially the places he'd been, laughed with every fibre of their being.

But Sadie Bliss did.

It was strangely soothing in the cocoon of the cab.

'Right,' she said. 'Of course not. World renowned, multi-award-winning photojournalist who's been in every war zone on the planet in the last decade. But nothing here to see, folks, move along?'

'Okay, how about not a lot I want to talk about?'

Sadie regarded him for a moment. His jaw was clenched just beneath his cheekbone, his brow was scrunched. 'We made a deal,' she reminded him.

'Oh, well, in that case...'

She didn't miss the sarcasm in his arid tone but she wasn't going to be put off by it either. 'Tell me about your parents. I'd appreciate a tale of divorce and woe if you have one?'

Kent glanced at her to gauge her sincerity. She seemed fairly matter-of-fact. ''Fraid not. Two parents, both still together and very much in love. An older sister. Standard Australian suburban upbringing.'

Sadie liked the sound of that. 'They must be proud of you,' she murmured.

He shrugged. 'Worried mostly.'

The minute he'd taken off for the Middle East over a decade ago his family had worried. He didn't know how many times his mother had called the foreign affairs department if he missed a scheduled call in, but he was pretty sure she had a direct line at one stage.

And then, since the accident, they'd been even more concerned.

'I suppose you were an angelic child,' Sadie mused. 'Straight As. House captain. School newspaper. Valedictorian.'

Kent burst out laughing. He couldn't help it. She was so far wide of the target she was practically off the page. 'No. I think my mother once described me to one of my many school principals, in my presence, as a horrible little shit.'

Sadie blinked. At the admission and his laughter. It was just as delicious as last night. Low and easy, it transformed the spare planes of his face into a pallet of lines and creases. It softened his mouth and twinkled in his eyes. 'And were you?'

He glanced at her. 'Guilty as charged.'

Sadie wasn't quite sure what to say. He certainly didn't look contrite. He'd just described an idyllic childhood—one she would have killed for. What on earth had motivated him to behave in such a way that his own mother would disparage him?

'Because they didn't understand you and you were trying to prove something or some other lame excuse that horrible little boys make to justify their behaviour?' she asked sweetly.

Kent laughed again but it was more brittle. 'No. I guess I just always craved adventure. Wanted to know what was beyond the end of my street. Outside my town. Over the sea. On the other side of the world. I'm afraid I became a bit of a hell raiser as I chafed against the bonds of my perfectly nice, domesticated, suburban life.'

Somehow Sadie could imagine that. Especially with the whole buzz cut and bristles he had going on. It seemed more in line with the whole *he-man* thing than the safe middle-class life he'd just described.

'So you what? Broke some rules, got caught shoplifting, maybe smoking behind the bike sheds? Some trouble with the cops?' She snuck a look at him. 'Caught a venereal disease?'

Kent almost choked at her suggestions. 'Hell, no,' he spluttered.

'No to the venereal disease?' she asked innocently.

He pierced her with a quelling look. 'No to any of them.'

'Well, what then?' she demanded.

Kent looked back to the road as Sadie's mouth pouted the question at him. 'I wagged school. Constantly. Spent my time at the arcade or swimming at the local creek. I did crazy things like jumping off buildings and sticking my hand into an ants' nest and climbing to the top of an electricity pylon.'

Sadie blinked. 'Why would you do those things?'

Kent looked at her. 'Because someone dared me to.'

'Oh.'

She'd never really understood boys. She hadn't had a brother—or not one that she'd known as she was growing up anyway. And her father had always seemed a bit of a mystery to her. The same went for the men she'd dated. Even the ones she'd slept with. She'd understood them as sexual beings but the rest was a mystery.

Even Leo, probably the least he-man guy she'd ever known, had this stubborn male pride about him.

Ego, she supposed some psychologists would call it.

'They sound kind of dangerous.'

Kent nodded, his eyes fixed on the road. 'I always had something in plaster. My poor mother became an expert at taking out stitches. A couple of times she even threatened to put them in herself, with no local anaesthetic.'

'Maybe she should have?' Sadie suggested.

He chuckled. 'I do believe my father proposed it on several occasions.'

'So...rattling around in war zones? That took care of the adventure cravings?' she asked. She was pushing it but it was a natural segue and he finally seemed conducive to being pushed.

'Yes.' Kent sobered a little as he realised he'd answered a question that had strayed off topic.

'Are you going back?' she asked.

There was a beat where he looked as if he was going to answer her and Sadie held her breath. Then he reached into his chip packet, pulled one out and tossed it into his mouth.

He glanced at her. 'How do you know Leo?'

Sadie gave him a grudging smile. He'd retreated back behind his line. And she had absolutely no intention of coming out from behind hers.

They were back to the beginning again.

An hour later Kent pulled the vehicle into a petrol station to stock up on more calorie-laden essentials. They'd passed that time in silence again, his MP3 player firmly plugged into his ear canals.

He hadn't asked her any questions about her childhood and Sadie felt a little miffed.

Surely he was a little interested in *her* childhood?

'I bought extra,' Kent announced as he dumped a plastic bag between them.

She was wearing pretty much the same type of outfit as yesterday—cut-offs and a loose polo shirt. He wasn't quite sure what she was trying to achieve in denying her curves the artistic outlet they deserved but he'd hate to see them starved into oblivion.

Sadie shot him a sweet smile through gritted teeth as the vehicle got back onto the highway. 'Imagine my surprise,' she said as she bit into a carrot stick with a loud crunch.

Of course the crunch of breaking wafer biscuit as he bit into a chocolate bar was far more satisfying. Especially followed by a waft of something sweet.

Chocolate?

Sugar...

A smear of caramel clung to that beautiful full lower lip and Sadie turned away from the decadent scene. Kent Nelson eating a chocolate bar should come with an obscenity warning!

She munched on a handful of carrots sticks and ignored him for a while. They staved off the grumbles but were hardly satisfying. Kent licking his lips in her peripheral vision did not help.

'So, you want to hear my story now?' she asked.

Kent didn't look at her as he shook his head. 'Not really.'

Sadie blinked at his rejection. The implication that she wasn't remotely interesting stung. And besides, she needed to keep him talking, not least of all because the silence was driving her crazy. 'But you told me yours.'

He shrugged. 'I like hearing mine.'

Narcissist. 'It's only polite to listen to the other person's story, you know? It's called conversation.'

Kent eyeballed her. 'I don't suppose there's any way you're letting this drop, is there?'

Sadie gave her head a firm shake. 'Nope.'

He took a deep breath. *Fine.* 'So tell me, how was it growing up? Blissful?'

Sadie ignored the wisecrack. It wasn't as if she hadn't heard it before. She looked out of her window at the dry yellow-green scenery flashing by. 'Not so much, as it turned out. My dad up and left when I was twelve and got himself a new family. With his secretary. Spreading the bliss…as you do.'

Kent whistled. 'Ouch.'

Sadie nodded. Ouch all right. She still remembered the day he'd left. Coming home from school to her mother crying. Trying to comprehend what had happened. That her father had been so unhappy he'd left her. Just walked away. The years of trying to hold onto him, trying to make him love her all for nothing.

'Do you have a relationship with him?'

'Of sorts,' she murmured. 'I have two half-brothers. Twins. I see them, ergo I see him.'

Kent thought about how close he was with his own father. 'That seems kind of…distant.'

'Well… I never really quite measured up. He was a bit of a jock who'd wanted a boy. Someone he could take to the footy and the cricket. And—' she lifted a shoulder '—he got me. Who liked to read. And draw. And daydream. I'm afraid I was a bit of a disappointment. I spent a lot of years trying to be who he wanted me to be but I never quite got there and then the twins came along and…'

Kent nodded. 'He had someone to take to the footy.'

Bingo. 'Yes.'

Not even the engine of the Land Rover, loud by modern standards, could drown out the wistful note in Sadie's voice. 'And your mother?'

'Mum's great. She's been a rock. Through everything. She could have become bitter, but she wasn't. She just got a part-time job and supported me in everything I wanted to do. When I went to art college she took on a second job to pay my tuition.'

Kent looked at her. 'Art college?'

Sadie nodded as she transferred her attention back to the blur of the outback. 'I wanted to be an artist for a while.'

She shook her head even as she said it. What had she been thinking?

Kent flicked his gaze to the road, then back to her. 'What medium?'

Sadie ironed the flat of her palms down the fabric of her fake cammo cut-offs. 'Painting.'

'What happened?'

She twined a finger into her hair. *I met Leo.* 'I wasn't really that talented.' She shrugged. 'I dropped out.'

Became someone else's muse instead.

Kent frowned at her nonchalance. There was a hell of a lot more to that story!

None of which he wanted to know.

'So you became a journo? A bit different from painting, surely?'

'Not really. I paint my pictures with words now. I like it. I like the facts of it, the clearly defined boundaries. Art is all about interpretation. You must know that,' she said dismissively, looking up at him. 'Reporting deals in definites, in absolutes. I like the structure.'

She did. She really did.

Art for her had been a double-edged sword. So tied in with her emotions, her well-being, it had been hard to separate out. It had felt like possession.

Which was, as Leo had pointed out, insane when her talent didn't justify it.

It had certainly destroyed her relationship with him.

'Don't you miss the creativity?'

Sadie shook her head. 'Words are creative,' she countered.

Kent shot her a *come-on-now* look. 'You know what I mean.' He'd thought for a long time he never wanted to get behind a camera again, but the urge had returned with gusto.

Sadie sighed, fixing her gaze on distant hills. 'Painting took over my life. Or rather striving to be good enough took over my life.' Leo had been a hard taskmaster when she'd gone to live with him and trying to get it right had been impossible. 'I'm afraid if I took it up again I'd be back in that place. I don't think I can have one without the other.'

'Well, that sounds intense,' he murmured.

'Trust me—' she grimaced '—it was.'

Kent's fingers tightened around the wheel. 'Did you paint nudes?' he asked, wondering suddenly if that was where the Pinto puzzle pieces fitted.

Sadie pulled her gaze off the horizon, not that far gone that she didn't recognise he'd moved her into dangerous territory.

'Where should we stop for lunch, do you think?' she asked, pulling the map out of the glovebox.

They stopped for lunch at a truck stop near Blackall. Sadie ate a ham and salad roll but discarded the bun. Kent watched as she leaned forward slightly when his hamburger with beetroot and a fried egg arrived as if she was trying to absorb its mouth-watering aroma. He was also aware of her gaze as he brought it to his mouth and chomped into the juicy delight.

When the waitress delivered his lamington and large caramel thick shake to the table he thought he almost heard her whimper before she stood abruptly.

'I'll wait for you by the car,' she said.

Kent watched her go. Her wavy hair swung between her shoulder blades, her shirt hung loose around her waist and bottom, completely concealing everything down to the backs of her thighs. But every time she moved those curves moved with her and there wasn't one trucker in the joint that didn't watch her sway out of the door.

He continued to watch her through the glass sliding doors as she walked out into the heat of the midday sun and strolled towards the vehicle. She looked up at a massive road train semi-trailer thundering past. The guy driving was hanging out his window, leering and yelling something at Sadie.

Kent wasn't an expert lip-reader but he did pretty well with body language so he figured that when Sadie flipped the bird, the trucker had probably suggested she flash him a certain part of her anatomy.

He sucked the last of the thick icy shake up his straw and watched his fellow diners, who were looking wistfully at Sadie no doubt wishing that she'd complied with the lewd request.

The woman was a walking, talking hourglass. Why was she so hell-bent on straitjacketing her assets? Why did she want to starve them into submission?

Kent stood, throwing a tip on the table.

It was none of his bloody business.

Halfway between Barcaldine and Longreach they blew a tyre. Sadie was in a deep sleep when Kent's curse woke her.

'What's up?' she asked as he pulled off onto the side of the highway.

'Got a flat.' He turned off the engine. 'Sit tight. I'll have it fixed in a jiffy.'

Sadie blinked as lingering sleepiness tugged at her eyelids. Broken sleep made her irritable and his *he-man* condescension grated. 'What makes you think I can't have it done in a jiffy?' she grouched as he opened his door. 'I am perfectly capable of changing a tyre, you know?'

Kent raised his hands in surrender. 'You want to do it? Knock yourself out. I'm all for women's lib.'

If she wanted to get hot and dirty he wasn't going to stop her. Of course, she wouldn't be able to undo the wheel nuts but it might be fun watching her try.

Sadie jumped down to the ground and looked around. The scenery hadn't changed much for hours. Flat, dry, brittle pastures with the slightest tinge of green. And lots of sheep. It was quiet out here apart from the occasional rattle of a passing car.

'Where are we?' she asked when she joined him to look at the shredded back passenger tyre.

''Bout half an hour out of Longreach,' he said, kicking the flat in disgust. He'd put four new tyres on the vehicle before coming away. 'We'll get the tyre repaired there.'

He walked to the back and opened the doors. Sadie helped him move their gear onto the ground so he could access the spare tyre.

'How long will that take?' Making this trip any longer wasn't particularly thrilling.

'Hopefully they'll be able to do it for us straight away. Maybe a delay of an hour?' He located the wheel brace and handed it to her. 'Why don't you get started while I grab the spare?'

Sadie saw the challenge in his eyes and gave him a triumphant smile. A man who'd always wanted a son had been a useful person to have around when she was learning to drive—Sadie had changed many a tyre, thanks to her father.

She approached the job with a spring in her step. It would be good to teach *he-man* that she was a little more than a neurotic, food-obsessed girly.

And it was a perfect plan until she hit the first hurdle. None of the wheel nuts would budge. When Kent brought the spare around she was cursing and muttering under her breath, practically standing on the brace trying to shift one of the stubborn nuts.

'Would you like a hand?' he asked innocently.

She glared at him. 'Why on earth are these on so tight? You'd need to be Popeye on steroids to get them undone.'

He grinned. 'They tighten the nuts with a machine.'

'Well, that seems kind of stupid, doesn't it, if people can't get them off?'

He nodded, trying to be serious. 'Of course, maybe if you'd eaten a burger for lunch you might be feeling stronger.'

'I would have to have eaten an entire side of beef to be strong enough to take these suckers off.' She thrust the brace at him in disgust. 'Looks like it's a job for *he-man*.'

Kent suppressed the urge to cough at her forceful handing over of the tool. 'Step aside.'

Sadie watched, her pride soothed as Kent had to use significant grunt to shift the nuts. Still, he made pretty short work of the tyre change and was cleaning off greasy hands in less than fifteen minutes.

He had sweat and grease on his forehead and the testosterone cloud emanating from him was making her dizzy. She opened the back passenger door and handed him a bottle of cold water from the supply in the camp-fridge.

'Thanks,' Kent said, twisting the lid and guzzling half in one swallow before pouring some over his head.

Sadie's gaze followed rivulets of water as they trekked over the contours of his face, his mouth and down the tanned column of his neck.

She reached in and grabbed one for herself.

A breeze lifted her hair as she slaked her thirst and put out a few fires south of her throat. Lusting after Kent was just plain counterproductive. She had a job to do here and it didn't have anything to do with her sexy photographer.

She didn't need another complication.

Leo was complicated enough.

She lounged back against the vehicle, ignoring Kent, who was doing the same. She looked out over the outback vista instead. It seemed flat all the way to the horizon, interrupted only by the odd clump of trees and the occasional fence. The only population appeared to be sheep and the odd passing car.

There was something soothing about the isolation.

In the distance she saw the beginning of something that looked like a brown dust cloud barrelling along close to the ground and parallel with the road. 'What's that?' she asked.

Kent squinted to where she was pointing. It was too far away to see properly but, given that it was travelling at a rate of knots, it wouldn't be long before it was passing by. 'Not sure,' he said, reaching into the back passenger foot well and removing his camera bag.

He pulled out his camera, clicked on the zoom lens and looked through it. He smiled as the cloud took form and shape.

'Emus,' he announced.

Sadie stared as the cloud came closer and she could just make out individual figures. 'So it is,' she murmured. 'Wow, look at them go!'

A flock of about a dozen of the large, flightless birds was running helter-skelter, their powerful legs eating up the paddock, their feet kicking up dirt and dust, their soft feathers bouncing with each foot fall. As they got closer still Sadie counted ten of them.

Even with them way out in the paddock when they passed by, they were a magnificent sight. 'Where are they going?' she mused out loud.

'Who knows?' Kent shrugged as he snapped off a series of pictures. 'But they're in a hurry.'

They'd no sooner drawn nearer then they were past. 'That was amazing,' Sadie said, watching the cloud get smaller and smaller. 'I've never seen emus in the wild.'

He tisked. 'City chick,' he muttered as he continued to click away.

Sadie watched him as he peered through the lens—focused, centred. It reminded her of the picture she'd seen of him in New York, where the camera had seemed an extension of him. He stood, his whole body engaged in the process, as if he'd been born with a camera.

'When did you know you wanted to take pictures for a living?'

Kent ignored her, snapping until the birds were no longer distinguishable. When he pulled the camera away from his face he looked down at Sadie. His first instinct was to shut her down, as he had been doing, but the camera felt good in his hand, the pictures he'd just taken felt right and he remembered the first time so vividly.

'I was sixteen. My grandfather took me on a road trip to the Red Centre during the school holidays. His camera was ancient but it took amazing images.'

Sadie thought how nice it would have been to have had a grandparent in her life. 'That was nice of him,' she mused.

Kent snorted. 'I think my mother was at the end of her tether and Grandad feared there would be bloodshed. I think he was just trying to save his daughter's sanity.'

He smiled, remembering that momentous trip. How it had changed his life.

He put the camera to his face again and scanned the broad canvas before him. 'There was something about the light out there,' he said. 'The contrasting colours. I was hooked.'

Sadie watched him peering through his lens. 'I bet your mother was relieved,' she murmured.

Kent gave a short sharp laugh as he lowered the camera. 'Hell, yeah. She signed me up for a photography course as soon as I got back.'

Sadie sucked in a breath at the smile that transformed the harsh planes of his face. He really ought to do it more often. 'And you never gave her a spot of bother again?' she predicted.

He nodded. He had knuckled down. Once he'd found his calling he'd put his all into achieving his goal. 'Essentially,' he agreed as he returned his camera to its bag in the back of the car. 'The war zone thing kind of freaked her out.'

Sadie nodded. 'Mums worry. That's their job, I guess.'

Her mother had worried about her too. About how she'd tried so hard to be the boy her father wanted. Tried even harder to be the woman Leo wanted. She'd been especially concerned at Sadie's obsession with her figure.

Kent looked down at the pensive look on her face. She seemed to have gone somewhere far away, a little frown knitting her brows together, her teeth torturing that perfect bottom lip.

'Come on,' he said, stepping back from her. And her mouth. 'We better get this show on the road if we want to get to Mt Isa before this day is over.'

They got to Mt Isa at eleven that night after a couple of stops for photos. They'd passed the hours with minimal conversation despite Sadie's best efforts.

'How are you feeling?' Kent asked as he pulled into a petrol station. 'Tired?'

Sadie shook her head. Strangely she wasn't. Driving through the eerily flat landscape on a cloudless, practically moonless night had been weirdly energising. As if she were in a spaceship, floating through the cosmos.

'You want to see if we can make the Northern Territory border? It's another couple of hours but it'll cut the trip down tomorrow. We can pull off to the side of the road and catch a few hours' kip before moving on.'

Sadie regarded him for a minute. 'Pull over? And where do we sleep?'

'I'll take my swag up to the roof of the vehicle and sleep under the stars. You can doss down on the back seat if you like.'

She pursed her lips. 'Camping, huh?'

Kent shot her a derisive look. 'I'd hardly call it that. But it's something you should try at least once in your life.'

Sadie looked at him. At his mouth.

Her, him and a billion stars.

And his mouth.

'Okay.'

CHAPTER FIVE

'ARE YOU COMING up or not?'

Sadie stood with her hands on the bull bar as an outback night stretched dark and mysterious like a lucky eight ball above her head.

It was one a.m. and they were pulled over near the dust-encrusted sign that announced their entry into the Northern Territory. It was chilly and she shivered.

'Are you sure it's okay to walk on your car? Won't it get dinged?'

Kent shut his eyes, blocking out the pinpricks of light twinkling down at him. 'If it was one of those modern four-wheel drives, sure. But this thing wasn't built to crumple. It was built to deflect.'

Sadie eyed the bonnet dubiously even though she knew how sturdy it was from the way it handled. Walking on a car just didn't seem right.

'By my reckoning I have you by a good twenty-five to thirty kilos, Sadie Bliss, and it didn't buckle under my weight. Unless of course you want to stay on the ground there and fend off the spiders.'

Sadie's pulse spiked as she leapt onto the bull bar. Her gaze flicked from side to side. 'There are spiders?'

Kent opened his eyes and grinned at the strained note in her voice. 'Probably a few scorpions too, I'd say.'

Sadie shuddered. 'Now, see, this is why I don't camp. There aren't any scorpions at five-star hotels,' she griped.

'There aren't any up here either,' he said, too tired for hysterics.

Sadie flicked her gaze from the ground to the roof of the car where she could just make out the outline of Kent's body encased in his swag. 'Think I'll just use the back seat,' she said, even though the thought of having to put her foot to the ground was creeping her out.

'Up to you. But, just so you know, you're missing out on a truly spectacular experience.' The celestial display was utterly dazzling and Kent wished he'd brought his camera up with him. 'It'll blow your mind, city girl.'

Sadie rolled her eyes and muttered, 'Yeah, yeah, that's what they all say,' under her breath. Except sound travelled exceptionally well through a still outback night and she blushed when she heard Kent chuckle.

'Okay,' she announced in a louder voice as she hauled herself onto the bonnet. 'But I'm going to want my money back if you're getting me up there under false pretences.'

Kent saluted. 'Money-back guarantee.'

Sadie kicked off her ballet flats and felt the warmth of the engine heat her cool toes as she clamoured gingerly to her feet. She gave a slight bounce, testing the strength of the metal beneath, satisfied to feel absolutely no give whatsoever.

She scrambled up the windscreen, hanging onto the sturdy metal rungs welded to the roof completely enclosing it. *At least she wouldn't roll off the roof in her sleep!* She rather inelegantly hauled herself up over the top and crawled on her hands and knees towards Kent and her swag.

She didn't look at him as she climbed into her bedding and zipped it up to her chin. She squeezed her eyes shut tight, hoping that she could block him and their sleeping arrangement out altogether. She was immediately cocooned in fleecy warmth, tiredness injecting instant fatigue into her marrow. She moved around for a bit attempting to find a comfortable spot, thankful for the swag's padded lining on the unforgiving metal rooftop.

'Will you stop wriggling,' Kent grumbled. He was actually feeling tired and there was something soothing about being outdoors. He planned on taking full advantage.

Sadie stopped moving and opened her eyes as the illusion that she wasn't on a car rooftop in the middle of the night, in the middle of nowhere, with a virtual stranger was completely obliterated by his gruff command.

And then a billion stars and a crescent moon took over and everything else melted away.

They had stars in Sydney. She'd often been out on the harbour at night and had them twinkle down at her, but somehow they just hadn't been able to compete with the ones twinkling from the buildings that made up Sydney's iconic skyline.

Not so tonight.

Tonight a New Year's Eve fireworks display would have paled in comparison.

The inky blackness blazed and dazzled as the lights from billions of stars glowed seemingly just for her. They crowded each other out, a black and white kaleidoscope, and on the roof of the car in the vast nothingness of the outback night, where the line between heaven and earth didn't exist, Sadie felt as if she could just reach up and pluck one from the cosmos.

Looking up, she suddenly understood how Van Gogh must have felt when he'd painted his famous starry French sky.

She breathed out. 'Wow.'

'Indeed,' Kent agreed, staring into the inky dome with her. 'You want your money back now?'

Sadie shook her head slowly. 'They're like...diamonds or crystals or teardrops or...something... I don't have the words.'

Kent grimaced. Unfortunately he did. They were the diamanté on Sadie's pink thong.

All trillion of them.

Winking down at him.

'Wow,' he murmured, trying to divert his thoughts from her underwear. 'Sadie Bliss lost for words. Somebody call a doctor.'

Sadie smiled as her gaze roamed the sky. 'Shut up, Kent Nelson. You're ruining the moment.'

Kent chuckled. 'I'll make a camper out of you yet.'

Sadie ignored him as a sudden revelation dawned. She might not be able to find the words but she knew exactly how she could express the swell of emotion swirling inside her. The urge to paint, to replicate what she saw on canvas, flowed through her on a surge of energy that fizzed and bubbled in her veins like a slug of Moët.

She hadn't felt it in a long time. Not since Leo had told her she'd only been awarded the scholarship to the London Art College because the director owed him a favour.

'Don't you want to take a picture of it?' she said quietly, not wanting to disturb the preternatural hush of the sleeping outback.

Kent glanced at her, surprised by the awe, the emotion in her voice. Her lips were slightly parted, the waning light from the crescent moon laid gentle fingers across the plush pillows.

He nodded as he fixed his gaze firmly heavenward again. 'Yes,' he admitted. 'I'll make sure I get some before the trip ends.'

Sadie wasn't sure how long they lay there just looking at the sky. She'd have never thought a person could actually stargaze and lose track of time. But her fingers were tingling and her mind was buzzing. How could she capture all this? Do it justice?

How could he?

But then she remembered his photograph in the exhibition—its very starkness the key to its power—and knew if anyone could, he could.

She was conscious of him awake beside her. She could hear his breath. Knew somehow that he, too, was looking at the cosmic vista with the eye of a true artist.

'I saw *Mortality*,' she said into the night. 'In New York. A few months back.'

Kent's gaze that had been roaming freely screeched to a halt directly above him. He didn't say anything. He didn't move a muscle. He barely breathed. He hadn't wanted that photo, any of the crash photos, to go public but the families of the men who'd died had specifically requested that they be released. And he hadn't been about to deny them.

Still, he'd had no idea that out of that day forged in hell his photograph of a dying soldier would leave a lasting mark on the world.

It was what every photojournalist dreamed of, he supposed, but it was an honour he could do without.

Sadie turned her head to look at his silent profile. He had one arm flung above him, propping his head a little higher. His mouth was a bleak slash adding to the severity of the rest of his face. His gaze was trained steadfastly above.

'It was…amazing. Did you see how well the gallery had it lit?'

Kent shook his head. 'I never go to my exhibitions.'

Sadie blinked, surprised. As an art student she'd survived on dreams of attending her own exhibitions. 'Well, they did a great job. Although it doesn't need much, does it? It's so…stark. Such a…private image. I had to leave. I couldn't look at it.'

Kent didn't want to talk about the photo. Especially not with a woman whose definition of a hard day was the presence of a rather large spider.

'Goodnight, Sadie Bliss,' he said, rolling away from her.

Then Sadie was staring at his back wishing she'd never said anything at all.

Sadie was momentarily confused when she startled awake some time later, her heart racing. She wasn't sure of the time but the stars were still out in force. She wasn't even sure what had woken her. Then Kent whimpered beside her and she knew.

She raised herself up on her elbow, her pulse still beating madly as he shook his head from side to side in his sleep, baring his gritted teeth. His swag had ridden down exposing his T-shirt-clad chest. His breath sawed in and out, harsh and loud in the stillness of the night.

'Kent?' she murmured.

He didn't respond, still obviously caught somewhere deep and dark inside his head. The same place the shadows came from, no doubt.

'Kent?' she said, louder this time.

Still nothing.

Another distressed little cry came from somewhere at the back of his throat, his face twisting as if he were in physical as well as mental agony, and before she could form a rational thought she was reaching out for him, placing her hand on his chest.

'Shh,' she murmured, rubbing the flat of her palm against his chest, soothing him as she would one of her younger brothers. 'Shh.'

To her surprise, he quietened a little and she continued to gently pat his chest until the creases in his face flattened out, his beautiful mouth relaxed, his breathing settled.

She looked down at him as she absently patted him. What was going on inside his head? Was he reliving the helicopter crash that killed nine of the soldiers he'd been embedded with for almost two months? Was he hearing their cries? Did he see Dwayne Johnson's rosary beads and his grimy tear-streaked face every time he shut his eyes?

She had. For days after leaving the gallery it had played on her mind. And she'd only seen the photograph.

She hadn't been there when it had all gone down.

Had he talked to someone about it? Or didn't *he-men* believe in all that touchy-feely stuff?

Maybe he needed to, though. If he was suffering from PTSD it would be vital, surely? Even *he-men* needed help through such huge life upheavals.

The cool air swirling around her shoulders made her shiver and Sadie collapsed on her side, hunching down a little into her swag, keeping her palm anchored against his chest. She was reluctant to remove it despite Kent's now peaceful slumber. The steady thump of his heartbeat was firm and solid beneath her fingers, his chest expanded evenly and it was curiously reassuring.

Her gaze drifted to his face, relaxed now. She followed the hollows beneath his cheekbones to the beautiful symmetry of his mouth. Even slack with slumber it was utterly fascinating and for the first time in a long time she wished she had her sketch book with her. Once upon a time she'd never have gone anywhere without it.

And tonight with the stars and Kent's mouth she missed it desperately.

Movement in the distance caught her eye and she flicked her gaze just above his face to see the tail end of a shooting star heading towards the inky, barely discernible horizon.

She shut her eyes deciding what to wish upon. It should be something to do with Leo. A wish that he could see she had been a success without him. A wish that maybe he'd still want her. Just a little. That maybe he was still a little in love with her.

That he'd been pining for her.

But strangely on this night that Kent had given her she didn't want it to be about a man who had used her up and thrown her away.

So she wished Kent a dreamless sleep before drifting off herself.

Kent woke slowly to early daylight. The sun was still low and there was a heavy feeling against his chest. He gradually cracked his eyelids open, giving his pupils a chance to adjust.

It was quiet. So quiet. No muffled city traffic waking him. Not even insects to break the eerie morning stillness.

The sky, not yet fully warmed by the sun, was still a soft blue. He turned his head, inspecting the distant horizon. The line where the dome of the heavens met the arc of the earth was still a little hazy in the cool morning air. In an hour, when heat transformed blue sky and red dirt into almost unbearable vibrancy, the line would slash a distinct path between the two.

He looked down at his chest, surprised to find the heaviness there was a hand. Sadie's hand. He turned his head to look at her, his gaze meeting a river of hair, her back to him. He looked down at her hand again. No rings. No fingernail polish. None of those French manicures that every second woman seemed to sport these days. Just neatly trimmed nails, not too short, not too long.

Nothing fancy. Just like the rest of her.

Quite why she had her hand on his chest he wasn't sure. He knew from her loglike sleep in Cunnamulla she wasn't a restless sleeper. So why was she touching him?

And, more importantly, why was he just lying here not doing anything about it?

In the distance he could just make out the noise of a car approaching and as it got closer she started to stir. He froze as Sadie turned, rolled to face him, sighed, licked her gorgeous lips and then settled to sleep again.

All without moving her hand.

He held his breath as the car passed by without waking her and then he was looking right in her face, her plump mouth moist from the swipe of her tongue. The deep red rouge of it, like an apple amongst the creaminess of her complexion, looked lush and kissable. Her eyelashes fell lightly against her cheeks. Her wild wavy hair framing the lot as if she'd just been painted by Rubens himself.

He found himself wishing for his camera again. Wanting to capture the way the gentle morning light enhanced her too wide eyes and her too big mouth into something quite striking.

Wondering if that too big mouth of hers kissed as well as it wisecracked.

If it was as good a lover as it was a talker.

A louder engine roared in the distance just as things beneath the covers started to stir, snapping Kent out of his stupor.

What the hell was he doing?

He sat bolt upright, displacing her hand and waking her in the process.

'Come on, Sadie Bliss,' he said briskly as he kicked out of his swag. 'The day has started and I'm starving.' He ignored her groan. 'Let's hustle.'

An hour later, Sadie left Kent to another disgustingly unhealthy roadhouse breakfast as she headed for the amenities. Yes, she was starving, but she was seeing Leo today and she was doing that with the flattest stomach possible even if it meant depriving herself of food all day.

Plus she needed a shower. Badly.

The facilities were fairly basic and she thanked God she'd thought to bring her own shampoo and conditioner. Her hair was thick and did not take kindly to cheap products.

Still, even with hair products that cost a small fortune, Sadie despaired as she looked into the grimy mirror. She sucked in her cheeks in the vain hope that they'd look like they used to—all hollowed and model-like. She hunched her shoulders to enhance her collarbones. She pirouetted and craned her neck around to try and see if the size of her bum had reduced any in the last few days.

Even the minimiser bra she'd bought especially didn't seem to look as good in the cheap roadhouse lights as it had in the expensive Sydney department store.

If only she'd known about this trip a month ago—she could have at least done something earlier.

She'd spent a lot of the last few years imagining her first meeting with Leo again. How she would look, what she would say, how he would react. And she could already sense the reality and fantasy were hopelessly mismatched.

She'd wanted Leo to weep when he saw her. To rue the day he'd told her to go. To eat his words. Words that had struck right at her very core.

Who's going to want you, Sadie? You're nothing without me.

And she'd wanted to be smoking hot when he did.

She didn't care how vain, how girly that made her. How much it didn't make sense. Leo had worshipped her body, had immortalised it in dozens of his works, and she wanted to show him that she still had it.

That Sadie Bliss was wanted plenty.

She screwed up her nose at her reflection. Could she pull it off?

And what would she do if he crooked that imperious little finger at her? Because despite everything there was still a damaged part of her, the Daddy's girl, that craved his approval.

Sadie dialled the number Tabitha had given her as she made her way across to Kent, who was filling up the vehicle. Her heart was pounding in her chest as it rang in her ear and when it picked up her pulse spiked so quickly she thought she was going to faint.

Which turned out to be unnecessary given that it was Leo's PA who answered the phone. Kevin informed her Leo was painting and not to be disturbed, but that he would pass on the message that the *Sunday On My Mind* reporter was expected by mid afternoon.

'Is that *Leo*?' Kent asked as he returned to the vehicle after paying for the fuel.

She ignored his childish emphasis. 'They're expecting us.'

'Ready to go?'

Sadie nodded absently. As ready as she was ever going to be. No time now for losing some last-minute pounds.

This was the day.

'Your cup of tea is in the dashboard cup-holder,' he said as he swung up into the vehicle.

Sadie buckled up and they got under way. She sipped her tea and ignored her growling stomach and the light-headed feeling making her a little dizzy. She watched out of the window as the flat red earth and occasional scrubby bushland passed by in a blur, her mind preoccupied with seeing Leo again after three years.

Her enthusiasm of the last forty-eight hours to get Kent talking was non-existent today. She didn't even notice the jolts and rattles of the vehicle as it negotiated the far more potholed highway. Her mind was busy and her gut was gradually screwing itself into a tighter and tighter ball.

Kent, however, did notice the jolting and the shaking, particularly in the interesting way it manifested itself. Sadie's chest shifted and bounced in his peripheral vision, totally screwing with his concentration. His initial relief that she wasn't going to be Little Miss Nosey was quickly tempered. At least conversation might have kept his mind on something other than the way her breasts rocked and swayed in rhythm with the vehicle.

After two hours of complete silence from her, Kent couldn't stand it for another moment. Particularly when she was wound as tight as a bow string and frowning enough to give her wrinkles that no amount of youth serum would fix. Her thoughts were so loud he could almost hear them forming.

He gave a slight shake of his head as he opened his mouth to speak, not quite believing that he was the one initiating conversation. 'Penny for them?' he asked.

Sadie frowned as she turned towards his voice. It took a second for his question to register front and centre in her brain. 'Nothing,' she dismissed. 'Just…formulating some questions for the interview.'

'Then why are you frowning so much. He doesn't bite, does he?'

Sadie didn't answer as she thought about Leo's particular brand of scathing wit. Plenty of people had felt the sting of it. He wasn't a man who tolerated fools very gladly.

It was Kent's turn to frown at her silence. 'Does he?' he demanded. Photographing celebrities already felt like a sell-out. He wasn't going to pander to an overinflated ego, no matter how well regarded he was in the art world.

Sadie frowned again. 'What? Oh…no, he doesn't bite.'

Kent cocked an eyebrow. 'So you do know him?'

Sadie pulled her gaze away from the probing reach of his. 'How much longer do you think?'

Kent stood waiting at a petrol station in Borroloola his good foot resting up on the bull bar, a map spread over the red-dust-encrusted bonnet of his vehicle, studying the directions to Leonard Pinto's outback retreat. Sadie had insisted on stopping here even though they'd not long stopped at a roadhouse for lunch.

Well, at least he'd eaten lunch. She'd nibbled on a small apple and hadn't even finished it. But given her little speech from day one about her cast-iron bladder he was surprised she needed to use the bathroom again so soon.

Movement to his left snagged his attention and he turned his head to focus on the woman walking towards him. It took him a beat or two to realise it was Sadie.

He blinked.

She was wearing a dress. A flowing red dress with shoestring straps that showed the tiniest hint of cleavage. It outlined her thighs and fell in a fringed hem just below her knees.

It was hardly revealing, in fact it seemed to just skim everything. To hint but not reveal.

But the way it flowed against her body, moved against her curves, the way the red offset her hair and complemented her mouth and skin was nothing short of a marvel.

She drew level with him and asked, 'Does this look okay?'

Okay?

Kent felt as if he had a few short days ago in Tabitha's office—as if his eyes were poking out on springs. Up close he could see she'd enhanced her eyes a little with some dark kohl, had smeared some gloss on her mouth, big silver hoops hung from her ear lobes. Her raven hair flowed around her shoulders.

She looked like a gypsy and Kent struggled to keep himself from falling under her spell.

'Wow,' was about all he could manage when he realised he hadn't answered her hesitant enquiry. But it seemed to do the trick as a huge grin kicked her crazy big mouth up at the sides.

'Right answer,' she murmured. 'For a moment I thought you were going to say fine.'

He shrugged. 'I *was* toying with mighty fine.'

'Ah,' she smiled. 'You're learning.'

He smiled back. 'I didn't know we had to dress?'

'Just trying to make a good impression,' she quipped as she moved past him to the passenger seat, feeling more confident from Kent's positive reaction.

Kent blinked again. 'That ought to do it,' he muttered under his breath.

He started up the car and pulled out onto the road. The cab was full of a new fragrance. Gone was the smell of earth, diesel fumes, aged leather and axle grease. It smelled like passionfruit and something headier, something that reminded him of sex, and he doubted he'd ever get the aroma out of the upholstery.

Out of his head.

And it irritated him. Largely because he realised he'd spent three whole days not thinking about having sex with Sadie Bliss and now that was all he *could* think about!

Somehow, in such a short time, her smart pouty mouth and treacherous curves had managed to get under his skin.

In his peripheral vision he could see her foot tapping briskly on the floor. Or rather he could see the ripple effects as it vibrated through her thigh and wobbled through her chest.

A thigh and chest he suddenly wished he knew a hell of a lot better.

Damn it. Sadie should have flown. She should have insisted. *He should have insisted.*

Damn Tabitha Fox to hell!

'You seem nervous,' he said, because if he had to watch anything more shift on Sadie Bliss he was going to be the one to make it so.

Sadie jiggled her leg. 'I am.'

'First big interview?'

Sadie shook her head. 'No. I mean yes. It's my first big interview but that's not why I'm nervous.'

'Oh?' Kent continued, pleased to see she'd stopped her infernal jiggling.

Sadie looked at Kent, his eyes fixed on the road, his beautiful mouth a perfect slash in his perfect profile. She was so nervous she wanted to throw up.

So nervous she couldn't keep it to herself any longer. The need to share the burden of it all was upon her suddenly like a big black cloud.

'Leo and I used to be lovers.'

CHAPTER SIX

KENT WAS SO stunned by the admission he didn't see another massive pot-hole until they hit it and they both bounced in their seats as the whole cab rattled and shook. He'd suspected from the beginning she knew Pinto somehow and her *Leo* slip had confirmed it, but never in a million years would he have thought this.

Sadie glanced at Kent as he drove along without a word. *Back to the strong silent type again.* Not something she needed right now. She needed someone to give her a pep talk. To tell her that what happened in the past didn't matter. The clock had been reset and she would be fine.

God, anything would do, anything at all.

She just needed him to say *something*.

'Nothing to say?' she demanded after his continuing silence stretched her nerves to their limit.

Kent glanced at her, his brain still grappling with the bombshell. The number of questions he had probably outnumbered the stars in last night's sky but he wasn't going to get into this with her.

He looked back at the road. What she did with her life was her own concern. It was absolutely nothing to do with him.

He'd known her for three days and it didn't matter that she was sit-ting in his car in a dress that oozed sex or that he wanted to pull over and have his way with her because that was never going to happen. They were doing a job together and when it was done they'd probably never see each other again.

So, she had a thing for older guys. If she wanted to sleep with men twenty years her senior then good luck to her.

Or to them anyway.

'None of my business,' he said, trying not to think about the twelve years that separated them.

Sadie glared at him. Kent's lack of enquiry drove her nuts. She'd spent the last three days foraging for crumbs from him thinking it was just about his privacy, but maybe it was really that he didn't give a damn about anyone else?

'That's it? That's all you've got?'

Kent shrugged. 'Who you've slept with is nothing to do with me.'

'What, no, isn't he a little old for you, Sadie Bliss? Or, how the hell did that come about, Sadie Bliss?'

Kent sighed. Sadie obviously wanted to talk about it and, as much as he didn't want to know any more about her, there was a part of him that really, really wanted to know how a smoking-hot woman like Sadie ended up with a guy twice her age.

If Leonard Pinto had been buff and handsome he might have been able to see it, but Kent had seen the man's picture and he doubted good old Leo would ever be asked to pose for a centrefold.

'Okay, then, out with it,' he said. 'You obviously want to get it off your chest, so spill.'

Sadie looked out of the window, not in the mood to be humoured. 'It doesn't matter.'

Kent glanced at her petulant profile and felt as if he were back in high school. 'I'm not going to ask you twice, Sadie, so why don't you tell me all about it? Tell me how a man who must be at least twenty years older than you came to be in a sexual relationship with a much younger woman.'

Sadie turned to face him, her eyes blazing. 'It wasn't like that.'

Kent raised an eyebrow. 'Like what?'

'The way you're making it sound,' she snapped.

'Okay. So how was it, then?'

Sadie turned back to the window, watching the scenery flash by as she gathered her thoughts. 'I took one of his classes at art school.'

Kent snorted. If Sadie thought that made things sound better, then she was much more immature than he'd originally thought.

'So...he was your teacher? Isn't that against the rules?'

Sadie sent him a scathing look. 'I took the class for a term. We didn't get involved until six months later.'

'And how did that start? No, let me guess. He was impressed with your talent and offered to give you extra tuition.'

Sadie looked back out of the window. 'I went to one of his exhibitions and we got talking. He took me out for drinks afterwards.'

'And then he said come back to my place and take off your clothes, I want to paint you?'

Sadie ignored the sarcasm. 'He was the most articulate and witty man I'd ever met. Sophisticated. Urbane. And what he didn't know about the world and art and culture wasn't worth knowing. And he was interested in me. This older, interesting man who could have had his pick of women was interested in little ol' me.'

Kent frowned. Obviously her father's desertion had had a lasting impact on Sadie. 'Why wouldn't he be? You're an interesting person.'

Not to mention how very interesting she was to look at.

Sadie flicked him an *oh-really* look. 'Yes, I've noticed how you've been completely enthralled by my life.'

Kent shrugged. 'Don't take it personally. I've been pretty uninterested generally the last couple of years.' He swerved to avoid another crater-like pothole, then looked at her. 'I can't believe, though, that there weren't a veritable glut of men your age that were also interested?'

She nodded. 'Sure. In my E cups.' Sadie looked back out of the window. 'Guys my age tend to have conversations with my chest. Leonard didn't. He looked me right in the eye.'

Kent felt an instant spike of guilt at his own fascination with her chest, but at least he could take comfort from the fact that *every* part of her seemed to fascinate him.

God knew her mouth was becoming an obsession.

'So Leonard's gay? Or bi, I guess.'

Sadie gasped and turned to stare at him. Where in the hell had that come from? 'Were you dropped on the head as a baby?'

'Hey, nothing wrong with that,' Kent assured her. He could understand Sadie being attracted to someone who didn't objectify her. 'I'm just saying that any man who doesn't at least check you out can't be heterosexual.'

Sadie opened her mouth to blast him despite the traitorous part of her that felt curiously flattered. 'Are you implying that *all* men aren't capable of restraining Neanderthal behaviour and if they are then they must be gay?'

'Heterosexual men check out women, Sadie.' He shrugged. 'I agree it's appalling that some guys behave like morons and that subtlety isn't part of their repertoire, but we're pretty simple creatures really, genetically predisposed to appreciate the female form. It's just as natural as breathing.'

Sadie wondered for a moment if Kent had checked her out. In *that* way. And if so, when? She hadn't really noticed him gawking like the average male and he'd certainly never had one of those conversations with her breasts that annoyed her so much. In fact she'd have to say that Kent had displayed supreme lack of interest.

Annoyed at the direction of her thoughts when her mind needed to be on Leo, Sadie grappled to get back on the page. 'Trust me, he's straight,' she said icily, seeking and holding his gaze for a moment. 'Very, very straight. We had lots and lots and lots of sex.'

Which wasn't exactly true. Leonard had been more into oral sex and they'd had plenty of that but he'd not been great at reciprocating. Still, he'd stimulated her in other ways, intellectually and artistically, so his low sex drive hadn't ever been an issue.

Being his lover had transcended the physical.

Kent dragged his gaze back to the road as her doe eyes told him stuff he wasn't sure he was keen on knowing. He really did not want to be regaled with stories of Leonard Pinto's straightness.

Not as it pertained to Sadie anyway.

'So *did* he paint you?' he said, trying to shift the conversation.

Sadie nodded. 'Oh, yes. I became his muse. Gave up art school, moved in with him so I could pose for him whenever he wanted. All hours of the day or night. It was...exhilarating.'

And it had been. His obsession with her had been heady stuff. It had also been exhausting. Living with an arty temperament had its downside, especially when she was struggling to find time for her own art.

Still, she'd have never taken that part of her life back.

'He didn't paint anyone else for nearly two years.'

Kent heard pride soften her voice. It sounded a little co-dependent to him, but Kent couldn't blame the guy and a part of him hoped he might get to see one of those paintings.

He remembered wanting to photograph her this morning and, whilst he wasn't a fan of Pinto's nudes, Kent couldn't deny he was curious to see a master's take on Sadie's curvy perfection. Had Leonard managed to capture the perfectness of her imperfect features?

Although quite how Pinto managed to be so productive with Sadie living in his house and stripped naked a lot of the time he had no clue. He knew for damn sure there wouldn't be a lot of work going on if she was buck naked and posing for him!

His groin stirred and he clamped down on unproductive thoughts as he zeroed in on the most startling part of her story. 'You gave up art school?'

Sadie nodded. She'd cut herself off from everything, even her mother. Completely isolated herself. Weeks would go by without seeing another soul and she'd revelled in it, satisfied with being the centre of Leo's world, buying in to his control over her because she'd loved him and believed he loved her.

'I was never really good anyway,' she dismissed.

Kent blinked. That was the second time she'd written off her ability. 'Says who?' Art schools were notoriously difficult to get into—they only took talented students. It had taken him two years of applying before he'd been accepted into one to study photography.

'Leo.'

'And you believed him?'

Sadie rolled her eyes. 'He's Leonard Pinto. I think he knows a thing or two about talent, don't you?'

Kent thought good old Leo also knew a thing or two about manipulation. 'How old were you when you hooked up with Pinto?'

'Nineteen,' she said wistfully.

Kent paused as that info sank in. 'And he was?'

'Thirty-nine.'

Oh, yeah. *Leo knew which side his bread was buttered on.*

'What happened?' Kent asked. 'How'd it end?'

'Behind my back my mother gathered a portfolio of my work and put me up for a scholarship to my dream college in London. And I got it.'

Kent shook his head. And she *still* believed she didn't have any talent? 'I'm guessing Leonard was none too pleased to have his muse running away.'

Sadie looked away. 'I hadn't painted in over a year. Leo loved me, he didn't want me to fail. He was right to point out that I'd lost my edge. That I wouldn't last long there, that places like that require exceptional talent and dedication. That I'd probably only got in because of my association with him.'

Kent ground his teeth at Pinto's disingenuous actions. *Nice.* 'So you didn't want to go?'

Sadie shook her head. 'No. I did want to go. I'd been doing nothing for a year and I was getting restless. I just...'

'What?'

'It was hard. Leo saw it as a betrayal.'

Kent snorted. 'I thought he loved you.'

Sadie looked away. No. That had been her mistake. She had loved him. Leo had never loved her. 'I was torn and he told me the decision should be easy and as it wasn't that I should go.'

Kent didn't know what to say. Pinto sounded like a total arse. 'Did you go to London?'

Sadie shook her head, she'd been devastated by the whole thing. 'I needed to get away from art for a while. So I studied journalism instead. And here I am today coming full circle.'

'So, why does Pinto want you for the interview?'

Sadie shrugged. 'Curiosity probably. I think he thought I would fall apart without him. Whatever his agenda is, I'm determined to show him I didn't.'

Kent looked at her, then looked away. 'Well, that dress ought to do it.'

He slowed as he saw the sign for Casa Del Leone, the Pinto retreat, approaching, but not before he noticed that fabulous mouth break into a broad grin.

Neither of them spoke as they drove into the property. The house, complete with massive marble columns, looked as if it had been picked up from Ancient Greece and deposited by Zeus himself. It looked completely out of place in the middle of the Australian outback.

Kent whistled as he pulled the vehicle into the Grecian portico. 'It looks like a pimple on a pumpkin,' Kent said as he reached for his seat belt.

'Wait,' Sadie said, putting her hand on his forearm.

Kent frowned at her. 'What?'

Sadie looked at the imposing marble entryway and massive wrought-iron door, her heart suddenly pounding loud enough to shake the columns to their foundations. 'Do not let me get sucked in by him, okay?'

Kent's frown deepened as he looked at her hand on his arm. 'Please tell me after everything you've just told me, you're not still in love with him.'

Sadie shook her head. 'No... I don't think so.' Kent's impatient look spurred her to clarification. 'He was a big part of my life for a long time. He was like...an addiction or something. And addicts are never really cured, are they?' She chewed on her bottom lip. 'I'm afraid I'm going to get a taste and...fall off the wagon.'

Kent's gaze involuntarily followed the action of her teeth as they ate away her lip gloss. When he realised he was staring he dropped his gaze to her revenge attire. 'I think you're stronger than you think, Sadie Bliss.'

Sadie smiled at him, suddenly conscious of the warmth of him beneath her palm and the bunch of muscles in his forearm. She was surprised how good they felt. How the power of them did funny things to her insides.

He was so different from Leo. And not just in looks. Leo would never have calmly told her she was strong.

Leo had spent two years telling her she needed him.

'Come on,' he said briskly, because she was looking at him with those big doe eyes and the ridiculous urge to lean over and kiss her was growing stronger.

Neither of them needed that. Not now.

Not ever.

He undid his belt, her hand falling away. 'Let's do this thing.'

Leonard's PA greeted them at the door. 'Mr Pinto is in his studio and is not to be disturbed for another two hours. I'll show you to your rooms and then take you on a tour,' he said.

They spent the next two hours touring around the palatial house and grounds. Kent dutifully took photographs and Sadie asked all the standard questions. It was late afternoon when they were invited to *freshen up* and join *Mr Pinto* for pre-dinner drinks at six in the *saloon*.

Kent felt as if he'd just walked into the set of an Agatha Christie movie but he did as he was told, having a shower and getting changed into clean jeans and a casual skivvy. He took his camera with him as he headed for the *Gone With The Wind* staircase.

Sadie, who was still in her killer dress, met him at the top and they descended together. 'I feel like I should be calling you Scarlett,' he murmured.

Sadie laughed. 'Why, Rhett, I do declare...'

Kevin fixed them both a drink and they all made polite conversation whilst they waited for the guest of honour. Leo turned up twenty-five minutes later.

'Sadie!' he exclaimed from the doorway.

Sadie, who had been chatting to Kevin, rose to her feet, her heart pounding again as the man she'd once loved walked briskly towards her.

'Leo,' she murmured as he swept her into a hug.

Sadie shut her eyes and waited for the familiar intoxicating rush she'd always experienced just from his presence. When it didn't come she opened them to find herself looking directly into Kent's gaze. He was standing near the large floor-to-ceiling French doors across the other side of the room in her direct line of sight.

He winked at her and she found herself suppressing a smile as Leo held her for a little longer than she was comfortable with.

'My goodness,' Leo said as he finally released her and held her away at arm's length. 'I think you've been living the high life. Where have all those lovely bones gone, darling?'

Kent watched Sadie's smile falter and before he knew it he was striding towards them. The urge to punch Leonard Pinto in the face was one he was just able to suppress as he stuck out his hand and introduced himself.

'Ah, yes, Mr Nelson,' Leo said, grasping Kent's hand. 'Kevin mentioned that you were the photographer. It is indeed a great pleasure to meet you.'

Kent nodded. He supposed he should have returned the compliment, but Sadie's smile in his peripheral vision was so brittle he thought it might actually crumble off her face and, frankly, Leonard Pinto's handshake had been unimpressive.

Kevin handed Leo his standard gin and tonic and regaled Kent with his attempts at photography. Sadie listened to them on autopilot. She'd nibbled on an apple all day and the glass of white wine she was sipping was going straight to her head.

She tried not to let Leo's opening comment get to her—he'd never been a particularly sensitive man—but she'd starved herself for days and knew she looked damn good. Not rake thin as she had been, but good nonetheless.

Would it have killed him to have given her a compliment?

Leo laughed at a joke he'd told and Sadie ran her eyes over him. He hadn't changed. Maybe there was a little more grey in the wings at his temple, some more padding under his chin and around his middle, but he was the same. Tall and thin, with long arty fingers, curiously not paint stained as per usual, and bookish wire-rimmed glasses.

She waited for the rush of tangled emotions he'd always aroused and was relieved to feel nothing.

She switched her attention to Kent and his polite fixed smile. The comparison between the two men was striking. Kent was toned and broad and fit-looking compared to Leo's obvious indoor physique. Kent's spare, angular features were sharply contrasted with the gentle planes of Leo's.

Sadie had never placed any stead on looks but with the two of them together it was hard not to compare. Kent looked like a Rodin sculpture—all symmetry and fluid lines. Leo looked like a kindergarten art project—something that you cherished because of an association but not something you wanted to just look at for hours.

'The evening meal is served,' Kevin announced interrupting Sadie's reverie.

Kent watched Sadie nibble pathetically around the edges of her meal. It was all beautifully cooked by Kevin who seemed to be general dogsbody, but it just wasn't his thing.

Small servings, big plates, posh names.

By the end of it Kent was still starving.

And Sadie must have been ready to eat the table leg.

More polite conversation was made about the local area and the history of the house until Kevin took away the last plate.

'Would you like a tour of the studio now?' Leonard asked them as he stood.

Kent looked at Sadie, a half-query in his eyes. Personally he'd rather drive to the nearest steak restaurant and order the biggest Waygu they had.

'Sure,' Sadie said, standing also, her head spinning a little. She was curious to see what kind of space he painted in now, in this marble mausoleum in the middle of nowhere.

Leo, ever the charming host, regaled them with stories as he led the way towards the back of the house. He opened a large double wooden door, flicking a light on in the darkened room illuminating the space inside and out.

The first thing she noticed was that the studio overlooked the man-made lake Kevin had shown them earlier. The next was how clean it was. She knew Leo, she knew him well, and when he was in the middle of a project—the studio was always a shambles.

The third thing she only noticed when Kent said, 'Holy cow.' She turned to look up on the wall behind her to see what had his jaw dropping.

A giant nude portrait hung there. Of her. And for a moment all three of them just stood and looked at it.

'My best, don't you think, Sadie?'

Sadie nodded as she remembered how many hours she'd sat for this particular painting. She felt her cheeks flush as Kent's gaze continually darted over it. It wasn't the same as seeing her naked in the flesh, she knew, but it was still her up there, lying reclined in all her glory.

Kent couldn't believe what he was seeing. He'd hoped to see something like this. To see a true artist capture Sadie's likeness. But this portrait was shocking. The Sadie in the painting was a far cry from the woman he'd shared a car with for the last few days.

She was very thin. Her bones stuck out, her curves were non-existent and her breasts were much smaller.

He looked down at her, horrified. 'My God, were you ill?' he asked.

Leo blanched at Kent's blunt question. 'I beg your pardon,' he blustered. 'She was much healthier then. Look at that bone structure. Those angles. She's the very picture of female beauty, of what men desire in women. And she worked hard to look that good, didn't you, darling?'

Kent looked at Leo Pinto as if he'd just grown another head. Suddenly Sadie's eating patterns of the last few days, her '*It's complicated*,' made sense.

Leo had obviously been starving her for two years.

And facing him again as a successful, independent career woman must have taken a lot of courage.

Finally he understood her. Understood the celery sticks and the over-sized T-shirts.

And he understood why. Leo Pinto.

She'd loved him to the point that she'd become someone else for him.

And he'd let her.

Toxic bastard.

He looked at a silent Sadie, then back at the painting. He hated it on sight. She looked like his ballerina nudes.

Thin and androgynous.

She did not look like Sadie Bliss.

'I'm sorry, Mr Pinto,' Kevin interrupted from the doorway, a phone in his hand. 'It's your agent—he says it's urgent.'

Leo gave Kent a pained smile and ran his fingers down the back of Sadie's arm. 'I won't be a moment.'

Kent watched him go, then turned back to Sadie. She was looking at the painting with an inscrutable expression and he couldn't figure out whether it was admiration, indifference or revulsion.

'Are you okay?' he asked.

Sadie nodded absently, rubbing her arms, feeling suddenly cold and very light-headed. It had been interesting seeing the portrait again with time and distance on her side.

Interesting to see it through Kent's eyes too.

'You've been starving yourself to look like that?' he asked incredulously, jabbing a finger in the general direction of the portrait. 'You don't seriously believe that men find bones and angles attractive, do you?'

'I used to,' she said. 'Leo used to say I had the perfect face on the wrong body but that could be fixed.' Spots started to swim before her eyes as she dragged her gaze away from the portrait she'd once loved so much.

Kent watched as Sadie swayed and he grabbed her upper arms in alarm. 'You're not okay.'

Sadie nodded as his strong, frowning face swam before her eyes. 'Just a little light-headed,' she dismissed, but reached for his arms for extra anchorage.

'I'm not surprised. That's what happens when you don't eat anything. Come on, I have a Mars bar in my bag.'

Something told him there wouldn't be anything so common in *Casa Del Idiot*.

'No,' she resisted. 'Just give me a moment. It'll pass.'

Kent shook his head as he looked back at the painting. The woman staring back at him looked utterly miserable. Thin for sure, but where was the vibrant woman of sass and spark he'd come to know the past few days? 'That is a tragedy,' he muttered.

'Thanks a lot,' Sadie half joked, looking up into his face. He was still holding her, his scratchy-looking jaw line in profile. 'I was rather fond of my bony look.'

Kent looked down at her in alarm. Which was a mistake, because her mouth was so very, very near, her red dress like a beacon in his peripheral vision. That passionfruit smell enveloped him in a flurry of very bad ideas. He dropped his gaze to the plump pillows turned up towards him, thinking that thin was never a good look.

Not on bodies. Or mouths. 'Trust me, curvy looks way better.'

Sadie could feel the heat of his gaze on her mouth. She shifted her hands so they were lying more comfortably against his biceps. 'Leo always said that men lied about liking curves, that given a choice they'd choose skinny every time.'

Kent frowned. 'God, he's a pretentious arse.'

Sadie smiled, but Leo's words still stung after all these years. She traced a finger absently around the bulk of a bicep. 'He said no one would ever want me.'

Kent shook his head as her doe eyes blinked up at him. His pulse was pounding through his ears as her body swayed closer to his. He swallowed as desire bolted through his system. He shouldn't kiss her. Not in a client's house. And certainly not standing under a life-sized image of her in the buff. But she smelled so damn good and her lips were so damn near. Nearer as he moved his face closer to hers.

'He's wrong,' Kent muttered.

Sadie's breath quickened as his lips descended. She hung onto his words. Looking at her portrait again, listening to Leo's rapture over it had sucked her back into a turbulent time in her life, but this man—this potent virile he-man, the polar opposite to Leo in every way—was telling her something different.

He was going to kiss her in this room, in front of that painting.

And she needed it. She needed to be desired for the person she was now, not the one she'd been.

The air crackled around them as their lips met. Kent felt no resistance, just her body completely aligning with his and her incredible mouth opening to him on a little whimper that reached right inside his gut and squeezed.

And then it was gone as a much hotter, deeper, more urgent need consumed him. The need to claim, to conquer, to lead. He sucked in a breath, pushing his hands into her hair and his tongue into her mouth, feeling the tentative touch of hers grow bolder.

But then voices getting nearer started to intrude and Kent suddenly realised where he was. He pulled away, her little disappointed mew and moist pouty mouth almost bringing him to his knees.

'You okay?' he asked, when she opened her big grey eyes, now the colour of slate, his arms steadying her.

Sadie blinked and nodded as she heard Leo enter the room even though she wasn't sure she'd ever be okay again.

CHAPTER SEVEN

THE KISS KEPT Sadie awake long into the night. Nothing kept Sadie awake long into the night. Especially not something that probably didn't even last twenty seconds. It was practically over before it began but, man, did it have an impact!

It had certainly shot her flagging blood sugar into the stratosphere. And as she lay in the dark staring at the ceiling she felt as if she were still riding the sugar high.

It had been impossible to concentrate on Leo after the impulsive kiss. All she'd been aware of was the tingle in her lips, the fizz in her blood and Kent's brooding monosyllabic presence nearby. Had he felt as flummoxed as she had? Or was it just another gallant deed *he-men* performed every day for damsels in distress?

The kiss of life to revive flagging blood sugars and dented egos.

She had escaped as soon as possible to get away from Kent. To get away from both of them.

Two very different men who had both rocked her world.

Kent hadn't attempted to stop her or even follow, for which she was grateful. She needed some distance. To gain some perspective. Like the perspective she'd gained over Leo since being apart from him for the last few years.

Because she seriously doubted that one little kiss meant anything to

Kent, especially considering how very hard he'd tried to have absolutely nothing to do with her the entire trip.

Men flirted with her. It was just a fact of her life no matter how hard she dressed down and didn't try to draw attention to herself.

But not Kent. Kent had been blunt in his complete lack of interest.

Which only made the kiss more puzzling.

But it had been an odd moment. And straight afterwards he had looked as if he were contemplating hacking his lips off. Reading something into it would be a bad idea. It would be something the nineteen-year-old Sadie would have done. Latching onto anyone who flattered her and showed an interest in anything other than the contents of her bra.

Twenty-four-year-old Sadie used her head.

And it was telling her to get a grip.

After her restless night Sadie woke late. Kevin informed her that Kent had headed out about midnight to take photographs and wasn't expected back until after lunch. And that Mr Pinto would receive her in his studio at ten.

Sadie felt an immediate sense of loss. The memory of her starry night on top of Kent's Land Rover had stayed with her and the pull to see an outback night again, to see it as he saw it, through a lens, was undeniable.

And what was she supposed to read into his sudden walkabout? Was it his not-so-subtle way of saying that he didn't want to talk about what had happened?

That the kiss hadn't meant anything?

That it had been a mistake?

'Egg-white omelette?'

Kevin's question broke into her swirling thoughts. She shook her head, her hunger pangs dampened by her confusion. 'Just a cup of tea, please.'

Twenty minutes later she was knocking on Leo's studio door in a similar shoestring-strapped dress to yesterday, hinting and skimming in a deep ochre like the colour of the earth outside the oasis that Leo had built for himself. It buttoned all the way up the front with tiny black buttons. Her hair was clasped behind in a tight ponytail. Strappy sandals adorned her feet. Dark kohl emphasised her eyes and gloss drew attention to her mouth.

It had been tempting to interview him in her travel clothes just to see that annoyed little crease he got between his brows. But she was a professional and she was working, representing *Sunday On My Mind,* and she wouldn't compromise that.

And, in Leo's presence, her career was like a shield against his poisonous words from the past, so she was going to armour herself in the full uniform and hold her head up high.

Leo pulled the door open. 'Sadie!'

He pulled her towards him into an embrace, kissing her on the mouth before Sadie could take evasive action and lingering a little longer than was polite. She pulled back and noticed a fleeting look of confusion on his face before he ushered her in.

Light filled the room from the large windows and Sadie was struck again by how clean the studio was. She looked around for half-finished canvases stacked against the walls, drop sheets, preliminary sketches littering the ample bench tops. Even the familiar toxic chemical odour of paint, so inherent in his studio, was strangely absent.

'I've never seen your studio so sparkling before,' she remarked.

Leo shrugged. 'I've never allowed a photographer into my space before,' he said, indicating the studio looking even more cavernous with the usual chaos cleaned away. 'Can't have the public knowing what a pigsty I work in.'

Sadie noticed his very clean-looking hands again. The entire two years she'd lived with him Leo's fingers had rarely been without paint stains. 'Are you between projects at the moment?'

Leo nodded briskly. 'I've set up some chairs over by the windows,' he said, moving towards them. 'Will that be okay for the interview?'

Sadie followed him over to the two low bucket chairs separated by a coffee table upon which there was a carafe of water and two glasses. Kevin appeared as she sat down, handing Leo his usual gin and tonic, and enquired as to whether she wanted something else to drink. She declined and he poured her some water as she rummaged through her bag for her notebook and her tape recorder.

'Do you mind?' she asked as she set it on the table between them.

Leo shook his head. 'Not at all.'

Sadie felt ridiculously nervous as she started the interview. She knew the man intimately and it was hardly her first job, but she didn't want to stuff it up. Leo had told her she couldn't make it without him and it was imperative to prove she could.

She had.

Two hours later it was over and Sadie was exhausted from the polite pretence between them. Especially with Leo's continual efforts to sabotage Sadie's professionalism by spicing his answers with personal details of their past life together. Her nerves were at screeching point when she closed her notebook and pronounced herself satisfied.

Leo stretched back in the chair and looked at her for long moments. 'What are you doing, Sadie?'

Sadie contemplated pretending she didn't know what he was asking, but decided that playing coy wasn't her style any more. 'I'm doing my job,' she said as she stuffed the tools of her trade back in her handbag.

Leo stood and held out his hand to her. 'Come,' he commanded.

Sadie looked up at his outstretched hand and cocked an eyebrow at him. 'I beg your pardon?'

Leo sighed. 'Let me show you something.'

After a moment or two Sadie stood ignoring his hand. She let him usher her over, his hand at her elbow, to stand in the middle of the room facing the painting of her. Neither of them said anything for a moment.

'You belong here with me.'

Sadie felt the pull, the allure, of the painting even after all this time. Every brushstroke told a story of a time in her life when she'd been deliriously happy. When a man had cosseted her and celebrated her female form instead of lamenting it as her father had done.

'Look how beautiful you are,' Leo whispered.

His finger stroked the inside of her elbow and tears blurred in Sadie's eyes—she had looked good. But being back here with him beside her she also remembered his obsession with her body. And how she'd bought into it. As her stomach rumbled again she remembered those days when she would have killed for a cheeseburger and fries.

When not even his compliments could soothe the ache that continually gnawed at her gut.

When the diet pills and the caffeine and nights of no sleep as Leo painted her obsessively had left her strung out.

With distance she could recognise the insanity of it.

'I could help you get back to that, Sadie. Stay here with me. Let me paint you again.'

His voice was low and, oh, so familiar as his thumb continued to stroke her arm. Sadie fought against the illicit thrill of addiction. She shook her head. 'I have another job now.'

'I bet it doesn't measure up to being Leonard Pinto's muse. I need you, Sadie. We need each other.'

It was his utter arrogance that helped pull her back from the edge. A few years ago she'd revelled in that title; now it turned her stomach.

He might as well have said Leonard Pinto's plaything.

As if she were some doll he could manipulate into whatever position he wanted.

She looked down at his thumb still stroking her. The skin was pink as a newborn babe's and she could see the whorl of his fingerprint. *I need you, Sadie.*

She took a step away from him as realisation dawned, his hand falling away. 'Oh, my God. You're blocked, aren't you?' She looked around at the studio gleaming like a luxury car showroom. 'You're not in between projects at all.'

Leo looked at the floor. 'A small slump,' he dismissed.

'How long, Leo?' she asked his downcast head.

When he finally looked at her again she could tell he was steeling himself to lie. But then his shoulders sagged and he looked significantly more than twenty years her senior. 'I haven't painted anything decent since you left.'

Sadie blinked at his admission. She'd been gone for over three years. *That had to be killing him.*

Leo looked at her. 'You belong here with me, Sadie.'

He sounded like a petulant child and Sadie shook her head as she realised she was finally free of him. 'No. I belong to me. And I have a job that I love.'

'You *loved* posing for me.'

His interjection was almost a whine and she took pity on him. 'It's not a real career, Leo.'

'That didn't seem to bother you at the time.'

Sadie ignored his sarcasm and the truth of it. 'Journalism can take me places. I've been out for just a few months and already I have a shot at my dream job.'

Leo stuck his hand on his hip. 'Thanks to me. You've only got this shot because you slept with *me*. I warned you—you were nothing without me.'

Sadie reeled a little as the crudeness of his triumphant accusation sank in. He'd obviously been waiting three years to throw that one in her face. And it was true—she had scored this interview because of her association with Leo. But she wasn't the lost young woman he'd tossed away a few years back—she had a spine these days and his slights didn't have the power to hurt any more.

She certainly wasn't going to hang around listening to any more. 'Goodbye, Leo,' she said, turning away from him.

'Sadie, wait!'

She contemplated ignoring him, but the urgency in his voice pulled her up and she turned around.

'You walk away and you're walking away from that.' He pointed to the painting. 'You'll never get a shot at being her again.'

Sadie looked at the painting and finally saw what Kent had seen last night. Bones and angles and hollows. Leo had even painted her breasts smaller—artistic licence, as he was so fond of quoting. Suddenly she looked like just another skinny Hollywood starlet or skeletal model.

Like every ballerina he'd ever painted.

It didn't look like her.

'I don't want to be her, Leo. I like me. I like the me I am now.'

She stalled for a moment, realising the words that had just fallen out were utterly true. Time, distance and Kent's kiss had put some things into perspective.

'I like to eat good food and drink good wine and I love junk food as well! I like those little tiny marshmallows on my cornflakes for breakfast and hot dogs and, damn it all, I think Twisties should be a food group.'

Leo shook his head. 'You don't mean that,' he said.

Sadie nodded. 'I'll tell you a secret about that girl, Leo. She wasn't happy. Not really. She just thought she was.'

Sadie couldn't look at the painting a moment longer. All she could see now was how starved for affection she'd been.

And she just wasn't that girl any more.

She turned on her heel and left. Left Leo standing in the middle of his studio gawping like a landed fish.

She took the stairs two at a time to her room and threw her things in her bag. As she headed out again she noticed a sketch pad and a box of sketching pastels on the bedside table. She fingered them lovingly—Leo was a creature of habit. He'd always kept stashes of them everywhere so he'd have access when the muse struck.

No doubt they were here because he'd thought they'd end up in bed together.

On a whim she picked them up and shoved them in her bag. Then she turned straight back around. She reached the front door just as Kent was entering. He looked so good, so *he-man*, so not *arty*, she almost threw herself straight at him.

But the wariness in his gaze as he took in her bag stopped her. 'We're leaving,' she said.

Kent blinked. They were supposed to stay another night with Sadie getting a plane to Darwin in the morning. He wasn't sure what had gone on in his absence but Sadie sounded pretty serious.

Hot but serious. That damn mouth he'd been thinking about all night set in a determined little line.

Just as the line of buttons down her front was taunting him.

'Give me five.'

She nodded. 'I'll wait for you in the car.'

Kent didn't ask any questions about Leo when he joined her in the promised five minutes. He just started the car. 'Where to?' he asked.

'Town,' she said. 'I need Twisties.'

Kent kept the food coming at a café in Borroloola and Sadie ate as if she were pregnant with twin elephants.

'Better?' he asked as she finally pushed away her plate and refused some more of his hot chips. It had given him immense satisfaction watching her load food into her mouth.

The painting of her in Leo's studio had been disturbing and he'd spent a lot of time out in the bush last night trying to scrub it from his brain. Understanding that the misogynistic idiot residing in Casa Del Leone was behind all her insecurities hadn't helped—seeing her eat did.

It also distracted him from the buttons.

And the kiss.

She nodded. 'I think I'm going to vomit, though,' she said as she rubbed her painfully full belly.

'Then my job here is done,' Kent mused as he sucked on his thick shake straw. She looked as if she'd been sprung from prison—or at least the chains from her past—and he was glad he was here to witness her first moments of freedom.

Sadie laughed, then groaned. 'Don't make me laugh or I really will throw up.'

Kent shrugged. 'You have tablets for that.'

'They're for motion sickness. Not gluttony.'

He laughed then and Sadie was relieved to see the wariness that had been in his gaze when they'd met at Leo's front door and on the silent trip into town seemed to have dissipated.

'What now?' he asked. 'Your flight doesn't leave until the morning. I can drop you at a hotel on my way out of town?'

Sadie shook her head. She didn't want to stick around any longer than she had to. 'You leaving for Darwin straight away?'

Kent nodded. 'It's about fifteen hours without stops for photos and a kip here and there.'

Sadie thought about it for a minute. Another night under the stars. With Kent.

Who had kissed her.

It didn't sound wise.

'Can I hitch a ride with you?'

Kent's gaze dropped to Sadie's mouth as the illicit request undulated towards him. He sobered as he dragged his eyes upwards. 'I didn't think you were keen to drive any further than you had to?'

Sadie nodded, noting the return of his wariness. And the way he'd looked at her mouth. Her heart started to beat a little faster. 'By the time my flight gets into Darwin tomorrow you'll already be there, right?'

'Probably,' he conceded.

'So it kind of makes sense to go with you.'

He nodded. 'It does.'

Which didn't stop him from knowing that being in a car with her for hours on end was not at all sensible. Nor was lying on a rooftop with her under the stars.

Not after the kiss.

'Please,' she asked quietly as his face remained in an uncompromising mask. 'I really just need to get as far away from Leo as possible.'

Well, now that reasoning he couldn't fault. If he had his way, he'd be on the other side of the planet to the man.

Sadie watched his features soften a little and quickly jumped in. 'I promise I'll be quiet as a mouse.'

Kent snorted as he pulled his wallet out and threw money on the table. 'I'll believe that when I see it Sadie Bliss.'

Sadie's vow of silence didn't last long in the car. 'About last night.'

Kent's grip tightened on the steering wheel. He flicked a glance at the dashboard clock. 'Ten minutes, Sadie, you're slipping.'

Sadie ignored him. She could feel the tension rolling off him and didn't want to spend fifteen hours absorbing the fallout. 'I think we need to talk about it… It's kind of the elephant in the car at the moment, don't you think?'

Kent shrugged. 'It happened. It shouldn't have. Let's leave it at that.'

Sadie blinked at the very neat summation of what had been going through her head. How surprising that Kent should be so succinct!

'It was just a kiss,' he dismissed as Sadie's silence worried him. 'It was a weird moment in a strange night.'

She nodded. It certainly had been. But it hadn't just been any old kiss. There'd been nothing friendly or brotherly about it. Nothing comforting. It might have been brief but for those few seconds she'd never felt so out of her depth.

'Stop it,' Kent said as the silence stretched loudly between them.

Sadie frowned. 'Stop what?'

'Stop humming the "Wedding March" in your head.'

Sadie glanced at him, alarmed. 'Don't flatter yourself, Kent Nelson. It wasn't that good,' she lied. 'I'm not into strong silent times. I like to be able to converse with a potential future husband, not have to bargain for every word that comes out of his mouth.'

'Good.' He nodded, satisfied.

She glared at him, feeling tenser than when she'd first opened her mouth. 'There, now, don't you feel better it's all out in the open?' she asked sarcastically.

Kent didn't deign to answer and not least of all because the answer was no. All she'd done was put the kiss front and centre when he had been almost successful in burying it with the other stuff in his *do-some-thing-about-it-later* box.

Sadie spent the next few hours feigning interest in the scrubby red-earth scenery but her brain was busy with other things. She couldn't work out whether she was more upset that he'd dismissed the kiss as nothing or that he'd kissed her in the first place. She certainly had relived it more times than was helpful when the man responsible for it and all its cata-clysmic glory was just an arm's length away, those lips of his tantalising her peripheral vision.

Lips that knew how to get down to business.

By the time the dash clock hit five she desperately needed a distrac-tion from the direction of her thoughts.

She glanced at Kent, his strong silent profile unchanged, an ear bud jammed in the ear closest to her. She reached over and pulled it out.

'Why haven't you done an interview since the accident?' she asked, her idea of a feature story on him returning.

Kent ignored her, not taking his eyes off the road. And to think her silence had lulled him into a false sense of security.

Sadie rolled her eyes. 'So we're back to ignoring me again?'

'If I thought it'd make a difference I just might.'

'You must have had offers,' she pressed when it became obvious he wasn't about to say anything else. 'It's a fascinating story.'

'Yes I have,' he said, gaze fixed on the white lines running up the cen-tre of the highway.

'And?' Sadie prompted.

Kent turned his head and looked her straight in the eye. 'It's no one's damn business, Sadie.' He looked back at the road. 'What happened to me is private—very private. It's not for general consumption.'

Sadie got the message loud and clear. But it was pretty obvious Kent needed to talk to someone.

'What if I interviewed you? I'm pretty sure Leo's on the phone right now to Tabitha revoking all rights to the interview material so I'm going to need a back-up plan.'

'You have the road-trip story,' he dismissed.

'She wants two for the price of one, remember, and getting sacked on my first job is not good on the CV. I can't let her down. I need to deliver.'

Kent nodded. 'That's true. Tabitha doesn't like to be let down.'

Sadie gave an internal groan. *Excellent.* 'Is that a yes?'

Kent wrapped his fingers more firmly around the steering wheel. 'My story is not for sale.'

Sadie heard the same ice in his voice he'd used for telling her he didn't fly. Regardless, she prepared to launch into a whole selling patter because the thought of letting Tabitha Fox down was not a nice one, but mostly because she knew it'd annoy him.

And at least when he was angry at her she wasn't thinking about kissing him so much.

But an awful clunk coming from the general direction of the engine put paid to any further chit-chat.

'What was that?' she asked, clutching the door handle.

Kent slowed the still-running vehicle slightly as he looked at his instruments. 'I'm not sure,' he said after a moment or two. 'The temperature gauge is climbing, though.'

His eyes sought the road ahead, looking for the best place to pull over.

Fifteen minutes later Kent had parked the Land Rover under some large gum trees on the relatively flat stretch of highway. The other side of the road was less hospitable with a large expanse of scrub stretching almost uninterrupted to the horizon.

'What's wrong with it?' Sadie asked as she joined Kent beneath the bonnet.

'I think I've blown the water pump.'

Sadie looked at the convoluted metallic pipes of the internal combustion engine. It might as well have been an alien spacecraft. 'That sounds bad.' She looked at him. 'Is that bad?'

'It'll need a new one and if we were in Sydney I could probably find a dozen mechanics within two city blocks that had one in stock. Maybe not so much out here.'

Sadie chewed on her lip. 'Oh.'

Despite the fact that his hands were covered in grease, all Kent could smell was that damn passionfruit aroma of hers. Combined with her fate-worse-than-death look it was just plain irritating.

'It's okay, Sadie Bliss,' he said as he pulled the bonnet down and wiped his hands on an oily rag. 'You're not destined to be stuck in the outback for ever. I'm sure there'll be a garage in Borroloola that will be able to help.'

He left her by the front of the car and grabbed the satellite phone from the front seat. In ten minutes he'd located a supplier in Katherine who would send a tow truck by nine tomorrow morning. He hung up the phone. 'Better get comfortable. We're here for the night.'

Sadie looked at him, alarmed. 'We are?' She looked around her wondering how many spiders chose to call this speck on the earth home.

He nodded. 'It's okay, I have camp gear in the back. I'll build a fire for now and we'll sleep up top like we did the other night.'

'Right,' Sadie said faintly.

Except they hadn't kissed the other night...

Kent set her up in a fold-out chair beneath the shade of a tree with her fully charged laptop and then came and went unloading stuff from the back of his vehicle and gathering firewood. In an hour he was lighting the fire. Sadie half expected him to drop a couple of rabbits at her feet and then set about skinning them.

'How's it going?' he asked, nodding at the laptop. 'Did you get everything you wanted for Pinto's feature?'

Sadie blinked, momentarily confused by the question because she hadn't been tapping away about Leo at all. Instead she'd been writing about him. About the strong, silent, tough-guy enigma that both baffled and intrigued her.

'Oh, yes, good, thanks,' she lied, shutting the lid. 'Plenty of info.' The earthy aroma of wood smoke spiralled out to meet her as the first plume hit the air. 'What about you? Are you happy with the pics you got on your little expedition last night?'

Kent nodded as he knelt by the fire, slowly feeding it. 'Yep.'

'Can I see them?' she asked.

Kent looked up at her, surprised. 'Sure. My camera bag's in the car.'

Sadie retrieved it and Kent showed her how to scroll back to the pictures he'd taken the night before. It seemed more complicated than something off the space shuttle, but eventually she got the hang of it.

'What did we do before digital cameras with delete buttons?' she mur-

mured as she viewed the images of the starry night and giant phallic ter-
mite mounds rising out of long grass and silhouetted in the moonlight.

'I wish I could see these bigger,' Sadie said, frustrated by the vast outback night condensed to one tiny image.

'USB lead in the camera bag—attach it to your laptop,' Kent said as
he threw bigger logs onto the fire.

Delighted, Sadie hooked up his camera to her laptop and scrolled
through the images again. She skimmed right through the ones of Leo
and his monolith, slowing down as she got to Kent's outback shots.

'These are amazing,' Sadie breathed in awe. 'They're going to look
spectacular in the feature.'

Kent nodded, more than a little pleased with the shots himself.

'How did it feel? Out there, taking them?' she asked.

Kent paused, surprised at her question. Surprised even more that he
wanted to answer it. 'It felt…good.' As if the part of him that had died,
or had at least been severely injured, was finally recovering. 'Familiar.'

Sadie realised she probably wasn't going to get any more from Mr
Silent and contented herself going through the shots a second time, pic-
turing them laid out in the magazine. When she was done she realised the
shadows had grown quite long and evening was just about to fall around
them. She shivered as the temperature suddenly seemed to plummet.

'Here,' Kent said, coming up behind her and plonking something
around her shoulders.

Sadie hunched into the warmth of the fleecy flannelette shirt, like
one of those cowboys always wore.

How fitting that Kent should own one.

'How does two-minute noodles and flambéed marshmallows sound?'
he asked as he sat on the groundsheet he'd laid down earlier.

Sadie laughed. 'Will we be singing "Kum-ba-yah" too?'

Kent grunted as he set the billy in the fire to boil the water for the
noodles. 'I don't sing.'

Sadie rolled her eyes. 'Don't sing. Don't fly. Don't talk. What do you
do for fun, Kent Nelson?' she teased.

Kent looked up at her encased in his shirt. Long shadows formed on
her cheeks from her eyelashes as the firelight played over her face and
the sky behind her slowly faded to a deep purple. He tried not to think
about the many fun things they could be doing right now.

Sadie held her breath for a second or two as the copper highlights flickered to life in Kent's gaze. And she didn't think it was from the fire.

'I flambé marshmallows,' he said.

He turned back to the billy and Sadie breathed again, the moment passing.

She asked him some technical questions to do with his photography, which got them through the noodles, but when she confessed to never having roasted marshmallows in a fire and she sat down beside him for tuition, things moved back to that state of awareness again and she knew he was feeling it too.

Kent laughed as he watched Sadie attempting to cook her marshmallow in the coals of the fire, too frightened to shove it right in and turn it into a little ball of flame. He couldn't believe anyone could get to their twenties and not have done something so simple and so damn good.

'You're doing it wrong.' He tutted as she pulled off a lukewarm marshmallow and popped it into a mouth already moist and sticky.

Not something that was good for his sanity.

Her cheeks were flushed by the heat radiating from the fire and she looked like a teenager.

'They're supposed to be like this,' he said, pulling his out from the fire glowing brightly in the night like a meteor burning up on entry. He blew on it gently, putting it out, then pulled it off the end of his stick and dropped it into his mouth.

Sadie watched the process, fascinated. Who'd have thought lips that would have been perfectly at home on a statue would also look just as good coated in gooey marshmallow? Last night it hadn't even occurred to her to analyse how he tasted. It had been too quick, too intense.

Now she couldn't think about anything else.

'Doesn't it taste burnt?' she asked, looking away as she realised she was staring.

He shook his head as he skewered another soft treat and held it above the coals. 'It tastes crunchy and then explodes in your mouth all hot and gooey.'

Sadie's mouth watered. And she was pretty sure it had nothing to do with the marshmallows.

Kent's marshmallow caught and he pulled it away, pushing the glowing orb her way. 'Here, just try it.'

Sadie shook her head. 'Won't it burn my fingers?'

Kent rolled his eyes as he blew on it and pulled it off. 'You're such a city girl.' He offered it to her quickly. 'Open up.'

Sadie shouldn't have opened up. But his fingers were pushing it towards her lips and his tiger eyes were daring her and the treat smelled hot and sweet and sticky.

So she opened up.

Big mistake. The crunch melted against her tongue and soft sweet goo spilled into her mouth. Her senses filled with sugar and him. Flames danced shadows over his stubbly cheeks as she sucked every sticky morsel from his sweet warm fingertips. She saw his pupils dilate in the firelight.

Kent froze as his fingers lingered on her mouth completely of their own accord. His gaze lingered too. How could it not when her mouth glistened all sweet and sticky? Beckoned, even, and he was suddenly wondering what her marshmallow mouth tasted like.

'Oh, hell,' he muttered as he dropped his head to find out.

CHAPTER EIGHT

SADIE MET HIM halfway, her heartbeat slow and thick as if marshmallow were running through her veins. His perfect mouth touched hers and there was nothing sweet and warm about it. It was hot and heady. Exploding inside her like a shower of sparks from the fire.

Heat shot to all her extremities. Lighting spot fires wherever it touched.

And she didn't care that they were in the middle of the bush or that they'd known each other for only a handful of days or that creatures lurked beyond the radius of the firelight.

She only cared about his hands in her hair, the brush of his thumbs at her temples, the heat of his mouth.

The harsh suck of his breath. The sweetness of lips. The deep rumble of his moan as her tongue found his.

And the driving imperative for more.

Her hands crept to his chest, bunched in his T-shirt, pulled him closer. She opened her mouth wider. Angled her neck back further. Kissed him harder.

Kent could feel Sadie trembling against him as their kiss raged out of control. Could feel the answering tremble in his gut. Every breath he took filled his head with her and lust beat like a jungle drum in his head, pounded through his veins, pulsed through his impossibly hard erection.

It was heady and addictive and he wanted more. He wanted her naked. Under him. Crying out his name.

All night.

And the one after that. And the one after that.

It was way too much, way too soon.

He tore his mouth away, his forehead pressed against hers, his breathing harsh in the vast outback evening.

Sadie mewed as her scrambled brain grappled with the abrupt disconnect. 'What?' she asked, her voice husky as she pulled back slightly, her hands dropping from his chest, her gaze locking with his.

Kent cleared his throat. 'This is…kind of out of control. It's heading pretty quickly in a direction you might not want it to go.'

Sadie frowned. 'I'm not sixteen, Kent. I know where this is heading.'

Kent swallowed as her gaze zeroed in on his mouth and the urge to kiss her again intensified. 'I can't offer you a relationship, Sadie.'

Sadie blinked. *Where in hell had that come from?* 'Just as well I only want to use you for sex, then.'

'Sadie,' he growled as his still rock-hard erection twitched.

Sadie ran her tongue over her lips, trying to savour the taste of him while he was being all adult. 'I'm not hearing the "Wedding March" if that's what you're worried about.'

Kent followed her tongue as it took a tour of her mouth. 'Don't do that,' he rasped as the action went straight to his groin.

Sadie heard the strain in his voice and smiled. 'What—this?' she asked, cocking an eyebrow as she sent her tongue around for a second swipe.

Kent felt every cell in his body tense. 'Sadie,' he warned.

'Or this?' she asked innocently as she reached for the packet of marshmallows, plucked one out and slipped it into her mouth.

'Mmm,' she murmured, shutting her eyes as she chewed, then deliberately pushed her hands into her hair, lifting it off the back of her neck before dropping it again and opening her eyes.

Sadie watched Kent's Adam's apple bob in his throat. She reached for another marshmallow, bringing it slowly to her mouth, touching it lightly to her lips before withdrawing it.

'You look like you could do with one of these,' she murmured, advancing it towards him, brushing it against his mouth.

Kent's lips tingled at the illicit gesture; he wasn't fooled by the innocence in her eyes or the soft baby pink of the offering.

It might as well have been shiny red because both of them knew it was an invitation to sin.

Their gazes locked as he opened his mouth and she gently pushed it in. 'Now this is my kind of fun,' she murmured.

She kept two fingers against his mouth as he slowly devoured it, admiring the way the fire illuminated the shadows of his face. When he was done he sucked her fingers into his mouth and removed the powdery marshmallow coating.

Then he hauled her into his lap and slammed his mouth against hers.

Sadie wasn't sure if she moaned or he did as sugar turned to spice but she gripped the front of his T-shirt as passion flared and their kisses became deeper, wetter, longer.

Desire squirmed in her belly, heated her thighs, tingled between her legs where the denim of his jeans rasped against her. She could feel the thud of his heart beating at one with hers.

The smell of wood smoke and man filled up her senses and their passion took on a primal quality. She rubbed herself against him. She wanted to strip off all her clothes and be naked with him, like the first man and woman.

As if they were the only two people on earth.

For one crazy moment out here in the middle of nature she even wished that this were her first time.

Kent was only vaguely aware of the cool air hitting his back as Sadie hauled his T-shirt up. Their contact was temporarily broken as he ducked out of it and he took the opportunity as he claimed her mouth again to shift, to tumble her onto the groundsheet, her hair spilling out around her head.

He propped himself on his side, his mouth leaving hers to explore lower, his hand coming to rest on her belly. He traced his tongue down her throat, dipping into the hollow at the base. She moaned and shifted restlessly, her body undulating in his peripheral vision, pushing her breasts up. His hand scrunched into the fabric of her dress as lust seared his groin with a fiery arrow.

He traced his tongue to her collarbone. Followed the path of her shoestring strap. Licked along the edge of her bodice. Dipped into the hint of cleavage.

She shifted again and her little whimper had him pulling back. He gazed down at her. Her eyes were closed, her beautiful full mouth parted. When her eyelids fluttered open her large grey eyes were cloudy with passion.

'I want to look at you,' he said as his hand drifted up over her breasts.

Sadie gasped, her eyelids flickering to half-mast as his fingers brushed an erect nipple.

Kent stopped his upward trajectory and brushed his thumb over the hard little bead he could feel scraping against his finger pad. 'You like that?' he murmured as Sadie gasped again and arched her back. He didn't give her a chance to reply as he dipped his head and put his mouth to the fabric, sucking hard.

Sadie hissed out a breath as she felt the pressure of Kent's tongue and the moistness of his mouth deep down in her centre. Her breasts had always been extraordinarily sensitive and she gripped his shoulder as he took his own sweet time with it. Her belly stirred and she shifted against the ground, each swipe of his tongue involuntarily arching her back. Her brain was utter mush when he finally lifted his head and turned his attention to her cleavage.

'These damn buttons have been taunting me all day,' he muttered as he popped the first one, then the next, then the next. His one-handed dexterity wasn't the best but he enjoyed the slow reveal of her pink bra with a familiar twinkling diamanté in the V of the cleavage.

Sadie's breath was ragged as she watched Kent patiently undo each button on her dress. *All forty of them.* He didn't appear to be in a hurry and when he finally parted the dress and it slithered off her body to pool at her sides he took his time, running his gaze over every centimetre of bare skin.

Sadie actually blushed.

She wasn't used to men taking their time or inspecting her so thoroughly.

'Kent.' She wasn't sure if it came out as eager or desperate but her whole body was humming with desire.

He dragged his gaze away from her body and looked down into her firelit face. 'You're beautiful, Sadie Bliss.'

Sadie's breath caught in her throat. 'You look pretty damn fine your-self,' she murmured.

Kent chuckled as he looked back down at two very magnificent breasts. Breasts he'd thought about a lot the last five days. He traced a finger up a creamy slope to the diamanté at the centre, then back down again. Goosebumps broke out on her skin and he looked at her. 'Cold?'

Sadie shook her head. 'I think I'm so hot I'm about to self-combust.'

He reached into the V and flicked open the front clasp, her large breasts spilling free. 'You can say that again,' he breathed reverently.

Sadie blushed at his scrutiny and tried to cover herself up out of habit. She'd spent a lot of years trying to disguise her breasts. For her father who'd wanted her to be a boy. For Leo who'd wanted them to be smaller. For her career so she could be taken seriously.

Kent pulled her arm away, planting it above her head as he stared at the perfection before him. 'Don't.'

She looked away from the wonder in his eyes, her belly squirming at his utter fascination. She'd seen that look too often when she'd got to this stage with previous partners. But in her experience they held more nov-elty value for men than forming any actual part of their sexual repertoire.

'They're too big,' she muttered as she stared into the fire, embarrassed.

'They're perfect.'

Sadie looked at him. 'Aren't you going to ask me if they're real?'

Kent shook his head as he cupped her breast where it naturally fell sidewards. 'Nope. These,' he said, stroking his fingers along the gener-ous side swell, 'are the real deal.'

And then, because he was practically salivating, he dropped his head and sucked a large round nipple deep into his mouth.

Sadie shut her eyes on a whimper that was almost primordial. His mouth was hot and her nipple even more so but it ruched as quickly as if Kent had placed an ice cube on it. She arched her back and he took it deeper.

Spots formed behind her eyes as he flicked his tongue and grazed his teeth across the sensitive nub. She cried out when he released it, from relief or frustration she wasn't sure, but it was short-lived as he bent to suckle the other, his fingers moving to continue the torturous posses-sion of the one recently released.

Heat started to ripple in little pools deep inside her belly and she lifted her hips restlessly as she cried out, 'Kent.'

Kent lifted his head, desire pounding thick and sludgy through his veins. She looked utterly sexy with her head tossed back, her mouth parted and he quickly claimed it, plundering the soft recesses, soothing her whimpers with his tongue even as he stoked them higher by fondling and kneading her breasts.

'Oh, God,' Sadie whispered as Kent once again abandoned her mouth in favour of a nipple. She sucked in a breath, arching her back as his warm mouth closed over her and his fingers created havoc with the other.

Sadie couldn't think. She could barely breathe as she rode the intense sensations battering her body. The ripples spread further to her thighs and radiated to her buttocks as the world became just Kent—his bare broad shoulders and his hot, hot mouth.

She was sure she was drooling.

She was definitely very, very ready.

Kent pulled away to look at the moist peak he'd just been savouring glisten in the firelight. 'God, Sadie,' he groaned. 'I could do this all night.'

Sadie had a brief moment of clarity when she knew she'd never survive a night of this before he lowered his head to the closest nipple and the world went hazy again.

She cried out as his teeth grazed the tip, her muscles inside contracting hard at the sheer eroticism. Heat flooded into her pelvis. Her thighs grew heavy. Her belly tensed. She was barely aware of his hand finally relinquishing its torture of the other nipple as the ripples grew stronger, more rhythmic, syncing in with the swipes of Kent's tongue.

Kent's head spun at the desperate keening cries coming from somewhere at the back of Sadie's throat. Her arousal was heady and his erection throbbed at every appreciative little whimper. Her nipples were hard and tight against his tongue, a stark contrast to the warm gooey marshmallow from before but no less sweet.

His hand stroked down her abdomen, swirling around her belly button, brushing lower, her soft sighs playing like a cheer squad in his head.

His fingers brushed the edge of her underwear, soft and gauzy, the little diamanté that had taunted him that night in the bathroom hard as the nipple in his mouth. He moved lower still, tracing his fingertips

down over the outside of the fabric, the weave of the filmy material im-
printing on his fingerprints.

He followed the heat down, down, down as his tongue rolled over and
over the peak of her taut nipple, his teeth grazing lightly with each pass.
His finger dipped into the seam that parted her, whispering against the
little nub engorged with sex, heat and lust.

Sadie bucked. One second his mouth was creating delicious havoc and
the next, with just one brush of his finger, her world came apart. Release hit at warp speed, coalescing into a ball of heat and light and pressure right at her very core. The ripples became a tsunami and exploded
through her internal muscles in spasms of almost unbearable pleasure.

She cried out his name into the night as her climax not only shook her,
but felt as if it shook the very foundations beneath her. The stars above
her head twisted into pretty kaleidoscope patterns just before her lids
shut them out and she gripped his shoulders to keep her earthbound.

It took a moment for Kent's lust-drunk brain to realise what was happening. His hand stilled and he lifted his head as he looked down into
her firelit face as she gasped, her eyes shut tight, her head rocking from
side to side.

Watching Sadie Bliss shatter into a million pieces was the sexiest thing
he'd ever seen.

He'd never been so turned on in his life.

He'd lost his virginity at nineteen and he'd prided himself on always
leaving a woman satisfied, but never in all the years since had a woman
been *this* responsive.

He watched every last nuance of her climax as it rippled through her
face from her scrunched brow to her parted mouth. He held her as her
cries settled, her face relaxed and her eyes slowly opened, coming into
a slow dazed-looking focus on his.

He smiled down at her. 'Why, Sadie Bliss, that's one hell of a party
trick,' he murmured.

Sadie's brain scrambled to come back on line as her cheeks warmed.
She saw amusement flickering in his gaze and shut her eyes again. She
wanted to die. She wanted the earth to open up and swallow her. The
man had barely touched her and she'd shattered into a thousand pieces
like some seedy porn queen.

The exact behaviour every guy she'd ever been with had expected from a woman with a body like hers.

'I'm sorry,' she said, opening her eyes, pushing against his arms, desperately trying to pull the edges of her clothing together, suddenly ashamed of her nudity.

Kent frowned as she struggled to sit up. 'Sadie,' he said, firming his arms around her a little.

Sadie shook her head, panic setting in. She needed to get up, to cover up. To have a shower. To curl up in her bed and stick her head under the pillow. 'Let me up,' she demanded, pushing against him again.

Kent heard the note of alarm in her voice and instantly rolled back. 'Sadie, it's fine,' he said as she vaulted upright, scrambling to her feet, grasping at the edges of her clothes, keeping her back to him.

Sadie shook her head, her legs barely supporting her as her useless trembling fingers tried to button the dress. 'I'm sorry,' she said, battling with the insane urge to cry as the buttons refused to cooperate. 'I'm… they're very…sensitive and it's been a while.'

Sadie cringed even as she said it. What possible excuse was there to come in two seconds with someone who was practically a stranger? God knew what he thought of her.

Kent frowned. He couldn't for the life of him work out what was so awful about the situation. 'Why are you apologising?'

Sadie shut her eyes as the buttons defeated her. Keeping her back to him, she quickly shrugged out of his shirt, her dress and bra and then climbed back into the fleecy warmth of flannelette.

Kent, still hard, twitched at the glimpse of her bare thonged buttocks, another diamanté winking in the firelight where the back waistband was intersected by a thin vertical strip connecting the front with the back.

'Can we please just forget this happened?' she muttered, pulling the shirt edges together firmly across her chest, knowing buttons were still beyond her.

She really didn't want to talk about this.

Kent watched as his shirt enveloped the backs of her thighs and the view was snatched away.

'Look at me, Sadie.'

Sadie hugged her waist and contemplated melting into the dark outback night. Anything seemed preferable to facing him after her completely wanton behaviour.

Even the spiders and scorpions seemed a reasonable risk.

How many could there be?

But, there were times for putting on her big girl pants and this was one of them. She hugged her waist harder as she turned to face him. 'I'm sorry,' she said again, looking at the ground.

Kent stood but stayed where he was. Sadie looked as if she was going to bolt off into the bush at any moment and he didn't want to scare her. 'You should never apologise for enjoying sex, Sadie. Never.'

He cringed as soon as he said it. He sounded just like his high-school sex-ed teacher and the last thing he needed to do now with Sadie looking utterly mortified was to come across as if he were the mature voice of reason and she were a child.

Especially considering what had happened was very, very adult!

Sadie looked at him incredulously. 'We didn't even get to the sex bit.'

He didn't understand. How could he? She felt as if she needed to clarify. To put the experience in context.

'I'm sorry,' she apologised again, returning her gaze to the ground because the firelight on his chest was doing funny things to nerves still hypersensitive to stimuli. The low crackle of the campfire and the trill of insects were the only witness to her discomfort.

'I know I probably just came across as inexperienced but it's not that... Men don't ever usually...not really anyway, you know...take the time with...to...you know...with...them...' she tightened her arms across her chest and cleared her throat '...and you did. So, sorry I...you know... got there...a little...early.'

Kent frowned. Was she saying what he thought she was saying? 'I don't understand? Are you saying that the men you've been with haven't appreciated your...assets?'

Sadie blushed at the incredulity on his face. She suddenly preferred it when they weren't talking. But given what had just happened, they couldn't pretend they were just travelling companions any more.

And she really needed him to understand her rather over-the-top reaction to a bit of heavy petting.

She tossed her hair. 'Oh, they appreciate them well enough. Like a status symbol, you know? Check out my phone. My car. My girlfriend's knockers. But when it gets down to…the business…they usually get pretty neglected.'

Kent frowned again. 'Are men on the dating scene intellectually impaired these days?' He could have spent all night fondling her breasts.

Especially when she was so goddamn appreciative!

Hell, he could get off on her getting off alone.

Sadie shook her head, ashamed at the words that were forming there. At the horrible truth of them. About what they said about her more than an indictment on the men she'd been with.

Of what she'd put up with.

'Men form an impression of me…of what I'd be like in the sack… because of my bra size. They want pneumatic Barbie but sex is usually more about them than me.' Certainly it had been for Leo, but love had blinded her to that until tonight. 'I sometimes feel like I'm starring in some kind of wham-bam-thank-you-ma'am porn movie where it's all about looking the part and the end result rather than the journey.'

Kent looked at her, horrified. 'So you just let them?'

Sadie shook her head, frustrated as she transferred her gaze to the fire, trying to think of a way to explain it. 'Don't get me wrong. I enjoy sex, I like…the end result. It's not bad…it's just not…' She didn't know how to explain it other than the truth, which she hadn't realised until tonight with Kent.

She looked at him standing in nothing but his jeans, the warm yellow light shading the fascinating musculature of his abdomen in interesting shadows.

'Like tonight. Like the journey mattered more.' She held his gaze. 'I'm sorry it just…happened.'

Kent shook his head. 'Don't be sorry. I've never been so turned on in my life.'

Sadie swallowed. His voice was deadly serious and her belly contracted. She saw the flare of heat in his eyes, which she didn't think had anything to do with the fire. She was acutely aware of their state of undress. Of what they'd been doing just a few minutes ago.

'Oh, God,' she said, clutching the two edges of the shirt tight at her cleavage as she realised that, whilst she might be pretty damn satisfied, he'd been left in the lurch. 'You must be…' she blushed. 'Do you want to…? I mean, I can help you with…'

She took a step towards him feeling like a virgin again as her gaze dropped to the area between where his hands bracketed his hips.

Was there a discernible bulge there?

Kent held up a hand. 'It's fine. I'm pretty sure I won't die from going without,' he said drily.

She took another step, appalled at leaving him hanging. And also feeling the heat starting to stir again as she wondered what he could possibly do with other parts of his anatomy if he could do what he'd done with his mouth. 'Oh, but—'

Kent stepped back, shaking his head. 'No, wait. I'd rather just…look at you. Can I?'

Sadie glanced at him warily. 'What do you mean?'

'I'd like to look at you,' he said throatily. 'At the firelight on your skin.'

Sadie tightened her hold on the shirt. Night had well and truly fallen around them now and the glow of the campfire was the only light. The road was silent. It was just them and the stars.

Kent held out his hand, his heart pounding in his chest. Sadie had been hiding her body because a few lousy men didn't know how to treat a woman. He wanted to show her she had nothing to be ashamed of and there was one way he knew how to do that better than any other.

Sadie swallowed. He looked so serious, but her insides had turn to mush at his husky request and whilst he was looking at her as if she were the only woman in existence she'd probably do just about anything he wanted.

She took his hand and let him pull her down to the groundsheet until they were sitting cross-legged opposite each other, close but not touching.

'Do you mind?' he asked as he reached over for his camera bag.

Sadie felt everything deep down inside her squeeze. He wanted to photograph her?

Posing, she knew.

Posing, she could do.

But in this medium? With this man? Who'd known her for five days but had still managed to give her the most intense sexual experience of her life?

It was equal parts titillating and scary.

She nodded, not trusting her voice.

Kent dipped in and pulled the camera out. He looked through the lens at her face as he made some adjustments, knowing without a doubt as he studied her features that he had his mojo back.

Her eyes were cast downwards and her hair had fallen forward. She made no attempt to push it back, as if she was deliberately trying to hide.

Suddenly she looked right at him, her knuckles white as they gripped his shirt tight across her chest at the lapels. 'What do you want me to do?'

'Whatever you want,' he murmured as he snapped off the first shot.

He watched as she sat awkwardly beneath the eye of the all-seeing lens, snapping away. The fire glowed on one side of her face, throwing the other side into relief. He concentrated on the shadows, how they shaded her profile, her eyelashes, her cheekbones, the pout of her mouth, the jut of her chin.

Sadie tossed her head and looked right in the lens finally. A little frown knitted her brows together.

'You'll get wrinkles,' he murmured.

Sadie poked her tongue out at him and said, 'Hey,' when he captured it in a split second.

He chuckled and she smiled. Suddenly self-conscious, she scrunched her hair, fluffed it a bit. 'This is what I used to look like,' she said, forming a little moue with her mouth and sucking in her cheeks as Kent clicked.

Kent shuddered at the image from Leo's studio wall. 'You looked terrible.'

Sadie scrunched her face. 'Gee, thanks.'

Kent caught the scrunch with a quick press of a button. 'I mean it, Sadie, you looked like you had a terminal illness.'

Sadie looked at him through his camera, a little frown between her brows. She'd held Leo's images of her up in her mind for so many years as the idyll of feminine lure, had lived in its shadow, it was surprising to realise it wasn't actually true.

'So...the painting...' she hesitated '...didn't work for you?'

Kent dropped the camera to look at her. 'You want to know what works for me? Let your shirt go, Sadie. I'll show you.'

Sadie's breath stuttered to a halt in her throat for a few seconds. Things shifted deep inside her and she was suddenly incredibly nervous. Portraits took weeks, months. Film was instant. There was something about the immediacy of a camera, the up-close intrusion of the lens, that made her want to run for the hills.

She tossed her head. 'So you're not really any different from Leo, then? You also want me to strip off my clothes for your art?'

Kent could hear the quiver in her voice and see the resentment on her face. He hated the comparison to that misogynistic bastard, but he shook his head calmly. 'I want to look at you. See you. As you are. Not my *interpretation* of you. Just you. In all your amazing, curvy glory. I want to show you.'

Sadie could feel herself blushing beneath the intensity of his gaze, the copper flecks glowing in the firelight.

Could she just be her?

'You're beautiful, Sadie. Let me show you.'

Sadie swallowed. His request whispered to her on the still night air and oozed into all those places that had ever harboured doubts about her body. She could feel the chains of Leo's conditioning loosen.

Could Kent be right?

Was *this* Sadie Bliss, *the real one*, beautiful?

She looked down as she slowly let go of the shirt, her hand falling in her lap, the edges parting slightly. The chill had started to encroach as the fire dwindled and it stroked cool fingers over the hint of exposed cleavage.

Kent exhaled slowly as he caught a glimpse of creamy flesh. His erection made an instant resurgence but he didn't say a word, just put the camera back to his face and started snapping again. She didn't move for a while, her hair falling forward masking her face, and he didn't ask her to, just snapped away, being patient, waiting for her to make the first move.

Sadie glanced up at him through her hair, the constant click and whirr of the camera loud between them. She rolled her shoulders back a little, exposing more of her chest, her nipples beading despite still being covered. She looked at the lens more directly.

'I better not see any of these on the Internet,' she joked.

Kent smiled as he clicked. 'That's the beauty of the delete button.'

Sadie pushed her hair back behind her ear, the shirt lifted and opened some more.

'Lay back a little,' Kent murmured, his voice husky as his erection surged against the confines of his jeans.

Sadie felt his words go right to her pelvic floor. She waited a beat before complying. Placing her palms flat on the groundsheet behind her, automatically thrusting her chest outwards. She heard the snap, snap,

snap and dared a little further, shaking her hair as she fell back onto her bent elbows.

'Like this?' she asked. The shirt gaped open covering only the tips of her breasts now.

Kent swallowed. 'Fabulous,' he croaked.

Sadie bent both her knees up and tipped her head back, shrugging her shoulders as she did so, rippling the shirt right off her breasts, fully exposing them. Her nipples were painfully tight from cold and the illicitness of their nature shoot.

'This okay?' she murmured, shutting her eyes as the warmth from the fire heated one side of her body.

Kent dropped the camera from his face momentarily. She looked as if she were moon-baking, her face raised to the heavens in silent supplication. 'Perfect,' he murmured, the camera forgotten as he drank in the creamy palate of skin bathed in a yellow glow.

Sadie lifted her head and looked at him, at the heat in his gaze. She felt suddenly liberated baring her all to him. Flaunting her body instead of trying to de-emphasise it.

Thankful more than he'd ever probably know that he'd rescued her from a mindset that had held her prisoner too long.

She parted her lips and gave him a Mona Lisa smile. Her heart beat a little faster as she let the leg closest to the fire flop to the side, the movement shifting deliciously through her torso. 'What about this?' Her underwear was laid bare to him and she watched as his gaze dropped to check it out.

Kent swallowed as she lay almost completely exposed to his view. The diamanté decorating her pink thong winked at him as his gaze fanned upwards, over the gentle rise of her belly, up to the swell of her breasts, the nipples standing hard and proud beneath his gaze.

She looked so damn perfect he wanted to eat things off her.

Twisties. He wanted to eat Twisties off her.

He ignored the direct order coming from his pants to cease and desist with the camera already and get down to business. Sadie was looking at him with power in her gaze, with pride, and he was determined to give her this moment. He picked up the camera and snapped away again, recording every delectable dip and curve.

'You should never hide any of this, Sadie. You're glorious. You should be proud of it. Embrace it.'

Sadie was officially turned on knowing he was watching her intently through the lens, his gravelly words soothing to an ego that had been battered and bruised for a long time. She shifted her still-bent leg until the foot was resting on his calf, then she slowly traced her big toe up to his knee and down his thigh before coming to rest on the bulge behind his zipper.

'What about this?' she asked, her voice husky as she idly traced her toe over the hard ridge.

Kent dropped the camera, shutting his eyes as he sucked in a breath at the erotic torture. He cracked open his eyes as he placed a stilling hand on her foot. 'Ever done it on the roof of a car?'

Sadie smiled as she pushed the ball of her foot against the hard length of him. 'I don't think those swags are conducive to fooling around in and it's getting pretty cold.'

Kent's erection surged against the pressure. 'Lucky for us they zip together.'

'Really?' Sadie smiled. She withdrew her foot and in one fluid movement got to her feet.

'That's a yes, then?' He smiled, enjoying the view as he looked up at her. His shirt had never looked so damn good. It was completely open, exposing both breasts and the jut of her hard nipples. That fascinating pink gauzy patch at eye level.

'Hurry,' she tossed over her shoulder as she headed towards the vehicle.

Kent watched her go, firelight at her back, starlight at her front. He picked up his camera. 'Sadie,' he called.

Sadie half turned and smiled at him as he snapped the perfect silhouette. His shirt was half off her shoulders, the starry night an amazing backdrop.

'I'm getting naked in ten seconds and it's cold over here,' she said as she continued on her way.

Kent didn't need to be told twice.

CHAPTER NINE

KENT WOKE WITH a start in the middle of the night to a noise. The first thing he saw was Sadie's concerned face looking down at him. He knew without having to ask that the noise must have come from him.

'You okay?' she asked. She'd gone to sleep with her head resting on Kent's shoulder and his head thrashing had woken her a few seconds ago.

Kent raised his head, blinking a couple of times as he looked around, trying to clear the clinging debris of his recurrent bad dream.

He sometimes wondered if he'd ever be okay again.

'Sorry.' He grimaced, his head falling back down.

Sadie resumed her position, snuggling into his side, tucking her head into his shoulder. He smelled good—like wood smoke, soap and man. Her palm sat against his chest and she could feel the accelerated thump of his heart. She shivered as he traced his fingers up and down her bare arm.

She didn't say anything for a while, content after their exhaustive roof-top session to lay snuggled against him under the stars.

'You have bad dreams?'

Kent's caress stilled momentarily before starting again. 'Yes.'

Sadie wasn't fooled by the evenness of his tone. His thudding heart told another story. 'You had one that first night, too,' she said. She waited for him to say something and when nothing was forthcoming she glanced at his profile. 'Is it about the accident?'

'Yes.'

Sadie gently rubbed her palm along the pillow of a sturdy pec. 'I'm guessing you don't talk about it much?'

'Nope.'

'Maybe you should talk to a professional?' she suggested gently.

'Nope.'

Sadie's hand stilled on his chest and she rolled up onto her side, propping her head in her hand. 'Oh, dear,' she mused, watching his mouth in the moonlight. 'Are we back to the beginning again?'

Kent dropped his hand from her shoulder and looked at her. 'I'm not telling some strange shrink my problems.'

Sadie heard a world of pain and denial behind his vehement rejection of help. 'So don't,' she said, finally giving into the urge to trace his mouth with her finger, pulling it away when he shook his head from side to side to displace it. 'Talk to me about it instead.'

And before he could say no to her face she dropped down beside him again, placing her head on his shoulder, his hand automatically coming to rest there again.

Kent looked up at the stars, conscious of Sadie's naked body draped all warm and pliant against his. Every breath he took was filled with a special mix of cool outback and her and immersed him in memories from their fun beneath the covers not that long ago.

There was something extraordinarily generous about Sadie Bliss. She was a giver. And that had obviously cost her in life. She'd been a very generous lover. Making him laugh, making him want, making him hope more than he had since the accident.

All he'd wanted for two years was to feel better and here on a rooftop in the middle of nowhere, under a canopy of stars, he doubted he'd *ever* felt better.

She had sat in front of his camera tonight and bared more than just her body to him. She'd been naked and vulnerable in the truest sense of the word.

Maybe he could reciprocate?

'I hear Dwayne Johnson crying out for his mother.'

The words fell into the cold night air, stark and tinged with anguish, dragging Sadie out of a drowse. It had been quiet for so long, Sadie had assumed he'd drifted off or just wasn't going to talk about it at all.

For a moment she wasn't even sure what she should do or say. But then her hand automatically smoothed along his chest from one nipple to the other and she said, 'That must be difficult.'

Kent was relieved when Sadie didn't try to go all amateur psychologist on him. A few days ago he wouldn't have even contemplated telling her, worried that an intrusive, chatty, stacked twenty-four-year-old would go all Freudian on him.

But he'd learned a lot about Sadie Bliss in the last couple of days. She was much more than an arachnophobic girly.

'It's not every night,' he said. 'But it's…disturbing when it happens.'

Sadie pressed a kiss to his shoulder without conscious thought. She couldn't even begin to imagine the trauma Kent had been through. 'Tell me about *Mortality*.'

Kent tensed. 'That bloody picture,' he murmured.

'You don't like it?'

Kent shook his head. 'You told me that when you saw it, in New York, you couldn't look at it because it was too private.' He shrugged. 'That's the way I feel about it too.'

'So how'd it make the cover of *Time*?'

'A journo friend of mine handed the camera over to my editor when I was in emergency surgery. I lost some days immediately after the crash. They operated four times in thirty-six hours and it was all a bit of a fog. The pictures were the least of my worries. When I finally came to my senses they were all over the media.'

'Couldn't you have them withdrawn?'

He nodded. 'I tried, but Dwayne's parents asked me if I would reconsider. They wanted the world to know that their son had died defending his country.'

'Bit hard to say no to that,' Sadie mused.

Kent chuckled at her understatement, surprised that he could laugh amidst it all. He gave her shoulder a squeeze. 'Yes.'

Sadie lay there absorbing the information for a while. 'At the risk of annoying you…' she said tentatively, not wanting to kill the mood. Obviously Kent talking about this torrid time in his life was not an easy thing but something was bugging her. 'I know you think I talk too much and—'

'Just say it, Sadie,' Kent interrupted on a sigh as tension crept into his belly muscles.

Sadie could feel the cosy mood evaporating but she'd come too far to back out, and if she was the only person he ever spoke to about this then maybe it was up to her to ask the difficult question. The question that had crowded into her brain when she'd first laid eyes on the photograph in that swanky New York gallery.

'I don't understand...how you even...took the photos in the first place?' There was more silence from Kent so she pressed on. 'I mean you were injured, right? Trapped in the body of a crashed helicopter, pinned by your ankle? Men you'd been embedded with for two months were dead and dying.' She pushed herself up and looked down at him. 'How do you stay on task when there's chaos around you?'

Keeping his cool in a situation had never been an issue for Kent. He'd cut his teeth in war zones. It was hard for anyone who didn't live that kind of life to understand.

He didn't look at her as he answered.

'It's my job to snap pictures when all around me is going to hell.'

Sadie would have to have been deaf not to hear the defensive tone in his voice. 'I'm not judging you, Kent. I'm just...curious.'

Kent grappled with telling her politely to mind her own damn business and the strange urge to talk to her. She'd been about the only person he'd ever met who hadn't tried to blow smoke up his arse about *Mortality*. She'd told him how unsettling the image was and he had the feeling she might just understand.

'I didn't want to take the damn pictures,' he finally muttered, looking at her. 'I was trapped. I could smell jet fuel and smoke. I was pretty sure I was about to die in a fiery inferno or by a bullet in the head from the guys that had shot us down.'

Kent wasn't sure if it was the last remnants of the campfire, but he swore he could still smell the smoke. How many times had he woken with the acrid stench in his nostrils?

'My leg hurt like hell. The very last thing on my mind was to snap off some pictures.'

Sadie raised her hand and gently brushed it over his eyes, his cheeks, his mouth. 'But you did?'

Kent nodded, remembering that day in all its Technicolor horror. 'The pilot, Johnny Lieberman, he was also trapped up front. He asked me if I was taking pictures.'

Sadie remembered that the pilot had died a few days later in an ICU in Germany from the wounds inflicted by the crash.

'I said no. *No, I'm not taking bloody pictures.* I couldn't believe he was even asking. I wasn't even sure where my camera was at and frankly I didn't care.'

'But you found it?'

'Johnny was adamant that I should. In fact, he ordered me to do it. Not that he could but he did anyway. Said people should know about this part of war. That helicopters crashed, that good men died. That hearing about it on the news and seeing a burnt-out shell after everything was cleaned up was different from looking at pictures taken in the middle of hell.'

Sadie traced his lips with her finger. 'So you took them.'

He nodded. 'I couldn't see a lot from my vantage point. Wreckage and desert and sky.'

'And Dwayne Johnson.'

Kent nodded. 'He'd been thrown clear so I had a...' Kent shut his eyes as the young soldier's cries played through his mind again. 'A really clear shot of him. I could see the life ebbing from his eyes through the lens. He was calling for his mother. He was frightened and I didn't want him to die alone. I tried to get out, to free myself.'

Sadie could only imagine how frantic Kent must have felt. 'But you couldn't,' she whispered.

The stars above him suddenly blurred, developing auras as if it had been raining in heaven, and it took him a moment to realise the moisture was in *his* eyes. He blinked rapidly. 'All I could do was take pictures.'

Sadie looked down into his face. She could just make out a shimmer of moisture in their copper-brown recesses. She kissed him lightly. What else could she do? How was someone supposed to go through such a trauma and come out the same person at the end? For some things there were no words—just comfort and consolation.

'I'm so, so sorry,' she murmured against his mouth. Kissing him again.

Kent kissed her back, pushing his hands into her hair as he pulled her head down onto his mouth hard and fast, all the anguish and pain and frustration he'd felt over the last two years injected into the moment. Her lips tasted sweet and he wanted to get lost in her, in her mouth, her body, her moans and her sighs.

To not think for one night about Dwayne Johnson and a photo that still haunted him.

To affirm life.

He shifted, rolled towards her, rolled her under him as she opened her mouth to him, opened her legs to him.

He plundered her mouth as his hands moved lower, feeling her buck as he skimmed a breast and stayed to rub his thumb over the rapidly ruching nipple.

'Condom,' she muttered as she wrapped her legs around his waist, felt the thick hard bulk of him butting against her.

Kent blindly reached for the box inside her backpack that she'd brought up with her earlier and was stashed near their heads.

Where the hell was it, damn it?

'Hurry,' Sadie muttered in his ear as the temptation to have him drive into her then and there beat like insect wings inside her brain. She was ready, he was ready and she wanted to take him away somewhere far removed from an Afghan desert.

Kent finally located the box, grabbed a foil packet out and quickly donned the protection. Sadie reached for him and he settled back into the cradle of her pelvis, kissing her long and hard as he pushed deep inside her.

She cried out, the sound primal in their own rooftop Eden. Her fingertips bit into the flesh of his shoulders as he ground into her, each thrust driving higher and harder, pushing her closer. His mouth left hers, seeking a nipple, sucking it into his mouth as he rocked into her.

Kent lifted his head and groaned as his building climax dug fiery fingers deep into his buttocks, his arms anchored either side of her trembling as they held him up.

'Yes, yes, yes,' Sadie whispered as she too felt the bubble rising inside her.

He buried his face in her neck as everything spiralled out of control.

He tried to hold it back, to hold them in the moment where things hung on a precipice between pleasure and completion, but the primal call was too strong for him and he let the wave sweep him away as she tightened around him and joined him in the maelstrom.

Sadie woke again as the sky was just starting to lighten. The stars were still out but waning as obsidian faded to velvet. Kent was sleeping, the first violet hues of dawn lying gently against his number-two stubble and beautiful mouth. She wanted to wake him but, between an insatiable sex drive and an obviously exhausting dream, his night had been disturbed enough.

She felt around her for his shirt which had been discarded somewhere in the bedding, finally locating it down by her foot. God alone knew where her thong was. She had a feeling Kent might have tossed it over the side.

The air still felt cool and she dragged the shirt on, doing up three buttons as she sat up, the sky too resplendent to miss. She reached behind her into her bag, pulling out the sketch pad and pastels she'd taken from Leo's, inspired again as she had been the other night under the stars when she hadn't had access to materials.

She sat with her back to Kent facing the road and the uninterrupted view in that direction. All that could be heard as the morning lightened to soft baby blues was the scratching of the pastels on the paper as Sadie sketched like a woman possessed, hurrying to capture the moment that night faded and dawn encroached before it was lost to her for ever.

She was so utterly absorbed in the process she didn't even feel Kent stir until he was behind her, pressing a kiss into her neck, peering over her shoulder.

She shut her eyes as he rumbled, 'Good morning,' in her ear.

She sighed, snaking a hand behind her and anchoring it around his neck, her fingers stained with a multicoloured chalky residue. She settled against his broad naked chest as his arms encircled her waist.

She felt stiff from sitting hunched over the sketch pad and she stretched a little as she said, 'Morning.'

Kent looked down at the sketch pad, the drawing arresting him immediately. It had captured the essence of an outback dawn with the vivid colours and swirls around the fading stars similar to those used by Van Gogh in his famous starry night painting, and yet there was something uniquely contemporary Australian about it.

It was an incredible blend of old world charm and modern boldness. It was simply stunning.

'Sadie...' He shook his head. 'That's...amazing.'

Sadie blushed at the compliment. 'It's just a sketch,' she dismissed, used to disregarding her work.

Kent shook his head. 'No, it's not. It's...a work of art.'

Sadie gave a half-laugh. She liked what she saw, and creating it had felt incredible, but she could see its flaws and felt the old doubts return. Could hear Leo's *you're not talented enough* mantra in her head.

'I couldn't not,' she said absently, looking down at the sketch. 'When I woke up and saw the sky, I couldn't not capture it. I *had* to do it.'

Kent heard the surprise in her voice. 'Well, that says a lot, doesn't it?' he murmured.

Sadie frowned as she half turned to look at him. 'What does it say?'

'You're an artist, Sadie Bliss. And whatever the hell you're doing with this journalism gig is just wasting your time. You were obviously born to do this.'

Sadie shook her head as she turned back to the sketch. 'No. I'm not good enough.'

Kent tightened his hand around her belly. 'Says who? Leonard Pinto?'

Sadie shrugged. 'The man does have an eye for art.'

Kent felt irrationally angry that one man could screw with a woman's head so much. 'Leonard paints women who look like boys. I think his eye is seriously off. I also think he knows *exactly* how talented you are but he didn't want to let you go.'

Sadie wanted to deny it but hadn't she come to the same conclusion yesterday? That he'd wanted his muse back and he was prepared to go to any lengths to get it?

Kent gentled his hands against her and lightly circled his thumbs over the curves of her hips. 'Sadie, you are *incredibly* good. Don't you think you owe it to yourself to explore that a little more?'

Sadie shut her eyes as his words of praise, aided and abetted by the brush of his thumbs against her skin and the scrape of stubble at her neck, seduced her.

A fledgling ray of possibility sparked to life inside her and she shied from it. Art had made her incredibly happy. And incredibly unhappy. Could she go back to that roller coaster again?

She pushed the illicit thought away, stamping on its lure. It wasn't something she could decide on a whim. Certainly not on a car rooftop with a man who had already muddled her senses a little too much.

'I think,' she said, injecting playfulness into her tone, 'you're just saying that to get in my pants, Kent Nelson.'

Kent smiled as he nibbled at the place where her neck met her shoulder. She was obviously changing the subject but he had to give her points for her method.

'Well, now, that'd be kind of hard considering I pitched them somewhere over the side last night.'

Sadie smiled, letting herself get lost in the sexiness of his voice, taking her away from the serious stuff for a while. 'Kent Nelson,' she murmured. 'Are you suggesting I'm not wearing any underwear?'

Kent chuckled as he trailed his hand from her hip downwards. 'Well, now, why don't I check?'

Sadie shut her eyes as he confirmed what they both knew very quickly.

'Mmm,' he murmured, his other hand travelling north as his tongue traced patterns on her neck. 'You feel good.'

Sadie bit her lip as his hand cupped a breast. She tried to turn but he tightened his arms around her.

'Shh,' he said. 'Lean back and enjoy.'

Not an offer she could refuse.

The tow truck arrived at nine as promised and before they knew it they were sitting in the front of a poorly sprung truck next to an ancient local who chatted away merrily. A local who was thankfully oblivious to the fact that Sadie's fingers kept brushing lightly against the firm bulge behind Kent's zipper. And the way Kent's fingers caressed the swell of her breast under the guise of a casual arm slung over her shoulder.

It was a long, sexy, three-hour journey back to Katherine.

When they got into town Sadie opted for a café to do some work on her laptop whilst Kent saw to the vehicle. But not before he'd dragged her into the deserted toilets at the garage, pushed her against the wall and kissed her senseless, promising retribution for the torture she'd put him through.

Which made it difficult to concentrate on the story for Tabitha. So instead she spent her time in the café madly journalling the last few days with Kent. Words, like the strokes of the pastels this morning, flowed freely and she wasn't sure how much time had passed when a pair of worn jeans came into her line of vision.

She looked up from her screen and Kent smiled at her.

'I called your name twice. The story's shaping up nicely, then?'

Sadie tried not to look guilty as she smiled back at him. 'I think Tabitha will be happy,' she lied. 'Is the Land Rover ready?'

He nodded. 'Have you eaten?'

'Three cappuccinos, a muffin and a burger with the lot.'

Kent laughed at the sparkle in her doe eyes. 'Good. I'll order something to go and then we can hit the track.'

They were heading north to Darwin fifteen minutes later.

'Let's play I Spy,' Sadie said as she opened the packet of Twisties Kent had purchased back at the café.

Kent rolled his head to look at her briefly before looking back at the road. 'You think because we bonked like bunnies last night that I'll do anything for a repeat performance?'

Sadie grinned as she bit down on the cheesy snack, flavour exploding in her mouth. 'Yep.'

He laughed. *She was right.* 'You think I'm that easy?'

Sadie shrugged, examining a fat orange finger of pure carbohydrate. She brushed it against her mouth and sucked it slowly in. 'I could make it worth your while.'

Kent's gaze snagged on the orange dust clinging to her mouth. 'We're not talking about hand feeding me Twisties here, are we?'

She smiled as she plucked another out of the bag and licked it before she popped it into her mouth. 'Nope.'

'You're talking trading sexual favours?'

'Yep.'

'I *love* your dirty mind.'

Sadie laughed. She *loved* how he looked at her—as if he'd already stripped her naked.

Leo had looked at her as if he could fix her.

Kent looked at her as if she was already perfect.

'I spy with my little eye, something beginning with…' she pulled another Twistie out of the packet and poked it into her cleavage '… T,' she said, looking up when she was satisfied with the placement.

Kent's breath hitched in his chest as saliva coated his mouth. He was reminded of how he'd thought about eating Twisties off her body last night and he was hard in under ten seconds. 'How about we play truth and dare instead?' he suggested, his voice rough and low.

'Truth and dare,' Sadie mused as she placed a second in her cleavage.

'I dare you to strip down to your underwear and stay that way until we get to Darwin.'

He held his breath as he waited for her reply. The Sadie from a couple of days ago would have flayed him alive at the suggestion. Hell, the Kent from a couple of days ago would never have suggested it. But this Sadie, hell-bent on decorating herself in snack food, looked as if she was up for something totally spontaneous.

He certainly was.

Sadie felt her breath thicken in her throat and her nipples bead at his indecent proposal. 'Sure. But I dare you not to touch. Think you could manage that?'

Kent's pulse wooshed through his ears. She looked so damn sure of herself and he was torn between being the dare-taking kid of old who'd do anything to win and knowing that, if she really did get down to her underwear, it would only be a matter of time before he folded.

He nodded. 'Absolutely.'

Sadie smiled at the bob of his throat. 'Okay, then.'

Kent tried really hard to concentrate on the road, but it was difficult with Sadie shimmying out of her clothes in his peripheral vision. In under a minute she was sitting in some hot-looking red and black matching underwear—Twisties protruding from her cleavage.

Sadie tossed her clothing on the floor and smiled at him. 'I give you—' she looked at the clock '—five minutes.'

Kent kept his eyes firmly trained on the road. 'Easy,' he scoffed.

'Yes.' She smiled as she shoved another lurid orange finger into her bra. 'I know.'

Kent tapped his foot as the minutes slowly ticked by and Sadie shoved more Twisties everywhere. Her hair, her bra straps, snuggled against her nipples, her belly button.

At four minutes and thirty seconds she pulled the band of her knickers out and dropped one down the front, closing it with a snap.

'Right!' Kent said, indicating abruptly as he took the car cross country, right off the road. 'You win.'

The three-hour trip took about double that by the time he'd relieved her of all the hidden food and licked all the Twistie dust off her and she'd eaten a few off him. It was early evening when they drove into the outskirts of Darwin.

Kent looked at Sadie as she stared out of the window. She'd been curiously quiet the last hour or so. 'Cat got your tongue, Sadie Bliss?'

Sadie turned and smiled at him. She'd been conscious of their time running out and it was making her wistful. 'I didn't think you liked me chattering?'

'Since when did that stop you?'

Sadie ignored him. Since their relationship, or whatever the hell it was now, had moved to another level, since they'd both got to know each other a little better, she didn't feel a blinding need to fill up the silence.

The silence was companionable. Maybe that was the sex. Whatever— it wasn't awkward for her any more.

'Airport?' Kent asked a moment later. 'Or night in a swanky hotel and airport in the morning?'

Sadie felt her heart rate pick up a little. One last night with Kent. She wasn't foolish enough to believe this was the start of something. As addictive as Kent could be, he had issues to get sorted. So did she. She needed to sort out what she wanted to do with her life and she didn't need the distraction of him.

She didn't want to trade one addiction for another.

'What, no spiders? No scorpions?'

Kent grinned. 'How will we manage?'

'Lead the way.'

* * *

Half an hour later they were opening the door to the executive suite at the Esplanade Central. Sadie brushed past Kent and threw herself on the cloudlike, king-sized bed, flapping about as if she were making a snow angel on the stark white bedding.

'Ah-h-h, bliss,' she murmured.

Kent looked at Sadie all stretched out and shook his head. 'Not yet.'

Sadie sucked in a breath at the undiluted lust she saw in the copper flecks of his eyes. She lifted her foot and placed it on his thigh. 'I need a shower first. I smell like Twisties.'

Kent's pulse tripped at getting Sadie wet all over. 'Good idea.' He pulled his T-shirt over his head. 'Get naked,' he said.

Sadie laughed even as the sight of his chest did funny things inside hers. 'I just need to put my laptop on charge,' she said.

He unzipped his jeans. 'Hurry.'

Sadie watched him as he headed to the shower until he disappeared from sight. Maybe getting on a plane tomorrow was going to be a little harder than she thought.

She vaulted off the bed at the unsettling thought. She grabbed her laptop out of her bag and set it up on the desk in the room, plugging it into the nearby power point. She opened the lid and pulled up the document from earlier. She took her memory stick out of the pouch in the laptop bag and was about to insert it when Kent called, 'Sadie Bliss, get your delectable butt in here now or I'm coming to get you.'

Sadie turned around to find a naked Kent standing in the doorway to the bathroom. She hadn't seen him naked and vertical and he really was a sight to behold. Even his deformed ankle didn't detract from his overwhelming masculinity. Her belly flopped and her heart did a painful squeeze.

She dropped the memory stick on the table and swallowed against her suddenly parched throat.

'Well, when you put it like that,' she said, mission forgotten as she kicked out of her shoes and lifted her T-shirt off as she walked towards him.

Kent grinned as he took three paces into the running shower, feeling the warmth hit the back of his neck, watching as Sadie entered the bathroom in just a tiny scrap of red and black fabric at the apex of her thighs, a foil packet between her teeth. His semi-arousal turned to full blown as she looked him straight in the eyes whilst she stripped the scrap away.

And when she stepped into the shower cubicle and sank straight to her knees he knew Sadie Bliss was going to be very hard to forget.

CHAPTER TEN

KENT WAS STILL grinning as he left Sadie washing her hair in the shower fifteen minutes later. This really wasn't how he thought this assignment was going to turn out.

He'd been prepared to tolerate it.

Tolerate her.

To have just pushed her against the shower tiles and had his way with her was not what he'd envisioned after their first not-so-promising shower incident in Cunnamulla.

Well, not seriously anyway.

His stomach growled and he remembered why he'd been kicked out of the shower. He picked up the room service menu off the bedside table and headed for the phone to order. He sat at the desk and dialed, shifting the open laptop to make room for the menu. Sadie's discarded memory stick sat next to it and he picked it up as he said, 'Hello,' into the receiver.

He had a brief conversation as he flicked through the menu ordering wildly inappropriate things that would probably give Tabitha apoplexy when the bill came in.

Champagne. Strawberries. Oysters. Cheese platter.

The fancy chocolate pudding with a warm gooey centre. He had definite plans for that.

His gaze fell on the laptop screen as he absently turned the memory stick over in his hands while the call taker repeated his order. The header *Kent Nelson, Mere Mortal* caught his eye and his grin faded.

He read the two paragraphs on the screen, then dropped the stick as he scrolled down further, replying automatically to the woman on the other end of the phone and hanging up, not hearing or caring if the order was correct.

He read it all—all two thousand words—his heart beating faster, anger simmering with every one. Everything he'd said, everything that had happened between them, was there. And more. Her observations. Her opinions.

Her pop psychology.

Stuff that he hadn't even begun to grapple with. Had shied from even thinking too hard about.

By the time he got to the end—*Kent Nelson is an enigma but no man is an island*—he was so mad he wanted to break things.

Sadie came out of the shower wrapped in a fluffy gown, towelling her hair. 'Did you order something?' she asked his back. 'I'm starving.'

Kent stood and turned to face her. 'You're writing a story about me?' he demanded.

Sadie frowned at the steel in his voice and the return of the hard lines of his face. She hadn't seen them for a couple of days now and had forgotten how austere they could be. 'No.'

He stepped aside and pointed to the laptop screen. 'I think you are.'

Sadie gasped as she realised what she'd done. She shook her head as she walked towards him. 'It's not what it looks like.'

Kent slashed his hand through the air, pulling her up short. 'I told you my story *was not* for sale. This stuff is private.'

Sadie struggled to understand how the day had gone to hell so quickly. One moment they were in the shower and she was thinking she could get used to all that single-minded intensity of his, particularly when he was buried deep inside her, and the next he was looking at her with ice in his eyes.

Back to square one.

Sadie dropped the towel, her hair hanging in damp strips around her shoulders. 'I'm not doing a story on you. I'm just…journalling.'

'It sure as hell reads like a story,' he snapped. 'Did Tabitha put you up to this?' he demanded. 'She's been trying to get me to do an exclusive for months.'

Sadie took another step towards him but halted as he held out his hand. 'Tabitha has nothing to do with this. It's just me putting my thoughts and feelings down. I have absolutely no intention of doing anything with it. You can delete it right now if you want.'

Kent turned, leant over the keyboard and hit Control A. The article highlighted before his eyes and he hit the delete button.

He only wished it felt as satisfying as it looked.

Sadie watched her work disappear in dismay. Those words might have come easily but no writer liked to lose work. Sure, she could write them again, but they'd never be as perfect as they had been.

She propped her hands on her hips. 'Happy now?'

'Do you have a backup?' he asked.

Sadie nodded. 'On the memory stick.'

Kent picked up the stick. He gave her a wide berth as he rounded her and headed for the bathroom. Once inside he avoided looking at the shower cubicle as the memories of their soapy encounter returned. He strode to the toilet, opened the lid, tossed the stick in and flushed it.

'It's okay,' Sadie said derisively when he stormed out a moment later, his limp more obvious than it had been in days. 'There wasn't anything important on there.'

Kent ignored her as he hefted his bag onto the bed and pulled out some clothes. Her apparent lack of concern over the loss of the article hadn't mollified him.

Had she been interviewing him all along? Was that what all the incessant questions had been about? Had she been taking notes the entire five days? Did she think that she could bat those incredible lashes at him and he wouldn't mean what he'd said yesterday—*God, was it only yesterday?*—that it was no one's damn business?

He'd thought she'd been joking about her interviewing him. Obviously not.

Sadie watched as he dressed quickly in jeans and a T-shirt, the flash of a naked back and buttocks when he dropped the towel having a funny effect on her pulse despite their current state of animosity. 'I'm not doing a story on you, Kent.'

Kent sat on the bed and stuffed his feet into his shoes. Whether she was or wasn't just wasn't the point any more. This debacle was a salient reminder of why he'd kept himself to himself.

He'd let Sadie Bliss and her treacherous curves get way too close. Her conjectures in the article had been searing and insightful and even now he shied from them.

He didn't want or need her inside his head. What the hell did someone in their mid-twenties know about stuff like this?

He'd come out here to get his photographic mojo back. Not to lose his head over a woman and certainly not to get it head shrunk by one either.

There were things he had to come to terms with, he knew that. But he was doing that to his own timetable.

She was wrong—this man was an island.

The uninhabitable kind.

He stood and looked at her. 'This was a mistake.'

Sadie blinked. 'What was? This hotel room? Sex in the shower? Sex on the roof of your car? Our night under the stars? Making me believe that I shouldn't be ashamed of my body? Talking about the accident? Or just the whole damn trip?'

Kent nodded, his jaw locked. 'All of it.' He should never have taken the assignment in the first place. He should have kept her at a distance.

His blunt admission rocked her back on her heels; she was surprised by how much it hurt. Okay, he was pissed at her. She got it. But did he really regret everything that had happened? Apart from this sticky end, which she would no doubt analyse ad nauseam in the coming months, she didn't have a one. Kent had helped her think differently about herself—about her body and her art.

And for that she would be for ever grateful.

'For the last time, I was not writing a story about you.'

Kent folded his arms across his chest. Okay, he believed her. But he doubted she was being honest with herself over her true reasons and that was cause for concern.

'Well, who were you writing it for?' he asked. 'Because if it was just for you then I think you may be a little...fixated on me.'

The last thing he needed was Sadie Bliss making his life difficult after they parted ways with some obsessive girly crush.

The last thing he needed was Sadie Bliss full stop.

'We had great sex, Sadie. But don't delude yourself—there can be nothing else.'

Sadie was speechless for a moment at the sheer ego on the man. She wished she could tell him it wasn't that good, but unfortunately she couldn't.

She could however assure him he wasn't the only man in the world. A girl had her pride.

'I hate to be the one to break this to you but I'm pretty sure you do not own the only penis-of-amazing-powers in the world and I'm *damn* sure I can get on with my life without pining for it.'

Although she'd probably think about it a little more than was healthy.

'Besides which,' she added, 'if you think all we had was sex, then maybe you're a little deluded. You shared stuff with me I'm betting you've never told anyone else. I can get sex and, thanks to you, I'll be sure to hold my future partners to a higher standard, but where are you going to find someone you can talk to, Kent? Because you *really* need to talk to someone.'

Kent glared at her, his face stony. He did not want to get into a conversation about his state of mind. That was especially none of her business. 'This is *not* about me, Sadie.'

'So you're just going to have nightmares for the rest of your life?' she demanded. 'You're going to hear poor Dwayne Johnson calling for his mother every time you shut your eyes?'

'I'll deal with my stuff,' he snapped. 'I just want to make sure you aren't spinning castles in the air because of our physical...intimacy.'

Sadie snorted. Kent had opened up so much from the guy he'd been at the beginning of the trip, but right now he'd taken a huge slide backwards. He couldn't even recognise they'd been more than just physically intimate. That there'd been emotional intimacy as well.

And he was running for the hills.

'Why on earth would I want to be involved with a man who is so guarded, so...' she floundered around looking for the most apt description that didn't involve mentioning how far up his backside his head was jammed '...deep in his man cave, I feel like I need a miner's lamp and pick whenever I talk to him? Relationships shouldn't be that hard, Kent.'

He nodded, his lips terse. *His work here was done.*

'Good,' he said, brushing past her and heading for the door. 'At least we agree on something.'

He was desperate to put as much distance as possible between him and her damn robe belt that was loosening and flashing glimpses of her cleavage. It made him want to throw her on the bed, which was not conducive to walking away.

To ending it.

Whatever *it* was.

Sadie turned and watched him limp away. 'Where are you going?' she asked.

He opened the door. 'Out.'

And then there was just Sadie left looking at a closing door, her heart beating wildly. She sank onto the end of the bed, her brain trying to catch up. Twenty minutes ago she'd had a screaming orgasm in the shower. Now Kent was gone and there was a heavy feeling in her chest and a growing urge to cry.

She stood. She would not cry. She'd cried over her father and cried over Leo.

She would not cry over a man she'd known for five days.

She walked on shaky legs to the telephone, ignoring the open laptop taunting her.

If only she'd shut the lid!

Maybe instead of scaring him off she and Kent would be talking right now about seeing each other some more. Because she hadn't been ready to say goodbye just yet and she was pretty damn sure, after that shower, he wasn't either.

She dialled the airport and changed her flight.

Six months later...

'C'mon.' Leila banged on the bathroom door. 'It's opening night and the gallery will be crowded.'

Sadie looked at herself one last time in the mirror. Why she was fussing she didn't know. He never went to gallery events, he'd told her that.

In fact she wouldn't normally be going either. Now she was a full-time student again she couldn't afford the big ticket price—she'd even had to take on a flatmate, Leila, to make the rent. But when two tickets had mysteriously turned up and Leila, a photography major, had spied them, Sadie hadn't had the heart to deny her.

And, truth be told, she was curious.

Sadie had already seen some of it, of course. The dozen photographs printed with her Leonard Pinto feature had been magnificent. But this exhibition, *Centre Attraction*, was the complete outback series and, being Kent's first exhibition of new work, had garnered a true buzz in the art scene.

It had been billed as *the* show to see.

'How do I look?' she asked Leila as she opened the door, her fingers absently stroking down the front of her retro fire-engine red dress. It dipped at the cleavage, nipped at the waist, clung to the hips and flared around the calves in an elegant fishtail.

'Woohoo, baby,' Leila crowed. 'I'd do you.'

Sadie laughed, the stress bunching her neck muscles instantly easing. Leila was out and proud and very much in a couple but her flattery was just what Sadie needed tonight. 'All right,' she said. 'Let's *do* this thing.'

Kent almost choked on his beer when he spotted Sadie sashay into the gallery. He hadn't been sure she'd come even with the tickets he'd sent her. And he certainly hadn't expected her to make such an entrance. The eyes of every straight man with a pulse tracked her path from the door to the bar area.

She'd come a long way since awful power suits and baggy T-shirts.

The gallery was crowded and he was stuck in a corner with some of Tabitha's cronies, but he watched her as she did the rounds of the displays. She chatted to the woman she'd arrived with and seemed to make polite conversation with other patrons who were admiring the exhibits as well.

None of them shone as she did.

Watching her felt like coming out of a fog and he realised he'd missed her even more than he'd thought. He'd wanted to see her, to show her his work that she'd been so much a part of. Particularly the centrepiece. He was proud of it and wanted her to be proud of it too.

But he hadn't expected everything to finally make sense by just looking at her.

Yes, he'd thought about her every day. Missed her every day. But this was more. So much more.

She was two exhibits away when he politely excused himself from the group of people he'd been barely paying attention to anyway.

Sadie stood in front of a photo of emus mid-dash across a western sky. The bounce of their soft feathers and the dust kicking up around their powerful legs gave the photograph a sense of motion and urgency. She remembered him taking the pictures. Telling her about his grandfather.

She studied it for a while as she waited for the crowd to clear from around the next piece. She'd been surreptitiously looking for him but he'd obviously been true to his word.

'Oh, my God.'

Sadie turned at the urgent tug on her arm administered by Leila. She wasn't too concerned though—Leila had been goggle-eyed all night, each photograph seemingly more fantastical through her rose-coloured glasses than the last.

'Sadie, is that you?'

Sadie frowned at her friend's face, then looked up at the photograph that had everyone's interest. It took a few seconds to compute what she was looking at and then everything inside her seemed to crash to a halt.

Her brain synapses. Her cellular metabolism.

The beat of her heart, the breath in her lungs.

It was the one he'd taken of her the night of the campfire. Where she'd stood and he'd called her name and she had looked back over her shoulder at him. It was a stunningly visual shot. Her face in shadow, her semi-naked body silhouetted in soft yellow light against a starry sky.

The caption read—*Sadie In The Sky With Diamonds*.

Beside it, enlarged and framed, was her sketch. The byline proclaiming her as the artist.

When she'd got home from Darwin she'd realised she'd left her sketch book in his car but hadn't bothered to contact him about it. A part of her had wanted him to have it, to have a tangible reminder of what they'd shared—*emotionally*, not physically.

Sadie could feel heat rising in her cheeks as she looked at it now. How could he share something so personal? How could he?

She'd believed him when he'd told her how very much he hadn't wanted *Mortality* to be shared. Had he not thought she'd feel the same way about this?

'You like?'

Sadie started at the oh-so-familiar tone. She turned to find him standing behind her, his mouth, beautiful as ever, so very, very close.

Her heart started again at the sight of him. It had been *so* long and he looked *so* good. Just as she remembered from the last long six months of thinking about him. Of sketching him.

Only better.

The dark suit blunted his *he-man* edge to a different kind of sexy and her belly clenched.

But it didn't change what he'd done or the sudden block of emotion welling in her chest. Her heart pounded in her ears as she shook her head. 'How could you?' she whispered, then pushed past him.

Away, she had to get away.

It was much harder for Kent to make his escape from the gallery than it had been for Sadie. He'd just caught a glimpse of her climbing into a taxi before someone blocked his view and it had been another twenty minutes before he'd managed to get away.

He guessed running out on your own exhibition was pretty poor form, but he'd only been there tonight hoping she'd show up.

And now she was gone, he didn't want to be there either.

He just wanted to be with her.

Luckily he knew the way to her flat and by the time he'd parked an hour had elapsed since she'd run from him.

'Sadie,' he called, knocking on her door. 'I know you're in there. Open up!'

Sadie, sitting in her daggy track pants and shirt, jumped at the harsh command. Her hand shook as she raised the glass of red wine to her lips.

Kent belted louder this time. 'I'm going to knock all night if I have to, Sadie!'

Sadie glared at the door. It was tempting to let him go for it. Mrs Arbuthnot from next door called the police if a cat meowed too loudly outside her door at night.

But she *was* pretty mad at him. And she did need to talk to him about pulling the photo from the exhibition. She stormed over to the door and pulled it open. 'You've got a bloody nerve,' she said, turning on her heel and stomping back into the lounge room, leaving him standing on the doorstep.

Kent shut the door after him and followed her at a more sedate pace, finding her waiting for him, arms crossed, grey eyes stormy, spoiling for a fight.

'I want it pulled,' she said straight up.

'Sadie—'

'No. You were supposed to delete those pictures. I did not give you my permission to use a *half-naked* picture of me in an exhibition that thousands of people will see.'

Kent undid his jacket buttons and thrust his hands on his hips. 'But a fully naked portrait is perfectly fine?'

'What other ones have you used?' she demanded, ignoring his jibe. The portraits were consensual and he knew it. 'Have you uploaded them somewhere? Damn it, Kent, they're private and I want them back.' The words were familiar and a thought suddenly hit her. 'Oh, my God, that's what this is about, isn't it? This is payback for that stuff I wrote. For the last time, Kent, it *was not* a story!'

'Sadie,' Kent said, holding up a placating hand, trying not to be turned on by how gorgeous she was all het up, her hair flying around her head, her eyes burning, her chest rising and falling in an agitated rhythm.

'They're burned to a disc. I kept meaning to send them to you but I couldn't bring myself to part with them. I wouldn't share them with anyone.'

Sadie snorted. 'Just half of Sydney!'

'It's one photo, Sadie. No one knows it's you.'

'*I* know it's me!' she snapped. 'And let's not even mention the fact that you reproduced and displayed *my* artwork, without *my* permission!'

'The two pieces belong together.'

Sadie gaped. He didn't even look a little contrite, standing in her lounge room oozing sex and confidence in his important artist suit. She hadn't really expected to see him tonight and she resented how damn good he looked.

And how her traitorous body didn't seem to care that he'd just exposed something between them that had been intimate and private. He might as well have stripped her naked in front of everyone at the gallery.

'Why?' she demanded.

'Because it's a stunning image. The pick of all the photos I took on our road trip. Maybe one of the best of my career. And to apologise.'

Sadie blinked. 'Apologise?'

'For being such a prat in Darwin.'

'By being an even bigger prat now?' She gaped.

Kent saw the two spots of colour up high on her cheekbones and wanted to drag her into his arms so badly he had to grind his feet into the floor to stop himself from following through.

Sadie didn't look as if she was quite there yet.

He took a steadying breath. 'If you don't like it I'll have it withdrawn.'

Sadie sat down and took a gulp of her wine. She needed fortification. 'It's got nothing to do with not liking it,' she said slowly through clenched teeth.

'Okay,' he said, hands still on his hips as he looked down at her. 'Explain it to me. It's not like you haven't posed nude before, Sadie.'

'It's got nothing to do with that.' She glared up at him. 'That picture represents a very personal moment you and I shared. And I know you're Mr I-don't-need-anybody and no doubt *he-men* pander to women with poor self-image every day, but it means something to me. I feel about it the way you feel about *Mortality*. That photo is an intensely private moment. Not for public viewing. It's not my body I want to protect. It's the moment.'

Kent sat down on the coffee table behind him, his legs stretching out, almost touching hers. He was encouraged when she didn't attempt to move away. 'I'll have it withdrawn first thing tomorrow,' he murmured.

Sadie looked into the multi-hues of brown that made up his eyes. 'Thank you.'

Kent nodded, his heart thudding as her gaze locked with his. 'It's good to see you, Sadie Bliss.'

She shook her head. 'Don't.'

He half smiled. 'Don't what?'

'I'm not going to fall into bed with you because you turn up on my doorstep all sexy and apologetic. I'm still mad.'

He chuckled then. 'I missed you.'

Sadie sipped at her wine, determined not to give him an inch. 'Yeh, well, I haven't missed you,' she lied.

'I've thought about you every day, Sadie. And I've pretended that's a lot of things—fond memories, lust, friendship—but I saw you tonight and I knew it was more than that.' He dropped his gaze to her full mouth that had parted as she listened. He wanted to kiss her so badly he could almost taste her. 'You're under my skin, Sadie Bliss.'

Sadie's internal muscles undulated deep down inside her at his words and his sudden intense look. It would be so easy to just throw caution to the wind and hurl herself at him, but after six months apart she knew two things.

She was head first in love with him. And the Kent she knew couldn't handle that.

'I'm back at art school,' she said as his gaze returned to her face. 'I'm loving it. For the first time in my life I really know what I want to do. I'm actually my own person. I love you, Kent. I think I have from the moment you let me drive the Land Rover.'

She paused. Her pulse was beating triple time but the admission had been surprisingly easy to make.

'But I can't take on your stuff. I need to be in a relationship where I can talk with the other person, where no subject is off limits, no words are left unsaid. Where I can talk whenever I want to. I have a lot to say.' She smiled at her own joke. 'I'm prepared to do some hard yards but I need to know that you're going to meet me halfway.'

Kent knew what she was saying was true. 'How did you get to be so wise so young?' he asked.

Sadie smiled around her wine glass. 'Misspent youth.'

Kent placed his hands on his knees. 'I've been seeing a psychologist for the last four months. It's been...hard at times. But it's helped. I've started to write a memoir about the time I was embedded. I even went on a commercial flight just recently. The dream doesn't come so much any more.'

He paused. Smiled at her. 'Now all I usually dream about is you.' She smiled back at him and he felt encouraged. 'I can't promise I'm going to be happiness and light twenty-four seven but my life didn't make sense for a long time and then you came along and, briefly, it did. I don't know how our future is going to pan out, Sadie—I'm so happy that you're pursuing your art dream and at some stage I'm going to want to take another overseas assignment—but I know that whatever happens I want you in it. I love you, Sadie.'

Sadie considered him over the rim of the glass, her heart beating frantically at words that were like music to her ears. The man who had taught her to embrace who she was, to glory in it, was telling her he loved her.

'That's all I need,' she murmured.

Kent held her gaze. He wasn't sure what that meant. Or whose move it was.

Sadie sat forward, placing her wine glass on the table beside him. 'So,' she said, resting her bent elbow on her knee and propping her chin on her palm, 'these dreams? Do I have my clothes on?'

Okay, Sadie's move. He grinned. 'Not often.'

'Are they…graphic?'

Kent nodded. 'Usually.'

She reached for his tie and started to untie the knot. 'I think you're going to have to demonstrate,' she murmured.

Kent nuzzled her temple, her ear, her neck. 'I'm good at demonstrating.'

Sadie slid the tie out from the collar with a loud zip. She stood, his tie dangling from her finger. 'Well come on then, let's get started.'

She held out her hand and he took it.

* * * * *

Bushfire Bride
Marion Lennox

Dear Reader,

Bushfires in Australia are terrifying and catastrophic, but they're also unavoidable if our native forests are to regenerate. The blackened landscape means death and destruction—but it also promises new life.

The forest near my home was destroyed two years ago and afterward I drove across the charred landscape with despair. Now my dog, Harry, and I walk through the newly regenerated forest with joy.

Rachel, my heroine in *Bushfire Bride,* has also felt despair, but the Cowral Bay bushfire (as well as the Cowral Bay doctor!) brings her joy and laughter and a new beginning. As with our bushfire, the destruction signals a new beginning for a whole community.

This book is a celebration of life after catastrophe. I hope you love reading it as much as I loved writing it.

Warm regards,

Marion Lennox

PROLOGUE

THE THIN BLUE line rose and fell. Rose and fell. Rose and fell.

How long does love last?

The young woman by the bed should surely know. She sat and watched now as she'd sat and watched for years.

'I love you, Craig,' she whispered, but there was no answer. There was never an answer.

Dappled sunlight fell over lifeless fingers. Beloved eyes, once so full of life and laughter, stayed closed.

The blue line rose and fell. Rose and fell.

'I love you, Craig,' she whispered again, and blessed his face with her fingers. 'My love...'

How long does love last? For ever?

CHAPTER ONE

'SHE MAY BE beautiful but I bet she's stupid.'

Dr Rachel Harper's hamburger paused midway to her mouth. Tomato sauce oozed onto her T-shirt, but her T-shirt was disgusting already. The sauce was the same colour as her pants. Hey—she was colour co-ordinated!

She was also distracted.

'Look at her hair,' the voice was saying. 'It'd cost a fortune to keep it like that, and what for? She's a blonde bimbo, Toby, mark my words. A gorgeous piece of fluff.'

'But she's got lovely legs.' The child's words were a thoughtful response to the man's deep rumble. 'And she's got really nice eyes.'

'Never be taken in by appearances, Toby,' the deep voice decreed. 'Under that gorgeous exterior, she's nothing but a twit.'

Enough! Rachel might be a reluctant protector, but she was here to defend and defend she would. She hitched back the curtain and faced the world.

Or, to be precise, she faced the Cowral dog show.

The pavilion was packed and she'd retreated with her hamburger for a little privacy. The cubicles behind each dog weren't big enough to swing a cat—or a dog—but at least they were private.

Who was criticising Penelope?

'Hey!' she said, and a man and a child turned to stare. She wiped a smudge of tomato sauce from her chin and stared right back.

Penelope's detractor was in his mid-thirties, she guessed.

Maybe he was a farmer? That's what he looked like. He was wearing moleskins and a khaki shirt of the type that all the farmers around here seemed to wear. His curly black hair just reached his collar. He had deep brown, crinkly eyes and, with his deeply tanned skin, he looked...

Nice, Rachel decided. In fact, if she was being critical—and she was definitely in the mood for being critical—he looked more than nice. He looked gorgeous! The small boy beside him was aged about six, and he was a miniature replica. They had to be father and son.

Father and son. Family. The man was therefore married. Married? Why was she wondering about married?

She gave herself a swift mental swipe for thinking of any such thing. Dottie had been doing her work too well. Why would Rachel possibly be interested in whether a complete stranger had a partner?

She was here with Michael.

But, then, who was she kidding? She was interested in anyone but Michael—married or not. The fact that she was married herself didn't—couldn't—matter. Dr Rachel Harper had reached her limit.

'I need to show Penelope to gain championship points,' Michael had told her one day at Sydney Central Hospital, where they both worked, and Dottie had pushed her to go. 'Get a life,' she'd said. 'It's time to move on.'

So she'd allowed herself to be persuaded. Rachel had imagined an hour or two displaying a beautiful dog, a comfortable motel in the beautiful seaside town of Cowral and the rest of the weekend lazing at the beach. Maybe Dottie was right. She'd had no holiday for eight years. She was exhausted past imagining. Maybe Dottie's edict that it was time to move on was worth considering.

But Michael's dream weekend had turned out to be just that—a dream. Reality was guilt. It was also a heat wave, a motel that refused to take dogs and an entire weekend guarding Michael's stupid dog from supposedly jealous competitors.

Where was Michael? Who knew? She sighed and addressed Penelope's critics.

'Penelope's been bred from two Australian champions,' she told the stranger and his child, and she glared her very best putting-the-peasants-in-their-places glare.

'She's a very nice dog,' the little boy said. He smiled a shy smile up at Rachel. 'Can I pat her nose?'

She softened. 'Of course you can.'

'She might bite,' the man warned, and Rachel stopped smiling and glared again.

'Stupid dogs bite. Penelope's a lady.'

'Penelope's an Afghan hound.'

'So?'

The man's lips twitched. There was laughter lurking behind those dark eyes and the beginning of a challenge. 'So she's dumb.'

Rachel brightened. A challenge? Great. She'd been here too long. She was bored to screaming point. Anything was better than retreating to her soggy hamburger and yesterday's newspapers.

In truth, what she was aching for was a fight with Michael but he wasn't here. However, this man was the same species—male—and the laughter behind his eyes told her he was fair game.

'You're not only rude,' she told him, her gaze speculative. 'You're also racist.'

He raised his brows and his brown eyes creased into laughing disbelief. 'You're saying she's smart?'

'She's a sweetheart.' Rachel gave the great white hound a hug and then winced as a smear of ketchup soiled the dog's immaculate coat. Whoops. Michael would be out with his pistols.

Where was Michael?

'You don't need to take my word for it,' the man was saying. A small crowd was gathering now. The judging heats were over; final judging wasn't for another two hours and things were slow in the dog shed. Rachel wasn't the only one who was bored. 'There's tests for dog intelligence.'

'You're going to implement the MENSA quiz?'

'Nothing so complicated. Lend me a piece of your hamburger.'

'Lend... Hey, get your own hamburger.'

'It's in the interest of scientific research,' he told her. 'My daddy's a doctor,' the little boy said, as if that explained everything.

'Yeah? Doctor of what?' Rachel grinned down at the kid, beginning to enjoy herself for the first time all weekend. 'It sounds a sneaky way to get some of my hamburger.'

'It's a simple experiment,' the man told her, refusing to be sidetracked. 'See my dog?'

The stalls and their associated sleeping quarters were raised almost three feet above the ground. Rachel peered over the edge. A lean, brown dog of indeterminate parentage gazed back at her. As big as a collie, the mutt was all legs, tail and eyes. As Rachel gazed down at him, he raised his back leg for a weary scratch.

'Charming,' Rachel said. 'Great party trick.'

'Digger doesn't do party tricks.'

She nodded in sympathetic understanding. 'I guess you need to be house-trained to be let into parties.'

The man's grin matched hers. War hadn't just been declared—the first shots had been fired. 'Are you implying Digger's not house-trained?'

'Seeing is believing.' This was OK, she decided. For the first time since she'd been conned into coming to this last bastion of civilisation, she was having fun. Guilt could be forgotten—for the moment. Penelope against Digger. It was a crazy conversation. She wasn't sure how it had started but she didn't intend to stop. 'Breeding will out,' she declared. 'There's been more gone into Digger's breeding than your mutt's.'

'My mutt's name is Penelope,' she said haughtily. 'And she's no mutt. She comes from long line of Australian champions. Whereas your mutt...'

'Digger also comes from a long line of champions,' the stranger told her. He smiled again, and it was a heart-stopper of a smile. A real killer. 'We're sure there's a piece of champion Border collie in there somewhere, and a champion kelpie...'

'And a champion dachshund?' Rachel watched as Digger's tiny pointy tail stuck straight up. 'Definitely dachshund.'

'That's silly,' the little boy said. 'Dachshunds are long and flat and Digger's high and bouncy.'

'Right.' She was trying not to laugh. Both the man and the boy were entrancing. Two gorgeous smiles. Two sets of deep, dark eyes ready to spring into laughter. She was bored out of her brain and this pair were a diversion sent from heaven.

'So what do we do with my hamburger?' she asked, and the man's smile deepened. Honestly, it was a smile to die for.

'We put it under a feed dish.'

Rachel raised her eyebrows, then shrugged and handed over her burger. A fair amount of ketchup came, too.

The man looked down at his hand—ketchup with hamburger attached. Ugh. In truth it had been a very soggy hamburger and Rachel wasn't all that sorry to lose it. 'You like your burgers well sauced?'

'Yes,' she told him, and went back to glowering.

'My Dad says tomato sauce has too much salt and salt's bad for blood pressure,' the little boy ventured.

'People who say rude things about dogs are bad for blood pressure,' Rachel retorted, and there was a general chuckle from their growing audience. 'So what are you intending to do with my hamburger?'

'Watch.' The man stooped and placed a piece of hamburger underneath an upturned dog dish. Then he stood back and let Digger's lead go slack.

'Dinner,' he said.

Digger looked up at him. Adoring. Then the skinny, brown dog gazed around the crowd as if ensuring each and every eye was on him. He sniffed, placed a paw on top of the dish, crouched down, pushed with the other paw... The dish toppled sideways to reveal the piece of hamburger.

Digger looked around again as if awaiting applause. It came. He received his due and then delicately ate the hamburger.

Uh-oh.

'Now it's Penelope's turn.'

'She'll get dirty,' Rachel said, and there was a trace of worry in her voice. Penelope might be lovely, but her opposition was seriously smart.

'We'll put it up on her platform.' The stranger's smile was growing broader. 'I'll even wipe the ketchup off. Or maybe you could do it on your T-shirt.'

Ouch! 'Watch your mouth.'

Another grin, but the entire pavilion was watching now and he didn't stop. He placed the dish in front of Penelope's nose. He broke a second piece of hamburger, showed it to Penelope and popped it underneath.

He backed away and left her to it. Penelope sniffed. She sniffed again. She whined.

She lay down in front of the dish. She stood up and barked. She shoved the dish sideways with her nose and barked again.

Nothing happened. She lay down and whined, pathos personified.

'So your dog's hungrier than mine,' Rachel told him with a touch of desperation, and there was general laughter. 'You must starve Digger.'

'Do I look like a man who'd starve a dog?'

No. He didn't. He looked really nice, Rachel decided, and she wished all of a sudden that she wasn't in soiled jeans and sauce-stained T-shirt, that her mass of deep brown curls were untangled and not full of the straw that the organisers had put down as bedding, and that she looked...

Oh, heck, what was she thinking of? This guy had a kid.

She was here with Michael and... 'Rachel, are you feeding Penelope?'

Unthinkingly, she'd raised the feed bowl, and Penelope was launching herself into the hamburger as if there was no tomorrow.

'Um... Michael.'

Michael, silver-haired, suave and in charge of his world, was elbowing through the crowd and his face was incredulous. No one messed with Michael's instructions. Pedigree dog food only. 'What on earth do you think you're doing?'

'I'm proving Penelope's intelligence,' she told him, chin jutting. Enough was enough and she'd had more than enough of Dr Michael Levering.

Back at Sydney Central, Michael had seemed witty and charming and, as one of Sydney's top cardiologists, he was extremely eligible. His invitation to go away with him for the weekend had half the staff in Casualty green with envy, and her friends and her family had finally pushed her to accept. 'Come on,' her mother-in-law had told her. 'This is your chance. You know it's time you moved on. A romantic weekend with a gorgeous bachelor... Rachel, love, you take some precautions and go for it!'

Precautions. Ha! That was the last thing she'd needed. They were supposed to be sharing dog duty. That was another joke. Michael had said he'd sleep in the car because he was too tall to fit in the dog box, but she was starting to have serious doubts about what car he'd slept in. When he'd appeared this morning, ten minutes before Penelope had been due to appear in the judging ring, he'd looked far too clean to have slept in any car. Then he'd said he'd had to make an urgent telephone call. She hadn't seen him again. So what had he been doing all this time? She looked at him suspiciously, checking for damp hair. If she could prove he'd been swimming while she'd dog-sat, she was going to have to kill him.

'Our dog's more intelligent than yours,' the little boy piped up, and Michael stared down at the child in distaste.

'What are you talking about?'

Rachel flinched. This weekend was definitely not going to plan. Sexy? Eligible? Ha! This man was a king-sized toad.

'I'm Toby McInnes and this is my dad,' the little boy told him, oblivious to the anger in Michael's voice. 'My dad's Dr Hugo McInnes. Who are you?'

Michael opened his mouth but Rachel forestalled him. She knew what would come out and it wouldn't be pleasant. 'This is Michael and I'm Rachel,' she told the little boy. She watched Hugo's grip tighten on his son's hand and she didn't blame him; she was moving into protection mode herself. 'Penelope is Michael's dog.'

But Michael had moved on. He was talking only to Rachel. 'Did you know there are bushfires out of town?'

'Bushfires?' Rachel knew nothing of any bushfires. She hadn't been out of the pavilion all day.

'They're a long way from here.' The man—the doctor?—called Hugo was gazing from Rachel to Michael and back again. His initial anger at Michael seemed to have faded and he now looked as if the whole scene held great interest for him.

'The fires are threatening to block the road,' Michael snapped. He shoved Penelope away from him and the big dog practically fell over. Fast thinking was not Penelope's strong point. She whined a little and nuzzled Rachel, and Rachel gave her a hug. Stupid or not, she was still a very nice dog.

As company went, if Rachel had a choice between Penelope or Michael, Penelope was definitely preferable.

'Rachel, there's an emergency back in town,' Michael was saying. 'Bushfires or not, I need to leave. There's a helicopter on the way to collect me.'

'A helicopter?'

A helicopter. Coming to collect Michael. Rachel focused.

She really focused.

Michael was clean-shaven. He was wearing immaculate slacks and a crisp white shirt—and a tie for heaven's sake. And his hair... She couldn't stop staring at his hair. He looked like he'd just emerged from the shower.

The dog pavilion didn't run to showers. Rachel hadn't seen running water for twenty-four hours. She stank of Michael's dog.

What was the bet Michael had just come from the beach via a shower? Via a motel.

She'd reached her limit. His talk of helicopters wasn't making sense but she didn't care.

'Did you sleep at the motel last night?' she demanded, and Michael paused.

'No, but—'

'Do you own a red Aston Martin?' Hugo asked, politely interested.

'Yes.' Michael suddenly looked flustered. Understandably. He was used to deference and subservience. He wasn't finding it here.

'That fits,' Hugo was saying. 'You look the sort of guy who owns an Aston Martin. I did a house call at the motel at two this morning. Arnold Roberts was suffering badly from gout. He had the adjoining suite to yours. We inspected your car from stem to stern while we waited for his analgesic to take effect.' He smiled from Rachel to Michael and back again—as if he was being really, really helpful. 'We were wondering who'd bring a car like that to a place like this and now we know. I'll tell Arnold it belongs to an Afghan owner and all will be clear.'

He was laughing, but Rachel hardly noticed. Her fury was threatening to overwhelm her.

'You slept at the motel?'

Michael heard her anger then. Everybody did.

'I thought you cancelled,' she said carefully. 'When they wouldn't let us bring the dog.'

'They rang me later and said it was too late to cancel—they were keeping my deposit,' Michael muttered. He had the grace to look a bit shamefaced, but only for a moment. He regrouped fast. With an ego the size of Michael's it was easy. 'And by then you'd agreed to sleep here. For heaven's sake, Rachel, you know how small the car is. Do you want me to hurt my back?'

'Yes!'

'Look, it's immaterial anyway,' he told her, moving right on. 'It's just as well I had a decent night's sleep as it happens. Hubert Witherspoon's had a heart attack.'

Hubert Witherspoon? The name had its desired effect.

Rachel's fury was deflected—for the moment.

Hubert Witherspoon was probably the richest man in Australia. He owned half the iron ore deposits in the country. What the man wanted, the man got.

'He wants me,' Michael told her. 'What—?'

'The Witherspoon family aren't risking road blocks due to bushfire. They've sent a helicopter to take me back to Sydney.' He glanced at his watch. 'It should be landing right now and they want me to leave immediately. Can you show Penelope for her final judging and bring her home afterwards?'

Hubert Witherspoon...

Hubert's death would be a national catastrophe—at least for the financial markets. It should have made Rachel's eyes widen in awe.

It should have made her do whatever Michael wanted. But—Michael had been swimming. He'd slept in a motel. In a bed.

While she'd been sitting with Penelope, feeling just dreadful about leaving Sydney. For such a reason...

'You want me to show Penelope?' she managed, and he smiled, the smooth, specialist-to-junior-doctor smile that had persuaded her to come on this weekend in the first place. Why did it make her think suddenly of snake oil?

'You've been watching the other dogs being shown,' he told her. 'You saw how I handled Penelope this morning.' He checked Rachel from head to toe with a judge's critical eye. 'Penelope will be fine. You might want to get yourself cleaned up a bit first, though.'

If she didn't slug him it was only because they were surrounded by a score of onlookers, but it was a really close thing. Somehow she managed to keep hold of a shred of dignity. A scrap. 'Right.' She took a deep breath. 'You want me to drive all the way back to Sydney by myself?'

'Of course. Unless the bushfires block the road. I'll understand if you're delayed.' He tossed her the car keys and she was so astounded she caught them. But that was all she was doing.

'No.'

'Rachel...' His tone became patient-consultant talking to slightly stupid junior. 'You know I can't be replaced. Hubert needs a cardiologist and he needs the best.'

'I have hay in my hair,' she muttered through gritted teeth. 'I can't show a potential Australian champion.'

'Yes, you can. You just need a—'

He got no further. She lifted the car keys and threw them right at his freshly shined shoes. 'Your dog, your problem. I'm going home,' she told him, one syllable at a time. 'I'll hitchhike if I must, but I'm not touching your car.'

'Rachel—'

'Stuff it. Stuff you.'

'But Hubert—'

'Hubert can die for all I care, but he won't die because you're not there. He's over eighty, he's grossly overweight and there are at least five cardiologists in Sydney who are as qualified as you are to care for him.'

'You know that's ridiculous.'

'I know nothing of the kind.'

'Can I make a suggestion?' It was Brown Eyes. Hugo. But Rachel wasn't in the mood for interruptions. She wheeled and gave him a look to kill.

'Butt out. This is my business.'

He held up his hand, placating. 'Whoa…'

'I'm out of here.' She leaned back into the cubicle, grabbed her overnight bag and hauled it out. It was a fine gesture which didn't come off quite as planned. She hadn't snibbed her bag shut, and it flew open. Out tumbled her spare jeans, her toilet bag—and a bra and a couple of pairs of very lacy, very scant panties.

They were Dottie's offerings. Her mother-in-law. 'You never know what's going to happen, dear,' she'd told her. 'And I do so want you to be prepared.'

Dottie was right. You never did know what was going to happen, but one thing Rachel did know. She'd been a fool to ever agree to come here. She closed her eyes as her belongings tumbled everywhere. A bra flew past Digger's nose. He snagged it and held on, seemingly bemused.

Everyone was bemused.

Dear heaven, let the ground open under her. She had to get out of here.

'The dog can keep it,' she said with as much dignity as she could muster, stuffing the rest of her gear into her bag and fighting a wave of burning mortification. 'He's so smart he can probably work out how to wear it.' She pulled the remains of her bag shut, tugged the shreds of her dignity around her and stalked toward the door.

They watched her go, Hugo with laughter in his eyes and Michael with his jaw somewhere around his ankles.

She didn't care. If she didn't see any one of them again she'd be delighted. She was getting out of here.

She didn't make it.

She stalked out of the pavilion, took a couple of deep breaths and regrouped for a moment to try and figure out the location of the main entrance to the showgrounds—and a dogfight broke out just behind her.

CHAPTER TWO

SHE STOPPED.

Of course she stopped. The sound of the dogfight was unmistakable, the vicious, ear-splitting snarls breaking through everything else.

And then a high-pitched scream of human terror.

She'd have to have been less than human to ignore it. She turned and stared, as did everyone else close enough to hear.

The dogfight was at the entrance of the pavilion she'd just left and it wasn't a fight—it was a massacre. A faded old cocker spaniel, black and white turned to grey, had been held on its lead by his teenage owner but the pit bull terrier had no restraint and it was intent on killing. The dogs were locked in mortal combat, though the cocker clearly had no idea about fighting—no idea about how to defend himself. The spaniel's owner—a girl of maybe fifteen or so—was the one who'd screamed in terror. She was no longer screaming. She was trying desperately to separate them. As Rachel started forward—no!—the girl grabbed the pit bull's collar and hauled. The dog snarled and twisted away from the spaniel—and bit. 'No!'

Rachel was screaming at her to stop—to let go. She was running, but it was a good fifty yards back to the entrance to the pavilion.

The man—Hugo—was before her. The dogs were everywhere—a mass of writhing bodies with the girl beneath...

She had to get them apart. The girl would be killed.

Rachel dived to grab a collar to pull the pit bull from the girl, but her arm was caught.

'Keep back!' Hugo's harsh command had the power to make her pause. He was reaching for a hose snaking across the entrance and he hauled it forward. 'Turn it on.'

She saw instantly what he wanted and dived for the tap. Two seconds later the tap was turned to full power. The massive hose, used to blast out the mess in the pavilion after showtime, was directed full at the dogs.

Nothing else could have separated them. The blast hit the pit bull square on the muzzle and drove him back. The hose turned to the spaniel, but he was already whimpering in retreat, badly bitten by the pit bull, while Rachel launched herself at the prone body of the girl.

'Her leg...' she breathed.

The girl's leg was spurting bright arterial blood, a vast pulsating stream. Oh, God, had the dog torn the femoral artery? She'd die in minutes.

The dog had lunged at her upper leg and the girl had been wearing shorts! Dear heaven...

'Someone, get my bag. Fast! Run!' Hugo was shouting with urgency. 'The car's by the kiosk.' Car keys were tossed into the crowd—swiftly, because Hugo's hands were already trying to exert pressure. Rachel was hauling her T-shirt over her head. They needed something for a pressure pad—anything—and decency came a very poor second to lifesaving.

She shoved the shirt into Hugo's hands and Hugo wasn't asking questions. He grabbed the T-shirt and pushed.

'Kim, don't move,' Hugo was saying, and with a jolt Rachel realised he was talking to the girl. He was good, this man. Even *in extremis* he found time to tell his patient what was happening. 'Your leg's been badly bitten and we need to stop the bleeding. I know it hurts like hell but someone's gone for painkillers. Just a few short minutes before we can ease the pain for you, Kim. I promise.'

Could she hear? Rachel didn't know and she had to concentrate on her own role. Hugo would want a more solid pad than one T-shirt could provide. She stared up into the crowd. 'Michael,' she yelled. Hugo was too busy applying pressure to haul off his shirt and he needed something to make a pad. And Michael could help with more than a shirt. He had the skills.

But Michael was gone.

It couldn't matter. 'Take mine.' A burly farmer had seen her need and was hauling off his shirt. She accepted with gratitude, coiling it into a pad.

Out of the corner of her eye she saw her overnight bag, sprawled and open in the dust where she'd dropped it as she'd lunged for the tap. More clothes. Great. As Hugo looked up, searching for whatever she had, she handed him a pad. She made another with what was in the bag. Then she shoved the pad hard down over his and pressed. He pressed with her. Even their combined effort wasn't enough to stop the flow.

'I need forceps,' he said grimly. 'My bag...'

'Clive's gone to fetch it,' the farmer told them, hovering over both doctors as they worked, his face ashen with concern. 'He'll be back any minute. He's the fastest runner.'

'Good.' They were working together, their hands in tandem. Hugo was breathing fast, using all his strength to push tighter, and Rachel realised that she was hardly breathing at all. *Live. Please.* It was a prayer she'd learned early on in her medical training, and had used over and over. Skills were good but sometimes more was needed.

Luck?

Still the blood oozed. 'Push down harder,' Hugo told her. 'Don't move off the wound.'

'I'm not moving,' she said through gritted teeth. The bite resembled a shark bite—a huge, gaping wound that, left untended, would release all the body's blood in minutes.

Even if tended...

She was pushing down so hard it hurt.

'I need forceps.' Hugo's voice was growing more urgent as the situation became more desperate. 'Damn, where's my bag?'

'Here.' A youngster, a boy of about sixteen, was bursting through the crowd, carting a bag that was three times the size of any doctor's bag that Rachel had ever seen. A country doctor's bag.

'Haul it open.'

The boy flicked the bag open and Rachel's eyes widened. Forceps. There were several and they were sitting on the top as if prepared for just this emergency. She lifted a hand from the wound and grabbed the first pair.

'We're not going to stop this without clamping,' she muttered. 'The femoral artery has to have been torn to explain this.'

He accepted her medical knowledge without a blink. 'I agree. Clive, take a shirt and clear as much blood as you can while we work. Let's go.' He grabbed forceps himself and then looked across at her. 'Ready?'

She took a deep breath. This was a huge risk. They needed the pad to stop the spurting, but the only way to stop the bleeding altogether was to remove the pad and locate the source. They had only seconds to do it or the girl would die beneath their hands.

'OK.' She took two deep breaths. 'Now.'

They lifted the pad away from the wound. The blood spurted out and they were working blind, searching in the mess that was the girl's leg.

Where in this mess was the artery? Dear God, they had to stop it.

'Take the swab right away, Clive. Just for the moment,' Hugo said. 'Be ready to replace it.'

And in the tiny millisecond before the wound refilled with blood... 'There!' Rachel pushed in and grasped, and the forceps linked to the torn artery. She clicked them shut—and the pumping died.

Not enough.

There were more. As well as the femoral artery, two or three minor vessels had been torn. They could kill all by themselves.

Hugo's forceps clamped shut on another blood vessel and the flow abated still further. Another pair of forceps was in Rachel's hands and Hugo had another.

She was working like lightning. Without the pads there was no pressure—the blood simply pumped out.

'Gotcha.' Another one was under Hugo's forceps. He clamped.

And another. And that was it.

The blood was still oozing, but slowly now. The pumping had stopped. It'd be flowing from the ripped veins but they'd done what they had to do. For now.

'We need to continue with pressure,' she said, and sat back as Hugo set to work with another shirt, forming another pad. They'd been lucky. Trying to find the blood vessels in these conditions...

Yeah, they'd been lucky—but this man was good!

Hugo was tying the pad firmly around the leg. He gave her a curious glance. There was still urgency but they were working with minutes now rather than seconds. They'd blocked off the blood supply. Now they needed to prevent shock setting in. They needed to replace fluids and they needed to save a leg that no longer had a blood supply.

'Pete, ring the ambulance,' Hugo snapped into the crowd. 'Tell them I want plasma and saline on board and if they're not here in thirty seconds I'll have their hides. Dave, can you and a couple of the men find those damned dogs and deal with them before we have another disaster? Toby... Where's Toby?' He looked out into the crowd, searching for his little boy. 'Myra, can you take him?'

'The first two are already being looked after,' someone said. 'The vet's got the cocker and a couple of guys have gone after the pit bull. The ambulance is on its way.'

Which left Toby.

A middle-aged woman stepped from the crowd of horrified onlookers and took Toby's hand. The child had been standing white-faced and shocked as Hugo and Rachel had worked. 'Come on, love,' she told him. 'Come with me while Daddy looks after Kim.'

Kim...

Rachel looked up to the girl's deathly white face. Kim's eyes were open but it wasn't clear whether she was conscious or not.

'You'll be OK, Kim,' she told her, taking the opportunity to take the girl's hand in hers. What she'd most need now would be reassurance. Not panic. 'We needed to hurt you a bit to stop the bleeding but we're both doctors. We know what we're doing. The bleeding's stopped now.'

The girl's eyes widened. She was conscious. 'Mum... Knickers...'

'Someone find the Sandersons,' Hugo ordered. 'It's OK, Kim. We'll find your mum and dad now, and Knickers is with the vet. You know Rob will look after Knickers just as I'll look after you.'

The flaring panic in the girl's eyes subsided. They were winning. Kind of. For now.

But...was one of the reasons the bleeding had eased because the blood pressure itself had dropped?

'She hasn't lost too much,' Hugo muttered, and Rachel realised he was thinking the same as she was.

Too much blood...

There was certainly a lot. Rachel herself was covered with a spray of gore. She was wearing only a bra above the waist and she looked like something out of a vampire movie. Paramedics were supposed to wear protective clothing, she thought ruefully. If Kim had any sort of blood-borne disease, then she and Hugo were now also infected.

They couldn't care. Not now.

Hugo was swabbing the girl's arm and Rachel moved to get a syringe. By the time Hugo had the line ready she was prepared.

'Five milligrams morphine?'

'Yeah, and then saline. We need plasma. Hell, where's the ambulance?'

It was here. There was a shout and then someone was pushing through the crowd. A couple of ambulance officers. Rachel almost wept with relief. They'd have plasma, saline—everything Hugo needed.

They'd take over. This wasn't her place. She could go back to being a horrified onlooker.

But...

'Your husband's a cardiologist?' She'd gone back to applying pressure as Hugo inserted an IV line.

Her husband? She stared blankly and then realised who he was talking about. Michael, her husband. What a thought! But now wasn't the time for fixing misconceptions. 'Yes.'

'Thank God for that.'

'Sorry?'

'I'm the only doctor in town,' he told her. 'Can you ask someone to find him? He'll be able to help.'

'He was catching the helicopter back to Sydney,' Rachel said blankly.

'There's a helicopter's taking off now,' a voice said helpfully. 'You can hear it.'

He'd left? Michael had left?

Maybe he hadn't even noticed what had happened. Rachel had stalked out and it'd be just like Michael to have left as well. He'd have heard the dogfight but he wouldn't have turned to investigate. She knew him well enough after this weekend to know he wouldn't deviate from his chosen plan for anyone.

'He's taken the helicopter?' Hugo searched the crowd to find the farmer who'd been the first to offer his shirt. 'OK, it'll have to come back. Matt, get onto the radio. Get the chopper returned here. Tell the pilot we need priority. Kim needs emergency surgery if we're to save this leg. She needs vascular surgeons. We need to evacuate her—now!'

'Will do,' Matt muttered, and ran.

There was a crowd of about twenty onlookers around them now, but it wasn't the sort of crowd you saw in city accidents, Rachel thought. There was horror on everyone's faces. They all knew Kim. They were all desperate to help. Rachel was the only woman who'd stripped to her bra but she knew without asking that each and every one of these women would do the same and more if they needed to. Their care and concern were palpable.

Then Kim's parents were there, running toward their daughter across the showgrounds. Their fear reached the group on the ground before they did, but Kim had drifted into unconsciousness. The combination of shock, blood loss and painkillers had sent her under. Good, Rachel thought as her mother disintegrated into tears, sobbing onto her chest. The horror on her parents' faces would only have made things worse.

Enough. There was nothing more she could do now. One of the paramedics had taken her position, keeping pressure on the wound. She rose. A buxom woman in floral Crimplene put her arm around her and held. Rachel wasn't complaining. She was grateful for the support.

'Who are you?' Hugo asked. He was adjusting a bag of plasma, the ambulance officers were helping. Rachel wasn't needed.

'Rachel. Rachel Harper.'

'You're a doctor?'

'Yes.'

'You're not a vascular surgeon, I suppose?'

'I wish.' She knew exactly what he was thinking. A vascular surgeon was what they needed, urgently. The chances of saving Kim's leg were incredibly slim. 'But Michael has the skills. And he's still in range.'

He'd be upset at being called back but he had no choice. 'OK.' He stared up at her for a moment longer, his intelligent eyes assessing. Each knew what the other was thinking. They couldn't voice it here—not in front of Kim's parents—but if the femoral artery wasn't repaired fast, Kim would lose the leg if not her life.

They needed the helicopter. They needed Michael. Kim's future depended on it.

There was nothing Rachel could do, though. For now she was no longer needed.

Mrs Keen, the lady in the Crimplene, ushered Rachel into the showground caretaker's residence. As the ambulance screamed its way to the hospital she was already under hot water while Mrs Keen tut-tutted about the state of her clothes.

'And the clothes in your bag are no better,' she told Rachel through the bathroom door. 'One of the men brought your bag over but you've dropped it, and then used everything to stop the bleeding. Oh, my dear, there's blood on everything.'

That was a minor worry. For now Rachel couldn't care. She let the hot water steam away the gore and she worried about the girl. Worried about the leg.

Michael would be really angry at being recalled. He'd hate to miss out on the Witherspoon case.

It couldn't matter. He wouldn't have heard the dogfight, she decided. Michael Levering saw only the things that affected him. He was needed in Sydney for a prestigious patient and Rachel wasn't doing what he wanted. He'd have simply turned on his heel and stalked away. As for Rachel and Penelope—others could pick up the pieces. If Rachel didn't take his expensive dog and his expensive car back to Sydney, well, Michael had the money to send a lackey to the country to collect them later in the week. Dog-show organisers were hardly likely to let Penelope starve and even if they did...

Penelope was just a possession. 'Damn the man.'

She was shaking, a combination of anger and reaction to the whole situation. They'd been really, really lucky to save Kim's life.

Michael would be back. The helicopter would have returned by now and, dislike Michael as she did, she had to concede he possessed the skills she didn't. He was an incredibly competent vascular surgeon. He might not have noticed the dog fight but if they planned to evacuate Kim on his helicopter, he would, of course, treat her. And with Hugo as back-up...

She washed the last trace of blood from her arms as Mrs Keen's face appeared around the door. Her cheeks were crimson with embarrassment and distress.

'My dear, I'm sorry to disturb you but you're needed back at the hospital. Dr McInnes has just rung. The helicopter's refused to turn around,' she told her. 'Dr McInnes says he has to operate now or she'll lose the leg, and you're all the help he has.'

'It's not a publicly owned chopper.' Harold Keen, the showground caretaker, drove her to the hospital in grim-faced anger. 'It seems it belongs to the chap that had the heart attack—Hubert Witherspoon. His man's the pilot. He's under instructions to take your young man to Sydney and there's no way he's turning back.'

'But Michael's on board. Surely he can overrule.'

'I don't think he has any say in the matter.'

Rachel stared straight ahead. She was wearing one of Doris Keen's Crimplene dresses. She'd hauled a comb through her hair, but her curls were still dripping. She was wearing a pair of Doris's sandals. She was heading to a tiny country hospital where they were facing surgery that was a nightmare.

Help!

'I suppose someone's looking after Penelope,' she said in a small voice, and Harold looked her over with evident approval.

'Your dog's fine,' he told her. 'There's any amount of folk looking after her. You look after Kim and we'll look after you.'

'Thank you.' She felt like she was about to cry. Damn Michael. Damn him. He had the skills she didn't. He had the helicopter she needed.

He was gone.

'It's no use being angry. We just have to get on with it.'

Hugo was already kitted out for surgery in green theatre gown, cap and slippers. The nurse had ushered Rachel straight through to the theatre. She glanced around and her heart sank. This was a tiny surgery, set up for minor procedures. Not the major trauma that was facing them now.

She swallowed and looked up, and some of her panic must have shown in her face.

'What's your background?' he asked, his voice gentling a little.

'I'm a registrar at Sydney Central. Emergency medicine. I don't... I don't have the surgical skills to cope with this.'

'But you're the reason we were able to clamp the arteries so fast,' he told her. 'So you saved Kim's life in the first place. It's just a matter of finishing what we started.'

Yeah, right. 'You're planning on rejoining the femoral artery?'

'If we can—yes.' He shook his head. 'It may be unlikely we'll succeed but we have to try. I've been on the phone to specialists in Sydney and we don't have a choice. By the time we get her evacuated to Sydney the leg will be dead. If we don't try then she loses the leg. It's as simple as that. I'm assuming you can give an anaesthetic?'

He wasn't expecting her to operate. That was such a relief her knees almost buckled right then.

'Yes.' If he was prepared to be heroic then so was she. This was heroic surgery, she thought. Damn fool surgery. The outcome seemed almost inevitable but he was right. They had to try.

'It's not as bad as it seems,' he told her. 'We have a video link to Sydney. Joe Cartier, one of the country's leading vascular surgeons, has agreed to help us every step of the way. I've hauled in Jane Cross, a local who plays at being a film-maker. She's setting up computer equipment and she'll video while we operate. She can do really intricate close-up stuff so everything I do goes straight down the line to Sydney and I get immediate feedback.'

He'd organised all this while she'd been in the shower? 'I... You're not a surgeon?'

'I'm a family doctor,' he told her. 'I'm two hours away from back-up. I'm everything. If you weren't here—if I didn't have an anaesthetist— then I'd count this impossible. But we have enough going for us now to hope. So what are we waiting for? Let's go.'

Afterwards, when Rachel was asked to describe what had been done, she'd simply shake her head. How they did it... It was impossible. All she could describe were the technicalities, and they were impressive enough.

They had a speaker-phone mounted just beside the table. Every sound they made went straight down the wire to Sydney.

Jane Cross, a woman in her forties, looking crazily incongruous with theatre garb covering a purple caftan and a mass of jangling earrings dangling beneath her theatre cap, directed a video camera straight at the wound.

'You promise you won't faint?' Hugo had asked the middle-aged woman as she'd set up the equipment, and Jane had regarded Hugo and Rachel with incredulity. Even with a hint of laughter.

'What, faint? Me? When I've got a captive audience? I intend to faint at least three times and I'll probably throw up too, but later. Not until I've done my job.'

She was wonderful, Rachel decided. She was right there behind Hugo's hands, but somehow she had the skill and the sensitivity to stay clear enough for his fingers to do their work.

The pictures she took were via a digital video camera linked to video conferencing equipment. In Sydney Joe Cartier had a clear view—and Hugo was asking questions every step of the way.

Rachel couldn't help him at all. She had her own battles. She wasn't a trained anaesthetist—she'd done basic training but that was all—and Kim was so severely shocked that just keeping her alive was a major battle.

She worked with a phone link, too. They'd run out of phone lines but Jane's partner, a dumpy little woman in jeans and sweatshirt, sat in a corner of the theatre where she didn't have to see—her stomach was evidently not as strong as Jane's—and relayed Rachel's questions down the line to an anaesthetist in Sydney.

'Minimal anaesthesia for such a shocked patient,' the specialist told her, working her through a careful, haemodynamically neutral induction method. He worked through her needs with her and Rachel wondered that such a small hospital could meet the requirements he snapped down the phone.

It could. For a tiny hospital Hugo had brilliant equipment. It was stunning that they had sufficient blood supplies on hand, but there was so much more. Rachel had blood on request, she had plasma, she had saline and a team outside the theatre was warming all the fluids before she even saw them.

The fluids weren't the only thing being heated.

'Keep the patient warm at all costs,' the anaesthetist barked down the phone, and warmed blankets appeared like magic to cover every part of Kim's body that Hugo didn't need to work on. After that one instruction Rachel didn't need to worry about warming—the blankets were replaced every few minutes by freshly warmed ones handed through the door. There must be a hive of industry out there.

It was an amazing scene. As well as the unseen industry outside, they had two nurses working with them in the theatre.

Elly was a competent middle-aged woman, white-faced and shocked because she was best friends with Kim's mum, but that fact wasn't allowed to get in the way of her professionalism. Then there was David, a ginger-headed kid who looked like he was hardly old enough to be qualifiedbut was magnificent under pressure.

They were all magnificent under pressure, Rachel thought. The whole town.

And Hugo...

What was being asked of him was unthinkable. His concentration was fierce—he didn't lift his head. He concentrated as she guessed he'd never concentrated in his life.

Where was the laughing man at the dog show? Gone. He'd been replaced by a pure professional—a professional being asked to work well past his level of training.

This was nightmare stuff. The specialist at the end of the phone could only guide—there was no way anyone could help Hugo manoeuvre the fine particles of tissue back into being a viable blood supply.

Rachel, concentrating fiercely on an anaesthetic that was taking her to the limits of her ability, could only wonder. If Hugo hadn't been there, could she have done such a thing? No, she thought honestly. Hugo had obviously done far more extensive reading and studying in this area than she had. The questions he asked the specialist showed keen intelligence and an incisive knowledge of what he was trying to achieve.

The man was seriously good.

And he was succeeding.

Even when the femoral artery was somehow—amazingly—reconnected and the first surge of pink started to appear in the lower leg, he didn't relax. His questions to the unknown Joe in Sydney seemed, if anything, to increase. He worked on and on, tying off vessels that were damaged beyond repair.

He completed the vascular surgery, took a deep breath, and a plastic surgeon came on the line, guiding him through the complex steps in closing such a wound to give a decent cosmetic outcome.

They were worrying about appearances, Rachel thought jubilantly, watching the colour seep back into Kim's toes and making sure the heart line on her monitor stayed steady as blood pressure stabilised. They were worrying how she'd look in the future.

They were winning!

And finally—finally, after hours without lifting their heads—the team in Sydney let out a cheer down the phone lines.

'Well done, Cowral,' they told them. 'Unless you have any more big dogs menacing the populace, we'll leave you to it.'

And to the thanks of the entire theatre team, the telephone lines went dead.

The theatre fell silent. Rachel was still concentrating. Hugo was placing dressings around the wound and she had to concentrate on reversing the anaesthetic, having Kim reestablish her own breathing. But the satisfaction...

She glanced up and the joy she felt was reflected in every face in the room.

Except Hugo's. He looked sick. The strain Rachel had been under had been immense—the strain Hugo had felt must have been well nigh unbearable. He'd won, but at a cost.

She'd worked as a team member for long enough to know that it was time for someone else to take charge. And she was the only possible option.

'David, take over the dressing,' she ordered. 'Hugo, leave the rest to us. We don't need you here any more.' He'd been under more pressure than any doctor should face and now, job done, reaction was setting in with a vengeance.

'I'm OK.' But the hands holding the pad were suddenly shaking. His fingers had seemed nerveless for hours, skilled and precise past understanding. It was more than understandable that reaction should set in now.

'Go and tell the Sandersons their kid will keep her leg,' she told him. 'Kim's parents will still be worried sick. Go.' Kim was taking her first ragged breaths. One of the nurses had given them the news some time ago that their daughter would be fine, but they wouldn't believe it until they'd heard it from Hugo.

And Hugo needed to tell them. Hugo had achieved the impossible. This was his gift.

The theatre team agreed. David lifted the tape from Hugo's nerveless fingers and started applying it. Job done. 'You're being kicked out of Theatre, Dr McInnes,' the young nurse told him, giving his senior a cheeky grin that was still flushed with triumph. They were all high on success. It was a fabulous feeling. 'The lady's told you to leave and what the lady wants the lady should get. Don't you agree?'

Hugo stepped back from the table. He gave Rachel a long, assessing look and then his face broke into the beginnings of a crooked smile.

'I guess. We owe the lady big time.'

'There you go, then,' Rachel said with a lot more placidity than she was feeling. 'Pay your debt to us all by getting out of here.'

'If you're sure.'

'I'm sure.' And then for some reason she couldn't fathom she put her hand on his arm. It was a fleeting gesture—of congratulation?—of comfort? She wasn't sure but she knew that she was compelled to do it.

Her hand stayed. He looked down at her fingers resting on the sleeve of his theatre gown and his face twisted into an expression she didn't recognise. For one fleeting moment his hand came up to cover hers. Warmth flooded between them—and something else. Something she couldn't begin to recognise.

'You're right, Dr Harper,' he said softly, so softly she could hardly catch the words. 'I need to get out of here.'

He left. The two nurses wheeled Kim through to Recovery and Rachel was left with Jane, the lady with the video, and Pat, the lady on the floor holding the mobile phone.

They'd never met until three hours ago and they were grinning at each other like fools.

'That was fantastic,' Rachel said, and if she couldn't keep her voice steady, who could blame her? 'Jane, I have no idea how you filmed that without fainting.'

'Fainting isn't what I felt like,' Jane admitted. 'What I felt like was far more messy. But I figured I could do the messy stuff afterwards when no one needed me and, hey, guess what? Now I don't feel like it at all any more.'

'You realise you guys saved Kim's leg.' The video recording and computer link had meant the specialists on the end of the line had been able to watch them every step of the way and Pat's relayed instructions had given Rachel every skill she'd needed.

'We all saved Kim's leg,' Pat decreed. She rose and came across to give her friend a hug and then the two of them hugged Rachel. This wasn't something that'd happen in a big city hospital but it was an entirely appropriate action here. A great action. 'We make a fantastic team,' Pat said roundly. 'We're so glad you're here now, Dr Harper. Something tells me Dr McInnes is going to need the best team he can get.'

The words somehow broke through her exhaustion. They didn't make sense. What was Pat saying? Something about Hugo needing a team? Surely that need was past.

'Why now?' she asked. 'Why would Hugo need me any more now?'

'A really solid medical team is exactly what we're going to need now,' Pat told her. 'The wind's swung around. Word came through as we were on our way in here. The fire's blocking the highway. There's no way in and there's no way out, and the fire's getting bigger by the minute.'

Rachel walked through to the sink and hauled off her theatre gown without even thinking. She was so tired she could hardly stand. She ran cold water over her wrists and then splashed her face, trying to haul her tired mind into gear.

She was stuck in this town?

'Well done, you.' The voice behind her made her jump and she turned to find Hugo in the doorway. The exhaustion in his face matched hers.

'Well done, yourself,' she managed. He'd startled her.

More... He unnerved her.

He really did have a gorgeous smile, she decided.

Crooked but nice. And the way he'd touched her...

No. She didn't want to think about the way he'd touched her.

What was a doctor like Hugo—a doctor with such skills—doing in a place like this? The surgery he'd just performed had been amazing. He should have trained in surgery. He could be one of the country's finest.

'I like Cowral,' he told her, and her eyes widened. 'What...?'

'You were thinking what's a nice boy like me doing in a place like this?' he told her, and he was so near the truth that she gasped.

'I don't... I wasn't...'

'It's what all city doctors think. Why on earth would anyone practise in such a remote area? But I think that Cowral's fantastic. I'm here through choice. While you, Dr Harper, are truly stuck.'

At some time since she'd kicked him out of the operating suite he'd hauled off his theatre gown. Underneath he was wearing moleskins and a casual shirt similar to the ones he'd been wearing at the dog show, though without the gore. Somehow he'd found time to change before surgery. He was transformed again, she thought. Doctor to farmer.

Doctor to farmer? What was she thinking? she wondered. She was finding it hard to concentrate on what mattered.

The fires. Being stuck here. Craig...

Oh, God, she shouldn't be here.

She was here. She was trapped. Without Craig. 'The fires are bad?'

'The fires are a problem,' he told her. He was splashing cold water on his face as if he needed to wake himself up, and his voice was muted. 'The burn's in the national park. There's no private property threatened but the neck of land into town has been cut. When the fire shifted, every-one who wasn't local got out of town before the road closed. You were in Theatre when the evacuation call came through. We didn't give you that option.' He rubbed his face on a towel and then looked at her. Re-ally looked at her. And his voice softened. 'I'm sorry, Rachel, but you're stuck here for the duration.'

She swallowed and tried to think through the implications. 'We could get helicopter evacuation,' she said at last, and he nodded. Still watch-ing her.

'We could. If it was urgent. But Kim's no longer an urgent case. Are you urgently required back in Sydney?'

Was she urgently needed?

No, she had to admit. At least, not by the hospital. As of last Friday she was officially on holiday. The trip to Cowral had been intended to be a weekend away followed by two weeks of lying in the sun. Back in Sydney, though. She'd have lain on Bondi beach so she could still visit Craig morning and night.

Craig needed her.

No. Craig didn't need her. She needed to get her head around that, once and for all.

She couldn't. But the reality was that no one would complain if she wasn't back in Sydney for the next few days, least of all Craig. She may as well admit it.

'Um...no.'

'That's great,' he told her. 'Because I may just need you myself.'

Hugo needed her. Great.

Everyone needed Rachel. Everyone always had. So what was new?

Dear God, she wanted to go home. Craig...

She didn't have a choice. She was here. With Hugo.

While Craig was... Craig just was.

CHAPTER THREE

RACHEL WALKED SLOWLY back to the showgrounds, dragging her feet in too-big sandals. She'd told Hugo she needed to see to Penelope. Kim's parents were needing more reassurance. He'd been distracted and she'd slipped away.

He had enough to worry about without her worries.

Which were considerable.

It was just on dusk. The evening was still and very, very warm. The sound of the sea was everywhere.

Cowral was built on a bluff overlooking the Southern Ocean. The stars were a hazy sheen of silver under a smoky filter. To the north she could see the soft orange glow of threatening fire. It was too far away to worry about, she thought. Maybe it'd stay in the national park and behave.

Meanwhile, it'd be a great time for a swim. But she had things to sort. Penelope. Accommodation.

Sleep!

Michael's Aston Martin was parked at the entrance to the showgrounds and she looked at it with a frown. She'd thrown the car keys back at Michael. Were they in his pocket right now as he did his heroic lifesaving thing back in the city, or had he left the keys in Penelope's dog stall? It was all very well standing on one's dignity, she thought ruefully, but if he'd taken his keys then she'd be walking everywhere. She didn't like her chances of hot-wiring an Aston Martin.

Meanwhile... Meanwhile, Penelope. Rachel pushed open the wire gates of the dog pavilion and went to find the second of her worries.

Michael might have taken his car keys but he hadn't taken his dog. Penelope was right where Rachel had left her, sitting in the now empty dog pavilion, gazing out with the air of a dog who'd been deserted by the world.

'Oh, you poor baby.' She hugged the big dog and hauled herself up into the stall to think about her options. 'I haven't deserted you, even if your master has.'

Penelope licked her face, then nosed her Crimplene in evident confusion.

'You don't like my fashion sense either?' She gave a halfhearted smile. 'We're stuck with it. But meanwhile...'

Meanwhile, she was hungry. No. Make that starving! She'd had one bite of a very soggy hamburger some hours ago. The remains had long gone.

Penelope didn't look hungry at all. 'You ate the rest of my hamburger? Penelope licked her again.

'Fine. It was disgusting anyway, but what am I supposed to eat?' She gazed about her. The pavilion was deserted.

Michael hadn't left his keys.

Her bag was over at the caretaker's residence where she'd showered. She could walk over there and fetch it, but why? The contents of the bag were foul. She had her purse with her—she'd tucked it into a pocket of the capacious Crimplene. She needed nothing else.

Wrong. She needed lots of things. She had nothing else.

So... She had her purse, a dog and a really rumbling stomach.

'I guess we walk into town,' she told Penelope. The only problem was that the hospital and the showgrounds were on one side of the river and the tiny township of Cowral was on the other.

'We don't have a choice,' she told the dog. 'Walking is good for us. Let's get used to it. The key to our wheels has just taken himself back to Sydney and we're glad he has. Compared to your master... I hate to tell you, Penelope, but walking looks good in comparison.'

* * *

Cowral was closed.

It was a tiny seaside town. It was Sunday night. All the tourists had left when the roads had started to be threatened. Rachel trudged over the bridge and into town to find the place was shut down as if it was dead winter and midnight. Not a shop was open. By the time she reached the main street the pall of smoke was completely covering the moon and only a couple of streetlights were casting an eerie, foggy glow through the haze.

'It looks like something out of Sherlock Holmes,' Rachel told her canine companion. 'Murderer appears stage left...' She stood in the middle of the deserted street and listened to her stomach rumble and thought not very nice thoughts about a whole range of people. A whole range of circumstances.

Murder was definitely an option.

Her phone was in her purse. She hauled it out and looked at it. Who could she ring?

No one. She didn't know anyone.

She stared at it some more and, as if she'd willed it, it rang all by itself. She was so relieved she answered before it had finished the first ring.

'Rachel?' It was Dottie's bright chirpiness sounding down the line. Her mother-in-law who'd so wanted this weekend to work. 'Rachel, I hope I'm not intruding but I so wanted to know how it was going. Where are you, dear?'

Rachel thought about it. 'I'm standing in the main street of Cowral,' she said. 'Thinking about dinner.'

'Oh...' She could hear Dottie's beam down the line. 'Are you going somewhere romantic?'

'Maybe outdoors,' Rachel said, cautiously looking around at her options. 'Under the stars.' She looked through the smoke toward the sea. 'On the beach?'

'How wonderful. Is the weather gorgeous?'

Rachel tried not to cough from smoke inhalation. 'Gorgeous!'

'And you have such gorgeous company.'

Rachel looked dubiously down at Penelope. 'Yes. Yes, I do.'

'You know we so wanted you to have a good time, Lewis and I. There's no chance of extending your time there, I suppose?'

'Actually, there may be,' Rachel told her. She explained about the fires and the road being cut. 'There's nothing to worry about but…we may be held up here for a few more days.' There was no reason to explain that 'we' meant Rachel and an Afghan hound. Not Rachel and a gorgeous hunk of eligible cardiologist.

But her words were just what Dottie wanted to hear. 'Oh, my dear, that's lovely.' She could hear Dottie's beam widen. 'Unless the fires are a real problem?'

'They don't seem to be.' Australians understood about bushfires. Most national parks burned every few years or so—they needed to burn to regenerate—and as long as they didn't threaten townships they weren't a worry. Dottie clearly thought this time they'd been sent from heaven.

'Dottie,' she said cautiously. 'Craig…'

'You're not to worry. We told you and we meant it. His father and I have taken right over as we should have long ago. As you should have let us.'

'But—'

'You concentrate on yourself,' Dorothy told her. 'You concentrate on your future. On your romantic dinner under the stars. That's an order.'

And the phone went dead. Great.

She stared at it. Her link with home.

She should be back in the hospital right now. Why wasn't she? Craig…

Don't think about it. Think about now. Now what?

If there was no dinner to be had in Cowral then she needed to think about her next need. Sleep. Accommodation.

Cowral Bay's only motel—the place where Michael-the-rat had slept last night—was on the other side of the river. She'd walk back over the bridge, she decided. She'd leave Penelope in her dog box in the pavilion and book herself into the motel. Hey, maybe the motel even had room service.

By the time she reached the motel her feet, in her borrowed sandals, were screaming that she had blisters. She'd bother with taking Penelope back to the pavilion later, she decided, so she tied the dog to a tree and walked into Motel Reception. To find no room at the inn.

'Sorry, love,' the motel owner told her, casting a nervous glance at

Rachel's dubious apparel. 'There's fire crews from the other side of the peninsula trapped here now and they've booked us out.'

'Do you have a restaurant?' Rachel asked with more hope than optimism, and was rewarded by another dubious look and another shake of the head.

'Everyone's closed. The Country Women's Association are putting on food twenty-four hours a day for the firefighters in the hall over the bridge but you don't look like a firefighter.'

Rachel swallowed. 'No. No, I don't.'

'Are you OK, love?' the woman asked. Her eyes narrowed. 'You don't need one of them women's refuge places, do you? I could call the police for you if you like.'

Great. That was all she needed. A girl had some pride but Rachel was really struggling to find it here. She took a deep breath and pulled herself together.

Maybe women's refuges had food? Good grief. What was she thinking?

'Um, no. Thank you.' She fished in her purse and found a couple of coins. There was a candy dispensing machine by the counter and the sweets looked really inviting. 'I'll ring a friend, but meanwhile I'll just buy a couple of these...'

'I'm sorry, love,' the woman told her. 'The machine's broken. The technician's due tomorrow—if he can get through the fires.'

Rachel walked outside and untied Penelope. Then she considered, trying really hard not to panic.

Panic seemed an increasingly enticing option.

She'd go back to the hospital, she decided. Hugo had said he needed her. How much? He was about to be put to the test. 'If you need me you'll have to house and feed me,' she'd tell him.

'No. Feed me first,' she corrected herself. And Penelope?

Maybe she couldn't expect Hugo to take on Penelope.

She'd take her back to the pavilion.

Bad idea. It had been almost an hour now since Rachel had collected Penelope. Penelope had been the last dog to leave and the showground caretakers had done their duty. At some time while Rachel had walked into town and back again, the high wire gates had been bolted closed.

The caretaker's residence was in the centre of the grounds, well out of shouting distance.

Rachel put her head against the cyclone wire and closed her eyes. Great. Just great. The whole situation was getting farcical.

Where was this women's refuge?

'This has to go into the record books as the most romantic weekend a girl has ever had,' she told Penelope, but Penelope looked at her with the sad eyes of an Afghan hound who hadn't been fed.

'You ate my hamburger,' Rachel told her. 'Don't even think about looking at me like that.'

She sighed. Her stomach rumbled a response. She put her hand on Penelope's collar and started trudging toward the hospital.

There was the sound of vehicle behind her—a big one.

She moved onto the verge.

A fire truck came around the bend on the wrong side of the road. It veered onto the grassy verge and she had to jump for her life.

If she'd been one whit less angry she might have been hit, but her reflexes were working fine. Rachel was tired and hungry and worried, but there was still a vast well of anger directed at Michael and herself and her circumstances. When the fire truck swerved around the bend on the wrong side of the road it was almost as if she expected it.

She yelped and leapt, and as the truck screeched to a halt she found herself sprawled ignominiously in the grass at the side of the road with Penelope somehow sprawling on top of her.

Great. What else could possibly happen to her? She lay and addressed herself to a clump of grass right under her nose.

'Beam me up, Scottie. Where's a spaceship when you need one?'

'Are you OK, miss?' The horror in the voice above her had her pushing herself up from the road. She might be mad as fire but no one here deserved to think they'd squashed her.

'I'm fine.' She rolled over, shoved a startled Penelope off, hauled her Crimplene down to something akin to decency and tried to look fine. 'Honest.'

'Oh, heck...' The man had reached her. He'd been driving the truck. Behind him his fellow firefighters were climbing down from the cab to see what was wrong. The engine was still running and the truck lights were illuminating the road. 'I could have killed you.'

'It's your lucky day. You didn't.' She tried a smile and the muscles almost worked. Sort of.

They were gathering round her now, a bunch of men and women with black-grimed faces, fire uniforms and hard hats. They looked exhausted. They were looking at her with concern.

She must look a real candidate for her women's refuge, she thought, and the concept was looking more and more appealing. If there was a women's refuge somewhere around here that would take her with an Afghan hound, she'd be in there like a shot.

Or maybe... She gave Penelope's backside another shove... Maybe even without an Afghan.

'We're really sorry,' the fireman told her, and she tried focusing on the man before her. He looked scared to death. 'I guess you weren't expecting hikers,' she told him. 'It's too dark to walk off the road.' She hauled herself upward. Someone gave her a hand which she accepted with gratitude. Then she looked more closely at the man before her. Under the soot there were cuts and scratches, blood as well as grime. He looked dreadful. 'Are you OK?'

Stupid question, really. It was absolutely obvious that he wasn't. 'I just...' He wiped his hand across his eyes. 'My eyes... The smoke...'

And he'd been driving.

'You need to go to the hospital,' she told him.

'That's where we're going. There was a shed—the farmer told us it was used for storing hay so we made an attempt to save it. What he forgot to tell us was that he stored fuel in there as well. The thing went up with a bang that scared us almost as much as we scared you. But that's all the damage, thank God. There's a few of us with sore eyes, but we're thinking that we've been lucky.'

Lucky or not, they looked shocked and ill. Rachel's personal problems were set aside in the face of these peoples' needs. 'You should have been treated before you drove.'

'Doc's been busy,' someone said. 'We heard up on the ridge that he couldn't come up. He's been caught up with a dogbite or something.'

Of course he'd been caught up. And there was no one else, Rachel thought. He was on his own.

Except for her. Hugo had her, whether he liked it or not. And a fat lot of use she was, she thought ruefully, hiking round the country with her crazy Afghan hound, looking for food and for shelter as if she were destitute. It was time she hauled herself together and started being useful.

'Tell you what,' she said, brushing gravel from her knees and trying to stop her knees from doing the shaking they were so intent on. 'Let's all go to the hospital. I'm a doctor and I'm needed there. But if it's OK with you...' She managed a shaky grin as she looked around their smoke-filled eyes which were now tinged with disbelief. A doctor in Crimplene... But she wasn't going down that road. Explanations could take hours.

'Indulge me with something I've always wanted to do,' she told them. 'I'm a country girl from way back. Once upon a time I even drove my dad's truck at hay-carting so I have my heavy vehicle licence. So all you have to do is say yes. Let me drive your fire engine.'

Which was how Dr Rachel Harper, MD, dressed in glorious Crimplene and Doris Keen's sandals, with gravel in her knees, nothing in her stomach and dog hair all over her, got to drive the Cowral Bay fire truck with a bunch of ten disgustingly dirty and slightly injured firefighters and one potential Australian champion Afghan in the back.

You told me to have a weekend to remember, she silently told her absent mother-in-law as they headed for the hospital. Well, Dottie, I'm doing just that.

Hugo wasn't at the hospital, and Rachel was aware of a stab of disappointment. But at least the nurses knew her from that afternoon when she'd helped with Kim. They greeted her as a friend, and the orderly took over Penelope's care as if she was no trouble at all.

'You've come to help, miss,' he told her as the firefighters milled around the emergency room, and it was obvious to everyone that Rachel needed to turn into a doctor again. 'You're very welcome. I'll give your dog some dinner, shall I?'

Dinner... Yes!

'Actually, I—'

But dinner wasn't her destiny. 'It's great that you're here.' David, the ginger-haired nurse who'd helped with Kim, was looking more flustered than he had that afternoon. 'One of our old farmers had a stroke an hour ago. Dr McInnes had to go out there in a hurry and here's all these guys needing checking. Can I give you a hand and we'll see what we can do together?'

She worked for an hour. It was solid medicine but straightforward, washing out eyes, checking bruises and cleaning scratches. One of the women was suffering slightly from smoke inhalation and Rachel decreed that she be admitted, but the oxygen alleviated the symptoms almost immediately. Great. She worked steadily through on. Minor stuff.

Except the man who'd been driving the truck. He had a sliver of something nasty in his eye as well as a cut that was deep enough to need stitching. But it was the eye she was worried about.

Rachel shoved her rumbling stomach aside and focused. She dropped in fluorescein—a yellow stain—and examined the eye through the ophthalmoscope. And worried. 'Can we X-ray?' she asked David.

'Sure.'

The X-ray came back—still worrying. She pinned it against the light and fretted some more as the door opened behind her.

'Problem?'

She turned and it was Hugo. For a moment—for just a moment—it was as much as she could do not to fall into his arms with relief. She'd pushed hunger and exhaustion and shock away but the events of the day were catching up with her. She was really close to breaking point.

Falling into a colleague's arms wasn't exactly professional. She got a grip. Sort of. Mental slap around the ears. She hauled herself into as much of a medical mode as she could muster.

'There's a foreign body just at the edge of the cornea,' she told him, turning back to the light-box and attempting to concentrate on the image. 'There was fuel in metal drums that exploded while they were trying to save a shed. This looks like a sliver of metal, embedded in the cornea but not penetrating. His sight's blurred but maybe that's just the reaction to the pain and a bit of debris that's on the surface. The eye won't stop watering. There's a couple of nasty lacerations around the eye itself that'll need stitching but it's the metal I'm worried about. It's very near the optic nerve. If he moves while I'm trying to manoeuvre it out... Well, I don't think I can cope with this under local anaesthetic.'

Hugo nodded. He crossed to stand beside her and they stared at the screen together.

'It's not touching anything crucial. I think we could do it.' He stared at it a bit longer. 'Maybe you're right, though. It's going to be fiddly.'

'But under a local anaesthetic?'

'I'd rather not.' He looked down at her and smiled. 'Like you, ophthalmology isn't my speciality. It looks straightforward enough as long as he doesn't move, but there's a bit of repair work to do and I'm not super-confident. Eyes aren't my area of expertise and if I have to fiddle and curse I'd prefer that the patient was sedated while I did it.'

'That makes two of us.' She looked at the X-ray some more and even managed a shaky smile. 'We couldn't evacuate him to the city?'

'It's a very small sliver. It's not penetrating. Evacuating means bringing a helicopter from the city and visibility is making things dangerous.'

'Yes, but—'

'But we do have two doctors,' he went on inexorably. 'Even if one of them looks like she just came out of a welfare shop.'

'From a home for battered women actually,' she said with dignity. 'I've had one offer to take me there in a squad car already tonight.'

'Have you?' The ready laughter she was starting to know flashed into his eyes. 'The fire guys tell me they nearly ran you down.'

'Yeah, but then they let me drive their fire engine,' she told him. 'Which was really cool.'

The deep smile lurking in the back of his eyes strengthened into the beginnings of something that looked like pure admiration. And surprise. She flushed but his eyes were sliding down to her legs, breaking the moment. He'd seen her bloodstained knee. 'That graze wants washing.'

'And we all need dinner and a sleep and it's not going to happen,' she told him, still strangely flushed. What was it with this man that had the capacity to unsettle her? She had to move on. 'Our firefighter has an empty stomach which means he's ready for anaesthesia now,' she told him. 'His eye isn't going to get better on its own. If we're going to operate there isn't a better time than now. Is there?'

'Nope.' He sighed. 'I guess not. Lead on, Dr Harper. Do you want to operate or do you want to do the anaesthetic?'

'I'm choosing anaesthetics,' she told him. 'Two anaesthetics in one day! I think I'm starting to specialise.'

* * *

It took longer than they had thought it would.

By the time they finished and the firefighter was recovering in the ward, neatly stitched, foreign body removed and intravenous antibiotics preventing complications, Rachel was swaying on her feet. She hadn't felt it at all while she'd been in Theatre—adrenaline again, she supposed— but when she emerged she sagged. Her stocks of adrenaline must be at an all-time low. She crossed to the sinks and held on, and if she hadn't held on she would have sunk to the floor.

It'd pass. She'd worked exhausted in the past. After nights on duty when Craig—

No. Don't go there.

In a minute she'd start considering the complications surrounding her but for now...

For now she held on.

'Hey.' Hugo had hauled off his gown and was watching her, his eyes narrowing in concern. 'Are you OK?'

She thought about it. OK? People kept asking her that and the concept was ludicrous. 'If you're offering to take me back to my women's refuge, the answer is yes.'

'Women's refuge...'

'Any sort of refuge,' she muttered. 'As long as it serves dinner. Bread and dripping would be fine. Come to think about it, bread and dripping would be fantastic.'

'You're hungry.'

'You stole my hamburger—remember?'

'So I did.' He was looking at her as if she'd just landed from outer space. 'That was—what—eight hours ago?'

'It feels more. And I didn't eat it then. Penelope finished it for me. Someone took her off to feed her when I arrived. I bet she's had a really good meal. Doggos or something. Something really delicious.'

'What did you do between operating on Kim and now?' he asked and she rolled her eyes.

'I walked. I walked in these really stupid sandals which, by the way, are about ten sizes too big. I walked back to the pavilion to find Michael hadn't left me the keys to his car. I brought his stupid dog from the pavilion and I walked into town searching for a cafe' to discover the whole place has shut. It's like a ghost town. I walked back to the motel to discover the place has been booked out by the Boys' Own Fire Brigade and their restaurant doesn't serve meals. And their candy-vending machine is broken. I walked back to the showgrounds to discover the gates had been locked. I started to walk back here but the fire engine nearly ran me down. I came in here, I washed out a few eyes, I sewed up a gashed leg and now I've operated on an eye. So... I think maybe I've reached my limit. I'm wearing Doris Keen's Crimplene, my feet hurt, my stomach's empty, I don't even have a dog box to sleep in and I'm very, very close to hysterics.' She eyed him with caution. 'And if you dare to even twitch the sides of your mouth with the suggestion of laughter, Dr McInnes, I intend to lie down on the floor and give way to a full-scale tantrum. They'll hear me back in Sydney.'

'I'm not...' His mouth definitely twitched but it was hauled back under control fast. 'I'm not laughing.'

'I don't believe you.'

'I'm definitely not.' He bit his lip, pushed the laughter resolutely to the backburner and eyed her with a certain amount of caution. 'OK. It appears you need some help. Where shall we start?'

'Food,' she told him. 'As bad as that?'

'Worse.'

'Let's go, then.' He smiled. 'It fits with what I need to do,' he told her. 'I'm hungry, too.'

'You haven't had dinner?'

'One of my very elderly patients had a stroke. I've been out there with her. She died an hour ago.'

'I'm sorry.'

'Don't be,' he told her. 'Annie was a ninety-six-year-old farmer. She's run her own farm since her husband walked out on her sixty years ago. She didn't miss him a bit. She's had a great life; she was healthy and happily living in her own home until the end, and I wish all endings could be as happy.'

'Mmm.'

It was a happy ending. But his words had caught her unawares, twisting her thoughts back to where her thoughts always ended.

Craig...

She swallowed. She looked down at her hands and found her hands had clenched into fists. Craig...

For some stupid reason her eyes were filling with tears.

Which was ridiculous. Surely she should be used to this by now. It was just that she'd never been away. For eight years...

Food. She needed food. That's why she was reacting like this. Hugo was watching her with concern and she blinked and sniffed and got on with it.

'Sorry,' she told him. 'I was just...reacting to the day or something. Did you say you knew where we can find some food?'

He was still watching her, still with that look that said he saw far more than she wanted him to, but he accepted that she needed to move on.

'We'll give you a few biscuits and cheese to keep the wolf from the door while I wash your knee first,' he told her. 'I need a medico with two good legs—not with one infected. Then we find Toby. Toby's down at the town hall, and that's where the food is. There's a fire effort happening in town and the locals are either out on the front or working to support them. Even at this late hour there'll be food. So we'll collect Toby and feed you. Two birds with one stone.'

She blinked back the last of her emotion and managed a grin.

'Lead on, then,' she told him. 'Two birds, did you say?

I'll eat them both.'

That he'd noticed the embedded gravel in her knee amazed her. The Crimplene was flapping around her calves and her knees were hardly exposed. Maybe one of the firefighters had told him.

Or maybe he'd just...noticed? He was that sort of a doctor, she decided as he carefully scrubbed the surface and then checked that each particle of gravel had been removed. It'd be hard to do it herself. But it was also hard to sit still and watch his bent head as he concentrated on what he was doing. His fingers were the fingers of a surgeon, she decided. He was skilled and careful and...kind?

He unnerved her. She didn't understand the emotions he engendered and she wasn't sure that she wanted to.

'Th-thank you,' she murmured as he put a dressing in place over the damaged skin.

He smiled up at her. 'Think nothing of it, ma'am. I owe you one.'

'Why?'

'I disparaged your dog.'

'Penelope's Michael's dog,' she said before she could help herself, and he gave a rueful little smile.

'So she is. But isn't there something in the wedding vows that says with all your worldly goods? Doesn't that include Afghan hounds?'

Hugo still thought she was married to Michael. She stared down at the band of gold on her left hand and gave a twisted smile. Married. To Michael. Ha!

But it wasn't the time or the place to disillusion him.

What was the point?

Besides, biscuits and cheese weren't nearly enough.

'We need to move on,' she murmured, and he cast her a look that was curiously questioning. And curiously understanding.

'Fine,' he said, and he let his fingers stay on the dressing on her knee for just a fraction of a moment longer than he had to. Long enough to impart...what? Comfort? Understanding? She didn't know.

'Fine,' he told her. 'Let's move on.'

They checked on Kim first. Rachel's stomach couldn't get any louder than it already was, and when Hugo suggested it she agreed. There were some things still more important than food, and seeing Kim safely asleep was one of them.

'She woke a couple of hours back,' Hugo told her. 'But she went back to sleep almost immediately.'

Her body would be so shocked that she'd sleep for days, Rachel thought, and she was sleeping soundly now. Kim's mother was by her side, sitting holding her hand. Doing nothing. She was simply watching.

It was enough.

'Kim shows every sign that she'll be fine,' Hugo told the woman as Rachel watched from the doorway. He lifted the base of Kim's bedsheet to reveal two sets of very pink toes. 'Her circulation's almost back to normal. She's on maximum intravenous antibiotics. Her obs are great. She looks as if she's going to have very little permanent damage. We'll do more nerve tests in the morning but she wiggled everything when she woke and had full sensation. Your husband was watching. Did he tell you?'

'He did.' Mrs Sanderson's face creased in fierce concentration. Concentrating on control. 'I was home getting some things for her when she woke.' Her fragile control broke and her voice choked on a sob. 'I shouldn't have left...'

'Kim needed her things.'

'I mean... I shouldn't have left her at the showgrounds. She wanted to show Knickers. If I'd thought the Jeffreys could be stupid enough to let their dog off the lead... I just didn't realise...how easy it is to lose someone. We came so close.'

'But not close enough,' Hugo said gently, his hand on the woman's shoulder. 'She'll be fine.' He smiled down into her tearful face. 'Tell me how Knickers is.'

It was the right thing to ask. It made the terror recede. The woman gulped and gave him a watery smile. 'Knickers is good.' She took a big breath and searched for calm. She'd been to the brink, Rachel realised. This day would live with her for ever. 'The vet says he'll be OK, though my husband is saying it'll cost more to have Knickers fixed than Kim. We can't claim a cocker spaniel's expenses through medical insurance.'

Hugo grinned. 'See? I'm cheap at half the price.' He smiled, a comfort smile Rachel was starting to recognise. 'Now, what about you going home and getting some rest? We've sedated Kim fairly heavily so I'd be surprised if she woke before morning.'

'I might just watch for a little more,' the woman whispered. 'If it's OK. I just want to watch...'

She just wanted to watch her breathing, Rachel thought. She knew. To sit there and watch a chest rise and fall...

She bit her lip and Hugo turned and saw.

He thought it was the hunger, though. He must do. There was surely no other reason for it. She could see she had him confused and she fought to remove her expression. The stillness of her face...

'I need to take our Dr Harper for a feed,' he told Mrs Sanderson. 'We'll leave you to your vigil. But don't exhaust yourself. Kim will need you in the morning, if only to prevent all her friends from visiting in the first five minutes. Keep up your strength.'

'I will.' The woman smiled through tears. 'Thank you both. We were so lucky...'

* * *

'We *were* really lucky,' Hugo said as they headed out to the parking lot together. 'We were hugely lucky to have you here to help us. We still are.'

Rachel said nothing at all.

The local hall was where the action was. It was set a block back from the main street, but even so Rachel wondered how she could have missed it when she and Penelope had walked into town. Hugo turned the corner and bright lights shone out through open doors. Even at midnight there were dozens of cars parked outside and people were spilling out onto the pavement.

'So this is Cowral Bay's night life,' she said faintly, and Hugo grinned.

'It doesn't get any better than this. Come and meet Cowral. Oh, and I'd take a deep breath if I were you. I suspect you've been voted an honorary local now, like it or not.'

She had. From the moment she walked in the door she was welcomed as a friend. A lifesaver. She'd treated the firemen and she'd treated Kim.

Now she could tell why the pavilion had been locked and darkened—why the town itself had seemed abandoned. Everyone was here. Doris Keen was busy making sandwiches but when she saw Rachel she dropped what she was doing and came forward, her arms outstretched.

'Oh, my dear, we were that worried. We didn't know where you'd got to. We assumed you'd gone home but then Charlie found your husband's car and it was still locked. We searched, but then the fire brigade boys came in and they said you'd gone back to the hospital and you've been working so hard...'

Everyone was assuming Michael was her husband, Rachel thought. She'd been with him. She wore a wedding ring.

It didn't matter. Let them.

She tried to think of Michael with some degree of caring. Had he managed to save Hubert Witherspoon? She didn't know and she didn't much mind. For a moment she almost felt it in her to be sorry for him. He'd left and he'd missed out on...this. This hubbub of caring.

Penelope.

The dog flashed back into her mind and she gave a guilty start. Her dog... Michael's dog was back at the hospital. She half turned, but Hugo was before her.

'Our hospital orderly has taken Penelope home for the night,' he told her. 'Jake's wife has a poodle. We figured they'd get on fine.'

What was it with this man? He had the ability to read what she was thinking almost as she thought it. The feeling was really, really unnerving.

'This lady's a real champion,' someone said behind her, and she recognised one of the men who'd been on the fire truck. There were scores of firefighters here. This must be their refuelling station before they went back to the fire or turned in for the night.

'She's a hungry real champion,' Hugo said from behind her. His hand was on her shoulder and for some reason it was a huge support. His warmth gave her shaking legs strength. Somehow his presence made this welcome feel real—as if she was part of all this.

But it wasn't real, she told herself a little bit desperately. It was an illusion. She was most definitely not a part of this. She cast Hugo an unsure glance and pulled away from under his hand.

But then she missed it when he released her. She missed...the contact? The link?

What?

'Daddy!' a voice yelled out from the other side of the hall and a tousle-headed, pyjama-clad Toby came bounding through the crowd of locals to greet him. Hugo reached out and caught him, swinging him high in the air.

'Tobes. Why aren't you in bed?'

'Mrs Partridge made me have an afternoon sleep,' Toby said, with all the indignation of a small man whose person has been significantly violated. 'She said we'd all had a nasty shock and she needed a lie-down, too. So I went to sleep. And now I'm wide awake and Mrs Partridge's helping me make lamingtons for the firefighters to eat tomorrow. Can we stay for a while, Daddy?'

'Yes, we can,' he told him, hugging him close. 'Far be it from me to interfere with lamington-making. And we need to wait for Dr Harper to be fed.'

'Why?'

'Because we're taking her home to stay with us.' To stay with them? He had to be kidding.

He wasn't. 'There's nowhere else.'

Full to the brim of Irish stew, fresh bread rolls and Toby's magnificent lamingtons, Rachel was tucked into Hugo's capacious car with as much room for argument as if she'd been a parcel.

'But why?'

'You've already discovered the motel's full. There's a couple of beds at the hospital but we need them. While this fire's burning I want all resources left free for emergencies. Toby and I have a big house at the rear of the hospital and there's two spare bedrooms.'

'But your wife...'

'I'm a widower,' he said bluntly. 'But I'm trustworthy.' He put on his most trustworthy smile and she had to smile.

'No, but—'

'Exactly. No buts. Can you think of anywhere better?' He smiled across at her and his smile had her insides doing strange things. Very strange things indeed. This was no trustworthy smile. It looked exactly the opposite.

But he was still speaking. She had to concentrate. 'There's no women's refuge to be had,' he was saying. 'Despite the rumours. The dog pavilion's closed for the night and something tells me you weren't very comfortable there last night anyway. And the park benches are exceedingly hard. So it's us or nothing.'

'We really want you to stay,' Toby announced from the back seat. 'Me and Digger like you. Even though your dress looks funny.'

'Gee, thanks.' She fingered the Crimplene and wondered how it was that the Crimplene was the least odd thing in the succession of things that had happened to her today.

'We'll do something about that tomorrow,' Hugo announced. 'But for now, we'd be very pleased if you took up our offer of accommodation, Dr Harper. What about it?'

What about it? There was only one answer to that. She had no choice.

'Yes, please,' she said, and decided then and there that arguing was out of the question.

Things were entirely out of her hands.

CHAPTER FOUR

THE HOUSE THEY took her to was a big old timber home in the same grounds as the hospital. It had wide verandas all around and a garden that in the dim light cast by the hospital nightlights looked overgrown and rambling. Digger was lying on the front steps. When they arrived he rushed down to greet them, his whole body quivering in delight. Hugo pushed open the front door, Rachel walked inside as he followed, carrying Toby—and she stopped still in astonishment.

This wasn't a home. It was an artwork. A magnificent artwork.

Like something out of *Vogue*, it had been furnished with exquisite taste. In rich reds and golds, every piece of furnishing was richly ornate and highly decorative. The floor was sleekly polished with gorgeous Persian rugs scattered at artistic intervals. There were elegant pieces of sculpture, carefully placed. The settees and chairs were colour coordinated with dainty matching cushions, artfully arranged. Heavy brocade curtains were held back, looped and looped again with vast gold tassels that hung to the floor.

Good grief!

This wasn't a doctor's residence. It wasn't a child's residence.

It was frankly...scary.

But Hugo seemed oblivious, both to his surroundings and to her reaction. 'Toby, would you show Dr Harper where she'll sleep?' he asked.

'I'll put the coffee on.' He disappeared in the direction of the kitchen while Toby towed her through to the back of the house.

The further she went the more awful it became.

'This room's where my daddy sleeps and this is where Digger and I sleep,' Toby told her, and Rachel had glimpses of two rooms with the same amazing furnishings. He towed her further. 'You can have this room or this room.'

It made no difference which. Gorgeous brocade beds with hugely rich furnishings. Huge gold bows of something like velvet with threads of something shining and metallic hung at each corner of the bed. The beds looked like they took half an hour of intense concentration and a degree in interior design to make each morning!

Ugh.

'Do you and your daddy like...um...really decorated houses?' she asked, as Toby stood and waited for her verdict.

His small face furrowed in concentration. 'Why?'

'Your whole house is sort of...frilly. And red. And gold.

You guys must really like red and gold, huh?'

'I like purple,' Toby told her.

'So Daddy likes red and gold?'

'I think he likes blue.' Toby considered some more. 'Or maybe yellow. Mr Addington at the bank has a really yellow car and whenever my dad sees it he whistles and says what a beauty.'

'So why is your house red and gold?'

'My mummy decorated the house,' Toby told her. 'My mummy died just after I was born. Daddy was really sad.'

'I guess he would be.' Rachel's face softened. 'Losing your mummy would be really hard.'

'Yeah, but I didn't know her,' Toby said with the blunt pragmatism of a six-year-old. 'My daddy says Aunty Christine looks like her. The photos are a bit the same. And Aunty Christine loves this house. She comes in here and looks at it and cries.'

Oh, great...

'Aunty Christine says Digger shouldn't come into the house because he messes it up but Daddy said he put his foot down over that, whatever that means,' Toby told her. 'And I want a Darth Vader poster on my bedroom wall 'cos Daddy and I love that movie, but Aunty Christine says my mummy would hate it and I mustn't even ask Daddy because it'd make him sad. Do you think it'd make him sad? Or is it something else he'd put his foot down about?'

'Maybe.' This wasn't a conversation she should get drawn into, she decided. Not when she'd known these people for not much more than two minutes.

There was lots of background here that she didn't understand.

But at least she had a bed, she decided, brightening. An amazing bed. She'd had a truly excellent meal. She could put up with a little red and gold opulence.

She sat down on the bed. It gave under her weight. She gave a tentative bounce and the bed bounced back.

The symmetry of the covers was ruined. Great.

'Do you do much bouncing?' she asked Toby, and he looked like he didn't know what she was talking about.

'You ruin the covers if you bounce,' he told her. 'Aunty Christine says so. She says don't move things. Don't touch. She says Mummy would have everything perfect.'

Rachel's eyes widened. What an extraordinary statement. 'But... bouncing's fun. I'm sure your mummy would want you to have fun.'

'Aunty Christine would growl at me if I bounced on my bed.'

'Would she growl at you if you bounced on mine?'

Toby thought about it. Deeply. 'I guess she wouldn't,' he said at last. 'You're a grown-up. She couldn't growl at you.'

'I'd like to see her try.' She'd never met the unknown Aunt Christine but already she held her in aversion. And Hugo... What had they created? A shrine to a dead wife and sister when it should be a home.

She knew—who better?—that life was to be lived by the living. For the living. Not for the dead.

It could all be taken away so quickly...

Enough. She bounced again. And smiled at Toby and moved along so that there was room beside her. 'Want to try?

'Yes,' Toby said, and went to join her. They bounced.

Digger, watching from the doorway, ventured further in, looking as stunned as it was possible for a goofy dog to look.

They continued to bounce.

Digger started to bark and Toby giggled and bounced higher.

It was great. Stupid but great.

It had been one heck of a day. Rachel's emotions had been pushed to the limit. She didn't know what she was doing here. She didn't have a clue what was happening to her, but for now...for this minute there was just one crazy time, a tousle-headed child who looked as if he didn't get enough laughter in his life and Rachel. And Rachel knew she definitely needed more laughter. More bouncing.

If the springs broke, she'd pay for them, she decided. If the tassels frayed. If the gilt was tarnished. Some things just had to be done, and they had to be done now. She had hold of Toby's hands and they were bouncing in unison as Digger barked a crazy accompaniment on the side.

'What on earth...?'

She looked over to the doorway. Hugo was watching them. Stunned. 'What on earth do you think you're doing?'

She refused to give up the moment. Not yet. She'd had a very big day and so had Toby. A vision of Toby's face as he'd watched them work on Kim came back to her. It was too much horror for a six-year-old to be put to bed with. He needed to sleep with bouncing.

'We're bouncing, Dr McInnes,' she told him, then gripped Toby's hands tighter and bounced again. 'Care to join us?'

'You'll break the bedsprings.'

'I'll pay for them,' she said nobly. 'I'm donating one set of bedsprings to the common good. I need a bounce and so does Toby. I'm sure you do, too.'

'I wouldn't fit,' he said faintly, and she grinned.

'That's what you get for showing your guest to a room with a single bed.'

'Daddy's got a bigger bed,' Toby volunteered, midbounce. 'Can we can go there?'

Digger barked again as if he thought that was a truly excellent idea.

'My bed's for sleeping in,' Hugo told them, and Rachel grimaced.

'How boring.'

'The kettle's boiled. Do you want a drink?'

Rachel considered. She bounced a couple of times and looked down at Toby. He bounced with her and met her look—co-conspirators. Co-bouncers. 'Do we want a drink, Toby?'

'I'd like some hot chocolate,' he told her, and bounced again.

'That sounds good.' Another bounce. 'Maybe we could stop and bounce again tomorrow night.'

'Are you staying for two nights?'

She cast a sideways glance at Hugo and bounced a bit more. 'I may,' she told him. 'If I'm not kicked out because of my bouncing habits. I think I'm needed.'

'Because of the fire?' Toby asked, and she nodded. 'Because of the fire. And because...maybe because you guys could do with a bit of bouncing. Like me.'

What was happening here?

Hugo prepared three mugs of hot chocolate and listened to their laughter. He'd backed out of the room fast.

Why?

He didn't know. Confusion, he thought. He was definitely confused. The sight of one crazy doctor, gorgeous in her borrowed Crimplene, holding his little son and bouncing as if she were six years old, too...

Confusion summed it up, he thought. She was like no one he'd ever met.

She was...gorgeous?

She was also married. She was wearing a band of gold very definitely on the third finger of her left hand. She was attached to a creep called Michael.

How attached? Married attached.

But, then...he wore a wedding band as well. Why?

Habit, he guessed. Beth had been dead for almost six years now.

So why did he keep wearing the ring?

The vision of Christine came into his head. Beth's older sister. Christine, who came in every day and cared for Toby, fussed over this house, made sure Toby had a memory of his mother.

Christine would marry him. He knew that. She was just waiting for him to move on from her sister.

So he wore a wedding ring.

'It's time you got over it,' Christine had told him, but he wasn't ready. He hadn't been ready to marry Beth. He hadn't wanted to marry anyone.

The memory of his parents' loveless marriage was always there— his mother, cool and calculating, with eyes only for things of monetary value, and his father who'd had eyes only for women he could bed. He himself had been raised to be self-contained, aloof and indifferent, and only Toby had ever been able to get under his skin.

The thought of Rachel came back into his vision.

Bouncing. Christine would never bounce. Not in a fit.

Neither would Beth, his ex-wife, have bounced. Neither would his mother.

Rachel was...different.

But Rachel had a husband. He thought back to the silverhaired cardiologist he'd met so briefly. The man might be odious, but he was obviously an extremely wealthy and well-connected doctor, and they were married. So Rachel might be bouncing in his spare bedroom with his small son but she had a husband and an Afghan hound and a life back in the city.

So stop thinking of her like...what? Like his father thought of women?

No. It wasn't like that. This was something he had never felt before—in truth, he'd never known he could feel this way. Ever. But he was certainly feeling, and the problem was—he couldn't stop to save himself.

The hot chocolate was excellent. Exhausted, glowing with exertion from their bouncing, Rachel and Toby enjoyed it equally. Hugo watched them as he'd watch two kids with their play lunch, and Rachel looked up and caught his eye and said, 'What?'

'What do you mean—what?'

'What are you grinning at?'

'I was just thinking you and Toby look of an age.'

'Toby is very mature for six.' She set her mug down on the table and rose to her feet, which all of a sudden didn't feel too steady. It had been a roller-coaster of a day and she was rolling downward to sleep. 'And I'm sure it's Toby's and my bedtime. Toby had an afternoon nap. I didn't even have a nap last night.'

'Why not?'

'It'd take far too long to explain,' she said with dignity. She eyed him with indecision. 'I suppose you wouldn't happen to have a spare toothbrush, would you? My gear's still at the showgrounds.'

'Not only a toothbrush.' He grinned. 'While you and Toby were bouncing I made you up a sleeping kit. One pair of pyjamas, slightly large, one brand-new toothbrush and a comb. Everything else you need you'll find in the guest bathroom.'

She swallowed. Heck. It was a small enough gesture, but it was enough. The man was thoughtful.

The man smiled!

The man was seriously gorgeous.

'Goodnight, then,' she said, and there was a distinct tremor in her voice.

His smile died and their eyes met. Something passed between them that was indefinable but it was still...there.

But there was nothing to say. To try and bring it into the open—this thing...

Impossible.

'Goodnight,' he said, and she knew he was thinking no such thing. He was thinking exactly what she was thinking.

Impossible!

What was it with her?

Hugo stood and watched while Rachel walked away from him down the corridor to her bedroom. Her door closed behind her but he stood and watched for a very long time.

What was it?

'Dottie?'

'My dear, why are you ringing at this time of night?'

'I'm checking.' Rachel was tucked into her opulent bed, her cellphone resting on her pillow. 'I just need... Dottie, I need to know...'

'You know he's just the same. He always will be just the same, whether you're here or not. Now, are you somewhere nice with that nice young man?'

'I...' Rachel bit her lip. That nice young man. Maybe she could apply the adjective to Toby. 'Yes,' she said. 'Yes, I am.'

'Has he taken you somewhere gorgeous?'

She smiled at that. This, at least, was an easy question. 'It's all red and gold brocade,' she whispered. 'And incredibly luxurious. Dottie, you should see the bed.'

There was a moment's silence. And then Dottie spoke again, deeply satisfied.

'Then why are you wasting time on the phone talking about it?' she demanded. 'You put your phone down this minute and go and make the most of it.'

Make the most of it? That was a joke.

Rachel put the phone down and pulled up her covers but in the end she did make the most of it. Or she did what she most needed to do.

She slept.

Digger was barking.

Rachel surfaced to sunlight streaming in over her bed.

She blinked, trying to figure out just where she was. Memory came flooding back. She stretched out in her toobig pyjamas and thought this wasn't such a bad place to live if you took away the brocade. And the tassels. And the particularly ghastly cupids staring dotingly down from the mantelpiece.

Her bedroom was facing east. She'd hauled back the dreadful crimson drapes the night before and now she could see right out to the ocean beyond. Why the bedroom had drapes she didn't know, unless the local cows were nosy. There were cows in the paddock beyond the house, the sea was beyond the cows and beyond the sea was the horizon. A smoky haze was filtering the light but it still looked great. Her apartment at the hospital looked out at a brick wall.

Maybe she could move to the country when Craig... Yeah, right. Get a grip.

Craig.

She groped under her bed for her purse, checked the time—it was eight o'clock, far later than she usually slept even after huge nights on call!—found her phone and dialled home. Some things were automatic.

But some things weren't needed. Or wanted.

'What are you doing, ringing again?' Dorothy sounded cross that she'd contacted her. 'I told you not to and I meant it. Rachel, leave it be. I can't tell you how delighted we are that you're having a good time.'

'But Craig?'

There was silence. Then: 'You know very well how Craig is, dear. I told you. Lewis popped in before breakfast and he's stable. As he always is. Rachel, it's no use ringing.'

'But you will let me know...'

'Rachel, love, nothing's going to change and you know it. You go back to whatever it is you're doing,' her mother-in-law said gently. 'Stop ringing. Move on. Get yourself a life.'

A life. Right. Dorothy thought she was having a nice romantic time.

She looked down at herself, dressed in what she guessed were Hugo's spare pyjamas. Blue and yellow stripes. Very fetching.

She looked at the bedside chair where Doris's Crimplene lay waiting.

'Which?' she said to herself. 'Romantic choice, eh? Which would Cinderella wear, and where's my fairy godmother when I need her?'

Hugo and Toby and the plump, round-faced lady she'd seen taking care of Toby yesterday were all having breakfast. Oh, and Digger. The lady was just setting down a plate of scraps under the table. This was clearly doggy heaven.

It was Rachel heaven. She sniffed. Bacon. Coffee. Toast.

Some things were irresistible. She hitched up her pyjamas and hiked right in.

'Hi,' she said, and tried not to look self-conscious. 'Hi,' said Toby, while the lady and Hugo just looked.

'No comment is required,' she told them. She glared at Hugo—at the lurking laughter she could see behind his eyes. 'Don't even think about it.' She held out her hand to the bacon lady, while the other still clutched her waist. 'I'm Rachel.'

'I'm Myra Partridge,' the lady told her, taking her hand and gripping it with warmth and real friendliness. She eyed Rachel's outfit in concern. 'They're not the doctor's pyjamas?'

'I have no idea,' she told her. 'They're the ones the doctor kindly gave me last night. All I know is that they're not this doctor's pyjamas. They're threatening to slide, but I've decided that they still look better on me than Doris Keen's frock does.'

'Oh, my dear...' Myra's lips twitched. She was in her late fifties, Rachel guessed, with eyes that said she smiled most of the time. She reached into a kitchen drawer and proffered a safety pin—which Rachel accepted with real gratitude. 'I saw you in Doris's frock last night. Doris rang a while back.'

'If she wants her frock back, she's welcome to it.' Rachel thought about it. 'Though she might want to come and get it. I can't see myself hiking over to her place in these.'

'Sit yourself down.' They were all smiling now as she stuck the safety pin in place—all three of them. The kitchen felt great. Here the opulence and over-decoration were toned down by the sheer domesticity of cooking and the dog under the table and smiling people. There were pots and pans and...

'Pancakes?' Rachel said faintly.

'I thought you'd all be hungry.' Myra beamed. 'The doctor's been out since dawn.'

'Has he?' Rachel's smile slipped. She looked across the table at Hugo. 'Problems?'

'Kim's running a fever. Not too bad. I'm hoping it's nothing. I've upped the antibiotics to maximum. And a couple of the fire crews have been working through the night. I checked them as they came in.'

'He'd be doing something else if it wasn't Kim and the fire crews,' Myra said comfortably. 'He's always gone at dawn. I come in and look after the wee one...'

'Until Aunty Christine comes in and takes me to school,' Toby told her. 'Mrs Partridge would take me to school and I want her to, but Aunty Christine makes Dad let her.'

She wasn't buying into any family argument. Not yet. 'Well, lucky you to have two ladies to escort you.' She wriggled herself around in her pyjamas, testing the security of the pin. She let go the waist and did a little test jump—her hands hovering just in case, while Hugo, Toby, Myra and Digger looked on, fascinated. They were doomed to disappointment. The safety pin held. She sat herself down and reached for a pancake, deeply satisfied. 'You were going to wake me up for some of these, right?'

Hugo was looking at her with a very strange expression. 'Um...right.'

'I wanted to wake you up hours ago,' Toby announced. 'But Daddy wouldn't let me.'

'You have a very kind daddy.' Rachel beamed. 'Just as long as he lets me share his pancakes and his bacon and coffee. Very kind indeed.'

* * *

Clothes. That was the most important thing.

'Doris dropped your bag off an hour ago,' Myra told her. 'But she's kept your clothes. There's stains…'

'I don't want to know about them,' Rachel said firmly, thinking about the last time she'd seen them and deciding if she never saw them again it'd be too soon. 'There's nothing wrong with Crimplene and flannelette.'

'Digger saved your bra,' Toby told her, and she faltered.

Her bra. The last time she'd seen that had been…

Whoops!

'Flannelette and Crimplene and lacy black bras are hardly professional,' Hugo told her, and Rachel managed a sickly sort of smile.

'Um…no. Not your white-coated doctor image, huh?'

'No,' he said faintly, and her grin widened. Hey, it wasn't he who was doing the discomposing. It was suddenly Hugo who was discomposed. She had Hugo McInnes out of his comfort zone, which felt…good.

Definitely good, she decided. He made her discomposed.

It was nice to have him a little discomposed in return.

But he was about to discompose her again. 'I think we have the problem sorted,' he told her.

'Mmm?' She was into a mouthful of bacon. Yesterday's hunger was still fresh enough to make her really appreciate her food and this was seriously good.

'Christine's bringing you some clothes.'

She thought about it. 'Christine.' She looked at Toby. 'Red and gold Christine?'

They all knew what she meant. There were three smiles. But Hugo was rising, pushing back his coffee-cup. 'She's very good. I don't know where we'd be without her. And she's not red and gold at all. She has a style all her own.' He glanced at his watch. 'She should be here in a few minutes to take Toby to school. I need to do a house call. If it's OK with you, Rachel, I'll collect you in an hour and take you out to our nursing home. I was hoping you might be able to help.'

He paused as if what he was asking was an impertinence, but she wasn't in the mood for worrying over impertinence. 'Of course I'll help. If I'm trapped here I may as well be useful. But how?'

'The fires are worsening.' He motioned to the window and the haze between there and the sea seem to be thicker. 'They're not threatening the town yet but the crews are working hard to keep it like that. And most of the crews are made up of volunteers with differing levels of fitness—as well as differing levels of common sense. There are lots of medical problems. I need to go up to the ridge.'

'So you'd like me to do the coughs and colds and the like while you do the hero stuff?'

'Would you?'

'Of course I would.' She grinned at him. There was something about this man that made her want to smile—even when she was offering to do his mundane work for him while he did the exciting stuff. 'Though I guess that means I don't get to drive fire trucks any more.'

His smile matched hers. 'I heard about your fire-truck driving. Very impressive. But still...' His eyes smiled at her—linking them—warming parts of her she hadn't known were cold. Crazy. But...nice? 'You're hardly dressed for fire-truck duty.'

She looked down at her pyjamas and pouted. 'What's wrong with these? I reckon I'd look pretty snappy behind the wheel of a fire truck in flannelette pyjamas.'

'Your safety pin would never hold.' He chuckled, and the strange link was broken. For now. 'OK. Let's negotiate the duty roster when we're organised. When you're wearing something a bit more doctor-like. Meanwhile, I have to go. Myra, can you—?'

He was interrupted in mid-sentence. The back door swung wide— and in walked Christine.

It wasn't hard to pick her. Rachel looked up from her bacon and she knew straight away who this had to be.

The lady was seriously lovely. She also wasn't decorated at all. She didn't need to be. What had Hugo said? 'She has a style all her own.'

She certainly did.

She was tall, with flame-coloured hair swept up into a sleek knot, the hair itself seeming to tug the flawless complexion free of any lines.

No lines would dare come near this woman. She was wearing cropped black pants to calf length, a tiny white top, strappy black sandals and a silver bracelet that must have cost a fortune.

She looked as if she belonged in an inner-city art gallery, Rachel thought, with only one very fast rueful glance down at her pyjamas. She thought back to the people she'd seen yesterday at the Cowral show. This woman didn't fit.

'Hello, all.' The woman's greeting was bright and warm. She smiled straight at Hugo, though, Rachel noticed, and Toby didn't look up from his breakfast. 'Are you ready, Toby?'

You can see he's still eating his breakfast, Rachel thought, but she didn't say so. The question seemed to be rhetorical. Christine had dropped a carry bag on the floor and was reaching for the coffee-pot. 'Heaven. You make the best coffee, Hugo.'

'Harrumph.' Myra rose and stumped over to the sink and Rachel wondered who had made the coffee. By the expression on Myra's face it wasn't hard to guess. Maybe it didn't matter, though. Christine had moved on.

'You're the new doctor?' Christine sank into the chair Myra had just left, as if it was her right, and turned her attention to Rachel. 'So you're Rachel. I've heard all about you.' She motioned to the bag. 'There are some clothes I purchased for you from our local discount store. I hope they're what you want, Hugo?'

They're what Hugo wanted?

Rachel raised her brows at Hugo and he attempted a smile. He looked a bit uncomfortable.

'I phoned Christine and told her you were in trouble.'

'Who, me?' Rachel tried hard to sound nonchalant. 'I like pyjamas.' Discount store, hey? Obviously she'd been categorised by Crimplene. She swallowed her last piece of pancake and smiled at all of them.

Discount store.

Maybe she should put that aside. There were undercurrents here that she clearly didn't understand. Undercurrents that were maybe more important than her pride.

Toby was concentrating fiercely on his pancake and wasn't looking at anyone. Myra was looking angry. What was going on?

It didn't matter. This wasn't her place and these people had nothing to do with her. In a couple of days the fires would die down and she'd be out of here.

'The clothes are all here.' Christine swept a manicured hand at her bag and smiled at Hugo, and Rachel thought, Unconcerned or not, I'm with Toby here. His little nose was practically in his toast.

But she knew her manners. 'Thank you, Christine,' she told her. 'Have you bought them? How much do I owe you?'

'I'll pay,' Hugo said, but Christine put a hand sweetly on his arm.

'It's fine, dear. The Mathesons, who run the discount store, know you're stuck. They won't charge you.'

Hugo was stuck?

Gee, she was having fun here, Rachel thought—or she didn't think.

She rose and lifted Christine's obnoxious bag. She hated it already, even though she hadn't opened it. 'I'll pick up my bill from...who did you say? Mathesons? If I really need this,' she told them. 'Otherwise I'll return it. Thank you anyway, Christine. Now, if you'll excuse me...'

She huffed at the lot of them. Toby looked up at her and she caught the six-year-old's eye and gave him a tiny sideways wink.

Then she sailed from the room with as much dignity as a girl in too-big pyjamas could muster.

'They're horrible.'

They were all gone—Toby and Hugo and Christine. Christine to take Toby to school and Hugo to do his house call. Rachel peered out into the kitchen where Myra was washing the dishes. The housekeeper turned and Rachel looked at her with despair in her eyes.

'I can't wear these.'

'Sorry?' The housekeeper wiped her hands on the dishcloth and looked Rachel up and down. Rachel was wearing Doris's Crimplene again.

'Look!'

She held up a pair of black trousers. Plain. Dead plain. Voluminous with a heavy vinyl belt. She held up a neat white cotton blouse. Another identical blouse. A plain black cardigan. Black flat-soled sandals.

'At least Doris's Crimplene has flowers on,' she wailed. 'And Hugo's pyjamas have stripes. Myra, I may be stuck here, but these are awful.'

'Christine only wears black and white,' Myra said dubiously, coming forward and taking the offending garments away from her. 'Only...'

'Only Christine's clothes are beautifully cut and really, really stylish and these clothes are built to fit anyone! Anyone at all. Or no one. These are burial clothes, Myra.'

Myra cast her another dubious glance. 'You don't think maybe you're going over the top here?'

'No.' Rachel's chin jutted. 'I may be stuck here but I refuse to look like Christine's welfare case while I'm here.'

'You don't wear black, huh?'

'No way.' It was the one thing she had in life—her clothes. She wore happy clothes, the sort of clothes that'd make Craig smile if he...

No. She wasn't going down that road, but she didn't wear black. Ever.

'You're wearing pink,' she told Myra, and if she sounded a bit like a sulky teenager she couldn't help it.

But Myra was smiling. 'Tell you what. I've finished the dishes,' she told her. 'I'm officially off duty until Toby comes home from school. We have an hour before Dr McInnes returns.'

'So?'

Myra glanced at her watch. 'It's not yet nine and Eileen Sanderson doesn't usually open until ten. But if it's for you...'

'Eileen Sanderson?'

'Kim's mum.'

'Oh, no. I can't—'

'She owns Cowral Bay's only decent dress shop and it's great. Expensive but good.'

'But she'll be with Kim.'

'She's home. I saw Brian, her husband, swap shifts with her a couple of hours ago as I was coming here and she lives next door to the store.'

'But she'll be asleep.'

'Not Eileen.'

'I can't—'

'Rachel, you saved her daughter's life,' Myra told her. 'You helped the firefighters last night. There's not a soul in Cowral Bay who wouldn't drop everything to help you right now.' She frowned and looked again at the black, shapeless trousers. 'Except maybe Christine.' And she tossed her dishcloth aside with a determined throw, grasped Rachel by the hand and towed her out to her car.

Hugo drove home an hour later, his thoughts overwhelmed with what lay ahead.

The fire was worse. The forecast was for a strong northeast wind, which would bring the fire down from the ridge. Already the town was shrouded by a pall of smoke so heavy Hugo had to put on his headlights.

There'd be heat exhaustion as well as fire-related injuries, he thought grimly. It was already scorchingly hot. If the fire grew worse... If there were emergencies...

He needed back-up.

He was set up here as a single doctor. Usually—well, sometimes— one doctor was enough. In a sleepy fishing village there was no need for a huge medical presence. Few doctors wanted to practise in such a remote area and the swell of campers during summer wasn't enough to tempt medics wanting a high income.

Normally Hugo didn't mind working alone—he even liked it—but his radio was telling him a quarter of the state was under threat from fire. That meant relief medical teams wouldn't be forthcoming even in an emergency. There was only him—but now at least there was Rachel as well.

But if the road cleared just for a few hours...

She'd be out of here, he thought grimly. She had a husband and the world's stupidest dog and a city career. She was a fine doctor—hell, she had the skills he desperately needed in a partner—but she'd be out of here.

The road was still cut, though, he thought, and as far he could see that was the only bright spot on his horizon. He had a captive worker and she'd said she'd work.

A captive worker...

He thought of Rachel as he'd last seen her. In those crazy pyjamas. His mouth twitched and his bleakness lifted a little. She was here. She had said she'd work. Now, as long as Christine had fitted her out in some sensible clothes...

He pulled into the driveway, looked down at the list of things he still had to do this morning and went to find his colleague.

He walked through the screen door and stopped dead. Good grief!

Rachel was sitting at the kitchen table, helping Myra pod peas. She'd obviously reclaimed Penelope. Penelope and Digger were lying side by side under the table looking extraordinarily pleased with each other, but that wasn't where Hugo's attention was caught and held.

Rachel was only five-four or so—a good eight inches shorter than he was—but what she lacked in height she made up for in impact. This morning in his pyjamas she'd looked amazing. But now...

She was wearing bright yellow leggings that stopped at mid-calf, and a white overshirt that looked as if it had been splashed by daubs of yellow paint. Her shirt was rolled up, businesslike, but there was nothing businesslike in the way it was unbuttoned to show enough cleavage to be interesting. Very interesting! So interesting he could hardly take his eyes away.

What else? He could scarcely take her in. Apart from the cleavage… Her riot of shining brown curls was caught back with a wide yellow ribbon and her feet were ensconced in gold and white trainers.

'Christine never gave you those clothes,' he said faintly, and she chuckled.

'Good guess. Mrs Sanderson's a darling and she has such taste. I returned the clothes Christine brought me. I'm very grateful but they just weren't me.' She held up a shoe and admired it. 'And gold and white trainers…how practical are these?'

'Very practical,' he said weakly, and she grinned. She rose and looked expectantly out to the car.

'Are we heading out to the nursing home now?'

'You're not wearing that outfit to the nursing home?'

'Why ever not?'

'I'm thinking of their hearts. I don't think I'm carrying enough anginine,' he said, and she chuckled again. She had the nicest chuckle…

'You're telling me the oldies won't like my clothes?'

'I have no idea,' he managed. 'I do know they'll never have seen anything like it in their lives.' He looked down at her amazing shoes. 'You don't think gold and white in this ash might be just a little impractical?'

'They'll wash. I'm not putting Doris's sandals back on for quids. They may be sensible but I don't do sensible.'

'So I see.'

The oldies not only loved Rachel's clothes—they loved Rachel.

In this heat and smoke-filled atmosphere, the ills of a group of sixty frail retirees could be depended on to keep Hugo busy for half a day, but only a couple of problems were serious. Hugo expected to do the tricky stuff himself while Rachel took a routine clinic, but Rachel had no sooner been introduced to the sitting room in general, and the nurse in charge in particular, than she balked.

'Tell me why you're staying?'

'I have a couple of bed-bound patients I'll check before I go.'

'You're telling me that I can't check them? That you don't think I'm competent?'

'No, but—'

'Then you're not needed anywhere else?'

'Of course he is.' Don, the nursing-home charge nurse, a beefy, bearded giant, was clearly amused by the strange tension between the two. And the way Hugo kept glancing at his colleague as if he couldn't believe his eyes. 'I've had a call from the hospital already saying there's another couple of firefighters need looking at, and they've just admitted Harry Peters's kid, who fell off the back of the fire truck and broke his arm. They want you back there, Hugo.'

'I can't just leave you here,' Hugo said, frowning at the jonquil-yellow apparition in front of him.

'Why not?' The jonquil-yellow apparition raised herself up on her jonquil-yellow toes and glared. 'Are you saying you're a better doctor than I am?'

'No, but—'

'Then take me to the patients you're worried about, talk me through what needs to be done and then get out of here. No more buts. You're wasting time, Dr McInnes.'

Wasting time?

No one had ever accused Hugo McInnes of wasting time.

Ever. It was all he could do not to gasp.

'Go on, then.' Don was clearly intrigued and enjoying himself. 'What are you waiting for, Hugo?'

He hardly knew.

CHAPTER FIVE

IT WAS HARDER work than she'd thought it would be.

Rachel had been working in an emergency department for the last four years, coping with emergencies. These weren't emergencies. She had to scour her brain for the things she'd learned in basic training—how to dress and treat leg ulcers, how to look after a man who was suffering long-term effects of the cortisone he'd taken after suffering rheumatoid arthritis for forty years, how to ease the passing of an old lady—ninety-eight, her bed card said, but she was still able to smile and grasp Rachel's hand in greeting—a lady who might only have days left to live.

Rachel had asked Hugo to let her do this, so he had left her to it. She hadn't realised until he'd gone that it had been quite an act of faith. Of trust.

'I'll come back and collect you at lunchtime,' he'd told her, and had gone off to see to his town patients and his firefighters. He was needed.

So was she. She couldn't think about Hugo. She had enough to con-centrate on herself.

But the oldies were lovely. They helped her all the way.

Don was at her side, and everyone knew the routine.

'Dr Hugo uses that sort of dressing,' she was told by a patient, the very elderly Mrs Collins, before Don could open his mouth. She cast him a sideways grin and started wrapping Mrs Collins's ulcer with the dressing the old lady had pointed at.

'Do I get the feeling this place would run on its own if we weren't here?' she asked.

'We learn to be self-sufficient,' Don told her. 'There's days when Hugo can't come.'

'When he's on holidays?'

'When there are emergencies in the town he can't come,' Don told her. 'Only then. Our Dr McInnes doesn't do holidays.'

'What, never?'

'He last took a holiday three years ago.' Don bent and helped her adjust the dressing. Mrs Collins, eighty-nine and very, very interested in this yellow doctor, was listening avidly as she was treated. 'I don't think he knows the meaning of the word holiday. Christine takes Toby to New York to visit his grandmother during school holidays—paid for by Hugo—and that's it.'

'It sounds a pretty dreary life.'

'It's a better life now than when he was married,' Don said bluntly. 'Some marriages are the pits.'

Hmm. 'Should you be saying this to me?' Rachel raised her eyebrows at the bearded nurse and Don grinned.

'Nope. But if we can't gossip, what's the use of living?

Isn't that right, Mrs Collins?'

'That's dead right.' Sheila Collins's old eyes perused Rachel and suddenly she leaned over and grabbed her hand. She held it up.

'You're married yourself?' she demanded, and Rachel met her look square on.

'Yes.'

'Not separated or anything?'

'No.'

'So when this fire is over and the road's cleared, you'll go back to your husband.'

There was only one answer to that. 'Of course I will.'

The old lady's look was steady. News must travel fast in this town. Everyone was really well informed. Frighteningly well informed. 'They say you were fighting with your husband at the dog show. They say he's a creep and a bully. And he left our Kim for dead.'

'No one here knows my husband,' Rachel said steadily. 'First impressions…'

There were places Rachel wasn't prepared to go. No one needed explanations. 'No one here knows him,' she said again.

'Stay out of her space, Sheila,' Don said sternly. 'Or you just might get iodine on those legs.'

Sheila's eyes narrowed. She stared at Rachel for a moment longer and then gave a cackle of laughter. 'Oh, sure. I guess it'd serve me right if I do. But it's not just me who's curious. She wants to know about our Dr McInnes as much as we want to know about her.'

'Then tell her.' Don was in his fifties or maybe a little older. He looked contented, Rachel thought. He looked like a nurse who'd spent his life caring for people in a small town—and who was content to do so for as long as he could. The feeling was suddenly…nice. Living in Cowral would be a good life, she thought. She'd never considered country medical practice. Maybe she…

Maybe after… No.

'Our Dr Hugo made a bad marriage,' Sheila told her, and Rachel forced herself to concentrate. Not that that was very hard. Sheila was right. She really did want to know.

'Why?'

'He didn't have much of a home life, our Doc Hugo,' Sheila said. 'His mother was a right little cow—only after what she could get. She lit out for the city as soon as she could and we never saw her again. But Hugo used to come down here. Old Dr McInnes had been here for as long as anyone can remember, and whenever his mother wanted to get rid of him—which was often—Hugo used to come down to stay. He loved his grandpa. Then the old man had a stroke soon after Hugo qualified as a doctor, and Hugo came for good. I don't think he had much choice. He came because he loved the old man and then he was sort of stuck.'

So he hadn't come through choice…

'He was really unsettled at first.' Don took over the tale then. They were a pair, Rachel thought—the nurse who looked like he'd be more at home on a logging truck than in a nursing home, and the ancient lady whose bright eyes gleamed with intelligence. And…mischief? 'The old man was ill for a couple of years,' Don continued, with only a sideways glance and a twinkle to show he knew exactly what Rachel was thinking. 'Hugo was here, helping him. It must have been a huge shock after practising medicine in Sydney.'

'But then he met Beth,' the old lady chipped in. 'Christine and Beth. They came down here to paint. Their parents were divorced. Their father had a fishing shack here so living was cheap. They had nothing to bless themselves with, but they thought they were the best thing since sliced bread. Their mother has a studio in New York and that's how they dressed—like they'd just walked off the streets of Manhattan. They complained because no one knew how to make decent coffee.'

'They were exotic and they were gorgeous,' Don added. 'They were also really, really expensive. Their paintings were incomprehensible and pretty soon they latched onto the idea that one of them should marry our doctor.'

'And of course he was so bored that he fell for it,' Sheila told her. This was a story told in tandem. The fact that there seemed to be some urgency about it was strange, but that was the way Rachel was hearing it. Maybe it was the way she was meant to be hearing it. 'He was feeling trapped by the needs of this community—by the needs of his grandfather. Beth was gorgeous and reminded him of a life he'd left behind. And after his parents' example I don't think he knew what a decent marriage was. So he married her. And had Toby.'

'Damned stupid...' Don shook his head. He looked sideways at Rachel as if figuring out how much to tell—and then obviously decided that, unprofessional or not, he was going to tell anyway. 'It was never going to work. Beth married Hugo for all the wrong reasons and personally I don't think Hugo knew the right reasons to marry, either. Neither of them really knew what marriage was. Beth filled that house with all that weird stuff. She spent a fortune but still it didn't make her happy. She left him twice. Then, when she found she was pregnant, she walked out for ever. She wanted an abortion but he hated the idea. She compromised by leaving him. No, I know it doesn't make sense but, then, Beth didn't make sense to herself. She wasn't living with Hugo when Toby was born. She was living with some painter up in Sydney.'

'But still bleeding him dry,' Sheila added.

'And then she died.' Don looked sick at the memory. 'She had eclampsia. Apparently she and the guy she was living with were drinking too much. She didn't care about the baby—but it wasn't Toby who ended up suffering. She ignored the symptoms until she was far gone. Toby was born by Caesarean section but it was too late and that left our Hugo feeling dreadful. Guilt. He hadn't tried to make her come home. And Christine made the guilt worse.'

'Christine,' Rachel whispered.

'Of course, Christine.' Don shrugged. 'She stays on in this town because that's where she owns a house but she hates the place. Her paintings don't sell. She spends any money she gets on stupid things. You'd feel sorry for her if she wasn't so damned...superior. She's got no money of her own. She lives here and she won't let anyone forget Beth. She makes Hugo's guilt worse. "My Beth", she keeps saying as she shoves that shrine of a house down their throats. "We must never forget Toby's mother." The fact that they fought like cat and dog when Beth was alive...'

'She wants to marry Hugo.' Sheila was totally absorbed in her tale. Her ulcers were almost completely bandaged now but the old lady had a captive audience until they were finished and she wasn't letting go. 'And little by little she's wearing him down. Hugo has to let Toby spend time with Christine. It's the only contact the kid has with his mother's family. And she guilts him into keeping that house just as it was. '

Enough, Rachel thought, beginning to feel just a little desperate. The bandages were in place. This was entirely improper—doctor gossiping about another doctor with that doctor's patients and a nurse. Rachel rose to her feet and tried to look determined.

'I'm sure I need to see someone else.'

'No matter who you see they'll tell you the same thing,' Sheila retorted. 'Our Dr McInnes is being railroaded into marriage with another like the first. And she's not even a decent artist. What she does is horrible.'

Rachel was left wondering what was horrible. The thought of such a marriage—or Christine's artwork?

Maybe she knew.

'How did it go?'

Hugo collected her half an hour after he'd said he would. He'd been delayed by a minor crisis, he told her, but the look on his face told Rachel it hadn't been minor. He looked strained past endurance.

'What's wrong?' she asked, but he shook his head.

Whatever it was, he didn't intend to share it.

'How did you manage at the nursing home?' he asked, changing the subject with more bluntness than tact.

She hesitated but his face was shuttered. This was a man accustomed to working on his own, she thought. He carried the responsibility for this town's health on his shoulders alone.

She could share but only as much as he wished her to share, and maybe it wasn't fair to push when she was here for such a short time.

So she concentrated on now. On the present.

'I love your oldies,' she told him. 'I now know not only their medical histories but also the history of everyone in Cowral.'

He managed a smile at that. 'Including mine?'

'Of course, including yours.' She settled into the passenger seat of his comfortable old family sedan and smiled across at him. She wanted him to smile. She wanted to take that look of strain away from around his eyes. 'How can you doubt it?'

'So...' He grimaced. 'Have they worked out your love life yet?'

'Mine?' She raised her eyebrows at that. 'I don't have a love life.'

'You have a husband.'

'That's right,' she said, and somehow kept her voice steady as he looked across at her.

'A husband. A love life. They're not the same thing?' Were they? Once they were. A long time ago...

'Where are we going now?' she asked. He wasn't the only one who could change the subject. It was high time to move on from what was suddenly dangerous ground.

'I'll drop you at home for lunch and a rest while I—'

'While you keep working.'

'That's the plan.'

She shook her head. 'Nope. As plans go, it sucks.'

'Sorry?'

'I slept this morning while you worked. I've done a whole three hours' work while you, I suspect, have done about six. So why is it that now I get to be bored while you play doctor?'

He thought about it. 'You don't have to be bored. You could take Penelope for a walk.'

'I walked my feet off last night. I don't intend to walk anywhere for six months.'

'Then what do you want to do?'

'Have lunch now and then do something useful,' she said promptly. 'If I'm trapped in your house for the whole afternoon I might be forced to do something dire—like strip the brocade wallpaper from the living room.'

It had been the wrong thing to say. His face sort of set. 'Whoops,' Rachel said, not sounding in the least contrite.

'Don't tell me you like brocade.'

'I'm very grateful to Christine,' he said stiffly, which was a strange answer to a question that had hardly been asked. 'I'm grateful to Christine, too,' she told him, refusing to be dismayed into a guilty conscience 'But I'm not wearing brocade because of it. Or even the clothes she chose.'

'You'll hurt her feelings.'

'Really?' She looked at him in disbelief. 'Is that why you stick with the brocade? You really think that she'd be devastated if you said, "Thank you, Christine, you're very thoughtful but I don't like red and gold brocade. I like yellow."'

He frowned. 'What are you talking about? I don't like yellow.'

'Toby says you like yellow.'

'I don't.'

'You don't like Mr Addington's yellow car?'

The corners of his mouth twitched. The look of strain eased a bit and Rachel found herself smiling inside. Good. 'Who told you about Mr Addington's car?' he demanded.

'Toby. You do like it?'

'Of course I like it. It's a Ferrari.'

'Is that all you like about it? You'd like it better in red and gold?' She cocked her head to one side. 'Michael's Aston Martin is red. I hate that car.'

He raised his brows at that. Seemingly intrigued. 'So what is it with you and Michael? You hate his dog. You hate his car. You fight with the man in public and he abandons you in a town with a bushfire threatening.'

How did she answer that? She couldn't. She managed a shrug. 'So?'

The coldness of her tone didn't deflect him. He was still being nosy. 'I don't see that you have much of a marriage, Dr Harper.'

Should she tell him? No, she decided. His reaction to such a story was a complication she could do without. She hated telling people. She hated the way their faces shuttered down with shock and disbelief.

It was so much better to use Michael as a scapegoat. A pseudo-husband to hide the reality of pain. It was none of Hugo's business after all.

'I don't hate Penelope,' she told him, concentrating on the least of her issues with Michael. 'Whatever gave you that idea?'

'You don't love her!'

'She's sort of…goofy.' She grinned, moving right on. Steering fast from very dangerous personal relationships. 'Come on, Dr McInnes. Share your work with me. Don't sentence me to an afternoon with my goofy dog and your brocade walls.'

'I was planning to go out to the fire front,' Hugo told her. 'There's a command post out there. The teams are starting to show effects of smoke inhalation, heat exhaustion, burns. And the adrenaline isn't letting them stop.'

'Can I come with you?'

Those mobile eyebrows rose right up again. 'In those clothes?'

She looked down at herself. 'Maybe not,' she agreed cautiously. 'Maybe Mrs Sanderson could find me something a wee bit more suitable.'

'Maybe we'll grab a sandwich and then drop by the fire station,' he told her, the smile she was beginning to know and to love resurfacing from behind his eyes. 'I don't think even Mrs Sanderson does a couturier line in yellow firefighting apparel.'

The fire front was closer than they had expected.

Cowral Bay was on a spit about five miles from The Narrows, the mile-wide strip of land connecting Cowral to the mainland.

The Narrows were covered in mountainous bushland and all of it was burning. Hugo had expected to drive through to the far side of the first ridge, but there were roadblocks just as the land started to rise, and he was waved to a command post that had been brought further south.

'Hell.' Hugo pulled off the road and they stared together up at the ridge. The wind had died a little, which meant the billowing smoke was spiralling skyward and they could see flames bursting up over the mountains.

And for the first time, Rachel got nervous.

Up until now the fire had been a sort of backdrop to her real worries.

It was the reason she was stuck here and nothing else. Australians were accustomed to bushfires and this was a bushfire. In bush.

But maybe it could turn to something worse?

She stared down at herself. The officer manning the fire station had equipped her with heavy-duty overalls and big leather boots, and she carried a hard hat. She'd looked at herself in the mirror and had hooted with laughter. But now...now she wasn't laughing.

'This is big,' she whispered, and Hugo looked over at her and nodded.

'We lost a firefighter this morning.'

'You lost...'

'The wind changed,' he told her. 'He was trying to backburn and he'd gone too far from his team. He was cut off and there was nothing anyone could do to save him. They brought his body down just before I came to find you.'

She swallowed. No wonder he'd looked strained. 'Why didn't you tell me?'

'I just did.'

There'd been no need, Rachel thought. Or there had been a need—a desperate need—but Hugo had been on his own for too long to realise it. Sharing trauma, talking about it, was the only way to cope in emergency medicine. But Hugo coped alone. Somehow.

'What can I do?' she asked in a small voice, and he looked across at her, assessing.

'If you really want to help...'

'I said I did, didn't I?' she snapped, suddenly angry. 'I'm a member of your medical team, Dr McInnes. A team. You're not on your own. Get used to it.'

'I didn't mean...'

'Just use me,' she said wearily. 'Use me.'

He cast her another strange look. But the situation was dire. It was true. He did need her.

'The team who were with Barry when he died...they're still out there. They're due to come in at two. I'd like to see them all. There'll be real trauma. None of them would come off duty until their shift changed but I said I'd be available.'

'And you want teams to be briefed?'

'Last year in bushfire season I had a volunteer go home after suffering smoke inhalation. He didn't tell anyone he was having trouble breathing, then started coughing uncontrollably. By the time I saw him it was almost too late. I want the dangers spelled out to everyone, whether they've heard it five times or not. I want them to know to keep fluids on board. The professionals—even the well-trained volunteers—have been augmented now by helpers who mean well but haven't got two clues as to personal safety. They're working in teams but they get good ideas and go off by themselves. The guy this morning… He's in his sixties and he runs—ran—the local hardware store. He thought he knew it all. The fire chief has taken it hard. He's taken the volunteers through the safety drill but I want the medical bits spelled out in words of one syllable. I don't want any more deaths.'

'I can do that.'

'Make it sound dire,' Hugo told her. 'There's no second chances out there.'

'I can do dire.' She nodded. There was no laughter between them now. There was only medical need.

Which was how, half an hour later, overalled and booted and wearing her hard hat for heaven's sake'We wear them all the time when we're on duty,' she'd been told. 'It's a habit that makes sense not to break.'—Rachel found herself lecturing to a group of people who looked as out of place as she was.

Hugo was with the team of firefighters who'd lost their friend. She was with everyone else. Trying to sound knowledgeable. And authoritative.

She did. It was amazing what you could do when needs must.

'You stay hydrated,' she ordered. 'You carry water all the time. You never remove your hard hat. Ever. You keep your protective clothing on no matter how hot you get. You feel unwell for any reason, you get back here. For *any* reason. You start to cough, I want you back at base. You get any chest pain, a sore throat, your legs start aching—anything at all—you get back here fast. There's no medals for heroics. If you put your life at risk you'll put your whole team at risk. Now, before you go I want you to run past me individually and tell me a really brief medical history, and if there's anything at all you're vaguely worried about, you tell me now. You hear? Now!'

'She's amazing,' one of the firefighters told Hugo.

Miriam was one of the semi-trained volunteers. She'd been on the front line with Barry and she was suffering a nasty burn on her hand as well as shock from that morning's trauma. Hugo had what he needed to treat her on the spot but, having cleaned and dressed her burn, he was sending the woman home. Now they stood together in the clearing, watching Rachel assessing her firefighters thirty feet away. Each catching their breath before they moved on.

'She is amazing,' Hugo agreed. They could hear her voice, raised in authority. 'Bossy!'

'You'd think she'd been trained to do it.'

'Be bossy?' Hugo smiled. 'Maybe she has.'

'I wish I'd been a bit bossy,' Miriam said, and there was a load of bitterness and regret in her voice. 'Barry knew what we were told to do. We were just mopping up after backburning. If anything gets away, call for help, we were told, but when it flared he started fighting like a madman. The rest of us were retreating and he took it as a personal challenge. Then it was all around him. If I'd been a bit bossier...'

'Barry wouldn't have taken it from you,' Hugo said gently. Miriam was usually a clerk in the shire offices. She was so out of place here it was almost ridiculous. 'He'd never take orders from someone without authority.'

'He'd have taken orders from your Rachel,' Miriam told him. 'You just have to hear her. She seems...in charge.'

She did.

But what had Miriam said? 'Your Rachel...'

His Rachel. The words were unnerving. Miriam had meant them to denote that he and Rachel were a team but, looking across and seeing Rachel, it seemed almost more than that. She was listening to an elderly man who was telling her exactly why he should be allowed to fight the fires. Sam Nieve. Hell. It was obvious to anyone the man couldn't firefight. Hugo half rose to intervene but he didn't need to. He couldn't hear what she was telling him, but the man's shoulders didn't sag. Instead, his chest puffed out, he removed his helmet and he departed with an air of increased importance. His little car took off in the direction of the town and Hugo gave a sigh of relief.

Sam had a heart condition. He was the last person they'd want on the fire line but he was almost as stubborn as Barry. How had she convinced him?

If anyone could, Rachel could, he thought. The lady was amazing.

His Rachel?

No. The lady was married. The lady was…taken.

They worked solidly for three hours, but then it was time to return to the town. Hugo had patients in hospital and he had a clinic to run. He needed to return. The teams had changed over, the off-duty firefighters had gone back to the town to sleep and the on-duty members were lined up against the fire front.

The doctors would be needed again at change-over—or earlier if emergencies arose—but maybe because of the work they'd done, there'd be less chance of an emergency.

They could only hope.

'You did really well,' he told Rachel as they drove homeward, and she flushed.

'If we're forming an admiration society, can we make it mutual?'

'Nope. What did you tell Sam to make him give up his plans to fight fires?'

'You really want to know?'

'Yeah.'

'I used you.'

He raised his brows and grinned. 'You used me?'

'I told him you'd lost two patients in two days and there wasn't room in the funeral parlour for a third. I also told him if you lost someone else you'd be in for a breakdown and it'd be on his head if the town lost its doctor.'

'Gee, thanks very much,' he said faintly, but she hadn't finished yet.

'I told him brute strength wasn't all that was needed here. I told him that if the fire worsened, it was really important that everyone's roof is clear and they have their hoses ready. There are lots of people who are just blind when it comes to this type of thing.' She grinned, ignoring the fact that his brows had hit his hairline. 'I suspect, in fact, that Mr Nieve's own personal gutters around his roof are not as clean as they should be. I seemed to hit a nerve. Anyway, I suggested he contact the local school and borrow a few of the older kids and do a house-to-house check.'

Hugo whistled, seemingly totally astonished. 'Well done, you.'

'It's true,' she said gently. 'What's true?'

'You really don't want any more deaths.'

'What do you think?'

She looked at him, considering. 'I'm all for them,' she said at last, teasing for a smile. 'More deaths mean fewer patients and patients mess up your consulting rooms faster than anything I know.'

He laughed with her, but there wasn't a true smile behind his eyes.

'The two deaths...' she probed gently, and waited. He needed to talk, she suspected. There wouldn't be a lot of professional support in this one-doctor town.

And it seemed like it was professional support he was uncomfortable with.

She didn't let him off the hook. She waited and finally he shrugged and started to speak.

'Last night's death was expected,' he told her. 'It was Annie's time, but I was fond of her for all that.' He gave a twisted smile. 'Annie started making me chocolate cakes when Beth died and we've had a weekly chocolate cake ever since. And Barry... Barry was a pompous little prig who didn't deserve what happened to him. He has a sweet little wife and a couple of obnoxious kids who'll miss him for ever.'

Silence. More silence.

'It's hard, this country practice,' Rachel said at last. She was combing pieces of debris from her hair with her fingers. She'd taken her hard hat off before she'd got back in the car, which had been a mistake. The air was thick with falling ash, and most of it seemed to have ended up in her hair. 'You get attached.'

'Something you don't do?'

'It's not all that easy getting attached when you work in emergency medicine,' she agreed. 'I keep track of some patients but not many.'

'So when you finish up a shift, the day's over.'

'Pretty much.'

'It'd be a great life,' Hugo said softly, and Rachel didn't miss the note of bitterness in his voice.

'What, so you'd really like to swap?'

'I'd just like to turn off sometimes,' he told her. 'This town... I came here for a few years to look after my ailing grandfather and I've never been able to leave.'

'Because you can't get anyone else to replace you?'

'Partly.'

'And partly what else?' She'd twisted sideways to watch him. They were nearly back in town now—their time for intimacy was almost over and she regretted it. She liked this big, gentle man with the laughing eyes. She liked him a lot. It seemed such a shame that he was meant for...the likes of Christine?

She'd seen the way Christine had looked at Hugo. Hugo may have married one sister but by the look in Christine's eyes and by the accounts of local gossip he was destined to marry the other.

But Hugo wasn't talking about Christine. Or he was, but only in that she was part of the tapestry of Toby's life. 'Partly because my life is here,' he told her. 'Toby's life. The people here love him. He has Myra and Christine and...so many people. He has the freedom of the place— there's not a soul in Cowral Bay who doesn't know who he is and watches out for him.'

'And in return you watch out for them,' she said softly.

He was concentrating on turning into the hospital car park but it wasn't the concentration that was causing the set look around his mouth. He cared. He'd certified the deaths of two of Cowral's own in the past twenty-four hours and it had bitten deep.

Rachel saw deaths most days. She worked in a big city emergency department.

Two deaths wouldn't affect her like this.

Maybe they should. Maybe she should be more involved.

She was involved enough. How could she be any more involved than she was right now?

She should be home...

'It must be amazing,' Hugo said, 'to leave work at night and be free to go to the movies, go out to a restaurant—do anything you want.'

He had to be kidding. If he knew how much she hated eating out... And when had she last gone to a movie? Going to movies on her own sucked. 'I have responsibilities,' she said stiffly, and he nodded.

'Of course you do. Penelope. Michael.'

'Michael's not—'

'You're right. Michael's none of my business.' He cut her off as he switched off the engine. 'But I'm interested. What do you do with the rest of your life? How do city doctors without kids operate? It's a world away from what I know.'

'You did it once.'

'It's so long ago I've forgotten. I wouldn't mind remembering.'

Remembering what? He was talking about the giddy social life Michael enjoyed, Rachel knew, and that was so far away from her own experience that it was ridiculous. She closed her eyes. What was the point in explaining? There wasn't one. This man had enough on his shoulders without burdening him with her personal tragedy.

'You wouldn't be interested,' she said flatly. 'And you have work to do. Is there anything else I can do to help?'

He looked at her and once again she had the feeling he saw more than she wanted him to. But he couldn't know. How could he possibly know about Craig?

He didn't. Of course he didn't. He was shaking his head, moving on.

'You've done enough.'

'You're doing clinic?'

'For a couple of hours.'

'So Toby and I will see you at dinner.'

'That's right. So you can take your overalls off, Dr Harper, and turn into a guest again. Exercise your dog or something.'

'Right.'

'I'll see you later.'

End of conversation. But he was still watching her. His eyes still held hers.

He should turn away, she thought. He should get out of the car.

He didn't. They were somehow...locked?

It was a strange sensation. Stupid. Senseless. He had things to do. She was a married woman and they had no link.

They did have a link. They were just looking at each other. Seeing...

Seeing past the fac,ade. Seeing what was really behind it. She stared into his face and she could see the battering this man had suffered over the years. The loneliness. The wanting.

How could she see that? She didn't know. But see it she did, and if she could read so much in his face, how much more could he read in hers?

This was ridiculous. She had things to do. Dogs to walk.

Hours to fill before she saw him again.

Ridiculous!

Somehow Rachel managed to break the moment—break the link. She climbed from the car and slammed the door with more force than was needed. The slam was a statement. 'I'm going to take a shower,' she told him, and if her voice wasn't quite steady there wasn't a darned thing she could do about it. 'I'll see you later.'

She walked away, leaving Hugo staring after her.

CHAPTER SIX

HE DIDN'T HAVE a clue what was going on.

Hugo worked his way through half a dozen patients and maybe it was just as well there was nothing serious, because his attention was definitely elsewhere. Or maybe it'd be better if there was something serious, he decided. Maybe his thoughts needed to be hauled right back to work. Not on some slip of a doctor whose eyes made him smile. Whose smile made him chuckle...

Whose smile made him twist inside.

How long had it been since someone had made him feel like this? Some woman?

Never, he thought as he carefully wound wet bandage around Tom Harris's arm. Tom had fallen and broken his forearm while clearing undergrowth around his house when the fires had started four days ago. Hugo had put the initial plaster on loosely because of inflammation but the arm had settled now and it could be fixed more securely into its casing.

Tom, though, was a man of few words. He didn't want to chat, so Hugo's attention stayed right where it was. On Rachel.

Why was it on Rachel?

She was married, he told himself. Happily married for all he knew. Sure, the man she'd been with at the dog show had seemed a creep, but the nicest of women found partners in the strangest of places. She hadn't said a word about her marriage being unhappy.

Maybe she couldn't. Maybe the man was violent.

No.

He thought back to his medical training, to the one question he'd been told could predict violence in marriages in almost every case. He'd used it time and again with sometimes astonishing results.

'Is there any time in the last couple of years where you've felt afraid of your husband?'

He thought of Rachel and he knew instinctively that she'd shake her head if he directed his question at her. She'd been angry at Michael at the dog show but she hadn't been afraid of him. She'd flung those car keys at him with such force that the memory still made him smile.

'You thinking of the new lady doctor?' Tom asked, and Hugo nearly dropped his bandages.

'No. I was thinking how good this arm is looking.'

'People don't smile like that thinking about a sixty-year-old fisher-man's broken arm,' Tom said dourly, though there was the hint of laugh-ter in his eyes.

'Why not? You have a very nice arm,' Hugo tossed back, and Tom's face creased into reluctant laughter.

'Yeah, and yours is sexy and all as well,' he retorted. 'But I bet our Rachel has a sexier one.'

Our Rachel... How quickly had the community taken her as one of its own?

'The lady's married,' Hugo snapped before he could stop himself, and Tom's grin broadened.

'So I'm on the right track, then.'

'Look—'

'It's nothing to do with me, mate,' Tom told him. 'I'm just here to get an arm fixed. You're the one who has to go home tonight and sleep in the same house. Married or not.'

Hugo shook his head, thoroughly confused. 'I can't...'

'Yeah, you can,' Tom said encouragingly, knowing exactly what he was thinking. Like it or not. 'Or you can at least try.'

* * *

It was well past dinnertime when a weary Hugo arrived home. What a day, and there was still a ward round to do before he could sleep. Even so, he was aware of a lifting of his spirits as he walked from the hospital across the lawn to the house. It'd be different tonight. Rachel would be there.

She certainly was. He walked in the back door and instead of a formally set table, with Myra waiting to serve up chops and three vegetables—her standard fare, to be expected at least three times a week—he walked in to find Rachel packing an enormous picnic basket. Toby was sitting on the table, poking things into its depths, and his small face was lit up with excitement.

'We're going to the beach for tea,' he told his father before Hugo could open his mouth. 'Or for your tea and an after-tea picnic for us. Rachel says it's so hot and stuffy that if she doesn't get a swim she'll expire.'

'She will, too.' Rachel was back in those extraordinary yellow clothes again. Her wonderful clothes. 'And the dogs are going stir-crazy.' She gestured to the two dogs, who were lying on the floor eyeing the picnic basket with a devotion that said they'd already tested the contents. 'Have you finished for the day, Dr McInnes?'

'I need to do a ward round before—'

'I've done your ward round,' she told him before he could finish. 'Elly talked me through every patient in the hospital and there's no need for you to see any of them again tonight.' She corrected herself. 'You might like to look in on Kim to check that her obs are still OK before you go to bed, but as of twenty minutes ago they were fine. There's no change in the fire crews for another two hours, and things seem relatively settled. The wind's forecast to strengthen tomorrow, which means havoc might break loose, so Toby and I figured we might have some fun while the going's good. That's now.'

'The nursing home—'

'Yep. There are a couple of oldies who need checks. Mrs Bosworth's breathing is cause for concern. I've told Don we'll stop in on the way.'

'The way...'

'To the beach.'

She tossed a bag of grapes into the picnic basket and beamed at him, expectant. So did Toby. The dogs looked up and wagged a tail apiece and he could swear they were beaming, too.

'I can't,' he said faintly, and Rachel's beam slipped immediately. He found himself staring at a lady with her arms crossed, schoolmarm-like, and a martial glint in her eye.

'Why ever not?'

'If I'm needed—'

'You're needed at the nursing home and Toby and I have agreed we'll watch television in the oldies' sitting room while you do the doctor bit. Or vice versa, but Mrs Bosworth's anxious and she's asking for you.' She smiled. 'You must have something in your bedside manner that I don't.' Her smile faded. 'Or Hazel Bosworth knows you and it's a familiar face she needs when she's frightened. But after that... The smoke's not so bad that it'll be awful. We have cold sausages. We have cold drinks and fresh bread and some of Toby's wonderful lamingtons. Your bathing costume's already packed and we're already wearing ours under our clothes, so what other objections would you care to make?'

Hugo couldn't think of any. He couldn't think of any at all. How long since he'd had a picnic on the beach?

'Please? Can we go, Daddy? Can we go?' Toby was jiggling with excitement. Under the table Penelope and Digger were jiggling as well.

'Yes,' he said promptly, before he changed his mind and got sensible. 'Yes, we can.'

Why not?

The nursing home was quieter than they'd expected. 'Most of the residents have seen scores of bushfires in their time,' Don told them. 'They're not panicking.' He gave a rueful smile. 'Most of them gave up their households of precious possessions when they came in here. It makes a difference when there's not so much to lose. Even Mrs Bosworth... Her breathing's dreadful, Hugo. She has emphysema and we can't get the smoke out of the atmosphere. She's so sick. But when I told her I was going to call you she said not to bother—that the doctors would have more than enough to cope with tonight, and if she died then it was her time. Age puts a different perspective on things.'

Not just age.

It was experience, Rachel thought as Hugo disappeared to see to Mrs

Bosworth's breathing problems and she settled to wait with Toby. Once upon a time in another life she'd collected porcelain. She remembered Craig coming home from football, bouncing in the front door full of his triumph, shouting to her. Whizzing her round in triumph, crashing one of her porcelain statuettes off the hall table.

She'd been angry.

Dear God, she'd been angry.

The porcelain was long sold. It had been many years since Rachel had seen anything more important than people. Life.

Now.

This minute.

Mrs Bosworth was settling. Hugo was emerging, discussing her condition with Don. The oxygen rate was up to maximum now and he'd given her a relaxant. Fear was making her breathing faster, causing more problems.

Because, of course, there was fear. Possessions could be abandoned. But not so life.

Sometimes life was wonderful.

Life was now, Rachel thought with quiet satisfaction as they reached the shoreline. Tomorrow might well be ghastly, but for now...for now there was this moment.

The locals had too much sense to be sitting on a smoky stretch of beach. Everyone not directly committed to the fire effort was supporting those who were. Tired people chose to stay indoors.

But now was too good to waste.

The tension eased from Hugo's tired mind almost as soon as his toes touched the sand.

The wind had miraculously dropped to almost nothing. The fine haze of eucalypt-filled smoke was even soothing. If there hadn't been the possibility that it might threaten the town when the wind came up, he could almost enjoy it.

Or maybe he could enjoy it anyway. How long since he'd hauled off his shoes and spent the evening on the beach?

He wouldn't have thought to do it. Rachel had thought of it. Rachel...

'Maybe we won't light fires to warm our sausages,' Rachel was suggesting, as the dogs went careering like mad things along the shore, and Hugo could only agree.

'Wise idea. One spark and we'd have every hose in town pointed straight at us. There are people on the lookout right now. Sparks drift for miles and are a threat all by themselves.'

'The town won't burn, will it, Daddy?' Toby asked, and Hugo hauled himself together. He'd been sounding too solemn.

Maybe he'd been sounding too solemn for far, far too long.

'No. The town won't burn. There's no wind at all tonight so the back-burners can really get things under control.' He took a deep breath. For now—for this small fragment of time—he could forget about fires. He could even—amazingly—forget about medicine. He could concentrate on what was important. 'Let's eat,' he suggested, and he could feel the tension easing out of him still more.

Rachel was smiling again, as if she knew that some invisible barrier had been broached. But it seemed she wasn't pushing.

'I'm swimming first,' she told him. 'Toby and I snacked while we waited for you. You have a sausage or two and join us—but don't eat too much. It'd be a shame to have to wait your requisite half an hour because you were scared of cramps.'

'That's an old wives' tale,' he said, and she raised mocking eyebrows.

'It's the medicine my granny taught me. Are you saying my Granny's medicine—and therefore my medicine—is wrong?'

He thought about that. He thought about the way he was feeling. Free. Almost light-headed. There was an anticipation in his heart that had nothing to do with common sense and everything to do with the way this lady smiled. Dr Rachel Harper's medicine.

'No, but—'

'Good,' she told him, her smile showing him she was aware of the fact that he was confused and she intended enjoying it. 'Mind your sausages, Dr McInnes. Toby and I are going for a swim.'

So Hugo sat and ate and watched his small son and this strange city doctor cavort in the shallows.

Rachel was the strangest creature, he decided. She was part girl, part woman. Part professional doctor, part kid who was searching for fun and laughter.

There was so much about her he didn't understand.

The hardest thing of all was to reconcile her marriage to Michael. To a doctor who'd risked a girl's life...

Hugo was under no illusion that Michael couldn't have redirected the helicopter. He would have heard the impassioned plea to return. He'd have heard how desperately ill Kim was. Hugo himself had talked to the pilot and he'd heard the pilot turn and talk to Michael. It had been Michael the helicopter had come to collect: to have forced him to stay in the air would have been nothing short of abduction. Michael therefore must have been complicit in the decision not to bring the helicopter back to take Kim to safety.

And Michael was married to Rachel. Rachel, who was gorgeous.

'Hey, Toby, spin,' Rachel was calling. Waist deep in the shallows, she had Toby high in her arms and was spinning him like the sails of a small windmill. She spun and spun while the dogs barked and barked and Hugo couldn't stop himself from grinning in delight.

Enough. He'd eaten enough.

'One more sausage and I'll cramp,' he told himself, and strolled into the water to join them. At the water's edge he paused, laughing at the expression of joy on Toby's face as he whirled faster and faster. Hugo chuckled out loud—and then his chuckle died.

Rachel and Toby had shed their outer clothes at the water's edge. From where Hugo had sat thirty yards up the beach, Rachel had looked beautiful. In her crimson, one-piece bathing suit, cut to reveal every gorgeous curve, she'd been glowingly lovely.

But closer...

Closer there were scars.

He stared, caught by the incongruity of it. By the questions. The fine white lines were the marks of a skilled plastic surgeon. Hugo could see that. But no skill could entirely cover the trauma Rachel's body must have once endured.

When? A long time ago, he thought, looking at the way the scarring had faded—fine lines blending into her nearperfect skin.

She was laughing and whirling and she and Toby turned to face him, glowing with happiness.

He didn't get his face in order fast enough.

She stopped whirling and set Toby down on his feet.

Carefully. 'What?' she said.

'You've been hurt.' He spoke without thinking and then could have kicked himself. He could have said nothing. He should have. He could have pretended he hadn't noticed.

A non-medical person might not have noticed.

No. She was so lovely that any man would look at Rachel long and hard. The fine lines of scarring didn't detract from her loveliness but they were unmistakable.

'Car accident,' she said shortly, answering his question before he'd voiced it. 'Eight years ago.'

A car accident. Of course. He gave himself another mental kick. Why had his thoughts gone straight to this Michael character he was starting so stupidly to dislike?

These weren't the type of scars that were the result of battering from an aggressive husband—and anyone could see that Rachel wasn't a battered wife. She was probably a hugely contented wife who occasionally threw car keys at her husband. Wives did that.

Beth had thrown more than car keys at him!

But what was he thinking of? He was still staring at Rachel as if he were stupid.

'I'm sorry,' he told her. 'I didn't mean to stare. It must have been some accident.'

'It was.' She looked as if she was about to say more and then closed her lips together, tight.

'Internal injuries? Fractures?'

'You name it, I had it.' She shrugged. 'It was a long time ago. Bodies heal. Mostly.'

There was a depth of bitterness in her words that he couldn't help but hear. Maybe someone had died in the accident? Someone she loved? But the blank look on her face was a shield all by itself. Keep off, the look said. Don't go there.

So he didn't. Even though he badly wanted to. It was none of his business.

'It looks like you've had some great corrective surgery,' he managed, and her smile came flooding back. There was relief there and the beginnings of laughter.

'I have, haven't I?' For heaven's sake, was she laughing at his discomfort? 'There's a wonderful plastic surgeon in Sydney who calls me his masterpiece. I sometimes get the feeling he'd like to hang me on his wall for show and tell!'

Rachel was so damned courageous. He just had to look at that scarring to know the trauma that lay behind it. And that brief look of pain had told him there was even more... 'You are a masterpiece,' he said softly, and she flushed.

She wasn't giving in to her discomposure, though. She moved right on to discomfit him further.

'You know, you're not too bad yourself.' She scooped Toby up into her arms and twinkled. 'What do you reckon, Toby? Don't you think your dad has the greatest six-pack you've ever seen?'

'Six-pack?' Toby was giggling, entranced.

And entranced was a good way to describe his father. Hugo was enchanted by this vivacious slip of a girl. She was soaking wet, her soft brown curls were lying in dripping tendrils around her face, her eyes were dancing...

'You know six-packs,' she told Toby, seemingly unaware of the riot she was causing in Hugo's solar plexus. Or somewhere. Some nerve centre he'd hardly been aware he possessed. 'Six-packs are cans of beer tied up together. You look at your daddy's chest and tell me if it doesn't look just like that?'

Good grief!

It was as much as Hugo could do not to blush. He swallowed, tried to think of something to say, couldn't, so did the only thing he could think of.

He dived straight under the water and left them alone.

He stayed out of their way for about a quarter of an hour. It's the equivalent of a cold shower, he told himself, and that was what he needed. He swam and he swam, using the rhythm of his strokes to try and settle his brain.

What was happening to him? Rachel was a married woman. She was a colleague who'd been trapped here by the fire. As soon as the wind changed and the fires burned back on themselves she'd be out of here. He had no business to think of her as he was thinking.

He had no choice. He was definitely thinking. He swam.

* * *

It had to end some time. It had been a huge day and a man could only swim so far, regardless of what demons were driving him.

Toby and Rachel had taken themselves up the beach and were engaged in building the world's biggest sandcastle. As Hugo towelled himself dry and strolled up the beach to join them, Rachel shifted back to admire their handiwork. She glanced up at his face—which he was still trying to control—and she chuckled.

'Hey, don't get your knickers in a twist by a comment on a six-pack.' She grinned. 'It's what we women put up with all the time. That was the female equivalent of a wolf whistle.'

He stared. 'Sorry?'

Her smile widened as his discomfiture deepened. 'Sorry yourself. OK, I'm sorry about the six-pack remark but you did get personal first.'

'So I did,' he said faintly. 'So I guess I'm sorry, too.'

'Actually, I'm not sorry,' she said with a sideways, very thoughtful look. 'For the expression on your face—it was well worth it.'

Had it been worth it? He stared down at her and she smiled back, enigmatic and lovely and thoroughly confusing.

It couldn't last. He might be directionless but Rachel at least was focused. Toby was lifting a football from the bottom of the picnic basket and was kicking it across the sand without much hope.

'Given up on the sandcastle?' Rachel asked him. 'Yeah.' The little boy looked down at his plastic football and sighed. 'I brought this with me tonight 'cos Bradley Drummond says I can't drop-kick. I gotta learn how to dropkick and Dad can't drop-kick for nuts.'

'You can't drop-kick?' Rachel stared at Hugo, amazed. 'I played basketball,' he said in explanation, and she looked at him as if it wasn't an explanation at all.

'I can't believe it. A man who plays basketball... What use is a six-pack in basketball?'

'Hey!'

'Say no more.' She wiped her hands on non-existent trousers, and wriggled her shoulders—a player prepared to launch into a tackle. 'A basketball player... Good grief. Toby, lad, give me the ball.'

'Can you drop-kick?' he asked shyly, and she nodded. 'I was taught by the best. My husband was the world's absolutely top drop-kicker. Or so he told me and who am I to doubt it? And he taught me.'

'Gee,' Toby, said, impressed.

'Gee is right. So there you go. Drop-kick lessons coming up. And you, Dr McInnes, stop worrying and have some dinner,' she told him. 'You've hardly eaten anything.' She flashed him a look that was almost a warning. 'Sausages and lamingtons and grapes. Eat. For heaven's sake, Hugo, let's keep life simple.'

Keep life simple? He didn't know what she was talking about.

Or maybe he did, but he sure as heck didn't want to admit it.

It had gone way past being simple but at least it was peaceful. Miraculously his cellphone stayed silent. It might be the calm before the storm but for these few hours there seemed no medical need, and no need at all for them to rush their picnic and head for home.

With their drop-kick lessons completed to their mutual satisfaction, Rachel and Toby turned their attention back to food. They polished off sausages with gusto.

'It's our second dinner,' Rachel declared, 'and it's much nicer the second time around.' They ate their fill of lamingtons and finished off with a Thermos of coffee, with lemonade for Toby, and then Toby snuggled down on beach towels beside them and drifted toward sleep. One six-year-old had had a truly excellent day.

'We don't do this often enough,' Hugo said ruefully, running his fingers through Toby's sand- and salt-stiff hair. But he wasn't totally focused on his son. He was still letting Rachel's words drift around his head. *My husband was the world's absolutely top drop-kicker.* He didn't like it.

He didn't want to think about Rachel's husband.

And it seemed Rachel's thoughts were travelling on a similar route.

'Christine doesn't like the beach?'

'Christine?' His gaze jerked to hers, startled. 'What's it got to do with Christine?'

'She is the lady you intend to marry,' Rachel said gently, and watched his face.

He said nothing.

Christine... That relationship had been on the backburner for so long that he hardly knew. When had it started? This assumption that he'd end up with his sister-in-law?

He didn't know when it had begun. She'd just been there. Even when Beth had been alive, Christine had done the organising, acting as go-between in their increasingly turbulent marriage, suggesting, steering...

Oh, there had been nothing untoward in their relationship during the marriage. There was nothing untoward in it now. It was just drifting...

Toward marriage? Maybe. And why? Because it was easier. Because the town was waiting.

Christine was waiting.

'It's been six years,' Rachel said softly. 'Isn't it about time you married the woman?'

'Who told you we were getting married?'

'Christine did,' Rachel told him. She glanced down at Toby who was sleeping now, deeply unconscious. 'Tonight. When I told her we were coming to the beach. I was told in no uncertain terms to keep myself to myself. I've never actually been given the scarlet woman treatment before, but I copped it tonight.'

For heaven's sake. Hugo's face set in anger. Of all the stupid... She had no right.

Did she have a right?

He hadn't given her reason to think otherwise, he admitted to himself. Lately, Christine had taken to kissing him goodbye, and a few weeks ago he'd let himself kiss her back. Not as he'd kissed her in the past, brother-in-law to sister-in-law, but more. Man to woman.

Hell, why?

He knew why. He'd needed to so much. Just to feel the touch of a woman in his arms.

But it had still felt wrong, even though Beth had been dead these six years. So he'd pulled back. Apologised. But Christine had smiled and he'd known that she was waiting.

And he hadn't said no. He hadn't said it could never work. In truth, he'd been wondering...

Six years was a long time and this was a tiny town. In this confined environment he couldn't look at a woman without that woman getting the wrong idea. Affairs were impossible. He was so damned lonely and he was hungry... He wasn't hungry for Christine, he conceded to himself, looking at the woman in front of him and accepting what was becoming clearer by the minute. He was hungry for Rachel.

Rachel was unavailable. What had she said about her husband? *The world's absolutely top drop-kicker...* There was a wealth of affection in the way she'd said it that had been unmistakable.

Maybe Christine was all there was. 'So you are going to marry her?'

Rachel was watching him with the air of an inquisitive sparrow. Furious, with himself as well as her, he started to haul the picnic things together.

'I think it's time we took Toby home.'

'Toby's asleep. He can't be any more asleep at home than he is right now. And you haven't answered the question.'

'It's none of your business.'

'Mmm, but I thought we'd agreed we'd already been impolite. We may as well keep going, don't you think?'

'No,' he said, goaded, and she smiled. 'You started it.'

He had, he conceded, with his talk of her scarring. But he had no intention of continuing.

Rachel had no intention of stopping.

'Toby doesn't like Christine much,' she told him. 'Neither does Myra. Do you think Christine would soften with the brocade-remembering-Beth thing if you married?'

'Look—'

'I wouldn't want to live with it.' She stretched her legs out full length, admiring her sandy toes. She had beautiful crimson toenails.

Very distracting toenails.

'I can see why you'd want to, of course!' she conceded. 'She's lovely. Is Christine very like your wife was?'

'Will you cut it out?' He was half laughing, half angry. 'Why don't we talk about you for a change?'

'Like what about me?' She was still admiring her toenails. 'Like what is it between you and your husband? You were fighting like cat and dog at the weekend. It can't be much of a marriage.'

The laughter left her face. She'd been teasing him—it had been lighthearted banter—but suddenly there was no banter left. There was a long silence. Then...

'No,' she said at last, and she spoke so softly he had to strain to hear what she was saying. 'No, I don't have much of a marriage.'

He shouldn't go further. He should stop this potentially hurtful conversation right now.

He couldn't. The devil—or something—was driving him.

He had to push.

'Yet you're criticising me for potentially making a loveless marriage?'

'Whoa...' Her eyes flashed at that. 'I didn't say a word about a loveless marriage,' she retorted, spirit re-entering her voice with a vengeance. 'I may not have much of a marriage but I surely went into it with love.'

'Yet you want out?'

The conversation had become suddenly so intense he could hardly breathe. Hell, how had this happened? He watched her face and her eyes were blind, as if she was consumed by panic.

'I'm out now, aren't I?' she whispered. 'Dear God, I shouldn't be, but I'm out.'

He didn't know what was happening. He didn't understand. All he knew was that he'd hurt her somehow, and hurt her badly. 'Rachel, don't look like that.'

'Look like what?'

'Like there's something inside you that's tearing apart.'

'I'm not... It's not...'

Her hands were fumbling, trying to collect the picnic things together, but he could see she wasn't thinking of what she was doing. Her hands weren't connected to her thoughts and her eyes were still so pain-filled that he found himself reaching out, grasping her fingers between his. Holding...

She didn't pull away. She didn't move.

How long they stayed there he could never afterwards tell. The night was creeping in through the smoky haze. The sun had slipped unnoticed, behind the mountains, behind the distant fires. The beach was deserted.

All was still, apart from the soft hush, hush, hush of the waves slipping into shore, one after the other.

Endless.

Time was nothing. There was nothing. This had started as comfort—hadn't it?—but now it was more. Deeper. For this moment there was just this man and this woman and a meeting that neither could understand, that neither wanted, that simply was.

Still their hands held. It was their eyes doing the talking, searching, locked to each other and discovering in each a link. A bond. An aching need and a knowledge that in each other pain could be assuaged.

The moment stretched on.

He should break his hold. He should release her hands, pull back...

But still his eyes searched hers and with every moment that passed the need to do more became increasingly compulsive.

Inescapable.

One man. One woman. One moment.

He pulled her into his arms and he kissed her.

What was she doing here? Rachel hardly knew. All she knew was that the moment Hugo's fingers touched hers, her mind shut down to everything that wasn't him.

Toby was asleep. The dogs were far off, fruitlessly chasing gulls in endless circles around the beach. There were no witnesses to what was happening here.

There was no problem with witnesses. No one would gainsay her this pleasure. Dottie had told her that as she'd packed the gorgeous lingerie and pushed her out the door to what she'd thought would be a romantic weekend with Michael.

Only it would never have worked. Even if Michael had been...nice, she could never have let him near her. The guilt had still been with her. The overriding bitterness at what could have been.

But all of that was lost the moment Hugo's hands touched hers. He pulled her into him and as his mouth claimed hers and as she melted effortlessly into him, all she felt was joy. Oh, the pleasure. The aching wonder. Eight years of sorrow and loneliness were all dispelled in this one kiss. In this meeting of bodies, one with the other.

It was a kiss, but it was so much more than a kiss. It was a melting of barriers, a moving forward, a reaffirmation of life itself.

She couldn't pull away. She knew she should but she hadn't the strength. Rachel, who'd been so strong for so long, was falling now as she hadn't let herself ever fall. She'd been alone and now...she was home. She was where she belonged. Hugo was kissing her and she was moving from an old life into a new, like a butterfly emerging from a faded and torn chrysalis to begin a new life.

Hugo.

Life or death. Living or dying.

I choose...life.

The dogs disturbed them. The flock of gulls they'd been chasing finally wheeled out to sea. Delirious with excitement, the dogs came hurtling up the beach, soaking wet. They landed on the picnic rug and proceeded to shake what seemed gallons of seawater over everyone.

Including Toby. He woke and whimpered a little. Hugo pulled away for an instant and it was enough. To let reality in.

To let Rachel's reality sink in. What was she doing?

And there they all were—the old doubts, the fears and the loneliness and the endless future. They hadn't disappeared. They'd been subsumed by the moment but they were still there.

The pressure of Hugo's mouth was still on her lips. She put her fingers up to touch them but Hugo was before her. Toby had stirred and settled, the dogs had wheeled away again and he was catching her fingers in his lovely big hands, and there was such a look of tenderness on his face that she must surely melt...

'Rachel...'

'No,' she faltered, and pulled away. Reluctantly, he released her. He watched her, his eyes calm. Something had changed for him, too, she thought frantically. He *knew*.

He couldn't know. He mustn't. 'Rachel, what's wrong?'

'I'm married,' she said, and there was such a blunt finality about the words that the look of tenderness shuttered down on his face as if it had never been.

'You said...you wanted out.'

'I didn't.' She was hauling herself together now—somehow. She had to get off this beach. She had to get away from this man.

She had to leave.

'I don't want—' he started, but she was before him. 'Neither do I.' She was close to tears. Here she was, lying again. She wanted Hugo so much that she was tearing apart and she could feel herself disintegrat-

ing. 'I-it's almost dark,' she stammered. 'You have to check Kim. I…
I'm tired. I need my bed. Please, Hugo, can we go?'

She rose and hauled her beach towel around herself like a shield. It was
stupid. Nothing could protect her from what she was feeling. Nothing.

'Can we go?' she whispered again. 'Please, Hugo. I don't need this.
I can't… I can't.'

And there was nothing for them to do but to leave.

There was nothing for Hugo to do but to look at her with hungry eyes
and a hopeless heart.

Kim was fine when he arrived back at the hospital, but Hugo took his
time with the injured teenager. He hardly knew why. Kim was deeply
asleep. Her exhausted parents had finally decided to cease their vigil and
leave their daughter in the nurses' care. Hugo could have simply glanced
at the observation chart and left, but instead he carefully checked the
wound, unwinding the bandages and surveying his handiwork with care.
David, the ginger-haired nurse who was in charge tonight, watched with
thoughtful appreciation.

'You know she's fine. I checked the leg myself a couple of hours ago.
No temp, the leg's as pink as the other one, she's having pain but it seems
to be settling—even her parents are relaxing now. Why not you, Dr
McInnes?'

'I'm relaxing,' Hugo snapped, and David grinned. 'Yeah, and I'm a
monkey's uncle. You're tense as all get-out. You're not expecting any
dramas here, are you?'

Hugo looked down at Kim's face. The fifteen-year-old was sleeping
soundly, exhausted from the effects of trauma and relaxing deeply into
the drugs he was using for painkilling. She looked…fine. No, he wasn't
expecting any trauma here. Thanks to Rachel.

What was Rachel's story? Why did he need to know?

'She'll be OK,' he managed, but David was still watching him.

'You're avoiding going home?' David asked softly, and Hugo winced.
Was he so transparent?

'No.'

But David didn't believe him. He was a fine nurse and part of that
was that he read people well. 'There's nothing here for you to do,' he
told Hugo, his eyes still thoughtful. 'The last of the fire crews rang in

half an hour ago. Because there's no wind up on the ridge, there's been no dramas at all—not even a bad case of smoke in the eyes. You can go home to bed, Dr McInnes.'

'Yeah.'

'And you ought to.' David was watching him with an intensity that Hugo found unnerving. 'The forecast for tomorrow is horrible. If they don't hold the firebreaks...'

'The town will be safe. The river...'

'The river will hold it this side. But the other side...'

'You know the plan is for everyone to get over here and stay.' Hugo shifted uneasily, thinking it through. Forcing his mind away from Rachel and onto the urgency of what lay ahead. 'People's homes are insured. They've had warning to leave. They'll come.'

'People do damned stupid things. Get yourself to bed, Hugo.' David's voice was suddenly rough with concern. 'You know you're going to be needed.'

'I'll be fine.'

Silence. Then... 'At least you have Dr Harper.' David's eyes were still probing. 'Rachel,' he amended, and watched Hugo's face twist. David looked even more thoughtful. Hmm, the expression on his face said. Was that the way the wind blew, then?

It wasn't up to Hugo to enlighten him. 'Yeah, at least I have Rachel,' he snapped, and shoved his hands deep into his pockets and glared.

'So go to bed and thank your stars you have her while you do,' David told him.

'Right.' He was right. Of course he was right. Go to bed and be thankful...

To bed. To sleep? That was a joke!

And Rachel?

She lay awake and thought about Craig.

But she didn't ring Dottie.

CHAPTER SEVEN

RACHEL WAS AWAKE before he was. As Hugo appeared in the kitchen for breakfast just after six, Rachel burst through the screen door, a dog attached to a leash in either hand.

She stopped short when she saw him. Discomfited. The dogs bounded across the kitchen to greet him and he bent to hug them. Giving himself time to collect himself.

The dogs were great. Afghan and mongrel were becoming fast friends.

Michael would have kittens. Aristocracy mixing with the hoi-polloi. Ouch.

Michael. There he was, thinking about Michael again. Why the hell couldn't he keep himself from thinking about Michael?

Rachel was wearing short shorts, and a crop top and sandals. She was all bare legs and glowing face and shiny hair.

How could he not think of Michael? He had to get himself together.

'Hi,' he tried, and waited. 'Hi.'

'You've been to the beach.' That much was obvious. The dogs were damp and sand-coated, and Penelope the Afghan had such a look of bliss on her dopey face he almost felt sorry for her that she had to return to the city. To Michael.

There he was again.

Rachel had to return to the city to Michael. The thought was enough to make the beginnings of his smile fade completely.

'I couldn't sleep,' Rachel told him, and the tension escalated by about a mile. She hadn't been able to sleep. Neither had he. Because...

What was he thinking of? Heck, he had better...more serious things to think about than why Rachel hadn't been able to sleep.

Like a bushfire.

'It's bad,' Rachel told him, moving on before he could. 'The wind came up before the sun did. The dogs and I could see the flames rising higher on the ridge while we waited for the sunrise.'

How long had she been on the beach? It didn't matter. It couldn't matter. Move on...

'Crisis today,' he said, and turned his back to put on the kettle. He was wearing his boxer shorts and nothing else. That was what he always wore while he ate breakfast and why his lack of clothes bothered him now he didn't know. 'What precautions are we taking?' she asked, waiting for him to finish at the sink so she could pour bowls of water for the dogs. Then she turned her attention to toast, as though she was completely unaware of him.

How could she be unaware of him? he thought savagely. He was climbing walls here! In her shorts and her tiny crop top that left nothing to the imagination, he was so aware of her that everything else was blotted out completely.

Like the little matter of a town threatened by bushfire. 'We're setting a safety zone up on the beach,' he managed. 'Maybe you saw...'

'There were people on the beach, setting up equipment, as I was leaving. The safety zone's changing from the hall?'

'Yeah. This side of the river can act almost as a safety zone by itself—it's been really well cleared. But if the fire turns firestorm...'

'Firestorm?'

'That's what frightens us,' he told her. 'We can cope with a fire that comes at us fast but a firestorm is something else. If it's burning so fast it starts sucking oxygen before it, then it creates its own energy. It becomes a vortex, consuming all. We'll move medical supplies down to the beach and essentials to protect a crowd. If the fire looks like escalating then everyone goes there. We'll evacuate the hospital—everyone—and we hope like hell.'

'Won't they send back-up from the mainland?' Rachel asked in a small voice, and he frowned. She sounded scared. He hadn't meant to scare her—but maybe he was a bit scared himself.

'I've been lying in bed, listening to the radio reports,' he told her. 'With this north wind after days of such heat, half the state's threatened. Every fire service is looking after its own, and the state troops are needed for the cities where most lives are at risk. So we're on our own.'

And despite the dangers the town was facing today—despite the uncertainty—he was suddenly distracted.

We're on our own.

The words jabbed deep.

He was on his own, he thought drearily as he sat on the other side of the table and ate cereal as she ate her toast. She was only feet away from him but she was so distant. So lovely.

She was married. And he had a fire to think about.

Patients. Medicine. The future...

Right.

They ate on in silence, each deep in thought. And neither willing to share.

Toby arrived before they finished eating, hiking into the kitchen in his Bob-the-Builder pyjamas and blessedly breaking a tension that was well nigh unbearable.

'Hi,' he said.

'Hi, yourself.' Hugo smiled at his young son, grateful to have someone break a silence that was becoming way too difficult. Impossible. 'Breakfast?'

Toby scorned to answer such a dumb question, but his small face lit at the sight of Rachel and he launched himself onto her knees. She hugged him round the middle and he beamed.

'Can I have my toast here, Dad?'

'Why not?' Toast on Rachel's knees. If Hugo could...

No! He needed a cold shower—and he'd just had a cold shower.

He rose and made toast and handed it to his son without saying a word, while Rachel and Toby chatted like old friends.

'I need to go,' he said, more to himself than anyone else. 'Myra will be here soon.'

'Do you want me at the hospital or down at the beach?' Rachel asked, balancing her coffee around Toby's breakfast.

'Can you do standard clinic?'

She winced at that. 'Yeah, right. As if anyone's going to check in with coughs and colds today.'

'Someone needs to be there.'

She looked at him for a long moment, weighing what he'd just said. She was trying to decide whether to challenge him—whether to bring to the surface the real issue here, which was that he needed room in his head. She was infringing on that, just by being. She knew it. He needed to work alone.

'You know where to find me if you need me,' she said at last. 'Don't hesitate.'

'I won't.'

'Is the fire going to burn the town down?' Toby was sitting more firmly on Rachel's lap now, regarding his father with huge eyes. He'd claimed Rachel as his own, but he still needed his daddy.

'The fire won't burn the town,' Hugo said, and Rachel put her arms around Toby and hugged him again.

'I think today you should stay home with Myra or with me,' she told him. 'And I'm guessing Myra might want to stay on her own farm. Maybe we could pack a suitcase with all the most important things you and Daddy have. Hugo, give me a list and, Toby, you can make a list, too. Then if it gets really smoky we can take the suitcase down to the beach and we won't have to worry about the smoke making everything smell.'

'Will we take the dogs, too?'

'Of course we'll take the dogs.' She looked down at the two dogs who were slumped in soggy and sandy happiness over her feet. 'How could we let them get smoky?' She smiled up at Hugo. 'Off you go, then, Dr McInnes. Make a list and leave it for us, then you go and save the world and Toby and I will save Penelope and Digger and Toby's teddy-bear and your photo albums and whatever else we can find that's worth saving.'

'Right.'

Whatever was worth saving? Hugo made a list, which was really—stupidly—short, then made his way to the hospital. And all he could think of was...

Save me.

* * *

Christine arrived at eight-thirty to collect Toby for school and was annoyed to find he wasn't coming. 'He's staying with me for the morning,' Rachel told her, and Christine gave her a look that was meant to turn her to stone and huffed to the hospital to find Hugo.

'I went to collect the kid—'

'Toby,' Hugo said mildly. He was packing equipment into the back of his car. He needed a full operating suite. On this day he couldn't depend on any one place to stay safe, but he could always run his car into the shallows and operate from there. If he had to. 'The kid's name is Toby.'

'Don't be stupid,' Christine snapped. 'I know what his name is. Hugo, what's going on?'

'Rachel's offered to take care of Toby. Myra wants to stay home today—understandably. Her farm's under threat as well as the rest of the town. Toby's nervous about going to school and Rachel's offered to care for him.'

'He'll be safe at school.'

Christine wasn't offering to care for Toby herself, Hugo noticed. He only had half his mind on what she was saying. The rest of his thoughts were on the contents of the cooler he was packing into his car. Did it contain every drug he could need? Had he forgotten anything important?

'So why isn't he going to school?' Christine's anger was palpable and he made himself concentrate.

'The school's happy for every child with parents available to care for them to stay home.'

'Rachel's not a parent.'

Hugo paused. He straightened and looked at Christine, really seeing her. She was brittle this morning. Tight.

'No. She's not.' He met her gaze full on.

'There's something between you and Rachel,' Christine snapped, and Hugo shook his head.

'No.'

'But you want there to be something.'

'She's married.'

'You still want there to be.'

There was only one answer to that. 'Yes,' he said gently. He paused but the thing had to be said. 'Christine, what's between us... It's happened so gradually that I've hardly noticed but it's there...the expectation that we'd start a relationship.'

'We have started a relationship.'

'No.' He shook his head. 'Christine, what's between us is no more a basis for a relationship than what was between Beth and I. I've made a mistake. Rachel... Well, it's true she's married and there's no future for us but it's made me see that you and I can never work.'

'Because you'll find someone like Rachel.'

'No.' He closed his eyes. 'I can't find anyone like Rachel. But even knowing there's someone like her in the world...it makes a difference.'

'So I've been hanging around in this one-horse dump for nothing.'

'I thought you were here for your art.'

There was a long silence. Then... 'The fire will make great pictures,' she admitted. 'And the publicity...it'll give me a market.'

'There you go, then.' He hesitated but it might as well be said. 'Be honest, Chris. That's all that's ever mattered to you—and to Beth. The art. Things. Not people.'

Silence. She half turned, ready to leave angry, but he held her with his eyes. And continued to hold.

Finally she smiled, a crooked little smile that was half mocking, half furious. 'Damn you, you know us too well. Me and Beth...'

'You love your art. People are second.'

'We could have worked out a great relationship.'

'Yeah. I practise medicine while I pay for your paints.'

She shrugged but the crooked smile stayed. 'It was worth a try.'

He shook his head. 'No. It wasn't. Christine, it's time I did things a bit differently. I think it's even time I moved on from brocade. Meanwhile, I have a fire-ravaged community to care for.'

She looked at him for a long moment and then shrugged again. A shrug of release. 'Fine. I have things to paint. But you know she'll never have you. She's married to some wealthy medical specialist in town. Why could she possibly be interested in you?'

Why indeed? No reason at all.

Christine turned on her heel and walked away and Hugo stared after her and thought, I've just tossed in a future because of a slip of a doctor who has nothing to do with me. Nothing.

And everything.

* * *

The fire threatened for most of the morning, but that was all it did. Threaten. Reports coming into the town were that the line created by backburning was holding. The temperature soared but the wind seemed to rise to a certain velocity and stay. Holding.

Rachel worked through the myriad minor ailments presenting at the clinic. There were so many she had to concede that Hugo had been right in asking her to take over. Asthmatics were having appalling trouble with the smoke, and people who'd never had asthma in their lives had it now. The town's older residents, their capacity to retain body equilibrium with sweating compromised with age, were in real trouble. Rachel admitted two elderly men to hospital, and Don rang through wanting advice for another in the nursing home.

'The ash in the air is messing with our air-conditioning,' he told her. 'The oldies are suffering enough already and we need to have them fit to evacuate.'

'You're planning on evacuating?'

'Hugo's down on the beach, setting up a full medical centre in case,' Don told her. 'The real problems will be when this wind changes. It'll strengthen before any change and that's what Hugo's most worried about. It's what we're all worried about.'

So she should be worried, too. Rachel gave him the advice he needed, replaced the phone and looked out the window. There was nothing to see. The smoke had thickened to the stage where visibility was down to about ten yards.

Toby was settled out in the waiting room, playing with a train set. He seemed perfectly content to be there, watched over by Ruby, Hugo's receptionist, but within calling distance of Rachel. Unless she was actually examining patients, she left the door open so she could make eye contact. Every now and then he'd look up and make sure she could see him, and then he'd glance over to where the giant suitcase was sitting in a corner.

He had Rachel. He had his precious belongings. Penelope and Digger were out on the veranda, in sight. So... Hugo was out in the wide world but this link made it OK.

For now.

'Rachel!' It was a call over the intercom. Rachel had just seen her last patient but the call made her sink back into her seat. Elly, the hospital charge nurse, sounded worried. 'Rachel, are you there?'

'Yes.'

'Can you come through to the hospital? Fast? There's a baby fitting. Katy Brady, the baby's mother, is bringing her in now but she sounds as if she's unconscious already.'

A fast word of explanation—thankfully, Toby was a doctor's child and knew what the word emergency meant—and Rachel ran, leaving the dogs and Toby with Ruby. She reached the hospital entrance as a rust bucket of an ancient Ford screeched to a halt in the entrance.

'It's Connor Brady and his mother, Katy,' Elly told her as they hauled open the car door, but there was no time for more. The young mother almost fell out of the driver's seat. The baby was slumped over his mother's knee. Katy was obviously a teenage mum—young to the point where she was scarcely out of childhood herself. She was wearing frayed jeans and a tiny crop top with tattoos peeking out from underneath. Her hair hung in dreadlocks down to her waist.

But it wasn't Katy that Rachel was looking at.

Connor Brady seemed about six weeks old and he was in dire trouble. The baby had been lying across his mother's knees and one look told Rachel what the trouble was—and what was the cause of what was happening. She put her hand on the child's forehead and winced at what she felt. Fever. The baby's temperature must be over forty.

And he was wrapped—tightly wrapped—in blankets! 'My baby...' Katy was sobbing, almost incoherent in fear, but Rachel already had him, hauling away the blankets as she lifted the little one from the car. The baby was limp, his eyes rolling back in his head as if he'd been convulsing for far too long.

'I need Dr Hugo,' the girl wailed, but Rachel wasn't listening. She was doing a fast assessment, looking for telltale signs of a meningococcal rash, checking for neck stiffness, searching...

Thankfully there was nothing.

'Get me scissors,' she told Elly. Damn, there were buttons and ribbons everywhere and she wanted these clothes off fast. There were no signs of a rash that she could see, and the little one's neck was moving freely. The likely cause of this was a simple fever combined with heat. 'Elly, run me a sink full of cool water.'

As the girl stumbled out of the car and reached for the baby. Rachel met her fear head on. 'I'm a doctor,' she told her. 'Katy, I'm pretty sure that your baby's convulsing because he's hot. We need to get him cool straight away.'

'Give him to me.' The girl was reaching out for her baby in instinctive protest at losing contact, but Rachel was already moving toward the hospital entrance, carrying the baby with her.

'Come with me,' she told Katy. 'Talk to me as I work.

How long's he been like this?'

Her confident tone must have broken through. The girl hiccuped on a sob and then tried to talk.

'He's...he's got a cold. I asked Dr McInnes for antibiotics but he wouldn't give me any. Then this morning he was so stuffed up and the radio said we might be evacuated so I wrapped him up really well and started packing, but then I came back to his crib and he was...he was all rigid. Then when I picked him up he went sort of limp.'

Rachel had reached the emergency room now. She hadn't stopped—Katy had stumbled along beside her as she'd taken Connor inside. Now she had him on the examination table and was attacking the crazy layette, peeling it away like an unwanted skin. A really thick skin. Bootees, jacket, nightgown...

The baby's body was so hot.

'When you found him, did you put him straight in the car?' She was turning to the sink where Elly was already running water, but she was still questioning the frightened child by her side. The girl needed comfort but the need to establish a time frame was more urgent than comfort.

'What?'

'How long's he been fitting?' she asked directly. 'When did you phone?'

'I phoned as soon as I saw him. I picked him up and he was really odd and I was so scared I just called.' The girl hiccuped on a sob.

'The call came through eight minutes ago,' Elly told her. 'I rang you straight away.'

'How long had you left him in the cot? Could he have been fitting for a while before you found him?'

'No.' The girl was trying desperately to focus, sensing it was important. 'Just for a moment.' The last of the baby's clothes fell away to reveal a tiny limp body. 'Just two minutes at most. I wrapped him and put him down and went to get his carry-cot and then he was like this.'

So he'd been fitting for probably no more than ten minutes. But ten minutes convulsing still meant a risk of brain damage. They had to get him cool.

'What's the problem?'

It was Hugo. He'd entered unseen behind them, taking in the scene before him as he strode into the room.

'Convulsion,' Rachel said shortly, without turning. She'd lifted the baby to the sink and shoved her elbow in to check the temperature, but Elly knew her stuff. The water had the chill taken off but that was all. It was cool to the touch. Rachel lowered the little one right in, up to his neck. The remains of his clothing and all.

'Sponge water over his head,' she told Elly. 'Hugo, I need diazepam.'

He didn't question her need. 'Coming,' he replied, and disappeared.

'Come on.' The baby lay unresponding in her hands.

Please...

It was a silent prayer, said over and over in her years working in Emergency. Sometimes it worked. Let this be one of those times. *Please...* 'Come on, Connor.'

And, as if on cue, she felt a tremor run through the little body. Another. The baby stiffened. Arched.

Was it more of the same? A further convulsion? The eyes were still unfocused.

'I need the diazapam.'

'It's here.' Hugo was back with her. Rachel lifted the baby's slippery little body for a moment as Hugo carefully administered the drug.

Their heads bent together over the tiny child. Elly had stepped back to give Hugo room to manoeuvre. He discarded the packing, then started scooping water over the little head.

Come on. Come on.

They were willing this thing together.

And it worked. Connor's body gave a long, long shudder—and his little eyes opened. Connor stared up at the strangers above, his little mouth dropped open, his chin wobbled—and he gave a feeble, feeble wail.

It was the sweetest sound. Rachel let her breath out—how long had she been holding it? Almost since she'd seen the baby. She looked up at Hugo and saw her joy reflected in his eyes.

'He's back.'

'We have success,' Hugo said softly. 'Well done, you.'

'Lucky me,' Rachel whispered. Hugo was continuing to scoop water over the tiny, fuzzy head but the wail was building strength as young Connor realised the indignity of his position. To have this outcome was a gift. A blessing. She looked over her shoulder at the young mother. Katy was quietly sobbing, mascara running in two ugly lines down her cheeks. 'Will you hold him in the water, Katy?' she said softly. 'He sounds like he wants his mother.'

'I can't...' The girl choked on a sob. 'He shouldn't be sick. I wanted an antibiotic but Dr McInnes wouldn't give it to me. He wouldn't...' She sank down on a chair and put her head in her hands and Rachel signalled to Elly to take her place with the baby. With a questioning look at Hugo—and an answering nod—she stooped and took the girl's hands in hers, pulling them away from her tear-drenched eyes and forcing her to look at her.

'Katy, antibiotics wouldn't have helped. Connor's cold will get better all by itself. It's a combination of fever and this heat that has caused the fitting.'

'The baby book said keep him warm when he has a cold,' Katy said defiantly. 'It said it. I read...' She sniffed and tried a glare that didn't come off. 'I read everything.'

'You don't have someone who can give you advice?' Rachel frowned. 'Is there a baby clinic in town?' In the city there were clinics specifically set up for very young mothers who didn't have the support that an older woman might be capable of finding for herself.

'No.'

'There's not the staff available for a baby clinic,' Hugo said grimly from behind her. Connor's cries were escalating and he needed to raise his voice to be heard. 'I do my best but we need another doctor.' He hesitated. Then added, 'What about you? How do you feel about staying in town and helping set a baby clinic up? Plus the rest.'

'I wouldn't mind,' Rachel said before she could help herself, and suddenly she was looking at Hugo and he was looking back at her.

With unspoken thoughts...

But this wasn't the time—or the place.

'We need to move on,' Hugo said, and there was real reluctance in his voice. 'I'm sorry but we need to move fast. The fire's broken through the firebreak.'

'What does that mean?'

'That we evacuate,' Hugo told her. 'Now.'

'My baby...' Katy sobbed, and Hugo looked down at the thrashing, screaming infant and grinned.

'You know, Katy, I reckon your baby might be the least of our problems. We'll dress him in a nappy and nothing else. There's shade down at the beach. If he gets hot then you take him into the shallows. In fact, sitting in the shallows seems a fine idea for everyone. It's your job to keep Connor cool, Katy, while we look after everyone else.'

Later Rachel could only remember the next few hours as chaos. Ordered chaos, but chaos for all that. But the township had been gearing for this event for two days now and when they moved they moved fast.

Firefighting became a lower priority. Once the firebreaks had been breached everyone moved into protection mode. All firefighters were pulled out of the hills—it was pointless and dangerous to stay there. Every able-bodied person was assigned a job. Volunteers went from house to house, ensuring people had left, checking that everything that could be done had been done, then the town was left to fend for itself.

Sam Nieve was in his element. He was the elderly man with the heart condition Rachel had sent home from the fire front. Now he was in charge of what he termed the home guard. He'd taken his role very seriously— he had lists of houses with every occupant, and by the time Rachel and Hugo reached the beach, Rachel accompanying Kim's stretcher and Hugo supervising the other two seriously ill hospital inmates, he was set up at a makeshift desk, crossing off the name of every town inhabitant.

He'd even set up planking so that every person who arrived at the beach was forced to walk past his desk.

'This way I know who's still in their houses,' he told Hugo, and there was no mistaking the pride in the man's voice. 'There's only three I'm still worried about. Miss Baxter, who's got a gammy leg and won't leave because she loves her garden. Les Harding, who's worried about his crazy feral cats. And Sue-Ellen Lesley. I've sent a couple of teams to bring in

Miss Baxter and Les and as many of his cats as they can catch. There's only Sue-Ellen left to worry about.'

'You didn't send a team to fetch her in?' Hugo asked. The hospital stretchers were being set up far down the beach. The idea was that if the fire grew to firestorm status then people could back into the shallows. Every blanket in the town had been collected and was already lying sodden, waiting to cover a needy head.

Kim's stretcher had already been taken down. In a moment Rachel would go down and readjust the drips that the girl still needed, but Hugo had stopped by Sam's desk and so had Rachel. She saw the concern etched on Hugo's face and was immediately worried.

'Sue-Ellen won't come if a team of people arrive,' Sam said, casting an uncertain glance up at Hugo. 'I tried to tell her the danger but she slammed the door in my face.'

'Have you seen her today?' Hugo asked shortly, and Sam shook his head.

'Not since yesterday. Gary Lewis went up there last night but she wouldn't let him in either. He's been on the radio, worrying about her, but there's nothing I can do.'

'How did she seem?'

'Erratic. Jumpy. Angry.' The two men were looking at each other and their worry was mirrored in each other's eyes.

'Problem?' Rachel asked, and Hugo nodded.

'Sue-Ellen has schizophrenia. She's normally good but something like this can throw her. I saw her last week and she was coping well but...'

'I asked if she was taking her pills,' Sam said. 'She told me to go to hell.'

'She'd say that even if she was taking them.' Hugo had turned and was staring up into the hills. As if he could see anything. The idea was ludicrous. The smoke was whirling around their faces and visibility was practically zero. The fire trucks had parked on the sand and were surrounding the temporary township in a ring—fire trucks in a semi-circle with the sea at their backs. There was safety here. But not for Sue-Ellen. 'You know she hates interference.'

'I was a mate of her dad's,' Sam said heavily. 'I know she stops taking her pills from time to time and I know it used to scare her old man.'

'Where is she?' Rachel asked.

'Out the back of the town,' Hugo said. 'She has five acres.'

'Of overgrown bush.' Sam shook his head. 'I'm not sending anyone else out there. Not now. If she won't come, she won't.'

'She might come for me.'

'Yeah, and you'll put your head in a noose because of a bloody schizo...'

But Hugo's face had set in anger. 'Sue-Ellen's a great woman.' He looked at Rachel as if he was seeking her approval. By the look on Sam's face he knew he wouldn't get approval from him. 'She used to play with the state orchestra before she became ill.'

'And now she sits up there with her damned goats, getting madder and madder,' Sam muttered, but Hugo shook his head.

'She runs angora goats. She spins and weaves and plays...'

'And talks to herself.'

'I'm wasting time.' Hugo hesitated. 'I'm the only person she trusts.'

'Where are her people?' Rachel asked, dismayed.

'Her father died five years back. She went out for a while with Gary Lewis, one of the local firemen, but she fretted that her medication was making her stupid. She made Gary leave her be, and since then she doesn't let anyone else close.'

'You can't get up there.'

'There's still time.' They turned to look northward but, of course, there was nothing. An impenetrable layer of smoke. The wind was pushing ash through the air. Rachel could taste it. She opened her mouth to speak and a fine film of ash landed on her tongue. Instead of speaking, she ended up coughing.

'There's surgical masks,' Hugo said shortly. 'Get one on. You need to be fit. Rachel, I want everyone here wearing them. Can you...?'

'Can I what?' But she knew already what he was going to ask.

'Can you take over? I need to go.'

'There's Toby.' She stared at him helplessly. Myra had collected Toby when the order for evacuation had come and now Toby was splashing happily in the shallows with his mates from school. To them this was still a game. Long may that last. 'Hugo, let me go.' She placed a hand on his arm, suddenly urgent with anxiety. 'I don't have anyone. I can go.'

'You have a husband.'

'Who doesn't need me.' There, she'd said it, and even as she said it she acknowledged it was the truth. Dottie was right. 'But Toby needs you.'

'You don't know the way. And Sue-Ellen doesn't trust you. There's no one else Sue-Ellen will come with. I'll be all right. There are dams in her home paddock. We'll make it in time.'

'Risk your life for a schizo...' Sam was bristling in indignation.

'She's not a schizo,' Hugo said wearily. 'She's a fine musician and she's a lovely person and she's my patient. I should have gone out there myself last night.' He stared helplessly at Rachel. 'I need to go. Can you cover for me here?'

Their eyes met. He knew what he was asking, she thought. He knew.

But he had to go. She knew this man well enough even after such a short time to understand that his need was absolute. Toby had an aunt. Toby had a town full of caring people.

The unknown Sue-Ellen had no one. Except Hugo.

'Of course you need to go,' she whispered, and watched his face change. 'I understand. Go, then, but go fast and only go on the understanding that you'll come back safe. Promise me?'

'I...'

'Promise?' She reached out and grasped his hands, her voice suddenly urgent. She met his eyes and hers locked with them and held. 'Hugo, you must.'

He stared down at her for a long moment and his gaze fell to their clasped hands. His mouth twisted into an expression she couldn't begin to understand.

'I promise,' he said, and he pulled her to him and kissed her hard on the lips. It was a fast and brutal kiss, a kiss born of fear and of want and of pure adrenalin. Then he was pushing her away, his eyes bleak.

'Take care of Toby,' he said as he turned and ran into the smoke. 'Keep the town safe for me until I come back.'

CHAPTER EIGHT

'HE'S GOT TIME,' Sam said uneasily. He was watching Rachel, watching the stricken look in her eyes. He didn't understand all of what was going on here but he understood enough. 'The fire's coming through fast but there's no hint of firestorm yet. If he's sensible...if the wind stays at its current force...'

Only, of course, it didn't.

Ten minutes after Hugo had left, the wind strengthened from strong to gale force, ripping across the crowded beach with a force that was terrifying. The blast of hot air before the fire was almost overpowering. Rachel was stooped over a stretcher. Bridget McLeod had turned a hundred the week before. The heat was making her badly dehydrated and Rachel was setting up a saline drip. As the searing wind blasted across the beach, the woman pushed her away.

'There's others need you more. Leave me be.'

'There's no need to be noble,' Rachel told her, trying not to sound panicky behind her mask. 'We're organised for this.'

She finished what she was doing and straightened, trying to see through the swirling smoke. But the townsfolk were prepared. A heat like this couldn't last. The gale-force wind would blast through with frightening force but, because of the beach, they could survive. After the initial fire front, firefighting operations could begin again.

But for now… The little populace were hauling blankets over their heads, following orders that had been drilled into this fire-prone town since their childhood. Those who couldn't walk were being carried into the shallows.

'Toby.' Rachel turned to find Myra at her side. Myra had Toby in her arms with blankets wedged between them.

'There's nothing more you can do, lass. Stay with us during the worst,' Myra said, and there was no choice. Two firefighters had hold of Bridget's stretcher and were carrying her into the shallows, the old lady already covered with a soaking blanket. The rest of the stretchers were lined up where the waves broke lightly over patients' feet. Every patient had an allocated carer, each with sodden blankets.

Toby was whimpering with fear.

The noise from the fire was almost deafening. 'Take care of Toby,' Hugo had said.

Hugo.

Oh, God, Hugo…

She couldn't think of him, now. She mustn't.

The people of this tiny town were huddled in the shallows. She could scarcely breathe. There was nothing to do except survive.

Somewhere out there was Hugo.

'If I survive, so must you,' she whispered to herself as she dropped to her knees in the shallows. Toby crawled from Myra's arms to hers and clung. They had their blankets right over their heads, a sodden canopy to stop the shower of burning ash falling directly onto them. The fire was a roaring inferno. Despite the pall of smoke she could sense the flames—a wall of fire bursting down from the mountains. The air was being sucked up. The oxygen. It was so hard to breathe…

'I want my daddy,' Toby whimpered, and Rachel held him close and whispered into his hair.

'So do I,' she murmured. 'So do I. But Daddy's gone to see a patient. He'll be back soon. Please…'

'Sue-Ellen?' Hugo was out of the car, holding woollen wadding over his face to augment his mask as he raced toward the burning house. Vision was down to almost nothing—the fire was all around him. The trees overhead were roaring with flames.

It had caught. The back of the house had caught.

On this side of the house at least there was a little shelter. The house itself was stopping the worst of the blast. So far. Hugo was coughing, retching. Yelling. Thinking fast.

Maybe she'd gone to the dam. Maybe. It was the obvious place.

Surely she wouldn't still be in the house? 'Sue-Ellen...'

Something hit his legs—something alive. He looked down to see a half-grown collie pup whining in terror. Scratching at the door. Whining again...

Dear God.

The dog's body language was unmistakable. She was inside.

For something that had threatened for so long, it was over with a speed that was frightening all by itself. One minute the population of Cowral was crouched in the shallows while the fire blasted its way right over their heads. The next the front had moved on. The air was still choked with smoke and debris but the roaring receded. The feeling that the very air required to breathe was being sucked away was replaced by the same choking, thick sensation that had been with them most of the day.

With the passing of the front the wind dropped. The fire had made its own wind. A vortex. That's what the firefighters had said could happen and now Rachel believed them.

Toby was still cradled in her arms. Myra was beside them, their bodies a threesome of contact with the waves splashing over them in a rhythm that had been crazily undisturbed by the fire.

Rachel pushed back her blanket and peered cautiously out.

Around her everyone was doing the same—a field of grey, sodden ghosts arising from the ashes. Katy and her baby. The ancient Bridget, hauling back her blanket herself and peering out with an interest that belied her hundred years.

Casualties?

Sam was beside her, pushing himself out from underneath something that looked like a vast eiderdown. His wife was beside him. Sylvia Nieve still had a head full of hair-rollers and as she pushed back the eiderdown she gave them a cautious pat. Making sure of what was important.

'Did everyone get to the beach?' Rachel asked, and the cold feeling of dread in the pit of her heart felt like a lump of lead.

'Elaine Baxter and Les Harding arrived just as it hit,' Ian told her. 'One of the men got bitten by one of Les's cats. The cats are here in a cage—if someone hasn't drowned them.'

'But Hugo...?' she asked.

'He didn't come back. He'll have been well into the hills when it hit.'

'Seeing his patient,' Rachel said swiftly, as Toby turned a fearful face toward Sam. She had to stay calm. Hysterics would help no one. 'There was a lady who's ill up in the hills and your daddy has gone to look after her. And I need to go, too. Toby, can you stay with Myra while your daddy and I keep on working? I'll see anyone here who needs help and then... Sam, how long do you think before we can get through to Sue-Ellen's place?'

'I'll check with the fire chief,' Sam told her.

'As soon as it's safe to move, let me know,' Rachel told him. She gave Toby a hard hug, as much to reassure herself as to reassure Toby. 'Hugo might... Hugo might need help.'

'The chief'll send a tanker.'

'I'll come, too.'

She worked solidly on the beach, coping with breathing difficulties and myriad minor injuries while she waited for the fire chief to declare it safe to travel through the town to Sue-Ellen's farmlet beyond.

'I can't believe how lightly we've got off.' The chief, a grizzled man in his fifties, pushed back his hard hat and wiped his forehead as he surveyed the clearing beach. 'The storm sucked everything up in its path but we've done such a good clearing job around the town that we've only lost four houses. And they were holiday accommodation where no one followed orders to clear.'

Once the firestorm had passed, the townsfolk streamed back to their homes in time to put out spot fires and stop the fire from taking hold. Now the main front had reached the point where land became sea. Cowral was still surrounded by a ring of fire but increasingly the town looked safe.

But Hugo...

'Can we go?' Rachel finished wrapping a burned arm with a sterile dressing. A burning branch had been flung into the shallows at the height of the fire—it must have been blown for a quarter of a mile—but the child who'd been hit was already aching to get back to the excitement. Rachel clipped the dressing, gave the boy's parents a rueful grin and turned back to the fire chief.

'You don't want to go with us, Doc,' he told her. 'I've got Gary Lewis on the truck already—he's been out on the front and when he found out Sue-Ellen didn't make it to the beach he nearly went berserk. There's one of you emotionally involved.'

'And you're not?'

He met her look square on. And sighed. 'Yeah,' he admitted. 'Of course I am.'

'Then what are we arguing over?' She was dressed in her firefighting gear. Toby was safe with Myra. There was no one else needing urgent treatment. And somewhere out there was Hugo.

She definitely needed to go.

But still the fire chief hesitated. 'Doc...'

'What?'

'You're not seeing this at its worst,' he told her. 'The river's blocked the worst of the blast here. If we were right before the front...'

She gazed at his grim face and saw the message he was trying not to tell her. 'You're telling me there's little chance Hugo's survived?'

'The boys are trying to clear the road now,' he told her. 'We'll let you know.'

'No.' She straightened her shoulders in an unconscious brace position. 'I'm a doctor. He... They may be hurt.'

His eyes met hers. Giving her the truth. 'To be honest, Doc, the chances are that they're a lot more than hurt.'

'I know. But if not... I'm bringing medical supplies and I'm coming.'

Sue-Ellen Lesley lived five minutes' drive out of town but it took two fire crews half an hour to reach it. Once outside the town boundaries there was thick bush—or what was left of thick bush. Now there was simply smouldering fire.

Eucalypts burned fast. The trees were already starting to smoulder rather than flame and the smell of burning eucalyptus oil was overpowering. Branches had dropped across the road. Trees were down. Every obstacle they reached had to be dealt with slowly—flames put out and the wood cooled enough to shift. Two fire crews worked in tandem, with a water tanker ferrying water as needed.

By the time they reached the tiny farmhouse where Sue-Ellen lived, Rachel was almost ready to scream.

'You sure you're not needed back in town?' The fire chief's face was grim as they rounded the last corner. Rachel had been working as hard as any of his team, joining the hard manual labour that had been needed to clear the road. She was working as one of his crew but there were personal issues here. He could see it. The set look on her face had him worried.

He was worried anyway. One of his boys was emotionally involved with Sue-Ellen and Gary was making himself sick with worry. And as well as Sue-Ellen... Well, this was Doc McInnes. Hell.

'If I'm needed, they'll contact me,' Rachel told him shortly. 'Elly knows where I am, and the radio network is still operational. But there's nothing back in town but heat exhaustion and dehydration, and Elly and Don and David can cope with that.'

'But—'

'Don't fight me on this,' she told him. 'We're wasting time. Just get there.'

And then the farmhouse was in view. Or what was left of the farmhouse.

Nothing.

The tiny farm cottage looked almost as if it had been vaporised—sucked into thin air with only a smouldering slab remaining where the house had once stood. Even the chimney had collapsed in on itself and was now a low mound of crumbling, smoking brick.

Nothing could have survived this. Hugo...

Rachel caught her breath. There was a car parked beside the wreck. Or what was left of a car.

A big old family sedan. Hugo's car.

Rachel was out of the truck before it stopped. Staring.

Her heart was somewhere else. Gone. A lifeless thing with no meaning. There were tears streaming down her face and she didn't check them. She couldn't.

Hugo.

And then a shout. From Gary, the giant of a young firefighter who was so worried about Sue-Ellen.

'Over here. He's over here. In the dam.'

Gary, who obviously knew the lie of the land, had spared not even a glance for the burnt-out shell of the house where it was obvious nothing could have survived, but he'd moved swiftly toward a bank over to the left. Now he stood on the rise and yelled back to them.

'They're over here. They're in the dam. Doc with about thirty bloody goats and a dog and Sue-Ellen. They're alive.'

Hugo was alive, but Sue-Ellen barely qualified. He'd heard them come but he could do nothing. The girl in his arms needed all his attention. Her eyes were wide but what she was seeing was invisible to him. She was drifting in and out of consciousness. Her blood pressure was way down and her pulse was thready and weak.

He needed equipment. He needed help.

The grass at the verge of the dam was still smouldering.

He couldn't move.

So he lay, supporting Sue-Ellen, partly submerged in the water. Beside them, her half-grown collie lay and whined and whined, and around them Sue-Ellen's beloved angora goats shifted in anxiety.

The girl in his arms stirred and seemed to focus. 'I...can't...' she whispered.

'You don't need to do anything, Sue-Ellen,' he told her, trying hard to keep his voice reassuring and steady. 'You've done it all. Your goats are fine. You've saved your pup. You're burned but not too badly. You'll be OK. People are coming. We'll both be looked after. Your goats. Your dogs. All of us.'

She was no longer listening. She'd dropped again into unconsciousness.

He closed his eyes and when he opened them Rachel was slithering down the bank toward him.

His Rachel.

'I haven't been able to help. I haven't had anything to work with,' Hugo told her. The fire crew had laid a thermal blanket over the mud at the side of the dam. Gary—appalled beyond belief—had lifted Sue-Ellen's limp body from Hugo's grasp and laid her tenderly on the bank. Someone else had run for Rachel's equipment. Now they were working fiercely in tandem.

Severe burns. Shock. Smoke inhalation. Why hadn't they been able to get here earlier? Rachel thought fiercely as she checked blood pressure. Eighty over fifty. Hell.

'Gary, look after Hugo,' she ordered. As one of the few professional firefighters, Gary would know basic first aid, but Hugo was having none of it. He brushed Gary aside and reached for the IV equipment.

'I'm fine. I haven't been able to help but I can now.'

'Are your hands burned?'

'No.'

'Your voice is rasping.'

'I'm not burned. It's just from smoke inhalation.'

'Well, then...'

'Leave it.'

She cast a doubtful glance at him but his look was grim and determined. She had the sense to let it be, moving to Sue-Ellen's mouth, tilting her chin so her jaw dropped open. 'I checked,' Hugo said briefly. 'There's no obvious burns to her mouth. The pharynx isn't swollen.'

'Lucky.' Rachel placed a stethoscope on Sue-Ellen's chest while Hugo accepted the bag of saline from Gary and swabbed the girl's bare arm. IV access would have to be ante-cubital—through the elbow—because of deep burns on her hands. She was still deeply unconscious.

'Oh, God, she's dying,' the young firefighter whispered, and Rachel found time to glance up at him.

'You sound like you love her,' she said gently, and the young giant nodded. They were working together to rip away clothing and place the bags of saline.

'We used to go out with each other. When she was diagnosed with schizophrenia she called it off. Said it was unfair to me. I came around last night to see if she needed help and she told me to clear off. But she didn't want me to. I could tell. And then today I was caught out with the fire truck and couldn't check. Hell. I didn't know... I didn't know...'

He hadn't known how much he loved her, Rachel thought, with the sudden insight of someone who'd been down just that road.

'She'll be right,' she said gently. 'Gary, can you find us more blankets from the truck? I know it's crazy but the water will have chilled her and we need her warm. You'll find the sheets I brought——they look like a cross between plastic and tin foil. And I have sheets of clingwrap. I want them, too.'

The firefighter nodded, grateful to do anything. Anything!

He disappeared at a run.

'We need to contact air ambulance services,' Hugo said in a voice that was growing more ragged by the minute.

'I already have.' It was the fire chief, appearing over the dam bank with his radio receiver still in his hand. 'One of the state's medical evacuation helicopters is available. Apparently our firestorm has upgraded us. Cowral's become a priority and the chopper will be here in twenty minutes.'

'If we can keep her alive,' Hugo muttered, and Rachel shook her head.

'There's no doubt.' She had an oxygen mask on the girl's face and already Sue-Ellen's complexion was deepening under the grime to something that looked more healthy. As if on cue, the girl stirred and moaned.

'Morphine,' Rachel murmured, reaching behind her for her bag, but it was Hugo who administered it. He was shocked and battered but he was working on autopilot.

'Let me go. Let me go...' It was a thready whisper but she was starting to fight them.

'Haloperidol?' Rachel queried, and Hugo nodded. If Sue-Ellen was schizophrenic then the whole combination of events might well be enough to push her over the edge. Sedation was imperative.

The fluids were flowing freely now. Rachel took another blood-pressure reading and breathed a bit more easily.

'A hundred and ten, seventy. See, Hugo? We'll do it.'

'You'll do it,' he muttered. 'I couldn't do it without you.

Hell, Rachel, I had nothing.'

'Because your car went up in flames,' she said brusquely. 'It could be said you had an excuse. I don't think the medical board is going to strike you off for losing your doctor's bag. And you did save the patient.'

Gary arrived back, sliding down the bank with a bunch of blankets. He looked worried sick.

'Let's find the extent of these burns,' Hugo said. He was starting to sound in control a bit——just a little. He lifted Sue-Ellen's palms and grimaced. Rule of palm... Take the area of a size of a palm print and measure how many palm prints were burned on the girl's body. Twenty? Thirty? They were looking at something like thirty per cent burns.

'We need that fluid coming in fast.'

'We have it,' Rachel replied.

'Have we got dressing packs?'

'We have everything we need.' She'd carried her bag with her, and she flipped it open. As Hugo started gently separating burned fingers—imperative in these first few minutes—she started sorting, handing Hugo sachets of specially formulated gel to soak the burns, then gauze to place over them before they wrapped the whole area in clingwrap. It was imperative to get the area sterile and air-free.

At what cost came the time spent in the dam? What infections were in the ash- and mud-laden water? But at least it meant she had a chance.

And a chance was what she most needed. As Gary stooped over Sue-Ellen and her eyes fluttered open and found Gary...as Gary lifted her hand to his face and held...just held, Rachel thought Sue-Ellen had everything she needed right here. Right now.

She was injured almost to death.

But she had her love and one look at Gary told her that it would take more than schizophrenia or bushfires to part them again.

And all of a sudden Rachel was blinking back tears.

Of...envy?

'She was in the house.'

Hugo was sitting in the mud on the dam bank, his head in his hands. Behind them the whirr of the helicopter was fading into the distance.

They'd lifted Sue-Ellen from the dam bank, warmed her shocked body, covered her burns with antiseptic gel and the thin plastic burn wrap and continued her on intravenous fluids. They'd given her as much morphine as they could. Then they'd loaded her into the medical evacuation helicopter where a team of skilled medicos were waiting to take her to Sydney.

Gary had gone, too. It hadn't been discussed.

She had every chance of survival, Rachel thought as she watched the chopper disappear into the distance. Although the burns to her legs and hands were too extensive to be treated in a small country hospital, they shouldn't be extensive enough to be life-threatening. Not with the prompt treatment she'd had and the fact that in an hour she'd be in the best burns unit in the state.

And the schizophrenia? With love and devotion she had a good chance of a stable life. Gary wasn't about to be pushed aside again, for however noble a motive, Rachel thought.

And here… Already the goats were emerging from the water, starting to forage over burned ground. Amazingly, they even looked as if they were finding things to eat.

The goats might be back to business as usual but Hugo wasn't. He was sitting on the dam bank, looking sick. Rachel sat down beside him, hauled Pudge, Sue-Ellen's pup, up onto her knee and held the shaking dog. With her free hand she took Hugo's and held that, too. Tight.

'Hugo…'

He looked dreadful. While they'd worked over Sue-Ellen he'd been efficient, doctor in medical mode, but as the chopper left the fight seem to have drained out of him.

'Hugo,' she whispered again, and he stirred, as if trying to rouse himself from a dreadful dream.

'The house had started to burn before I reached her,' he said at last, wearily, as if hardly conscious that Rachel was beside him. 'She must have gone back in. I yelled out and I could hear her inside the house, screaming for Pudge. Screaming. But Pudge was outside. The pup came to greet me as I pulled up, desperate. As if he knew his mistress was inside.'

'So you went in.'

'Of course.' He winced and Rachel looked down at the hand she was holding. There were blisters there. Burns. He'd been wearing protective clothing and that was intact, but there were spot burns on his hands and on his face.

He'd been through hell.

She pulled back on her hand, afraid she was hurting him, but his grip tightened.

'But you found her,' she said softly, and he nodded.

'I found her in the back bedroom and the curtains were burning. The window had exploded inward. And she had bare feet. Bare feet!'

'Hugo—'

'I should have come last night. I should have thought of Sue-Ellen then.' He groaned. 'Hell, I should have—'

'You're one man,' she said gently. 'I went to the beach.'

'There was no danger last night. And other people checked. Gary loved her and he checked. She sent him away. There was nothing else you could do. You know that.'

'But today—'

'Today you came. You came in time. They're saying on the beach that Sue-Ellen refused to evacuate. Do you think she would have evacuated if you'd ordered her to? You're not omnipotent, Hugo. You're human. You're a doctor and a really fine one at that, but you're still human.' She took his palms into her hands and looked down. He was burned but not too badly. Still... Her face twisted. Dear God, he'd come so close. 'You're a lovely, lovely man,' she whispered. 'The best... Oh, God, Hugo if I'd lost you...'

He wasn't hearing. He was still with Sue-Ellen.

'I thought she was stable,' he said bleakly. 'Sensible. Last time I saw her... I was out here three days ago when the fires first threatened. She talked about evacuation plans. So why didn't I check?'

'Because you can't be everything to everyone,' she said softly. Then, because she couldn't bear to watch the pain in his eyes any more, she took his face in her hands and kissed him—softly, on each eyelid in turn. 'Sue-Ellen made her own decision not to leave her animals. That's her responsibility. Back at the beach... Sam called her a schizo—a mental case—and if that's the way you regarded her then, yes, you were responsible for her because she wasn't responsible for herself. You should have locked her up and taken total control. But you said she was a person capable of her own decisions.'

'Yes, but—'

'But nothing.' Rachel's voice was urgent now. She could see the self-loathing in Hugo's eyes and she wasn't having any of it. He was hurt, this man. She could put bandages on his hands but it wasn't enough. What hurt more than a heart?

'Sue-Ellen knew the dangers. Sam and Gary both said she'd been warned. She chose to stay.'

'She was ill.'

'Would you have locked her in a mental institution?'

'No, but—'

'But nothing. Sue-Ellen lived independently and she was hurt, making that life for herself. I won't have you blaming yourself, Dr McInnes.'

He looked up at her, and the beginning of an exhausted smile crossed his face. Just a trace.

'Bossy, aren't we?'

'It's what I do best,' she said softly, and smiled back at him.

Hugo gazed up at her. Really looked. His burned hand came up and brushed the curls from her face. They were tumbling every which way from under her hard hat.

She'd be smoke-grimed, she thought—black with soot and sand and smoke. But Hugo's eyes were holding her and his fingers traced her cheekbone gently—a feather touch.

'You're so beautiful.'

'Beautiful and bossy?' she asked in a voice that wasn't quite steady.

'That's the one. Rachel…'

'What?'

'I need to kiss you,' he told her.

And what was a girl to say to a request like that?

She kissed him.

More than that, she gave her heart. Right there and then. Or maybe it had been given in those awful moments on the beach, under the sodden blanket with the fire roaring overhead, thinking that somewhere out here was Hugo. Her love…

Her love.

There was another love. Craig. That hadn't disappearedit never could. There was still commitment, still pain, but it didn't stop this flowering that was happening within her right now.

Dottie had said it was time she moved on. Put Craig behind her. But it wasn't like that. She hadn't been able to put Craig behind her for eight long years.

And she couldn't now. She didn't need to.

Because Craig was still with her. Craig was a part of who she was, a part of her loving. She held Hugo's dear, scorched face in her hands and she kissed him with all the love in her heart and she knew that this was no betrayal.

This was an extension of loving. A wealth of love. Broadening, expanding her heart, to take in Toby and Cowral and Penelope and Digger and Sue-Ellen and maybe a few crazy goats clustered around and a confused pup called Pudge.

And Hugo.

She kissed him and found herself melting. Not just her lips. Her whole life, melting away and reforming. Regrouping. Stronger, richer, deeper.

Love…

He tasted of fire. He tasted of heat and want and aching need.

He tasted of… Hugo.

Her fingers held him, curled into his hair, clinging, letting his mouth devour her, knowing that for him this kiss was as affirmation of life as well as love.

Knowing for him this was the only way to move forward. Through love.

Love was…here. Love was now. Love was Hugo.

There was no time for each other. Not now.

They held each other for as long as they could, desperately taking what they most needed from this precious contact. But, of course, there was more needed of them this day than the care of Sue-Ellen.

The fire chief stood behind them and coughed and waited.

He'd given them space. He was a wise man and he'd seen their need. He'd directed his team away from them as the chopper left and had given them as much time as he could, but needs were breaking through.

'Doc…' He coughed a couple of times and tried again. 'Doc…'

They broke apart. Sort of. Battered and filthy, they sat in the mud and looked up at him, and the fire chief gave them a grin which said the incongruous picture they made was hardly lost on him.

'Geez, whatever turns you on, Doc,' he said to Hugo. 'Me, I like my missus in a sexy negligee but if you like 'em covered with soot—well, each to his own. But kinky is what I call it.'

Rachel blushed. She blushed from the roots of her hair to the tips of her toes and she tried to haul away, but Hugo was having none of it. His hand tightened around her waist and he grinned.

'Sexiest lady I know.'

'Isn't she just.' The fire-chief's grin broadened. 'We'll have her up on our calendar next year, hard hat included. Look, I'm sorry to disturb you...'

'You'd think we could have a bit of privacy,' Hugo complained. He seemed suddenly almost jovial. 'We've searched so hard to find it. And here we are with only thirty goats, one dog and twenty odd firefighters as an audience.' His smile faded, just a bit, but it didn't leave his eyes completely. 'Don't tell me. Problems?'

'No major ones.' The chief wiped his eyes with the back of his hand and something suspiciously like moisture smeared his cheek. 'We've been so bloody lucky. It's amazing. But...'

'But?'

'One of the teams down at the river are saying some of the guys are suffering from smoke inhalation. And the publican's wife...she tried to hook up the hose as the first of the heavy smoke hit the town but she was working blind and she fell over the tap. She sounds like she's broken her toe.'

A broken toe...

'Is that all?' Hugo asked in voice that was none too steady.

'That's all, Doc,' the chief told him. 'For now. You guys might have time to continue this...discussion later if you need to. But for now I'm afraid Cowral wants you both to be doctors.'

Hugo smiled and turned back to Rachel. To his love. 'Can we be doctors for a bit?' Hugo asked her. He held Rachel close and the expression in his eyes told her all she ever needed to know about this man. There was no need for anything else. Just Hugo. His feel. His touch. His eyes.

And the way he looked at her.

'What do you think, my love?' he whispered. 'Can we be doctors for a bit?'

'As long as we stay being more than just doctors underneath,' she answered, her eyes smiling and holding and loving. 'As long as we stay just as we are.' And then her smile broke into a chuckle of love and laughter and joy. 'Only maybe a little bit cleaner.'

They worked then, through the rest of that long, long day. Because, of course, it wasn't just firefighters with smoke inhalation and Maddie Forsyth's broken toe. The town was in firefighting mode. There were minor burns everywhere. Exhaustion. Dehydration. Stress.

Hugo and Rachel worked together and separately. They saw an endless stream of patients, one after another. The little hospital was a clear-
ing-house through which most of the town's population passed at some
time during the day. Toby was there from time to time, brought in by
Myra just to see that Daddy and Rachel were still there. Still fine. Toby
and Myra came with three dogs. Because of course they couldn't leave
the shaky Pudge at the farm. Hugo had scooped him up and carried him
into town beneath his firecrew jacket and had handed him over to Myra
to fuss over. Amazingly, the two big dogs seemed to sense the little dog's
distress and now Pudge was the centre of a two-dog, housekeeper and
small boy circle of protection. By his second visit into the hospital the
puppy's tail was starting to wag again.

'I'll telephone Melbourne and tell them to pass the news on to Sue-
Ellen,' Hugo told Rachel as Myra herded her charges outdoors again.
'It'll do her more good than medicine.'

In the middle of all this...he could find time to think laterally about
Sue-Ellen. That was what country practice was all about, Rachel thought
as she returned to washing ash out of a firefighter's eyes. Country practice was medicine from textbooks—plus the rest.

It was healing—just for her.

They worked far into the night. The townsfolk had gone home from the
beach. The wind died, and about ten o'clock the hoped-for change blew
through softly from the south. The air temperature dropped to almost
cool and there was a spattering of blessed rain.

But still they worked. A team had been organised to go from house
to house, checking, not for spot fires now but on people's health. The
elderly and those at risk had had a day where they'd been tested to the
limit. They could go home now and maybe collapse with exhaustion,
stress, smoke inhalation, minor injuries...

So everyone was checked. Cowral looked after its own. And as each
problem was reported, it was passed on to the medical team.

At two a.m. Rachel finally arrived back in the kitchen of the doctors'
residence. Myra had taken Toby and all three dogs out to her place for the
night. There were casseroles sitting on the kitchen table—of course—but
Rachel was beyond eating. She sat and stared at nothing. At nothing at all.

And fifteen minutes later Hugo walked in.

He was as exhausted as she was. He appeared at the screen door and his face was grey with fatigue. She rose and looked at him. Just...looked. And what passed between them...

It was a vow. It was confirmation of all they had come through that day.

It was the start of their life together.

'Rachel,' he said at last, and it was as if it was a blessing. 'Hugo,' she whispered, and walked straight into his arms.

There was no time then for anything but love.

There was no time for talking. No time for anything but filling this aching, searing need. Holding. Finding their rightful place.

They showered together because to do otherwise was to waste time. Their filthy clothes were shed together—clothes that on any day but this one would have had both doctors struck off the medical register as disgraces to the medical profession. But no one had minded their clothes. They'd been doctors first and foremost. They'd seen to the town's medical needs.

But now...the need was past. The town's needs. There was time now for their own needs.

Time to become lovers.

There was no hesitation. No questions. There were only answers.

Their bodies met in joyful wonder. They washed each other under the stream of warm water, soaping, smiling, learning each other's bodies in this, the most intimate act of cleaning. Soaping off the layers of grime to reveal bodies that were already known and loved.

His hands were smoothing the soap over her skin and it was the most erotic of sensations. She had the flannel and was rubbing his back, but her body was falling forward, leaning into him, letting her mouth touch his...

Tasting. Wanting. Needing!

The need was mutual. All-exclusive.

It was as if this man and this woman had been meant for each other—destined—from the beginning of time.

And then they were together in Hugo's big bed, dry and warmed but still naked, gloriously naked. Skin against skin, holding, holding, narrowing the gap, merging...

Man and woman becoming one.

* * *

It had been so long.

Had it ever been this good? Rachel didn't know. She couldn't think. She couldn't compare. What had been between Rachel and Craig was another time. Another life. It had been precious—was still precious—but it was a thing apart.

This was now. This man, her beloved Hugo, holding her as if he loved her.

He did love her. She knew it and she gloried in it. Craig would not gainsay her this love. Because she loved Craig she knew, with a surety that was a part of her own heart, that she had his blessing. She could feel it.

Her body was doubly blessed.

Dear heaven, the feel of Hugo. The wonder. His big hands were holding her as if she was the most precious thing in the world. His warmth, the smell of him, the taste...

The way her body moulded around him. Opened. Welcomed. He came into her, and their mutual need was overwhelming. The wonder...

The joy.

They slept. How could they not sleep after this day? Their exhaustion was absolute. Sated with loving, they slept entwined, and Rachel fell into a sleep as deep as she'd ever been in.

Ever since the accident—ever since that dreadful day—her sleep had been troubled, disturbed, as if she'd had to stay awake for the next disaster. There would be another disaster. Her world had been pulled from under her feet and she couldn't trust.

She couldn't sleep.

But now...in this man's arms, she slept. Let tomorrow bring what it may. For now there was only this man and his arms and his body and his love.

And Hugo?

It had never been like this with Beth. He'd drifted into marriage with Beth as he'd nearly drifted into marriage with her sister. Stupid. Stupid, stupid.

Yet how could he have known it had been stupid? He'd never known it could be like this. He woke about dawn and his fingers twined gently through Rachel's tumbled curls. How could he have suspected there was loving like this in the world?

This wonderful woman. This…blessing.

She stirred in sleep, her eyes half opened and she smiled at him. His heart twisted inside him and he gathered her to him with such tenderness. The most precious thing…

Rachel.

Her eyes closed and she snuggled into him. Her breasts moulded to him. He felt desire stir, but exhaustion was still there. Desire could wait, he thought with a growing joy. It could wait an hour or two. There was all the time in the world. This was his Rachel. Rachel…

Murmuring her name into her hair, he drifted back to sleep.

The phone woke them.

It was late. At least eight. The sun was streaming across the brocade quilt. He'd get rid of it, Hugo thought, and then joyously, yes! He'd get rid of every piece of brocade in the house.

This day was the first day of the rest of his life. His life with Rachel.

She was waking beside him, her eyes fluttering open, smiling, reaching up to touch his unshaven chin.

The phone was ringing. Rachel.

Medical imperative. Answer the phone. He smiled back at her and then answered the phone.

A woman's voice, urgent with need.

'Is Rachel there? Dr Harper? She's not answering her cellphone. I need to speak to her.'

'Sure.' He heard the fear and reacted. His eyes sent Rachel an urgent message and handed her the phone.

Rachel took the receiver and listened. 'Dottie.'

She was suddenly wide awake, pushing herself up in bed, oblivious of the fact that she was naked. A sunbeam was streaming across her creamy breasts.

Dear God, she was beautiful!

But her voice sounded concerned.

'No, Dottie, we're fine. I'm sorry. I should have rung you last night. I might have known you'd see it on the news reports. No. The town's been left basically intact. We're safe.'

'No.'

'No.'

Then her voice softened with dread. 'But he can't…

Dottie, he was stable…'

She listened some more and then put her lips tightly together. Her eyes closed as if in pain.

'Of course I'll come,' she whispered. 'Of course. Just as soon as I can get there.'

The line went dead. Hugo lifted the receiver from Rachel's suddenly limp grasp and laid it back on the cradle. Then he turned and took her hands in his.

'What is it, Rachel?'

She opened her eyes and stared at him but she wasn't seeing him. She was seeing something a long way away. In the far, far distance.

'It's Craig,' she whispered. 'Craig?'

'My husband. He's dying.'

CHAPTER NINE

SOMEHOW, WHILE HUGO helped Rachel put her belongings together and practically force-fed her toast and arranged for someone to drive her... somehow he got it out of her.

'Craig and I were in a car smash eight years ago,' she said, her voice laced with pain. 'We were med students together. We'd gone out together since school. Dottie, Craig's mum, is practically my mum. We were so close. We got married and everything was perfect and then some drunk driver smashed into us on a blind bend when we were coming home from one of Craig's football matches. The drunk was on the wrong side of the road and there was nothing Craig could do to avoid him. I was hurt. Craig... Craig was hardly touched. Except for a blow to his head. One blow. One blow and he was unconscious. And he never woke up.' Her voice broke on a sob and Hugo held her mug of tea to lips that were tight with the shock of past hurt and hurt still to come.

'So Michael... The guy at the dog show?'

'He's a schmuck,' she said. 'Dottie said I should get away. Have some fun. And I met you.'

He took a deep breath. Did some fast thinking. Last night he'd made love to a woman he'd thought was in an unhappy marriage. Now...

Things had changed. She'd changed.

And his head... He was having trouble getting it around this.

But the pain on her face was real and dreadful and it needed to be addressed now.

'Rachel, I'm really sorry.'

She pulled herself together then. Sort of. 'Sorry? I'm not.' She gave him a fleeting, hurting smile. 'How could I be sorry for last night? It was the most wonderful...' Her voice broke, but she managed to go on. 'Hugo, it was fantastic. The best. I could never, ever regret it. But you do see that I need to go.'

'Of course you do.' It tore him apart that he couldn't put her in his car and drive her to Sydney himself but, of course, he couldn't. The town still had medical imperatives.

At least the road was open. Rain in the night had cleared the route out of town. He'd put out a call and someone would drive her all the way to Melbourne. He could arrange that at least.

But he couldn't leave. 'Rachel...'

'I know.' She swallowed the last of her tea and stood, looking down into the dregs at the bottom of the mug. 'I know. I'm sorry, Hugo. I'm sorry, love...'

Hugo worked for that day—long hours of minor crises. He worked the next. The day after that...

The day after that he could bear it no longer. He talked to Myra and to Toby, contacted a locum service and found some help and went to town.

The thin blue line rose and fell. Rose and fell. Rose and fell.

How long does love last?

The young woman sat and watched as she'd sat and watched for years.

'I love you, Craig,' she whispered, but there was no answer, as there'd never been an answer.

Dappled sunlight fell over lifeless fingers. Beloved eyes, once so full of life and laughter, stayed closed.

The blue line rose and fell. Rose and fell. Faltered.

'I love you, Craig,' she whispered again, and blessed his face with her fingers. 'My love...'

How long does love last?

Maybe for no longer than a breath?

* * *

Hugo stood at the ward door and watched Rachel. She was sleeping. Her bright curls were tangled on the white coverlet. Her hand held his. Her face rested on his chest.

Hugo's eyes moved to the monitor and stilled. The heartbeat was fast and irregular. He watched.

He'd learned so much over the last few days. Questions that should have been asked of Rachel had been answered by the consultant he'd called.

'Eight years in a coma. He was a strong young man, Hugo, with nothing but a bleed into the brain to maim him. We thought he could live even longer than this. There's been no end in sight. But a few months ago he suffered a clot...'

'Deep vein thrombosis?'

'You know it's not uncommon in cases like this. The body's so inactive... We thought maybe we'd lose him then. I think his parents and Rachel said their goodbyes. But he rallied. And Rachel went on waiting.'

'Rachel...'

'I've known Rachel since she was a medical student,' the consultant said bluntly. 'She and Craig were a great pair—lovely creatures with the world at their feet. Since the accident it's as if someone's blown Rachel's flame out. She's clever, she's an extraordinary doctor but every night she sits by Craig's bedside and she simply...well, she simply is.'

'She must have loved him.'

'It's so hard to move forward,' the consultant said gently. 'Without a death. Dottie and Lewis, Craig's parents, well, after the clot they seemed to let go. They pushed Rachel. She was making the first tentative steps. And now... The clots have reappeared. One's sitting in his lung. This is the end, Hugo. The end of a very long story.'

So now Hugo stood at the door and watched her. He simply...watched her.

As she'd watched Craig for all these years. With all the love in her heart.

She'd gone for coffee.

It had been one hell of a day. The emotions in Rachel's tired mind were threatening to overwhelm her. How could this happen? While she was falling in love—for the second time—her first love was deciding to slip away from this world.

She didn't feel guilty. She couldn't. How could she? In a sense it was because of Craig that she'd fallen so heavily for Hugo. The love she felt for both men was mixed up, intertwined.

Because she loved Hugo, her love for Craig couldn't die, regardless of what happened to the man in the bed. The man she'd loved for ever.

But she couldn't think of Hugo now. He was still there in the background—a warmth and a joy in the back of her mind, a vast tenderness that filled the cold and the emptiness that had been with her for so long.

But for now there was only Craig. His breathing had become shallow. There was a pneumonia that wouldn't clear. It was his time.

Time to let go.

She filled her coffee-mug in the relatives' kitchenette at the end of the ward and walked slowly back to the small room where Craig lay by himself. And stopped short in the doorway.

Hugo was there. Hugo was sitting in the chair beside Craig's bed and he was speaking.

'Mate, I have no idea whether you can hear me. The jury's out on brain injury—on this dying business. How much you know. How much you can sense. But I figured...the way I felt I had to come. I had to talk to you. You have the right.'

Rachel stepped back. He hadn't heard her return. She leaned against the wall of the corridor and she closed her eyes. And listened while Hugo spoke to Craig.

While one love spoke to another.

'I don't know how much Rachel has told you, but I'm Hugo McInnes. I'm a country family doctor. I'm a widower, with a kid and a dog, and I'm thirty-five years old. And I'm in love with your wife.'

And I'm in love with your wife. It was such a bold statement that Rachel drew in her breath. She swallowed. And she waited.

'It sounds pretty dreadful, doesn't it?' Hugo said, and paused. 'I never thought I'd say that to someone I think of as a friend. That I'm in love with your wife. But maybe it's because that's the way I think of you that I can say it. As a friend.'

There was a long pause then. Out in the corridor Rachel set her coffee-mug down on the floor. Her fingers were trembling. A couple of nurses walked past and looked at her in concern but she waved them on. He'd come...

'Craig, you and Rachel have loved each other for a long time. I know that.' Hugo's voice was soft but pervasive, reaching where she strained to hear. 'I know that. I can see it in Rachel's eyes. I can see how deep your love was. After all this time...part of Rachel is you. Well, now I've fallen for her—fallen for her in a big way, maybe as hard as you ever fell. But, of course, it's different. I'm not loving a girl straight out of school. I'm loving a woman who's been loved before—who's loved before. Who's become what she is because some guy a long time ago made her smile. Lit up her world. Took her in his arms and loved her and made her feel that anything was possible when love was around.'

Hugo hesitated, as though finding difficulty in finding words. The right words. But somehow he kept going.

'I've never felt like that,' he said at last. 'I drifted into a marriage that was a bit of a disaster. My wife died and that made me feel even more self-contained. Like love—married love—was something you read about in romance novels. Not something that changed the world. Only then I met Rachel.'

Another silence. Then...

'She's really something,' he whispered. 'She's the best. You and Rachel must have been amazing. And what Rachel's grown to be...because of you...

'You know,' he said, his voice still soft, 'that's why I'm here. To tell you that you're a part of Rachel. And because of that... I guess you'll be a part of our family. You'll be with us. You'll live on.'

Rachel's eyes were filling with tears. She lifted a finger and wiped them away but more followed. Still he spoke.

'It sounds corny, doesn't it?' Hugo was saying ruefully. 'Lives on for ever in our hearts. It's true, though. I've finally figured this love thing out. The more you have the more you seem to get. The more you give, the more it grows around you. Because you loved Rachel and she loved you...she's reached out and she's enveloped us. Me. My kid—did I tell you that? I have a six-year-old called Toby who thinks your Rachel is the best thing since sliced bread. Rachel's promised to teach him to kick a football. She says you taught her that. Your football...living on in my kid.

'And there's more.' He was smiling. Rachel could hear it in his voice. 'We have a couple of dogs. Digger—he's mine. He's a mutt. And there's Penelope. She belonged to some creep we met and didn't like. I'm about to give the guy an offer he can't refuse because our family's too small. We need at least two dogs. We have another—Pudge—who's staying with us while someone else we know and love recovers from an injury. There'll be more. Rachel is the sort of woman who'll keep an open door to strays, and I'm with her there. And there'll be kids.'

Rachel drew her breath in at that. The tears dried. She was smiling. Stupidly she was grinning. The nurses passed her again and she grinned at them like a fool and they looked at her like she was demented.

It didn't matter. What had he said? How could she forget? *There'll be kids.*

'We'll have babies,' Hugo said softly. 'At least, I hope like hell we'll have babies. I haven't actually discussed this with Rachel yet but, hey, this is the equivalent of girls' talk with a bloke. We can say anything in here, right? Right. Well, having babies… Before Toby was born I thought one was enough, but he's twisted himself round my heart like you wouldn't believe. And if it was Rachel's kid… Your kid…'

Out in the corridor Rachel drew in her breath once again. 'You see, there's the thing,' Hugo said apologetically. 'Because if we have another kid then I'm going to be thinking that he, or she, is part of you. Any baby we have would seem your gift to us. You've given me the gift of love. The gift of Rachel. I'll never forget it, mate. I'll never forget you. You'll be held in our family in all honour. If we have a boy then there's no doubt what he'll be called. I'm not sure how we can swing Craig into a girl's name…' Rachel heard the smile in his voice. 'Maybe we'll just have to keep on trying until we get a boy. It'd be fine with me. As long as it's fine by you.'

Rachel's eyes were closed. The emotions surging around her heart were threatening to overwhelm her. She leaned hard against the wall—she needed its support to stop herself falling over. It seemed as if the whole world had stopped breathing. The silence went on for ever. And then…

'Well, that's all I wanted to say,' Hugo murmured. 'I needed to get that off my chest. You've got things to do. Breathing to concentrate on.' Rachel peeped forward and saw Hugo's hand lift Craig's and hold it. Two big hands, men's hands, intertwined. It was all she could do not to cry out at the sight of it. Her breathing started again, ragged and filled with tears.

'And you have dying to face,' Hugo whispered. 'I'm sorry, mate, that you can't live. I'm that damned sorry—and if giving up Rachel's love would bring you back to us I'd do it in a minute. But the guys in consultant suits are telling me it won't happen. So I'll say goodbye. I'll leave you to your parents and to Rachel. But know… Know, mate, that in our house—in any home that I'm lucky enough to build and share with your wife—you'll be honoured and you'll be loved for ever.'

It was five minutes before Hugo left the ward. When he came out into the corridor there was no one to be seen.

Just a mug of cold coffee lying abandoned on the polished floor.

CHAPTER TEN

ASHES TO ASHES. Dust to dust.

The wind blew gently across the mountain graveyard. Rachel stood silent as the coffin was lowered into the waiting ground. Lewis and Dottie stood on either side of her, holding her, united in a grief that had been agonised and raw eight years ago but was now muted—a soft and wondrous goodbye. These three who still loved Craig. Who would always love Craig.

In the end, it was good. This tiny graveyard… It was near to the place where Craig had been born—a tiny country cemetery where the wind keened around the mountains and a man could see for miles.

Where spirits could at last be free.

This was a good place for Craig to come to rest. His grandparents, his great-grandparents, a babe who would have been Craig's brother if he'd been born at term…they were all here.

His body was where it belonged and Craig lived on in those who loved him.

Rachel hugged those holding her—this man and this woman who'd been by her side for so long.

'It's OK,' she whispered, and Dottie smiled through her tears.

'It surely is.' Dottie blinked back tears and looked across at her husband—and Lewis released Rachel and came around to take his wife in his arms.

'Well done, lass,' Lewis said. He was a big gruff man who'd loved his son with an intensity that was even greater than his passion for the football he'd once played. He hugged his wife but he looked over her head at Rachel. 'And now it's time for you, girl, to move on.'

'Move on...'

'Your young man.' Lewis kissed his wife gently on the top of her head and then Dottie and Lewis both turned and smiled at her. 'Your Hugo.'

'My Hugo?'

'He's here,' Lewis said, and motioned out to the road where the track led down the mountain to the tiny township below. And there was Hugo. He was standing by his car. He didn't approach the mourners. He simply stood. Waiting. 'He's here,' Lewis said simply. 'It's time you went to him.'

Rachel closed her eyes, and when she opened them they were smiling at her. Dottie. And Lewis.

And Hugo.

There was nothing left to do here. Nothing at all. She gave her in-laws one last hug—one last smile—and then she crossed the graveyard and walked into the arms of her love.

CHAPTER ELEVEN

As WEDDINGS WENT, it was a pretty good wedding.

Toby knew about weddings. He knew the bride was supposed to look gorgeous. Well, Rachel looked gorgeous. Brides were supposed to be white and lacy and Rachel was lacy enough to be entirely satisfactory. Not too fussy, though, he decided. She had no veil or train. Her dress was made of white silk, Myra had told him. It was sort of bare around her shoulders with a floaty kind of skirt and bare feet. It was pretty nice, Toby decided—for a bride.

He wasn't sure about her feet, though. Bare toes. Weren't brides supposed to wear high heels? Still, that'd be pretty stupid on the beach where they'd decided to hold the ceremony. The ceremony was taking place on the exact spot where Rachel had taught him to drop-kick, the exact place where the townspeople had sheltered from the fire.

They were waiting for the ceremony to start. A couple of oldies from the nursing home were setting up a sound system. They were fiddling with knobs and Don was helping. It seemed like they were having a bit of trouble, but it didn't matter. Everyone was smiling and waiting, as though they had all the time in the world.

Which was fine for them, but Toby's football was up in the car. If he'd known he'd have to wait he could have brought it down for a quick kick.

He was a fantastic drop-kicker now. Rachel was all right at teaching him drop-kicking, he guessed—for a girl. She was better than his dad. But Lewis was... Well, Lewis was ace. He and Dottie, who refused to be called anything but Lewis and Dottie, seemed to spend a heap of time here now. They loved Cowral. They loved Toby.

Which was fine by Toby. He loved Lewis and Dottie right back.

Life had expanded considerably for Toby.

Everyone he knew was on this beach. Such a crowd...

That was part of the reason they'd decided not to have the ceremony in Cowral's tiny church. There'd be people who wouldn't fit and who could miss out?

Myra was standing beside him. Toby was holding the ring and Myra was a bit worried that he'd drop it. As if he would.

Myra was looking a bit distracted, Toby thought, looking at her with affectionate appraisal. She'd spent the morning grooming the dogs to within an inch of their lives. Penelope looked gorgeous—well, she always did, though not quite so gorgeous now that Hugo and Rachel and Toby spent so much time on the beach. But Digger had come up respectably, too.

Knickers was here as well, with a great red bow round his neckKnickers, the cocker spaniel, whose fight seemed to have started this whole chain of events. The black and white spaniel had recovered completely. So had Kim.

The girl was sitting hugging her knees on the sand as they waited for the ceremony to begin. Her dog was snuggled beside her. They looked great.

Pudge looked great, too, Toby conceded, moving on to the next dog in the pack of assorted canine guests. Pudge was still spending time with them, even though Sue-Ellen had returned. She'd been back in town for a few weeks now, staying in the hospital while her feet slowly healed. The townsfolk were rebuilding her cottage.

And one of the firefighters was with her. Gary. Toby had overheard Dad telling Rachel that maybe this was the best thing that could have happened to Sue-Ellen. Rachel said Gary was big and kind and besotted. He'd carried Sue-Ellen out of the dam with her burnt feet, he'd visited her in Melbourne, he was pushing her wheelchair now and Rachel and Dad thought things were looking really interesting.

Dad said Gary even liked goats.

There were all sorts of interesting things happening in Cowral at the moment. Myra said the fire had started people thinking how transient life was—whatever that meant. Myra said it had something to do with being happy. Being happy now.

She said it also meant what was happening to Aunty Christine. She was here with that man. Michael.

Michael had come down one day soon after the fire to collect Penelope. He'd blustered in, really angry, saying there was no way Penelope could stay. And then he'd met Christine. Christine had been in their kitchen when he'd arrived. She'd been angry about Dottie and Rachel redecorating Toby's bedroom, so she'd been in the mood to yell, too. Anyway, Michael had yelled at Rachel, and Christine had yelled at Dad and then Michael and Christine had gone somewhere to complain some more and Rachel and Dad had grinned and Dad had said, 'Well, well, wonders will never cease.'

And it seemed Penelope could stay. Because of the mess at the dog show she hadn't got enough championship points to keep her place in the state's Afghan hound hierarchy, which meant Michael didn't want to breed from her—which was just fine by Rachel and Dad. Dad said any puppies of Penelope's would risk having a kangaroo loose in the top paddock and Rachel had giggled and agreed.

What was keeping them? They were taking so long. Gee, if there was just time to get his football...

But the oldies behind the sound system had finally succeeded. The sound system crackled into action and music blared out across the beach.

What was the song? Toby knew it. He knew it! It was a bouncing song! And everyone else in town knew it too, because in seconds the whole town was singing about great balls of fire at the top of their lungs.

Everyone was laughing as Rachel walked down the sandy beach. Lewis held her arm, as proud as any father, and Dottie fussed over her dress, but it was Hugo Rachel was watching. Hugo who was waiting, with so much love in his eyes that even Toby could see it.

It was very satisfactory, Toby decided. He liked his dad looking like that. Soppy but good.

Then the tune ended and another started. Softer. Lovely. 'It's Bach's "Sheep May Softly Graze",' Myra whispered, her eyes glistening with unshed tears. 'Because they've come home to each other.'

Home. Here. Everyone was gazing at the shallows where once a township had sheltered to be safe and now a man and a woman were meeting each other, taking fingers in hands and turning together to make these, the most sacred of vows.

Toby even forgot his football.

With this ring, I thee wed.
With my body I thee worship.
From this day forth.
I now pronounce you...man and wife.

'I love you,' Hugo whispered, and Rachel looked into the eyes of her second and most precious love and she whispered them back.

'I love you,' she whispered. 'Hugo McInnes, I love you for ever.'

Ace, thought Toby. It had gone off exactly as it should. Great vows! No one could wiggle out of this one.

Not that he thought they'd want to. Rachel and his dad were looking at each other with the goofiest grins. Matching grins. Any minute now... Yep, here it was. Yuck! The kiss. If it had to be done, then it had to be done, he supposed.

But he wished they'd get on with it.

There was football to be played. Wedding cake to be eaten.

Life to be lived.

Right now.

* * * * *

A Father In
The Making

Ally Blake

Having once been a professional cheerleader, **Ally Blake**'s motto is "Smile and the world smiles with you." One way to make Ally smile is by sending her on holidays, especially to locations that inspire her writing. New York and Italy are by far her favorite destinations. Other things that make her smile are the gracious city of Melbourne, where she now lives, the gritty Collingwood football team and her gorgeous husband, Mark.

Reading romance novels was a smile-worthy pursuit from long back, so with such valuable preparation already behind her, she wrote and sold her first book. Her career as a writer also gives her a perfectly reasonable excuse to indulge in her stationery addiction. That alone is enough to keep her grinning every day!

Ally would love for you to visit her at her Web site www.allyblake.com

Books by Ally Blake

Dear Reader,

If you drive not so very far north of Melbourne, braving congested traffic and suburbia as far as the eye can see, you will eventually find yourself on a long winding road leading you to a whole new world.

Think wombat holes hidden in tall grass, fallen logs that double as homes to families of wild rabbits and yabby-filled dams, which are the haunts of families of gray kangaroos. From abundant hilltop farms, panoramic views reveal the smudge of the city skyline to the south, tracts of clear-cut green pastures to the west, distant eucalypt-scattered hills to the east and sweeping, burnt umber sunsets the likes of which you have never seen....

And though in my many visits to the region I have never met a Laura Somervale—singing her heart out to an audience of magpies as she hangs the washing on her wonky old clothesline—or seen such a magnificent property as Kardinyarr, nor a town quite like quirky Tandarah, the great Australian Outback hovering on the very edge of Melbourne offers inspiration enough to make them seem entirely possible!

Happy reading,

Ally

www.allyblake.com

To my friend Mel, for a trillion different reasons, with an extra hug thrown in for the loan of the gorgeous view from the corner of her desk way back at the beginning of all of this.

CHAPTER ONE

RYAN PULLED OFF the winding country road onto a long gravel driveway
and slowed his car to an idle. A weathered wooden sign at the turn read
Kardinyarr. He looked to the return address on the letter laid flat on the
passenger seat of his car. Youthful handwriting on lavender stationery,
dappled with fairies, smudged with tears, scrunched into a ball, and flattened again, told him that this was the place. Kardinyarr was where he
hoped against hope to find her. Though she had written the letter several years earlier, Ryan had only stumbled upon it that week, and it was
all he had to go on.

He gunned the engine, his tyres skipping and jumping over the uneven dirt track. He slowed again as a family of grey kangaroos bounced
at the same pace along the other side of the neat wire fence, before leaping onto the road, hopping in front of his car, and bounding up the rise
to his left and disappearing over the other side of the hill.

'Well, that's not something you see every day,' he said.

Ryan ignored the 'Private Road' sign at the first gate and drove up
the hill. At the fork in the drive he pulled left, coming to stop under a
sprawling banksia tree in the front yard of a rambling brick home.

The CD of a keynote speech he had given at a recent economic summit in London, an addendum to a university-level economics textbook
he was in the final stages of editing, came to a sharp halt as he switched

off the car engine. His mind otherwise engaged, he had barely heard a word of the familiar oration on the two-hour drive from Melbourne, but the deep well of silence that now filled the car was deafening.

So this was Kardinyarr House; the last home his little brother had known. Backlit by the light of the setting sun, proudly situated atop its windy hill, it was just as Will had described it all those years before. A black corrugated roof and matching shutters framed the clinker brick. A neat veranda laced with black wrought-iron trim hugged the house, rendering a pretty finish to the sturdy structure.

Ryan's recent hasty research told him it had been left vacant in the years since Will's passing, the foreign owners of the property keeping the acreage as an investment rather than an operating farm. As such, Ryan had expected scattered leaves, debris on the veranda, and obvious decay. However, the place seemed neat and tidy. Maintained. Welcoming.

Will had e-mailed the family when he had first arrived at Kardinyarr.

There is no place like it. The colour, the light. The fresh air gets under your skin.

Ryan opened the car door and took in a deep breath of clean country air. Will had been right. There was nothing quite like the mix of scents bombarding him—sweet pollens, swirling dust, and hazy country heat that seemed to have a scent all of its own. The acrid smell of car fumes that he'd left behind in Melbourne faded to a memory.

'Okay, Will,' Ryan said aloud. 'It's charming here. I get it. But so charming as to shoulder out all other options in your life?' Ryan shook his head.

Kardinyarr was meant to have been a brief stop on Will's winter back-packing trek around the country. But from the chain of information Ryan had uncovered in the last few days he believed that if his brother had not been killed, he might never have left at all. All because of the girl in the crumpled lavender letter.

Ryan grabbed the offending document, folded it carefully, and placed it in the top pocket of his shirt. He hopped out of the car, instinct caus-ing him to lock it. A wry smile tugged at his mouth. He hadn't seen an-other living soul for five kilometres, bar the kangaroos and a half-dozen cattle standing under the shade of a widebranched gum. *You can take the boy out of the city...*

The pleasant breeze tickling at his hair dropped suddenly, and he heard a noise coming from the other branch of the gravel drive. Opera. It had the sharp scratchy timbre of a record, and in the now still air it carried past him and beyond, echoing in the gullies either side of the hilltop. He swished a buzzing fly from his face and looked to the broken wooden gate that had long since been swallowed by lily pillies, climbing vines, and a lush Japanese maple.

On the other side of that gate he hoped to find the woman who had written that long-ago, tear-smudged letter. Perhaps she could tell him why his infuriating little brother had been offered the world, and refused it.

Laura's head bounced up and down in time with the music.

She loved days like these: a little cloud cover to take the edge off the summer heat, but not enough to stop the differentiation of light and shadow playing across the Kardinyarr hills. Once she had hung the washing, and finished dinner, she had a slot in her evening for a too hot bubble bath. The very thought had her happy as a kookaburra!

The record player was turned up loud enough to create a hanging-out-the-washing soundtrack. She hummed along with the orchestra and sang aloud in makeshift Italian to the magpies lined up on her roof gutters, tragic operatic hand movements and breast-thumping included. Okay, so she was no Pavarotti, but what did the magpies know?

Enough, it seemed, as soon they skedaddled, flying off in muddled formation to land in a gum tree further along the hill. 'Come on guys!' she shouted. 'You'll usually put up with a great deal when you know there's honeyed bread in it for you!'

The song finished, another began, and Laura went back to her chore. She grabbed a heavy white cotton sheet and lobbed it over the clothesline, thinking she would teach them a lesson. 'No honey on your bread today. So there!'

Ryan pushed his hands deep into his jeans pockets as he walked up the gravel drive.

Once, Will had e-mailed their sister, Sam.

I have never felt so alive. You guys have to come out here. You have to come and see what I mean. Only then will you understand why I plan to stay.

But they hadn't come. They had all been too busy. His sister Jen as first violin of the Sydney Symphony Orchestra. Sam with her young family and her selffunded quilting magazine, with its monthly worldwide readership in hundreds of thousands. And his parents, wildlife documentary film-makers, who spent all their time in faraway jungles.

Within a fortnight of that e-mail having been sent, Will had been buried back in their home town of Melbourne. It had been a drizzly winter's day, with a hundred people watching over him—or so Ryan had later been told.

Past the broken wooden gate and atop the short rise, a small transformed worker's cottage came into view. Multi-coloured flowers bordered the full-length portico, trying desperately to cling to life in the dry conditions. A water tank sat rust-free against the near wall. The fence was neat and the grass was short, but in need of rain. And through the white sheets flapping on the old-fashioned circular clothesline, Ryan caught sight of an ambiguous female form. *Laura Somervale.*

What would she be like, the woman for whom Will had given up an Oxford scholarship? Would she be quiet and bookish? Would she be artistic and soulful? Or would she simply be a girl? A country girl who had caught the eye of a lonely, mixed-up, directionless city boy? Would life have worn her down, or would there still be a glimmer of the girl with the fairy stationery? What sort of woman could make a Gasper turn his back on all that?

Some kind of woman, Ryan thought sardonically, for here she was, doing it again. She had drawn him out of his perfectly civilised world of five-star hotels and nightly political debate over cocktails, and into her world of dirt and heat and flies, with a page of tear-smudged words written many years before.

The circular clothesline turned and Ryan glimpsed a flash of sun-kissed auburn curls.

She's adorable. And sweet. She makes me laugh. She makes me feel ten feet tall. This is her home, and, as such, it feels like my home too.

A wry smile crossed Ryan's mouth. Will must have known exactly the response his realist big brother would have given to such poetic musings; which was why he had never let Ryan in on the exact nature of his feelings about the girl he'd met at Kardinyarr. Will had saved the deep and meaningful outpourings for their sister.

'Adorable' Ryan didn't need. Answers. Information. Reason. Those things he could tie off in a neat, contained system, once he'd closed the page on the question still buzzing in the back of his mind after all this time. *Why here, Will? Why?*

As Ryan neared, he realised that the woman behind the flapping white sheet was singing...almost. Occasionally the notes coming from her and the notes coming from the speakers matched, but due more to random luck than skill. It was unabashed, full-tilt, and indescribably terrible.

He slowed. Perhaps he ought to have called first. Meeting her like this would be like talking to someone with parsley caught in their teeth. Did you mention the fact and embarrass them? Or ignore it and pretend it wasn't there? As Ryan tussled with his decision, the woman pulled herself around the heavy damp sheet until she was revealed fully to him, and he couldn't have switched direction if a bushfire had sprung up between them.

Auburn curls twirled long and thick down her back, tied into a low loose ponytail with what looked like a pink shoelace. The setting sun shone straight through the cotton of her simple floral sundress, highlighting a longlimbed, youthful figure hidden beneath.

The wind picked up, whipping from out of the gully at the rear of the property and across the hilltop. It was enough to knock Ryan sideways, but the woman's feet remained steadfastly planted as she reached up to peg a pillowcase to the line. The wind blew about her knees, the thin fabric of her dress clinging to her. Her curling ponytail flapped in a horizontal line before sinking into a thick wave down her back when the wind settled.

She bent down to gather another sheet, one bare foot kicking out behind her for balance. As she came back upright she returned to full voice, head thrown back, hips swaying as the music reached a blazing crescendo.

'Now, how do you like that, Maggie?' she called out, turning on the spot, arms outstretched, her dress spinning high revealing a pair of smooth, tanned legs.

This was Laura Somervale? This vivacious creature was brooding Will's mystery dream girl? This happy-go-lucky woman had written words of honest, teardrenched pain and longing to a family she had never met?

It was suddenly too much. What had he been thinking of, jumping in the car with nothing more than an overnight bag and cannon-balling out to the middle of nowhere to find her? He should have used her example and written.

He stepped backwards, but the crunch of his riding boots on the gravelly earth sounded loud in the now still air. Like a hiker who had stumbled upon a scorpion, Ryan stopped still with one foot cocked against the ground.

The woman spun from the hips and stared him down with eyes the colour of the creamy-gold grass at her feet.

The afternoon sun shone into her face, casting a glow over her naturally bronzed skin. And, since his breath had long since escaped his lungs, Ryan said nothing as he returned her silent stare.

Laura held up a hand to shield her eyes from the setting sun as she looked over the stranger who had wandered unexpectedly onto her small patch of the world.

All thoughts of Pavarotti and too hot bubble baths slipped from her mind to make way for a pleasing combination of tight, dark curls and eyes as blue as the wideopen sky above. The stranger's shoulders were broad enough to carry a bale of hay, his long legs were encased in taut new denim, and strong muscled forearms appeared below the rolled-up arms of a new chambray shirt. There was even something faintly familiar about his steady blue gaze but, considering all the other visual enticements on offer, she couldn't put her finger on it. Either way, the gent was so nicely put together he could have been a poster boy for country living.

But parked under the banksia tree in front of big, beautiful, empty Kardinyarr House next door, was the gent's car. She had been singing so loud she hadn't even heard it arrive. The car was black, sporty and expensive, and covered in fresh dust. The dust made her smile. No matter that he wore the local uniform, and wore it extremely well, this guy was no local. Clothes too new. Car too flash. Haircut too neat. He had city boy written all over him. Laura was a born and bred country girl, so it was unlikely this guy had ever meandered through her life before.

So who is he? she wondered. Some lost tourist looking for directions?

Or a strip-o-gram organised by Jill, her friend and resident busybody? Ha! If only!

Nah, he's a salesman, she decided. In that flash car, with those trying-to-look-like-a-cowboy-clothes, he was equipped to charm his way into selling something to somebody. She then noticed the length of the stranger's shadow. Whatever he was selling, the sooner he was gone the better. The tiny window she had later in her day, time in which to soak in that too hot bubble bath, relax, maybe even read a chapter of the thriller that had been collecting dust on her bedside table, was slipping away the longer she dilly-dallied.

'Hello, there,' she singsonged.

He gave her a short nod, tipping his hand to an imaginary hat as he did so. *Ooh, too smooth.*

'Am I interrupting you?' he asked. His voice fitted the rest of him to perfection. Persuasive, elegant, and deep as the gully slipping away behind him.

'It's probably best you have,' she answered. 'Or I would never have had all this washing on the line before the sun sets.' *Hint, hint. I'm a busy woman with no time for salesmen, devastatingly handsome or otherwise...*

'You weren't talking to someone?' he asked, missing her point as he looked past her to find the elusive Maggie.

Her grin turned to a grimace. To be caught singing was one thing. To be caught talking to the birds was quite another. Living atop her beloved hill, she had been without daily adult contact for far too long. 'Only the magpies,' she admitted with a shrug, but naturally they had not remained in sight to prove her tale.

His deep blue eyes crinkled at the edges, hinting that a decent smile played thereabouts on occasion, but no smile creased his handsome face just yet. 'Do they talk back?'

'Not in so many words,' she said. 'But we have an understanding. They listen to me sing and I thank them with food. Honeyed bread is their culinary preference.'

'Ah, so you buy their affection?'

'It seems to be the only way I can get any nowadays.' *Oh, Laura, did you seriously just say that?* 'Any audience willing to listen to me sing—Puccini in particular,' she qualified. 'Not affection. I get plenty of affection without having to pay for it.'

Just shoot me where I stand, please, she begged anyone listening in to her thoughts. The intent gleam in the stranger's intense blue eyes had her gabbling. Or maybe it was the fact that most of the guys around those parts were wizened, bow-legged, and married, and this one seemed to be a very nice combination of anything but. Then again, perhaps it was the still distant possibility that the guy was a strip-o-gram that had her in a flap. *What the heck?* she thought. *I have the music going if he has the moves!*

Ryan was speechless. An in-demand public speaker, he modified the thinking of powerful people every day: politicians, special-interest groups, people a lot bigger and scarier than this auburn-haired spitfire.

Sweet? This woman was a heck of a lot more interesting than plain old sweet. Her eyes told the tale before she even opened her mouth— she was direct, sassy, and visibly attentive. But, then again, perhaps this wasn't Laura Somervale. Absurdly, Ryan's pulse quickened at the theory that perhaps this was a complete stranger, some glorious, undiscovered creature he had chanced upon all on his own.

And then he remembered the inflammatory letter burning a hole in his shirt pocket. Oh, this was she. This creature with her bare feet and tumbling curls was the girl who had spilled her broken heart onto girlish lavender paper. *Now who's being a poet? Come on, smart guy, stop delaying the inevitable and fess up,* his conscience implored. *Just tell her who you are and what you know.*

The woman's feet caught up with her hips as she turned fully to face him, and he saw that her spare hand gripped a set of little girl's pink overalls.

The words in the lavender letter, which until that moment had seemed somehow unreal, crystallised in that moment. A little girl. Ryan's heart thundered so hard his ears rang from the blood-rush. She had a little girl.

'So, now that you have been witness to me embarrassing myself on several levels,' the woman said, 'I'm sure you can find it in yourself to tell me what you're doing here.'

'I came by way of Tandarah,' he said, evading the question, needing the extra time to control his breathing again. 'The woman who runs the Upper Gum Tree Hotel sent me here.'

Suddenly the strip-o-gram fantasy was not nearly so ridiculous after all. Laura felt her cheeks warm. She even had to clear her throat. 'Jill Tucker?' she said. 'Short silver hair? Mischievous gleam in the eye?'

The man nodded. 'She sent me up here as I'm looking for Laura Somer-vale.'

Well, if he was a salesman he was exceedingly customer-specific. Laura dropped the hand shielding her eyes long enough to swish it about, presenting herself to him like a prize on a game show. 'Well, now you've found me what are you going to do with me?'

When he didn't answer straight away, simply watching her with that relentless, memorable blue gaze, Laura did as she was wont to do when faced with an unsettling silence. She stumbled in with both feet a-tapping.

'Have I won the Lotto?' she asked. When he still didn't flinch, she blundered on. 'No? Well, I don't need aluminium siding on the house, I only buy the local weekly newspaper, and I am perfectly happy with my long-distance phone plan—especially since everyone I know lives hereabouts.'

His slow blink proved he was selling none of the above. But a curious smile kicked at the corner of the wannabe-cowboy's lips. Just as she'd expected, it was an engaging smile, a tempting smile, and a smile that gave her heart-rate an entirely satisfying kick.

Laura changed her mind about the salesman angle and decided her run of bad luck had ended and God was offering her one big, juicy payback in the form of a dashing man. Instruction sheet attached—feed three square meals a day, does have expensive tastes, but likes to give back rubs and draw too hot bubble baths three times per week.

'Now, this has been a fun way to spend the last few minutes,' she said, 'but why don't you put me out of my misery and just tell me what I can do for you?'

He swallowed, shifting his weight until it was evenly distributed on both shiny new riding boots. 'Ms Somervale, my name is Ryan. Ryan Gasper. I am Will Gasper's brother. I know it's been a long time coming, but I have come in response to your letter.'

Laura watched in stunned silence as in seeming slow motion he pulled a crumpled piece of lavender notepaper from the pocket over his heart and held it towards her. 'I have come to find out if what you wrote in your letter is true. Are you the mother of Will's child?'

Ryan Gasper, Laura repeated in her mind. *Wannabe cowboy, city gent, heaven-in-a-pair-of-blue-jeans is Ryan Gasper!*

Her mind went over all fuzzy, as her memories skipped and tumbled back through the years to the last time that name had been foremost in her mind…

She stood, sheltered, hidden by a weeping willow, a good twenty metres behind the congregation at the edge of the cemetery, feeling like Alice gone through the looking glass.

In her pale pink sundress and her borrowed tweed coat, her pink headband holding back her mass of curls, which had gone wild in the drizzly Melbourne weather, she felt out of her depth, like a kid playing dress-up, hoping the adults wouldn't notice she didn't really belong.

The hundred-odd people huddled together against the cold were a who's who of the Australian social set. Even she, a girl from the bush, recognised the multitude of television personalities and politicians alike. They were all dressed up in glamorous black, in hats, in designer sunglasses. The only hat Laura had ever owned was a twenty-year-old Akubra of her father's, bumped and bruised by years of wear while working the land.

Standing apart from the throng, she clutched a letter in her cold hand: a letter laboured over, cried over, written longhand, on stationery she had received a couple of years before on her sixteenth birthday. Fairies danced in the top corner of the page and hid behind toadstools along the bottom rim. She hadn't really paid attention when writing on it; she had only given in to the burning need to get her despairing words onto paper.

She rested a protective arm across her flat belly. It would not be flat for much longer. Talk between the young mothers in Tandarah came back to her. Stretch marks. Bladder problems. Varicose veins. She was eighteen, for goodness' sake! How had her life turned so completely in the last two months that she had ended up here?

But what choice did she have? What with both her parents gone, these people were the only family her child would know—this overwhelming, well-to-do, influential, formidable group of people standing watching over the casket of heavy wood that contained their son, their brother.

Through gaps between the sea of black coats, Laura watched as the casket slowly sank into the rain-drenched ground. From nowhere, the disturbing strains of a solo violin wafted over the gloomy scene, and her heart grew so heavy with sorrow she could barely breathe.

Will. Dear, sweet Will. He had been so unassuming. So gentle. So uncomplicated. One would never have guessed that he came from such a family. But in the last few days she had found out the truth of it. She had read the small notices of condolence in every newspaper in the country. Devoured them. Clipped them and kept them in a precious shoebox beneath her bed back home. Somehow it had helped her live outside of herself, outside of the poignant realisation that she was pregnant, and that the father of her unborn child had been killed before he even knew.

Laura made an effort to place as many of the mourners as she could—anything to take her mind off the weight in her heart. The violinist had to be one of the sisters—Jen. The younger of the sisters, Samantha, was very pregnant herself, and married to a television actor. Will's parents, the elegant couple standing either side of the minister, were award-winning film-makers.

But where was the elusive elder brother? The one Will talked about more than the rest. Ryan. The workaholic perennial wanderer, the oft-published, world-renowned economist who travelled the world at the whim of foreign governments in order to advise them on economic policy. Will's hero.

The family moved forward, each to throw a blood-red rose atop Will's coffin, but no young man came forward with Will's sisters and parents. As far as Laura could tell, illustrious big-brother Ryan was not there.

She had come this far, catching a bus, a train and a tram, alone, to get there, to be present when her young friend was lowered into the ground. Ryan Gasper had the means, the money, and the time. How could a man not move heaven and earth to be at his own brother's funeral? And how could Laura bring her only child into a family such as that? So scattered. So civilised. So impenetrable.

Laura looked to the letter in her hand, now crunched into a tight ball in her shaking palm. She smoothed it out again and slipped it deep into the pocket of her borrowed coat. She would post the letter on the way back to Tandarah, and then it would be up to them to make the next move.

'Until then,' she whispered, her words forming a cloud of steam in the chill winter air. 'I think it's fair to say it's just you and me, possum.'

Eighteen years old, and all alone in the world bar the tiny speck of life inside of her, Laura turned and walked away without looking back...

Ryan watched Laura's warm, open face slowly crumble and turn paper-white. She didn't move, didn't blink, and didn't even seem to notice when the pink overalls left her limp hand and fluttered to the dusty ground.

'You're *Will's* brother?' she whispered, her previously chirpy voice now thin and faraway. Wisps of dappled hair had fallen from their restraint and curled across her forehead. Without all the bluster and noise she suddenly looked very frail. Delicate. And terribly young. He took a step her way, for fear she might swoon.

'Ms Somervale?'

She made no move, as though she had not heard him. 'Laura? Are you all right?'

When she swallowed, her lips trembled. Then her haunted gaze locked in on the letter in his still outstretched hand. Her hand flew to her mouth and her teeth clamped down on the length of her index finger. Ryan knew not if she was stopping herself from crying out or biting down hard to cover up a deeper pain elsewhere inside of her. And then, just when Ryan was about to reach out and gather her against him—anything to stop the unnerving trembling that he had caused—she did the incredible: she managed to muster up a smile.

'You're Will's brother,' she repeated, and this time it was a shaky statement, not a question. 'Ryan. The economist, right? I'm sorry I didn't recognise you. Will never did carry pictures of any of you. And you weren't at his funeral.'

Did that mean she had been? He'd had no idea. His family must not have either. Astonishing. She had been in their midst all those years before, and none of them had known. 'Ms Somervale, I'm not here to cause you or your...family any trouble. I've come because...'

Why had he come? To find the child she had written to the Gaspers about in her letter? Absolutely. But after that he was running on gut instinct alone.

He reached down slowly, so as not to startle her, and picked up the pink overalls. 'I need to know, Ms Somervale.' He handed them back to her and saw understanding dawn upon her face.

She took a great breath, as though gathering her scattered trains of thought, nodded, and her bottomless golden eyes fluttered back up to meet his. 'The Upper Gum Tree,' she said, coming out of some sort of trance. 'The hotel in town where you met Jill Tucker. Six o'clock tonight.'

Before he even had the chance to ask her what made the Upper Gum Tree at six o'clock so special, a voice called out from deep within the cottage.

'Mu-u-um!'

'Coming, possum!' she called back, her flashing eyes begging that he keep his attention on her and nowhere else. But it was a hopeless demand as suddenly the owner of the pink overalls and the shouting voice came skipping out of the cottage.

The crackling record, the whisper of the breeze, even the vibrant vision of a barefoot Laura Somervale slipped away as every ounce of Ryan's being focused on the little girl. She had Laura's oval face, healthy glow, and dishevelled curls. But the Gasper traits were unmistakable. The intelligent blue eyes. The square jaw. Even the way she bit at the inner corner of her mouth was a habit his sisters had never overcome.

There was no longer any doubt in Ryan's mind. Laura Somervale had given life to his brother's child.

The little girl was holding a crayon drawing in her hand, and she stopped short when she saw that her mother was not alone. 'Mum?' This time her voice was not so resolute.

Laura's glance flicked towards the little girl, her voice neutral. 'Go back inside, Chloe.'

Chloe. Ryan spun the name around his mind several times. *Chloe Gasper. No, surely not. Chloe Somervale.* 'Get Chimp's dinner ready. I won't be long. Okay?' No matter that she was trying desperately to sound all right, they heard the strain in her voice. Chloe nodded, and looked over at Ryan. He gave her his best effort at a friendly smile, but her face creased into an uncertain frown before she hustled back inside.

'Please, Mr Gasper,' Laura said, her own voice firming with each word. 'Meet me at the Upper Gum Tree Hotel at six tonight. We can talk there.'

And then she turned and walked away, leaving Ryan with little choice but to do as she asked.

Feeling Ryan Gasper's now staggeringly familiar gaze burning into her back, Laura picked up her washing basket, spun on her numb feet and hurried inside, the smile she had fashioned fast sliding into oblivion.

Will's brother had come, and he had her letter. No wonder she'd thought she had seen him somewhere before. He didn't look at all like Will, who had been barely nineteen, lean and lanky, with streaky blond hair when she had known him. But the something that had tugged at her subconscious was the fact that his deep, dark eyes were as vividly blue as her own daughter's.

In the intervening years since Will's funeral she had never heard back from his family, reasonably deducing that they either didn't believe her, wanted nothing to do with her, or simply didn't care. Truth be told, the more years that went by, the more that suited her just fine. But now here *he* was. The dashing, determined, older brother Will had yearned to equal, to emulate and, on the flipside, to disoblige as much as humanly possible. The brother who had not even deigned to show up at his funeral.

Laura shook her head to clear the returning fuzz. None of that mattered now. What mattered was that the time had come for Laura to share her darling little girl. He had said he wasn't there to cause her any trouble. Maybe. Maybe not. If he thought for a second that he could take Chloe away...

Laura's chest tightened as adrenalin kicked in. No matter how cool and self-assured Ryan Gasper's voice was, no matter how bewitching his gaze, how tempting his smile, or how Will had worshipped him, she didn't trust him as far as she could throw him. This was too important. The way she handled this, the way she handled him, would be *the* most important situation of her life.

'Mum!' Chloe called again. She bundled into the room, her strawberry-blonde ringlets pulled back into messy pigtails. 'Who was that man?'

'A friend,' Laura said, taking care how she approached the subject with Chloe. She instinctively chose not to create any sort of preconceived image of him. She had always taught Chloe to make up her own mind about people, not to listen to gossip.

She dumped the basket of wet clothes, with the dusty, dirty overalls splayed across the top, sat on the couch, tugged her daughter onto her lap, and held on tight. Too tight. Thankfully, Chloe didn't struggle away as she sometimes did when Laura became *mushy*.

'Now, what have you got there, possum?' Laura asked, her voice running on back-up power.

'I have to draw a picture of my family for school.' Chloe held out her crayon drawing of a house, a couple of animals, and a trio of people. 'I have you and me, Chimp and Irmela,' she said, referring to their pet fox terrier and overweight jersey cow respectively. 'And Jill is at the front gate. Is that enough?'

It always has been enough until now, Laura thought. 'I don't think you've missed anybody.'

'Well, Tammy is putting in all of her cousins. Even the ones who live in Scotland.' Chloe twisted on her lap to look her in the eye. 'Do I have any cousins in Scotland?'

Laura opened her mouth to say no, of course she didn't, but then she thought of the man in the black shiny car. Chloe might very easily have cousins all over the world, for all she knew.

From the moment Laura had posted her letter she had put the shoebox full of old clippings about Will under her bed, and had quite specifically *not* gone out of her way to hear about the Gasper family. But it seemed the time had come for her to peek at the world outside of her community, to find out about Chloe's extended family—and she had until six o'clock to figure out how to go about it.

Well, she had until six o'clock to finish the laundry, cook dinner, check Chloe's homework, finish the pies for the Country Women's Association meeting that night, *and* to figure out how she was going to handle the arrival of Ryan Gasper. The too hot bubble bath was so far down the list it dropped and fell away.

Once Chloe was ensconced back at the desk in her bedroom, Laura picked up the phone and dialled the Upper Gum Tree Hotel. When Jill answered the phone she all but blubbed with relief. 'Jill, it's Laura. We have a problem. I need you to set aside a table for me, and I need it to be discreet.'

CHAPTER TWO

THE UPPER GUM tree hotel bustled with activity. Barflies lounged at the bar. Families conversed at a smattering of snug round dining tables. Local teenagers played snooker. And Ryan sat all on his lonesome in a secluded high-walled booth at the back of the room.

By the time six o'clock came and went he was onto his second beer and a young boy at the next table had taken a liking to him. The kid continued to stare over the top of the booth, and Ryan had no idea how to get rid of him.

He'd never had much experience dealing with kids. He had been nine years old when Will was born, and in boarding school by the time Will was three. By the time Ryan had left for university and beyond, they had spent little time together; Will, so quiet and shy, and intensely studious, had been practically a stranger to him. And to Jen's and Sam's kids he was merely cool Uncle Ryan, who brought presents whenever he came back from overseas.

But now he had another niece—a walking, talking remembrance of his little brother—and for some reason he felt an obligation to get to know this one properly. Half of him was energised by the prospect, and the other half wanted to wring Laura Somervale's pretty little neck for not trying harder to track his family down.

What reason could she possibly have for telling them about the little girl and then never contacting them again? It would have made more sense if she had never tried to contact them at all. It didn't add up, and as a guy who worked with checks and balances he planned to stick around at least until it did.

Perhaps she had simply found herself a new father for her daughter in the meantime. A strange sort of uncomfortable heat formed in Ryan's gut as he realised that she could even be married. Affianced. Living with someone. He hadn't counted on having to get through another man as well as Ms Somervale. He dearly hoped that he still wouldn't have to. Either way, if Laura Somervale didn't show in the next five minutes he was heading back out to the little weatherboard worker's cottage and he wasn't leaving until he had his answers.

Ryan gave in and crossed his eyes back at the kid who was still staring him down. He poked his tongue out and even added a humped back for good measure.

'So, did you find our Laura all right?' a female voice asked. Ryan uncrossed his eyes to find a short, round lady with boyish grey hair and bright button eyes leaning against the edge of the booth, beaming down at him. Jill Tucker. He had a feeling the woman knew exactly how he had found Laura, and what had transpired word for word.

'Yes, thanks,' he assured her with an unadorned smile. 'She was right where you told me she would be.'

'Of course she was,' she said, and her own smile grew larger. 'She's lived there since she was born. A dear girl, Laura. Would do anything to help any of us in a pickle, and if anyone ever dared to hurt her, or her little possum, they would have to deal with the rest of our town as well. Can I get you something to eat while you wait?'

Ryan blinked. It seemed Miss Somervale was not the only one who could so adeptly change tack mid-spiel.

Perhaps the idiosyncrasy could even be considered part of the local dialect.

'I'm happy with my beer,' he said. 'Thanks, anyway.' Jill gave him a sympathetic smile before moving on to the next table. Before he even had the chance to take another sip, he was struck by the intoxicating scent of freshly baked apple pie. He had a famously sweet tooth, and the scent was so delicious he actually sniffed the air as a pair of cake boxes slid across his bench. In their wake came Laura Somervale. He was fairly sure it was her...

Gone were the messy curls, pulled back under a red bandana, and the graceful cotton dress had been replaced with an excessively frilly white shirt. She looked over her shoulder at the little boy peering over the next booth. 'Liam, your dessert is getting cold.'

The little boy disappeared from sight. Just like that. Wow. He would have to remember that trick. As she sat, Ryan opened his mouth to ask why she had gone to such trouble to dress in disguise, but when their eyes met he was rendered speechless yet again by the most startling difference from her earlier appearance. The sexiest dark smudges of eyeliner framed her pale brown eyes, making them glitter like gold. A searing flash of awareness overcame him. Had the flash come from him or from her?

'Sorry I'm late,' she said, her voice as crisp and curt with him as it had been with the little boy, Liam, and he figured any sort of responsiveness had been his alone. 'I had to get Chloe settled in at a friend's place first.'

So she hadn't left Chloe at home. She had sequestered her away somewhere unknown. No matter how promising her words, how valiant her smile, this woman was not as calm and trusting as she made out.

'So there's no one else at home who could have looked after her tonight? Your husband, perhaps?'

Laura coughed out a sorry laugh. 'Hardly,' she said, flapping a ring-free hand under his chin. 'Chloe and I are perfectly happy on our own.'

And, just like that, the uncomfortable lump in Ryan's mid-section faded away.

'Where are you staying?' she asked, shifting her weight on the soft leather seat.

'I have a room upstairs.'

'Nice?' she asked, still not looking him in the eye. 'Not sure. I haven't seen it yet. I came straight here from your place.'

'Oh, I just can't stand this,' she said suddenly, scrunching her eyes tight and banging her fists on the old wooden table.

Ryan's hands zoomed out to catch his glass of beer and stop it from overturning.

'I'm not bred for small talk,' she said, her voice earnest, her expression pleading. 'I'll be honest. Your being here scares the living daylights out of me.'

Ryan tried to disregard the divine scent of apples and sugar, and something else—an unexpectedly exotic perfume wafting from the direction of the woman in the equally exotic costume. 'You have no reason to fear me, Laura.'

'I have every reason!' She snapped her mouth shut, her fists closing tight atop the table. She seemed to collect herself, to temper her anguish. When she looked back at him from beneath her smoky lashes he knew she had found the calm in the eye of the storm.

'I had no brothers or sisters,' she continued, her voice now more controlled, though a tiny vibration gave her away. 'I have no aunts or cousins, distant or otherwise.

I understand that there are other people out there who are family to Chloe. You. You are her family. As such, you are the answer to her very dreams. And at least a very tiny, small but noisy part of me is relieved that you have finally come. But, at the same time, you also represent *my* very greatest fear. Losing her.'

Her anxious words brought about the image of tear stains on lavender paper, and he found it hard not to stare as he reconciled the heartfelt prose on that page with the plucky woman three feet from him now. Her honesty in that letter had amazed him, even while the news shocked him. Several years on, she was just as unwilling or unable to hold back her feelings as she had been then, and just as able to surprise him in person as she had been in print.

'I need to know your intentions,' she said. 'I can take it. I might not like it, but I can take it.'

His intentions? It was such an old-fashioned term but, coming from this wide-eyed country girl, it fitted. Though it made him feel like a rogue, he gave her the only truth he could. 'I don't exactly know.'

Her golden eyes glinted back at him in the low light. 'You're going to have to give me more than that if you think we can take this matter further.'

'What more do you want?'

'Proof that you are as nervous as I am.' She leaned forward, pinning him with her candid stare. 'I am an even mix of morbid embarrassment and stiff terror right now. When you wandered up onto my property, in your clean shirt and your new jeans, you must know I didn't for a second expect you to be…well, you. If you had, in fact, been a male stripper it would have shocked me less.'

'A male what?'

Laura bit her lip to stop herself from saying anything else she oughtn't. She filtered back through all the things she had mentally accused him of being, including an aluminium cladding salesman, but, no, the male stripper idea she had managed to keep to herself. Until now. She fluffed a hand over her face to try and divert him from her terminal case of foot-in-mouth disease.

She did want Chloe to meet her uncle. *Really* she did. For Chloe's sake how could she not? She was trying to think outside of her own selfish desire to keep her contented little existence intact because the big picture of Chloe's life meant so much more. Even though none of his superstar family had ever cared enough to write, to call, or to ask if Chloe was okay, she had to give him a chance. But, even so, there was a noisy little voice in her head that told her that *he* in particular was dangerous. Not cruel. Not insensitive to her fears. But somehow dangerous to her precariously balanced contentment. For a girl who felt as though a wonderful life was never quite within her grasp, she had no idea how to deal with a perpetual winner like the one seated before her.

'Stick to the subject, Mr Gasper. Why now? Why after all this time have you come?'

'*Your* letter brought me here, Ms Somervale.'

Her cheeks warmed as she thought of the words she had written in that letter. The words of a hormoneriddled, deeply sad, terrified, lonely and desperate teenager. But before she had a chance to ask to see the letter, which of course she would shovel into her mouth, chew and swallow so that no one else would ever know it existed, a shadow passed over the table. She looked up to find a man in dark trousers and a grey pullover smiling down at them.

'Hi, there, Father Grant,' she said, saving her request for when they were alone again. She glanced over at Ryan and had no idea how to introduce him. Friend? Hardly. Chloe's uncle? She could barely believe it herself, much less say it aloud. Male stripper in the making? Now, that would probably cause less gossip in town than any of the other options on offer!

'Dress rehearsal tonight, Laura?' Father Grant asked. Laura only then remembered her get-up. Oh, Lord! While Mr Perfect sat there looking so flawless, in his blue button-down shirt that did distracting things to his bluer than blue eyes, *she* was decked out in a mass of white frills and tight purple pants, with knee-high black boots jiggling skittishly below the table.

'Pirates of Penzance,' she blurted, for Ryan's benefit, flicking at a ruffle. 'The Country Women's Association is putting on the musical and I am playing the Pirate King.'

Ryan must have thought she was utterly insane, coming to meet him in such a get-up. And for singing to magpies. And for batting her eyelids at a stranger while all on her own out in an isolated Outback property... If he *were* intent on finding reasons to take her daughter away, he would surely have the beginnings of a list already.

'Isn't that a singing part?' Ryan asked. Father Grant nodded. 'It is.'

Laura saw Father Grant shoot Ryan an ironic smile, and she all but harrumphed in response.

'The musical was all Laura's idea,' Father Grant continued. 'The local CWA are raising money for drought aid for local farmers who have been hit pretty hard over the last couple of years. Last year they did *Chicago*, and Laura's Matron Mama Morton brought down the house!'

'I'll bet it did,' Ryan said.

Laura didn't need to look at him to know that his face would be the picture of disbelief at Father Grant's kind words. She kept her head down as she picked at a flake of old paint on the tabletop.

'Our Laura is involved with numerous community projects,' Father Grant continued. 'She is President of the PTA and a volunteer firefighter, as well as infamous for undercharging for catering every event we throw in town. I don't know what we would do without her. Or little Chloe. They are family to all of us. We've just up and adopted them since Laura's dear father passed—haven't we, Laura?'

'Of course, Father Grant. You're the best.'

'Now, I'd better be off. Enjoy your meal.' He shot them a parting smile and Laura let out a shaky breath, thankful she had not had to introduce her companion.

'He seemed nice,' Ryan said. 'He certainly had a lot of good things to say about you.'

Laura brushed the praise away. 'Mr Gasper, if we keep beating around the bush like this I am likely to explode on the spot. Mr Gasper—'

'Call me Ryan, please.'

There was something in his voice, something low and intimate, that had her forgetting what she had been talking about in the first place. 'I just…' She took a moment to swallow. 'I know that this moment had to come. I only wonder why, seven years after the fact, that silly little letter of mine has sent you out looking for us.'

'I only just found your letter, Laura,' he explained. 'A couple of days ago. As the fates would have it, your letter never came to our attention at the time in which you sent it.'

Oh, God! Had they truly never known about her? About Chloe? She had never, not even once, thought that might be the reason why they had not come looking for her.

'I'm back in Australia for an extended stay for the first time in years,' he continued. 'At my family's request I have been cleaning up Will's effects. Seven years having passed since Will…died, no financial records need be kept any more. I discovered your letter unopened in amongst the great host of condolence letters.'

'Unopened?' Laura repeated, still coming to terms with Ryan's bombshell.

'At the time, my family received so many condolence letters—from friends, acquaintances, readers of my sister's magazine, fans of my parents' documentary films, even many of your neighbours. My family read as many as they could, but after a couple of weeks found they couldn't keep up. It was too much. Too hard. In the end they posted a half-page thank-you note in the *Australian* newspaper to all who had Will in their thoughts.'

Laura noticed Ryan's dulcet voice was unnaturally even. Though he held eye contact with her the whole time, the poor man was struggling just as she was with the situation. Nevertheless, she fought back the desire to take his fisted hand in hers, to unpeel his tightly clenched fingers and rub some warmth back into them.

'Mum and Dad went back to Brunei to finish the film they were working on,' he said. 'Jen was already back on a musical tour of the United States. And Sam had just had her second child and couldn't cope with the task. All of Will's correspondence was forwarded to our family accountant, who kept on track with bills and tax correspondence, and simply filed everything else. When cleaning out the files this week I found one folder with several unopened letters. Including yours.'

Laura realised he hadn't included himself in the list of people available to read the letters and look after the formalities. Where *had* he been when his family had needed him? she wondered. Why hadn't he been at the funeral? But she heard the steady thread of regret in his voice that he was trying so hard to mask. So she let it go. 'And...and your family?' she asked, when she found her voice again. 'Your sisters and parents? Do they know about me?'

'Only Sam. She was with me when I found your letter, and would have come too if not for having three kids under ten herself. As to the others, no. Not yet. We thought it better to find out if you had—'

He stopped, and for the first time was discomfited enough to look away.

'If I had gone through with the pregnancy?' she finished for him, biting down the bitter taste the very thought brought. But it wasn't his fault. He was only being honest. 'And now that you know that I did?'

He looked back at her, the deep, steady blue gaze creating patches of warmth on her skin wherever it touched.

'Well, now I think it would be best for Chloe to get used to me first,' he said, 'before the whole Gasper gang descends upon her. We can be formidable as a united front.'

A tiny portion of the tension in Laura's shoulders eased. Surely, if that was his ultimate plan, he would have brought the might of the Gasper clan down on her with a vengeance? It seemed there was a streak of compassion within the self-assured outer shell.

The bell over the door jingled as a group of chattering women in pirate garb jumbled into the restaurant. Their beady, kohl-smudged eyes searched the restaurant.

Ryan felt the chance to get to his own questions slipping away. Somehow, with her smoky eyes and bold honesty, her bare feet and knee-high boots, her glossy curls and red bandana, she had managed again and again to keep the conversation as one-sided as she pleased. She had found out his side of the story and he still knew nothing of hers. He wondered if it was entirely accidental, or whether, despite all her *I really want you to meet Chloe* promises, she would be happier if that never eventuated at all.

'That lot are looking for me,' Laura said. 'I'm sorry to leave this hanging mid-air, but I do have to go.'

She stood, and he grabbed her hand. 'So when do I get to meet her?' he asked.

Laura stared at their entwined fingers for a few moments before her glittery golden eyes swung to face him, her head cocked to one side.

'Chloe,' he clarified. 'When do I get to meet her properly? I hoped that was what this secret meeting was all about.'

'Half the town is at this restaurant, Mr Gasper,' she said. 'This meeting is hardly a secret.' He knew then that she was wilfully misunderstanding him. Her obstructiveness was no accident. Behind the pretty eyes, this woman's mind had not stopped ticking all night.

If he could figure a way through her labyrinthine thinking, maybe he would end up on her side rather than three steps behind. At least now he knew what made the Upper Gum Tree Hotel at six o'clock on a Sunday night so special. She'd figured that if he was going to make demands, she would have *half the town* as witnesses.

'Well, obviously my presence here is not a secret. Why else would I have had people lining up to give you glowing testimonials?'

She made to protest, then seemed to realise what Father Grant's speech had been about. So that at least hadn't been her doing. A soft blush crept across her cheeks—a pretty blush, seriously becoming, distracting enough for him to forget what he was accusing her of in the first place. 'That had nothing to with me,' she said, giving his hand a light tug. 'Though I have some idea who to blame.'

Realising her hand was still in his, he let go, the feel of smooth skin slipping across his palm momentarily unsettling. *Enough!* he scolded himself. He stood, determined to get them back on an even footing.

'It's a meeting secreted away from the one person for whom the meeting is most important,' he said, his voice stern and implacable. 'Make a time. Set a date. Now. Or I may decide not to believe all your promises that you do want me to meet Chloe. How about tomorrow morning?'

She blinked, and he saw the moment her ticking mind switched into overdrive. 'Tomorrow is Monday. She has school.'

'What about after school?'

'Pony club. Then violin practice.'

Violin. Just like Jen. She had known he was an economist. Did she know about Jen, too? Could that have prompted the choice of instrument? The thought warmed him more than he thought sensible. 'And dinner time?' he asked, determined not to let her sway the conversation again.

'She has homework. And her bedtime is eight o'clock.'

She was relentless. He bit back a smile.

'Soon,' she promised, obviously realising as much herself. 'But on my terms. She's a cluey kid, outrageously bright, and even more sensitive for it. We need to tread carefully.'

He nodded. She could have been describing Will at Chloe's age. 'So when?'

The twittering sound of pirate-garbed women grew louder behind him, and when Laura all but melted with relief he knew he was too late. 'Saved by your merry men,' he said under his breath, and she had the good grace to blush even more.

'Laura!' one of the women called out. 'If you're not ready to rehearse we could grab a quick shandy?'

'No, no, no. I'm done here,' Laura said, moving into the protective haven of the colourful group.

'Laura is such a darling,' one of the ladies said out of the blue. 'I can't read so well any more, so she always helps me with my lines.'

Ryan had a feeling she had been *helped* with her current lines as well. 'Does she, now?' he asked, unable to stop the smile tugging at his mouth.

'I was overseas last spring when my daughter fell ill,' another said, after getting a nudge in the ribs. 'And, even though spring is the worst time for Chloe and her asthma, she and Laura made the long trip via my daughter's house every day to get her little ones to school.'

Ryan could tell Laura wanted to slap a hand across each of their mouths, but she just stood back and let them vent. It reminded him of a passage from one of Will's e-mails to Sam, which she had shared with him when they were going through Will's papers:

The people here are amazing, Sam. Kind, generous, selfless, opinion-ated, and meddlesome! You can't scratch your nose without somebody know-ing about it. And you can be sure that within the day everyone in town will know about it too. I thought it might be infuriating, but it's not. It means that there are people who care about you. So, no matter how far away we all actually live from one another, we know that we are never really alone.

It seemed that Will had been right on the money. The town knew exactly who *he* was, and had turned up in force to make sure he knew exactly who Laura was too.

'Our Laura is an angel,' the ringleader said. 'Esme, seriously, that's enough,' Laura murmured.

'From what I have heard tonight,' Ryan butted in, 'I would say sainthood is not far away.'

The ladies all grinned back at him, knowing they had all successfully played their parts in the night's hastily organised small play.

'Will you be coming to see the musical?' Esme asked. 'You never know your luck,' he responded with a wink, and with that the three grey-haired pirates left in a twitter, and he and Laura were again left alone in the room full of people. 'So,' he said.

'So,' she returned. 'I'd better go after them. If I'm not there within a minute they'll be back for shandies. And their husbands will all be onto me first thing in the morning complaining that the play is just a front for the Country Women's *Drinking* Association.'

She reached over and grabbed her cooling apple pies, turned and walked away. It seemed their meeting was over.

'Isn't the Pirate King a male part as well as a singing part?' he called out curiously, not yet wanting the encounter to end.

Laura spun on her knee-high black boots but kept walking away from him. 'Not so many males in the Country Women's Association,' she explained.

'Isn't that discriminatory?'

'So join!' she said, throwing out her hands. 'Be my guest. You can even take my part.' She tore off the bandana and a mass of auburn curls spilled onto her shoulders. She fluttered the bandana towards him, and when he didn't accept the offer she spun about and walked away.

'I'll see *you* tomorrow,' Ryan warned.

'I don't doubt it,' she called, as she waved the bandana over her shoulder and headed out of a side door, slamming it behind her.

Ryan stood staring into space. The image of those tight purple pants would take some time to dissolve from his memory. But all he had was time. For the first time in...for ever he had nothing planned: no jobs lined up, no reports to complete, only the final edits on the textbook with the complementary CD to turn in to his editor. He slid back into the booth and nursed his now warm beer. Chatter and laughter from the other patrons filtered back into his awareness. And he was left...wanting.

The last sentence of Will's e-mail to Sam came back to him.

...no matter how far away we all actually live from one another, we know that we are never really alone.

Had his brother really felt so alone in the great hustle and bustle of Melbourne? Had he needed his scattered family around him that much? And had living around these people really made all the difference?

Ryan remembered the last time he and Will had spoken, and tried to see if he had missed the signs of Will's isolation even then...

Ryan's hotel room phone rang. He was on his way to a black-tie function in the piazza in front of the Pantheon in Rome. He thought about not answering, but a quick glance at his watch showed he had time.

'Ryan Gasper,' he answered.

'This is a collect call from Tandarah, Australia,' the operator said in English, with a strong Italian accent.

'I'll accept,' Ryan said, slumping down onto the side of his bed. 'Will, is that you?'

'Yeah.' His little brother breathed out.

'Excellent. So, are you coming? I'm off to Paris in three days, so I can just meet you there. My PA back in Melbourne is ready to book everything the second you say yes.'

'Well, actually, bro,' Will said, his voice so heavy and glum Ryan pretty much knew what was coming before he even spoke, 'that's what I was calling about. I'm not coming.'

Ryan rubbed his hand across suddenly tight eyes. 'You can't possibly tell me you've had a better offer.'

'Actually, I have.'

For the briefest of moments Ryan's heart skipped a beat. 'You've taken the scholarship offer at Oxford?'

'Umm, no. You see, there's this girl...'

Ryan leapt off the bed and strode back and forth across the room, as far as the telephone cord would allow. 'Will, do we have to have this conversation again? You don't know how good you have it, kid. I don't know how many more times any

of us can stick our necks out for you. You can't keep turning away the opportuni-
ties we have created for you.'

'But, bro, this is an opportunity I have created for myself.'

'Considering who you are, I would hazard a guess she is the opportunist in
this scenario.'

'That's way harsh, bro, and so far off the mark it's funny. Maybe you should
give up the Paris thing and come visit me instead. Meet her. See this place. It's
phenomenal.'

'Be serious.'

Will's exasperation broke through. 'God, you just don't get it, do you? I can
never be you! Out here I feel like I don't have to be, either. I can be somebody new.
Somebody I like.'

The red light on Ryan's phone began to flash. His taxi was waiting downstairs.
'Look, Will, I have to go. Just tell me you're still considering Paris, okay?'

A deep heartfelt sigh wafted down the phone line. 'Sure,' Will said. 'Okay.'

'I'll talk to you again in a couple of days, and by that time I hope to hear bet-
ter news. Take care.'

Ryan hung up the phone, his whole body thrumming with frustration. It hurt
so much that the kid was letting this time slip through his fingers. The last thing
he wanted was for his little brother to look back on his wasted youth with regret.
He should have been studying, travelling, networking, embracing the world—not
some hick chick in the middle of the Outback.

He picked up his keys, slipped his wallet into the hidden pocket in his tuxedo
jacket and left. Next week. Next week when he was in Paris he would call him
back and try to talk some more sense into the kid.

Of course by that stage Will would probably be done with the whole farming
dream. He would have become bored with the girl and decided to become a fire-
stick twirler in Byron Bay.

Tremendous...

Coming back to the present, Ryan caught Jill's eye at the bar and she
came straight over.

'Another beer?' she asked.

He shook his head. 'But there is something else you can do for me.'

She raised an eyebrow and waited. 'Who is the local real-estate agent?'

'That would be Cal Bunton.'

'Let's get Cal Bunton on the phone, then, shall we? Let him know I have some business I need to conduct. It has to be tonight, but I will make it worth his while.'

CHAPTER THREE

THE NEXT MORNING Ryan knew better than to park his car beneath the flowering banksia in front of Kardinyarr House. The day before it had dropped spiky red petals all over the roof of his car, leaving a horrible sticky residue it had taken him a half-hour to clean away.

He parked his car beside the house, got out, and, stretching his arms over his head, walked the last few metres to the edge of the yard, until he could see over the rise to the gully at the rear of the property.

Kardinyarr: two-hundred hilly acres of grazing land that had grabbed his brother so tight he had been willing to give up a very different sort of life for it. And for her. Clouds brushed large patches of shadow across the huge, dusty green parcel of land. Ghost gums collected in majestic pockets on the hilltops. Hardy lantana and sturdy low-lying scrub wound in a curling thick mass alongside a meandering creek in the gully below. It was so quiet he could hear leaves skittering across the roof of the house, the windows creaking against the buffeting breeze. What he could *not* hear was traffic, or televisions, or barking dogs.

It *was* picturesque, just as Will had described in his e-mails to Sam, just as he had tried to tell Ryan on the telephone that night in Rome. But Ryan needed more. He wanted to understand. Needed to understand. Because it seemed that until he could reconcile Will's decision to stay, he couldn't let him off the hook, couldn't let him go.

Ryan headed back to the car and pulled a couple of bags of groceries from the passenger seat just as Laura drove up the driveway in her old grey hatchback. She skidded to a halt at an angle in the middle of a patch of grass, leapt from the car, and stormed towards him. Today's cotton sundress was white with ripe cherries. Today's ponytail was tied back with a proper red ribbon. Today she wore flat white sandals that kicked up clouds of dust as she raged over to him.

'What? No purple pants?' he asked.

She ignored him, just as he'd expected her to. 'I just ran into Cal Bunton, dropping his daughter off at Chloe's school, and he told me what you've done.'

And there he'd been, wondering how he would tell Laura the good news, when he should have guessed she would know before the ink had even dried on the contracts. He hitched the grocery bags onto his hip, shut his car door, pressed the remote lock, reminded himself he really didn't need to do that any more, and then headed towards the house.

'I have been pleasant,' Laura raved, stamping along behind him. 'Heck, I haven't made nearly as much of a fuss at your landing on my doorstep without any warning as I could have. Now you have gone and *bought* Kardinyarr and you're moving in? Just like that?'

'Well, not quite just like that,' Ryan said, balancing the groceries precariously as he reached into his jeans pocket for the front door keys. 'A quick settlement suits both buyer and seller, so Kardinyarr should be mine within the fortnight. Until then I'm leasing the place from the Callaghans.'

'But how could you?'

'It seems that I had to. I will have a good chance of actually *meeting* your daughter this way. Unless, of course, she'll be at school, or slumber parties, or busy with super-important first grade homework for evermore.'

Laura blithely ignored his sideways barb. 'Cal Bunton also said you were asking his advice on running livestock. Are you seriously thinking of working this place?' *Nice move,* he thought. *If you can't win the argument, change the subject.* 'I seriously am.'

'But what do you know about running a farm?'

Without looking over his shoulder, he opened the door and headed inside his empty house. 'I know a lot about agriculture. In fact, the paper I was brought to Australia to present focused on the importance of the cotton industry in South East Queensland to the Australian economy. Nothing like harnessing the best natural resources the world has to offer to keep our economy chugging along nicely.'

Only once he'd reached the kitchen and placed the groceries on the empty bench did he realise she hadn't followed. He poked his head into the hall to find her fuming out on the grass. He threw his keys onto the bench and walked back to the doorway.

She threw her arms out in frustration. 'Well, so long as you can learn what you need to know from a chat with a bunch of cronies around a conference table, you're laughing!'

'I'm also about halfway through reading *Running Livestock for Dummies*, and I am finding the cartoons and pie charts most helpful.'

She blinked, obviously trying to decide if he was, in fact, serious. She started to shuffle from one foot to the other, scrunching her once neat and tidy dress into tight fists.

'But I would be happy to take any advice you wish to impart,' he said, knowing it would get her goat even more.

'Oh, rack off,' she blurted.

And he laughed. Really laughed. She looked so sweet, all dolled up in her enticing little outfit, but beneath the pretty face and the county-girl candour she was as spicy as they came. 'I have never met an adult so hyperactive,' he said. 'Can I recommend Vitamin B1?'

She crossed her arms and he knew she couldn't calm herself even if she wanted to. 'While we are sharing *advice*, Kardinyarr is *no* place for a hobby farm!'

'I have no intention of setting up a *hobby farm*, Laura. I don't believe in doing anything halfway. Never have. All or nothing is the only way to live. I have a feeling you share that sentiment.'

'Well, that's just fine and dandy,' she said, her voice suddenly eerily calm. 'But I should warn you we've had city gents come out this way before, and they *never* last past six months.'

Will. The name slammed into Ryan's thoughts, and he saw the second it slammed into Laura's as well. Will had not lasted *two* months before the harsh reality of life at Kardinyarr had killed him. A brown snake. His clever brother, with his whole future out there, just waiting for him to grab a hold, had died from a tiny little snake bite. Laura's mouth dropped open, her whole face fell, and he felt the apology as surely as if she had said it aloud. 'Just come inside, Laura. I make no promises about being here six months from now, but until then I'll still need to find a home for all my groceries, and I'm sure you would just love to tell me where to put them.'

Her mouth snapped shut, her contrition warring with her fighting spirit. Then her gaze flickered and rambled down his form, taking in his clean fingernails, his pressed jeans, his shiny boots. When it slithered back up to meet his eye, he knew... Her spirit had won.

'I'm sorry, *Cowboy*,' she said, her voice lingering on the final word, 'but I don't think you could last six *weeks* before the bright lights of the big city called you home.'

'Clothes do not maketh the man, *sweetheart*.'

She grew red in the face as he returned with his own endearment. 'Then why not just stick to a suit and tie? Unless you're trying to convince people otherwise.'

Touche'. Oh, she was good at this. But he wasn't done yet. 'Haven't you heard the phrase, "Dress for the job you want, not the job you have"?' *Gotcha!*

That was enough to have her huffing off back to her car and careering up the driveway to her own house. He would have liked to follow, if only to know what she was accusing him of this time, but another car had just pulled in behind his. It was a dusty van with 'Tandarah Antiques' written in scrawling ye olde script on the side. 'Mr Gasper?' the driver said as he hauled his heavy bulk from the front seat of the van. The name 'Bill' was stitched into his shirt.

'That's me—Bill.' Ryan shook the big man's sweaty hand, and gave a short nod to his cohort in the passenger seat.

'So, where do you want the credenza?'

'I'm sorry. The what?'

'The credenza.'

'Nope. I still have no idea what you are saying, mate. You'll have to try translating that into *male speak*.'

'A great hunk of wood in which you keep the family china.' The delivery guy looked down at his folder. 'Kardinyarr House. For R. Gasper from S. Gasper-Jackson.'

Aah. He had called his sister Sam the night before, to update her about young Chloe and to let her know his plans for Kardinyarr and obstinate

Laura Somervale. She had insisted on sending him a housewarming gift purchased from a store in Tandarah. Something with a *country flavour*, she had promised, as though living in a sprawling home on two hundred acres wasn't *country* flavoured enough. But it was good of her, nonetheless. A token gift to show she understood his sabbatical and approved.

'Oh. The *credenza*. Umm, in the dining room?' He wished he had paid more attention to the multitude of home renovation shows on TV. But Bill seemed satisfied by his response, so he must have subconsciously picked something up along the way.

Ryan was momentarily distracted by a flicker of lace curtain from inside the cottage next door. He had asked Sam to hold off telling his parents and their sister Jen about Chloe. And Laura. His family were overwhelming enough in grander circles much less in a quiet haven such as this. But they would come. They were just those sort of people. Tolerant. Understanding. Adaptable. In that regard, *he* was the Gasper born of a different mould. He liked things the way he liked them. He didn't know if he had it in him to compromise, though Laura Somervale was certainly out to make him try.

He looked over to the cottage again. Yep. Definite curtain-flicking going on over there. With a small smile, Ryan followed the hulking great credenza-whatsit into his new home.

Mortified that she had been caught staring, Laura stormed into her kitchen, looking to lose herself there.

As a teenager, living alone with her dad, she had learned early on that if she wanted to eat anything more exciting than scrambled eggs she would have to cook it for herself. She had soon found the kitchen was a place in which she could daydream, where she could whisk away her gravest demons and cook up her most sublime fantasies. At that moment she felt a great desire to beat the heck out of something.

Within fifteen minutes of unmeasured pouring, gratifying egg-cracking and manic batter-whipping, she had a chocolate cake baking in the oven. The bulk of her vexation exhausted out of her, she leant against the kitchen bench and stared out of the window. She looked down the length of her slim five-acre block, past the undulating paddock with its fallen trees—home to a new family of rabbits—past a line of fruit trees which would be ripe for the picking any day now, past the low-lying dam where Chloe's plump pet cow, Irmela, was taking a drink beneath the shade of a tree, and out into nothingness.

It seemed Ryan Gasper was not going to be hoodwinked into vanishing out of her life. Soon she would have to sit Chloe down and have *the* conversation she had been preparing herself for since the day her little possum was born.

Laura's ribs suddenly felt too tight in her chest. With a hearty sniff, she headed to the bedroom to change. She stopped when she caught sight of herself in the mirror at the end of the hall. Her hair was falling from its constraint. Her dress was crushed and a patch of cocoa stained one hip. Darn it! It was one of her nice dresses. She had only been popping out to drop Chloe at school, but she had dressed up in more than her usual old jeans, T-shirt and flip-flops. Why? In case she bumped into *him*, that was why. She had to look good for him. She had to look like a good mother. His family had power. Influence. She had a fair idea that if they wanted to whip Chloe away from her they would know the right person to talk to.

She leaned forward and pinched some colour into her cheeks. 'Argh!' she growled at her reflection. 'Of course you did not dress up to look like a good mother. You are a single mother, wasting away on a hill top, miles from the nearest anybody, and one smile from some hot city boy sends you to the far reaches of your closet in search of something girly to wear. You are pathetic!'

Then she remembered she was no longer miles from anybody. For the first time in several years she had a neighbour. And not just any neighbour, not just any hot city boy, but Ryan Gasper.

Though she didn't want Chloe to have a preconceived idea of the man, Laura didn't have that luxury. During her short time with Will she and he had talked and talked and talked. Whereas most of Laura's talks had been about how she felt about losing her father, most of Will's talks had concerned his relationship with his all-too-successful big brother. Through Will's eyes she had come to imagine Ryan as whip-smart, confident, and larger than life. Everything that at that time she wasn't. So much so that even now his name still brought about a chemical reaction inside of her.

'Add opinionated, irritating, and utterly frustrating!' she yelled into the mirror.

She undid the zip of her dress with more effort than necessary, whipped the dress over her head, threw it at the dirty-clothes basket in her room, grabbed her faded old jeans and her oldest, plainest T-shirt, and dressed herself back as Laura Somervale, farmer's daughter.

And if anybody had a problem with that, they could take it up with her!

A knock sounded at Ryan's front door. He put away the last of his dry groceries, wiped flour dust from his palms and approached the front door, feeling more invigorated than he ought to at the thought of sparring with Ms Somervale yet again. He opened the door, but it wasn't Laura.

'Morning, Jill,' he said, and even he heard the regret in his voice. *Badly done, Ryan.*

'Were you expecting somebody else?' Her sharp gaze shot across the way to the small cottage next door, to the house with the fluttering curtains.

'Not at all. Especially considering nobody bar you, Cal Bunton, the previous owners and my sister have been told I'll be staying here.'

She reached out and slapped his face softly. 'You are a dear boy for even pretending to think that would be the case. Now, invite me in. I come bearing fruit!'

She pulled back a teatowel covering the basket in her arms to reveal an abundance of banana muffins.

'Come on in.' He stood back to let her pass. 'You have beaten my furniture here, so I can't offer you a seat. All I can offer is a viewing of what I'm told is a credenza.'

'Lead the way.'

He did as he was told, escorting Jill into the dining room where she stared at the sideboard with wide eyes.

'Now, that's impressive!' she exclaimed.

Ryan stood beside her and crossed his arms. 'It really is, isn't it? Somebody cut down a forest to build that thing.'

'Mmm. I'm glad to see the place filling up with life again, Ryan. I'll bet Laura will be just as thrilled to have somebody living here after all these years.'

Ryan knew he could have won a lot of money taking that bet. 'You think so, do you, Jill?'

'Sure. She loves this place like nobody else.' She fluttered a hand around the all but empty space before it sank to her side.

Ryan had a sudden feeling he was being railroaded. He felt a big empty pit open up inside of him and almost didn't want to ask. 'And why is that?'

'Lady Laura has looked after the upkeep on this place for years, knowing the overseas owners didn't give a hoot. It was nothing more than a nest egg for them. But for her? So many memories. For years she's kept Kardinyarr up to nick, even organising tradesmen to look it over each spring. We always kind of hoped she would win the Lotto, so she could make an offer on the place.' Now the song-and-dance act made even more sense.

He was turning into Laura's every nightmare rolled into one.

'She is the jewel of the region and she has lain dormant for all too long. So if you don't do right by her, the whole town will lynch you for sure,' Jill said, with a huge grin spread across her face.

Ryan wasn't so sure if Jill was now talking about Kardinyarr, or the lady who had kept it looking rosy for so many years. He decided to take Jill's words at face value. 'I have no plans to tear the place down, Jill, or subdivide, or deck it out in modern furniture. I'm sure you can pass that on to the good folks of Tandarah for me.'

'Excellent. I'll quote you on the specials board at the Upper Gum Tree.'

Ryan laughed, but he had a feeling that Jill had it in her to follow through.

'You weren't kidding, were you?' she said, wandering through the rest of the house, spying the fact that he didn't have a fridge or a microwave. All he had in the kitchen was an old kettle. On the floor of the lounge room he had laid out a comforter, pillow, and sheets borrowed from Jill's hotel, and an overnight bag, which he'd had with him when he first arrived.

'But who needs a table, right?' Jill said. 'Out here we make do. Follow me.'

Jill led him out to the back veranda, where they sat, legs dangling over the edge, and shared the still warm muffins. He wasn't doing anything much—he wasn't making plans, or forging budgets, or negotiating agreements—but he was enjoying himself immensely. This wasn't a bad way to spend a morning.

'Did you grow these yourself?' he asked through a mouthful of banana muffin.

Jill's grin returned. 'Don't tell anyone, but it's a packet mix! Laura is the chef in the region. Give her a bite of any dessert and she can reproduce it blindfolded. So, as I figure it, there's no reason in competing.'

'I love your reasoning. And I like your muffins—home-grown or not.'

'And I like you, Ryan Gasper, though I probably should not. Considering who you are, on so many levels, I am sure I ought to be extremely wary of you.'

She looked over at him with a gaze so intense Ryan knew lesser mortals would quite easily crumble to sand at her feet. 'Promise me you are not going to be a fly-by-night farmer. That would be too sad. Not nearly enough dashing young economists with cheeky glints in their eyes around these parts.'

'I know of at least one person who thinks there is one too many of me in town already.'

Jill gave him a squeeze on the shoulder. 'Nevertheless, she will do her best to broker a peaceful accord between you for Chloe's sake—because she's too kind for the likes of you and me.'

Jill dragged herself to her feet with a great heaving sigh. 'Take advantage of that goodness and there are a million places I could bury you out here and you would never be found. Keep the muffin basket. If you're here long enough to see me again, you can give it to me then.' Then she was gone. Off the veranda and around the side of the house before Ryan had a chance to disassemble her words.

He uncurled his lanky frame from the edge of the veranda and rounded the house in time to see Jill take off in her rusty, once-white ute. She crunched the gears and drove down the long sloping driveway in a swirl of dust.

It seemed the people of Tandarah had nothing but good to say about Laura Somervale. And they went out of their way to say it too. Ryan wondered if his own friends would go to the same lengths to say they believed in him. Since all of his friends lived thousands of miles from one another, in cities all around the world, the best he would ever hope for would be the odd dissolute telegram.

But what did he expect? He had been deliberately gung-ho and adventurous all his life. Taking advantage of every opportunity. Travelling wherever the dollar and the city lights shone brightest. That didn't leave much room for putting down roots.

And perhaps he had not been the most supportive brother Will could have wished for. Jeez, even after Will had died he had kept working. Ryan rubbed a rough hand over his face, massaging his eyes as he imagined the remainder of his family, huddled against the cold on that windy, wet, Melbourne winter's day...

Ryan sat in the window of his hotel room in Paris, staring through the drizzly sky over the grey rooftops to the tip of Notre Dame's spiralling spires, hazy in the distance.

When he blinked, his focus shifted. The grey raindrops trickling down the windowpane made it look as though he was crying. But on that day no tears came.

On that day, ten thousand miles away, on the other side of the world, in a small private cemetery in Melbourne, Australia, his younger brother was being buried. Ryan didn't feel tears. He felt utterly at a loss.

Will had been such a smart kid. A student with immense aptitude. A kid with a scholarship to study commerce law at Oxford. But a kid who, without blinking, had turned it down. Will had had no goals. No gumption. He never had.

Being several years older, and a heck of a lot more streetwise, Ryan had done his best over the years to guide him, to offer advice, even to use his own political influence to get Will interviews, to get him noticed, to get him on track.

He had, even as recently as a week earlier, offered to buy Will a ticket to Paris— a ticket to join him at the World Economic Summit where he was set to give the keynote speech. He had hoped that his success, a glimpse of his own energetic lifestyle, would inspire his brother to grab hold of the opportunities life had afforded him and not look back.

But, no. Will had preferred to live like a hippy in some Outback town and he had been happy to stay there, living off his Christmas money for ever if he could manage it. All for the sake of some girl. Some farm girl he'd just met.

Ryan had revelled in the intensity of his frustration. He'd wanted to take Will by the scruff of the neck and shake some sense into him. But now it was too late. Will was gone. Dead. All that latent talent wasted. All that wonderful, fruitful, eminent Gasper blood spilled into the earth.

Frustrated to the point of fury, Ryan lashed out a punch at the drizzly windowpane, and the glass cracked and smashed. He didn't even feel the pain, didn't even know he had injured himself until the first blood-red drop landed upon his pale grey suit pants...

Ryan stretched out his hand, staring at the long scar across his knuckles. He had refused stitches at the time, preferring to bandage the wound himself. It hadn't healed as well as it could have, and he could still feel it sting on cold days.

Ryan looked over at the cottage next door, the flickering curtains now still. Maybe now was the time to put past mistakes behind him. With this new project, this new house, this new family member, maybe he had been given the chance to prove that when it came to the crunch, a 'fly-by-night' tendency wasn't his defining characteristic.

CHAPTER FOUR

LATE MONDAY AFTERNOON Ryan had still heard no word about the rest of his furniture, which Sam had organised to send up from his apartment in Melbourne, but he did receive a phone call to say Betsy had arrived. He hadn't seen her in a couple of months and, so, rather than his usual one-off visit every few weeks, he had some real time to spend with her.

Marking his place in his book—which was *not*, in fact, *Running Livestock for Dummies*, but close enough that he did not need Ms Somervale catching him reading it—Ryan grabbed his keys and headed out. Jogging down the front steps, he pulled up short when he found a visitor in floral jeans, pink sneakers and a *Little Mermaid* T-shirt playing jump rope in front of his house. His breath hitched as a pair of cool blue Gasper eyes looked back at him. *Chloe.*

He looked up at the cottage next door but saw no sign of Laura. 'You must be Chloe,' he said.

The little girl spun around as she skipped. 'And you must be Mr Gasper.'

Ryan shot a glance towards the quiet cottage. 'Did your mother tell you who I was?' he asked, feeling a mite sneaky but more than a mite interested in her answer.

She nodded, skipping-rope thumping rhythmically against the dirt.

'Mum said that you come from the city, and that you will be living in Kardinyarr House for now.'

Huh. Unless the little girl was editing her mother's words, it seemed that Laura Somervale was above spreading her *spicy* feelings towards him to her daughter. 'And before she told me to go play with my skip rope,' Chloe continued, 'I heard her on the phone, telling Auntie Jill that even though you fill out a pair of blue jeans just fine, that doesn't make you a real farmer.' Ryan bit back a laugh. So, smart-mouthed Laura Somervale liked the way he filled out his jeans. Ryan felt himself grow at least an inch taller at the notion.

'What did my Mum tell you about *me*?' Chloe asked. Ryan paused, suddenly finding himself on rocky ground again. 'She did say that you are a heck of a horsewoman.'

'I won a blue ribbon a couple of weeks ago.'

Ryan imagined her sitting atop a pony, blue ribbon pinned to her chest. He wished he had been around to see that, to see the smile spread across that earnest little face. 'Well, Chloe, now we know so much about each other, I think it would be all right if you called me Ryan.'

She nodded again, and this time there was even a hint of a smile, with a sweet dimple on her right cheek. 'Good, because I would laugh if I had to say Gasper all the time.'

His own smile slipped. 'Why would that make you laugh?'

'Because Gasper is my middle name.'

Well, Laura Somervale certainly hadn't told him that. 'Gasper was my dad's last name,' Chloe continued. 'He lived in your house before I was born. He came from the city, too.'

Ryan had no idea how to broach the minefield of statements that Chloe had so innocently blurted out.

Again he looked to the cottage, but there was no hint that Laura was aware the two of them were chatting. He suddenly wished for some curtain-flickering, or some atrocious singing by the clothesline.

Then Chloe came out with a jaw-dropper. 'My friend Tammy says that her mum said that you're my uncle.'

'Whoa!' What to say? If Laura thought he had overstepped the boundaries she would surely snap him in two. This would take some fancy dancing. 'Did you...? Have you talked to your mum about that?'

Chloe shook her head. 'I forgot until now.'

'Well, how about you and your Mum have a longer chat about me when she gets off the phone.'

'They're chatting about something I'm not allowed to listen to so she sent me outside. I told her I'm old enough to know everything.'

'Mums are usually pretty good at knowing when little girls are ready to know everything.'

'I guess.' Then, after barely a pause, she asked, 'Do I have any cousins in Scotland? My friend Tammy has cousins in Scotland. Mum says Scotland is cold and green, and that the men wear skirts. I've never seen a man wear a skirt. Do you wear skirts?'

Yep. Definitely Laura Somervale's daughter, he thought, marvelling at Chloe's fluctuating speech pattern. At first he had found it too fast to follow; now he found it downright endearing. Not wanting to fall prey to her conversational trickery, he reached out, scuffed her hair, and said, 'You never know your luck. Now, maybe you should check if your mum is off the phone.' Chloe shrugged mid-skip. Ryan was surprised to find he was genuinely loath to leave her sight, but he had pushed his luck long enough. 'It was nice to finally meet you, Chloe *Gasper* Somervale. I hope we can chat again soon.' With that, he turned and jogged towards his car. 'Where are you going?' Chloe asked, her rope not stopping as she skipped alongside him. 'I'm going flying,' Ryan said.

That stopped her short. Her skipping-rope slumped at her pink sneakers and her head tipped to one side as she looked at him as if he was making up stories. All serious and untrusting. All Somervale.

He crouched down until he was at eye level with her. 'You know the airstrip out back of the Mackay place?'

Chloe nodded.

'Well, I have my very own plane parked over there right now. Her name is Betsy, and I'm more excited than a kid at a funfair about seeing her again.'

Her hands shot to her hips. 'You have no such thing!' she said, and again she looked so like her mother.

'Have you ever been in a plane?' he asked.

'Once. Jill drove us into Melbourne, which took two hours, then we flew to Sydney to meet a doctor for my asthma, and that took an hour. We were home again the same day. He gave me a new puffer that tastes the worst.'

'Well, my plane isn't a big white jumbo, like that plane, it's more like the size of a truck. It's a Cessna Skyhawk 172R, an all-metal, single-engine piston, high-wing monoplane with a four-person seating capacity.'

Chloe blinked at him. 'Our plane was red.'

And then he remembered. He wasn't making conversation with some political flunky at a cocktail party—he was speaking to a six-year-old. It seemed that Ryan hadn't developed a way to communicate with people that much younger than himself overnight, after all.

'You went in a red plane? Now, *that* is impressive.

Red planes are always the fastest, you know.' He hopped in the car and wound down the window. 'I'll see you later, Chloe.'

'Okay, Ryan.'

He drove down the dirt driveway, and in his rear-vision mirror he could see the little girl standing there watching him. She gave a sweet little wave, and only then did he realise how fast his heart was thumping in his chest.

Laura had the phone tucked beneath her ear as she whipped a bowl of egg whites and sugar. She watched as Ryan Gasper's dusty black sports car trawled down the bumpy front drive and turned right onto the main road away from town.

'You came visiting next door, Jill,' she accused down the phone, 'and you didn't even pop in here to say hello. Don't deny it. I saw your ute.'

'I had to get home to my cats,' Jill lied. 'So, have you spoken a reasonable word to him yet?'

'How can one be reasonable when one is caught singing to birds? Or when one is dressed in purple pants? Or when one is so outraged at being duped by some guy with more money than sense that one can barely speak English, much less reasonable English? Did you have any idea what he was cooking up with Cal?'

Jill's laughter echoed down the phoneline. 'Of course. I know everything. Now, don't tell me you are planning on hiding from him for the rest of your life.'

'Jill, he will not be here for the rest of anybody's life. Did you check out his clothes? All brand-new. All expensive. He doesn't belong out here.'

'I hardly noticed. Those bluer than blue eyes having blinded me to much else,' Jill said. 'Except, of course, those glorious dark curls. My word!'

'Okay. I get where you're going with this. But, unlike you, I have no choice but to look past them. He's my Will's brother.'

Laura heard Jill's pause, and knew she wouldn't like what was coming next.

'Laura, I'm too old and cranky to let that slip through. I have *never* heard you call that young man *your* Will. Not when he was alive and traipsing after you like a lovesick puppy, and not since. What's up?'

Laura whisked all the harder, but said nothing. 'Don't look at this stranger and only imagine his back as he walks away, Laura. Not every man who comes into your life is going to leave you all alone.'

Laura stopped whisking and the mixing bowl sank to the bench. She put a hand to her temple to rub away the sudden spinning in her head. It seemed Jill was not going to be any use in relocating the man next door.

Laura peered out of the kitchen window but Chloe was out of her sight. Panic welled in her throat. How long had Chloe been gone? Her daughter knew better than not to check in every ten minutes or so. What if she fell ill? What if she got hurt? What if Ryan had found her scampering about outside, had seen his opportunity and taken her off in his dusty black car...?

The phone had begun to slip out of Laura's hand when suddenly Chloe came scurrying into the backyard with a tennis ball to throw for Chimp, who was busy sniffing a bunch of weeds in the corner of the yard.

She took a deep breath, swallowed down the huge lump of panic that had all but overwhelmed her, and rerouted the conversation before Jill took her to places she had no intention of going. 'Jill, this is one man I would be glad to see the back of. What if...what if he decides to contest for Chloe? What if his family decides they want to take her away from here? From me?'

'Then we will rain fire down upon him the likes of which he has never imagined. You are safe. Chloe is safe. Give yourself a break, and give the urban cowboy next door a break as well. The guy has no furniture, for goodness' sake. All he has is an old kettle, which one of your tradesmen must have left behind by mistake, and he's all alone out here—more alone than you have ever been. Face it, kiddo, he's a member of Chloe's family, a member of our little community, and neither I nor anyone else in Tandarah is going to disenfranchise him. We need men with brains and muscles to help in the fire season.'

Jill's words hit their mark. If she continued being so openly against Ryan it wouldn't do her any good. The people of Tandarah would take him under their wings, as they always did lost souls. And that was what he was. Laura had glimpsed hints of the hidden pain that he had not been able to cover up. Jill was on to something there. This was a guy who was after more than a meet-and-greet with a new family member. But wondering how much more had Laura concerned to the point of sleepless nights. Until he had worked out his demons, in whatever way worked for him, it seemed she had no choice but to play happy neighbours and happy families with the slightly puzzled, entirely enigmatic *wunderkind* next door—or die trying.

Ryan took his time completing his pre-start, post-start, taxiing checks and run-ups. The local flight tower cleared his flight plan from the Mackay Airfield, east over Mount Bulla—which at this time of year would be dry and barren, without snow or the people snow brought to the region—then back around home again. A one-hour flight all up; it would be enough to get himself and Betsy used to the new run.

He took off, his back slamming into the seat with only a fraction of the power felt on a commercial flight, but the thrill was the same. The freedom. The comforting hum of the engine. The view of never-ending clear blue sky. There was nothing in the world like it.

He flew a large loop around the area, tilting his wing to check out the low lie of the local town, then crossed the hills and valleys of his new home. The house perched on top of the hill looked magnificent. Proud. The fact that it was to be his gave him an unexpected rush. The flush of ownership, of the challenge ahead. It had been so long since anything or anyone had challenged him the same way, and he found himself relishing it.

Maybe that was why he'd had such a love-hate relationship with his brother—his greatest challenger. The one person in his life who'd told him no on a regular basis. He missed that. He missed him. Perhaps even more so now. Will would have turned twenty-six this year, and Ryan wondered what sort of a man his brother would have become. Would fatherhood have changed him? Would it have forced him to take responsibility? If given the chance, would feisty Laura Somervale have made a man of him?

Ryan glanced down at the worker's cottage next door. From this height he only now realised how isolated Laura's place was. The next nearest house, bar his, was over the hill and far away—and she had lived out there for several years, raising a child on her own. Talk about a challenge.

Ryan circled the adjoining properties again, recognising the washing flapping on the cottage clothesline, and the spray of floral colour around the edge of the house. Her small fenced-in yard was neat and golden green, whereas the remainder of the surrounding landscape and the bulk of Kardinyarr looked barren and dry, as though her cottage was an oasis in the desert. After several minutes there was no sign of the lady of the house, and he was unexpectedly disappointed.

He tilted his wings back horizontal and headed back to the airstrip. He had plenty of work to do to get the staid old farm back into full working order. And spying on the nubile neighbour was not part of the plan. All he wanted from her was the chance to build a relationship with her daughter—and to wipe the smug smile from her face when his farm became a success.

That evening, as Laura pulled the washing off the line, she saw Ryan out on his back veranda, an old frayed workbook in one hand and a steaming mug in the other. Typical. All the men she had known would have lived on packet soup rather than learn to cook for themselves. Then she remembered Jill's comment that his furniture had not yet arrived, and that in fact he had no other choice.

She felt a tug of guilt as she remembered those first nights in the cottage on her own, after her father had passed away. Jill and other locals, people with families of their own to tend to, had run a constant line to her door with enough food to keep a cattle station full of people living for a month. Her whole life since then she had been passing on the favour, paying them back for their small kindnesses, and she planned to do so as long as she had strength in her cooking arm to do it.

That was what country people did, they looked out for one another. Yet, knowing that, she had left Ryan rattling around in the big house with no word on when he would get to meet his niece. She was a horrible person, a horrible neighbour, and a horrible mother. Penance would be the only way through.

She remembered the cake she had baked earlier in the day for no reason in particular other than the need to cook. In a funny way the cake was Ryan's fault, and it was still sitting uneaten in her fridge.

Laura headed into the kitchen as Chloe came scampering into the room.

'What are you doing?'

'Making a peace-offering,' Laura said, tearing off a measure of cling-wrap and tucking it over the edge of a crockpot full of leftovers.

Chloe scrambled up onto the kitchen stool. Her nose crinkled. 'Is that Tuna Mornay? I *hate* Tuna Mornay.'

'Since when?' Laura asked.

'Since Tammy hates Tuna Mornay.'

Laura cracked a smile. 'Well, then, lucky for you, this Tuna Mornay is not for you.'

'Who's it for?'

'It's for Mr Gasper next door.'

'Oh, Uncle Ryan.'

Laura stopped her fussing and stared at her daughter. 'Excuse me?' she exclaimed, surprised any words had managed to slip through her suddenly rubbery lips. 'How did you come to call him by that name?'

Chloe's face dropped, as if she knew she had been caught out. 'He and I were talking this afternoon about Scotland, when I was, um, exorcising Chimp—'

'Exercising,' Laura corrected automatically. She clenched her hands to stop herself from throwing the Tuna Mornay straight down the sink. 'What did he tell you, possum?'

'He said that he doesn't wear skirts.'

'Okay. But how do you come to call him Uncle Ryan?'

'Today at school Miss Tilda and some of the teachers were whispering about the fancy black car they had seen parked outside the Upper Gum Tree. I told Tammy I had seen that car next door, and Tammy said that her mum said that…'

Laura waved her hands in front of her face to stop the flourish of words. 'Okay, okay—I can see where this is going.'

So Ryan hadn't spilled the beans. The wonderful world of small-town gossip had got there first. *Stupid Laura!* She should have known. Though it had been so very long since she'd had to put up with any of that sort of guff, it simply had not occurred to her that Chloe might become a victim of the rumour mill. That had been a downright dangerous assumption—especially when concerning the emotional welfare of her child.

Laura ignored the food on the table, crouched down onto her haunches and looked her little girl in the eye, all the while laying a hand on her brow to check her temperature and watching the pace of her breathing with a practised eye. Everything seemed all right.

Now, how to explain all this to a six-year-old? *Here goes.* 'You know how you were asking me about cousins in Scotland yesterday, for your family-picture homework?'

Chloe nodded. 'I handed it in this morning.' Suddenly her bottom lip began to tremble.

'I know, possum. I know this is all very confusing.' The last thing she wanted was for her happy little girl to have undue stress brought upon her. She took Chloe's hand and led her to the couch.

'No, it's not. I get it. Ryan is my dad's brother. Come from a long way away because he wanted to meet me. Tammy explained all that. It's my picture.' She stopped for a little sniffle. 'I handed it in this morning. And when Tammy told me about Uncle Ryan I asked Miss Tilda for it back, so I could fix it. I told her it wasn't finished. But she said that I'd had time enough in the last week to get it done.'

Laura bit down on the run of nasty words that she wished to let forth. Miss Tilda was twenty years older than Laura, and twice her size, but she wouldn't know what hit her the next morning at school when the president of the PTA came to visit!

Laura ran a soothing palm over her daughter's golden curls. 'How about we have our own project instead? You can draw *me* a family picture, and you can put anyone in the picture you like. And, instead of this one being handed in to Miss Tilda, we can get it framed and we can hang it on the wall here.'

Chloe gulped down the last of her tears and her sniffles ceased. 'Framed?'

'You betcha! Now, let's back up a step. Mr Gasper says he doesn't wear a skirt? I don't know about that!' Chloe's mouth twisted as she fought back a smile, and Laura's heart twisted right along with it. Laura had told Ryan that she and Chloe were perfectly happy on their own. Mostly that was true. But during those moments when her little girl was clever, or funny, or downright stupefying, Laura often found herself turning to share an adoring smile, a knowing wink, with someone who wasn't there.

'I'm heading over to Kardinyarr House now,' she said.

Chloe leapt down onto the floor and ran to the front door. 'Can I come with you?'

Laura smiled at her effervescent little girl, and said, 'Wherever you are is where I want to be.'

She followed Chloe outside to feed the guy-next-door, half hoping he would choke on her tuna and on her cake.

Ryan shifted his weight from one numb bottom cheek to the other. The hardwood stairs leading away from his back veranda weren't built for long sittings. He rubbed his eyes, encouraging them to refocus into the distance after a couple of hours of close reading.

The scuffle of boot on gravel caught his attention. He looked across the yard to find Laura coming towards him with Chloe tumbling and cartwheeling behind her. There was something slow and deliberate about her gait that had his wariness factor on full alert.

'Good evening, Mr Gasper,' she said, her voice low enough to set his nerves on edge.

'He likes to be called Ryan!' Chloe said.

'So I've heard,' his neighbour said, her eyes flaring. She then winked at her daughter, her face softening with affection, and Chloe grinned back. It was the first real smile he had seen Chloe give, and it was as though the sun had risen all over again.

'Ryan—or *Cowboy*. I'll answer to both,' Ryan interjected. Laura's eyes widened a fraction at his effrontery, but he just stared right back. She was simply going to have to get used to him. Especially since he had developed such an immediate fondness for her daughter, one he had every intention of cultivating. The food in Laura's arms suggested she was going to try to be civil. Unless, of course, it was laced with rat poison.

'Is that for me?' he asked.

'Jill told me you had nothing, and she would never forgive me if I let you starve to death. I've brought you a fork and a plate so you can eat now.'

'Why don't you come in and share it with me?' At her obvious reticence, the rat poison theory took hold. He stepped back against the doorway and waved an arm inside his home.

Chloe took a step forward, but Laura clicked her fingers and the little girl understood. With a world-class pout, she ran down the stairs and back to the cottage.

Laura's mouth tightened and her voice dropped to a whisper, even though her daughter was long since out of hearing range. 'I was going to invite you over for dinner tomorrow, to meet Chloe for real, but it seems the two of you have beaten me to the punch.'

Ha! Ryan didn't believe she had been planning to invite him anywhere—unless it was to take a long walk off a short plank. He reached down to take the plates from Laura's grip and laid them on the floor, out of reach. 'She found me. I was heading out, and suddenly she was just there, skipping. Apparently you had sent her outside so she couldn't listen in on your secret women's business with Jill.'

Her mouth dropped open, then snapped shut again. 'So it's my fault you met her without my permission, without my protection?'

The little kick in her voice ultimately sent him over the edge—the delicate, barely there, sizzling tone that made itself felt deep down inside of him. He hadn't done anything wrong through this whole process, but she made him feel as if he was treading on her toes at every step. All he'd asked was to meet Chloe—face to face, uncle to niece. The more she baulked, the more he would push his own case. 'Well, yes, Laura,' he said. 'It *was* entirely your fault.'

Her back stiffened, and her pouting lips thinned into a taut line. But the fire in her eyes could not be quenched. This woman was all heat, wavering from warmth and sunshine to spicy and ablaze. But there was no husband in the wings. Not even for the sake of her little girl. Surely there would be any number of strapping young farm boys willing to escort her to a country dance or two? Unless she still held a torch for a beau from long ago.

Ryan's stomach clenched painfully at the thought, and it blindsided him completely. Was that a pang of jealousy? Bad news. He had spent a lifetime dousing the envy he felt for the ease with which everything had come his brother's way—grades, offers, opportunities. He had no right to wonder if Laura had been as easy as everything else in Will's life. She was none of his business. Only Chloe was his business.

'I am not the enemy here,' he said, deciding it was in his best interests to be conciliatory. 'I know my presence is unexpected, but it was unexpected to me as well. In a parallel universe I would be on a plane right now, heading for Las Vegas, looking forward to a month's stay at a top hotel on the strip, all on the dollar of a major US bank. But instead I have made the choice to stay here.'

As he said it, he knew that it was true. He was going to make a go of Kardinyarr. For the sake of all the times he had told his brother no, this time he would stay for real. Better late than never? For the sake of the bruise obscuring his heart, he certainly hoped so.

'I'm staying, Laura. In order to get to know Chloe.

And to get to know you—the woman for whom my brother was willing to give up the world.'

Something shifted in Laura's uninterested and disbelieving countenance. A raw edge flashed across her expressive eyes. And there was his answer. Even the mention of Will's name gave her heartache. There was no danger in their continued acquaintance—not on her part, at least. So long as he could focus on Chloe alone, and disconnect himself from her mother's dominating energy, from the gentler pull of the passionate young girl in the fairy notepaper, he would be fine. They would all be fine.

He just had to be tough with himself. 'Come on in, Laura,' he said. 'I make a killer espresso.' So much for being tough with himself.

'Espresso?' she asked, one fine auburn eyebrow kicking into a point. It was sexy enough for him to need to draw new breath. Sexy? Where had *that* subversive little word come from? 'A regular cup of tea is more than enough to tempt this country soul.'

'Okay,' he said. 'So it's not really espresso. I plan to have a crack at plain old instant black coffee, made in an old kettle that has seen better days.'

She blinked. Once. Twice. And he thought perhaps she would acquiesce. He hoped she would. Maybe they could get to know each other a little better. Just two adults, sitting down and chatting...on the floor by his credenza...? But then she shook her head and took a step away.

'Another time, then?' Ryan offered. Laura sent him a tight smile but made no answer. Eventually, with a small wave, she left, following her daughter's path back to the cottage.

Ryan watched her the whole way—watched the sway of her jeans-clad hips, the swing of her curled ponytail. He took in a deep breath and realised his heart-rate was flying. Every run-in with the woman had him feeling as if he had just drunk one of his favoured espressos.

The smell of the food got to him. He sat down on his back stairs and ate the delicious tuna concoction straight from the bowl as the sun set over his property—while trying to convince himself he was not acting like some teenager with an inappropriate crush.

CHAPTER FIVE

THE NEXT DAY at school Laura worked up a perfectly good head of steam, tracked down Miss Tilda, explained a thing or two about Chloe's family situation, then accepted a job catering for Miss Tilda's upcoming birth-day celebrations, quoting a price that would barely make her a profit. She was a sucker, no doubt about it.

'Laura Somervale! Just the woman I was looking for.' Jesse Bunton—Cal's wife and Tammy's mother—popped her head through the car win-dow just as Laura was about to pull away.

'Morning, Jesse,' Laura said through a stiff smile. 'My daughter has been telling stories about you.'

'Oh,' Jesse said, bringing a hand to her innocent heart. 'I hope they're all good.'

'Not really. I realise the whole town knows about my new neighbour. But can I trust you to pass on the word to be careful about what Chloe and her friends overhear? I don't need her to be upset by anything, or anyone.'

'Oh, of course,' Jesse blustered. 'If I ever inadvertently said anything to make our little Chloe anxious I would never forgive myself.'

Laura nodded her thanks, knowing the word would be all over town, quick-smart, that she was on the warpath against any sort of gossip that made its way to the classroom. But she also knew by the twinkle in the school mum's eye that she wasn't off the hook. 'Was there something else, Jesse?'

'Well, since you brought him up, we were hoping to find out a little more about that new neighbour of yours.'

'Who's we?' Laura asked, peering past Jesse to find half a dozen other local school mums inching into a circle around her.

'Spill, Laura!' one called out, gaining confidence. 'What's he like?'

'Is he straight?' Jesse asked. 'Is he single? Is he staying?'

Considering they were all married, she didn't know what the big deal was. Well, okay. She knew. Ryan Gasper was gorgeous. He was empirically, undeniably gorgeous. Compared with the usual assortment of tubby, balding, old-before-their-time lot who lived within a twenty-kilometre radius, Ryan Gasper was a rare dream-boat. A rare dream-boat who had invited her in for coffee the evening before, and for a brief moment there had been something in his eyes that had made her think he was after more than a companion for hot beverages. But for her to be even thinking that he might see her that way was ridiculous. Dangerous, detrimental to achieving the 'happy neighbour' relationship she had decided she would need to foster, and ridiculous.

'Apart from the fact that he is Chloe's uncle, and that he has bought Kardinyarr,' she said, keeping her voice even, 'all I know is that he won't say no to free food.' Perhaps that was playing a tad unfair. Once that snippet of news got around he would have more visitors than he would know what to do with. He would barely have time to leave the kitchen, much less come a-visiting the house across the way. Laura bit back a wicked smile. 'So you've had dinner with him already?' Jesse said, sending a meaningful grin to the others. 'Good for you!'

'Well, no,' Laura backtracked. 'I've baked him Tuna Mornay and a chocolate cake, but that's all.'

'So he's tried one of your cakes? The guy has no chance!' The ladies all laughed along with Jesse.

'No. Uh-uh. You've got the wrong idea…' But with every sentence she was digging a deeper hole for herself. They were as bad as Jill, matchmaking in their spare time. And if this lot were happy to say it to her face, she wondered what the rest of the town were saying behind her back. All she could do was continue supplying no ammunition for their ideas;

they would realise her life was as conventional as theirs, and talk would fizzle. She had discovered that, in time, it always did.

'Do stop by at my place when you visit Kardinyarr,' she said, before gunning the engine and heading off.

Ryan spent the morning getting dirty at the Minbah livestock markets. He trawled the unique bazaar from one end of the car park to the other. Families sold every mower part one could ever need out of the back of Kombi vans. Local kids manned tables full of their old toys, selling them off without remorse or entanglement at a dollar a piece. The cocktail scent of human sweat and animal waste was indiscriminate, but the energy of the place more than made up for it.

The livestock auction was held in a square wooden barn, taller than it was wide, with a dressage ring in the centre, surrounded on three sides by slap-hazard rows of wooden seats rising to a man's height from the roof. Ryan spent some time talking to a couple of vendors, and made himself known to Doc Larson, the local veterinarian, before deciding on the mix of beasts he wanted, and by the time their place in the queue was reached his palms were damp with nerves.

The room was stifling, the crowd noisy, but the auction process was meticulous.

This is what it's all about, Ryan thought. Buying and selling. Market forces. Capitalist economics. This was exactly what he had been talking about for the last twenty years without ever having lived it at the most elementary level.

Arriving back at Kardinyarr, he was eager to harness his enthusiasm—and the surplus of ideas regarding international trade and primary industry rocketing through his mind. He grabbed his laptop and went to make himself a cup of coffee, then realised that, though he had enough powdered milk to last him three months without a fridge, he hadn't bought any coffee or any sugar. So, with a mug filled with crisp, tinny tank water, he sat on the back steps, his laptop resting on the step above, and set to getting his thoughts down.

The next two hours flew. His fingers were cramped from pounding the keyboard with more vigour than he ever had before. *And* he was starving.

Before he had the chance to change his mind, he grabbed the empty Tuna Mornay tray—the cake tin still held enough of the heavenly cake for him to keep hold of it a little longer——then he jogged out through the back door and across the patch of grass that led him to the cottage next door.

He passed by an overturned bicycle, Chloe's discarded skipping-rope, and the washing line with newly washed clothes hanging damp and long in the hot, heavy, windless air. He cleared his throat and knocked on the open back door. 'Anyone home?'

He could hear noises from inside the house, music playing quietly on a stereo——he recognised it as 'In the Hall of the Mountain King', from *Peer Gynt*——and kitchen noises, cooking noises. And then the smell hit him. Sugar. Fruit. Pastry. He drank deeply of the most delicious mix of smells he had ever known.

Intrigued, he opened the unlocked fly-screen door and entered. The small entrance was cluttered. Several pairs of Chloe's shoes were piled up in the corner, and a square of mud-splattered welcome rug encouraged him to wipe his feet. A hall table littered with mail——some opened, some not——held a huge vase of dried wild flowers in the centre, all but hiding an antique mirror residing behind it. Several mismatched photo frames littered what was left of the table space. He'd leaned in to have a closer look when the lady of the house popped her head around the doorway.

'Ryan!' she called. 'I thought I heard somebody.'

He snapped up straight, sprung snooping, his feet scuffling on the floor like a naughty schoolboy. 'I hope you don't mind. I let myself in.'

He held out the casserole dish and she took it.

'You may as well have the grand tour now that you've made it past the guard dog,' she said.

Ryan followed Laura's line of sight to find a miniature fox terrier snuffling at the toecaps of his boots. He squatted down and offered his hand to the creature for a smell. After a few tentative sniffs the dog's body began to wriggle, and he earned himself a happy yap. 'Who's this?' Ryan called out.

'Chimp,' Laura said from further away. 'We should be a registered zoo, with the odd assortment of animals we've adopted over the years. It's one of the many nice things about living on so much land.'

Ryan followed her voice. Rounding the small entranceway, he found himself in the body of the house. An overstuffed floral lounge suite filled the living space.

A dining-room table was littered with trays, muffin cups, and sheets of aluminium foil. A record player—an actual old-style record player—rocked gently in one corner, spilling Grieg through a pair of ancient mission-brown speakers. An open-plan kitchen with a window overlooked Laura's undulating land and their shared front driveway. A doorway led to what must have been the bedrooms and bathroom.

It was...cosy. Warm. Snug. But it was about a quarter of the size of his new home, and smaller even than some of the serviced apartments he had been put up in when in some of the larger cities. The Vegas hotel room he had given up would have fitted her house twice, and he would have been staying there alone.

'Why Chimp?' he asked, skirting around a rug with a rocking-chair in the corner until he came up against the kitchen bench.

Laura switched off the tap and dried her hands on her apron. 'Chloe's wanted a chimpanzee since the day she first saw one on television.'

Ryan followed the wave of her hand to find what must have been a twenty-year-old black and white box on top of a lamp-table against the wall. The thing was so old it was probably worth more now to a collector than it would have been when first bought.

'After some negotiating a couple of Christmases ago,' Laura continued, 'we settled on a pup named Chimp.' She shot him a glance warmed by memories of her daughter. 'Now, come to think of it, I would put money on the fact that Chloe always wanted a dog and used all the leverage she could muster.'

'Clever girl, eh?'

'You have no idea.'

A familiar click and whir filled the silence as the needle went back to the beginning of the record. Ryan simply waited, looking over the woman before him as though time stood still between songs.

Silhouetted by the sunlight spilling through the wide kitchen window, Laura looked as alluring as all-get-out. Again, she wore a dress, pale blue this time, with a floaty skirt, tight middle, and thin shoulder straps. A plain white apron was pulled tight around her waist, cinched at the back in a large bow. Her clear brown eyes, the colour of bushland grass after a long drought, looked back at him—steady, strong, unwavering.

No wonder Will had been smitten. Even at eighteen she would have been something else to behold. She was undeniably the most unashamedly feminine woman Ryan had ever met—all soft curves and curling hair, with long limbs and a pretty face, smooth lips, skin quick to blush. Yet she had a complicated mind and a smart mouth that grabbed him deeper than her merely aesthetic delights ever could.

A faint crackle heralded the beginning of the record and the fine strains of Grieg released Ryan from his consideration of Laura's entirely natural loveliness.

'Chloe's at school still,' she told him, her voice slightly wavering.

Was she nervous, having him alone in her house? Rather than sending him running it made him all the more determined to stay. 'I knew that.'

'So why did you come over?' she asked more slowly. 'Just to bring back the Tuna Mornay dish?'

You wish. He bit back his response and searched for a reason that would make her relax. He retraced his steps. Out of her warm kitchen. Away from her cluttered entrance. Outside of her inviting doorway. Back to his empty house with his half-empty pantry. 'I was hoping to borrow some sugar.'

He expected to be shot down in flames by some entirely deserved barb from a woman who knew how to deliver them. But instead she laughed. Her slender throat worked as the delightful tinkle of laughter escaped her throat. 'You're kidding me.'

'I'm not,' he continued with a shrug. 'I don't know that I have ever shopped before for groceries enough to fill a pantry, and I overcompensated on odd things, like flour, and forgot basic things like coffee and eggs.'

'That's priceless,' she said, her laughter gone, but her face still creased by a smile. 'Now, go on and sit.'

After the moments it took for him to disengage himself from her unexpected warmth, he looked around for the dog.

'Chimp is outside, chasing the magpies,' she said. 'I was talking to you, Ryan. Sit. Stay. I'll make you a proper coffee.'

Not daring to push his luck, he pulled up a kitchen stool and sat, leaning his elbows against the bench and trying to quell his suddenly growling stomach. 'So, what's with all the aluminium foil?' he asked, motioning to her flour-covered apron and the two dozen trays littering her workspace.

'Tonight is a get-together of the local chapter of the Country Fire Association.'

'Is there any local group for which you are not a volunteer?'

She shrugged. 'I do what I can. I am not entirely philanthropic; I've been hired to cook for this event as well.'

'Is catering really that lucrative?'

At that statement she stared him down. 'I more than *cater*, Mr Gasper,' she said, her voice overbrimming with confidence. 'I can do things with sugar and flour that you have never experienced. Even in your big-city cafe's.'

'Maybe you've been into the wrong cafe's. I'm sure I could show you a couple that would blow your mind.'

'Could you, now?'

'Why not?' he said, feeling as if he was pushing against some sort of diminishing boundary. 'Maybe one day I'll take Chloe into town for a play date, and maybe we'll invite you along.'

She watched him from behind her long lashes. 'Well, maybe I'll accept your invitation,' she said. She turned back to the sink and began washing out a bowl full of strawberries, and he decided then and there that he liked it much better when they were moving towards each other than when she was pulling away. 'So, when were you last in a big-city cafe'?'

After a brief pause she turned back to face him, wiped her wet hands on her apron, cocked a hip against the bench and looked him straight in the èye. 'It was the day of your brother's funeral. I had some time before my train was due to take me home and I had a sudden need for piles of chocolate. The just as strong need to be out of the rain meant that I stumbled into the first open cafe' I found. The pastries were fair, but I knew I could do better.'

Listening to her talk about that day, Ryan felt a deep hard pressure against his lungs, festering, compounding, until he could think of nothing else. She was so cool and tough, but Ryan had to fight the desperate need to clear his throat and look away.

'So why weren't you there?' she asked.

'Where?' he asked, his voice regrettably ragged, but he knew what she meant.

'At Will's funeral.'

Ryan searched through the array of possible answers. He'd been busy. He hadn't been able to get a flight in time. It had been too late to pull out of his commitments in Paris.

'I was angry with him,' he said, surprised at the words spilling from his own mouth.

He ran fingers over the pale scars on his knuckles, formed when he had smashed the window in his hotel room. His chest again grew tight with memories, and tighter still as he awaited her response. Would that be the end of it? Would she never more look at him with those brief flashes of inescapable curiosity, as if she wanted to know more, to know him deeper, as he wanted to know her? Would she write him off completely for being so callous?

But, instead, she gave him an accepting smile and said, 'I know *exactly* what you mean.' Jill was right; Laura was far too kind for the likes of him.

'When my dad died suddenly, a few years ago, I was furious,' she explained. 'I was so angry with him for leaving me alone, for not giving me the chance to let him know how much I was going to miss him. And I was angry with all the good people of Tandarah because, in my blinkered grief, I knew they couldn't possibly know how I felt. Most of all, I was angry with myself for being so angry. I am a pretty happy-go-lucky person, but during those first weeks I thought I would never remember how to be happy again.'

An easy smile slid across her face, and he knew that those feelings had long since been reconciled. Despite being a single mother, living from hand to mouth, she was in a much better place than he was.

'Tell me a nice memory you have of Will,' she said, as though sensing his melancholy.

A nice memory, eh? They'd clashed so often, he wondered if he could. He shuffled through his memories for something he thought Laura would appreciate.

'When he was a kid,' he said at length, 'he would lie out on the trampoline, staring at the stars, until somebody remembered he was out there and dragged him back inside.' He shook his head, diffusing the memory. 'I always wanted to light a fire under him, to get him animated, but at the same time I envied him that level of serenity.'

'Chloe can look through picture books for hours on end,' Laura interjected. 'I *never* had that sort of patience at her age. I still don't. I constantly have to be moving, doing something, talking, walking, cooking or singing, for fear if I stop I might never want to get started again.'

'Yep. I've been there.'

'But Chloe has the ability to simply *be*. As did Will.' She shrugged. 'It's a gift.'

The more he knew about her, the more Ryan believed Laura was the one with the gift. She had an amazing resilience, and an ability to smile through anything. 'How did you get past the anger?' he asked.

'Too hot bubble bath therapy went a long way,' she said, with a cheeky twinkle in her eye, before turning back to her strawberries.

The sudden image of Laura in a deep spa bath, her hair pinned high on her head, damp curls stuck to her neck as she lay up to her chest in bubbles, was enough to have Ryan shift himself on the seat. 'Enlighten me.'

'Happy to. The first thing you should know is that the joys of the too hot bubble bath are all in the timing.'

'All in the timing,' Ryan repeated, committing the information and the accompanying image to memory.

'For example, a couple of months ago I was down by the dam, reeling in the hose after watering my plum trees, when I was caught in a sudden sun shower. By the time I made it back up to the house I was soaked through. What better way to warm up than with a too hot bubble bath?'

Now Ryan had to fight off the image of Laura running through the rain, her clothes soaked to her skin, sun glinting off her hair. 'Tell me more.'

Laura glanced over her shoulder at the sound of his suddenly uneven voice, but when he merely smiled politely back, she continued.

'Okay... Ummm... When I dropped Chloe off at her first ever day at school, I came home to find I had nothing to do. No dinners to cater, no phone calls to make, no clothes to wash. Nothing. After a too hot bubble bath, I got back into my pyjamas and ate nothing all day but half a round of brie, an entire block of chocolate and left over, two-day-old, reheated fried rice. That was perfect timing.'

She spun to face him, her skirt twirling before settling in soft folds about her legs. She took a bite of a strawberry, her teeth biting down and her lips drawing the succulent flesh into her mouth. She threw the stem into the sink, licked her fingers, then continued, wholly unaware of Ryan's escalating enchantment.

'Oh, and then there was one beautiful afternoon I discovered the consummate hanging-washing-on-the-line soundtrack. I sang along with every song; the magpies weren't so impressed, but I had a ball. Suddenly through the damp white sheets I caught sight of a perfect cerulean blue sky and thought, Why have I been looking down all day? *Voila!* Perfect timing.'

Ryan laughed aloud as he realised how the conversation had turned. 'But, from what I remember, on that day some stranger bundled up in shiny boots and a not-so-shiny car and threw a spanner in the works.'

'That he did.' She nodded, her eyes sparkling. 'And, alas, that perfect time was lost for ever.' She smiled, creating an adorable dimple in her right cheek, and suddenly Ryan thought of Chloe. The little girl who had the same dimple. His brother's child.

He sucked in a cooling breath. What was he doing, allowing himself to become so captivated by a woman who had shared his brother's bed? The problem was, he couldn't help himself. There was something about her that had him entranced, intrigued, covetous of any feelings she had ever had for any other man.

'Sincerest apologies,' he said, meaning it. He wished he had never denied this dazzling woman a moment's pleasure.

'Apology accepted,' she said, something in the timbre of her voice making him think she wasn't wholly unaware of his train of thought. 'But only because that is the beauty and the bane of the too hot bubble bath. I revere it all the more for its rarity.'

'Thank you for sharing that with me.'

'No biggie.' She lifted a shoulder, then her gaze sharpened as she pointed a finger at him. 'But it wasn't only too hot bubble baths that helped me cope. If your bother had not turned up when he did, if he had not been willing to listen to my blathering with an outsider's kind ear, it might have been a very different story.'

Again, Ryan's gut kicked with a horrible stab of foolish envy. *Next subject.* 'So, how are you going to prove to this city boy that you are such a cook?' he asked.

'The chocolate cake and Tuna Mornay weren't enough?'

'Not even close,' he lied. The memory of the flavours and textures had his tastebuds watering in response.

She smiled again, drawn in by his challenge. 'How do mini-mincepies and chocolate-covered strawberries sound?'

'It sounds like a goal well worth shooting for.'

She reached over and grabbed the percolator from inside a cupboard. 'And coffee, right? Black with sugar?' Seeing that she had no bench space left on which to put the coffeepot, Ryan snapped to attention. He leapt off the stool and was by her side in a flash. 'The one thing I can make is a cup of coffee. So, you do your magic over there, and I will make a brew. Deal?'

Big amber eyes blinked up at him, and Ryan had a funny feeling that nobody had ever offered to make her coffee in her own home before. Any man would be lucky to have this creature waiting for him at home, all wrapped up so sweet in one of her cotton dresses, but he had the growing feeling she had never been spoilt as she deserved to be.

But what if he had known Laura back then? If he had done as Will had asked and come to Kardinyarr and seen the reason why Will had been willing to give up Oxford, to reject Paris, would he have understood? Would he have left Will to his own devices and stopped pushing? Or would he have taken one look at young Laura Somervale and flipped over her himself? He kicked himself for never making room for the possibility that his brother might be onto something good for himself until it was too late.

Damn Will for dying! Ryan thought. *Damn him for leaving this woman all alone. And damn him for creating such a captivating picture of this woman, and this place, in his e-mails that the minute Sam showed them to me I had had no choice but to come all the way out to the middle of nowhere to see what the fuss was all about.*

He reached out and took a hold of the percolator and coffee bag. His fingers brushed against hers for a fraction of a second and she jerked away as though burnt. Desperate to find somewhere to put her hands, she bunched her fingers into fists at her sides then flattened them against her skirt. It was enough to make him long to touch her again. How would she react if he brushed his knuckles along the smooth curve of her cheekbone...?

'Coffee would be...helpful,' she said, taking a step back towards the sink, her voice unbelievably husky as she looked into his eyes. 'Thank you.'

Ryan nodded and did as he was asked. But as soon as the hot water and coffee were happily becoming acquainted, he turned and leant his back against her bench, watching her knead out a slab of freshly mixed pastry. Her back was to him as she finished off the food portion of their meal, and he soon became entranced by the big white bow of her apron.

All he had to do was reach out and grab one end, and the whole thing would slip undone...

She glanced over her shoulder and caught him staring. Her wheat-gold eyes flashed, her soft cheeks warmed, and it was all he could do to stop himself from dragging her into his arms and kissing her until her pupils became dark and heavy and her limbs grew languid. He watched, fascinated, as she swallowed down a great lump in her throat, and her eyelashes battered against her cheeks. At length, her gaze tore from his and landed upon the bubbling percolator. She reached out for it as though it was a lifeline.

'Uh-uh,' he chastised. 'That's my job.' When she didn't move, he gave her a little bump with his hip and she skittered back to the safety of the sink. 'So, my part of the cooking deal is almost done, how about you?'

He risked a glance and found her watching him, her gaze hooded, her thoughts far away. But she blinked and was back with him before he knew it.

She tried a smile, but it went no further than her pale pink lips. 'Sure. Of course.' Wiping her hands on her apron again, she then slipped on a pair of oven mitts and opened up the top oven.

The mix of aromas that hit Ryan knocked him for six. 'That smells incredible.'

The smile lighting her profile this time was real. 'My own mince pie recipe. The secret ingredient is the plums.'

'Well, it's not a secret any more.'

'Are you going to be making them any time soon?'

'Ah, no. Even if I did have the utensils, I wouldn't have a clue what else to put in, bar the plums, so your secret is safe with me.'

'That's what I figured.'

'Hey,' he said rounding on her with arms crossed across his chest. 'I'll have you know that I can cook a very little.'

'What's your speciality? Three-minute noodles? Egg on toast? Frozen pizza?'

'Actually, all of the above. Plus a couple that you will never know about.'

'Oh, and why's that?' Her smile now reached her eyes, and he swore there was now an almost flirtatious swing in her hips as she carried the pies past his straining nose and over to the edge of the sink.

'Because you are laughing at me,' he said, watching her every move with extra attention. 'So now you will just have to lie awake at night trying to guess.'

'Ryan, I can assure you the minute my head hits the pillow I will be fast asleep. You moving in next door will do nothing to change that. Shall we eat outside?' she asked, loading another tray of pies into the oven before placing a few on a white dish for them to enjoy.

Ryan glanced around the busy room. 'Either there or on the floor.'

'If you insist on being churlish you'll get nothing.' This time Ryan had to lick his lips they were so suddenly dry. 'Off to bed without supper?' he asked.

Her face dropped, as though she'd only just realised that they had in fact been flirting outrageously for some time. But he wasn't going to let her off the hook again. It was her turn.

'I am a mother,' she said by way of apology. 'Sorry. I find myself telling off the local vet if he doesn't wipe his feet at the front door. It's pathological.'

It's adorable, Ryan thought, but he knew that saying it aloud would only strain the capricious confidence that had begun to blossom between them.

'Bring the coffee?' she requested over her shoulder.

Ryan did as he was told, and followed her through the front door and out to the portico where a wroughtiron table and chairs sat in one corner by a pretty garden sprouting with new flowers.

'Yoo-hoo!'

Their two heads snapped in the direction of Ryan's front door. It seemed he had a visitor.

'Oh. That's Jesse. Cal Bunton's wife,' Laura said, her voice and her eyes so filled with regret Ryan bit back a curse. 'I kind of told her that you were in need of feeding.'

'Mr Gasper!' Jesse called out, her voice coming louder and closer. 'Don't be shy. I know you're here. I can see your divine car!'

'You should go,' Laura said, her arms still filled with the tray of delicious pies. 'We can do this another time.' His mouth twitched. He knew exactly why she had told Jesse Bunton he needed feeding. To keep him busy so she wouldn't have to. He had stupidly been thinking she was flirting, when the whole time she had been politely marking time until somebody else took him off her hands.

He pulled away to stand in the bright sunshine of her front yard, leaving her shaded in the doorway. He imagined she looked sad, disappointed to be sending him away. But he was a wilful man, and in his life he had imagined many things that simply weren't there.

'Thanks for the almost-lunch, Laura. It was enlightening,' he said, before turning and jogging away.

Over the next couple of hours the line of cars, utes and four-wheel drives kicking up dust on their communal driveway was out of control. Laura didn't know whether to be thankful that she had brought the town's women to Ryan's rescue, or if she wanted to wind back the clock and see what might have happened if Jesse hadn't blundered along.

That night the Country Fire Association was going to have a feast the likes of which they had never seen: glazed tartlets, homemade jam doughnuts, Pavlova piled high with fresh fruit and whipped cream, all things sweet and succulent. Anything that might help whisk away the disturbing tension coursing through her overripe body.

Something had been cooking between Ryan and her. Something friendly—and more than neighbour-friendly. But, alas, her own hubris in daring the local women to come out to Kardinyarr and see that nothing was happening between them had ended up preventing something happening between them.

Of course that was for the best. Being hospitable towards Chloe's uncle was one thing, but being *friendly* was another. It didn't matter that she was undeniably drawn to his easy confidence. It didn't matter that every time she felt his eyes upon her she warmed from the inside out. It didn't matter because she knew Ryan had come to Kardinyarr in search of family, not in search of a complicated connection with the mother of his newfound niece.

Laura thought back to the last time she had spent concentrated time in a man's company. She had cherished Will for the comfort he had given her when she'd needed it most, but she had never felt as if she was walking on hot coals whenever he came within five feet of her.

Will's shrewd big brother was in a whole other league. Where Will had been a young man, all at sea, Ryan was a man of action who knew exactly what he wanted and made no bones about going after it. But what had that afternoon been all about if it hadn't been about him letting her know in a million subtle ways that he wanted her? A touch here. A look there. A delicious shiver ran down Laura's spine until she scrunched her toes into the floor mat below her bare feet. There was something about him that meant so long as he was sleeping in the house next door she would never again fall asleep the minute her head hit the pillow.

By the time she had taken up every spare surface in her lounge room, with twice as much food as the CFA could possibly eat, a pair of moving trucks had trundled up the dirt drive. Through the window, she watched Ryan jog over to meet the trucks. There was much backslapping and laughter as he set to, helping the men carry piles of furniture into Kardinyarr House. Laura saw a bed for each room, at least a dozen dining chairs, lounge suites for both the formal lounge and the sitting room... Did that really mean he was thinking of staying? Her heart leapt. She slapped it down. But it was too late. Dangerous feelings had crept up on her when she was determinedly looking the other way. She wanted him to stay, for if he left now she would miss him. She would miss the look in his eye when he spoke of his brother, the way he listened when she prattled, the way he watched her when he thought she wasn't paying attention.

Damn Jill and her meddling, Laura thought. *Damn Will for building Ryan up so brilliantly in my imagination. And damn Ryan himself for the little-boy-lost look in his eyes, and for making me believe that somehow I am the only one who can help him find whatever it is he is looking for...*

CHAPTER SIX

'CHLOE!' LAURA CALLED out later that night, when dinner was almost on the table. Her ears pricked for a loud, frustrated *Wha-a-at?* But the response did not come.

'Chloe!' she called again, louder this time. Still nothing. Her chest constricted. Chloe knew not to go further than calling distance, and she knew why—especially when the flowers were in bloom, the ground was more dust than soil, and when the wind had picked up more than a whisper.

Laura jogged through the house, checking each room as she went, but Chloe was nowhere to be seen. She ran out of the house and called across the gully. She strained her ears to hear her daughter's voice, to pick up a noise, a scent, anything, her instincts stretched to their limits. And then she heard it. Laughter. Coming from the direction of Kardinyarr.

Her heart thudding against her ribs, Laura found Ryan crouched by a fence halfway down the hill, hammer in hand, fixing a broken paling. Chloe stood by him, holding onto a tin of nails, chattering away blithely about her day at school. Chimp lay next to a new red toolbox, munching on an old bone. While Ryan concentrated on not putting a nail through his thumb he listened, looking Chloe's way every few moments, and asking questions every time her speech came to a halt.

Laura watched as Ryan held out a hand for a nail, holding up his thumb and forefinger to show Chloe the size he was after. With her tongue half hanging out of her mouth, Chloe scoured the tray until she found the right one, and when Ryan grinned his thanks she just glowed.

Laura's heart lurched. Troubled as she was by her own mixed-up feelings towards Ryan Gasper, she hadn't thought this whole thing through to its logical conclusion. Of course Chloe would fall for the guy. She'd never had a solid male influence in her life, and then one day this prime specimen fell from the sky into her lap. Laura sensed a whole heap of trouble brewing. If—no, *when*, Ryan headed back to his real life, Chloe would be too young to understand why she had been left behind.

'Chloe,' Laura called out, her voice gruff. Her daughter jumped out of her skin. 'Didn't you hear me calling you?'

Ryan stood and turned from his work to face her. Her blood warmed instantly at the sight of him, dressed down in an unfamiliar chocolate-coloured T-shirt, snug, shabby button-fly jeans, aged sneakers, and a red baseball cap worn backwards the better to see his work at hand. Beads of sweat lay across his brow, between clumping, damp dark curls, and his skin already looked a shade more tanned from the kiss of a couple of days of sun.

Laura growled at herself and tore her disobedient gaze away from the man to the imperilled little girl at his side. She put her hands on her hips, raised an eyebrow, and waited for Chloe to explain herself.

'I was outside the back door playing when I heard Ryan's hammer. I asked if I could help and he said that was fine.' Chloe looked to her partner in crime for reassurance, and he came to the rescue.

'Without my little helper here I'm sure this job would have taken me twice as long.' He ruffled Chloe's curls and she beamed up at him.

Laura turned on him. 'That's all well and good. But your little *helper* here has a deal with her *mother*. Don't you, Miss Chloe?'

Chloe bowed her head, her tiny shoulders slumping. 'When at home I am not to go any further than shouting distance, or I have to check in every ten minutes.' Then her head sprang up. 'But I was with Uncle Ryan! So if my breathing became bad he would have helped me.'

Ryan's gaze flicked from mother to daughter. 'Your breathing?' he repeated.

'Chronic asthma,' Chloe explained, mimicking the words of her many doctors. 'If I have an attack, I could die. My asthma is so bad even with regular use of my reliever and preventer puffers nothing is certain.'

Ryan pushed away from the fence, as though distancing himself from Chloe's dire words. 'I... Really? She did mention asthma the other day, but I had no idea it was that serious.'

'I just need her to be nearby. To know she is safe,' Laura snapped. 'You understand now why I have tried to take my time with all of *this*?' She waved her hand about, taking in him, her, and the house behind them. *Don't mess about playing happy families with my little girl unless you mean it.*

Ryan's sneaker-clad foot kicked at a lonely tuft of grass. 'Yeah,' he said, the word emerging slowly from his mouth. 'Yeah.'

He looked so appalled, and Laura felt instantly guilty for being so abrupt. It wasn't his fault that Chloe hadn't followed the rules. It wasn't his fault that Chloe had flitted to him like a moth to a flame. It wasn't his fault that both Somervale women were becoming dangerously used to the fact of him being there.

'She hasn't had a full-blown attack in months,' Laura said, softening her temper. 'So long as we take care she might never again.'

He reached out and laid a gentle protective hand across Chloe's shoulders. 'Just don't go so far again without letting your mum know, okay?' he said.

Chloe leant into his embrace and Laura fought the cry of anguish that rose in her throat. Instead, she held out her hand and Chloe tumbled over into her arms for a forgiving hug.

I am sorry, Ryan mouthed over Chloe's head.

It's not your fault, Laura mouthed back.

Ryan tore the cap from his head, wiped at the sweat on his forehead with the back of his gloves, then tugged the cap back on the right way around. Gloves.

'Where on earth did you find those?' she asked, her sudden outburst drawing all eyes to Ryan's gloved hands.

He held out his hands palm-up. 'I found them in the front shed. Are they yours?'

'No. They were my father's,' Laura said, her voice sounding as though it was coming from far away. She reached out and ran a finger along Ryan's open palm, the sensation of worn old suede so familiar. 'Funny, I looked for them everywhere after he died.'

'Would you like them back?'

Laura shook her head. 'No. I'm just happy to know that they're still about, still working on Kardinyarr's fences. He ran cattle on Kardinyarr land right up until the heart attack took him.'

'Then I guess there is symmetry in the fact that these old gloves are still achieving the same ends today,' he offered, his voice soft and kind.

'Mmm, and a day of working those fences without gloves and your girly-soft city-boy hands would never be the same again.'

Ryan's strong gloved fingers suddenly closed over her own soft hand. 'You do enjoy taunting me, don't you, Ms Somervale? I think it comes as naturally to you as breathing.'

Laura's cheek twitched. 'I'm afraid it does.' Taunting him felt darned good. Fighting with him gave her more of an endorphin rush than laughing with almost anybody else. Sparring with him made her feel wilful, resilient, fascinating. It had been a long time since she had felt that way about herself.

Chloe clearing her throat broke the exquisite mood that had settled over the two of them. 'Can we finish the fence now you're here?' Chloe asked. 'I do have other things to do, you know!'

Laura coughed back a laugh. The girl was barely six, yet she was already showing signs of becoming a right little teenager. Laura was not looking forward to the day Chloe discovered boys were for kissing rather than for swapping footy cards and collecting tadpoles. As such, she slid her hand from Ryan's rough grasp.

'What do you have to do tonight?' Laura asked, and Chloe backed down enough to look sheepish.

'Miss Tilda said that my letter As need work. I didn't like her saying that in front of all the other kids. So by the end of term I plan to have the best letter As in the whole class.'

Ryan and Laura shared a smile, and again it hit her exactly how much she missed not having someone in her life to share moments like these. Special, unique Chloe moments. Chloe's first word. Chloe's first step. The first terrifying midnight rush to the doctor when she'd thought Chloe would never take breath again. These were moments she had lived through alone. Jill had heard everything after the fact, in their daily phone chats, but it wasn't the same. Having someone else to bear witness felt terribly precious.

Dangerous, she corrected. Because though this man was invested, though it was likely he would be in their lives from this day on, it would be on the periphery. Somehow, she was no longer afraid that Ryan would try to take Chloe from her. Despite her warnings to herself she totally trusted him. But now she felt the cold curl of dread for the day he *would* leave them both.

'Chloe, how about you head in now and practise your As. I'm sure Ryan won't mind.'

'But who will get the nails for him?' Chloe asked. 'Your mum can do that,' Ryan offered promptly.

Laura had been about to say he was a big boy and could handle himself, but now she was caught. 'Of course I will, possum,' she said. 'Now, off you go. We'll be done here in a minute.'

'Okay!' Chloe cried out, before skipping happily back to the house, with a less energetic Chimp sniffling along in her wake.

Laura spun to lean on the fence a good arm's distance from Ryan. The sounds of evening whispered in her ear. This was her favourite time of day. Right when the sun had disappeared beneath the hill, the brilliant orb having reached out its last gasp of too bright light, casting a kaleidoscope of colour across the undulating horizon. The tall, fine eucalypts on the next hill cast disproportional shadows into the gully below. The temperature dropped five degrees in as many minutes. Night was close on sunset's heels.

She glanced sideways to find Ryan looking out over the land with the same wistful expression.

'Nice outfit,' she said, having to break the loaded silence.

Ryan looked down to his scuffed shoes, then back up at her with a crooked grin. 'What? These old things?'

He looked so darned good in those old things her breath hitched and she had to look away. 'Did you raid the second-hand store in town?' she asked.

'Nah. Along with furniture and appliances, my sister Sam packed up some old clothes stored in my apartment in Melbourne. You like?'

She shrugged. There was certainly no need for him to know quite how much she liked. 'In that get-up you could almost pass for a local.'

'I'll take that as a compliment.' He grinned and held out two fingers about an inch apart. 'I would like a nail this long, please.'

Laura found the right nail and dropped it into his gloved palm. 'So, have you decided who is going to benefit from this fixed fence?' she asked. 'Has *Running Livestock For Dummies* got some sort of close-your-eyes-and-point game included?'

'Goats,' Ryan said, taking a nail between his teeth and banging it into a new paling. 'I picked them out at the Minbah market.'

'Goats?' Laura repeated, carefully removing her gaze from the muscles in his tanned forearm, which clenched with every hit. 'Not horses? Not cattle? Not something more overtly...manly?'

Ryan's eyes narrowed as he kept his focus on the nail between his gloved fingers, but his grin only broadened.

It seemed the guy was perfectly secure in his own manliness. More was the pity, because Laura was becoming more and more certain of it herself.

'So what sort of...*goats* did you have in mind?'

'Angora,' he said, with no small amount of pride in his voice.

'What do you know about Angora goats?'

His grin eased into a comfortable smile. 'About as much as I know about cattle or horses.' His bright blue gaze shot her way, creating a ball of fire in her stomach. Laura bit her lip. 'I have a mother and two sisters who can't get enough of Angora,' he said, in between hammer hits. 'I know there is a huge demand for natural fabrics on the Australian fashion scene, and that there is a huge demand for Australian fashion overseas. I know that I can run a small flock on my own, with hired help only at shearing time, and I know that I already have wool buyers lined up across the country and throughout Asia.'

Laura dared not open her mouth for fear that she would come up with nothing more insightful than *duh*. Ryan's growing smile showed that he knew it too.

'So what do you reckon, Ms Somervale? Will I be a farmer yet?'

She felt him getting comfortable, loose-limbed, as if he was born to lean on that fence, and she felt her own need to kick him right out of that comfort zone and back to his side of the fence. Gathering her wits, she pierced him with her fiercest glare and said, 'Nah.'

He shot her a quick glance from the shade of his cap before changing the subject. 'So, why didn't you tell me that you had your eyes on Kardinyarr for yourself?'

Surprised completely, Laura swore beneath her breath.

'Bloody Jill Tucker! Jill told you, right? She can't keep her nose out of this, can she?'

'Out of what?'

'Out of my business,' she said, fudging over the specifics somewhat. 'I never really thought it would ever happen. It was a pipedream, really. Some girls want to be a rock star...'

'You wanted this house and land,' he finished. 'Don't panic. I have no plans to poison your water tanks or knock down your fences in the middle of the night. Unlike *some people*, I am somewhat used to my plans not working out the way I hope they will. It pays to be philosophical about these things.'

'*Some people* being me, right? You think I am used to things working out exactly as *I* planned? As it turns out, Miss Smarty Pants, I do know what it feels like to be told no. And it's not that easy to move on.'

There was something hard in his voice that had her wondering who had denied him. A business associate? A woman? Will? It was Will. That was why he was angry with him. Because if Will had said yes to going to Paris he would not have been walking through the long grass by the gully, he would not have disturbed the deadly brown snake, and he would still have been around today...

She was suddenly aware of how close they were standing. Had she shifted closer to him or he to her? The arm's width distance was now less than a foot. She could feel warmth streaming from his body. She looked up at the stars. *When had they arrived?* she wondered, realising it had fallen dark.

'I have ignored my own rule long enough,' she said. 'Chloe isn't within shouting distance. I had better go. Are you all right for dinner?'

Ryan held a hand to his stomach. 'Thanks to your welcome wagon, I was given six—yes, *six*—pot-roasts today. I will be fine for dinner for the next month.'

'Excellent.' She shot him a quick salute before backing away from his enveloping warmth. 'Goodnight, Ryan.'

'Goodnight, Laura.'

Ryan let out a long slow breath as Laura disappeared within the shadows leading up the drive.

'What are you doing, Gasper?' he asked himself aloud. 'You are asking for trouble, that's what you are doing.'

He reached into the back pocket of his jeans and found Laura's letter. He had kept it on him since the day he'd found it. As first it had been as though if he let it go he would lose the last tenuous link to his brother. But now, the more real the woman in the letter became, the reason for keeping the letter close had changed.

He brought the paper to his lips and imagined he caught a wafting scent. But there was nothing there—only the memory of a woman who smelled so sweet, as though covered in a permanent layer of sugar from her cooking, so sweet it made him ache.

He tucked the letter back into his pocket. The letter that had made him come all the way out to Kardinyarr. And it wasn't just about the information within; it was about the words, the passion, the hope, the wonder—and the woman who had written them.

So what if he had bought the house his brother had loved? That did not give him any right over the woman as well. He was a guy who'd lived out of a suitcase all his life. He was a guy who had told his younger brother to live as he lived, finding companionship wherever he laid his hat, not wanting or needing it to last longer than the weeks or months he stayed in one city. So what right did such a guy have to admire, to want, to long for a woman like Laura?

The laughable thing was that before he had even come, before he had even laid eyes on either of them, he had already been intrigued to distraction by the place—and by the woman. Now that he was getting to know them both, he knew that his imaginings had not even come close to how extraordinary they both were.

Ryan threw his hammer into his shiny new toolbox, grabbed the box, and stormed back to the big house, where the impassive pleasures of fine new furniture and a freezer full of pot-roasts awaited him.

Laura managed to keep out of Ryan's way over the next couple of days. After dropping Chloe at school, she worked her regular part-time shifts at the local post office. Her nights were also full, with Tammy's birthday party one night, and her own *Pirates of Penzance* rehearsal another. So she could fortunately keep Chloe's time with her new champion to a minimum as well.

The peculiar thing was, every time she sneaked her tired little girl home after dark, and she came upon the lit windows of Kardinyarr

House, Laura felt joy. She knew it was because every night the windows remained lit was another night Ryan Gasper had lasted. Having a neighbour was enormously comforting. Having him as a neighbour meant that her comfort came with an unpredictable edge.

One evening she found a parcel wrapped in newspaper and string on her welcome mat. She unwrapped the package to find her father's worn, battle-scarred suede gloves. The note with them read: *Symmetry be damned. Keep these safe. R.* The next morning, on the way to dropping Chloe at school, she had left a fresh batch of mini-mince pies on his doorstep, in thanks.

By Friday mid-morning, she had shuttled Chloe to school, cleaned the house, and hung the washing. So by the time Ryan's goats arrived, Laura was crazy with cabin fever. She was used to walking the hills and valleys of her neighbour's farm on a daily basis, and since he had come along she had been stuck in the house, pottering, cooking, and thinking herself in never-ending circles.

She peered out of the kitchen window as the livestock truck trundled up the drive. When it rounded the side of the house she couldn't see any more without leaning herself bodily out of the open window. So she grabbed her gardening gloves and a small spade and hustled outside, where she found an excellent vantage point atop an old fruit crate by the huge lemon tree at the edge of her property.

Her mouth fell agape when she caught a glimpse of Ryan's flock. Not one to start with seeds planted in the ground, he had acquired a seriously healthy, fully-grown herd, which would produce an ample yield of wool. From the looks of it, three of the females were pregnant. Nothing like serious start-up money to get a farm turning a dollar.

Once her curved-up T-shirt was overbrimming with lemons, she ran inside and set to work.

Ryan looked up from gazing at his flock to find Laura striding towards him. He had been expecting her the moment the truck arrived, and wondered what had taken so long.

Rather than her usual sun dresses, she wore faded jeans, moulded tight to her lean curves, and a pale yellow fitted T-shirt. Her curls were tied back into a highswinging ponytail, again with one of Chloe's pink shoelaces. The knees of her pants were smeared with dirt and grass stains, and her cheeks were pink from the sun. Her eyes had faint remnants of eyeliner smudged around the edge, making Ryan think she must have had another *Pirates of Penzance* rehearsal the night before. It also made him think how unfairly sexy smudged eyeliner could be on a woman. She looked healthy as sunlight, farm-fed and golden.

'Howdy, ma'am,' Ryan said with a friendly neighbourhood smile when she arrived, doing his best to cover up the fact that she had him entirely unhinged. 'What you got there?'

She lifted a Thermos by way of hello. 'Lemonade. It's a scorcher today, and I thought you could use some.' She rested the Thermos on the railing and poured him a glass. The chilled drink created instant condensation on the outside of the aluminium cup.

He licked his lips as he held out a hand, but looked at her through narrowed eyes. 'Is it homemade?'

She tilted her pretty head to one side. 'Naturally. And using my own lemons.'

'Ms Somervale, I think that they are in fact *my* lemons. The tree trunk is on my side of the fence.'

She glared over at the tree in between their yards. 'You know what?' she said, 'I think you might be right.' Then, easy as you please, she lifted the aluminium cup to her own lips, gulped down the lemonade, then screwed the cap back onto the Thermos without offering him a drop.

'Tease,' Ryan said with a grin, though the clear cool sheen to her lips and the near scent of lemon on her breath tormented him in more ways than one.

'So how's it all going?' she asked, mirroring his stance and lifting one foot onto the bottom rail of the fence, leaning her forearms along the top rail, pulling her jeans tight across her backside.

'Excellent,' Ryan said, unable to hide the longing in his voice.

Laura's eyes narrowed a fraction before flickering over to the placid flock of snowy goats, already attacking the low-hanging leaves of a nearby eucalypt. 'They're precious,' she said.

Their big droopy ears, along with the soft, curling fleece flopping over their eyes and the appearance of a constant smile on their mouths, did give them a sweet, dopey expression. However, Ryan decided to ignore her emasculating jibe.

'They look hot, too,' she said. 'Maybe they would like some lemonade.'

She stepped up on the fence as though she was going to jump over and join them, but Ryan grabbed a hold of her belt loop and tugged her back to the ground. He pulled his hand away before he gave in to any further temptation to touch the smooth line of skin peeking out above the top of her jeans. She kept her eyes on the flock, but he could tell she was grinning from ear to ear. 'They'll be shorn by the end of the month,' he told her, sticking with the conversation topic though his thoughts were on anything but. 'If I don't get to them soon they'll naturally shed, and I'll lose this half-year's fleece. But right now I'm just letting them get used to the place.'

'They'll love it here.'

'I hope so. I paid a mint to an independent breeder for those three females, and they are ready to drop their kids. Then, come autumn I'll stick my top buck in a field with the dozen other mature breeding females and I'll let him have his way with them.'

'How nice for him.'

That earned her a sideways grin. 'They don't seem too upset about it,' he promised. 'If you watch them long enough you'll find the gals are lining up already. He's a stud. Literally.'

'Of course he is. I wouldn't have expected any less from you.' Laura stumbled over her *faux pas*. 'From you…in your choice of stud…goat. Oh, you know what I mean!' She tried to glare at him, but couldn't pull it off with her ruby-red cheeks.

'I know just what you mean,' he agreed, deciding to give her a break. 'Now, local girl, tell me it's going to rain, and soon.'

'It's going to rain and soon,' she echoed, deadpan. 'Excellent. So I guess I should cancel my order for water to be delivered to fill up all my tanks?'

'I wouldn't go that far.'

'Mmm. I wouldn't like to have to do it again every month. It would really cut into my profit margins.' He sensed her glancing his way.

'Wow,' she said. 'You *look* like a real farmer, and now you're starting to *sound* like a real farmer.'

An instant grin stretched across his face. 'The minute I start to smell like a real farmer, you'll let me know?'

'I'll be letting the whole town know.'

He laughed, the sentiment swelling inside of him and radiating warmth to his fingers and toes. In the couple of days out of her company he had almost managed to convince himself he had been imagining the extent of the sparks between them. But now he could almost see the buzz in the air. The energy made him feel as if he could run the perimeter of the property without losing breath.

'I think I am trying to tell you that it's not as easy as looking the part,' Laura said, unexpectedly serious. 'A lot of people try it and simply can't handle the life. If it doesn't work out, and you do leave, don't feel bad.'

She glanced up at him as though gauging his reaction. 'Laura, I know you want the house for yourself, but that is a tad transparent.' He had meant to be joking, but she swallowed in response, hard.

'When I want to be transparent, Ryan, you'll know it,' she said. 'I'm just saying if it all turns bad, and you decide to leave us, you shouldn't feel like a big fat loser.'

He watched for her reaction, and she didn't laugh it off as he'd expected. No, there was more than teasing going on behind her golden eyes.

'And you would be there to buy me out, I assume?' She flicked her ponytail and lifted her fine chin a fraction. 'Of course I'd get first dibs. So you'd better tell me the minute you're ready to give the place up.'

What was going on? This time she wasn't baiting him. The only way that made sense was if she was actually troubled by the thought of his leaving. 'Laura, if I ever leave this place, you will be the first to know.'

She smiled her thanks, but it was a feeble effort, not even remotely reaching her eyes.

'Now, tell me, neighbour,' he said, deciding to herd the conversation in the opposite direction, to see what else she might give away. 'Since you are obviously so taken by the look, sound, and scent of farm boys, is there some local with his eye on you?'

'Oh, I'm sure there are dozens—hundreds, even.' Her words were thick with sarcasm. She smiled up at him, but there was a question behind the smile. A question Ryan had no intention of answering then and there.

'You mean that the folk in town didn't spill all the gory details about my social life the day you arrived?' she asked.

Ryan held her gaze. 'In fact, no. So why don't you tell me? Is there no big, hunky, overtly manly cow wrangler hoping to become Mr Laura Somervale?'

Her cheeks grew a pretty pale pink and her grin grew disarmingly crooked. 'Nah. Who has the time?'

'Surely there are plenty of local social events at which to, well, socialise?'

'I make my living catering, Ryan. At any local event I am always the one in the apron, with the sweat pouring down my cheeks, as I do the rounds with plates of hot hors d'oeuvres. I hardly make the most beguiling picture.'

'Oh, I don't know,' he said. 'Most guys would do well to find a woman who spends most of her day chained to the kitchen sink. The whole Fifties housewife thing can be a real turn-on.'

This time her glare was full-power. Much better. 'Not to me, of course.' He held a fist in the air. 'Go Women's Lib!'

'Oaf!' she said, and then began running a finger around and around the top of a nail in the fence. 'So, how about you? Is there an exotic yet understanding girlfriend awaiting you in some fabulous overseas locale?'

'Dozens. Hundreds, even,' he said, echoing her own wry retort.

'Really?' She watched him carefully, actually believing that *he* might be telling the truth. Did she really see him as some sort of Lothario? He didn't know whether to be put out or utterly flattered.

'Nah,' he said. 'Who has the time?'

She nodded, and this time her grin was real. Real and utterly arousing. He thought of the long line of beautiful women he *had* met and known in his working life. Elegant Parisians. Enchanting Florentines. Enterprising New Yorkers. Educated, clever, charming women, the lot of them. But none of them, not a single one, had made him feel the desire to decelerate. Not one had had such a deep love of their homeland that simply by being around them he'd felt it too. And not one had made him buy a house, on a farm, miles from a capital city or a members-only club, to instead spend his time with smelly goats and even smellier goat sellers. But this one had done all that and more.

Laura looked out into the field, where the trees dappled sunlight upon the patchy, dusty ground. The lemonade in her hands was beginning to feel slippery in her hot palms. As slippery as their conversation had become. What was she doing, talking to him about prospective lovers? She had succeeded in keeping him at arm's length these last few days, from her and from Chloe.

And within a millisecond of being within his vicinity she'd become a woolly-headed muddle.

She sensed Ryan watching her. She did *not* want to know what he was thinking, and had to bite her tongue to stop herself from asking. *She* was thinking that she very much liked the realisation that the dirt of the land was finding a way into the creases by his eyes, into the soles of his shoes, and into his heart.

He raised one dark eyebrow, smiled, and lifted his hand to shield her eyes from the sun. Laura spun the lid from the Thermos, poured a cup of lemonade, and offered it to him. She watched in mute fascination as he drank it, the column of his unshaven throat working in hard gulps as he downed the cold drink in one breath.

He finished with a satisfied, 'Aah,' wiped his mouth with the back of his arm, and then handed back the empty cup. For all his big-city charm and sophistication, at his core he was simply a fine man.

There was no longer any doubt in her mind. The picture Will had created in her mind all those years before, tempered by getting to know the real, live person, and knowing how much he adored her daughter, had her falling for Ryan Gasper. She was falling like a stone slipsliding to the bottom of a creek, slowly, inevitably, desperately, hoping a net would catch her before she fell all the way.

Ryan's brow furrowed and he smiled back at her, his straight, white, perfect teeth shining at her from within his gorgeous face. 'What?' he asked.

Maybe it was time to set a few things straight. If they were going to move one way or the other, forward or backward, to friendship or something else, she had to clear the way—for everyone's sake.

'Can I show you something?' she asked. 'Back at my place?'

He blinked back at her, a grin creasing his handsome face. Her heart skittered and leapt in her chest at the awareness of what he was thinking. Yep. It was past time she cleared the way.

'It's about Will,' she said, and was grateful when all temptation cleared from his eyes in an instant.

'Of course it is,' he said. She sensed his hesitation and she understood it. There was unfinished business between Ryan and his brother. She had thought so back then and she knew so now. She sensed it in the stiffness of Ryan's shoulders, in the tension in his voice, in the subtle torment in his steady blue eyes whenever Will's name was mentioned.

She wiped a damp hand on her jeans and held it out for him. 'Come on, Cowboy. It's time.'

He reached out and clasped his hand in hers. His large, warm hand was already lightly callused from the beginnings of the first lot of hard labour he had probably ever done in his life. A slow, steady new warmth swept up her arm, and she knew she was doing the right thing.

She headed towards the house, he followed, and she didn't let go. She led him inside, dodged Chloe's dirty shoes and the obstacle course of furniture, and made her way down the hall.

When they reached her bedroom doorway, Laura baulked. Had she made the bed? Yes, the floral comforter was neatly pulled back in place. Had she put her nightie and underpants in the laundry? Thank goodness, yes! She had hardly been expecting visitors when she'd readied herself. And never in a million years would she have expected this particular visitor.

She tugged. 'Go sit.'

Once Ryan was sitting on the edge of her bed, Laura got down on all fours on the floor, shimmied under the bed and pulled out an old shoebox. Once she had blinked the dust out of her eyes, and removed a piece of lint from her lower lip, she sat on the floor, one foot tucked beneath her, the other leg spread out sideways, the shoebox clutched between her hands.

'I kept all sorts of odd bits and pieces,' she explained. 'Will's things. For Chloe. One day, when the time is right, I want to have something real, something concrete, to connect her to her dad.'

'In case we never showed up,' Ryan finished for her, and Laura's heart contracted at the regretful twinge in his voice. 'Laura, you don't have to do this.'

'Yes, I do.' She had to, for him. He needed this. He might not know it, but the big strong man perched on the end of her neat bed needed to hear this. It was obvious to her that before he could really move on Ryan needed to know everything that had happened to Will while at Kardinyarr. Until then he was marking time. Entangled in the past. She only hoped she would be able to set him free, help him get past his misplaced anger towards Will, as Will had helped her get past hers towards her father. If Ryan weren't so embroiled in her plan, she knew he would appreciate the symmetry too.

Her hands shook as she pulled away the lid to reveal a neat pile of folded newspaper clippings, letters and knick-knacks—things she had not laid eyes on in years. She reached in and pulled the top one out. It was a clipping about the upcoming World Economic Summit in Paris, several years before. She passed it to Ryan and he took it, his eyes scanning the page until he found the one line about halfway down the page mentioning that, among the special guest speakers, top Australian economist Ryan Gasper would attend.

'He always bought the Melbourne newspapers just in case you might be mentioned in them. There's a couple of dozen more just like it in here.'

'How did you two first meet?' he asked, ignoring her statement as he seemed to stare right through the page. 'I was eighteen when my dad passed away. Within a week Will had taken out a month-by-month lease on Kardinyarr. He came strolling up the drive one day with nothing more than a lazy smile and a backpack.'

Laura shuffled and leant back against the bed, her knees tucked up against her chest, Ryan's feet resting side by side on the floor beside her. When he didn't say anything, she continued.

'From the second we met we hit it off. I needed to talk and he was happy to listen. He needed time to sort out his head, and the peace and quiet around here gave him that. He told me that my pies would be my fortune, and I believed him. I told him that so long as he followed his heart he would be fine, and he believed me. It was as though the fates had landed us together in that brief moment in our lives for a reason.'

And that was all we were, Laura thought. *Two lonely kids reaching out for emotional comfort through physical means.* She only hoped Ryan could see what she was trying to tell him without her having to say it aloud.

Ryan placed the old newspaper clipping carefully on the bed. 'He loved you, Laura,' he said, and it wasn't a question.

She shook her head, her curls making a shuffling noise against the bed sheets. 'No, not in the way that you think. I think in the end he put me on a pedestal, the same way he did you.'

A brief glance flickered her way.

'The way he spoke about you...' she continued. 'He worshipped you, Ryan. I think half of him thought he ought to be more like you—to work hard, to live big. But the other half wanted nothing more than to lie back on a trampoline and stare at the stars for the rest of his life. I often wonder if that's what he saw in me: if I was the girl least likely to turn his big brother's head, so he used me as the ultimate rebellion.'

She kept her head down as she played with the corner of an old letter in the shoebox, waiting in breathless silence for his reaction. But the last thing she'd expected him to do was reach out and run a hand over her hair.

'Don't do that to yourself, sweetheart,' he insisted, his voice raw with emotion. 'Maybe in the beginning he came all the way out here purposely walking steps I had never taken, but don't you *ever* think that *you* could be something so trivial as somebody else's insurrection.'

'It was just a fleeting thought,' she said. One that had crept up on her repeatedly over the years.

He didn't stop caressing her hair, and she didn't pull away. He tucked one stray curl after another into his palm, running them through his work-roughened fingers. Her eyes drifted closed as she allowed herself the decadent pleasure of revelling in Ryan's deft touch.

But there was more to say. 'That last week,' she said, her voice sounding softer, further away, almost like a purr, 'you invited him to join you in Paris.'

'I did.' His voice reverberated through his fingers, creating tingles in her scalp.

'I've figured out, from the things you have said, that you didn't know... he was planning to go.'

'He what?' Ryan's fingers stopped their digression through Laura's curls.

This was it. She sucked in a deep breath, a cool column of air chilling her from the inside out. 'That morning,' she said, referring to Will's last day, 'he was taking a final walk around the property to say his goodbyes.'

'Goodbyes?'

'He had told me he was leaving. He had told me that he'd thought about it and that he wanted to join you in Paris after all.'

Ryan leant forward, hiding his face in his open palms. She fought the urge to wrap her arms about his legs and hug away the hurt.

'Will...he told me about you,' Ryan said at long last, pulling one hand from his face to reach out to her. 'He told me he had met you. *I* told him to let you go, to move on, to spread his wings before he even thought about settling down. That's why I wanted him in Paris. To take him away from you. Laura, sweetheart, I am so sorry. It was all my fault.'

She spun on the floor to face him and his hand slipped to his side. 'No, but don't you see? I agreed that he needed to experience life. He was still so young at heart, and with such a young soul. I told him to try and see it your way, to give you a chance before he could ever really know if he wanted to take a different path in life from yours. He was coming to Paris, Ryan, because I asked him to leave.'

CHAPTER SEVEN

RYAN STARED AT LAURA, assimilating her bombshell. *She* had asked Will to leave. He felt as if he was on the verge of something—a breakthrough or a breakdown. Either way, he had to see her tale through to its very end.

'Did you love him, Laura? Did you love my brother?' His heart slammed against his ribs as he awaited her answer. If she told him yes, that despite everything she'd loved Will, then that would be that. He would leave well enough alone. But if in fact he had been wrong all along...

'I cared for him deeply,' she said, heeding her words. 'He helped me through the most rotten time of my life. But we were so young. Kids, really. Both alone and lonely. I think we both found a great deal of solace in each other's arms. But no, Ryan, I was never *in love* with him.'

With that, she spun about onto her knees and leant her lovely face into his palm. 'Ryan, please don't hate me. When he died, I almost fell apart. Two people so dear to me gone in such a short time—I felt like I'd never find my feet again. The day after Will died Jill found me dropped over the bath, too worn out to move. She took me to see Dr Gabriel in town, and that's when I found out I was four weeks pregnant. I didn't have the luxury to wallow, or to fade away. Having someone else to care for made me grow up quick-smart. And then you came along and made me remember...made me wonder if I treated him badly.'

Ryan snapped out of his trance. He cupped his hand beneath her dainty chin, making sure she was looking him in the eye as he spoke. 'Laura, sweetheart, you couldn't treat someone badly if you tried. If you had lessons. If you had someone coaching you on how to do it.'

'I need to know that I haven't hurt your feelings in telling you all this,' she said. 'It just felt like the right thing to do. To clear the air. So that we both know where we stand. I feel like we have forged a...friendship these last days, and I need to be honest with my friends.'

She amazed him. Talk about being a grown-up. He didn't know if he had it in him to be as forthright and honest as she was being right then. He knew he didn't have half her strength, unable as he was to tell her the extent of the feelings he had been fighting against for days.

Ryan ran his thumb over the softness of her cheek, and he knew he had wanted to touch her like this since the moment he'd laid eyes on her. He tucked his hand behind her neck, deep into the soft haven of her curls, making sure he held her eye contact the whole way.

'My turn to set some things straight,' he said, his throat so tight he felt as though he was swallowing razorblades. 'I don't think Will chose you because you were the least likely to turn my head, Laura. I think he knew how much I would admire your spirit, how readily I would react to your artless beauty, and even how much I would be fascinated by the charming cadence of your speech.'

She didn't break eye contact once. Amazing. 'You know that first day,' she said, 'when you wandered up onto my lawn in your new jeans and shiny boots? I thought you were pretty hot stuff too.'

Ryan couldn't stop the charmed laugh that escaped his throat. He reached out, tucking a stray ringlet back within the rage of curls at her neck. 'Chloe spilled the beans on that one already.'

'Why am I not surprised?' she said, her eyes bright and guileless. 'But you can't blame me. I'm a single mother, living all alone in the middle of nowhere. What was I supposed to think?'

He laughed aloud, the pleasure of it creating great relaxing waves down his length. 'I have never met anyone like you before, Laura. You are fearless.'

She shook her head. 'I am so scared right now I can barely catch my breath.'

'You? Scared? I don't believe it.'

'Believe it.'

The hitch in her voice drew his gaze from the silky softness of her curls back to her glittering eyes. And only then did he see it. Beneath the cheeky flare, beneath the frisky smile, was the slow-burning flame of an impossible attraction. Feelings she could no longer hide even though she knew she must. Feelings for him.

And what made it even worse was that he knew exactly how she felt. Affected beyond reason, he delved his hand deeper, sinking sweetly until it rested behind her warm neck. Then, as though it was the most natural thing in the world to do, he kissed her.

After the briefest moment of hesitation, Laura melted completely beneath him. Her soft groan was smothered as her smooth, warm lips melded perfectly against his. Her hand reached into the hair at his neck and she pulled herself up onto her knees, leaning her length against him, pressing her breasts against his chest, sliding her spare arm tight about his torso.

The immediacy of her need blinded him to all reason, and Ryan was soon swept from diffident and discovering into scorching and intense. Fire sparks danced behind his eyes as he slipped deeper and deeper under Laura's dazzling wave of explosive passion. His stomach muscles ached as he struggled to stem his powerful appetite. On a dull groan, he wrapped her up tighter in his arms.

One hand slipped straight beneath the cotton T-shirt to stroke the writhing velvet heat of the skin on her back, the other hand diving beneath the belt of her soft jeans, and the sensation as he felt the rounded bump of the top of her buttocks sent him spiralling into rapture.

Aeons later Laura came up for breath, and at the sudden wisp of cool air against his hot mouth Ryan saw himself clearly. What the hell was he doing? Taking advantage of her in a deeply sensitive moment, that was what!

He disentangled his arms from about her exquisite body and shot to his feet. 'I'm sorry. I don't know why—I shouldn't haveDamn it!'

'Ryan, really, it's okay,' Laura said, watching him with wide eyes. She hadn't pulled away because it had felt wrong! Though every nerve in her entire being had sprung to life, though as his warm lips had brushed against hers her whole body had jolted with electricity, though she had not been able to feel the ground beneath her knees, or even the clothes on her back, she had never felt more unwavering, more complete, more sure. But as Ryan paced back and forth, running ravaging fingers through his hair, it was obvious he did not feel the same way.

Laura swallowed down her disappointment. 'Ryan, stop. Please. We are both trying our best to fudge our way through a difficult situation here. Neither of us really knows what we are doing and we only have each other to lean on. Emotions are high. It's only natural that something like that would occur.'

And the fact that I have imagined that kiss, dreamed of how your lips would feel, sure doesn't help, she thought. Maybe she should just tell him that she wanted it too. Perhaps it would make it easier for him if he only knew how attracted to him she was. Still, if he hadn't figured it out from her consuming reaction to his kiss… This was more than chemistry. There had been plenty of opportunities for her to pursue relationships since Will. Some nice men had taken her on dates and whispered sweet nothings in her ear, but she had always been the one to pull away before she got too close.

So why didn't she just put up that wall—that big, hard, tough I-am-a-mother-and-nothing-else-is-as-important-as-that wall—and be done with it? Because she knew that some things were just as important as being a good mother. When Ryan looked at her he made her feel utterly female. Not like a cook, or a mother, or a daughter. But like a woman. And she was addicted. She wanted more. But the problem was, after all this effort at clearing the air, she still had no idea where *he* stood. He was taken with her, that she knew. But how much? Enough for him to push through any mental barrier in order to have her?

'Maybe you should add this letter to the collection.' Laura looked up to find Ryan holding out the letter she had written to his family all those years before. She'd thought he had brought it with him as evidence to prove he was who he said he was. But he still had it on him—it seemed—at all times.

'I can't take that.'

'Why not?' he asked on a heavy sigh. His chest still heaved as he tried to bring his breathing back to a normal pace.

'Because I try very hard not to remember writing the thing. I was young. Upset. Hormonal. Alone.'

'You were wonderful. If Chloe is going to have these precious me-

mentos of her father, I think she needs to see this as well. To see what a strong, amazing, generous, loving woman her mother is.'

If you think I am all those things, why did you pull away from my kiss as though you had been burned?

'Please. I am hardly any of those things. Amazing, sure. But the rest— I don't think so,' she said, trying for sassy.

Ryan reached out and took her hands, drawing her to her feet. She stopped babbling and gazed into his impassioned blue eyes. 'Joke all you want, Laura, but I am being utterly serious here. This letter... I have never read anything like it. Most people would not have the guts to present such a gift of knowledge to those who could take everything away from them. You didn't know us at all, and if Will told you anything, we must have seemed the most terrifying family on the planet.'

'When your sister played the violin at his funeral... I had never heard anything like it,' Laura admitted. 'I was pretty terrified that you guys had the means and the power to take Chloe away from me.'

'Yet you sent the letter anyway?'

She shrugged. 'Of course. I knew it wasn't about me. I would fight. I would survive. It was about Chloe. You are her family too. And I... I am glad you have found us. Finally.'

'Finally,' he repeated, and by the stormy look in Ryan's eyes Laura was sure he was about to pull her into his arms and kiss the breath from her lungs once more.

But he took a decided step away and she all but stumbled.

'I think it's time I headed home,' he said, his voice cool and distant. 'I want to spend some time with the goats to make sure they're settled. Introduce them to their water troughs and the dry shed and such.'

'Oh, okay.' Her whole body went slowly numb as she followed Ryan to her front door. She had been so hellbent on helping Ryan out of his blue funk that she had instead danced him blindly right into another. It seemed she had two left feet, as well as a terrible singing voice. Ryan bestowed upon her a strange half-smile before walking from her door, leaving her feeling as if she had gone ten rounds in a heavyweight fight. And she had no idea if she had won or lost.

Ryan couldn't sleep. The heat had reached the high thirties again that day, but the famously changeable regional temperature had dropped to half that in the last two hours. A change was coming through. He sat on the back veranda, watching the dark, cloud-filled sky, wishing for rain and reliving his startling afternoon with Laura.

The guilt that had plagued him for so many years no longer felt so crushing. Through Laura's optimistic eyes he even felt as though he understood his little brother more. Will had been a kid, exploring his own path, and doing pretty well in his search. Will had found a woman of value, he had supported her and learnt from her. Somehow, that one idea alone brought more comfort than he had felt in years. Laura had given him that, and Ryan saw, looking back, that that had been her intention the whole time.

But as to *his* relationship with Laura? He was more confused about that than ever. Had she shown him the shoebox as a way to get him to back off? To show him that her life was complicated enough as it was? Or had she been telling him that her heart was free? Her spectacular reaction to his kiss suggested it was the latter.

By two o'clock in the morning he needed a good excuse to get away from the house. He had barely lived in the place long enough to accumulate much rubbish, but he threw a light Mackintosh over his T-shirt, took his one bag of trash out to his big plastic wheelie bin, and set off. By the time he had rolled the bin the hundred metres to the front gate it had begun to pour—big, hard, fat splashes of rain.

It was too far to run for cover, and the only nearby shade was a tree by Laura's dam. But an obese cow already held her ground there, and he wasn't sure she would appreciate his company. So, instead, he just gave in to the downpour. He tipped his head back and drank in the cool drops. Heavenly drops which would hopefully fill his tanks, would fill his water troughs over the hill and give his gorgeous goats a fighting chance.

The goats must have heard his bumpy travels, as they were standing, bleating, at the fence when he jogged back up the hill. Of the pregnant goats, two still had great stomachs—but one did not. Some time that day she had dropped her young.

He swore beneath his breath before leaping over the fence. Mabel. The one without the large tummy was the one he had called Mabel. Her mid-section was stretched and flaccid, and she had dried blood below her tail. Even a city boy could tell she was no longer carrying.

'Bloody hell. What have you done, Mabel?'

The goat bleated at him and nudged his hand. According to Doc Larson's instructions, and the how-to book he had finished reading earlier that night, she seemed all right. She was upright, alert, mobile. But what about her kids? Where the heck were they?

Rain slashed across his field of vision. The halfhidden moon lit patches of high grass and missed dark puddles of gathering water. Where would she have dropped? It could be anywhere.

The dry. The front shed!

Ryan rushed through the thrashing rain to the shed halfway up the near hill. Inside, he found a litter of two laid out on a pile of straw. One, though weak, was healthy, pink and bleating. The other was still. Too still. This was not all about Will any more. It wasn't even about Laura Somervale and her adorable daughter. This was about life and death. In his ridiculous he-man pretence at fitting in he had taken on these strange creatures, and therefore it was up to him to look out for them. If this little one died... He swallowed down the thought.

But what to do? What to do?

Mabel had followed him in, and she set about nursing the crying baby, blithely ignoring the still one.

Remembering a mishmash of advice from his book and from the farmers at the Minbah market, he checked that the feed in the shed was still dry for the goats huddled inside. The last thing he needed was to lose his new flock to damp, mouldy feed. He opened up the bale and checked deep inside. It smelt sweet and felt dry. Good news.

Leaning on instinct, he tore off his Mackintosh, whipped off his warm, dry T-shirt, grabbed the still kid, and wrapped it up tight. He pulled the Mac over his head and, with the precious package under his arm, ran through the dark rain, keeping his footing on the slippery ground more through will-power than through clever footwork, until he'd run up the steps and into the warm house. He ran straight to the kitchen and turned on the oven to a low heat.

Unwrapping the little creature on the kitchen table, he lost himself for a moment. There was simply no evidence of life. No swelling breaths. No niggling noises.

The poor limp kid was cold as any stone. He carefully slid his hands beneath its torso and placed it on a hand towel, then on a tray in the oven. Leaving the door open, he sat upon the slate floor, cross-legged, and waited.

And waited. And waited. Topless and shivering. But he couldn't leave. Not yet. Not while there was still hope.

His own sneeze startled him several minutes later. And a soft mewling sound in his ear reminded him why he was sitting, soaking wet, on the cold kitchen floor.

The baby goat. It was alive. Eureka!

He turned off the oven and with slow, careful hands brought the goat into his lap. The towel on which the goat lay was warm and crispy, making Ryan realise how cold he really was.

He ran a finger down the little one's back, revelling in the feel of the skin and the muscles moving beneath his touch. He had saved its life. He wanted to run, scream, and wake the neighbours to tell them what he had done. He pictured Chloe's excited laughter at seeing a newborn kid take its first look at life. He pictured Laura's parting smile, careful and unsure. Maybe this would turn it around, bring back the easy camaraderie they had enjoyed before the shoebox had been opened. But it was the middle of the night. He would have to enjoy this moment on his own.

He carefully got to his feet, keeping the kid as steady as possible. He found an old moving box, and tucked her inside with a throw rug while he made a fire. Then he braved the rain again, found Mabel, and gathered a cupful of first milk. Without that, the kid still might not stand a chance. Sitting back beside the kid's makeshift nest, he soaked his finger and let the little one drink the elixir. After five minutes of sipping its way towards a healthy life, the goat shuffled in its makeshift bed, and even tried to stand on wobbly feet.

'Whoa, little one. Settle down. You have the rest of your life to be a grown-up. Now, I'll let you stay in here tonight, but tomorrow you'll have to face the big bad world. No use cosseting you from reality, as then you will never have the chance to grow big and strong.'

Post speech, he sneezed again, and this time he felt it all the way deep into his lungs. More exhausted than he could ever remember being, Ryan grabbed a cushion and another throw rug and curled up on the couch by the makeshift crib. And somehow, on what was one of the most mentally exhausting days of his life, he fell asleep, feeling as though the last of his demons were floating away with his dreams.

* * *

Laura let Chimp out for a run in the mud puddles early the next morning. The house next door looked all too quiet. The windows were closed up tight. The back screen door was shut. Ryan's boots were still on the back stoop. Moreover, the goats had gathered about the front shed, as though they too were waiting for the morning to begin. Something wasn't right.

Biting at her bottom lip, she fought the need to check up. Maybe after what had happened between them the day before he'd had a late-night bender and was sleeping off a hangover. What if all her soul-searching had scared him away? What if he had felt pressured by her reaction to his kiss? Maybe he'd decided to do a runner in the middle of the night? That was enough to send Laura sprinting over to Kardinyarr House.

'Knock, knock!' she called out, before slipping inside the unlocked back door. She walked slowly down the Kardinyarr House hallway for the first time since Ryan had moved in. A huge antique mirror had pride of place at the end of the hall. A Tasmanian oak dining setting and a stunning antique credenza filled the dining room perfectly. Stuffed leather sofas, deep red rugs, and a wall full of periodicals and textbooks littered the formal sitting room.

She would have expected all black, white and chrome from a city boy trying to fit his square life into a round country setting. But, no. It looked…beautiful. It looked as a home should. Ryan had a feel for the place. Or perhaps the place had a feel for him.

But right now the house felt eerily quiet. No noises came from the kitchen. No rustle of newspapers or general manly noises could be heard anywhere.

'Ryan?' she called, as she poked her head into the lounge room, but the word faded on her lips at the sight that met her.

Big, burly Ryan Gasper was curled up on an extralong lounge chair with a tiny newborn goat snuggled into the crook of his bare arm. He was naked, bar a pair of jeans and a throw rug covered him to his shins, big bare feet poking out the end. The remnants of a fire had burned itself out in the grate, so the room was cool.

His usually determined face was peaceful and smooth, his thick dark eyelashes rested against suntanned cheeks, and his mouth lay ever so slightly open as he slept. Oh, what a beautiful man…

Chimp must have followed her inside, as from nowhere he suddenly leapt up onto the couch, his muddy paws landing right on Ryan's stomach.

'Chimp, get down!' Laura whispered, but it was too late.

Ryan jackknifed, and his flailing feet tipped over a bowl of milk which had been sitting on the ground near the couch. 'What?' he cried out, his voice deep and sexy with sleep. 'What's going on?'

He stared at Laura with wild eyes, and she stared back, her hand covering her mouth to stop her laughter. He was hopping about on one foot, trying to keep the milk-splashed foot off the ground. Half his face was creased, red with the geometric pattern of the cushion imprinted on his cheek. He was shirtless, his glorious array of muscles tense as he held on tight to the tiny creature in his arms.

'Ryan, it's Laura.'

Ryan let out a huge sneeze that had Chimp running for cover. 'Why? What's wrong?'

Laura's gaze fell back to Ryan's strong arms. 'Why don't you ask Munchkin there?'

Brow furrowed, Ryan's head tipped downwards, and then remembrance of what must have been one strange night dawned on his face. 'She's alive,' he said, his voice almost a whisper. He ran a large finger delicately down the kid's soft back.

Laura swallowed. Hard. The look in Ryan's eyes was enough to have her melt on the spot. It was a goat, for goodness' sake! Livestock. A means towards profit maximisation. Not anything to goo and gah about! But there was just something about a grown man acting with such tenderness that got her where it mattered.

'And she's hungry,' she added, doing all she could to crack the delicate mood before she burst into tears or threw herself into his arms. 'How many young do you have?'

But Ryan looked so bewildered Laura stepped in further. 'Would you like my help to find out if there are any others?'

A smile creased his sleep-softened face, and he said, 'I would like that very much.'

'Right. Well. Good. Fine.' Laura struggled to remember what he would like very much as the tone in his voice was rather more provocative than she had anticipated.

But then the kid bleated, and Laura remembered. The livestock. A born-and-bred farm girl, animals she could cope with. She was still having trouble with big, gorgeous, half-naked men she had kissed until she'd all but passed out. 'Great,' she said, clapping her hands with vigour. 'It's a little cooler out today, so you'd better put on something warm before following me.'

Ryan looked around for somewhere to put the kid. *Put it on the floor!* Laura thought, but he had such a proprietary stance she knew he wouldn't bear such a suggestion.

'Oh, just give the thing to me!' she said, reaching out and cradling the infant in her arms.

Ryan padded off on bare feet, scratching his head as he wandered to his bedroom. The goat looked up at Laura with liquid eyes. Shaking her head, she tucked her fingers beneath its soft chin and looked right back.

'Ooh, you know just how to bat those lashes, don't you, Munchkin? You've got that big galoot right where you want him. Maybe you could teach me a trick or two.'

An hour later, Laura and Ryan had checked on the other newborns. Three more had dropped through the night, and all were well. It took some time for Laura to encourage Mabel to take little Munchkin on the teat, for by that stage she smelled more like Ryan than like goat. 'You have to be more careful with that next time.

You're just lucky that Mabel is a big softy. Munchkin could very well have been rejected.'

Ryan shrugged. 'So—then I would have fed her, and raised her as an indoor goat.'

Sitting there, watching the future of his farm growing before his eyes, he looked as happy as a pig in mud. A smile lay easily on his mouth, and his gaze skimmed over his flock. Laura fought the urge to pull a strand of hay from his hair. Heck, it looked so adorable in there, maybe she'd never tell him.

'Me and Munchkin against the world,' he continued. 'I would take her with me in the car whenever I went into town.'

She stared at him. The guy had gone cuckoo. Overnight he had shed his inhibitions and become...happy. She had heard him sneeze a couple of times; perhaps he was delirious with fever.

'The townsfolk would look at us as we drove past,' he continued, 'shaking their heads, but smiling all the while. "There goes Munchkin with that silly goat," they would say.'

And then Laura knew he was pulling her leg. She wasn't usually so gullible, but this man just knew how to push her buttons, ring her bells, and make her tremble... She shot to her feet. 'Well, it seems you're all sorted now. You and your goats seem happy enough, so I'll leave you to it.'

Ryan scrambled to his feet and ran his palms down the sides of his jeans. 'You don't want to come in for breakfast?'

'Not today.'

'Oh.' His disappointment was palpable—and tempting. 'But Chloe doesn't have school today, right? Why don't you both come over? This time I can cook for you.'

First he made her coffee, and now he wanted to cook her breakfast. Help! 'Not today. Chloe didn't have a good night last night; we've been up with a bad cough. I'd rather keep the excitement level at a low today. For her. Her excitement level.'

And mine, she thought. Even if Chloe hadn't had a bad night, Laura wouldn't have slept a wink as it was. She had been up most of the night, sitting on the window-seat in her room, wrapped in her comforter, thinking of the future. No matter how many times she played it out in her mind, when she thought about where they would all be in six months' time, when winter set in and living on the land was not so easy to love, for the life of her she could not imagine Ryan still living next door. Seeing him with Munchkin in his arms hadn't changed that. So no more mooning over him. No more falling under the spell of his relentless blue gaze. And definitely no more kissing! Her head was still kind of fuzzy from exhaustion, and she wasn't sure she could handle Ryan in such an endearing mood.

'Another time,' she said, hoping she could avoid the invitation for ever. She called to Chimp, who was busy trying to round up the goats, who were blithely ignoring him, and went home.

CHAPTER EIGHT

THE NEXT MORNING, Laura found Chimp hiding behind her mother's antique chaise-longue.

'It is a beautiful warm bath that will leave you feeling like a million bucks!' she insisted, as she dragged the dog into her arms. 'I never get the chance to have a hot bath, and here you are, refusing one!'

She set Chimp down in the lukewarm chest-high water in the laundry sink, hitched her old, worn tracksuit pants back up to a discreet level on her hips, and dived into the project at hand. Once he was squeaky clean, Laura put him on a towel on the floor. He instantly shook himself until she ended up with soapy water all down her front. She grabbed a corner of the cotton towel to dry her face, and when Chimp saw his opening he took off.

'Chimp—stay!' Laura called out, but Chimp was conveniently temporarily deafened by the water in his ears. She took off after him, following the trail of suds through the lounge room and out through the open front door. When she caught up to him Chimp was halfway across the yard and already rolling in a grass-free patch of dirt.

'Why, you little. '

Sensing imminent danger, Chimp raced off again, across the rest of the yard and through the gate, where he knew he was not meant to go without an escort.

'Chimp!' Laura tiptoed across the rocky ground in her bare feet. When she rounded the Japanese maple, she all but ran into Ryan. Her breath caught at the sight of him leaning against her front gate, in jeans and a cable-knit jumper, morning coffee cup in hand, one foot hooked up onto a tree stump.

Chimp stood behind Ryan, using him as a human shield, panting and watching her as though sensing the complete collapse of her authority.

'Hi,' Ryan said, his voice all laid-back gorgeousness that melted her inside and out.

'Hi,' she said back, casually crossing her arms over her wet T-shirt. She saw that his new jeans were fading, they even held a couple of stubborn stains and a tear in one leg. 'Were you waiting here for me?'

He shrugged. 'I knew you'd stick your nose out sooner rather than later. I wanted to see how Chloe was doing today.'

'Much better, thanks. She had a good night. It was probably the sudden change in weather that brought it on. Emergency averted. How's Munchkin?'

He stared at her for a few moments, his blue eyes baffled, and then realisation dawned. 'Oh, the baby goat! She's doing fine.'

'The kid,' Laura corrected.

'Hmm?' he said through a sip of coffee. 'Not baby goat, Ryan. It's called a kid.'

His face broke into a cunning smile. 'You couldn't let that go, could you?'

'I wouldn't want you making a fool of yourself in company.'

'That's rot. You love correcting me. The farm girl putting the city boy in his place. But, as a great man once said "a rose by any other name would smell as sweet".'

She hitched her drooping old pants back to her hips, and then recrossed her arms over her wet T-shirt. 'I can simply stop jumping in to help altogether, if that's what you want. No more saving you from yourself.'

'Sweetheart, I am counting on you to save me from myself.'

At Ryan's instant about-face, Laura's mouth snapped closed. There was more behind that comment than backpedalling. More behind his eyes than fun and games. Something had changed in him, but she hadn't a clue what. A very different kind of energy arced between them—an energy completely commanded by the man smiling back at her with a gleam in his eye.

'Speaking of making a fool of myself,' he drawled, 'I heard the Tandarah Mini-golf Championship is on this afternoon.'

Laura blinked.

Ryan blinked right back. 'It's like golf. Only smaller.'

'I know what mini-golf is. I'm just surprised that a big-city fella like you would be interested.'

'I'm more than interested. I plan to win.'

'Please! *I* have won the tournament the last two years, and *I* plan on making it a hat-trick.' As soon as the words were out of her mouth she knew—he had known that all along, and she had just fallen into his trap.

'Great!' he said, the half-smile splitting into a full-on beam, and she had to brace her knees to stop them from collapsing out from under her. 'No point in taking two cars. I'll pick you and Chloe up around eleven?'

'I don't know, Ryan...'

'I thought it was about time that Chloe and I did something social together. With you as chaperon, of course. She's feeling better; you're defending champion. So it's a date.' He backed away down the drive.

'Ryan, you can drive us to Tandarah, but I promise you it won't be a date.'

Unfazed, he shot her a little wave before bounding up onto his veranda and inside Kardinyarr House. This left Chimp without a shield. Laura reached down and grabbed the dirty, wet dog.

'He is just so exasperating!' she yelled to the fluffy white clouds. But they ignored her attempt to convince herself that exasperation was her prime emotion when it came to Ryan Gasper.

Laura had every intention of being dressed, ready and waiting, by Ryan's car by ten minutes to eleven. The less this whole escapade felt like a *date* the better. She had to let Ryan off the hook, move the friendship back towards neighbourly, so that when he had had his fill of getting to know her little girl, when he went back to his jet-setting lifestyle, she would not fall apart again and he wouldn't feel guilty for leaving.

But by ten minutes to eleven she had a towel holding up her damp hair, she could not find her lucky shoes, and Chloe was nowhere to be seen.

'Chloe!' Laura called, with her toothbrush in her mouth. 'Tell me you are ready!'

She stormed to the front door, and pulled up short to find Ryan standing on the other side of the flyscreen. Decked out in casual beige trousers and a navy designer polo shirt, he did things to her equilibrium—even with the softening effect of the mesh in between them.

'You're early!' she accused.

He pulled the door open and invited himself in. 'You're not,' he said. His blue eyes scanned over her makeshift hairdryer with blatant interest.

'Sure I am. I find the towel gives me better balance when I putt.' His gaze shot to her eyes, so filled with humour that she had to bite her lip to stop from grinning inanely back at him. 'If you think it's an unfair advantage, you could always give me a minute to lose it.'

His gaze flicked up to her turban, then back down again. 'Laura, it wouldn't make a lick of difference. You have all sorts of unfair advantages over the likes of me.'

'Oh,' she said, her voice ridiculously breathy. She could have kicked herself where she stood.

Chloe, barefoot, with her plaits already coming undone, bundled in from outside, with Chimp at her heels. 'Shoes, Chloe!' Laura demanded, stepping away from Ryan's concentrated presence. 'We are going in two minutes.'

'All right, already!' Chloe harrumphed, before skipping into her bedroom.

'Wait here,' she demanded of Ryan, before disappearing down the hall and out of his sight.

Ryan traipsed into the kitchen, where a tray of fresh scones lay cooling on the bench. Strips of crisp hot dough lay like rays of sunshine across the top of each. She couldn't possibly notice if one of them went missing...

Above the humming sound of a real hairdryer, Laura's voice boomed from down the hall. 'Ryan! If those scones look any different when I get out there, you will lose a hand.'

Ryan's fingers snapped back, away from temptation and into his trouser pocket. The woman was good!

When she came back, hair curling softly over her shoulders, Ryan remembered she was more than good. She was stunning.

Hipster denim jeans held up with a wide brown belt and an embellished pink top clung to a flawless arrangement of trim curves. Ryan almost called out in protest when she wrapped a lurid gold button-down shirt over her shoulders, hiding her stunning figure. But then, lest it drag about her knees, she tied the shirt at her waist, and she was delectable again. She grabbed a big cream sunhat and a soft handbag and joined him in the kitchen. 'Nice shirt,' he said, focusing on the only part of her get-up that didn't have him salivating more than he had been over the scones.

She spun on the spot so he could read the writing on the back. It read: *Tandarah Mini-golf Champion.*

'Impressive,' he said. 'Do you get to keep it when you lose today? Or do you have to pass it on to the next champ? That, of course, being me.'

Her eyes narrowed. 'I get to keep it. And today I will add another, the *third* I shall have hanging in my closet.'

'Mmm. Three shiny gold shirts made big enough to fit any self-respecting trucker. You need never go shopping for clothes again.'

'So stay home if the idea of winning one doesn't appeal,' she dared. 'The petrol tank in my car is full.'

He raised a hand to his heart and did his best to look contrite. 'Did you think I was being disparaging? On the contrary. I just think that shirt of yours would fit me a heck of a lot better than it fits you.'

Outwitted, she dropped her arms, searched in her handbag for her house keys and walked past him with her eyes dead ahead. 'Ask me nicely, Cowboy, and I might even let you try it on one day.' She grabbed the tray of scones, along with a small cooler from the fridge, her lean hips swinging saucily as she sauntered away. It was a view he could get used to. Purple pants, tight jeans; the colour didn't seem to make any difference to his libido. But it seemed it was a view he would have to get used to, as she seemed to walk away a heck of a lot more than she walked towards him.

'Chloe, we are leaving!' she yelled, and the little one materialised from goodness knew where, trussed up in overalls, pink sneakers, and with an odd assortment of clips in her hair, which were half falling out already.

'Can we take Chimp?' Chloe asked.

'Not today, possum. Pop him inside, and we'll bring him back a treat, okay?'

Ryan followed the girls out through the front door, silently taking the tray from Laura's hand so she could lock up.

Chloe looked up at him, her eyes squinting in the bright sunlight. 'Are we really going in your car, Ryan?'

'Yep. Is that okay?'

Chloe looked over at his black sports car, which was all but beige with dust. 'Sure,' Chloe said with a shrug. 'Though I do think it's the most ridiculous sort of car to have on a farm.'

Ryan burst into laughter, knowing exactly where the little girl had picked up that opinion.

'Chloe!' Laura chastised her, tucking her daughter behind her as they traipsed towards the car in question. A familiar blush crept up her cheeks.

Ryan crouched down to Chloe's height. He would never get used to her scent—a wonderful mix of strawberries, grass and baby powder. 'So, what sort of car do you think I should have instead?'

'Do I really get to choose?'

'I am happy to listen to your opinions,' he said, covering himself.

'Umm...' she said, poking a finger in her mouth as she thought deeply. She leaned against him and he felt something distinctly paternal swell within him. As if a pact had been made in that instant. He would uphold her instinctive trust to the end of time.

Her face lit up. 'You should get a pink Corvette. Like Barbie's. Tammy got one for her birthday. It's the coolest car ever!'

'Whenever you two are done yabbering,' Laura said from behind them, 'I have a tournament to win. And the jam and cream in that cooler will not last long in this sun.'

Ryan stood and looked over to find Laura watching them from beneath her large floppy sunhat. Her bottom lip had half disappeared between her teeth, as though she was trying to bite back a smile.

'Let's go! I don't want to miss the candyfloss!' Chloe called out, taking his hand in her small, hot, sticky grip. And, just like that, Laura's smile slipped away; she forcibly broke eye contact and glared at his car. 'Is there even enough space in the back seat of that contraption to fit a child, scones, and a cooler?'

'Well, just think how privileged you should feel in being the one to find out.' Ryan opened up, pushed the seat forward, and helped Chloe scoot into the back seat, then helped her with her seat belt. As she sat back, allowing him to take care of her, again he felt the dawning knowledge that he was mad about this kid. He swallowed hard as he slid the tray of food next to Chloe, wrapping it in its own seat belt as well, which had Chloe giggling.

'Your mum can hardly complain now, can she?' he whispered to her.

'I don't know about that,' Chloe said with a shrug. 'When she wants to, she can always find something to complain about. Like how she always ends up giving Chimp a bath. But I'm too short to reach the tub. And now you're next door she can't hang washing on the line in her underwear.'

'Chloe!' Laura warned her, and Chloe sank back into her seat, head down, hands clasped demurely in her lap.

Ryan pushed the passenger seat back into place, and left only just enough room for Laura to slip past him.

'Don't let me stop you,' he whispered, before she slid into the car.

She looked him in the eye, their faces mere inches apart. 'You think she has a smart mouth? You just try pushing me, Cowboy, and I promise I can tell you some things that will have your city-boy ears turning as red as a Kardinyarr sunset.' And then she was in the car, shuffling her cute backside into his bucket seat, making sure he knew how uncomfortable she was.

Not willing to give in without a fight, Ryan leant into the car and reached across her, his arm resting against her warm torso, pinning her to the back of the seat. 'Do you need help with *your* seat belt?'

She glared at him, but not before moistening her lips with a quick stroke of her pale pink tongue. 'No, thank you.'

He eased himself away and shut her door, a spring in his step and a whistle on his lips as he jogged around to the driver's side of the car, thinking that this day was going to be full of surprises.

Laura lined up the ball. A miniature Uluru lay red and ominous at the end of the fuzzy green trail. This was the big one. The clincher. If she got this in one shot, the hat-trick would be hers.

'Looks like there's a bump about halfway along,' Ryan whispered in her ear.

She and Ryan had been conveniently teamed as a pair—thanks, no doubt, to Jill, who owned the Tandarah Mini-golf links and thus was the organiser of the event. Laura stood up straight and glared at him, amazed she was so close to winning considering he had been playing mental games with her all day. 'You seriously think I need coaching advice from *you*? And where is it likely you will come today?'

'Umm…about eighteenth, at last count.'

'Last. Eighteenth is last, Ryan. So keep your advice to yourself.'

He held up two hands in self-defence. 'Hey, I was just trying to ensure that the gold shirt is yours. I have a vested interest in this, remember?'

'Oh?'

'You promised I might be able to try one on, one day. I figure the more shirts you have, the more likely that honour will come about.'

'Come on, Mum!' Chloe called out from the sidelines. Her face was painted to look like a tiger, and she stood arm in arm with Tammy.

Laura sent her daughter a big smile, all the while remembering the way her little girl had taken hold of Ryan's hand back at the car. Ryan's face had come over all hazy and devoted, and she had known all her grand plans had come to nought. While she'd been running around, trying to sort out everyone else's muddles, Ryan and Chloe had become smitten with one another. The danger she had sensed was always just around the corner had arrived with a bang.

She took a deep calming breath, which did nothing at all to calm her, then leant over and lined up her bright orange ball once more. Now she only had to get over the fact that Ryan was standing behind her, his eyes no doubt focused on her wriggling…club.

She cleared her mind, looked at the fake red rock, looked at the ball, imagined it was Ryan's smirking face, and hit.

The ball skittered and jumped along the bumpy path, hit the wall about halfway and slowly meandered along the painted concrete towards the tiny hole at the base of Uluru. The small crowd standing along the edge of the 'fairway' took in a collective deep breath, all eyes following the ball as it skipped, rolled, and plopped with a perfect clunk into the waiting hole.

The crowd cheered. Laura leapt into the air, and was soon enveloped in a pair of strong arms. She squealed, all breath slamming from her body as she was twirled through the air. All thoughts of winning faded away as she revelled in the sensation of warm arms—male arms, Ryan's arms—wrapped tight about her. When he finally put her down he didn't let her go. His arm remained proprietorially about her waist as everyone congratulated her.

'My partner. She couldn't have done it without me,' he said, eliciting laughs all around from the other players, and giving a perfectly reasonable excuse for the two of them to remain snuggled together.

She didn't believe it for a second. There was more behind Ryan's casually positioned arm than sporting partnership. But what could she do? Throw his arm away and look unkind? Wrap both arms about his heavenly waist and look out of control? Or continue as she was, smiling and laughing and pretending that the skin along her waist wasn't burning up under his easy touch.

After several minutes of seductive torture Laura had cause to uncurl herself from Ryan's embrace as she went up onto the makeshift dais to accept her new shirt. As usual, it was gold, shiny, and excessively big. But, as usual, it gave her a particular thrill to have won. To have thrown herself into the game and won. She didn't do something purely for herself often enough.

She looked out into the crowd to see Chloe jumping up and down, yelling loudly, one hand tucked happily into Ryan's arm. And, seeing that tableau before her, Laura knew then that she had been kidding herself. Winning the mini-golf tournament was fun, but if she were ever able to choose something for herself she would choose this. She would choose someone to share her life. Someone with whom to share Chloe's growth. Someone with whom to match wits, share smiles, and give warmth. Someone real, strong, and fascinating. Someone very much like Ryan Gasper.

The odds against her were stacked too high. Firstly, he had never stayed put in one place longer than a month in his whole adult life. And, secondly, he was still Chloe's uncle. The way he had chastised himself after their kiss proved he would never really be able to see her as just Laura—woman in love.

Not wanting Chloe, or Ryan, to see how much that picture clenched at her heart, she grinned convincingly down at them. They both grinned back, and her heart ached all the more.

After all of the awards had been given—pretty much ensuring that every participant went home with some sort of trophy—Laura skipped down the stairs and made a beeline for her daughter. When she was within a few feet she grabbed Chloe by the hand and did not stop walking, hoping they would simply lose Ryan within the crowd. She needed time away from his overwhelming company. Time to convince herself she wasn't in love with him. She shouldn't be. She couldn't be.

'Do you want that candyfloss now, possum?'

'Yes, please!'

Laura looked back, and the smile dropped from her face when she saw that Chloe was leading Ryan on a baby elephant walk through the crowd.

'Don't you have any other families to bug right now?' Laura asked, as they approached Jill at the candyfloss stand.

'Perhaps,' he said, his sexy smooth voice sending glorious but entirely unwanted shivers through her torso, 'but the sound of candyfloss was too good to pass up.'

'Too much sugar and you'll lose all your teeth before you're forty.'

'Rubbish,' he said, his perfectly healthy teeth gleaming at her.

'Two sticks, please, Auntie Jill,' Chloe said.

'I don't know that you can stomach two sticks of floss, Chloe,' Jill said.

'No! One is for me and one is for Uncle Ryan.'

'Okay, then. So, champ,' Jill said, looking at Laura, 'are we having fun?' Her gaze flickered to a point over Laura's shoulder, and Laura wanted to reach out and strangle her meddling friend.

'Bucketloads,' she said, through gritted teeth.

'I think beating me guaranteed that,' Ryan said, tucking in beside her, resting a hand on Chloe's shoulder.

Jill's eagle eyes took in the scene. 'I'll bet,' she said. She handed over the first stick of sugary pink floss to Chloe. 'Now, don't eat it too fast.'

'Thanks, Auntie Jill. I won't...'

Something in Chloe's voice caught Laura's attention. Sweat slicked Chloe's forehead, melting the face paint, and she was breathing with her mouth open.

'You okay, babe?'

Chloe nodded, eyeing the floss with wide eyes, but Laura was not to be deterred.

'Do you have your puffer?' Laura asked.

Chloe nodded again, but this time pulled the blue and white contraption from the pocket at the front of her overalls and took a deep breath of medicine.

'Better?'

'Better.' Chloe took a lick of candyfloss, ending up with half of it on her nose. 'I'm going to meet Tammy on the merry-go-round. Is that okay?'

'Sure. Have fun.'

'She can have my candyfloss,' Ryan offered. 'An old man like me has to look after his teeth.'

'Thanks!' Chloe said, before running away with both pink fluffy sticks in her hand to find her friend.

Ryan wondered if a six-year-old city kid would think herself too old for such a ride, whereas sweet Chloe Somervale still had much childhood left in front of her. It was comforting that there was a place in the world where kids still found pleasure in skipping-ropes, pet dogs, and fairground rides.

Ryan watched Laura as she watched her daughter run through the maze of adult legs towards her friend on the other side of the park. There was something about her that kept him hooked. Something soft beneath her sharp wit. Something warm behind her cool gaze. Something deep beneath the blustery fac͵ade.

'I'm going to head off and do the washing-up from the barbecue, Jill,' Laura said, once Chloe was out of her sight.

'Don't be silly. I have staff to look after that.'

'Let them play today. I'm happy to do it.'

'There are always Doc Larson's boys. They are terrified of me. If I say the word, they'll do it. I'll keep an eye on Chloe; you two go off and enjoy the sunshine together.'

Ryan could see Laura was on edge. Her toes curled and uncurled in her sandals, her hands continuously tugged at the tie of her gold winner's shirt.

'Yeah,' he said. 'I reckon you could do with some sunshine right about now.'

She turned on him, her eyes flashing. 'I get *sunshine* enough at home, thank you very much.' And then she seemed to realise what she had intimated. 'Oh, blow the both of you,' she blurted, and took off, presumably to work out her frustrations in the kitchen.

Ryan watched her storm away. 'I can't keep up with her. I don't think even the Energizer bunny could keep up with her.'

'Well, handsome,' Jill said, 'I tell you what; I'm having no trouble keeping up with the game at hand.'

'Game?' he repeated.

'It's not as though he moved out and you moved right in,' she said. 'Time has passed. Wounds have healed. Look at the situation with an open mind. You are a man, she is a woman, and there is a little girl in between whom you both love very much.'

Ryan turned and stared at Jill, ready to tell her to mind her own damn business. But she wasn't grinning inanely at him, like some busybody. She was dead serious.

'I don't consider the sort of thing you are talking about a game, Jill.'

'Neither does she. So don't let her run away,' Jill said. 'You'll regret it.'

But Ryan was already on his way, so he didn't have a chance to rebuff or agree. 'Wait up, Laura!' he called as he caught up to her.

'I'm busy.'

'And I'm handy with a teatowel.'

'Good for you.'

They reached the kitchen where the Upper Gum Tree Hotel met the mini-golf links. Ryan jumped forward and held open the door, then followed her into the blissfully cool and quiet room.

She twirled her long hair into a makeshift ponytail, grabbed a pair of elbow-length washing gloves, without even having to look where they were, and swished her hands under the tap water to find the perfect temperature. Then she threw a teatowel at him and he caught it.

'I like your friends,' he said. 'It's a pretty great community here.'

'They have their moments.'

'Meaning?' he asked.

'Well, Chloe came home upset from school the other day, because apparently you are not her uncle, you are an American movie star out here *under cover*. You are divorced and hiding from the law because you stole that ridiculous car of yours. And that's all just from Chloe's schoolmates.'

'Wow. I had no idea they'd found me out so soon!'

Her mouth twitched into a fleeting smile, but by the vigour of her scouring he knew it mattered to her that the three of them had become fodder for the town gossips.

There must have been plenty of talk when she'd first found out she was pregnant, and she'd had to bear it alone. Anger bubbled to the surface as he wished he could have been there to shield her from any talk.

From any hurt. But instead his presence here now was only bringing it all swarming back. 'I'm truly sorry,' he said.

She gazed back at him, her big pale brown eyes clear and bright. 'For what?'

'For putting you in a situation where you have to deal with gossip. Again. From what I've deduced, you have an amazing standing in this town. I only hope that my being here hasn't maligned the reputation you have worked so hard to uphold.'

'Don't be silly. Let them talk. My life is my own. What I get up to is my business. The people who I care about, who care about me, love me no matter what. The rest is just white noise.'

She was nobody's fool, and the most beguiling, surprising, courageous woman he had ever known. And the most fidgety. He wondered what it would take to make her stop, to halt time, to give her a moment to catch her breath. He had recently learned how liberating it felt to let his head roll back and drink the rain. He wondered how long it had been since she had allowed herself such an indulgence. Then there was the way she had reacted, the way she had melted and given in to her most basic de-sires when they had kissed... The time had come to find out many things.

'Have dinner with me, Laura,' he asked. 'A real date.' Without even looking at him she answered, 'No.

Nope. Can't. Won't.' But he could see that her hands had stopped washing and had gripped the sink.

Ryan reached out and tucked the tumble of curls over her shoulder. He didn't want her hiding behind her hair. 'You really can, Laura. I'm certain Jill, or Tammy's mum, will happily babysit Chloe. I can drive us into town. We order. We eat. We don't talk about Will. We don't talk about Chloe. We only talk about us, and this exceptional attraction be-tween us. Easy as pie.'

Laura shook her head. 'Pie isn't easy, Ryan. I for one should know. Sometimes it has apples, as well as blueberries, and it can be quite a big deal to get it just right. And that's not even considering the pastry.'

She was babbling. That was the last way to sway him from wanting to spend time with her. 'Well, let's defy convention,' he said. 'Let's make it easy. Man and woman go on date. One date. One evening together to see if we should even think about taking this thing between us further...'

Laura spun on her heels and pierced him with a wild glare. 'You just don't get it, do you? The answer is no. I can't go on a date with you.' She stumbled to a stop as she gathered her thoughts, and Ryan steeled himself. 'The fact is, it tears me up inside every time I see you fixing another fence or wrangling your goats. Because I know, in my heart of hearts, that though it's all fun and games right now, you *will* return to your real life. Right now you're benefiting from being here—reconnecting with Will, playing house, playing Mr Fix-it, playing dad, and playing with the farm-girl's helpless heart. But it won't last.'

'Laura, don't—'

'No, you started this, but now I have to finish it. The other morning, before I found you asleep with Munchkin, I thought you had gone. That you had left. And it... I couldn't breathe. My chest hurt so bad I didn't know what to think. The idea that someone else I...that another person in my life could leave so suddenly was too hard to take. I can't do it again. The risk is just too great. Because this time it isn't just about my risk, or my heart. I never want Chloe to have to experience the pain of abandonment. I will not let you do that to her.'

Whoa. Ryan had had no idea how deep her anguish ran. He loved Kardinyarr and her challenges more every day. But he wasn't going to lie to himself, or her. She had fair reason to worry. He still woke up every morning thinking through the daily itinerary of the convention he should have been attending in Las Vegas. He wondered what his mates were doing on the other side of the world as he rounded up his livestock. He was happy where he was, but would he never want to leave? He really couldn't say. But at least he was willing to have an open mind about it. He had learned that from his stubborn little brother: never say never.

'Laura, I won't let you push me away like this. I am not Will.' Even as he said it, Ryan knew it was the wrong thing to say. Her lovely face closed over and all thoughts were locked behind an icy glare.

'I know you're not. You are nothing like him. Will was undemanding, and kind, and he knew he wasn't perfect. Whereas you—you are invulnerable, and intoxicating, and you are too bloody perfect!'

He crushed his hands between his back and the sink, knowing that if he gave in to the urge to reach out to her she would as likely bite his fingers as not. 'Laura, nobody's perfect. I have done and said things in my life I wish I could take back.'

'Well, I haven't. I don't regret a thing I have done. Not a word I have said. I'm a good person. I go out of my way to make sure that I hurt nobody in my life. When I sent Will I was doing the right thing, the proper thing, in letting him go. I know it.' Her shoulders slumped, and his vibrant tempestuous Laura looked so small and so frail.

Putting aside all thoughts of his own safety, Ryan closed the gap between them and rested his hands on her shoulders, his fingers caressing the fine hollows beneath her neck. 'Sweetheart, don't do this to yourself. You can't help it if you are so utterly lovely that men fall over themselves to be with you. We have no control over our own hearts, much less over anybody else's.'

He turned her around and she didn't fight him. Using one finger, he lifted her chin so she had no choice but to look him in the eye. 'Laura, it's time to stop running. Only if you stop running can any of us hope to catch up with you.'

He could feel the warmth of her body radiating towards him, calling him, beckoning him. Then she looked at him. Really looked at him. Her eyes skittered, blinked, and then shone. And with a telling sigh she stood on tiptoes, slid her sudsy gloved hands around his neck, and kissed him.

Her kiss was so sudden it caught him off guard. His heart slammed against his ribs. Or perhaps it was her heart. Her ribs. Then just as suddenly his body came to life, every inch of him pulsing as her soft lips pressed against his, coaxing, imploring, summoning him to give in as she had.

He did as he was asked and let the commotion overwhelm him. He let her lead. Let her guide him beyond attraction to something deeper, more honest, and infinitely more fulfilling than he had expected from a woman who only moments before had been determined to deny him.

With a heavy groan he wrapped his arms about her small frame, lifting her until her toes barely touched the ground. She turned limp in his arms, the kiss softening and intensifying at the same time.

Ryan could barely breathe. He saw nothing behind his eyes, but he felt with each nerve in his body every whisper of her breath, every tremor down her length.

Giddy with pleasure, and slightly losing balance, he bumped Laura against the bench behind her and their lips slid apart. There they stood, looking into one another's eyes, their ragged breaths mixing as their lips rested mere millimetres apart. Dribbles of soapy water ran down his back, his raw nerves shivering in response. Ryan finally let her feet slide to the floor.

'I promised myself I wouldn't do that,' she said, and when she blinked two perfect shimmering tracks of silver slid down her cheeks.

'Oh, God, Laura...'

She lifted a finger and held it to his lips. 'Don't.'

Don't what? he wondered. Don't apologise? Don't tell her the depth of what he was feeling? Don't kiss her again?

The sound of voices outside permeated their warm bubble and Laura pushed him away, quickly straightening her clothes and wiping away her tears. But she could not wipe away all evidence of their kiss. Her lips were swollen and moist, her cheeks were too pink, and her eyes were round and shell-shocked.

Father Grant came blustering into the room with Chloe on his back. 'Laura, I found this creature making dirt castles outside with a couple of the local boys.'

When he saw the two of them, Father Grant stopped short. 'Oh, Mr Gasper. Good evening.'

'Evening, Father.'

'So, when do we get to meet the rest of your family?' Father Grant asked, filling the loaded silence as best he could. 'I am a huge fan of your sister's.'

'Jen would love to know that,' Ryan said.

Father Grant summoned up a decent blush. 'Ah, actually I meant Samantha. I am a closet quilter from long back. I do hope that now you've found us, you will be bringing the rest of your intriguing family for a visit.'

'There are more of them?' Chloe asked.

Laura held out her arm and, taking Chloe by a dirty hand, held her tight in front of her. 'There's more of them,' Laura said. Her voice was still shaky. 'Ryan has two sisters as well.'

'Wow!' Chloe said. 'I bet I have a bigger family than even Tammy now!'

Ryan knew Laura was using the little girl as a shield. She had told him in no uncertain terms that she hadn't wanted to kiss him again. No, not that she hadn't wanted to kiss him, but that she *wouldn't* kiss him. So she had thought about it. But instead of choosing to enjoy the raging, straining, impossible-to-ignore attraction that had grabbed hold of the both of them, she was desperate to renounce it. And for good reason.

What was he really thinking of, hitting on a single mother? Falling harder and harder for the mother of his brother's child? Maybe since he was the one with the least to lose it should be up to him to put an end to it.

If it was causing her that much distress, enough to bring tears to those big shining eyes, he had to stop. Stop the torrent of feelings that over-whelmed him every time he caught sight of her? No. But stop letting her know about it. That he could hopefully do.

She had cared enough for Will to let him go. Knowing it was her deep-est wish, he had no choice but to give her the same gift.

Chloe gripped her mother's arms, yawning with a wide open mouth.

'Time to go home?' he asked, his voice soft, letting them both off the hook.

Laura nodded. 'Can you let Jill know she might need Doc Larson's boys to finish up here, after all?' Laura asked Father Grant. 'It's time I took this one home.'

'Sure. Of course. You guys head home.'

'You ready?' Laura asked, looking down into her daughter's tired face with such easy love Ryan felt his heart squeeze in his chest.

He would drive them home, and for the next little while he would leave it at that. A couple of days without contact would surely staunch the fires.

Surely...

CHAPTER NINE

LAURA SAT TUCKED up on the window-seat in her bedroom, the curtain hooked behind her back so she could stare out of the window at the star-spangled night. How could she possibly have fallen in love with Will's brother? She twirled a piece of orange twine around her fingers as her mind buzzed and whirred, looking for an answer, a way out. How could she possibly have fallen in love with Will's brother?

The shoebox lay open on the seat at her feet. Newspaper clippings spilled over the cushion, as well as a dried wild flower Will had picked for her on one of their long walks around Kardinyarr. It felt like so long ago. And she could not even remember the significance of the twine, which she had found at the bottom of the box. Had that been in the box to start with? Or had she and Will created a long-forgotten memory around it?

She disentangled the twine and pressed it back into the box, along with the other bits and pieces that one day Chloe would hold dear—these simple treasures mapping the significant friendship between a couple of kids. But her love for Ryan was the love of a woman. She was in love with his strengths, and with his frailties. She was in love with the intensity of his wish to be a good man. She was in love with the way he adored her daughter. She was in love with the way he kissed. She was in love with his dark curls, with his beautiful blue eyes, with the way he filled out his fading blue jeans.

She'd meant to pull back, denying her feelings, knowing they did not serve either of them well. Kissing him again probably hadn't been the best way to achieve those ends. But, oh, what a kiss. Laura rubbed her lips together, closed her eyes, and relived those heavenly moments. She'd known the whole time she was wrapped in his strong embrace that it was the kiss of a lifetime. Heavenly. Perfect. And heartbreaking. It would never happen again. It had been enough to make her weep.

Uncurling her limbs, she slipped off the seat, let the curtain fall back into place and moved to her bed. Sleep was a fool's errand, but she should at least rest.

But just as she drew the sheet up to her chin she heard it.

A wheeze.

She was out of bed and at Chloe's side before the little one had taken her third strained breath. 'Chloe—wake up.' She gave her daughter a light shake, waking her from her troubled slumber.

Chloe's eyes shot open and her eyes all but bulged from her face. Laura brought her into a sitting position, grabbed the reliever puffer from beside the bed, and held it to Chloe's mouth. 'Here, possum, take a deep breath.' She repeated this four times, but the wheezing did not abate. The ventilator controlling the temperature, the moisture levels and pollens in the room was humming away happily, but it wasn't enough. She had Chloe take a second series of puffs, but it made no difference. Laura knew her daughter could not long survive such a lack of oxygen-fuelled breaths.

She ran to the phone and called Dr Gabriel, who lived twenty kilometres away. 'Come on, come on,' she begged into the phone as it rang and rang. With her spare hand, she tore off her nightie and slipped into a T-shirt and soft track pants, ready to go at a moment's notice. Dr Gabriel's mobile answered.

'Gabe, it's Laura. Chloe is having a pretty bad attack.'

'Laura?' She heard the stress in his voice from that one word and her heart-rate doubled. 'Cindy Mathews is having her baby at home. There have been complications. I can't leave.' There was a pause, then, 'Look, get in the car. Bring Chloe here.'

The Mathews farm was thirty kilometres past Doc's place. An hour's drive at least. Not good enough.

'Thanks, Gabe. But I don't know that there's time. I'll find another way to get help. You just concentrate on Cindy, and tell her from me that it's all worth it.'

'Shall do.' The good doctor hung up and Laura was left alone in her small stifling house, with her little daughter gasping for breath.

She ran a hand over Chloe's forehead, smoothing out her damp hair, trying to calm her as much as possible. 'It's okay, sweetie. Mummy's going to get you help.'

Laura squeezed her brain for a way out. A plan. She called on all her motherly instincts to find an answer.

'Mum...' Chloe called, her voice wheezing, on the verge of panic.

It was enough to kick Laura's instincts into overdrive. She grabbed her little girl into her arms, kicked open the front door and ran across the moonlit patch of dirt and dying grass to her last hope.

Ryan shifted in his sleep. A loud continued knocking came at his door and his eyes flew open. It occurred to him that the knocking had been going on for some time, and it was what had woken him in the first place.

Throwing off his hot sheet, he dragged his half-asleep body to the back door to find Laura standing in his door-way, in a pink T-shirt and track pants, her hair wild and curling about her face. His first thought was *gorgeous*... How could he possibly hope to deny his attraction to her?

But then he saw the terror in her eyes. Chloe lay sideways across her arms, her head tucked into her mother's shoulder. And the little girl was wheezing, pulling for breaths that just wouldn't come.

'She can't breathe,' Laura said, on the verge of panic. 'I can't lose her. Don't let me lose her, too.'

Ryan stepped forward to... He knew not what. To take the girl from her mother's arms? Never. To give the girl the breath from his own lungs? He figured that would not help, or Laura would have done as much already.

'What can I do?' he asked, feeling more helpless than ever in his life before.

'Your plane,' she said, her words spare and fast. 'You have to fly us to the Woondarah Hospital.'

Right. He could do that. 'Come in, come in,' he said, taking her by the shoulder and drawing her into his home.

Laura shook her head. 'We'll be at your car.'

With a curt nod, Ryan ran into his bedroom, whipped on a pair of jeans, shoved his feet into sandshoes and grabbed a shirt, slinging it over his shoulders without bothering to button it up. He grabbed the keys to Betsy, shut his front door without locking it, and then ran to his car.

Laura was already there, running soothing hands over Chloe's hair and making constant cooing noises. When she heard Ryan's footsteps, she looked up at him, and her eyes were frantic. Her long auburn curls whipped about her face. He had never seen anything more beautiful or more heart-wrenching. Staunching the hit of inescapable affection, he pulled open the rear door to the car, slammed it shut once Laura and Chloe were in place, leapt into the front seat, and tore off down the dirt driveway.

'How close is Woondarah Hospital to an airstrip?' he asked.

'Not at all. But there is a golf course right alongside it. Couldn't we land there?'

A golf course. Little chance of powerlines. His Betsy could handle a bush landing, no worries, so long as she had the landing distance and a well-lit runway...

Ignoring road rules, he was on his mobile to the Mackay place within the minute. He kept his voice low and calm as he explained the situation at hand, and was relieved almost to the point of tears when Frank Mackay agreed to get on to the local control tower, declaring Ryan's intention to pilot a low-altitude mercy flight from the Mackay airfield to Woondarah Hospital. Frank promised to have the permission and the flight plan ready when they arrived. Anything for that sweet Laura Somervale.

He shot furtive glances at Laura as his sports car ate up the short mile to the airstrip in record time. Her face was drawn. Her eyes were wide and unblinking. Her cheeks were pale and tight. She was petrified.

The car skidded to a halt by the side of the small plane, and Laura was out of the car before he was. Frank was waiting for them, and he talked Ryan through every step of the journey as they loaded up the plane. Frank assured Ryan that he had checked, and his airframe and fuel levels were appropriate—which saved him some time.

Ryan reached out, and Laura readily gave up her precious cargo into his waiting arms. He cradled Chloe's head as he slipped her into a seat and buckled her in. The poor little thing was shivering, cold, terrified. Ryan gulped down a lump in his throat as he pushed her damp curls from her sweating forehead. 'We're taking you to help, possum. It won't be long now.'

Chloe smiled at Ryan's use of her pet name, and he took that as a happy sign. With no time for gallant assistance, he leapt from the plane, grabbed Laura around the waist and hoisted her up into the back seat, ignoring the pleasure of her smooth curves against his palms. He slammed the door shut, wrenched open the door to the cabin and hopped in. He shot Frank a thankful salute, then the plane was rumbling to life.

He finished his post-start and pre-flight checks as he taxied to the downwind end of the runway. Precious minutes later, after performing essential idle-speed checks and run-ups, they were in the air. Once cruising he shot a glance over his shoulder. 'You okay back there?'

Laura nodded, though her eyes looked wide and fearful. He only wished he could go faster, harder, quicker, get her down sooner. But instead he slowed his reactions and followed procedure of Night Visual Flight Rules. It would get them there safe and sound, and that was more important.

He relayed information to Laura all the way there. Keeping her up to date on their estimated time of arrival, with his conversations with the hospital, with their altitude, everything. He only hoped it helped, that it felt as if they were getting closer.

Within fifteen minutes they were in sight of the hospital. He only hoped Frank's plan had worked. His eyes skittered over the ground ahead and he saw it. the pale glow of the hospital roof, with its helipad lit nice and bright. To the west of the hospital was the golf course, and there it was—the glow from thirty sets of car headlights, switched to full beam, pointing slightly into the wind so as not to blind him as they lit the ninth fairway for him.

As the fates had it, the Woondarah Golf Links had held a wedding reception that night and, upon hearing news of the mercy flight, every member of the party with a car had turned out onto the fairway to help.

Betsy landed like a dream, with the least amount of bumps he could have hoped for considering their makeshift runway. As the plane rumbled to a halt, its tyres kicking up great hunks of the perfect grass, Ryan saw an ambulance heading towards him. Inside would be a trauma crew, ready and waiting. He ripped off his headphones, leapt out of the plane and around, to help Chloe down.

He blanched. The little girl was colourless. She had stopped breathing. He held her limp form for only moments before the hospital crew took her from him and rushed her across the oval in the mini-ambulance to the hospital next door.

He dragged his eyes back up towards the plane, to find Laura slumped against the seat, tears pouring down her face. She was spent. He had never seen anything like it. Never experienced anything so...real.

He had avoided Will's funeral, sensing he would not cope. Knowing the sight of a coffin with his brother inside it would break him into a thousand pieces that would never be put back again. But this woman had been there. Within two months of losing her father she had pulled herself together enough to be there for Will.

He hadn't known what responsibility meant before he'd met her. It didn't just mean creating reports, giving speeches to ensure his findings were heard. It didn't mean accepting every talking engagement that ever came his way in an effort to change the world for the better. It didn't even mean telling someone when you knew they were wrong. Responsibility meant being there for another person. It meant looking out for their most urgent as well as their lesser needs. It meant looking out for their happiness and their well-being. It meant thinking of someone other than yourself.

Laura had lost too many loved ones already in her short lifetime, and now her daughter was in a critical condition. How she managed to remain lucid he had no idea. His heart was beating so fast he felt faint. And angry. And exhausted. And helpless. He itched to get onto his mobile and call his folks, and his sisters, just to hear their voices. Later. He would certainly do so later.

But in that moment he had no other choice but to reach up and take Laura in his arms, comfort her, ease her pain, carry her inside the hospital towards her healing daughter.

Ryan sat in the hospital waiting room, waiting, and watching the line of early-morning sunlight creep under the frosted-glass doors.

He tried to think if he had missed anything. Laura had given him a list of phone numbers, so everybody was up to date. Jill knew where they all were. Dr Gabriel had been assured they had made it okay. Doc Larson, the local vet, would call in on the goats, and would organise one of their closer neighbours to check up on them and feed them later in the day as well. Nice people.

All of them. He was practically a stranger to them, but still they'd banded together without pause to help.

His tired eyes misted over, and he'd almost managed to zone out the sounds of shuffling feet, sniffling patients, clanking utensils and the smell of antiseptic and floor cleaner, when he felt a small tap on his shoulder. He looked up to find a kindly nurse smiling down upon him.

'Mr Gasper?' He nodded.

'Ms Somervale hoped you might join her in Chloe's room.'

He stood, running his palms down the front of his jeans. 'Where do I go?'

The nurse pointed the way. Ryan took several deep breaths and went to find his girls.

Laura sat on a vinyl chair, her chin resting against her hands, which clasped Chloe's hands. Chloe looked so small in the big white bed. But though she looked pale, she was breathing of her own accord as she slept.

'Is she okay?' he asked.

Laura lifted her head and nodded. 'She stopped breathing for about a minute.' She shuddered. 'But the doctors performed their magic, and she's now breathing steadily. She fell asleep a few minutes ago.' Laura's eyes drifted shut. 'Maybe I should move into the city. But then again Melbourne has one of the highest concentrations of allergens in the world, so not Melbourne. But closer to a hospital at least. What do you think?'

She looked up at him with her big, beseeching eyes, and, though he gave his considered opinion to heads of state and to Fortune 500 companies every day, he had never felt as honoured to be asked in all his life. He crouched down next to her chair and laid a hand over hers, feeling her life force as well as Chloe's flow through him.

'Laura, stay. She loves Tandarah. That's her home.

And she came out of this just fine.'

'We can hardly rely on you being nearby with a handy plane any time this happens again.'

'Why not?'

She swallowed. 'Come on, Ryan...'

It all came back to her concerns in the kitchen at the Upper Gum Tree. Despite everything else, despite their pasts, despite their familial relationship, it all came to nought if he wasn't sticking around.

Laura's gaze locked onto his and held. He knew that she was think-

ing back and forth to the pros and cons of that occurrence. Having him
stay meant that Chloe would have family all around her. Having him stay
meant Chloe would be that much more safe living in her beloved town.
But having him stay would mean no more excuses. They could not hope
distance would temper the feelings they had for one another.

'Anyway,' he said, 'now is not the time to settle any of this. I've found
us a room. There's a motel a couple of blocks from here.' He knew she
was going to refuse, so he made it easier for her to say yes. 'Somewhere
to take a nap. A shower. Have some peace. You'll be no good to Chloe
when she wakes if you can't even gather the energy to crack your sunshiny smile.'

He reached out, tucking his hand beneath her ear and running his
thumb along the fine smile line on her cheek. It was enough to encourage the line to deepen as she managed a crooked smile. Ryan even imagined that she pressed against his palm. For a brief second he believed it,
believed that she rubbed her cheek against his hand before gently pulling away.

'Thanks, Ryan. A shower would be wonderful.'

An hour later, Ryan came in from the local twenty-four-hour market with
a bag full of staples. He had bought food, aloe vera tissues, and clean underwear for himself. He had planned to get some for Laura too, but that
had been beyond him, standing staring at a wall full of multi-coloured,
different-sized women's underwear. As soon as somebody else had begun
to trundle a trolley up his aisle he had choked and given up.

He went back to the motel with a plan to send her straight out shopping for them on her own, but when he arrived she was fast asleep on
the bed. She wore a white cotton robe. Her heavy auburn curls were
splayed out over the pillow. Her face shone from being scrubbed clean
and glowed pink from the warmth in the room.

Ryan quietly laid the bags on the kitchenette table and went into the
bathroom to clean up. He stopped short when he happened upon her underwear, which was drying on the shower rail. Fine, lacy, white—and
evocative. He did his best to ignore it. And the fact that it meant that
beneath the white cotton robe Laura was completely bare.

He looked at himself in the mirror. 'Okay, *Cowboy*. Hands off. She is
exhausted. Her daughter is in hospital. She took up your offer of a bed

and a shower only to be alert for her daughter, not for any other reason you might have in mind.'

Drawing in a deep, ragged breath, he walked out into the cosy room where Laura slept. Looking down upon her, he felt his promise to himself fast slipping away. The woman was a total beauty. With an attitude that said *hands off* but an innate sweetness that said *hold me*. Ryan fought harder than ever before against the mixed messages.

He sat down on the edge of the bed. The springs creaked, but she didn't even stir. Yet when Chloe's breathing had hitched earlier in the night she had heard it all. It was as though she knew her daughter was safe now, so she could sleep.

The sun had fully risen, and it filtered through a gap in the heavy orange curtains, spilling a glowing sliver of light across the bed and onto the bright bronze highlights in Laura's hair.

Unable to help himself, Ryan reached out and wrapped a clump of curls about his hand. The cool skein slipped softly over his fingers. He could smell the scent of the sweet pineapple juice she had drunk at the hospital easing from between her lips with her soft, slow breaths. 'Laura... Laura,' he whispered. 'Surely it's no accident that we have ended up here together. What if the many decisions in our lives have led us to this point for a reason? What if you were meant to meet Will to give Chloe life? And what if I was meant to find your letter only at the precise moment I was able to take the time to find you, and you were ready to give your heart to someone new? Did you ever think of that?'

She stirred, her body stretching, her limbs sliding across the bed as she woke. A small moan slid from her mouth as her eyes flickered open. Then she raised one thin arm to shield her sleepy eyes from the burgeoning sunlight.

'Hi,' she said, her voice husky and sexy as hell.

Ryan swallowed to wet his parched throat. 'Good morning, sunshine.'

Laura's mouth stretched into a long yawn, and midway through she took in her surroundings: beige wallpaper, orange curtains, double bed, a table with two chairs. The de'cor screamed small-chain motel. And then she remembered why. Chloe. Before she even moved off the bed, Ryan held up his mobile phone.

'I just called the hospital,' he said. 'She's still asleep and they don't expect her to wake for another couple of hours. So I reckon we have until about nine o'clock before we need to head back.'

Laura sat up, carefully tucking the robe about her thighs and across her chest, wondering how long he had been sitting on the end of the bed watching her. She had felt it in her sleep, which was why she had woken so languorous and warm.

She shook her head. 'I've rested enough. I think I'd prefer to have a quick shower and head back now.'

'Wearing what?' Ryan asked.

Laura looked over to her track pants and T-shirt, hanging over the back of a chair, then her glance slid to the bathroom door, behind which her lacy white underwear dripped tap water slowly onto the bathroom floor.

'You make a fair point,' Laura conceded, sinking her face into her palms. 'I'm not thinking straight right now.'

'That's perfectly understandable.'

'So what can I do for two hours with no dry underwear?' The minute the words came out of her mouth she wished she could take them back.

She waited for Ryan to take advantage, to crack a joke, to smile that cheeky smile that made her insides squirm. He wanted her. She knew that for a fact. And after the way she had thrown herself at him he knew she wanted him too.

But instead, after several moments of sustained eye contact, during which time Laura imagined too many ways to spend such time, Ryan stood and walked over to the table.

He grabbed two grocery bags and began to pull out all sorts of goodies. 'For now,' he said, holding up a packet of fresh bread rolls, salad ingredients and freshcut cold meats, 'we eat. And once we are full, and your underwear is dry, we can go back to Chloe revitalised and refreshed and ready to cheer her up so she won't even remember she's in a hospital.' He pulled a pack of playing cards and a funny-looking little fluffy bear from the grocery bags as well. 'It's all they had,' he apologised.

Laura shuffled over to the table, tucking one foot beneath her and taking hold of the fluffy bear. She buried her face into its soft fur. 'It's beautiful.'

She watched Ryan as he chopped and sliced, creating the most imaginative mountain of a sandwich she had ever seen. He had mentioned a cooking speciality once, and it seemed she was now being allowed to witness it. He slid the finished product her way, using a paper grocery bag as a plate. Then he sat in the chair next to hers and watched her take her first bite.

'Good, huh?'

'This is fantastic,' she said, with a mouthful of bread. 'That's pretty high praise coming from the best cook I have ever known.'

Ryan took a bite of his, and the two of them chewed in comfortable silence until they were all done. Laura moved to clean up, but Ryan pressed her back into her chair.

She watched him do the job that was usually hers, and thoroughly enjoyed the guilty pleasure of being waited upon. She felt spoilt. She felt cared for. She felt so much love for him she could barely contain herself.

'Where did you come up with this concoction?' she asked, her adoring eyes following him around the room. 'Living out of hotels, one has to come up with quickfix healthy meals or one will turn sumo-wrestler-sized from eating too much Room Service food.'

When he seemed convinced the room was clean he turned back to face her. 'And now for the next instalment in the get-Laura-ready game. How does a too hot bubble bath sound?'

Like a dream come true! 'Are you serious?'

He delved into his bag of magic tricks and pulled out a mermaid-shaped bottle of bubble bath. 'It was either this, or some grotesque monster that I am sure is meant to encourage naughty, dirty eight-year-old boys to bathe. This seemed more you.'

'It's wonderful. It's perfect. Thank you, Ryan,' she managed to choke out.

'Come on, sunshine.' He took her by the elbow, led her into the bathroom, turned on the bath taps, poured in half the bottle of suds, walked back out into the bedroom, and closed the door, leaving her with the memory of the most doting smile she had ever received.

She leant her head against the back of the door. *Thank you, sweetheart. Gorgeous, darling man,* she wanted to add. But, at the post, her legendary courage failed her.

Ten minutes later, Ryan's mobile rang. He answered it. 'Gasper!' a familiar voice called at the other end. 'James Carlisle,' Ryan said to the personal financial advisor to a British publishing doyenne.

'I was sure I'd hear the magical ding-ding-ding of poker machines in the background.'

'I'm not in Las Vegas, James.'

'You bailed? On Vegas?'

'Something came up back in Australia. Now, what can I do for you, mate?'

'It's time, buddy. It's only taken me four years, but I have convinced the big kahuna to meet with you. Now is your big chance to pitch the book idea you've been beating my ears with all these years.'

Ryan looked over at the closed bathroom door. He heard a splash of water as Laura shifted her body beneath the bubbles.

'Ryan? I need you on a plane tonight. She has a halfhour window in two days' time. She wants a face-to-face pitch. Think talk-shows, spin-off book deals… Your feet will never touch solid ground again!'

And then, through the bathroom door, Ryan heard Laura begin to hum. The tune was recognisable, somewhat, as the Pirate King's theme song from *Pirates of Penzance*. The next weekend it would be the big show. If he hoofed it to London he would miss it. Worse, he would miss her.

'I'm sorry, James,' he said. 'I'm going to have to decline.'

The pause on the other end of the phone was heavy with shock. 'You're kidding, right?'

'No, mate. I have another couple of projects I'm working on back here. They've reached critical mass. I can't leave.'

'Projects bigger than this one? They must be something else. Anything I can get in on?'

The thought of suit-and-tie James out in the paddock with his goats made him grin. He thought of Munchkin taking her first steps. He thought of Jill Tucker and her cheeky banter. He thought of the new article resting on his laptop back home——the one he had started to write the day he had come home from the Minbah markets. That article was fast turning into enough for a whole book in itself. A book he'd be excited to write. A book that needed many more months of hands-on research. Maybe years worth. Maybe a lifetime's worth.

He faced facts. For a guy who had lived in planes and high-rise hotels for the better part of his life, he found he actually loved the feel of solid ground beneath his feet. Will's words came swimming back to him.

This is her home, and as such it feels like my home too.

Kardinyarr was home because Laura Somervale was there.

'Not your kind of thing, James,' he said. 'But I'll let you know how I get on.'

'Do that, Ryan. Hope it all works out for you. Even though I now have to go and tell the big kahuna that the guy I've been raving about all these years has taken a better offer.'

At that moment Laura came out of the bathroom, all dressed, clean and hairdryer dried underwear hidden beneath her soft clothes, her hair up in the ubiquitous towel. Her face was pink and damp, and tiny curls crept from beneath the towel around her head. She continued to hum as she rubbed the moisture from her hair.

'It's the best offer this guy's ever had,' Ryan said. 'Good luck to you, then. I'll see you, Ryan,' James said.

'Count on it,' Ryan said, before hanging up the phone.

Laura turned at the sound of his voice. 'Was that the hospital?' she asked.

He shook his head. 'A friend overseas.'

'Anything important?'

'In the grand scheme of things?' He shook his head again. 'So, how was your bath? Too hot?'

She grinned, her whole face softening at the remembrance. 'Oh, yeah. I wouldn't care if my fingers and toes remained pruney for evermore. It was that good. And now that I have been thoroughly and undeservedly spoilt, let's go see my darling daughter and your darling niece.' She looked at him, her eyes imploring, as though half afraid he had another pamper session up his sleeve.

'Let's go get our girl.'

Laura clapped her hands together and, despite apparently promising herself that she would never kiss him again, planted a long hard kiss upon his mouth—a kiss filled with thanks, and desire, and so much more—before running back into the bathroom to dry her hair. And Ryan knew there was a lot he would do to get that reaction from this woman again. And again. And again.

CHAPTER TEN

ONE NIGHT, a week later, Ryan walked into a war zone. Dishes lined Laura's sink. Chloe's clothes were strewn across the back of every sofa. The range hood still ran, though it was obvious dinner was long since finished. And the record player creaked and groaned as it came to the end of a record.

Laura ran from out of a doorway, dressed in her pirate costume, those tight purple pants doing it for him yet again.

'Evening, Laura.'

She looked up and seemed to light up when she saw him. But then she blinked furiously, doing her best to staunch the fire. But he knew better than to worry. 'Oh, Ryan. I wasn't sure that you would... I haven't seen you much these last few days.'

'I've been busy,' he said.

She spun on the spot, lifting sofa cushions as though looking for something. 'Bah! Doing what?'

'All sorts of things I think you would approve of. Farm things. Including trading in my *ridiculous* car for a new Ute.'

That stopped her fussing. She glanced up at him, her heavily mascara-rimmed eyes staring at him. Unblinking, shocked, and, just as he had hoped, thrilled to bits.

'You...really? Your car is gone?'

'Not gone from the neighbourhood, I fear. I've heard on the grapevine that Doc Larson's boys were going to pitch in to buy the car together. So if you see it coming down the road towards you, look out.'

'Well, the grapevine is usually right.'

'Hmm.'

As she looked at him, she took in a deep breath, her whole chest filling and releasing. Her beautiful goldenbrown eyes glimmered back at him, and he knew she felt as breathless as he did. She blinked, looked away, and went back to her search with a vengeance. But he still knew better than to worry.

'Nevertheless, Mr Busy Man,' she said, 'you shouldn't just up and disappear like that. People worry.'

'People?' he asked.

'Chloe. Chloe has missed you.'

Her shoulders relaxed as she found a big, silver hoop earring. She stuck the pin into her ear as she bustled past him, doing all she could to ignore the inevitable electricity arcing between them. 'I am sorry. Can't talk now. Chloe is refusing to get dressed. And if I'm not there in the next fifteen minutes I am going to have a dozen ladies in pirate costumes going bananas.'

'You go. I still have to change and get ready yet. How about I take Chloe in a little while?'

Ryan thought she might hesitate, and he would have understood it if she had. If she agreed to leave Chloe in his care that would be the ultimate trust. But she merely smiled her great, glorious, sunshiny smile and he felt her trust light him from within.

'That would be much appreciated. The show starts at eight sharp.'

He nodded. 'That really means about twenty past, right?' he said.

Her gorgeous dimple showed itself before disappearing just as quickly. 'So it seems that you are starting to live on country time. Maybe we'll make a farmer of you after all.'

Sweetheart, you already have, he thought. 'Are you ready?'

She lifted a hand to her hair, felt the bandana still in place, and nodded. 'I've been ready for so long I can't remember if I'm really actually ready.'

'Go. Go on. We'll see you there in a little while.'

Laura grabbed her keys and her handbag and ran out through the door.

She snuck her head back in to say, 'I'm glad you're back, Ryan.' Then she ran off before he could tell her he felt the same way.

Ryan headed down the hallway to find Chloe lying back on her bed reading. He leant in the doorway. 'Ms Somervale?'

Chloe snapped to attention, her startled gaze flickering to the open doorway behind her. 'Ryan. Where…where's Mum?'

'Gone to the theatre.'

Her bottom lip jutted out as she took in this pearl of information. It seemed that her spat had not worked as she had hoped.

'So, how about you get dressed so we can go and watch her sing up a storm to raise money for the drought-stricken farmers.'

Chloe was about to open her mouth to say no, but then, somehow, the whole big picture came clear. 'That's why she's singing tonight?'

'Yep.'

'Kylie at school. Her family lost all their calves last spring,' she said. 'She had to borrow her older sister's shoes for school all year, and they were too big for her. Some of the other kids laughed at her, but I just thought it was sad. I made Mum give her some shoes of mine I knew would fit her better.'

Ryan tried very hard to keep the indulgent grin from his face. *Like mother like daughter,* he thought. No matter how hard Chloe was trying to throw a tantrum, she had too much goodness bred into her for it to really work.

'Well, then, you had better come along and cheer louder than anybody so that your mum can help other kids like Kylie. Okay?'

Chloe nodded. She hopped off the bed and pulled her jumper and rainbow tights from under the covers, whipped them on before Ryan had the chance to turn his back, then strutted out of her room and to the front door.

'Well,' she said, holding out her hand to Ryan when he strolled up slower behind her. 'What are we waiting for?'

Laura paced back and forth backstage.

The Tandarah Community Hall was fast filling up. It looked set to be another sell-out. And what with the clever pre-show games, raffles and door prizes her favourite economist Ryan had lined up, it was set to raise almost double the amount they had raised the year before.

The cling-clang sound of old piano keys wafted through the curtains, and she wrung her hands as she went through her lines quick-speed in her mind.

She peeked through the curtains every now and then to see if her fan club had arrived, and when she saw the familiar strawberry-blonde mop-pet sitting in the middle of the fourth row she relaxed no end.

'Laura,' Ryan's smooth voice said from behind her.

She fair leapt out of her skin! Okay. So she wasn't as relaxed as she had imagined. Her hand on her galloping heart, she spun around. 'Jeez, Cowboy! Don't sneak up on aOh.'

Her diatribe came to a screaming halt when she saw Ryan standing before her in a black suit, a self-striped white button-down shirt and a lavender tie. Without the encumbrance of his now regular baseball cap, his dark hair made him seem raffish and dangerous. And he held a bunch of juicy red roses in his arms.

'You look gorgeous!' she said, unable to stop the words from spilling from her nervous lips.

'So do you,' he said. He was looking at her in a way she had not seen before, as if he wanted to tickle her, or strangle her, or…something. Her already nerve-ridden insides flip-flopped all over the place.

She managed a slight shrug. Blown away by the effort he had gone to on her big night, she was too tongue-tied to make coherent thought, much less a sensible sentence.

'I have a surprise for you,' he said.

'Um, could it be the bunch of flowers in your arms?

Because I could pretend I hadn't noticed them.'

He seemed to only just remember they were there. His mouth twisted for a moment before he grinned at her. 'Nah. These are for some other actress.'

He placed the flowers on a card table at his side before reaching in-side his suit jacket, pulling out a collection of A4 papers and handing them to her.

'What's this?' she asked, too full of nervous energy to see the words straight.

'It's Kardinyarr.'

Her nervously jiggling leg slammed to a halt as she stared at him. 'It's who—what?'

'Settlement came through at midday today. Kardinyarr is all yours. Well, all Chloe's, actually. I have signed the property over into her name. With the proviso that the land is under our care until she turns twenty-one. I told you I'd been busy with farm stuff.'

Laura continued to stare. Kardinyarr. The guy had *given* her the home she had always dreamed she would one day be able to have for her daughter. The world beneath her feet wobbled precariously before the truth in Ryan's beautiful blue gaze brought her back down to earth.

'*Our* care?' she repeated, clinging to the words that had stood out the most.

'Well, I was hoping Chloe would let me stick around for a while. Build the place up to something really extraordinary so that she earns herself a nice little nest egg.'

'How long is a while?' she asked.

His heavenly blue eyes sparkled back at her as he said, 'As long as you'll have me.'

Laura knew the questions she was asking were only skimming around the issue. Was he really telling her he planned to stay? Or was she dreaming? She shook her head to clear the cobwebs. 'Are you sure about this, Ryan?'

'More sure than about anything I have ever done in my whole life. This is only the beginning, Laura. I plan to do a heck of a lot more to ensure Chloe has every chance in life. Every chance to do *whatever* it may be that *she* wants to do.'

Laura nodded. She saw the symmetry in his gift. He had never been able to be there for Will in that way. Never been able to give for the sake of giving. This amazing gift went a long way to healing that old wound. Kardinyarr. Every square inch of paddock, of lantana weed, of wombat hole, of splendid view, was to be in Chloe's family for evermore. Laura's dad would have been so thrilled. As would have Will.

She ached to bury her face against Ryan's freshly shaven cheek, to wrap herself in his warm arms, to leave this place and begin her life anew, knowing that Ryan really, truly planned on being there for as long as she would have him. And, if it was actually up to her, she knew exactly how long that would be. For ever...

Laura flapped the sheets of paper in front of her face to force back the suddenly brimming happy tears. 'Oh, no! You do realise that if I cry now this mascara is going to run all over my frilly white shirt and it will never be cleaned in time for curtain-up!'

'So don't cry,' Ryan said, and it was enough to make her laugh.

So, instead of crying, she did the other most natural thing in the world. She gave in to him completely. She threw herself into his arms. He rocked back on his feet to take on the kinetic wake, his arms reaching up to wrap around her so that the two of them didn't end up sprawled on the wooden floor.

His body was warm and hard beneath his lovely suit, and, wrapped close enough against him, she felt as if this was a defining moment in her life. Now *this* was a man who deserved her love, whether he knew what to do with it or not. The danger had dissipated; there was nothing but sanctuary in her foreseeable future—a future she could now see all too clearly with Ryan at her side. 'Hey, I'm not finished yet,' he whispered against her hair, his rumbling voice creating hectic shivers down her length.

She pulled away, making a big play out of checking that her ruffles had not been squashed. 'More surprises? I'm still wondering who the roses are for!'

'Way more surprises than that,' he promised. 'What's next? Did you buy Chloe a condo in the city?' she joked. He smiled. She melted.

Esme, one of Laura's pirate gang, cleared her throat to garner their attention. 'Sorry to interrupt, Laura, but it's three minutes to curtain-up.'

'Thanks, Esme. Ryan was just leaving.'

Esme smiled pertly at Ryan. 'Not from what I hear.' Then she tootled off to hang out with the other cast members who had begun to spill onto the stage.

Laura blinked and dragged her eyes back to the man at her side. 'Sorry. Now, three minutes means you have more like five minutes—so quick. Spill. What's your next surprise?'

'My sisters are both here.'

Now, that was the last thing she had expected! 'What? Here?' she shrieked. She spun around, whipped open the curtains, her eyes madly scanning the audience. She found Chloe sitting in between two gorgeous dark-haired women who were both leaning down and listening to her excited babble.

'My parents would have been here too, but they couldn't get a plane out of Brunei in time. They're on their way and should be here in a couple of days.'

Unfortunately she watched too long, and Chloe soon found her peeking through the curtains. She leapt up on the chair, waved madly, and shouted loudly enough for Laura to hear the words, *'That's my Mum!'* echo across the large room. The two dark-haired women zeroed in on her and smiled. Beautiful smiles. Elegant smiles. Smiles full of perfect Gasper teeth.

Laura waved briefly, then shoved the curtain back into place. 'Are you insane? I can't possibly meet them looking like this. And, oh, God! They're going to hear me sing! Even before I get the chance to wow them with my brilliant repartee, or impress them with my famous macadamia muffins, they will already have heard me sing! This is the worst surprise ever!'

Laura braved another peek, and soon realised that the whole row was in fact filled with dark-haired Gaspers. Gasper-in-laws. Gasper cousins. With her own little Gasper Somervale snuggled up in the middle of the lot of them.

'I wouldn't worry about all that, Laura.'

'Oh?' she shot back, hands on hips, staring him down. 'And why's that?'

'Your atrocious singing voice wasn't enough to stop me from falling madly in love with you.'

Of course the piano stopped tinkling, the cast members stopped twittering, and even the crowd seemed to fall silent at that precise moment. So Ryan's voice carried, his admission falling on at least a dozen pairs of ears apart from the one pair they were meant to reach.

Before Laura even had the chance to respond the Chinese whispers had begun. Before curtain-up, the whole town would know that Ryan Gasper, Will Gasper's brother, Chloe Gasper Somervale's uncle, was madly in love with their dear, sweet Laura Somervale.

'Could you repeat that, please?' Laura said, dragging her chin from its resting place somewhere near her chest. 'He is madly in love with you, honey,' Esme whispered, loud enough to set off a round of giggles in the front row.

'And his parents are coming into town,' one of the other pirate ladies repeated.

'To meet you,' Ryan joined in, his sexy grin focusing her on the subject matter at hand.

'And Chloe,' Laura said, going with the flow.

'And Chloe,' he agreed. 'But that could have happened any time they were next in town. I wanted my whole extended family to be here for the party.'

'Whose party? What party?'

'I wanted them to be here to meet you as soon as possible after I asked you to become my wife.'

'Laura!' Esme called out. 'One minute to curtain!' Laura flapped a mad hand at her friend and co-star, hushing her loudly.

'That's it,' Ryan said. 'I've had more than enough of fighting for your attention. Come here, you.' Ryan grabbed her around the waist with one arm and delved the other deep into her hair. All Laura's hand-flapping and shushing was instantly forgotten.

'Laura, from the strength, emotion and honesty in your letter I was half in love with you before I even set eyes on you and on your beautiful corner of the world. But since I have come to know you I have fallen deeper and deeper every second. I adore you. You light up my world. Laura, you are my home. If you even feel half the love for me that I feel for you, I hope that you can find it in your heart to consent to become my wife.'

The music started up. The curtains ruffled. A sliver of light from the spotlights split the stage. And Laura couldn't have cared less.

'Oh, Ryan,' she said, before lifting up on her toes and, with her kiss, showing Ryan in no uncertain terms just how much she adored him. Her tears spilled in great running rivers down her face as she gave up every inch of her heart and soul to the beautiful man in her arms.

Ryan was the one who pulled away. A hand shielding his floodlit eyes, he grabbed Laura around the waist and dragged her off-stage. When they reached the wings she was back in his arms, kissing him until she could barely think.

'Laura, though I would happily drag you all the way home right now, I fear the show must go on,' he whispered, his beautiful hot breath washing against her lips.

Laura pulled him back to her and kissed him to shut him up. The show could wait.

'I think I'm going to end up with more make-up on than you,' he murmured.

'So?' she murmured back. She was melting in his arms, and would have the chance to do so as much as she wanted for the rest of her life. What else could possibly matter more?

'Think of the poor drought-stricken farmers,' he said. That was enough to bring her back to the present. 'Oh. You're right.' She pushed him away, sending him jogging down the steps beside the stage. 'I love you too, Ryan,' she called out.

'I know, sweetheart,' he said, before she slipped back into the darkness.

Ryan sneaked through the dark hall, then along the row of chairs until he reached the middle of the fourth row.

'I never knew *Pirates* started with a guy in a suit and the Pirate King locking lips,' Ryan's sister Sam whispered as she swapped seats with him.

'Well, now you know,' he whispered back.

Chloe heard his voice and looked up at him with a huge smile. If he'd thought his heart was full to bursting before, now he knew that it had more room than even he had expected. He grabbed Chloe and pulled her up onto his lap. She spun around so that she was looking him right in the eye.

'You love my mum,' she said. 'I just heard.' Ryan could feel his sisters listening in intently.

'It's okay,' Chloe continued. 'I love her too. It's hard not to. Now, shush, here she comes. This is her best song.'

The Pirate King leapt onto the stage. Small, dainty even, and decidedly female. And the sexiest thing in purple pants Ryan had ever seen.

Laura sang her heart out. Her entire performance, every word, every song, she sang to him. Badly. Terribly, even. He had seen shows at the Met in New York, at the Arena in Verona, at the Opera House in Sydney. But never had he been so moved by any performance in his whole life.

He relaxed against the back of the rickety fold-up chair, his heart reaching out to the two women he knew would continue to surprise him and would continue to move him and love him for the rest of his life.

His girls. The Gasper Somervale girls.

* * * * *

Her Knight In
The Outback

Nikki Logan

Nikki Logan lives on the edge of a string of wetlands in Western Australia with her partner and a menagerie of animals. She writes captivating nature-based stories full of romance in descriptive natural environments. She believes the danger and richness of wild places perfectly mirror the passion and risk of falling in love.

Nikki loves to hear from readers via nikkilogan.com.au or through social media. Find her on Twitter, @ReadNikkiLogan, and Facebook, NikkiLoganAuthor.

Books by Nikki Logan

HARLEQUIN ROMANCE

Their Miracle Twins
Awakened by His Touch

The Larkville Legacy
Slow Dance with the Sheriff

HARLEQUIN KISS

How to Get Over Your Ex
My Boyfriend and Other Enemies
His Until Midnight

Visit the Author Profile page
at millsandboon.com.au for more titles

Dear Reader,

How far would you go to find someone you love? Would you sell your house? Quit your job? Hit the road in a clapped-out bus and pledge to visit every single town in your country until you find them?

A few years ago a close friend of my sister was reported missing, and through my sister's efforts to spread the word about him I fell into the online world of "The Missing." Life is completely excruciating for those who love a missing person. There is no closure, limited information, even more limited progress. Everyone's story has unique facets, but the one thing they all have in common is frustration and heartbreak at being so incredibly powerless.

Her Knight in the Outback began with those feelings. With one woman's decision to make finding her missing brother her absolute priority. It should be no surprise to learn that Eve is in a pretty poor psychological state herself when she first meets biker Marshall Sullivan. She's been on the road for months, hunting for her brother, and she's tired, emotionally devastated, but determined to go on.

The last thing she wants or needs is for one gorgeous man to distract her from her mission to find another.

Her Knight in the Outback is a story about a love that saves someone right at the moment they most need rescuing. I hope that you enjoy the very special romance that forms between a broken woman and her knight in shining...leather.

May love always find you.

Nikki Logan xx

For Mat

Acknowledgments

With enormous gratitude to
Dr. Richard O'Regan for his help
with the pharmaceutical aspects of this story,
which were integral to its resolution.
And with deepest respect and compassion
for the families of "The Missing."

CHAPTER ONE

IT WAS MOMENTS like this that Evelyn Read hated. Life-defining moments. Moments when her fears and prejudices reared up before her eyes and confronted her—just like a King Brown snake, surprised while basking on the hot Australian highway.

She squinted at the distant biker limping carefully towards her out of the shimmering heat mirage and curled her fingers more tightly around the steering wheel.

A moment like this one might have taken her brother. Maybe Trav stopped for the wrong stranger; maybe that was where he went when he disappeared all those months ago. Her instincts screamed that she should press down on her accelerator until the man—the danger—was an hour behind her. But a moment like this might have *saved* her brother, too. If a stranger had only been kind enough or brave enough to stop for him. Then maybe Travis would be back with them right now. Safe. Loved.

Instead of alone, scared...or worse.

The fear of never knowing what happened to him tightened her gut the way it always did when she thought too long about this crazy thing she was doing.

The biker limped closer.

Should she listen to her basest instincts and flee, or respond to twenty-four years of social conditioning and help a fellow human being in trouble? There was probably some kind of outback code to be observed, too, but she'd heard too many stories from too many grieving people to be particularly bothered by niceties.

Eve's eyes flicked to the distant motorbike listing on the side of the long, empty road. And then, closer, to the scruffy man now nearing the restored 1956 Bedford bus that was getting her around Australia.

She glanced at her door's lock to make sure it was secure.

The man limped to a halt next to the bus's bifold doors and looked at her expectantly over his full beard. A dagger tattoo poked out from under his dark T-shirt and impenetrable sunglasses hid his eyes—and his intent—from her.

No. This was her home. She'd never open her front door to a total stranger. Especially not hours from the nearest other people.

She signalled him around to the driver's window instead.

He didn't look too impressed, but he limped his way around to her side and she slid the antique window open and forced her voice to be light.

Sociopaths make a decision on whether you're predator or prey in the first few seconds, she remembered from one of the endless missing-person fact sheets she'd read. She was not about to have 'prey' stamped on her forehead.

'Morning,' she breezed, as if this wasn't potentially a very big deal indeed. 'Looks like you're having a bad day.'

'Emu,' he grunted and she got a glimpse of straight teeth and healthy gums.

Stupidly, that reassured her. As if evil wouldn't floss. She twisted around for evidence of a big damaged bird flailing in the scrub after hitting his motorbike. To validate his claim. 'Was it okay?'

'Yeah, I'm fine, thanks.'

That brought her eyes back to his glasses. 'I can see that. But emus don't always come off the best after a road impact.'

As if she'd know...

'Going that fast, it practically went over the top of me as it ran with its flock. It's probably twenty miles from here now, trying to work out how and when it got black paint on its claws.'

He held up his scratched helmet, which had clearly taken an impact. More evidence. She just nodded, not wanting to give an inch more than necessary. He'd probably already summed her up as a bleeding heart over the emu.

One for the prey column.

'Where are you headed?' he asked.

Her radar flashed again at his interest. 'West.'

Duh, since the Bedford was pointing straight at the sun heading for the horizon and there was nothing else out this way *but* west.

'Can I catch a lift to the closest town?'

Was that tetchiness in his voice because she kept foiling him or because hers was the first vehicle to come along in hours and she was stonewalling him on a ride?

She glanced at his crippled bike.

'That'll have to stay until I can get back here with a truck,' he said, following her glance.

There was something in the sag of his shoulders and the way he spared his injured leg that reassured her even as the beard and tattoo and leather did not. He'd clearly come off his bike hard. Maybe he was more injured than she could see?

But the stark reality was that her converted bus only had the one seat up front—hers. 'That's my home back there,' she started.

'So…?'

'So, I don't know you.'

Yep. That was absolutely the insult his hardened lips said it was. But she was not letting a stranger back there. Into her world.

'It's only an hour to the border.' He sighed. 'I'll stand on your steps until Eucla.'

Right next to her. Where he could do anything and she couldn't do a thing to avoid it.

'An hour by motorbike, maybe. We take things a little more easy in this old girl. It'll take at least twice that.'

'Fine. I'll stand for two hours, then.'

Or she could just leave him here and send help back. But the image of Trav, lost and in need of help while someone drove off and left him injured and alone, flitted through her mind.

If someone had just been brave…

'I don't know you,' she wavered.

'Look, I get it. A woman travelling alone, big scary biker. You're smart to be cautious but the reality is help might not be able to get to me today so if you leave me here I could be here all night. Freezing my ass off.'

She fumbled for her phone.

His shaggy head shook slightly. 'If we had signal don't you think I'd have used it?'

Sure enough, her phone had diminished to *SOS only*. And as bad as that motorbike looked, it wasn't exactly an emergency.

'Just until we get signal, then?' he pressed, clearly annoyed at having to beg. 'Come on, please?'

How far could that be? They were mostly through the desert now, coming out on the western side of Australia. Where towns and people and telecommunications surely had to exist.

'Have you got some ID?'

He blinked at her and then reached back into his jeans for his wallet.

'No. Not a licence. That could be fake. Got any photos of you?'

He moved slowly, burdened by his incredulity, but pulled his phone out and flicked through a few screens. Then he pressed it up against Eve's window glass.

A serious face looked back at her. Well groomed and in a business shirt. Pretty respectable, really. Almost cute.

Pffff. 'That's not you.'

'Yeah, it is.'

She peered at him again. 'No, it's not.'

It might have been a stock photo off the Internet for all she knew. The sort of search result she used to get when she googled 'corporate guy' for some design job.

'Oh, for pity's sake...'

He flicked through a few more and found another one, this time more bearded. But nothing like the hairy beast in front of her. Her hesitation obviously spoke volumes so he pushed his sunglasses up onto his head, simultaneously revealing grey eyes and slightly taming his rusty blond hair.

Huh. Okay, maybe it was him.

'Licence?'

A breathed bad word clearly tangled in the long hairs of his moustache but he complied—eventually—and slapped that against the window, too.

Marshall Sullivan.

She held up her phone and took a photo of him through the glass, with his licence in the shot.

'What's that for?'

'Insurance.'

'I just need a lift. That's it. I have no interest in you beyond that.'

'Easy for you to say.'

Her thumbs got busy texting it to both her closest friend and her father in Melbourne. Just to cover bases. Hard to know if the photo would make them more or less confident in this dusty odyssey she was on, but she had to send it to someone.

The grey eyes she could now see rolled. 'We have no signal.'

'The moment we do it will go.'

She hit Send and let the phone slip back down into its little spot on her dash console.

'You have some pretty serious trust issues, lady, you know that?'

'And this is potentially the oldest con in the book. Broken-down vehicle on remote outback road.' She glanced at his helmet and the marks that could be emu claws. 'I'll admit your story has some pretty convincing details—'

'Because it's the truth.'

'—but I'm travelling alone and I'm not going to take any chances. And I'm not letting you in here with me, sorry.' The cab was just too small and risky. 'You'll have to ride in the back.'

'What about all the biker germs I'm going to get all over your stuff?' he grumbled.

'You want a lift or not?'

Those steady eyes glared out at her. 'Yeah. I do.'

And then, as though he couldn't help himself, he grudgingly rattled off a thankyou.

Okay, so it had to be safer to let him loose in the back than have him squished here in the front with her. Her mind whizzed through all the things he might get up to back there but none of them struck her as bad as what he could do up front if he wasn't really who he said he was.

Or even if he was.

Biker boy and his helmet limped back towards the belongings piled on the side of the road next to his disabled bike. Leather jacket, pair of satchels, a box of mystery equipment.

She ground the gears starting the Bedford back up, but rolled up behind him and, as soon as his arms were otherwise occupied with his own stuff, she unlocked the bus and mouthed through the glass of her window. 'Back doors.'

Sullivan limped to the back of the Bedford, lurched it as he climbed in and then slammed himself in there with all her worldly possessions.

Two hours...

'Come on, old chook,' she murmured to the decades-old bus. 'Let's push it a bit, eh?'

Marshall groped around for a light switch but only found a thick fabric curtain. He pulled it back with a swish and light flooded into the darkened interior of the bus. Something extraordinary unfolded in front of him.

He'd seen converted buses before but they were usually pretty daggy. Kind of worn and soulless and vinyl. But this... This was rich, warm and natural; nothing at all like the hostile lady up front.

It was like a little cottage in some forest. All timber and plush rugs in dark colours. Small, but fully appointed with kitchenette and living space, flat-screen TV, fridge and a sofa. Even potted palms. Compact and long but all there, like one of those twenty-square-metre, fold-down and pull-out apartments they sold in flat packs. At the far end—the driving end—a closed door that must lead to the only absent feature of the vehicle, the bed.

And suddenly he got a sense of Little Miss Hostile's reluctance to let him back here. It was like inviting a total stranger right into your bedroom. Smack bang in the middle of absolutely nowhere.

The bus lurched as she tortured it back up to speed and Marshall stumbled down onto the sofa built into the left side of the vehicle. Not as comfortable as his big eight-seater in the home theatre of his city apartment, but infinitely better than the hard gravel he'd been polishing with his butt for the couple of hours since the bird strike.

Stupid freaking emu. It could have killed them both.

It wasn't as if a KTM 1190 was a stealth unit but maybe, at the speed the emu had been going, the air rushing past its ears was just as noisy as an approaching motorbike. And then their fates had collided. Literally.

He sagged down against the sofa back and resisted the inclination to examine his left foot. Sometimes boots were the only things that kept fractured bones together after bike accidents so he wasn't keen to take it off unless he was bleeding to death. In fact, particularly if he was bleeding to death because something told him the hostess-with-the-leastest would not be pleased if he bled out all over her timber floor. But he could at least elevate it. That was generally good for what ailed you. He dragged one of his satchels up onto the sofa, turned and stacked a couple of the bouncy, full pillows down the opposite end and then swung his abused limb up onto it, lying out the full length of the sofa.

'Oh, yeah...' Half words, half groan. All good.

He loved his bike. He loved the speed. He loved that direct relationship with the country you had when there was no car between you and it. And he loved the freedom from everything he'd found touring that country.

But he really didn't love how fragile he'd turned out to be when something went wrong at high speed.

As stacks went, it had been pretty controlled. Especially considering the fishtail he'd gone into as the mob of emu shot past and around him. But even a controlled slide hurt—him and the bike—and once the adrenaline wore off and the birds disappeared over the dusty horizon, all he'd been left with was the desert silence and the pain.

And no phone signal.

Normally that wouldn't bother him. There really couldn't be enough alone time in this massive country, as far as he was concerned. If you travelled at the right time of year—and that would be the *wrong* time of year for tourists—you could pretty much have most outback roads to yourself. He was free to do whatever he wanted, wear whatever he wanted, be as hairy as he wanted, shower whenever he wanted. Or not. He'd given up caring what people thought of him right about the time he'd stopped caring about people.

Ancient history.

And life was just simpler that way.

The stoic old Bedford finally shifted into top gear and the rattle of its reconditioned engine evened out to a steady hum, vibrating under his skin as steadily as his bike did. He took the rare opportunity to do what he could never do when at the controls: he closed his eyes and let the hum take him.

Two hours, she'd said. He could be up on his feet with her little home fully restored before she even made it from the front of the bus back to the rear doors. As if no one had ever been there.

Two hours to rest. Recover. And enjoy the roads he loved from a more horizontal perspective.

'Who's been sleeping in my bed?' Eve muttered as she stood looking at the bear of a man fast asleep on her little sofa.

What was this—some kind of reverse Goldilocks thing?

She cleared her throat. Nothing. He didn't even shift in his sleep.

'Mr Sullivan?'

Nada.

For the first time, it occurred to her that maybe this wasn't sleep; maybe this was coma. Maybe he'd been injured more than either of them had realised. She hauled herself up into the back of the bus and crossed straight to his side, all thoughts of dangerous tattooed men cast aside. Her fingertips brushed below the hairy tangle of his jaw.

Steady and strong. And warm.

Phew.

'Mr Sullivan,' she said, louder. Those dark blond brows twitched just slightly and something moved briefly behind his eyelids, so she pressed her advantage. 'We're here.'

Her gaze went to his elevated foot and then back up to where his hands lay, folded, across the T-shirt over his midsection. Rather nice hands. Soft and manicured despite the patches of bike grease from his on-road repairs.

The sort of hands you'd see in a magazine.

Which was ridiculous. How many members of motorcycle clubs sidelined in a bit of casual hand modelling?

She forced her focus back up to his face and opened her lips to call his name a little louder, but, where before there was only the barest movement behind his lids, now they were wide open and staring straight at her. This close, with the light streaming in from the open curtains, she saw they weren't grey at all—or not *just* grey, at least. The pewter irises were flecked with rust that neatly matched the tarnished blond of his hair and beard, particularly concentrated around his pupils.

She'd never seen eyes like them. She immediately thought of the burnt umber coastal rocks of the far north, where they slid down to pale, clean ocean. And where she'd started her journey eight months ago.

'We're here,' she said, irritated at her own breathlessness. And at being caught checking him out.

He didn't move, but maybe that was because she was leaning so awkwardly over him from all the pulse-taking.

'Where's here?' he croaked.

She pushed back onto her heels and dragged her hands back from the heat of his body. 'The border. You'll have to get up while they inspect the bus.'

They took border security seriously here on the invisible line between South Australia and Western Australia. Less about gun-running and drug-trafficking and more about fruit flies and honey. Quarantine was king when agriculture was your primary industry.

Sullivan twisted gingerly into an upright position, then carefully pulled himself to his feet and did his best to put the cushions back where they'd started. Not right, but he got points for the effort.

So he hadn't been raised by leather-clad wolves, then.

He bundled up his belongings, tossed them to the ground outside the bus and lowered himself carefully down.

'How is your leg?' Eve asked.

'I'll live.'

Okay. Man of few words. Clearly, he'd spent too much time in his own company.

The inspection team made quick work of hunting over every inch of her converted bus and Sullivan's saddlebags. She'd become proficient at dumping or eating anything that was likely to get picked up at the border and so, this time, the team only found one item to protest—a couple of walnuts not yet consumed.

Into the bin they went.

She lifted her eyes towards Sullivan, deep in discussion with one of the border staff who had him in one ear and their phone on the other. Arranging assistance for his crippled bike, presumably. As soon as they were done, he limped back towards her and hiked his bags up over his shoulder.

'Thanks for the ride,' he said as though the effort half choked him.

'You don't need to go into Eucla?' Just as she'd grown used to him.

'They're sending someone out to grab me and retrieve my bike.'

'Oh. Great that they can do it straight away.'

'Country courtesy.'

As opposed to her lack of...? 'Well, good luck with your—'

It was then she realised she had absolutely no idea what he was doing out here, other than hitting random emus. In all her angsting out on the deserted highway, she really hadn't stopped to wonder, let alone ask.

'—with your travels.'

His nod was brisk and businesslike. 'Cheers.'

And then he was gone, back towards the border security office and the little café that catered for people delayed while crossing. Marshall Sullivan didn't seem half so scary here in a bustling border stop, though his beard was no less bushy and the ink dagger under his skin no less menacing. All the what-ifs she'd felt two hours ago on that long empty road hobbled away from her as he did.

And she wondered how she'd possibly missed the first time how well his riding leathers fitted him.

CHAPTER TWO

IT WAS THE raised voices that first got Marshall's attention. Female, anxious and angry, almost swallowed up by drunk, male and belligerent.

'Stop!'

The fact a gaggle of passers-by had formed a wide, unconscious circle around the spectacle in the middle of town was the only reason he sauntered closer instead of running on his nearly healed leg. If something bad was happening, he had to assume someone in the handful of people assembled would have intervened. Or at least cried out. Him busting in to an unknown situation, half-cocked, was no way to defuse what was clearly an escalating situation.

Instead, he insinuated himself neatly into the heart of the onlookers and nudged his way through to the front until he could get his eyeballs on things. A flutter of paper pieces rained down around them as the biggest of the men tore something up.

'You put another one up, I'm just going to rip it down,' he sneered.

The next thing he saw was the back of a woman's head. Dark, travel-messy ponytail. Dwarfed by the men she was facing but not backing down.

And all too familiar.

Little Miss Hostile. Winning friends and influencing people—as usual.

'This is a public noticeboard,' she asserted up at the human mountain, foolishly undeterred by his size.

'For Norseman residents,' he spat. 'Not for blow-ins from the east.'

'Public,' she challenged. 'Do I need to spell it out for you?'

Wow. Someone really needed to give her some basic training in conflict resolution. The guy was clearly a xenophobe and drunk. Calling him stupid in front of a crowd full of locals wasn't the fastest way out of her predicament.

She shoved past him and used a staple gun to pin up another flier.

He'd seen the same poster peppering posts and walls in Madura, Cocklebiddy and Balladonia. Every point along the remote desert highway that could conceivably hold a person. And a sign. Crisp and new against all the bleached, frayed ones from years past.

'Stop!'

Yeah, that guy wasn't going to stop. And now the McTanked Twins were also getting in on the act.

Goddammit.

Marshall pushed out into the centre of the circle. He raised his voice the way he used to in office meetings when they became unruly. Calm but intractable. 'Okay, show's over, people.'

The crowd turned their attention to him, like a bunch of cattle. So did the three drunks. But they weren't so intoxicated they didn't pause at the sight of his beard and tattoos. Just for a moment.

The moment he needed.

'Howzabout we find somewhere else for those?' he suggested straight to Little Miss Hostile, neatly relieving her of the pile of posters with one hand and the staple gun with his other. 'There are probably better locations in town.'

She spun around and glared at him in the heartbeat before she recognised him. 'Give me those.'

He ignored her and spoke to the crowd. 'All done, people. Let's get moving.'

They parted for him as he pushed back through, his hands full of her property. She had little choice but to pursue him.

'Those are mine!'

'Let's have this conversation around the corner,' he gritted back and down towards her.

But just as they'd cleared the crowd, the big guy couldn't help himself.

'Maybe he's gone missing to get away from you!' he called.

A shocked gasp covered the sound of small female feet pivoting on the pavement and she marched straight back towards the jeering threesome.

Marshall shoved the papers under his arm and sprinted after her, catching her just before she re-entered the eye of the storm. All three men had lined up in it, ready. Eager. He curled his arms around her and dragged her back, off her feet, and barked just one word in her ear.

'Don't!'

She twisted and lurched and swore the whole way but he didn't loosen his hold until the crowd and the jeering laughter of the drunks were well behind them.

'Put me down,' she struggled. 'Ass!'

'The only ass around here is the one I just saved.'

'I've dealt with rednecks before.'

'Yeah, you were doing a bang-up job.'

'I have every right to put my posters up.'

'No argument. But you could have just walked away and then come back and done it in ten minutes when the drunks were gone.'

'But there were thirty people there.'

'None of whom were making much of an effort to help you.' In case she hadn't noticed.

'I didn't want their help,' she spat, spinning back to face him. 'I wanted their attention.'

What was this—some kind of performance art thing? 'Come again?'

'Thirty people would have read my poster, remembered it. The same people that probably would have passed it by without noticing, otherwise.'

'Are you serious?'

She snatched the papers and staple gun back from him and clutched them to her heaving chest. 'Perfectly. You think I'm new to this?'

'I really don't know what to think. You treated me like a pariah because of a bit of leather and ink, but you were quite happy to face off against the Beer Gut Brothers, back there.'

'It got *attention*.'

'So does armed robbery. Are you telling me the bank is on your to-do list in town?'

She glared at him. 'You don't understand.'

And then he was looking at the back of her head again as she turned and marched away from him without so much as a goodbye. Let alone a thankyou.

He cursed under his breath.

'Enlighten me,' he said, catching up with her and ignoring the protest of his aching leg.

'Why should I?'

'Because I just risked my neck entering that fray to help you and that means you owe me one.'

'I rescued you out on the highway. I'd say that makes us even.'

Infuriating woman. He slammed on the brakes. 'Fine. Whatever.'

Her momentum carried her a few metres further but then she spun back. 'Did you look at the poster?'

'I've been looking at them since the border.'

'And?'

'And what?'

'What's on it?'

His brows forked. What the hell *was* on it? 'Guy's face. Bunch of words.' And a particularly big one in red. MISSING. 'It's a missing-person poster.'

'Bingo. And you've been looking at them since the border but can't tell me what he looked like or what his name was or what it was about.' She took two steps closer. 'That's why getting their attention was so valuable.'

Realisation washed through him and he felt like a schmuck for parachuting in and rescuing her like some damsel in distress. 'Because they'll remember it. You.'

'Him!' But her anger didn't last long. It seemed to desert her like the adrenaline in both their bodies, leaving her flat and exhausted. 'Maybe.'

'What do you do—start a fight in every town you go to?'

'Whatever it takes.'

Cars went by with stereos thumping.

'Listen...' Suddenly, Little Miss Hostile had all new layers. And most of them were laden with sadness. 'I'm sorry if you had that under control. Where I come from you don't walk past a woman crying out in the street.'

Actually, that wasn't strictly true because he came from a pretty rough area and sometimes the best thing to do was keep walking. But while his mother might have raised her kids like that, his grandparents certainly hadn't. And he, at least, had learned from their example even if his brother, Rick, hadn't.

Dark eyes studied him. 'That must get you into a lot of trouble,' she eventually said.

True enough.

'Let me buy you a drink. Give those guys some time to clear out and then I'll help you put the posters up.'

'I don't need your help. Or your protection.'

'Okay, but I'd like to take a proper look at that poster.'

He regarded her steadily as uncertainty flooded her expression. The same that he'd seen out on the highway. 'Or is the leather still bothering you?'

Indecision flooded her face and her eyes flicked from his beard to his eyes, then down to his lips and back again.

'No. You haven't robbed or murdered me yet. I think a few minutes together in a public place will be fine.'

She turned and glanced down the street where a slight *doof-doof* issued from an architecturally classic Aussie hotel. Then her voice filled with warning. 'Just one.'

It was hard not to smile. Her stern little face was like a daisy facing up to a cyclone.

'If I was going to hurt you I've had plenty of opportunity. I don't really need to get you liquored up.'

'Encouraging start to the conversation.'

'You know my name,' he said, moving his feet in a pubward direction. 'I don't know yours.'

She regarded him steadily. Then stuck out the hand with the staple gun clutched in it. 'Evelyn Read. Eve.'

He shook half her hand and half the tool. 'What do you like to drink, Eve?'

'I don't. Not in public. But you go ahead.'

A teetotaller in an outback pub.

Well, this should be fun.

Eve trusted Marshall Sullivan with her posters while she used the facilities. When she came back, he'd smoothed out all the crinkles in the top one and was studying it.

'Brother?' he said as she slid into her seat.

'What makes you say that?'

He tapped the surname on the poster where it had *Travis James Read* in big letters.

'He could be my husband.' She shrugged.

His eyes narrowed. 'Same dark hair. Same shape eyes. He looks like you.'

Yeah, he did. Everyone thought so. 'Trav is my little brother.'

'And he's missing?'

God, she hated this bit. The pity. The automatic assumption that something bad had happened. Hard enough not letting herself think it every single day without having the thought planted back in her mind by strangers at every turn.

Virtual strangers.

Though, at least this one did her the courtesy of not referring to Travis in the past tense. Points for that.

'Missing a year next week, actually.'

'Tough anniversary. Is that why you're out here? Is this where he was last seen?'

She lifted her gaze back to his. 'No. In Melbourne.'

'So what brings you out west?'

'I ran out of towns on the east coast.'

Blond brows lowered. 'You've lost me.'

'I'm visiting every town in the country. Looking for him. Putting up notices. Doing the legwork.'

'I assumed you were just on holidays or something.'

'No. This is my job.'

Now. Before that she'd been a pretty decent graphic designer for a pretty decent marketing firm. Until she'd handed in her notice.

'Putting up posters is your job?'

'Finding my brother.' The old defensiveness washed through her. 'Is anything more important?'

His confusion wasn't new. He wasn't the first person not to understand what she was doing. By far. Her own father didn't even get it; he just wanted to grieve Travis's absence as though he were dead. To accept he was gone.

She was light-years and half a country away from being ready to accept such a thing. She and Trav had been so close. If he was dead, wouldn't she feel it?

'So...what, you just drive every highway in the country pinning up notices?'

'Pretty much. Trying to trigger a memory in someone's mind.'

'And it's taken you a year to do the east coast?'

'About eight months. Though I started up north.' And that was where she'd finish.

'What happened before that?'

Guilt hammered low in her gut for those missing couple of months before she'd realised how things really were. How she'd played nice and sat on her hands while the police seemed to achieve less and less. Maybe if she'd started sooner—

'I trusted the system.'

'But the authorities didn't find him?'

'There are tens of thousands of missing people every year. I just figured that the only people who could make Trav priority number one were his family.'

'That many? Really?'

'Teens. Kids. Women. Most are located pretty quickly.'

But ten per cent weren't.

His eyes tracked down to the birthdate on the poster. 'Healthy eighteen-year-old males don't really make it high up the priority list?'

A small fist formed in her throat. 'Not when there's no immediate evidence of foul play.'

And even if they maybe weren't entirely healthy, psychologically. But Travis's depression was hardly unique amongst *The Missing* and his anxiety attacks were longstanding enough that the authorities dismissed them as irrelevant. As if a bathroom cabinet awash with mental health medicines wasn't relevant.

A young woman with bright pink hair badly in need of a recolour brought Marshall's beer and Eve's lime and bitters and sloshed them on the table.

'That explains the bus,' he said. 'It's very...homey.'

'It is my home. Mine went to pay for the trip.'

'You sold your house?'

Her chin kicked up. 'And resigned from my job. I can't afford to be distracted by having to earn an income while I cover the country.'

She waited for the inevitable judgment.

'That's quite a commitment. But it makes sense.'

Such unconditional acceptance threw her. Everyone else she'd told thought she was foolish. Or plain crazy. Implication: like her brother. No one just...nodded.

'That's it? No opinion? No words of wisdom?'

His eyes lifted to hers. 'You're a grown woman. You did what you needed to do. And I assume it was your asset to dispose of.'

She scrutinised him again. The healthy, unmarked skin under the shaggy beard. The bright eyes. The even teeth.

'What's your story?' she asked.

'No story. I'm travelling.'

'You're not a bikie.' Statement, not question.

'Not everyone with a motorbike belongs in an outlaw club,' he pointed out.

'You look like a bikie.'

'I wear leather because it's safest when you get too intimate with asphalt. I have a beard because one of the greatest joys in life is not having to shave, and so I indulge that when I'm travelling alone.'

She glanced down to where the dagger protruded from his T-shirt sleeve. 'And the tattoo?'

His eyes immediately darkened. 'We were all young and impetuous once.'

'Who's Christine?'

'Christine's not relevant to this discussion.'

Bang. Total shutdown. 'Come on, Marshall. I aired my skeleton.'

'Something tells me you air it regularly. To anyone who'll listen.'

Okay, this time the criticism was unmistakable. She pushed more upright in her chair. 'You were asking the questions, if you recall.'

'Don't get all huffy. We barely know each other. Why would I spill my guts to a stranger?'

'I don't know. Why would you rescue a stranger on the street?'

'Not wanting to see you beaten to a pulp and not wanting to share my dirty laundry are very different things.'

'Oh, Christine's dirty laundry?'

His lips thinned even further and he pushed away from the table. 'Thanks for the drink. Good luck with your brother.'

She shot to her feet, too. 'Wait. Marshall?'

He stopped and turned back slowly.

'I'm sorry. I guess I'm out of practice with people,' she said.

'You're not kidding.'

'Where are you staying?'

'In town.'

Nice and non-specific. 'I'm a bit... I get a bit tired of eating in the bus. On my own. Can I interest you in something to eat, later?'

'I don't think so.'

Walk away, Eve. That would be the smart thing to do.

'I'll change the subject. Not my brother. Not your...' *Not your Christine?* 'We can talk about places we've been. Favourite sights.' Her voice petered out.

His eyebrows folded down over his eyes briefly and disguised them from her view. But he finally relented. 'There's a café across the street from my motel. End of this road.'

'Sounds good.'

She didn't usually eat out, to save money, but then she didn't usually have the slightest hint of company either. One dinner wouldn't kill her. Alone with a stranger. Across the road from his motel room.

'It's not a date, though,' she hastened to add.

'No.' The moustache twisted up on the left. 'It's not.'

And as he and his leather pants sauntered back out of the bar, she felt like an idiot. An adolescent idiot. *Of course* this was not a date and *of course* he wouldn't have considered it such. Hairy, lone-wolf types who travelled the country on motorbikes probably didn't stand much on ceremony when it came to women. Or bother with dates.

She'd only mentioned a meal at all because she felt bad that she'd pressed an obvious sore point with him after he'd shown her nothing but interest and acceptance about Travis.

facepalm

Her brother's favourite saying flittered through her memory and never seemed more appropriate. Hopefully, a few hours and a good shower from now she could be a little more socially appropriate and a lot less hormonal.

Inexplicably so.

Unwashed biker types were definitely not her thing, no matter how nice their smiles. Normally, the *eau de sweaty man* that littered towns in the Australian bush flared her nostrils. But as Marshall Sullivan had hoisted her up against his body out in the street she'd definitely responded to the powerful circle of his hold, the hard heat of his chest and the warmth of his hissed words against her ear.

Even though it came with the tickle of his substantial beard against her skin.

She was *so* not a beard woman.

A man who travelled the country alone was almost certainly doing it for a reason. Running from something or someone. Dropping out of society. Hiding from the authorities. Any number of mysterious and dangerous things.

Or maybe Marshall Sullivan was just as socially challenged as she was.

Maybe that was why she had a sudden and unfathomable desire to sit across a table from the man again.

'See you at seven-thirty, then,' she called after him.

Eve's annoyance at herself for being late—and at caring about that—turned into annoyance at Marshall Sullivan for being even later. What, had he got lost crossing the street?

Her gaze scanned the little café diner as she entered—over the elderly couple with a stumpy candle, past the just-showered Nigel No Friends reading a book and the two men arguing over the sports pages. But as her eyes grazed back around to the service counter, they stumbled over the hands wrapped around *Nigel*'s battered novel. Beautiful hands.

She stepped closer. 'Marshall?'

Rust-flecked eyes glanced up to her. And then he pushed to his feet. To say he was a changed man without the beard would have been an understatement. He was transformed. His hair hadn't been cut but it was slicked back either with product or he truly had just showered. But his face...

Free of the overgrown blondish beard and moustache, his eyes totally stole focus, followed only by his smooth broad forehead. She'd always liked an unsullied forehead. Reliable somehow.

He slid a serviette into the book to mark his place and closed it.

She glanced at the cover. *'Gulliver's Travels?'*

Though what she really wanted to say was... *You shaved?*

'I carry a few favourites around with me in my pack.'

She slid in opposite him, completely unable to take her eyes off his new face. At a loss to reconcile it as the under layer of all that sweat, dust and helmet hair she'd encountered out on the road just a few days ago. 'What makes it a favourite?'

He thought about that for a bit. 'The journeying. It's very human. And Gulliver is a constant reminder that perspective is everything in life.'

Huh. She'd just enjoyed it for all the little people.

They fell to silence.

'You shaved,' she finally blurted.

'I did.'

'For dinner?' Dinner that wasn't a date.

His neatly groomed head shook gently. 'I do that periodically. Take it off and start again. Even symbols of liberty need maintenance.'

'That's what it means to you? Freedom?'

'Isn't that what the Bedford means to you?'

Freedom? No. Sanity, yes. 'The bus is just transport and accommodation conveniently bundled.'

'You forget I've seen inside it. That's not convenience. That's sanctuary.'

Yeah...it was, really. But she didn't know him well enough to open up to that degree.

'I bought the Bedford off this old carpenter after his wife died. He couldn't face travelling any more without her.'

'I wonder if he knows what he's missing.'

'Didn't you just say perspective was everything?'

'True enough.'

A middle-aged waitress came bustling over, puffing, as though six people at once was the most she'd seen in a week. She took their orders from the limited menu and bustled off again.

One blond brow lifted. 'You carb-loading for a marathon?'

'You've seen the stove in the Bedford. I can only cook the basics in her. Every now and again I like to take advantage of a commercial kitchen's deep-fryer.'

Plus, boiling oil would kill anything that might otherwise not get past the health code. There was nothing worse than being stuck in a small town, throwing your guts up. Unless it was being stuck on the side of the road between small towns and kneeling in the roadside gravel.

'So, you know how I'm funding my way around the country,' she said. 'How are you doing it?'

He stared at her steadily. 'Guns and drugs.'

'Ha-ha.'

'That's what you thought when you saw me. Right?'

'I saw a big guy on a lonely road trying really hard to get into my vehicle. What would you have done?'

Those intriguing eyes narrowed just slightly but then flicked away. 'I'm out here working. Like you. Going from district to district.'

'Working for who?'

'Federal Government.'

'Ooh, the Feds. That sounds much more exciting than it probably is. What department?'

He took a long swig of his beer before answering. 'Meteorology.'

She stared. 'You're a *weatherman*?'

'Right. I stand in front of a green screen every night and read maximums and minimums.'

Her smile broadened. 'You're a weatherman.'

He sagged back in his chair and spoke as if he'd heard this one time too many. 'Meteorology is a science.'

'You don't look like a scientist.' Definitely not before and, even clean shaven, Marshall was still too muscular and tattooed.

'Would it help if I was in a lab coat and glasses?'

'Yes.' Because the way he packed out his black T-shirt was the least nerdy thing she'd ever seen. 'So why are my taxes funding your trip around the country, exactly?'

'You're not earning. You don't pay taxes.'

The man had a point. 'Why are you out here, then?'

'I'm auditing the weather stations. I check them, report on their condition.'

Well, that explained the hands. 'I thought you were this free spirit on two wheels. You're an auditor.'

His lips tightened. 'Something tells me that's a step down from weatherman in your eyes.'

She got stuck into her complimentary bread roll, buttering and biting into it. 'How many stations are there?'

'Eight hundred and ninety-two.'

'And they send one man?' Surely they had locals that could check to make sure possums hadn't moved into their million-dollar infrastructure.

'I volunteered to do the whole run. Needed the break.'

From…? But she'd promised not to ask. They were supposed to be talking about travel highlights. 'Where was the most remote station?'

'Giles. Seven hundred and fifty clicks west of Alice. Up in the Gibson Desert.'

Alice Springs. Right smack bang in the middle of their massive island continent. 'Where did you start?'

'Start and finish in Perth.'

A day and a half straight drive from here. 'Is Perth home?'

'Sydney.'

She visualised the route he must have taken clockwise around the country from the west. 'So you're nearly done, then?'

His laugh drew the eyes of the other diners. 'Yeah. If two-thirds of the weather stations weren't in the bottom third of the state.'

'Do you get to look around? Or is it all work?'

He shrugged. 'Some places I skip right through. Others I linger. I have some flexibility.'

Eve knew exactly what that was like. Some towns whispered to you like a lover. Others yelled at you to go. She tended to move on quickly from those.

'Favourites so far?'

And he was off… Talking about the places that had captivated him most. The prehistoric, ferny depths of the Claustral Canyon, cave-diving in the crystal-clear ponds on South Australia's limestone coast, the soul-restoring solidity of Katherine Gorge in Australia's north.

'And the run over here goes without saying.'

'The Nullabor?' Pretty striking with its epic treeless stretches of desert but not the most memorable place she could recall.

'The Great Australian Bight,' he clarified.

She just blinked at him.

'You got off the highway on the way over, right? Turned for the coast?'

'My focus is town to town.'

He practically gaped. 'One of the most spectacular natural wonders in the world was just a half-hour drive away.'

'And half an hour back. That was an hour sooner I could have made it to the next town.'

His brows dipped over grey eyes. 'You've got to get out more.'

'I'm on the job.'

'Yeah, me, too, but you have to live as well. What about weekends?'

The criticism rankled. 'Not all of us are on the cushy public servant schedule. An hour—a day—could mean the difference between running across someone who knew Travis and not.'

Or even running into Trav himself.

'What if they came through an hour after you left, and pausing to look at something pretty could have meant your paths crossed?'

Did he think she hadn't tortured herself with those thoughts late at night? The endless what-ifs?

'An hour afterwards and they'll see a poster. An hour before and they'd have no idea their shift buddy is a missing person.' At least that was what she told herself. Sternly.

Marshall blinked at her.

'You don't understand.' How could he?

'Wouldn't it be faster to just email the posters around the country? Ask the post offices to put them up for you.'

'It's not just about the posters. It's about talking to people. Hunting down leads. Making an impression.'

Hoping to God the impression would stick.

'The kind you nearly made this afternoon?'

'Whatever it takes.'

Their meals arrived and the next minute was filled with making space on the table and receiving their drinks.

'Anyway, weren't we supposed to be talking about something else?' Eve said brightly, crunching into a chip. 'Where are you headed next?'

'Up to Kalgoorlie, then Southern Cross.'

North. Complete opposite to her.

'You?' His gaze was neutral enough.

'Esperance. Ravensthorpe. With a side trip out to Israelite Bay.' Jeez— why didn't she just draw him her route on a serviette? 'I'm getting low on posters after the Nullabor run. Need an MP's office.'

His newly groomed head tipped.

'MP's offices are obliged by law to print missing-person posters on request,' she explained. 'And there's one in Esperance.'

'Convenient.'

She glared at her chicken. 'It's the least they could do.'

And pretty much all they did. Though they were usually carefully sympathetic.

'It must be hard,' he murmured between mouthfuls. 'Hitting brick walls everywhere you go.'

'I'd rather hit them out here than stuck back in Melbourne. At least I can be productive here.'

Sitting at home and relying on others to do something to find her brother had nearly killed her.

'Did you leave a big family behind?'

Instantly her mind flashed to her father's grief-stricken face as the only person he had left in the world drove off towards the horizon. 'Just my dad.'

'No mum?'

She sat up straighter in her seat. If Christine-of-the-dagger was off the table for discussion, her drunk mother certainly was. Clearly, the lines in her face were as good as a barometric map. Because Marshall let the subject well and truly drop.

'Well, guess this is our first and last dinner, then,' he said cheerfully, toasting her with a forkful of mashed potato and peas. There was nothing more in that than pure observation. Nothing enough that she felt confident in answering without worrying it would sound like an invitation.

'You never know, we might bump into each other again.'

But, really, how likely was that once they headed off towards opposite points on the compass? The only reason they'd met up this once was because there was only one road in and out of the south half of this vast state and he'd crashed into an emu right in the middle of it.

Thoughtful eyes studied her face, then turned back to his meal.

'So you're not from Sydney, originally?'

Marshall pushed his empty plate away and groaned inwardly. Who knew talking about nothing could be so tiring? This had to be the greatest number of words he'd spoken to anyone in weeks. But it was his fault as much as hers. No dagger tattoo and no missing brother. That was what he'd stipulated. She'd held up her end of the bargain, even though she was clearly itching to know more.

Precisely why he didn't do dinners with women.

Conversation.

He'd much rather get straight to the sex part. Although that was clearly off the table with Eve. So it really made a man wonder why the heck he'd said yes to Eve's 'not a date' invitation. Maybe even *he* got lonely.

And maybe they were now wearing long coats in Hades.

'Brisbane.'

'How old were you when you moved?' she chatted on, oblivious to the rapid congealing of his thoughts. Oblivious to the dangerous territory she'd accidentally stumbled into. Thoughts of his brother, their mother and how tough he'd found Sydney as an adolescent.

'Twelve.'

The word squeezed past his suddenly tight throat. The logical part of him knew it was just polite conversation, but the part of him that was suddenly as taut as a crossbow loaded a whole lot more onto her innocent chatter. Twelve was a crap age to be yanked away from your friends and the school where you were finding your feet and thrust into one of the poorest suburbs of one of the biggest cities in the country. But—for the woman who'd only pumped out a second son for the public benefits— moving states to chase a more generous single-parent allowance was a no-brainer. No matter who it disrupted.

Not that any of that money had ever found its way to him and Rick. They were just a means to an end.

'What was that like?'

Being your mother's meal ticket or watching your older brother forge himself a career as the local drug-mover?

'It was okay.'

Uh-oh…here it came. Verbal shutdown. Probably just as well, given the direction his mind was going.

She watched him steadily, those dark eyes knowing something was up even if she didn't know exactly what. 'Uh-huh…'

Which was code for *Your turn next, Oscar Wilde.* But he couldn't think of a single thing to say, witty or otherwise. So he folded his serviette and gave his chair the slightest of backward pushes.

'Well…'

'What just happened?' Eve asked, watching him with curiosity but not judgment. And not moving an inch.

'It's getting late.'

'It's eight-thirty.'

Seriously? Only an hour? It felt like eternity.

'I'm heading out at sunrise. So I can get to Lake Lefroy before it gets too hot.'

And back to blissful isolation, where he didn't need to explain himself to anyone.

She tipped her head and it caused her dark hair to swing to the right a little. A soft fragrance wafted forwards and teased his receptors. His words stumbled as surely as he did, getting up. 'Thanks for the company.'

She followed suit. 'You're welcome.'

They split the bill in uncomfortable silence, then stepped out into the dark street. Deserted by eight-thirty.

Eve looked to her right, then back at him.

'Listen, I know you're just across the road but could you…would you mind walking me back to the bus?'

Maybe they were both remembering those three jerks from earlier.

'Where do you park at night?' He suddenly realised he had no idea where she'd pulled up. And that his ability to form sentences seemed to have returned with the fresh air.

'I usually find a good spot…'

Oh, jeez. She wasn't even sorted for the night.

They walked on in silence and then words just came tumbling out of him.

'My motel booking comes with parking. You could use that if you want. I'll tuck the bike forward.'

'Really?' Gratitude flooded her pretty face. 'That would be great, thank you.'

'Come on.'

He followed her to the right, and walked back through Norseman's quiet main streets. Neither of them spoke. When they reached her bus, she unlocked the side window and reached in to activate the folding front door. He waited while she crossed back around and then stepped up behind her into the cab.

Forbidden territory previously.

But she didn't so much as twitch this time. Which was irrationally pleasing. Clearly he'd passed some kind of test. Maybe it was when the beard came off.

The Bedford rumbled to life and Eve circled the block before heading back to his motel. He directed her into his bay and then jumped out to nudge the KTM forward a little. The back of her bus stuck out of the bay but he was pretty sure there was only one other person in the entire motel and they were already parked up for the night.

'Thanks again for this,' she said, pausing at the back of the bus with one of the two big rear doors open.

Courtesy of the garish motel lights that streamed in her half-closed curtains, he could see the comfortable space he'd fallen asleep in bathed in a yellow glow. And beyond it, behind the door that now stood open at the other end of the bus, Eve's bedroom. The opening was dominated by the foot of a large mattress draped in a burgundy quilt and weighed down with two big cushions.

Nothing like the sterile motel room and single country bed he'd be returning to.

'Caravan parks can be a little isolated this time of year,' she said, a bit tighter, as she caught the direction of his gaze. 'I feel better being close to…people.'

He eased his shoulder against the closed half of the door and studied her. Had she changed her mind? Was that open door some kind of unconscious overture? And was he really considering taking her up on it if it was? Pretty, uptight girls on crusades didn't really meet his definition of uncomplicated. Yet something deep inside hinted strongly that she might be worth a bit of complication.

He peered down on her in the shadows. 'No problem.'

She shuffled from left foot to right. 'Well…'night, then. See you in the morning. Thanks again.'

A reluctant smile crossed his face at the firm finality of that door slamming shut. And at the zipping across of curtains as he sauntered to the rear of the motel.

Now they were one-for-one in the inappropriate social reaction stakes. He'd gone all strong and silent on her and she'd gone all blushing virgin on him.

Equally awkward.

Equally regrettable.

He dug into his pocket for the worn old key and let himself into his ground floor room. Exactly as soulless and bland as her little bus wasn't.

But exactly as soulless and bland as he preferred.

CHAPTER THREE

'THIS BUS NEVER stops being versatile, does it?'

Eve's breath caught deep in her throat at the slight twang and comfortable gravel in the voice that came from her left. The few days that had passed since she'd heard his bike rumble out of the motel car park at dawn as she'd rolled the covers more tightly around her and fell back to sleep gave him exactly the right amount of stubble as he let the beard grow back in.

'Marshall?' Her hand clamped down on the pile of fliers that lifted off the table in the brisk Esperance waterfront breeze. 'I thought you'd headed north?'

'I did. But a road train had jack-knifed across the highway just out of Kal and the spill clean-up was going to take twenty-four hours so I adjusted my route. I'll do the south-west anti-clockwise. Like you.'

Was there just the slightest pause before 'like you'? And did that mean anything? Apparently, she took too long wondering because he started up again.

'I assumed I'd have missed you, actually.'

Or hoped? Impossible to know with his eyes hidden behind seriously dark sunglasses. Still, if he'd truly wanted to avoid her he could have just kept walking just now. She was so busy promoting *The Missing* to locals she never would have noticed him.

Eve pushed her shoulders back to improve her posture, which had slumped as the morning wore on. Convenient coincidence that it also made the best of her limited assets.

'I had to do Salmon Gums and Gibson on the way,' she said. 'I only arrived last night.'

He took in the two-dozen posters affixed to the tilted up doors of the bus's luggage compartment. It made a great roadside noticeboard to set her fold-out table up in front of.

He strolled up and back, studying every face closely.

'Who are all these people?'

'They're all long-termers.' *The ten per cent.*

'Do you know them all?'

'No,' she murmured. 'But I know most of their families. Online, at least.'

'All missing.' He frowned. 'Doesn't it pull focus from your brother? To do this?'

Yeah. It definitely did.

'I wouldn't be much of a human being if I travelled the entire country only looking after myself. Besides, we kind of have a reciprocal arrangement going. If someone's doing something special—like media or some kind of promotion—they try to include as many others as they can. This is something I can do in the big centres while taking a break from the road.'

Though Esperance was hardly a metropolis and talking to strangers all day wasn't much of a break.

He stopped just in front of her, picked up one of Travis's posters. 'Who's "we"?'

'The network.'

The sunglasses tipped more towards her.

'The missing-persons network,' she explained. 'The families. There are a lot of us.'

'You have a formal network?'

'We have an informal one. We share information. Tips. Successes.'

Failures. Quite a lot of failures.

'Good to have the support, I guess.'

He had no idea. Some days her commitment to a bunch of people she'd never met face to face was the only thing that got her out of bed.

'When I first started up, I kept my focus on Trav. But these people—' she tipped her head back towards all the faces on her poster display '—are like extended family to me because they're the family of people I'm now close to. How could I not include them amongst *The Missing*?'

A woman stopped to pick up one of her fliers and Eve quickly delivered her spiel, smiling and making a lot of eye contact. Pumping it with energy. Whatever it took...

Marshall waited until the woman had finished perusing the whole display. '*The Missing*?'

She looked behind her. 'Them.'

And her brother had the biggest and most central poster on it.

He nodded to a gap on the top right of the display. 'Looks like one's fallen off.'

'I just took someone down.'

His eyebrows lifted. 'They were found? That's great.'

No, not great. But at least found. That was how it was for the families of long-timers. The Simmons family had the rest of their lives to deal with the mental torture that came with feeling *relief* when their son's remains were found in a gully at the bottom of a popular hiking mountain. Closure. That became the goal somewhere around the ten-month mark.

Emotional euthanasia.

Maybe one day that would be her—loathing herself for being grateful that the question mark that stalked her twenty-four-seven was now gone because her brother was. But there was no way she could explain any of that to someone outside the network. Regular people just didn't get it. It was just so much easier to smile and nod.

'Yes. Great.'

Silence clunked somewhat awkwardly on the table between them.

'Did you get out to Israelite Bay yet?' he finally asked.

'I'll probably do that tomorrow or Wednesday.'

His clear eyes narrowed. 'Listen. I have an idea. You need to travel out to the bay and I need to head out to Cape Arid and Middle Island to survey them for a possible new weather station. Why don't we team up, head out together? Two birds, one stone.'

More together time in which to struggle with conversation and obsess about his tattoos. Was that wise?

'I'll only slow you down. I need to do poster drops at all roadhouses, caravan parks and campsites between here and there.'

'That's okay. As far as the office is concerned, I have a couple of days while the truck mess is cleared up. We can take our time.'

Why did he seem so very reluctant? Almost as if he was speaking against his will. She scrunched her nose as a prelude to an *I don't think so*.

But he beat her to it. 'Middle Island is off-limits to the public. You can't go there without a permit.'

'And you have a permit?'

'I do.'

'Have you forgotten that this isn't a tourist trip for me?'

'You'll get your work done on the way, and then you'll just keep me company for mine.'

'I can get my work done by myself and be back in Esperance by nightfall.'

'Or you can give yourself a few hours off and see a bit of this country that you're totally missing.'

'And why should I be excited by Middle Island?'

'A restricted island could be a great place for someone to hide out if they don't want to be discovered.'

The moment the words left his mouth, colour peaked high on his jaw.

'Sorry—' he winced as she sucked in a breath '—that was... God, I'm sorry. I just thought you might enjoy a bit of downtime. That it might be good for you.'

But his words had had their effect. If you needed a permit and Marshall had one, then she'd be crazy not to tag along. What if she let her natural reticence stop her and Trav was there, camping and lying low?

'I'll let you ride on my bike,' he said, as though that made it better. As if it was some kind of prize.

Instantly her gut curled into a fist. 'Motorbikes kill people.'

'People kill people,' he dismissed. 'Have you ever ridden on one?'

If riding tandem with a woman in the midst of a mid-life crisis counted. 'My mother had a 250cc.'

'Really? Cool.'

Yeah, that was what she and Travis had thought, right up until the day it killed their mother and nearly him.

'But you haven't really *ridden* until you've been on a 1200.'

'No, thanks.'

'Come on… Wouldn't you like to know what it's like to have all that power between your legs?'

'If this is a line, it's spectacularly cheesy.'

He ignored that. 'Or the freedom of tearing along at one hundred clicks with nothing between you and the road?'

'You call that freedom, I call that terror.'

'How will you know until you try it?'

'I'm not interested in trying it.'

He totally failed at masking his disappointment. 'Then you can tail me in the bus. We'll convoy. It'll still be fun.'

Famous last words. Something told her the fun would run out, for him, round about the time she pulled into her third rest stop for the day, to pin up posters.

'There's also a good caravan park out there, according to the travel guides. You can watch a west coast sunset.'

'I've seen plenty of sunsets.'

'Not with me,' he said on a sexy grin.

Something about his intensity really wiggled down under her skin. Tantalising and zingy. 'Why are you so eager for me to do this?'

Grey eyes grew earnest. 'Because you're missing everything. The entire country. The moments of joy that give life its colour.'

'You should really moonlight in greeting-card messages.'

'Come on, Eve. You have to go there, anyway, it's just a few hours of detour.'

'And what if Trav comes through in those few hours?' It sounded ridiculous but it was the fear she lived with every moment of every day.

'Then he'll see one of dozens of posters and know you're looking for him.'

The simple truth of that ached. Every decision she made ached. Each one could bring her closer to her brother or push her further away. It made decision-making pure agony. But this one came with a whole bundle of extra considerations. Marshall-shaped considerations. And the thought of sitting and watching a sunset with him even managed to alleviate some of that ache.

A surprising amount.

She sighed. 'What time?'

'How long are you set up here for?'

'I have permission to be on the waterfront until noon.'

'Five past noon, then?'

So eager. Did he truly think she was that parched for some life experience? It galled her to give him all the points. 'Ten past.'

His smile transformed his face, the way it always did.

'Done.'

'And we're sleeping separately. You know…just for the record.'

'Hey, I'm just buying you a sunset, lady.' His shrug was adorable. And totally disarming.

'Now go, Weatherman—you're scaring off my leads with all that leather.'

Her lips said 'go' but her heart said *stay*. Whispered it, really. But she'd become proficient in drowning out the fancies of her heart. And its fears. Neither were particularly productive in keeping her on track in finding Travis. A nice neutral…nothing…was the best way to proceed.

Emotionally blank, psychologically focused.

Which wasn't to say that Marshall Sullivan couldn't be a useful distraction from all the voices in her head and heart.

And a pleasant one.

And a short one.

They drove the two hundred kilometres east in a weird kind of convoy. Eve chugging along in her ancient bus and him, unable to stand the slow pace, roaring off ahead and pulling over at the turn-off to every conceivable human touch point until she caught up, whacked up a poster and headed out again. Rest stops, roadhouses, campgrounds, lookouts. Whizzing by at one hundred kilometres an hour and only stopping longer for places that had people and rubbish bins and queued-up vehicles.

It was a horrible way to see such a beautiful country.

Eventually, they made it to the campground nestled in the shoulder crook of a pristine bay on the far side of Cape Arid National Park, its land arms reaching left and right in a big, hug-like semicircle. A haven for travellers, fishermen and a whole lot of wildlife.

But not today. Today they had the whole place to themselves.

'So many blues…' Eve commented, stepping down out of the bus and staring at the expansive bay.

And she wasn't wrong. Closer to shore, the water was the pale, almost ice-blue of gentle surf. Then the kind of blue you saw on postcards, until, out near the horizon it graduated to a deep, gorgeous blue before slamming into the endless rich blue of the Australian sky. And, down to their left, a cluster of weathered boulders were freckled by a bunch of sea lions sunning themselves.

God...so good for the soul.

'This is nothing,' he said. Compared to what she'd missed all along the south coast of Australia. Compared to what she'd driven straight past. 'If you'd just chuck your indicator on from time to time...'

She glanced at him but didn't say anything, busying stringing out her solar blanket to catch the afternoon light. When she opened the back doors of the bus to fill it with fresh sea air, she paused, looking further out to sea. Out to an island.

'Is that where we're going?'

Marshall hauled himself up next to her to follow her gaze. 'Nope. That's one of the closer, smaller islands in the archipelago. Middle Island is further out. One of those big shadows looming on the horizon.'

He leaned half across her to point further out and she followed the line of his arm and finger. It brought them as close together as they'd been since he'd dragged her kicking and cursing away from the thugs back in Norseman. And then he knew how much he'd missed her scent.

It eddied around his nostrils now, in defiance of the strong breeze.

Taunting him.

'How many are there?'

What were they talking about? Right...islands. 'More than a hundred.'

Eve stood, staring, her gaze flicking over every feature in view. Marshall kept his hand hooked around the bus's ceiling, keeping her company up there. Keeping close.

'Trav could be on any of them.'

Not if he also wanted to eat. Or drink. Only two had fresh water.

'Listen, Eve...'

She turned her eyes back up to his and it put their faces much closer than either of them might have intended.

'I really am truly sorry I said that about your brother. It was a cheap shot.' And one that he still didn't fully understand making. He wasn't Eve's keeper. 'The chances of him being out there are—'

'Tiny. I know. But it's in my head now and I'm not going to be able to sleep if I don't chase every possibility.'

'Still, I don't want to cause you pain.'

'That's not hurting, Marshall. That's helping. It's what I'm out here for.'

She said the words extra firmly, as if she was reminding both of them. Didn't make the slightest difference to the tingling in his toes. The tingling said she was here for him.

What did toes ever know?

He held her gaze much longer than was probably polite, their dark depths giving the ocean around them a run for its money.

'Doesn't seem a particularly convenient place to put a weather station,' she said finally, turning back out to the islands.

Subtle subject change. *Not.* But he played along. 'We want remote. To give us better data on southern coastal weather conditions.'

She glanced around them at the whole lot of nothing as far as the eye could see. 'You got it.'

Silent sound cushioned them in layers. The occasional bird cry, far away. The whump of the distant waves hitting the granite face of the south coast. The thrum of the coastal breeze around them. The awkward clearing of her throat as it finally dawned on her that she was shacked up miles from anywhere—and anyone—with a man she barely knew.

'What time are we meeting the boat? And where?'

'First thing in the morning. They'll pull into the bay, then ferry us around. Any closer to Middle Island and we couldn't get in without an off-road vehicle.'

'Right.'

Gravity helped his boots find the dirt and he looked back up at Eve, giving her the space she seemed to need. 'I'm going to go hit the water before the sun gets too low.'

Her eyes said that a swim was exactly what she wanted. But the tightness in her lips said that she wasn't about to go wandering through the sand dunes somewhere this remote with a virtual stranger. Fair enough, they'd only known each other hours. Despite having a couple of life-threatening moments between them. Maybe if she saw him walking away from her, unoffended and unconcerned, she'd feel more comfortable around him. Maybe if he offered no pressure for the two of them to spend time together, she'd relax a bit.

And maybe if he grew a pair he wouldn't care.

'See you later on, then.'

Marshall jogged down to the beach without looking back. When he hit the shore he laid his boots, jeans and T-shirt out on the nearest rock to get nice and toasty for his return and waded into the ice-cold water in his shorts. Normally he'd have gone without, public or not, but that wasn't going to win him any points in the *Is it safe to be here with you?* stakes. The sand beneath his feet had been beaten so fine by the relentless Southern Ocean it was more like squidging into saturated talcum powder than abrasive granules of sand. Soft and welcoming, the kind of thing you could imagine just swallowing you up.

And you wouldn't mind a bit.

His skin instantly thrilled at the kiss of the ice-cold water after the better part of a day smothered in leather and road dust, and he waded the stretch of shallows, then dived through the handful of waves that built up momentum as the rapid rise of land forced them into graceful, white-topped arcs.

This was his first swim since Cactus Beach, a whole state away. The Great Australian Bight was rugged and amazing to look at right the way across the guts of the country but when the rocks down to the sea were fifty metres high and the ocean down there bottomless and deadly, swimming had to take a short sabbatical. But swimming was also one of the things that kept him sane and being barred from it got him all twitchy.

Which made it pretty notable that the first thing he *didn't do* when he pulled up to the beautiful, tranquil and swimmable shores of Esperance earlier today was hit the water.

He went hunting for a dark-haired little obsessive instead.

Oh, he told himself a dozen lies to justify it—that he'd rather swim the private beaches of the capes; that he'd rather swim at sunset; that he'd rather get the Middle Island review out of the way first so he could take a few days to relax—but that was all starting to feel like complete rubbish. Apparently, he was parched for something more than just salt water.

Company.

Pfff. Right. That was one word for it.

It had been months since he'd been interested enough in a woman to do something about it, and by 'interested' he meant hungry. Hungry enough to head out and find a woman willing to sleep with a man who had nothing to offer but a hard, one-off lay before blowing town the next day. There seemed to be no shortage of women across the country who were out to salve a broken heart, or pay back a cheating spouse, or numb something broken deep inside them. They were the ones he looked for when he got needy enough because they didn't ask questions and they didn't have expectations.

It took one to know one.

Those encounters scratched the itch when it grew too demanding... and they reminded him how empty and soulless relationships were. All relationships, not just the random strangers in truck stops and bars across the country. Women. Mothers.

Brothers.

At least the women in the bars knew where they stood. No one was getting used. And there was no one to disappoint except himself.

He powered his body harder, arm over arm, and concentrated on how his muscles felt, cutting his limbs through the surf. Burning from within, icy from without. The familiar, heavy ache of lactic acid building up. And when he'd done all the examination it was possible to do on his muscles, he focused on the water: how the last land it had touched was Antarctica, how it was life support for whales and elephant seals and dugongs and colossal squid and mysterious deep-trench blobs eight kilometres below the surface and thousands of odd-shaped sea creatures in between. How humans were a bunch of nimble-fingered, big-brained primates that really only used the millimetre around the edge of the mapped oceans and had absolutely no idea how much of their planet they knew nothing about.

Instant Gulliver.

It reminded him how insignificant he was in the scheme of things. Him and all his human, social problems.

The sun was low on the horizon when he next paid attention, and the south coast of Australia was littered with sharks who liked to feed at dusk and dawn. And while there had certainly been a day he would have happily taken the risk and forgotten the consequences, he'd managed to find a happy place in the *Groundhog Day* blur that was the past six months on the road, and could honestly say—hand on heart—that he'd rather not be shark food now.

He did a final lazy lap parallel with the wide beach back towards his discarded clothes, then stood as soon as the sea floor rose to meet him. His hands squeezed up over his lowered lids and back through his hair, wringing the salt water out of it, then he stood, eyes closed, with his face tipped towards the warmth of the afternoon sun.

Eventually, he opened them and started, just a little, at Eve standing there, her arms full of towel, her mouth hanging open as if he'd interrupted her mid-sentence.

Eve knew she was gaping horribly but she was no more able to close her trap than rip her eyes from Marshall's chest and belly.

His *tattooed* chest and belly.

Air sucked into her lungs in choppy little gasps.

He had some kind of massive bird of prey, wings spread and aloft, across his chest. The lower curve of its majestic wings sat neatly along the ridge of his pectorals and its wing tips followed the line of muscle there up onto his tanned, rounded shoulders. Big enough to accentuate the musculature of his chest, low enough to be invisible when he was wearing a T-shirt. It should have been trashy but it wasn't; it looked like he'd been born with it.

His arms were still up, squeezing the sea water from his hair, and that gave her a glimpse of a bunch of inked characters—Japanese, maybe Chinese?—on the underside of one full biceps.

Add that to the dagger on the other arm and he had a lot of ink for a weatherman.

'Hey.'

His voice startled her gaze back to his and her tongue into action.

'Wow,' she croaked, then realised that wasn't the most dignified of beginnings. 'You were gone so long...'

Great. Not even capable of a complete sentence.

'I've been missing the ocean. Sorry if I worried you.'

She grasped around in the memories she'd just spent a couple of hours accumulating, studying the map to make sure they hadn't missed a caravan park or town. And she improvised some slightly more intelligent conversation.

'Whoever first explored this area really didn't have the best time doing it.'

Marshall dripped. And frowned. As he lowered his arms to take the towel from her nerveless fingers, the bird of prey's feathers shifted with him, just enough to catch her eye. She struggled to look somewhere other than at him, but it wasn't easy when he filled her field of view so thoroughly. She wanted to step back but then didn't want to give him the satisfaction of knowing she was affected.

'Cape Arid, Mount Ragged, Poison Creek...' she listed with an encouraging lack of wobble in her voice, her clarity restored the moment he pressed the towel to his face and disguised most of that unexpectedly firm and decorated torso.

He stepped over to the rock and hooked up his T-shirt, then swept it on in a smooth, manly shrug. Even with its overstretched neckline, the bird of prey was entirely hidden. The idea of him hanging out in his meteorological workplace in a government-appropriate suit with all of that ink hidden away under it was as secretly pleasing as when she used to wear her best lingerie to section meetings.

Back when stupid things like that had mattered.

'I guess it's not so bad when you have supplies and transport,' he said, totally oblivious to her illicit train of thought, 'but it must have been a pretty treacherous environment for early explorers. Especially if they were thirsty.'

She just blinked at him. What was he saying? What had she asked?

He didn't bother with the rest of his clothes; he just slung the jeans over his shoulder and followed her back up to camp with his boots swinging in his left hand.

'Nice swim?' Yeah. Much easier to think with all that skin and ink covered up.

'I've missed it. The water's so clean down here.'

'Isn't ocean always clean?'

'Not at all. It's so easy to imagine the Southern Ocean being melt straight from Antarctica. Beautiful.'

'Maybe I'll take a dip tomorrow.' When Marshall was otherwise engaged.

They fell to silence as they approached the bus. Suddenly the awkwardness of the situation amplified. One bus. Two people. One of them half-naked and the other fresh from a bout of uncontrollable ogling. As though her-on-the-bed and him-on-the-sofa was the only social nicety to be observed. There was a bathroom and TV space and…air to consider. She was used to having the bus entirely to herself, now she had to share it with a man for twenty-four hours. And not just any man.

A hot man.

A really hot man.

'Um. You take the bus to change, I'll just—' she looked around for inspiration and saw the quirky little public out-house in the distance '—check out the facilities.'

Oh, good Lord…

'Thanks. I'll only be a few minutes.'

Her, too. Most definitely. There was a reason she'd held out until she found a live-in transport with a toilet built into it. Public toilets in re-mote Australia were not for the faint of heart.

As it turned out, this one was a cut above average. Well maintained and stocked. Some kind of eco-composting number. It was only when she caught herself checking out how the pipework operated that she knew just how badly she was stalling. As if toilets were anywhere near that fascinating.

Come on, Read, man up.

Returning revealed Marshall to have been as good as his word. He was changed, loosely groomed and waiting outside the bus already. *Outside.* Almost as though he was trying to minimise his impact on her space.

He held his new bike helmet out to her.

'Come on.' He smiled. 'I promised you a ride. While we still have light.'

It took approximately twenty-five seconds for Eve to get over her con-cern that Marshall only had one motorbike helmet and he was holding it out to her. After that, she was all about survival of the fittest.

'I don't remember agreeing to this—'

'You'll love it, Eve. I promise.'

She glared up at him. 'Just because you do?'

'Because it's brilliant. And fun.'

No. Not always fun. She'd lost one and nearly two people she loved to a not-so-fun motorbike. Though that could just as easily have been a car, her logical side whispered. Or a bus. Or a 747. Tragedies happened every single day.

Just that day it happened to them.

'Think of it like a theme park ride,' he cajoled. 'A roller coaster.'

'That's not really helping.'

'Come on, Eve. What else are we going to do until it's dark?'

Apart from sit in the bus in awkward silence obsessing on who was going to sleep where…? She glanced sideways at the big orange bike.

'I'll keep you safe, I promise. We'll only go as fast as you're comfortable with.'

His siren voice chipped away at her resistance. And his vow——*I'll keep you safe*. For so long she'd been all about looking after her father and brother. When was the last time someone offered to look after *her*?

'Just slow?'

Of course there was small print, but it came delightfully packaged in a grin full of promise. 'Until you're ready for more.'

He seemed so incredibly confident that was going to happen. Her bottom lip wiggled its way between her teeth. She *had* always wondered what it would be like to ride something with a bit more power. If by *always* she meant after two hours of watching a leather-clad Marshall dominate the machine under him. And if by *ride* she meant pressing her thighs into his and her front to that broad, strong back, both of them hepped up on adrenaline. It was a seductive picture. The kind of picture that was best reserved for her and a quiet, deluded night in the bus. She hadn't imagined it would ever go from fantasy to opportunity.

He held the helmet out again.

'You'll slow the moment I ask?' she breathed.

'Cross my heart.'

Yeah, not really selling it. Everyone knew what came after that line…

But it was only when she was about to lower her hand away from the helmet that she realised she'd even raised it. What was she going to do, live in fear of motorbikes for the rest of her life? No one was even sure what had caused her mother's accident——even Trav, after he'd come out of the coma, couldn't shed much light. Tragic accident. Could have happened to anyone. That was the final verdict.

'You'll drive safely?'

Come on, Read, suck it up.

Sincerity blazed in his solemn grey gaze. 'I'll be a model of conservatism.'

How long had it been since she'd done something outside of the box? Or taken any kind of risk? She used to be edgy, back before life got so very serious and she took responsibility for Travis. And her risks had almost always paid off. That was part of the thrill.

Hadn't she once been known for that?

Here was a gorgeous man offering to wrap her around him for a little bit. And the price—a bit of reckless speed.

It had been years since she'd done something reckless. Maybe it would be good for her.

She took a deep breath and curled her fingers around the helmet's chin strap.

The KTM hit a breath-stealing speed in about the same time it took her to brave opening her eyes. The road whizzed below them in such a blur it was like riding on liquid mercury.

At least that was how it felt.

She immediately remembered the excitement of riding behind her mother, but her mother's bike had never purred like this one. And it had never glued itself to the road like the tyres on this one.

Maybe if it had, all their lives would have been very different now.

She pressed herself more fully into Marshall's hard back and practically punched her fingertips through his leather jacket from clenching it so hard.

'Is this top speed?' she yelled forward to him.

His hair whipped around above her face as he shook his head and shouted back. 'We're only doing seventy kilometres.'

'Don't go any faster,' she called.

She hated the vulnerable note in her voice, but she hated more the thought of hitting the dirt at this kind of speed. In Travis's case it had been trees but she felt fairly certain that you didn't need trees to be pretty badly injured on a bike.

Marshall turned his face half back to her and smiled beneath his protective sunglasses, nodding once. She'd just have to trust those teeth.

The roads of the national park were long and straight and the bike sat atop them beautifully so, after a few tense minutes, Eve let her death grip on his jacket ease slightly and crept them back to rest on Marshall's hips instead. Still firm, but the blood was able to leach back into her knuckles.

For a death machine he handled it pretty well.

Ahead, the road bent around a monolithic chunk of rock and he eased off the gas to pass it carefully. The bike's lean felt extreme to her and her grasp on his leather jacket completely insufficient, so her fingers found their way under it and hooked onto the eyelets of his jeans.

A few paltry sweatshop stitches were the only thing between her and certain doom.

While the engine was eased, Marshall took the opportunity to call back to her, half turning, 'Doing okay?'

Eyes front, mister!

'Stop staring down,' he shouted. 'Look around you.'

She let her eyes flutter upwards as he turned his attention back to the oncoming road. The entire park was bathed in the golden glow of afternoon light, the many different textures changing the way the light reflected and creating the golden equivalent of the ocean. So many different shades.

And—bonus—the speed didn't seem anywhere near as scary as staring down at the asphalt.

It was almost like being in the Bedford. Sans life-saving steel exoskeleton.

She didn't want to look like a complete wuss, and so Eve did her best to ease herself back from where her body had practically fused with his. The problem with that was as soon as he changed up gears, she brushed, breasts first, against his back. And then again.

And again, as he shifted up into fourth.

Okay, now he was just messing with her. She was having a difficult enough reaction to all that leather without adding to the crisis by torturing her own flesh. Leaning into him might be more intimate, but it felt far less gratuitous and so she snuggled forward again, widening her legs to fit more snugly around his. Probably not how a passenger was supposed to ride—the fact her bottom had left the pillion seat in favour of sharing his leathery saddle proved that—but that was how it was going to be for her first ever big boy's motorcycle experience.

And if he didn't like it he could pull over.

Minutes whizzed by and she grew captivated by the long stretches of tufted grass to her left, the parched, salt-crusted trees and coastal heath to her right and the limestone outcrops that practically glowed in the late-afternoon light. So much so that, when Marshall finally pulled them to a halt at a lookout point, she realised she'd forgotten all about the speed. Her pulse was up, her exposed skin was flushed pink and her breath was pleasantly choppy.

But she hadn't died.

And she wasn't ready for it to be over.

'I can see why she—why *you* like this,' she puffed, lifting the visor on her helmet and leaning around him. 'It's a great way to see the country.'

'Are you comfortable?'

His innocuous words immediately reminded her of how close she was pressed against him—wrapped around him, really—and she immediately went to correct that.

'Stay put,' he cautioned. 'We're about to head back.'

She leaned with him as he turned the bike in a big arc on an old salt flat and then bumped back onto the tarmac. As if she'd been doing this forever. And, as he roared back up to speed, she realised how very much in the *now* she'd been. Just her, Marshall, the road, the wind and the national park.

No past. No future. No accidents. No inquests. No Travis.

And how nice that moment of psychological respite was.

The light was totally different heading back. Less golden. More orange. And fading fast. He accessed a fifth gear that he'd spared her on the first leg and even still, when he pulled back in near the bus, the sun was almost gone. She straightened cold-stiffened limbs and pulled off his helmet.

'How was that?' he asked, way more interest in his eyes than a courtesy question. He kicked the stand into position and leaned the bike into the solid embrace of the earth.

'Amazing.'

The word formed a tiny breath cloud in the cool evening air and it was only then she realised how cold she was. The sun's warmth sure departed fast in this part of the country.

He followed her back towards the bus. 'You took a bit to loosen up.'

'Considering how terrified I was, I don't think I did too badly.'

'Not badly at all. I felt the moment when the fear left your body.'

The thought that she'd been pressed closely enough to him to be telegraphing any kind of emotion caused a rush of heat that she was very glad it was too dim for him to see. But he stepped ahead of her and opened the back of the Bedford and caught the last vestiges of her flush.

'How are you feeling now about motorcycles?'

His body blocked the step up into the bus and so she had no choice but to brush past him as she pulled herself up.

'It's still a death trap,' she said, looking back down at him. 'But not entirely without redeeming qualities.'

Not unlike its owner, really.

CHAPTER FOUR

'I WAS THINKING of steak and salad for dinner,' Eve said, returning from her little bedroom newly clad in a sweater to take the edge off the cool coastal night.

Lord, how domestic. And utterly foreign.

'You don't need to cook for me, Eve. I ate up big at lunchtime in anticipation.'

'I was there, remember? And while it certainly was big you probably burned it all off with that epic swim earlier.'

And Lord knew, between the lusting and the fearing for her life, she'd just burnt all hers off, too.

Preparing food felt natural; she'd been doing it for Travis for so many years. Moreover, it gave her something constructive and normal to do for thirty minutes, but Marshall wasn't so lucky. He hovered, hopelessly. After the comparative intimacy of the bike ride, it seemed ludicrous to be uncomfortable about sharing a simple meal. But he was, a little.

And so was she. A lot.

'Here.' She slid him a bottle opener across the raw timber counter of the Bedford's compact little kitchen. 'Make yourself useful.'

She nodded to a small cabinet above the built-in television and, when he opened it, his eyebrows lifted at the contents. 'I thought you didn't drink?'

That rattled a chuckle from her tight chest.

'Not in bars—' with men she didn't know, and given her familial history '—but I like to sample the local wines as I move around.'

She brought her solitary wineglass out from under the bench, then added a coffee mug next to it. The best she could do.

'You take the glass,' she offered.

He took both, in fact, poured two generous servings of red and slid the wineglass back her way. 'I guess you don't entertain much?'

'Not really out here for the social life,' she said. But then she relented. 'I did have a second glass once but I have no idea where it's gone. So it's the coffee mug or it's my toothbrush glass.'

And didn't that sound pathetic.

'You're going to need another storage cupboard,' he murmured, bringing the mug back from his lips and licking the final drops off, much to her sudden fascination. 'We're headed for serious wine country.'

'Maybe I just need to drink faster.'

He chuckled and saluted her with the mug. 'Amen to that.'

What was it about a communal glass of vino that instantly broke down the awkwardness barrier? He'd only had one sip and she'd had none, yet, so it wasn't the effects of the alcohol. Just something about popping a cork and swilling a good red around in your glass—or coffee mug—the great equaliser.

Maybe that was how her mother had begun. Social and pleasant. Until one day she woke up and it wasn't social any more. Or pleasant.

'So tell me,' Eve started, continuing with her food prep, 'did you have much competition for half a year in the bush checking on weather stations?'

He smiled and leaned across to relieve her of the chopping knife and vegetables from the fridge. 'I did not.'

It was too easy to respond to that gentle smile. To let her curiosity have wings. To tease. 'Can't imagine why not. Why did you accept it?'

'Travel the country, fully paid. What's not to love?'

'Being away from your friends and family?'

Being away from your girlfriend. She concentrated hard to keep her eyes from dropping to the bottom of the biceps dagger that peeked out from under his sleeve.

'Not all families benefit from being in each other's faces,' he said, a little tightly.

She stopped and regarded him. 'Speaking from experience?'

Grey eyes flicked to hers.

'Maybe. Don't tell me,' he nudged. 'You have the perfect parents.'

Oh...so far from the truth it was almost laughable. The steaks chuckled for her as she flipped them. 'Parent singular. Dad.'

He regarded her closely. 'You lost your mum?'

'Final year of school.'

'I'm sorry. New subject?'

'No. It's a long time ago now. It's okay.'

'Want to talk about it?'

Sometimes, desperately. Sometimes when she sat all alone in this little bus that felt so big she just wished she had someone sitting there with her that she could spill it all to. Someone to help her make sense of everything that had happened. Because she still barely understood it.

'Not much to talk about. She was in an accident. Travis was lucky to survive it.'

His fathomless gaze grew deeper. Full of sympathy. 'Car crash?'

Here it came...

'Motorbike, actually.'

His eyes flared and he spun more fully towards her. 'Why didn't you say, Eve?'

'I'm saying now.'

'Before I press-ganged you into taking a ride with me,' he gritted, leaning over the counter.

'I could have said no. At any time. I'm not made of jelly.' Except when Marshall smiled at her a certain way. Then anyone would be forgiven for thinking so.

'I never would have—'

'It wasn't the bike's fault. It's good for me to remember that.'

He took a long, slow breath and Eve distracted herself poking the steaks.

'A 250cc, you said. Not your usual family wagon.'

'Oh, we had one of those, too. But she got her motorcycle licence not long after having Travis.' Like some kind of statement. 'She rode it whenever she didn't have us with her.'

Which was often in those last five years.

'I think it was her way of fighting suburbia,' she murmured.

Or reality, maybe.

'But she had your brother with her that day?' Then, 'Are you okay to talk about this?'

Surprisingly, she was. Maybe because Marshall was a fellow motorbike fanatic. It somehow felt okay for him to know.

'Yeah——' she sighed '——she did. Trav loved her bike. He couldn't wait to get his bike permit. I think she was going to give him the Kawasaki. He'd started to learn.'

'How old was he when it happened?'

'Fourteen.'

'Five years between you. That's a biggish gap.'

'Thank God for it. Not sure I could have handled any of it if I'd been younger.'

It was hard enough as it was.

It was only when Marshall's voice murmured, soft and low, over her shoulder and he reached past her to turn off the gas to the steaks that she realised how long she'd been standing there mute. Her skin tingled at his closeness.

'New subject?'

'No. I'm happy to talk about my family. I just forget sometimes...'

'Forget what?'

Sorrow washed through her. 'That my family's different now. That it's just me and Dad.'

'You say that like...'

Her eyes lifted. 'That's the reality. If Trav is missing by force, then he's not coming back. And if he's missing by choice...'

Then he's not coming back.

Either way, her already truncated family had shrunk by one more.

'You really believe he could be out here somewhere, just...lying low?'

'I have to believe that. That he's hurting. Confused. Off his meds. Maybe he doesn't think he'd be welcome back after leaving like he did. I want him to know we want him back no matter what.'

Marshall's head bobbed slowly. 'No case to answer? For the distress he's caused?'

Her hand fell still on the spatula. For the longest time, the only sound came from the low-burn frying pan. But, eventually, her thoughts collected into something coherent.

'I ask myself is there anything he could do that would make me not want to have him back with us and the answer is no. So giving him grief for what he did, or why he did it, or the manner in which he did it... It has no purpose. I just want him to walk back in that door and scuff the wall with his school bag and start demanding food. The *what*, *why* and *how* is just not relevant.'

Intelligent eyes glanced from her still fingers to her face. 'It's relevant to you.'

'But it's not important. In the scheme of things.'

Besides, she already had a fairly good idea of the *why*. Travis's escalating anxiety and depression seemed blazingly obvious in hindsight, even if she hadn't seen it at the time. Because she hadn't been paying attention. She'd been far too busy shrugging off her substitute mother apron.

Thinking about herself.

She poked at the steak again and delicious juices ran from it and added to the noise in the pan. She lifted her wineglass with her free hand and emptied a bit into the pan. Then she took a generous swig and changed the subject.

'So, who is Christine?'

No-man's-land the last time they spoke, but they weren't spending the night under the same roof then. They barely knew each other then.

We barely know each other now! a tiny voice reminded her.

But they did. Maybe not a heap of details, but they knew each other's names and interests and purpose. She'd seen him half naked striding out of the surf, and she'd pressed up against him a grand total of two times now and had a different kind of glimpse at the kind of man he was under all the leather and facial hair. He struck her as...safe.

And sometimes safe was enough.

But right now *safe* didn't look entirely happy at her words. Though he still answered.

'Was,' he clarified. 'Christine was my girlfriend.'

Clang. The pan hit the stovetop at his use of the past tense. There was the answer to a question she didn't know she'd been dying to ask. Unexpected butterflies took flight deep in her gut and she busied herself with a second go at moving the frying pan off the heat.

'Recent?'

His strong lips pursed briefly as he considered answering. Or not answering. 'Long time ago.'

Yeah, the ink didn't look new, come to think of it. Unlike the one she'd seen under his biceps.

Which meant he could still be someone else's hairy biker type. That she was having a quiet steak with. Under a gem-filled sky. Miles from anywhere. After a blood-thrilling and skin-tingling motorbike ride...

She shook the thoughts free. 'Childhood sweetheart?'

Tension pumped off him. 'Something like that.'

And suddenly she disliked Christine intensely. 'I'm sorry.'

He shrugged. 'Not your doing.'

She studied the tight lines at the corner of his mouth. The mouth she'd not been able to stop looking at since he'd shaved and revealed it. Tonight was no different. 'So...there's no Christine now? I mean someone like Christine?'

His eyes found hers. 'You asking if I'm single?'

'Just making conversation. I figured not, since you were on a pilgrimage around the country.'

'It's my job, Eve. Not everyone out here is on some kind of odyssey.'

That stung as much as the sea salt she'd accidentally rubbed in her eye earlier. Because of the judgment those words contained. And the truth. And because they came from him.

But he looked contrite the moment they fell off his lips.

'You don't like talking about her, I take it?' she murmured.

He shook his head but it was no denial.

'Fair enough.' Then she nodded at his arm. 'You might want to get that altered though.'

The tension left his face and a couple of tiny smile lines peeked out the corners of his eyes. 'I couldn't have picked someone with a shorter name, huh? Like Ann. Or Lucy.'

Yep. Christine sure was a long word to tattoo over.

'It's pretty florid, too. A dagger?'

The smile turned into a laugh. 'We were seventeen and in love. And I fancied myself for a bit of a tough guy. What can I say?'

Eve threw some dressing on the salad and gave it a quick toss.

'She got a matching one I hope?'

'Hers just said *Amore*. Multi-purpose.'

'*Pfff.* Non-committal. That should have been your first warning.'

She added a steak to each of their plates.

'With good reason, it turns out.'

'Christine sucked?'

That earned her a chuckle. She loved the rich, warm sound because it came from so deep in his chest. 'No, she didn't. Or I wouldn't have fallen for her.'

'That's very charitable.'

He waved his coffee mug. 'I'm a generous guy.'

'So… I'm confused,' she started. 'You don't want to talk about her, but you don't hold it against her?'

'It's not really about Christine,' he hedged.

'What isn't?' And then, when he didn't respond, 'The awkward silence?'

'How many people end up with their first love, really?'

She wouldn't know. She hadn't had time for love while she was busy raising her family. Or since. More's the pity.

'So where did she end up?'

The look he gave her was enigmatic. But also appraising. And kind of stirring. 'Not important.'

'You're very complicated, Marshall Sullivan.'

His smile crept back. 'Thank you.'

Eve leaned across the counter and lifted the hem of his sleeve with two fingers to have a good look at the design. Her fingertips brushed the smooth strength of his warm biceps and tingled where they travelled.

She cleared her throat. 'Maybe you could change it to *pristine*, like the ocean? That way, you only have to rework the first two letters.'

Three creases formed across his brow as he looked down. 'That could actually work…'

'Or *Sistine*, like the chapel.'

'Or *intestine*, like the pain I get from smelling that steak and not eating it.'

They loaded their plates up with fresh salad and both tucked in.

'This is really good.'

'That surprises you?'

'I didn't pick you as a cook.'

She shrugged. 'I had a rapid apprenticeship after Mum died.'

She munched her way through half her plate before speaking again.

'Can I ask you something personal?'

'Didn't you already do that?'

'About travelling.'

His head tilted. 'Go ahead.'

'Do you...' Lord, how to start this question? 'You travel alone. Do you ever feel like you've forgotten how to be with somebody else? How to behave?'

'What do you mean?'

'I just... I used to be so social. Busy schedule, urban lifestyle, dinners out most evenings. Meeting new people and chatting to them.' Up until the accident, anyway. 'I feel like I've lost some of my social skills.'

'Honestly?'

She nodded.

'Yeah, you're missing a few of the niceties. But once you get past that, you're all right. We're conversing happily now, aren't we?'

Give or take a few tense undercurrents.

'Maybe you just got good at small talk,' he went on. 'And small talk doesn't take you far in places like this. Situations like this. It's no good at all in silence. It just screams. But we're doing okay, on the whole.'

She rushed to correct him. 'I didn't mean you, specifically—'

'Yeah, you did.'

'What makes you say that?'

'Eve, this feels awkward because it *is* awkward. We don't know each other and yet I was forced into your world unnaturally. And now a virtual stranger is sitting ten feet from your bed, drinking your wine and getting personal. Of course it's uncomfortable.'

'I'm not...it's not uncomfortable, exactly. I just feel really rusty. And you don't deserve that. You've been very nice.'

The word *nice* hit him visibly. He actually winced.

'When was the last time you had someone in your bus?' he deviated.

Eve racked her brain... Months. Lots of months. 'Long enough for that second wineglass to end up right at the back of some cupboard.'

'There you go, then. You're out of shape, socially, that's all.'

She stared at him.

'Let's make a pledge. I promise to be my clunky self when you're around if you'll do the same.' He drew a big circle around the two of them and some tiny part of her quite liked being in that circle with him. 'This is a clunk-approved zone.'

'Clunk-approved?'

'Weird moments acknowledged, accepted and forgiven.'

Why was it so easy to smile, with him? 'You're giving me permission to be socially clumsy?'

'I'm saying I'll understand.'

It was so much easier to breathe all of a sudden. 'All right. Sounds good.'

And on that warm and toasty kindred-spirit moment...

'Are you done?' she checked.

He scooped the last of his steak into his mouth and nodded.

'Hop up, I'd like to show you something.'

As soon as he stood up and back, she pinched the tall stool out from under him and clambered onto it. That allowed her to pop the latch on what looked to anyone else like a sunroof. It folded back onto the bus with a thump. She boosted herself up and into the void, wriggling back until her bottom was thoroughly seated and her legs dangled down into the bus.

'Pass the wine up,' she asked.

He did, but not before adding a generous splash to both their vessels. Then he hoisted himself up opposite her—disgustingly effortlessly— and followed her gaze, left, up out into the endless, dark sky over the Southern Ocean.

'Nice view.'

Essentially the same view as when they'd stood up on the Bedford's back step, just a little higher, but somehow it was made all the more spectacular by the location, the wine and the darkness.

And the company.

'I like to do this when the weather's fine.' Though usually alone.

'I can see why.'

The sky was blanketed with light from a gazillion other solar systems. The full you'll-never-see-it-in-the-city cliché. Eve tipped her head back, stared up and sighed.

'Sometimes I feel like I might as well be looking for Trav out there.' She tossed her chin to the trillions of unseen worlds orbiting those million stars. 'It feels just as unachievable.'

He brought his eyes back down from the heavens. Back to hers.

'It was such a simple plan when I set off. Visit every town in Australia and put posters up. Check for myself. But all it's done is reinforce for me how vast this country is and how many ways there are for someone to disappear. Living or dead.'

'It's a good plan, Eve. Don't doubt yourself.'

She shrugged.

'Did you do it because you truly thought you'd find him? Or did you do it because you had to do something?'

Tears suddenly sprang up and she fought them. It took a moment to get the choke out of her words.

'He's so young. Still a kid, even if the law says otherwise. I was going crazy at home. Waiting. Hoping each day would be the day that the police freed up enough time to look into Trav's case a bit. Made some progress. My heart leaping every time the phone rang in case it was news.'

Fighting endlessly with her father, who wanted her to give up. To accept the truth.

His truth.

'So here you are,' he summarised, simply. 'Doing something constructive. Does it feel better?'

'Yeah. When it's not feeling totally futile.'

It was too dark for the colour of his eyes to penetrate, but his focus fairly blazed out from the shadows under his sockets. 'It's only futile when it stops achieving anything. Right now it's keeping you sane.'

How did this total stranger know her better than anyone else—better than she knew herself?

Maybe because it took one to know one.

She saluted him with her wine. 'Well, aren't we a pack of dysfunctional sad sacks.'

'I'm not sad,' Marshall said, pretty proudly.

What was his story? Curiosity burnt, bright and blazing. The intense desire to *know* him.

'Nothing to say about being dysfunctional?'

'Nope. Totally guilty on that charge.'

The wind had changed direction the moment the sun set, and its heat no longer affected the vast pockets of air blanketing the southern hemisphere. They were tickled by its kiss but no longer buffeted, and it brought with it a deep and comfortable silence.

'So,' Marshall started, 'if I want to use the bus's bathroom during the night I'm basically in your bedroom, right? How's that going to work?'

She just about gave herself whiplash glancing up at him.

'Uh...'

The bus's little en suite bathroom was on the other side of the door that separated it from the rest of the bus. And from Marshall.

Groan. Just another practicality she hadn't thought through thoroughly. *That's because you just about fell over yourself to travel with him for a bit.*

'Or I can use the campsite toilet,' he suggested.

Yes! Thank the Lord for public services.

'It's not too bad, actually.' If you didn't mind rocks on your bare feet at three in the morning and spiders in the dark. 'What time do we need to be up?'

As soon as the words tumbled over her lips she regretted them. Why was she ending the moment of connection so soon after it had begun?

'The boat's coming at eight.'

And dawn was at six. That was two hours of daylight for the two of them to enjoy sharing the clunk-approved zone together. 'Okay. I'll be ready.'

He passed her his mug, then swung himself down and in and took it and hers and placed them together on the bench below. Eve wiggled to the edge of the hatch and readied her arms to take her weight.

'You all right?'

'Yeah, I do it all the time.' Though she just half tumbled, half swung, usually. Gravity fed. Completely inelegant. 'I don't normally have an audience for this bit.'

His deep voice rumbled, 'Here, let me help...'

Suddenly two strong hands were around her waist, pressed sure and hot against her midriff, and she had no choice but to go with them through the roof and back inside the bus. Marshall eased her down in a far less dramatic manner than she was used to, but not without bunching her sweater up under her breasts and leaving her stomach totally exposed as she slid the length of his body. Fortunately, there were no bare hands on bare skin moments, but it was uncomfortable enough to feel the press of his cold jeans stud against her suddenly scorched tummy.

'Thanks,' she breathed.

He released her and stood back, his lashes lowered. 'No problem.'

Instantly, she wondered what the Japanese symbol for 'awkward' was and whether she'd find that tattooed anywhere on his body.

And instantly she was thinking about hidden parts of his body.

She shook the thought free. 'Well... I guess I'll see you in the morning. I'll try and be quiet if you're not up.'

'I'll be up,' he pledged.

Because he was an early riser or because he wasn't about to let her see him all tousled and vulnerable?

Or because all the touching and sliding was going to keep him awake all night, too.

CHAPTER FIVE

IT HAD BEEN a long time since Marshall had woken to the sounds of someone tiptoeing around a kitchen. In this particular case, it was extra soft because the kitchen was only two metres from his makeshift bed.

He'd heard Eve wake up, start moving around beyond that door that separated them all night, but then he'd fallen back into a light morning doze to the entirely feminine soundtrack. You had to live with someone to enjoy those moments. And you had to love them to live with them. And trust them to love them.

Unfortunately, trust and he were uneasy companions.

He'd been in one relationship post-Christine—a nice girl with lots of dreams—and that hadn't ended well. Him, of course. Just another reminder why going solo was easier on everyone concerned. Family included.

Thoughts of his brother robbed him of any further shut-eye. He pulled himself upright and forked fingers through his bed hair.

'Morning,' Eve murmured behind him. 'I hope I didn't wake you?'

'No. I was half awake, anyway. What time is it?'

'Just after six.'

Wow. Went to show what fresh air, hours of swimming and a good drop of red could do for a man's insomnia. He sure couldn't attribute it to the comfort of his bed. Every muscle creaked as he sat up, including the ones in his voice box.

'Not comfortable?'

'Better than my swag on the hard outback dirt.' Even though it really wasn't. There was something strangely comfortable about bedding down on the earth. It was very...honest. 'I'll be back in a tick.'

The morning sun was gentle but massively bright and he stumbled most of the way towards the campsite toilet. Even with her not in her room, the thought of wedging all of himself into that compact little en suite bathroom... It was just too personal.

And he didn't do personal.

'I have eggs or I have sausages,' she announced when he walked back in a little later. 'They won't keep much longer so I'm cooking them all up.'

'Nah. I'll be all right.'

'You have to eat something; we're going to be on the water all day.'

'That's exactly why I don't want something.'

She stopped and stared. 'Do you get seasick?'

'Doesn't really fit with the he-man image you have of me, does it?' He slid back onto his stool from the night before and she passed him a coffee. 'Not horribly. But bad enough.'

'How about some toast and jam, then?'

She was determined to play host. 'Yeah, that I could do.'

That wouldn't be too disgusting coming back up in front of an audience.

She added two pieces of frozen bread to the toaster and kept on with her fry-up. If nothing else, the seagulls would love the sausages.

'Is that okay?' she said when she finally slid the buttered toast towards him.

'Just trying to think when was the last time I had toast and jam.' Toast had been about all his mother stretched to when he was a kid. But there was seldom jam.

'Not a breakfast person?'

'In the city I'd grab something from a fast food place near work.'

'I'm sure your blood vessels were grateful.'

Yeah... Not.

'Mostly it was just coffee.' The liquid breakfast of champions.

'What about out here?'

'Depends. Some motels throw a cooked breakfast in with the room. That's not always a nice surprise.'

'Well, this is a full service b & b, so eat up.'

Eating with a woman at six o'clock in the morning should have felt wrong but it didn't. In fact, clunk-approved zone moments aside, he felt pretty relaxed around Eve most of the time. Maybe because she was up-tight enough for the both of them.

'Marshall?'

'Sorry. What did you say?'

'I wondered how the boat would know where to come and get us?'

'They'll just putter along the coast until they see us waving.'

'You're kidding.'

'Well, me waving, really. They're not expecting two.'

'That's very casual,' she said. 'What if they don't come?'

'Then I'll call them and they'll come tomorrow.'

Dark eyebrows shot up. 'You're assuming I'd be happy to stay an extra night.'

'If not, we could just head back to Esperance and pick up the boat there,' he admitted. 'That's where it's moored.'

Her jaw gaped. 'Are you serious? Then why are we here?'

'Come on, Eve. Tell me you didn't enjoy the past twenty-four hours. Taking a break. Enjoying the scenery.'

Her pretty eyes narrowed. 'I feel like I've been conned.'

'You have—' he grinned around the crunch of toast smeared with strawberry jam '—by the best.'

She didn't want to laugh—her face struggled with it—but there was no mistaking the twisted smile she tried to hide by turning and plating up her eggs. Twisted and kind of gorgeous. But all she said was...

'So, talk to me about the island.'

The boat came. The *Vista II*'s two-man crew easily spotted the two of them standing on the rocks at the most obvious point of the whole beach. One of them manoeuvred a small inflatable dinghy down onto the still-est part of the early-morning beach to collect them.

The captain reached down for Eve's hands and pulled her up onto the fishing vessel and Marshall gave her a boost from below. Quite a personal boost—both of his hands starting on her waist but sliding onto her bum to do the actual shoving. Then he scrambled up without assistance and so did the old guy who had collected them in the dinghy that he hastily retethered to the boat.

'Thanks for that,' she murmured sideways to Marshall before smiling broadly at the captain and thanking him for real.

'Would you have preferred fish-scaly sea-dog hands on your butt?' Marshall murmured back.

Yeah. Maybe. Because she wouldn't have had to endure his heat still soaking into her. She already had enough of a fascination with his hands...

The next ten minutes were all business. Life vests secured, safety lecture given, seating allocated. Hers was an old square cray pot. Marshall perched on a box of safety gear.

'How long is the trip to Middle Island?' she asked the captain as soon as they were underway.

'Twenty minutes. We have to go around the long way to avoid the wrecks.'

'There are shipwrecks out here?' But as she turned and looked back along the one-hundred-strong shadowy islands of the Recherche Archipelago stretching out to the west, the question suddenly felt really foolish.

Of course there were. It was like a visible minefield of islands.

'Two right off Middle Island.'

As long as they didn't add the *Vista II* to that list, she'd be happy. 'So almost no one comes out here?'

'Not onto the islands, but there's plenty of fishing and small boating traffic.'

'And no one's living on Middle Island?'

Marshall's eyes glanced her way.

'Not since the eighteen-thirties, when Black Jack Anderson based himself and his pirating outfit there,' the captain volunteered.

Huh. So it *could* be lived on. Technically.

Eve turned her gaze towards the distant shadow that was becoming more and more defined as the boat ate up the miles and the captain chatted on about the island's resident pirate. Maybe Marshall's theory wasn't so far-fetched. Maybe Trav could be there. Or have been there in the past. Or—

And as she had the thought, she realised.

Travis.

She'd been awake two whole hours and not given her brother the slightest thought. Normally he was on her mind when her eyes fluttered open each day and the last thing she thought about at night. It kept her focused and on mission. It kept him alive in her heart.

But last night all she'd been able to think about was the man settling in just metres and a bit of flimsy timber away from her. How complicated he was. How easy he was to be around. How good he smelled.

She'd been pulled off mission by the first handsome, broad-shouldered distraction to come along. Nice. As if she wasn't already excelling at the Bad Sister of the Year award.

Well... No more.

Time to get back in the game.

'Eve?' Marshall's voice drifted to her over the sound of the outboard. 'Are you okay?'

She kept her eyes carefully averted, as though she was focusing on the approaching island, and lied.

'Just thinking about what it would be like to live there...'

They travelled in silence, but Eve could just about feel the moments when Marshall would let his eyes rest on her briefly. Assessing. Wondering. The captain chatted on with his semitour talk. About the islands. About the wildlife. About the wallabies and frogs and some special lizard that all lived in harmony on the predator-free island. About the southern rock lobster and abalone that he and his mate fished out of these perilous waters. About how many sharks there were lurking in the depths around them.

The promise of sharks made her pay extra attention as she slid back down the side of the *Vista II* into the inflatable and, before long, her feet were back on dry land. Dry, deserted land.

One glance around them at the remote, untouched, uninhabitable terrain told her Trav wasn't hiding out here.

As if there'd really been a chance.

'Watch where you step. The barking gecko is protected on this island.'

'Of course it is,' she muttered.

Marshall just glanced at her sideways. The fishermen left and promised to return for them in a couple of hours. A nervous anxiety filled her belly. If they didn't return, what would she do? How would she survive here with just a day's supply of water and snacks and no shelter? Just because Black Jack Whatsit got by for a decade didn't mean she'd last more than a day.

'So,' Marshall said after helping to push the inflatable back offshore, 'you want to explore on your own or come with me?'

Explore on my own—that was the right answer. But, at the same time, she didn't know anything about this strange little island and she was just as likely to break her ankle on the farthest corner from Marshall and his little first-aid kit.

'Is it safe?' she asked, screening her eyes with her hands and scanning the horizon.

'If you don't count the death adders, yeah.'

She snapped her focus straight back to him. 'Are you kidding?'

'Nope. But if you're watching out for the geckos you'll almost certainly see the snakes before you tread on them.'

Almost certainly.

'I'm coming with you.'

'Good choice. Feel like a climb?' She turned and followed his gaze up to the highest point on the island. 'Flinders Peak is where the weather station would go.'

He assured her it was only one hundred and eighty-five metres above sea level but it felt like Everest when you were also watching every footfall for certain death—yours or a protected gecko's.

Marshall pointed out the highlights to the west, chatted about the nearest islands and their original names. Then he halted his climb and just looked at her.

'What?' she asked, puffing.

'I'm waiting for you to turn around.'

They'd ascended the easiest face of the peak but it had obscured most of the rest of the island from their view. She turned around now.

'Oh, my gosh!'

Pink. A crazy, wrong, enormous bubblegum-pink lake lay out on the eastern corner of the island. Somehow everyone had failed to mention a bright pink lake! 'What is it?'

'Lake Hillier.'

'It's so beautiful.' But so unnatural. It just went to show how little she knew about the natural world. 'Why is it pink?'

'Bacteria? The type of salt? Maybe something new to science. Does it matter?'

'I guess not.' It was just curiously beautiful. 'Can we go there?'

'We just got up here.'

'I know, but now I want to go there.'

So much! A bit like riding on his bike, little moments of pleasure managed to cut through her miserable thoughts about Travis.

He smiled, but it was twisted with curiosity. And something else.

'What?' she queried.

'This is the first time I've seen you get really passionate about anything since I met you.'

'Some things are just worth getting your pulse up about.' And, speaking of which...

He stepped a little closer and her heartbeat responded immediately.

'Lakes and lizards do it for you?'

'*Pink* lakes and geckos that *bark*,' she stressed for the slow of comprehension. Right on cue, a crack of vocalisation issued from a tuft of scrubby foliage to their left. She laughed in delight. But then she caught his expression.

'Seriously, Marshall... *What?*' His focus had grown way too intense. And way too pointed. She struggled against the desire to match it.

'Passion suits you. You should go hiking more often.'

Her chest had grown so tight with the climb, his words worsened her breathlessness. She pushed off again for the final peak. And for the pure distraction of physical distress.

'I get how the birds get here,' she puffed, changing the subject, 'and the crustaceans. But how did the mammals arrive here? And the lizards?'

For a moment, she thought he wasn't going to let it go but he did, gracefully.

'They didn't arrive, they endured. Back from when the whole archipelago were peaks connected to the mainland. There used to be a lot more until explorers came along and virtually wiped them out.'

Eve looked up at a circling sea eagle. 'You can't tell me that the geckos didn't get picked off by hungry birds, before.'

'Yeah, but in balance. They live in *refugia* here, isolation from the world and its threats. Until the first cat overboard, anyway.'

Isolation from the world and its threats. She kind of liked the sound of that. Maybe that was what Trav was chasing when he walked out into the darkness a year ago. Emotional *refugia*.

She stumbled on a rock as she realised. Not a year ago...a year ago *tomorrow*. Not only had she failed to think about Travis for entire hours this morning but she'd almost forgotten tomorrow's depressing anniversary.

Her joy at their spectacular view drained away as surely as the water far below them dragged back across the shell-speckled beach where they'd come ashore.

Marshall extended his warm hand and took her suddenly cold one for the final haul up the granite top of Flinders Peak, and the entire south coast of Western Australia—complete with all hundred-plus islands—stretched out before them. The same sense of despair she'd felt when staring up at the stars the night before washed over Eve.

Australia was so incredibly vast and so incredibly empty.

So much freaking country to look in.

She stood, immobile, as he did what they'd come to do. Photographing. Measuring. Recording compass settings and GPS results. Taking copious notes and even some soil and vegetation samples. He threw a concerned glance at her a couple of times, until he finally closed up his pack again.

'Eve...'

'Are you done?'

'Come on, Eve—'

'I'm going to head down to the lake.' But there was no interest in her step, and no breathlessness in her words. Even she could hear the death in her voice.

'Stop.'

She did, and she turned.

'What just happened? What did I do?'

Truth sat like a stone in her gut. 'It wasn't you, Marshall. It was me.'

'What did *you* do?'

More what she didn't do.

'Eve?'

'I shouldn't be here.'

'We have a permit.'

'No, I mean I shouldn't be wasting time like this.'

'You're angry because you let yourself off the hook for a few hours?'

'I'm angry because I only have one thing to do out here. Prioritising Travis. And I didn't do that today.'

Or yesterday, if she was honest. She might have pinned up a bunch of posters, but her memories of yesterday were dominated by Marshall.

'Your life can't only be about your brother, Eve. It's not healthy.'

Health. A bit late now to be paying attention to anyone's health. Her own. Her brother's. Maybe if she'd been more alert a couple of years back...

She took a deep breath. 'Are you done up here?'

A dozen expressions ranged across his face before he answered. But, when he did, his face was carefully neutral. 'We have a couple of hours before the boat gets back. Might as well have a look around with me.'

Fine. He could make her stay...

But he couldn't make her enjoy it.

It took the best part of the remaining ninety minutes on the island but Marshall managed to work the worst of the stiffness from Eve's shoulders. He did it with easy, undemanding conversation and by tapping her natural curiosity, pointing out endless points of interest and intriguing her with imaginary tales of the pirate Anderson and his hidden treasure that had never been recovered.

'Maybe his crew took it when they killed him.' She shrugged, still half-numb.

Cynical, but after the sad silence of the first half-hour he'd take it. 'Seems a reasonable enough motive to kill someone. You know, if you were a bloodthirsty pirate.'

'Or maybe there never was any treasure,' she posed. 'Maybe Anderson only managed to steal and trade enough to keep him and his crew alive, not to accrue a fortune. Maybe they weren't very good pirates!'

'You've seen the island now. Where would you bury it if it did exist?'

She glanced around. 'I wouldn't. It's too open here. Hard to dig up without being seen by the crew.' Her eyes tracked outward and he followed them to the guano-blanketed, rocky outcrop just beyond the shores of Middle Island. 'Maybe over there? Some random little cave or hollow?'

'Want to go look?'

She turned wide eyes on him. 'I'm not about to swim fully clothed across a shark-infested channel to an outcrop covered in bird poo filled with God knows what bacteria to hunt for non-existent treasure.'

'You have no soul, Evelyn Read,' he scoffed.

'I do have one and I'd prefer to keep it firmly tethered to my body, thanks very much.'

He chuckled. 'Fair enough. Come on, let's see if the lake looks as impressive up close.'

It didn't. Of course it didn't. Wasn't there something about rose-coloured glasses? But it wasn't a total disappointment. Still officially pink, even once Eve filled her empty water bottle with it.

'You're not planning on drinking that?' he warned.

'Nope.' She emptied it all back into the lake and tucked the empty bottle into her backpack for later recycling. 'Just trying to catch it out being trickily clear.'

They strolled around the lake the long way, then headed back down to the only decent beach on the island. A tiny but sandy cove formed between two outcrops of rocky reef. The place the boat had left them. Marshall immediately tugged his shoes and socks off and tied them to his own pack, which he stashed on a nearby rock, then made his way out a half-dozen metres from where Eve stood discovering that the sand was actually comprised of teeny-tiny white shells.

'Water's fine...' he hinted. 'Not deep enough for predators.'

She crossed her arms grumpily from the shore. 'What about a stingray?'

He splashed a little forward in the waves that washed in from the current surging between the islands. 'Surfing stingrays?'

'Where lakes are pink and lizards bark? Why not?'

'Come on, Eve. Kick your shoes off.'

She glared at him, but eventually she sank onto one hip and toed her opposite runner and sock off, then she did the same on the other foot. Though she took her sweet time putting both carefully in her pack and placing the lot next to his backpack on the hot sand.

'Welcome to heaven,' he murmured as she joined him in the shallows. Her groan echoed his as her hot and parched feet drank up the cold water, too. They stood there like that, together, for minutes. Their hearts slowing to synchronise with the waves washing up and into their little minibay.

Just…being.

'Okay,' Eve breathed, her face turned to the sky. 'This was a good idea.'

He waded a little further from her. 'My ideas are always good.'

She didn't even bother looking at him. 'Is that right?'

'Sure is.'

He reached down and brushed his fingers through the crystal-clear water then flicked two of them in her general direction.

She stiffened—in body and in lip—as the droplets hit her. She turned her head back his way and let her eyes creak open. 'Thanks for that.'

'You had to know that was going to happen.'

'I should have. You with a mental age of twelve and all.'

He grinned. 'One of my many charms.'

She flipped her cap off her head, bent down and filled it with fresh, clean water and then replaced the lot on her head, drenching herself in salty water.

'Well, that killed my fun,' he murmured.

But not his view. The capful of water had the added benefit of making parts of her T-shirt and cargos cling to the curves of her body even more than they already were. And that killed any chance of him cooling down unless he took more serious measures. He lowered himself onto his butt in the shallows and lay back, fully, in the drink.

Pants, shirt and all.

'You know how uncomfortable you're going to be going back?' Her silhouette laughed from high above him, sea water still trickling off her jaw and chin.

He starfished in the two feet of water. 'Small price to pay for being so very comfortable now.'

Even with her eyes mostly shaded by the peak of her cap, he could tell when her glance drifted his way. She was trying not to look—hard—but essentially failing. He experimented by pushing his torso up out of the water and leaning back casually on his hands.

'Easy to say…'

But her words didn't sound easy at all. In fact, they were as tight as her body language all of a sudden.

Well, wasn't *that* interesting.

He pushed to his feet and moved towards her, grinning. Primarily so that he could see her eyes again. Her hands came up, fast, in front of her.

'Don't you dare...'

But he didn't stop until he stood just a centimetre from her upturned hands. And he grinned. 'Don't dare do this, you mean?'

'Come on, Marshall, I don't want to get wet.'

'I'm not the one with a soggy cap dripping down my face.'

'No, you're just soaked entirely through.'

And, with those words, her eyes finally fell where she'd been trying so hard not to look. At his chest, just a finger flex away from her up-turned hands.

'I'm beginning to see what Anderson might have liked about this is-land,' he murmured.

She huffed out a slow breath. 'You imagine he and his crew took the time to roll around in the shallows like seals?'

The thought of rolling around anything with Eve hadn't occurred to him today, but now it was all he could do to squeeze some less charged words past the evocative image. 'Flattering analogy.'

The *pfff* she shot out would have been perfectly at home on a surfacing seal. Her speech was still tinged with a tight breathlessness.

'You know you look good. That was the point of the whole submerge thing, wasn't it? To see how I'd react?'

Actually, getting cool had been the point. Once. But suddenly that original point seemed like a very long time ago. He dropped his voice with his glance. Straight to her lips. 'And how will you react, Eve?'

Her feminine little voice box lurched a few times in her exposed throat. 'I won't. Why would I give you the satisfaction?'

'Of what?'

'Of touching you—'

If she could have bitten her tongue off she would have just then, he was sure. 'Is that what you want to do? I'll step forward. All you have to do is ask.'

Step forward into those still-raised hands that were trembling ever so slightly now.

But she was a tough one. Or stubborn. Or both.

'And why would I do that?'

'Because you really want to. Because we're all alone on a deserted island with time to kill. And because we'll both be going our separate ways after Esperance.'

Though the idea seemed laughable now.

She swallowed, mutely.

He nudged the peak of her cap upwards with his knuckle to better read her expression and murmured, 'And because this might be the only chance we'll have to answer the question.'

Her eyes left his lips and fluttered up to his. 'What question?'

He stared at her. 'No. You have to ask it.'

She didn't, though he'd have bet any body part she wanted to.

'Tell you what, Eve, I'll make it easier for you. You don't have to ask me to do it, you just have to ask me *not* to do it.'

'Not do what?' she croaked.

He looked down at her trembling fingers. So very, very close. 'Not to step forward.'

Beneath the crystal-clear water, his left foot crept forward. Then his right matched it. The whole time he kept his glance down at the place that her palms almost pressed on his wet chest.

'Just one word, Eve. Just tell me to stop.'

But though her lips fell open, nothing but a soft breath came out of them.

'No?' His body sang with elation. 'All righty, then.'

And with the slightest muscle tweak at the backs of his legs, he tipped his torso the tiny distance it needed to make contact with Eve's waiting fingers.

CHAPTER SIX

DEAR LORD...

How long had it been since she'd touched someone like this? More than just a casual brushing glance? All that hard flesh Eve had seen on the beach—*felt* on the bike—pressed back against her fingers as they splayed out across his chest. Across the shadowy eagle that she knew lived there beneath the saturated cotton shirt. Across Marshall's strongly beating heart.

Across the slight rumble of the half-caught groan in his chest.

One he'd not meant to make public, she was sure. Something that told her he wanted this as much as she secretly did.

Or, as her fingers trembled, not so secretly, now.

Marshall was right. They weren't going to see each other again. And this might be the only chance she had to know what it felt like to have the heat of him pressed against her. To know him. To taste him.

All she had to do was move one finger. Any finger.

She'd never meant to enter some kind of self-imposed physical exile when she'd set off on this odyssey. It had just happened. And, before she knew it, she'd gone without touching a single person in any way at all for...

She sucked in a tiny breath. All of it. Eight months.

Puppies and kittens got touch deprivation, but did grown women?

Was that what was making her so ridiculously fluttery now? Her father's goodbye hug was the last time she'd had anyone's arms around her and his arms—no matter how strong they'd once been back when she was little—had never felt as sure and rooted in earth as Marshall's had as he'd lowered her from the bus's roof last night. And that had been fairly innocuous.

What kind of damage could they do if they had something other than *help* in mind?

How good—how *bad*—might they feel? Just once. Before he rode off into the sunset and she never got an answer.

Only one way to find out.

Eve inched her thumb down under the ridge of one well-defined pectoral muscle. Nervously jerky. Half expecting to feel the softness of the ink feathers that she could see shadowed through the saturated T-shirt. But there was no softness, only the silken sleeve of white cotton that contained all that hard, hot muscle.

God, he so didn't feel like a weatherman.

Marshall's blazing gaze roasted down on the top of her wet head, but he didn't move. Didn't interrupt. He certainly didn't step back.

Eve trailed her butterfly fingers lightly up along the line of the feathers, up to his collarbone. Beyond it to the rigid definition of his larynx, which lurched out of touch and then back in again like the scandalous tease it was.

Strong fingers lifted to frame her face—to lift it—and he brought her eyes to his. They simmered, as bottomless as the ocean around them as he lowered his mouth towards hers.

'Ahoy!'

Tortured lungs sucked in painfully further as both their gazes snapped out to sea, towards the voice that carried to them on the onshore breeze. Eve stumbled back from all the touching into the buffeting arms of the surf.

'Bugger all decent catch to be had,' the gruff captain shouted as he motored the *Vista II* more fully around the rocks, somehow oblivious to the charged moment he'd just interrupted. 'So we headed back early.'

Irritation mingled with regret in Marshall's storm-grey depths but he masked it quickly and well. It really wasn't the captain's fault that the two of them had chosen the end of a long, warm afternoon to finally decide to do something about the chemistry zinging between them.

'Hold that thought,' he murmured low and earnest as he turned to salute the approaching boat.

Not hard to do while her body screamed in frustration at the interruption, but give her fifteen minutes... Give her the slightest opportunity to think through what she was doing with half her senses and...

Marshall was right to look anxious.

But, despite what she expected, by the time the *Vista II*'s inflatable dinghy transferred them and their gear safely on deck, Eve's awareness hadn't diminished at all. And that was easily fifteen minutes. During the half-hour sea journey back to the campsite beach that followed—past seals sunning themselves and beneath ospreys bobbing on the high currents and over a swarm of small stingrays that passed underneath—still the finely tuned attention her body was paying to Marshall didn't ebb in the slightest.

She forced conversation with the two-man crew, she faked interest in their paltry fishy catch, she smiled and was delightful and totally overcompensated the whole way back.

She did whatever she needed to shake free of the relentless grey eyes that tracked her every move.

After an emotional aeon, her feet were back on mainland sand and the captain lightly tossed their last backpack out of the inflatable and farewelled her before exchanging a few business-related words with Marshall. Moments later, her hand was in the air in a farewell, her smile firmly plastered on and she readied herself for the inevitable.

Marshall turned and locked eyes with her.

'Don't know about you,' he said, 'but I'm famished. Something about boats...'

Really? He was thinking about his stomach while hers was twisted up in sensual knots?

'Have we got any of those sausages from breakfast still in the fridge?'

Um...

Not that he was waiting for her answer. Marshall lugged his backpack up over his shoulder and hoisted hers into his free hand and set off towards the track winding from the beach to the campsite. Eve blinked after him. Had she fantasised the entire moment in the cove? Or was he just exceptional at separating moments?

That was then, this was now. Island rules, mainland rules?

What gave?

Warm beach sand collapsed under her tread as she followed him up the track, her glare giving his broody stare all the way back from Middle Island a decent run for its money.

They polished off the leftover sausages as soon as they got back to the bus. At least, Marshall ate most of them while she showered and then she nibbled restlessly on the last one while he did, trying very hard not to think about how much naked man was going on just feet from where she was sitting.

Soapy, wet, naked man.

Had the bus always been quite this warm?

'I think I would have been better off washing in the ocean,' he announced when he walked back in not long after, damp and clean and freshly clothed. Well, freshly clothed in the least used of three pairs of clothes he seemed to travel with. 'Lucky I didn't drop the soap because I wouldn't have been able to retrieve it.'

'I think the previous owners were hobbits,' Eve said, determined to match his lightness.

He slumped down next to her on the sofa. 'The hot water was fantastic while it lasted.'

Yeah. The water reservoir was pretty small. Even smaller as it ran through the onboard gas heater. 'Sorry about that. I guess Mr and Mrs Hobbit must have showered at different ends of the day.'

Not usually a problem for a woman travelling alone. The hot water was hers to use or abuse. And that had worked pretty well for her so far.

'So what's the plan for tonight?' Marshall said, glancing at her sideways.

Lord, if she wasn't fighting off visuals of him in the shower, she was hearing smut in every utterance. *Tonight.* It wasn't a very loaded word but somehow, in this tiny space with this über-present man, it took on piles of new meaning.

'Movie and bed—' She practically choked the word off.

But Marshall's full stomach and warm, fresh clothes had clearly put the damper on any lusty intentions. He didn't even blink. 'Sounds good. What have you got?'

Apparently an enormous case of the hormones, if her prickling flesh and fluttery tummy were any indication. But she nodded towards one of the drawers on the opposite side of the bus and left him to pick his way through the DVD choices. The mere act of him increasing the physical distance helped dilute the awareness that swirled around them.

He squatted and rifled through the box, revealing a stretch of brown, even skin at his lower back to taunt her. 'Got a preference?'

'No.'

Yeah. She'd have preferred never to have said yes to this excruciating co-habitation arrangement, to be honest. But done was done. She filled her one wineglass high for Marshall and then poured filtered water into her own mug where he couldn't tell what she was drinking. Maybe if he was sedated, that powerful, pulsing thrum coming off him would ease off a bit.

And maybe if she kept her wits about her she'd have the strength to resist it.

He held up a favourite. 'Speaking of hobbits...'

Yes! Something actiony and not at all romantic. He popped the disc at her enthusiastic nod, then settled back and jumped through the opening credits to get straight into the movie. Maybe he was as eager as she was to avoid conversation.

It took about ten minutes for her to remember that Middle Earth was definitely *not* without romance and then the whole movie became about the awkwardness of the longing-filled screen kiss that was swiftly approaching. Which only reminded her of how robbed she'd felt out in that cove to have the press of Marshall's lips snatched away by the approach of the *Vista II*.

Which was a ridiculous thing to be thinking when she should be watching the movie.

Hobbits quested. Wraiths hunted. Dramatic elven horse chase. Into the forests of Rivendell and then——

'Are we in the clunk zone, Eve?' Marshall suddenly queried. She flicked her eyes to her left and encountered his, all rust-flecked and serious and steady.

'What?'

Which was Eve-ish for *Yes...yes, we are.*

'Did I stuff things up this afternoon by kissing you?'

'You didn't kiss me,' she managed to squeeze out through her suddenly dry mouth.

But that gaze didn't waver. 'Not for want of trying.'

A waft of air managed to suck down into her lungs. 'Well, the moment has passed now so I think we're cool.'

'Passed?' he asked without smiling. 'Really?'

Yeah... She was a liar.

'That was hours ago,' she croaked.

'I wouldn't know,' he murmured. 'Time does weird things when you're around.'

Her brain wanted to laugh aloud, but the fluttering creatures inside her twittered girlishly with excitement. And they had the numbers.

'I think you're being adversely affected by the movie,' she said, to be safe.

'I'm definitely affected by something.'

'The wine?'

His smile was as gorgeous as it was slow. 'It is pretty good.'

'The company?'

'Yeah. 'Cos that's been terrific.'

She let her breath out in a long, apologetic hiss. 'I'm being weird.'

'You're weird so often it's starting to feel normal.'

'It's not awkward for you?'

His large hand slid up to brush a strand of hair from across her lips. 'What I'm feeling is not awkwardness.'

There went the whole dry mouth thing again. 'What are you feeling?'

'Anticipation.'

The fantastical world on-screen might as well have been an infomercial for all the attraction it suddenly held. Their already confined surroundings shrank even further.

'Maybe the moment's gone,' she said bravely.

He didn't move. He didn't have to. His body heat reached out and brushed her skin for him. 'Maybe you're in denial.'

'You think I'm that susceptible to low lighting and a romantic movie?'

Sure enough, there was a whole lot of elven-human longing going on on-screen. Longing and whispering against an intimate, beautiful soundtrack. Seriously, why hadn't she insisted on something with guns?

'I think the movie was an admirable attempt.'

'At what?' she whispered.

'At not doing this…'

Marshall twisted himself upright, his fingers finding a safe haven for his nearly empty wineglass. His other hand simultaneously relieved her of her mug and reached past her to place it on the sideboard. It legitimised the sudden, closer press of his body into hers.

'Now,' he breathed, 'what were you about to say?'

Heat and dizziness swilled around her and washed all sense out to sea. 'When?'

'Back in the cove. Was it no?' Grey promise rained down on her. 'Or was it yes?'

Truly? She had to find the courage to do this again? It had been hard enough the first time. Though, somehow, having already confessed her feelings made it easier now to admit the truth. She took the deepest of breaths, just in case it was also her last.

'It wasn't no.'

Those beautiful lips twisted in a confident, utterly masculine smile. 'Good.'

And then they found hers. Hot and hard and yet exquisitely soft. Pressing into her, bonding them together, challenging her to respond. She didn't at first because the sensation of being kissed after so very long with no touch at all threw her mind into a state of befuddlement. And she was drowning pleasantly in the sensation of hard male body pressed against hers. And sinking into the clean, delicious taste of him.

But she'd always been a sure adaptor and it only took moments for her feet to touch bottom and push off again for the bright, glittery surface. Her hands crept up around Marshall's shoulder and nape, fusing them closer. Her chin tilted to better fit the angle of his lips. The humid scorch of his breath teased and tormented and roused her, shamefully.

Revived her.

God, she'd missed hot breath mingling with hers. Someone else's saliva in her mouth, the chemical rush that came with that. Tangling tongues. Sliding teeth. And not just any tongue, breath and teeth but ones that belonged with all that hard flesh and ink and leather.

Marshall's.

'You taste of wine, Weatherman,' she breathed.

His eyes fixated on her tongue as she savoured the extra flavour on her lips. 'Maybe it's your own?'

'I had water.'

He lifted back slightly and squinted at her. 'Trying to get me drunk?'

'Trying to fight the inevitable.'

His chuckle rumbled against her chest. 'How's that working out for you?'

Gentle and easy and undemanding and just fine with something as casual as she needed. Wanted. All that she could offer.

And so she gave him access—tempting him with the touch of her tongue—and the very act was a kind of psychological capitulation. Her decision made. Even before she knew she was making it.

She trusted Marshall, even if she didn't know him all that well. He'd been careful and understanding and honest, and her body was *thrumming* its interest in having more access to his. With very little effort she could have his bare, hot skin against hers and her fingertips buried in the sexy curve of all that muscle.

He was gorgeous. He was intriguing. He was male and he was right here in front of her in living, breathing flesh and blood. And he was offering her what she suspected would be a really, really good time.

Did the rest really matter?

One large, hot hand slid up under her T-shirt and curled around her ribcage below her breast as they kissed, monitoring the heart rate that communicated in living braille onto his palm. Letting her get used to him being there. Doing to her exactly what she longed to do to him. Letting her stop him if she wanted. But no matter how many ways he twisted against her, the two of them couldn't get comfortable on the narrow little sofa. No wonder he'd struggled to sleep on it last night. And all the while she had an expansive bed littered with cloud-like pillows just metres away.

Eve levered herself off the sofa, not breaking contact with Marshall's lips or talented hands as he also rose, and she stretched as he straightened to his full height.

'Bed,' she murmured against his teeth.

His escalating kisses seemed to concur. One large foot bumped into hers and nudged it backwards, then another and the first one again. Like some kind of clunky slow dance, they worked their way back through the little kitchen, then through the en suite bathroom and toward unchartered territory. Her darkened bedroom. All the time, Marshall bonded them together either with his lips or his eyes or the hands speared into her hair and curled around her bottom.

There was something delightfully complicit about the way he used his body to steer her backwards into the bedroom while she practically tugged him after her. It said they were equals in this. That they were both accountable and that they both wanted it to happen.

Below her socked feet, the harder external floor of the en suite bathroom gave way to the plush carpet of the bedroom. Marshall's hands slid up to frame her face, holding it steady for the worship of his mouth. His tongue explored the welcome, warm place beyond her teeth just as much as she wanted him to explore this unchartered place beyond the doorway threshold.

A gentle fibrillation set up in the muscles of her legs, begging her to sink backwards onto her bed. The idea of him following her down onto it only weakened them further.

'Eve…' he murmured, but she ignored him, pulling back just slightly to keep the bedward momentum up. It took a moment for the cooler air of the gap she created to register.

Her eyes drifted open. They dropped to his feet, which had stopped, toes on the line between carpet and timber boards.

Hard on the line.

Confusion brought her gaze back up to his.

'I don't expect this,' he whispered, easing the words with a soft brush of his lips. And, when she just blinked at him, his eyes drifted briefly to the bed in case she was too passion-dazzled to comprehend him.

She pulled again.

But those feet didn't shift from the line and so all she achieved was more space between them. Such disappointing, chilly space. At least the hot grasp of his hand still linked them.

'Marshall…?'

'I just wanted to kiss you.'

Ditto! 'We can kiss in here. More comfortably.'

But the distance was official now and tugging any more reeked of desperation so she grudgingly let his hand drop.

'If I get on that bed with you we won't just be kissing,' he explained, visibly moderating his breathing.

'And that's a problem because...?'

'This isn't some roadhouse.'

Confusion swelled up around her numb brain. 'What?'

'You don't strike me as the sex-on-the-first-date type.'

Really? There was a type for these things? 'I don't believe in types. Only circumstances.'

'Are you saying you're just up for it because it's convenient?'

Up for it. Well, that sucked a little of the romance out of things. Then again, romance was not why she'd put her tongue in his mouth just minutes ago. What she wanted from Marshall was what he'd been unconsciously promising her from the moment they'd met.

No strings.

No rules.

No consequences.

'I'm tired of being alone, Marshall. I'm tired of not feeling anything but sadness. I need to feel something good.' A guarded wariness stole over his flushed face and she realised she needed to give him more than that. 'I have no illusions that it's going to go anywhere; in fact, I need it to be short. I don't want the distraction.'

He still didn't look convinced.

'I haven't so much as touched another human being in months, Marshall.'

'Any port in a storm, then?'

God knew it would be stormy between them. As wild and tempestuous as any sea squall. And just as brief.

'We've covered a lot of ground in our few days together and I trust you. I'm attracted to you. I need *you*, Marshall.'

All kinds of shapes seemed to flicker across the back of his intense gaze.

'But I'm not about to beg. Either you want me or you don't. I'll sleep comfortably tonight either way.' *Such lies!* 'Can you say the same?'

Of course he wanted her. It was written in the heave of his chest and the tightness of his muscles and the very careful way he wasn't making a single unplanned move. He wanted what she was offering, too, but there was something about it that he didn't want. Just…something.

And something was enough.

Eve went to push past him, back to the movie, making the disappointing decision for both of them.

But, as she did, his body blocked her path and his left foot crossed onto carpet. Then his right, backing her towards the bed. And then he closed the door on the sword fights of Middle Earth and plunged them into darkness, leaving only the smells and sounds and tastes of passion between them.

CHAPTER SEVEN

EVERY MUSCLE IN Eve's body twinged when she tried to move. Not that she could move particularly far with the heavy heat of Marshall's arm weighing her down. But in case she somehow managed to forget how the two of them had passed the long night, her body was there to remind her. In graphic detail.

Languid smugness glugged through her whole system.

She gave up trying to softly wiggle out of captivity and just accepted her fate. After all, there were much worse ways to go. And to wake up. Right now, her brain was still offering spontaneous flashbacks to specific moments of greatness between them last night, and every memory came with a sensation echo.

Beside her, Marshall slept on in all his insensible glory. Buried face first in her pillows, relaxed, untroubled. It was very tempting just to lie here until lunchtime committing Sleeping Beauty to memory.

Although there was her bladder…

Ugh.

She took more decisive action and slid Marshall's arm off her chest, which roused him sufficiently to croak as she sprang to her feet. 'Morning.'

When was the last time she'd *sprung* anywhere? Usually she just hauled

herself out of bed and gritted her teeth as she got on with the business
of living.

'Morning yourself. Just give me a sec.'

Easing her bladder just a couple of metres and a very thin en suite bathroom wall away from Marshall was an unexpectedly awkward moment.
It seemed ridiculous after everything they'd shared in the past twelve
hours to have to concentrate her way through a sudden case of bashful
bladder. As soon as she was done and washed, she scampered back into
the toasty warm and semi-occupied bed.

'You're better than an electric blanket,' she sighed, letting the heat
soak into her cold feet.

'Feel free to snuggle in.'

Don't mind if I do. She was going to milk this one-night stand for every
moment she could.

Marshall hauled her closer with the same strong arm that had held
her captive earlier, her back to his chest in a pretty respectable spoon.

His voice rumbled down her spine. 'How are you feeling?'

Wow. Not an easy question to answer, and not one she'd expected
him to ask. That was a very *not* one-night stand kind of question. Thank
goodness she wasn't facing him.

'I'm...' What was she? Elated? Reborn? She couldn't say that aloud. 'I
have no regrets. Last night was absolutely what I expected and needed.
And more. It was amazing, Marshall.'

It was only then that she realised how taut the body behind her had
become. Awkwardness saturated his words when they eventually came.

'Actually, I meant because of today.'

She blinked. 'What's today?'

'One year?'

A bucket of icy Southern Ocean couldn't have been more effective.
The frigid wash chased all the warmth of Marshall's hold away and left
her aching and numb. And barely breathing.

Travis. Her poor, lost brother. Twelve months without a boy she'd loved
her whole life and she'd let herself be distracted by a man she'd known
mere moments by comparison.

She struggled for liberty and Marshall let her tumble out of bed to
her feet.

'I'm fine,' she said tightly. 'Just another day.'

He pushed onto his side, giving her a ringside seat for the giant raptor on his chest. She'd so badly wanted to see it last night but the room was too dark. And now she was too gutted to enjoy it.

'Okay...'

Mortification soaked in. What was wrong with her? How much worse to know that, for those first precious moments of consciousness, she hadn't even remembered she *had* a brother. She'd been all about Marshall.

What kind of a sister was she, anyway?

You wanted to forget, that little voice inside reminded her cruelly. *Just for one night. Wasn't that the point?*

Yes. But not like this. Not entirely.

She hadn't meant to *erase* Travis.

'It's a number,' she lied, rummaging in a drawer before dragging on panties and then leggings.

'A significant one,' Marshall corrected quietly.

She pulled a comfortable sweater on over the leggings. 'It's not like it took me by surprise. I've been anticipating it.'

Marshall sat up against the bed head and tucked the covers up around his waist ultra-carefully. 'I know.'

'So why are you making it into an issue?'

Ugh... Listen to herself...

Storm-grey eyes regarded her steadily. 'I just wanted to see how you were feeling this morning. Forget I mentioned it. You seem...great.'

The lie was as ridiculous as it was obvious.

'Okay.'

What was wrong with her? It wasn't Marshall's fault that she'd sought to use him for a bit of escapism. He'd fulfilled his purpose well.

Maybe too well.

'So, should we get going right after breakfast?' she asked brightly from the en suite bathroom as she brushed her hair. Hard to know whether all that heat in her cheeks was residual passion from last night, anger at herself for forgetting today or embarrassment at behaving like a neurotic teen.

Or all of the above.

A long pause from the bed followed and she slowed the drag of the bristles through her hair until it stilled in her hand.

'I've got to get back on the road,' she added, for something to fill the silence.

She should never have left it, really. She replaced the brush and then turned to stand in the bathroom doorway. Trying to be grown up about this. 'We both have jobs to do.'

What was going on behind that careful masculine expression? It was impossible to know. He even seemed to blink in slow motion. But his head eventually inclined—just.

'I'll convoy as far as the South Coast Highway,' he started. 'Then I'll head back to Kal. The road should be open by now.'

Right.

Was that disappointment washing through her midsection? Did she imagine that last night would have changed anything? She *wanted* them to go their separate ways. She'd practically shouted at him that this was a one-off thing. Yet bitterness still managed to fight its way through all her self-pity about Travis.

'Yeah. Okay.'

That was probably for the best. Definitely.

'Do you want me to take some posters for the Norseman to Kalgoorlie stretch? That'll save you doubling back down the track.'

It physically hurt that he could still be considerate when she was being a jerk. A twinge bit deep in her chest and she had to push words through it. Her shoulder met the doorframe.

'You're a nice man, Marshall Sullivan.'

His blankness didn't alter. And neither did he move. 'So I've been told.'

Then nothing. For ages. They just stared at each other warily.

Eventually he went to fling back the covers and Eve spun on the spot before having to face the visual temptation of everything she'd explored with her fingers and lips last night, and made the first excuse she could think of.

'I'll get some toast happening.'

Nice.

Just what every man wanted to hear from a woman he'd spent the night with. Not 'fantastic' or 'unforgettable'. Not 'awe-inspiring' or 'magnificent'.

Nice.

He'd heard that before, from the Sydney kids who had clambered over him in their quest to get closer to Rick and his chemical smorgasbord. From friends and girls and the occasional tragic teacher.

He'd always been the *nicer* brother.

But not the one everyone wanted access to.

Sticks and stones…

Problem was, Eve's lips might have been issuing polite compliments but the rest of her was screaming eviction orders and, though he'd only known her a couple of days, it was long enough for him to recognise the difference. He'd had enough one-off encounters with women to know *get out of my room* when he saw it. Despite all the brave talk last night, she was *not* comfortable with the aftermath of their exhausting night together.

And he was all too familiar with eyes that said something different from words. He'd had them all his life.

He'd been right in assuming Eve wasn't a woman who did this a lot; she was most definitely under-rehearsed in the fine art of the morning-after kiss-off. If he'd realised there'd be no lingering kisses this morning he would have taken greater care to kiss her again last night just before they fell into an exhausted slumber twisted up in each other.

Because Eve had just made it very clear that there would be no more kissing between them.

Ever.

He'd worked his butt off last night giving her the kind of night she clearly needed from him. Making sure it was memorable. And, if he was honest, giving Eve something to think about. To regret. Maybe that was why it stung even more to see her giving it exactly zero thought this chilly morning.

Wham-bam, thank you, Marshall.

Somewhere, the universe chuckled to itself as the cosmic balance evened up. That was what he got for usually hotfooting it out the next morning the way Eve just had.

Only generally to fire up his motorcycle, not the toaster.

What did he expect? Days wrapped up in each other's arms here in this ridiculous little bus while his remaining weeks on the project ticked ever closer to an end and her bank balance slowly drained away? Neither of them had the luxury of indefinite leisure. He wasn't stupid.

Or maybe he was…because Evelyn Read was definitely not a one-off kind of woman and some deep part of him had definitely hoped for more than the single night they'd both agreed on between kisses. Which meant it was probably just as well that was all he was getting. Eve had no room for another man in her single-track life.

And he was done being a means to an end.

He pulled yesterday's T-shirt back on and rather enjoyed the rumples and creases. They were like little trophies. A reminder of how the shirt had been thoroughly trampled underfoot in their haste to get each other naked. A souvenir of the disturbingly good time he'd had with her beyond her bedroom door.

'Don't burn it,' he murmured, passing into the tiny kitchenette intentionally close to her, just to get one more feel of her soft skin. His body brushed the back of hers.

Her feet just about left the floor, she jumped that fast and high. Then a sweet heat coloured along her jawline and her lips parted and he had to curl his fingers to stop himself from taking her by the hand and dragging her back to that big, warm bed and reminding her what lips were made for.

It felt good to torture Eve, just a little bit. It sure felt good to surprise her into showing her hand like that. To shake the ambivalence loose. To watch the unsteadiness of her step. She might call a halt to this thing just getting going between them but he wasn't going to go easily.

He kept on moving past her, ignoring the sweet little catch in her breath, and he stopped at the back doors, flung them open and then stretched his hands high to hook them on the top of the bus, stretching out the kinks of the night, knowing how his back muscles would be flexing. Knowing how the ink there would flash from beneath his T-shirt. Knowing how that ink fascinated her.

If she was going to drive off into the horizon this morning, she sure wasn't going to do it with a steady brake foot.

Yup. He was a jerk.

He leapt down from the bus and turned to his KTM, and murmured to the bitter cold morning.

'*Nice*, my ass.'

The bus's brake lights lit up on the approach to the junction between the Coolgardie and South Coast Highways and Marshall realised he hadn't really thought this through. It was a big intersection but not built for pulling over and undertaking lingering farewells. It was built for turning off in any of the four points of the compass. His road went north, Eve's went further west.

But the uncertain blink of her brake lights meant she, too, was hesitating on the pedal.

She didn't know what to do either.

Marshall gave the KTM some juice and pulled up in the turn lane beside her instead, reassuring himself in the mirror that there was no one on the remote highway behind them. Eve dropped her window as he flipped his helmet visor.

'Good luck with the rest of your trip,' he called over the top of his thrumming engine and her rattling one.

'Thank you.' It was more mouthed than spoken.

God, this was a horrible way of doing this. 'I hope you get some news of your brother soon.'

Eve just nodded.

Then there was nothing much more to say. What could he say? So he just gave her a small salute and went to lower his visor. But, at the last moment, he found inspiration. 'Thank you for coming with me yesterday. I know you would have rather been back on the road.'

Which was code for *Thanks for last night, Eve*. If only he were the slightest bit emotionally mature.

She nodded again. 'I'm glad I did it.'

Middle Island, he told himself. Yesterday. That was all.

And then a car appeared on the highway in his mirror, way back in the distance, and he knew they were done.

He saluted again, slid his tinted visor with the obligatory squished bugs down between them and gave the bike some juice. It took only seconds to open up two hundred metres of highway between them and he kept Eve in his mirrors until the Bedford crossed the highway intersection and was gone from view, heading west.

Not the worst morning-after he'd ever participated in, but definitely not the best.

He was easily the flattest he could remember being.

He hadn't left his number. Or asked for hers. Neither of them had volunteered it and that was telling. And, without a contact, they'd never find each other again, even if they wanted to.

Eve Read would just have to be one of those memories he filed away deep inside. He added *The Crusader* to his list of badly handled flings.

Except she didn't feel like a fling. She felt like forever. Or what he imagined forever must feel like. Crazy. He'd known her all of five minutes. So the lingering sense that things weren't done between them was...

Ridiculous.

The shimmering haze of her exhaust as she couldn't speed away from him fast enough told a very different story.

Trees and wire fences and road signs whizzed by the KTM in a one-hundred-and-ten-kilometre-per-hour blur. Plus a sheep or two.

Would he have stayed if she'd asked? If she'd crawled back into bed this morning and snuggled in instead of running an emotional mile? If he hadn't—like a freaking genius—brought up her most painful memory when she was half-asleep and vulnerable to his words?

Yeah. He would have stayed.

But it was the *why* that had him by the throat.

Eve was pretty but not beautiful, bright but not spectacular, prickly as a cactus and more than a little bit neurotic. She should have just been a charming puzzle. So what was with the whole curl-up-in-bed urge? He really wasn't the curl up type.

She's your damsel, man.

The words came burbling up from deep inside him, in his brother's voice. The kind of conversations they used to have way back when. Before they went down opposite off ramps of the values highway. Before Rick's thriving entrepreneurial phase. Certainly before Christine switched teams—and brothers. Back when Rick gave him stick for being a soft touch for girls in need of a knight on a white charger.

Orange charger, in his case.

Relief surfed his veins.

Yeah, this was about Eve's brother. That was all it was, this vague sense that leaving her was wrong. There was nothing more meaningful or complicated going on than that. He hated the helplessness he saw behind Eve's eyes and the flat nothing she carried around with her. It made him feel powerless—his least favourite emotion.

She's not yours to fix, Inner Rick nudged.

No, but was there really nothing more he could offer her than platitudes and some help with the posters and one night of sweaty distraction? He was a resourceful guy. He had connections.

And then it hit him...

Exactly why he'd chosen to place a woman he'd just met and a man he hadn't seen in ten years next to each other at the dinner table of his subconscious.

His brain ticked over as fast as his tyres ate up the highway. If a person was going to go off grid, they might ditch their bank accounts in favour of cash, stop filing tax returns and opt out of claiming against Medicare. But what was Eve the most cut up about—? That Travis was struggling with his panic disorder, alone. And what did people who were being treated for disorders do? They took drugs. And who knew everything there was to know about drugs?

Rick did.

Enough to have driven his kid brother away years before. Enough to have made a thriving business out of supplying half of Sydney with their chemical needs. Enough to have a world of dodgy contacts inside the pharmaceutical industry—legal and otherwise.

Marshall eased off the throttle.

That meant he was just one uncomfortable phone call away from the kind of information that the cops would never think to access. Or be able to. Not ethical, probably not even legal, but since when did Rick let something as insignificant as the law stand between him and his goals?

Of course it would mean speaking to his brother, but maybe a decade was long enough with the silent treatment. Lord knew, Rick owed him.

Marshall down-geared and, as he did, his rapid pulse started to slow along with his bike. The pulse that had kicked up the moment parting from Eve was upon him. Back at the intersection. A kind of anxiety that he hadn't felt in a long, long time—since before he'd stopped letting himself care for people.

The descending thrum of his blood and the guttural throb of his bike colluded to soak him in a kind of certainty about this plan. As if it was somehow cosmically meant to be. As if maybe this was why he'd met Eve in the first place.

Because he could help her.

Because he could save her.

That was all this was. This...unsettling obsession. It was his Galahad tendency. Evelyn Read needed *help*, not *him*. And he was much more comfortable with the helping part.

He hit his indicator and looked for a safe place to pull over. He fished around in the depths of his wallet for a scrap of paper he'd almost forgotten he still carried. Ratty and brown edged, the writing half-faded. Rick's phone number. He punched the number into his phone but stopped short of pressing Dial.

This was Rick. The brother who'd made his teenage years a living hell. Who'd lured his girlfriend away from him just because he could. The brother who'd been the real reason that most of his friends craved his company and half the teachers gave him special treatment. They'd all wanted an in with *The Pharmacist*.

Rick was the reason he couldn't bring himself to trust a single soul, even now. Rick had taken the lessons they'd both learned from their mother about love and loyalty—or absences thereof—and turned the hurt into a thriving new industry where a lack of compassion for others was a corporate asset.

He'd made it work for him, while his little brother struggled in his shadow.

It had taken him years to fortify himself against those early lessons. His mother's. His brother's. And here he was, straddling his bike and contemplating leaping off the edge of his personal fortress of solitude to help someone he barely knew. He'd kicked the door of communication closed between every part of his old life and here he was, poised to take to that door with a crowbar and crack it open again.For a virtual stranger.

No...*for Eve*.

And Eve mattered.

He thumbed the dial button and listened as the number chirped its ominous melody. Took three deep breaths as it rang and rang. Took one more as a gruff voice picked up.

Marshall didn't waste time with niceties.

'You said to call if I ever needed you,' he reminded his brother. 'Did you mean it...?'

Rick had been at first surprised, then wary, when he recognised Marshall's serious tone after so very long. But—typical of the brother he remembered—Rick took the call at face value and accepted the subtext without comment. He listened to the request, grizzled about the dubiousness of what he'd been asked to do, but committed to help. And, despite anything else he'd done in his life, Rick Sullivan was the personification of tenacity. If he said he'd get this done, then, one way or another, some time Marshall's phone would be ringing again.

End of day, that was all that really mattered. Eve needed results more than he needed to maintain the moral high ground.

Rick even managed to go the entire phone call without getting personal.

The leathers of Marshall's jacket creaked as he exhaled. 'Thank you for your help, Rick. I swear it's not for anything too dodgy.'

'This whole thing is dodgy,' his brother muttered. 'But I'll do it because it's you. And because dodgy is where I do my best work. It might take a while, though.'

'No problem.'

Eve had been waiting twelve months. What was one more?

'I might find nothing.'

'Understood.'

'And one day maybe you can tell me what we're doing. And who for.'

He tensed up, mostly at the suggestion that there'd be a 'one day'. As if the door couldn't be closed once jemmied open.

'What makes you think there's a "who"?'

'Because you don't get invested in things, brother. Ever. You're Mr Arm's Length. But I can hear it in your voice. This matters.'

'Just let me know how you go,' he muttered. Eve was not someone he would trust his brother with, even mentally. He wasn't about to share any details.

'So…you want to know whether she's okay?' Rick asked, just before they ended the call.

'Christine?' Speaking of not trusting Rick… A few years ago, he would have felt the residual hurt deep in his gut. But now it just fluttered to earth like a burnt ember. Maybe the history really was history now.

'No, not Christine. I have no idea where she ended up.'

That bit. That Rick hadn't even kept his prize after working so very hard to take it from him.

'I meant Mum,' Rick clarified. 'Remember her?'

Everything locked up tight inside Marshall. He'd closed the door on Laura Sullivan the same day he'd locked Rick out of his life. The two of them were a package deal. The moment she'd realised her enterprising oldest son was going to be a far better provider than the Government, she'd made her allegiance—and her preference—totally clear.

That wasn't something you forgot in a hurry... Your own mother telling you to go.

'No. I'm good.'

There didn't seem much else to say after that.

It took just a moment to wind the call up and slip his phone back into his pocket. He'd get a new number just as soon as Rick gave him the info he needed. But he didn't hit the road again straight away. Instead, he sat there on the highway, bestride his KTM, breathing out the tension.

You don't get invested in things.

Well, that pretty much summed him up. Work. Life. He had a good ethic but he never let himself care. Because caring was a sure way of being disappointed. Or hurt. Life in his brother's shadow had taught him that. And as life lessons went, that one had served him well.

Until now.

As Rick had readily pointed out, he was invested now. With Eve—a woman he barely knew. He was more intrigued and conflicted and turned inside out for a woman he'd known just days than the people he'd grown up with. Maybe because she didn't want anything from him that she wasn't prepared to own. She had no agenda. And no ulterior motive.

Eve just...was.

And maybe he'd found a way to help her. Or maybe not. But he sure wasn't going to be able to do it from here.

He'd just sent her off down the highway with absolutely no way of locating her again. No email. No number. No forwarding address. How many Reads might there be in Melbourne? He couldn't shake the screaming thought that this was the only moment he had left. Right now, Eve was rattling down a long, straight road that only went to one place. After that, she could head off in any of five different routes into tourist country and his chances of finding her would evaporate. Tension coiled inside him like a spring...

And that was when he knew.

This wasn't just about helping Eve. If it was, he could just take whatever information his brother dug up straight to the authorities. Let them do the rest. This wasn't just about some cosmic interference to help her find her brother. That unfamiliar, breath-stealing tightness in his chest was panic. And he didn't do panic because that implied caring.

He'd no sooner let himself care for someone than void a ten-year stalemate with his criminal brother to get something that might ease Eve's pain. Eve—a complex, brittle, single-minded angel. The most intriguing woman he'd met in…more than years. The woman who'd barrelled through his defences and wedged herself there between his ribs. Just below his heart.

Oh, crap…

From where he sat, he could see the endless stretch of highway ahead—north to Kalgoorlie, where he could pick up his work trail where he'd left it a few days ago. But, in his mirror, he could see the long straight run behind him, back to the four-way turn-off. Back to a one hundred per cent chance of catching up with the bus before it turned off the western highway.

Back to the possibility he'd been too cowardly to explore.

Back to Eve.

He started his engine, dropped his visor and let his eyes lift to the northern horizon. Towards work and the conclusion of this trip and his safe, comfortable life.

But then they dropped again to the mirror, and the road he'd just travelled.

Sure, she might tell him to get lost. And if she did, he would.

But what if she didn't…?

In the end, his hands made the decision before his head did, and a leathered thumb hit his indicator before pulling the KTM's handlebars right, out across the empty highway and then back onto the opposite shoulder.

Before he could second-guess himself, he gunned the accelerator and roared off towards the south.

Towards the unknown.

CHAPTER EIGHT

IT COULD BE ANYONE—that speck in the distance behind her.

Car. Bike. Truck. It was too small for one of the massive road trains that liked to thunder past at breakneck speed, but a smaller truck, maybe.

Eve forced her eyes forward and ignored the impulse to check again. Plenty of people drove this road into Western Australia's tourist region. People who had far more legitimate reasons to be heading this way than *he* did.

Marshall was heading north. Back to his weather stations. Back to reality.

Which was exactly what she should be doing. Middle Island had been a nice couple of days of escapism—for both of them—but they both had jobs to be doing.

And Travis was her job.

He always had been.

If the past couple of days had taught her anything, it was that she couldn't take her eyes off the prize—or the map—for a moment. Look how fast she'd been swayed from her purpose. Besides, Marshall couldn't get out of there fast enough this morning. Not once he saw her in full neurotic mode. He was probably congratulating himself right now on a bullet well dodged.

The speck in her rear-vision mirror grew larger. But not large enough to be a truck. A car, then.

Or smaller, her subconscious more than whispered.

No.

Why would Marshall return? He hadn't left anything behind in her bus—she'd checked twice. And their parting had been as unequivocal as it was awkward. And definitely for the best. She was on a mission and didn't need the distraction. No matter how compelling.

And boy, was he ever. He'd been an intriguing curiosity while tattooed and hairy. Clean shorn and well educated, he was entrancing. Naked, he was positively hypnotic. All the better for being a long, long way from her.

She glanced helplessly back at the mirror and her pulse made itself known against the fragile skin of her throat.

Not a car.

Her gaze split its time between looking ahead and looking back, then the forward-looking part became a glance and then a mere flick to keep the bus on a straight and safe line.

Plenty of motorbikes in the sea. Impossible to even know what colour this one was yet.

Her gaze remained locked on her mirror.

If it was orange—if it was *him*—that didn't have to mean anything. Their one night together had probably been so good because it was a one-off. No past, no future. Just the very heated and very comfortable present. Even if Marshall was coming back for a second go at last night, there was nothing that said she had to oblige—no matter what her pulse recommended.

No matter how enticing the promise of a few more hours of mental *weightlessness* he brought.

A dull mass settled between her shoulder blades. She couldn't afford to be weightless. Not until her journey was complete and Travis was home.

Her own thought tripped her up. She'd never thought about this journey being over. What she would do. Would work have her back? She'd resigned with notice, so there were no burnt bridges there, but could she go back to meetings and minutes and deadlines? Would she have the patience? What would she be like after it was all over? Could she be *normal* now that she knew how secretly cruel the world really was?

As for weightless... Would she ever feel that way again?

Or was that just another disloyalty to Travis? To be worrying about any of it?

She'd put herself first once before and look how that had ended. Travis had melted down completely the moment she took her eyes off him.

She glanced up again, just in time to see a flash of black and orange changing into the inside lane and then roaring up beside her.

All the breath squeezed up tight in her suddenly constricted chest.

He was back.

Marshall whizzed by on her right, then changed lanes into the vanguard position and weaved in the lane in a kind of high-speed wave. She took several long, steadying breaths to bring the mad thump of her heart back into regular rhythm.

Should she stop? Hear what he had to say?

No. If he wanted her to pull over he'd be braking, slowing her. But he was pacing her, not slowing her. Guiding her onward. Besides, not far now until the turn-off to the Ravensthorpe poster drop. If he had something to say he could say it there.

And she'd listen politely and when it came to the time to part again she'd try and be a bit more erudite than her poor effort this morning.

Two vehicles whizzed by in the opposite direction, marking their entry into tourist country. *Tourism.* That was what she and Marshall were doing, right? Exploring the unchartered country that was each other. Enjoying the novelty. But how many tourists sold up and moved to the places they visited? How many stayed forever? No matter how idyllic.

Right. Because the real world eventually intruded.

And her reality was Travis.

Marshall wiggled his motorbike again and seemed to be waiting for something. Did he seriously worry that she hadn't recognised him? She gave her headlights a quick flash of acknowledgement and his weaving ceased.

He placed himself squarely in the centre of their lane and let his bike eat up the highway.

And Eve did her best not to fixate on the strong breadth of his back and breathless imaginings about what it would be like to peel all that leather right off him.

The Bedford's front doors were as reluctant to open as Eve was to pass through them. But Marshall had made fast work of slinging the KTM onto its stand and pulling off his helmet. As he sauntered towards her on his thick-soled riding boots, he forked fingers through his thick helmet hair to ruffle it up.

Her first thought—on the clench of her stomach—was that finger-forking his hair was her job.

Her second thought—on the clench of her heart at the sound and smell of his creaking leathers as he stopped in front of her—was that she was completely screwed.

'Forget something?' she managed to squeeze out from the top of the Bedford's steps. More for something to say, really, because if he'd actually come back for his favourite socks she was going to be really crushed. She kept her body language as relaxed as was possible in a body ready to flee.

'Yeah,' he murmured, stepping up onto the bottom step, 'this.'

One gloved hand came up and lifted her chin as if he was holding a crystal flute and his lips brushed against hers. Then the brush got harder, closer. So...*so* much better. He turned his head and deepened the kiss, stroking his tongue into her mouth and against her own. Just when she'd thought no one would ever kiss her like that again.

She wavered there on the top step, the closest thing to a swoon she'd ever experienced.

'I didn't say goodbye properly,' he finally breathed against her astonished mouth. 'Now I don't want to say it at all.'

'You left,' she said between the head spins.

'But I'm back.'

'What about work?'

'What about it? There are plenty of weather stations still on my list. I'll just flex my route.'

What about my *work?* was what she really needed to be asking. Because how much of it was she going to get done with him around? If the past couple of days was any indication.

'You just assume I want to carry on where we left off?'

Just because she *did*... He wasn't to know that.

'I'm not assuming anything. If you send me away I've wasted...what... an hour of my time and a couple of bucks in fuel. Those are reasonable stakes.'

She pulled free. 'Charming.'

His grin managed to warm her right through, even as her heart screamed at her not to fall for it.

'Do you want me to go?'

She stared at him. Remembered how it felt to be with him. To be *with* him. And the thought of watching him drive off again was almost unbearable.

'I should,' she breathed.

'That's not a no.'

'No.' She stared at him. 'It's not.'

His puppy-dog grin graduated into a full, brilliant, blazing smile. 'Come on, then. Let's get some posters up. Time's a-wasting.'

He stepped down off the bus and held a hand out to help her. His eyes were screened by sunglasses but she could clearly see the trepidation still in the stiffness of his body. What she did next mattered to him. And that made her feel a whole lot better. She glanced at his outstretched hand. The unexpected chivalry excited and troubled her at the same time. She'd been jumping down off the Bedford's steps all by herself for eight months.

But just because she *could* didn't mean it wasn't a rare treat not to have to.

How would it feel to share this burden, just for a bit?

Would Travis understand?

After an age, she slid her bare fingers into his leathery ones and accepted his help.

But they both knew that taking his hand was saying yes to a whole lot more.

Marshall followed Eve as she chugged the Bedford into the biggest town in the Great Southern region behind the two-dozen cars that constituted peak hour in these parts. When she pulled up in a big open car park, Marshall stood the KTM and then jogged off to find something for them to eat. When he got back with it, she was set up and ready to go. Table and chair in place, bus sides up and covered in posters.

'I need to find the MP's office,' she announced. 'I'm getting low on posters.'

'Didn't you do that before?'

'Nope. Somebody distracted me.'

Yeah. He was probably supposed to feel bad about that. 'Too bad.' He winced.

'You don't look very sympathetic,' she admonished.

He just couldn't stop smiling. What was that about? 'MP's office was a few doors down from where I got lunch. I'll show you.'

Then it was her turn to smile. 'Thank you.'

She weighted down anything on her display that might blow away, grabbed a flash drive from her wallet and hurried alongside him. The door to the MP's office set off an audible alert as they entered.

'Hi there,' a friendly young woman said from behind the reception desk, addressing him. He looked straight at Eve, who slid the flash drive over the counter. 'Welcome to Albany.'

'Can you run off a hundred of these, please?'

The woman frowned and didn't touch the flash drive. 'What is it?'

'A missing-person poster,' Eve elucidated, but it didn't bring any hint of recognition. 'MP's offices are supposed to run off copies for free.'

A little explanation wasn't exactly an Open Sesame.

'Let me just check,' the woman said, stalling.

Eve looked as if she wanted to say more but his hand on her wrist forestalled it. A few moments later the woman came back, smiling, and chirped, 'Won't be long!'

Eve turned to the window and the port view beyond it and curled her arms around her torso.

Every day must have moments like these for her. When simple things like a bit of public bureaucracy suddenly reared up in front of her like a hurdle in her efforts to find her brother. No wonder she was so tired.

That kind of emotional ambush would be exhausting.

'Good morning,' a male voice said and Eve turned from her view.

An overly large, overly suited man with a politician's smile approached, hand outstretched. 'Gerald Harvey, MP.'

'Evelyn Read,' she murmured, sliding her fingers into his.

He followed suit. 'Marshall Sullivan.'

'You have a missing person?' the man asked and barrelled onwards before she could answer. 'I'm very sorry for your loss.'

'My loss?'

The statement seemed to stop Eve cold, and only the new colour in her face gave Gerald Harvey a hint that he might have put his finely shod foot in it. 'Your...uh...circumstances.'

Marshall stepped in closer behind her and placed his hand on Eve's lower back, stroking gently.

'Thank you,' she said to the man, more evenly than he would have expected based on her expression.

Harvey took the first poster that his assistant printed and read it aloud, rolling the name over his tongue like wine. 'Travis James Read.'

Just in case Eve didn't know who she'd been looking for the past year.

'Can't say I've seen him but someone might have. Are you circulating these in town?'

'All over the country.'

The man laughed. 'Not all over it, surely.'

Eve didn't waver. 'All over it. Every town. Every tourist stop.'

He stared as the poster in his hand fell limply over his substantial fist, and Marshall watched the interplay of disbelief and pity play over his ruddy face. Then it coalesced into kind condescension.

'That's a lot of posters.'

Brilliant. Of all the things he could have noted about Eve's extraordinary endeavour...

'Yes.'

'And fuel.'

Okay, enough was enough.

'Eve,' he interjected, 'how about we go back to the bus and I'll come back for the posters in fifteen minutes? You should get started. Don't want to miss anyone.'

Ironic, given her life was all about missing someone.

He thanked the MP and then bustled her out into the street, instantly feeling the absence of the tax payer–funded office heating. She didn't speak. Didn't confront him or rant. She'd turned inwards somewhere in that brief encounter and wasn't coming out any time soon.

He could endure the silence no longer than five minutes.

'Did I ever look at you like that?' he eventually asked as they walked back towards the main street. The mixture of pity and polite concern. As if she might not be all that mentally well herself.

His direct question dragged her focus back to him. Brown eyes reached into his soul like a fist and twisted. 'A little bit.'

Great. No wonder she'd taken a while to warm up to him. Maybe she still was.

'It's not crazy,' he insisted suddenly, stopping and turning her towards him. 'It's not common, sure, but what you're doing is…logical. Under the circumstances. I get it.'

'You do?'

He waved his hand towards her poster display of all *The Missing* as they approached. 'I imagine every one of their families would like to have the courage and commitment to do what you've done. To get out here and look, personally. To do something proactive. To know you've done as much as you possibly can.'

She tossed her head back in the direction of the MP's office. 'That reaction is pretty common.'

'People don't know what to say, I guess.'

She stared up at him. 'You didn't have that problem.'

Something bloomed deep inside on learning that she had forgiven him for whatever first impression he'd left her with. Enough to shrug and joke, 'I'm exceptional.'

The sadness cracked and her mouth tipped up. 'So you say.'

'Go,' he nudged. 'Get started. I'll go back and manage Mr Charm, and then I'll go find us a camping site after I've dropped your new posters to you.'

She seemed to do a full-body sigh. 'Thank you.'

'No problem. Back in a few.'

He turned back for the MP's office but only got a few steps before turning again. He was back beside her in moments.

'Wha—?'

It took no effort at all to pull her into his arms and tuck her safe and warm beneath his chin. To wrap his arms firmly around her so that nothing and no one could get between them.

How had it not occurred to him before now to hug Eve?

This was a woman who needed repeat and regular hugging. On prescription. And he was happy to be her spoonful of sugar. Her slim arms crept around his waist and hooked behind his back, and the rest of her pressed into his chest as she sagged into him. Stroking her hair seemed obvious.

Around them, the sounds of a busy coastal town clattered on.

But inside their bubble there was only the two of them.

'That guy was a dick,' he announced against her ear.

'I know,' she muffled into his chest.

'I'm sorry that happened.'

She wriggled in closer. 'You get used to it.'

'You shouldn't have to.'

'Thank you.'

He curled her in closer, resting his chin on her head.

'Um... Marshall?' she eventually mumbled.

'Yeah?'

'Aren't you going to get us a site?'

'Yep. Leaving now.'

Around them traffic did its thing and somewhere a set of traffic lights rattled off their audible alert.

'Marshall?'

His fingers stroked her hair absently. 'Hmm?'

'We're making a scene.'

He opened one eye and, sure enough, a couple of locals walked by, glancing at them with amused smiles on their faces.

He closed the eye again and tucked her in even closer.

'Screw 'em.'

'Gotta say, you have a strange idea of what constitutes a "camping site".'

'I'm funded to stay in motels.' Marshall shrugged. 'You might as well benefit.'

'Are all your *motels* quite this flash?' She leaned on the word purposefully because the waterside complex was more of a resort than anything.

'Well, no. But you put me up the last two nights so I have some budget savings. And there's hardly anyone else here out of season so you can take as much car park room as you need for the bus.'

Because she'd be sleeping in the car park while he spread out in the suite's big bed all alone?

She glanced at him. Maybe she'd misunderstood what his return meant. But she wasn't brave enough to ask aloud. Or maybe that was actually a really good idea. A tempestuous one-night stand was one thing but a second night—that needed some managing.

'Come on. At least check it out since you're here.'

She followed him up to the second storey, where the suite's balcony looked out over a parkland walkway below to the turquoise, pine tree—lined swimming bay that curled left and right of them. The rest of the suite was pretty much made of either sofa or bed. Both enormous. A large flat-screen TV adorned the walls between local art and something tanta-lising and white peeked out at her, reflected, through the bathroom door.

Her breath sucked in. Was that a...?

'Spa?'

'Yeah, I think so,' he said a little sheepishly. Had it suddenly dawned on him that this was all starting to look a little *boom-chick-a-wah-wah*? 'It came with the room.'

How long had it been since she'd soaked her weary body? And having a spa, or lounging on the sofa, or sitting on the balcony with a glass of wine didn't have to mean she was staying the night here. Her own bed was pretty comfy, thanks very much.

She glanced at the crack in the bathroom door again and wondered how she could ask him for access without it sounding like a come-on. Or an invitation.

As usual, Marshall came to her rescue with the lift of one eloquent eyebrow and the careful and chivalrous choice of words.

'You want first crack?'

It took her about a nanosecond to answer in the positive and about two minutes to sprint back to the bus and get some clean clothes. It was only as she took the stairs back up two by two that she realised what the bundle of comfortable leggings and track top in her arms meant.

They weren't going back out again tonight.

So, that meant room service for dinner. Nice and cosy, just the two of them.

Wow. Her subconscious was really going to make this tough for her. But the siren song of the bubbles was so strong she didn't care.

Bubbles. Heaven.

'It's a fast filler,' Marshall announced as she burst back into the room, more eager than she'd felt in a long time.

Oh, right...filling. Nature's brakes. Eve stood, a bit at a loss, shifting from foot to foot in the room's entryway.

'It has a shower, too,' he volunteered, bright light glinting in the grey of his eyes. 'You could get straight in and then just shower until the water level is high enough.'

She loved her bus, but its shower pressure was as weak as it was brief. The chance for a proper shower was overwhelming. 'Oh, my gosh, really?'

'Your face is priceless.' He grinned. 'You like a spa, I take it.'

'I used to have a jet bath,' Eve admitted to him. And then to herself, 'I miss it.'

Not that she'd given her big four-person bath much thought when she put her house on the market. Because brothers before bubbles, right? But—oh—how she missed the great soak at the end of a long, hard week. And out here where every week was long and hard...

'Go on,' he nudged. 'Get in there.'

Her thanks were practically a squeak as she slipped into the bathroom and closed the door behind her. She waited a moment too long to flip the lock—worrying how Marshall might read the click after such a long, silent pause—but decided to leave it. If he had something nefarious in mind, he'd had plenty of more isolated opportunities to perpetrate his crime. Not to mention the fact they'd already slept together.

Besides, sneaking into a woman's bathroom was beneath a man like Marshall.

He's a good man.

It took no time at all to get naked and under the thundering commercial shower as the water slowly rose up over her calves. Hot, hot water pounded down on her shoulders and back, then over her hair as she plunged fully under it.

Warm and reassuring and...home. The water brought with it a full-body rush of tingles.

Unexpected tears rushed to her support.

She'd been doing this so long. Being on the road. Was it okay to admit she was tired? That didn't have to mean she loved Travis any less, did it? The water thundered on and she lifted her face to let the fresh water wash away her guilty tears. Eventually, though, the spa reached a generous level of fullness and she killed the overhead stream and slid down into the piping-hot pool. Her groan was inevitable and the long sigh that followed the perfect punctuation.

When was the last time she'd felt so...buoyant? When was the last time she'd just closed her eyes and floated? The water's heat did its job and immediately soaked into muscles she'd forgotten didn't always feel this way, including a few that had only been aching since the marathon of last night.

Was it only twenty-four hours ago that she and Marshall had twisted up in each other's arms? And legs. And tongues. Like some kind of fantasy. Had it even really happened? If it had really happened, wouldn't he be in here with her? Not respectfully waiting on the other side of a closed—but not locked—door.

She lifted one hand to better position it and the cascading tinkle echoed in the silent bathroom.

'Marshall...'

'Yeah?'

Water splashed slightly as she started in the bath at the speed and closeness with which he answered. The door was right next to her head but he sounded close enough to be in here with her. Her eyes went to the mirror reflection of the door instinctively, but she knew before they got there what they'd find.

Marshall wasn't really the Peeping Tom type. If he wanted to look, he'd just knock and enter and stare at her until she was as much a hot puddle as the spa water around her.

Because he's a good man, and he knows what he wants.

So what was he doing? Just lurking there? Or did the suite have some kind of weird acoustic thing going on?

She cleared her throat gently. 'Are you busy?'

'Nope. Just unwinding.' Pause. 'Why?'

'I just thought...maybe we could talk.'

'Didn't you want to relax?'

'It's a bit...quiet.'

'I thought you'd be used to that after eight months on the road.'

Yeah. He had a point. Astonishing what two days of company did for a girl.

'Normally I'd have music in my bathroom.' Classical. Mellow.

That deep voice was rich with humour. 'You want me to sing something?'

The very idea added to her hot-water tingles. 'Talking will be fine.'

'Okay.' Another pause. 'What do you want to talk about?'

'I don't know. Where you grew up? Your family? Anything, really.'

The door gave a muffled rattle and Eve wondered if he'd leaned on it. She took the complimentary sponge from its packet and filled it with warm water, then squeezed it down her arms.

Rinse. Repeat.

The slow splashes filled the long silence and the steam started working on her pores. And her soul.

'I'm not sure my history will be particularly conducive to relaxation.'

The tightness in his voice paused her sponge mid-swab. 'Really, why?'

'My family's about as functional as yours.'

Dead, drunken mother and AWOL brother was going to be tough to top. But her curiosity was piqued. 'Where are they now?'

'They're still in Sydney.'

'That doesn't sound so very dramatic.'

'Growing up had...its challenges.'

Her sponging resumed. Eve closed her eyes and let herself tune in to the low rumble of his voice. 'Like what?'

Was that a resigned sigh through the door?

'My family weren't all that well off, but we didn't starve. We were okay.'

Uh-huh...?

'But it was the nineties. The decade of excess and success, and all that.'

Eve lay her head against the back of the bath and just listened.

'I have a brother, too, Eve,' Marshall went on. 'And poverty wasn't really his thing. So he took matters into his own hands and got quite... creative. Before long, the whole neighbourhood knew he was the go-to for whatever soft-core drug they needed.'

She opened her eyes and stared at the bathroom ceiling. After a moment she murmured, 'Your brother was a dealer?'

'An entrepreneur, according to him.'

Right. 'How long did that last?'

'Until very recently I couldn't have answered that at all. But let's just say business is as good as ever for Rick. I don't really see him any more.'

No wonder Marshall could empathise about Travis. He knew exactly what it was like to lose a brother.

'Whose decision was that?'

The only sound in the long, long silence that followed was the dripping of the shower into the spa.

'It's complicated,' he finally said.

Yeah, wasn't it always?

'I struggled growing up with Rick for a brother.'

'Because he was a criminal?'

'Because he was a hero.' He snorted. 'This was the back suburbs, re-member. Pretty rough area to grow up. People loved him, they loved what he sold and they scrambled to be part of his inner circle. And some-times that meant scrambling over me.'

There was something so...suppressed in his voice.

Eve lifted her head. 'Are you talking about girls?'

'Girls. Friends. Even a teacher or two with insalubrious habits.'

Oh, poor teenage Marshall. 'You resented him.'

'No, I loved him.'

'But you hated that,' she guessed.

'It meant I was no different to them. The sycophants. I just wanted to despise him and be done with it.'

So, there were many ways to lose a brother, then.

'Do you miss him?' she whispered.

'I did. For a long while. It felt like he was all I had, growing up. But I just focused my attention on my work and suddenly a decade had passed and I hadn't really thought about him at all. Or my mother. Or Chris-tine. Or what they were all doing together.'

She pushed herself up a little more. 'Christine is with your brother?'

'She was.'

The door rattled slightly again, but not the knob. Down lower. And that was when Eve realised how very close they were sitting to each other. Him sunk down onto the floor of the suite, leaning on the door. Her lying back in warm luxury.

And only a single thin wall between them.

No wonder Marshall was wary of people. And no wonder the tight pain in his voice. 'I'm sorry. I should have asked you about something else.'

'It's okay. I got myself out. It's history now.'

'How do you go from a bad neighbourhood to working for the Fed-eral Government?'

He laughed and she realised how attached she'd become to that sexy little chuckle.

'It will shock you to learn that meteorology is not the sexiest of the sciences.'

Not sexy? Had any of them *seen* Marshall Sullivan?

'But that meant there were scholarships going wasting, and one of them came to me. And it came with on-campus residency.'

'The scholarship was your ticket out?'

'At first, but soon I came to love meteorology. It's predictive. Stats and signs and forecasting. You always know what's coming with weather.'

'No surprises?' she murmured.

'I guess I was just looking for a life where you could spot the truth of something before it found you.'

Yeah. Given he'd been used by his earlier friends, cast off by his mother and then betrayed by his brother, maybe that wasn't surprising.

'It suits you.'

'Being a weatherman?'

'Busting the stereotype.' And how. 'I'm sorry I called you Weather-man.'

'I don't mind it as a nickname. As long as it's coming from you.'

'Why?' She laughed. 'What makes me so special?'

His answer, when it came, was immediate. 'How long have you got?'

The same kind of warmth that was soaking into her from without started to spread out from within. But she wrestled it back down. She couldn't afford to be feeling warm and fuzzy about anyone right now.

She made much of sitting up straighter in the spa bath. The bathroom equivalent of shuffling papers. 'Speaking of specials...what's on the menu tonight?'

Subtle, Read, real subtle.

But he let it go after a breath-stealing moment of indecision. 'Give me a second, I'll check.'

Good man, knows what he wants and compassionate.

Marshall Sullivan was just getting harder and harder to not like.

CHAPTER NINE

THIS WASN'T GOING to end well for him...

It had dawned on Marshall, somewhere between sitting at the bathroom door with his head tipped back against the timber and watching Eve tuck so enthusiastically into a bowl of Italian soup, that not everyone was rewarded for goodness. Any more than they were rewarded for doing the right thing.

Hadn't he got that by now?

But done was done. He'd made his choice and he was here. Only time would tell whether it was a crazily fatalistic or brilliantly optimistic decision. But since he was here and since she hadn't driven him off the road, he could use the time practically. He could try and get to know Eve a bit more. Understand her.

Maybe that way he could get a sense of her truth before it hit him like a cyclone.

'Can I ask you what happened with Travis?' he asked, passing his empty plate into the long fingers she reached out and starting at the most obvious point. 'When he disappeared.'

Her bright, just-fed eyes dulled just a little.

'One day he was there—' she shrugged '—the next he was gone.'

'That simple?'

'It wasn't simple.'

'Losing someone never is.'

He fell to silence and waited her out. It had certainly worked well enough on him while she was in the bath. He'd offered up much more than he'd ever shared with anyone else.

'She was drunk,' Eve finally murmured and he didn't need to ask who. 'She'd passed the few hours of Travis's Under-Fifteens hockey at the nearest pub. As far as anyone could tell, she thought she was okay to drive.'

Oh. Crap. Drunk and in charge of the safety of a fourteen-year-old boy.

'Was she an alcoholic?' That certainly explained Eve's moderate approach to liquor.

Her dark head slowly nodded. 'And the whole neighbourhood got to hear about it.'

He let his hands fall between his splayed thighs. Stared at them. 'That's a lot for a girl to handle.'

'It was a lot for all of us to handle,' she defended. 'Travis watched Mum die, Dad endured her reputation being trashed and I...'

'What did you do?'

'I coped. I got on with things. Took over caring for them both.'

'A lot of pressure.'

'Actually, it was okay then.' *Then...* 'It gave me something to focus on. Purpose.

'Dad pulled Trav out of school for the last few months of the year and that might have been a mistake. It took him from his friends, his sport, his structure. He lost his way a bit. He got back into it the next year and got okay grades but he was never cheeky and joyous again. I think we all just got used to the new, flat Travis.' She took a big swallow of water. 'Maybe we got used to a new *us*, too.'

Yeah. Numbness crept up on a person...

'It wasn't easy, those first couple of years. At first it was all about getting him out of the hospital, but then life had to... We had to just get on with it, you know?'

Yep. He certainly did know all about just getting on... Story of his life. But not everyone could do it. There were times *he* really wanted to just opt out. In some ways maybe he had.

'What changed? To make him leave?'

Her beautiful face pinched up slightly. 'Um...'

Whatever it was, it was hurting her.

'There was an inquest the year he went, and there was all this media interest in the accident again.'

'Years later?'

'A legal queue, I guess.' Her slight shoulders shrugged and he'd never wanted to hold someone more in his life. But she looked so fragile he worried she'd shatter. 'So much pressure on all of us again.'

He shifted closer. Leaned into her. 'He couldn't take it?'

Her head came up but she didn't quite meet his eyes. 'I couldn't. I desperately wanted to understand what happened but I couldn't go through it all again. Supporting Dad, mothering Travis. Just as things were getting normal. I just couldn't do it while we relived the accident over and over again.'

Suddenly her blazing need to find her brother began to make more sense.

'What did you do?'

'I went back to my own place. Replaced the dead pot plants with new ones, cleaned the gutters, threw out years of junk mail, started easing back into my own life.'

'And what did Travis do?'

'I didn't abandon them,' she defended hotly. 'I still visited, did sisterly things. But they were both men. They needed to step up, too. They agreed.'

He said nothing, knowing the question was almost certainly in his eyes. *But...?*

'Trav was finding it harder than any of us realised. The inquest brought it all back just as he might have started to become stronger. He turned eighteen, and drifted further and further from us emotionally.' She shook her head. 'And then he just left. Right in the middle of the inquest. We thought he'd just taken off for a few days to avoid the pressure but then it was a week, and then two. We finally reported him missing when we hadn't heard anything for a month.'

'You blame yourself.'

Her slim shoulders lifted and then sagged again. 'I wasn't there for him.'

'Yeah, you were. For years.'

'But I withdrew.'

'You *survived*. Big difference.'

Her tortured eyes lifted. 'Why wouldn't he talk to me? If he was struggling.'

Yeah—she'd been carrying that around a while; he recognised the signs of soul baggage.

'Eighteen-year-old boys don't talk to anyone about their feelings, Eve. I've been that kid.'

Old agony changed her face. He pulled her into his arms. 'You aren't responsible for Travis being missing.'

'That's what people say, isn't it,' she said against his chest. 'In this kind of situation. But what if I am?'

Okay, so she'd heard this before and still not believed it. A rough kind of urgency came over him.

'What if it had nothing to do with you and everything to do with a young boy who watched his mother die? On top of the day-to-day trauma of having an alcoholic for a mother. My own mother was no prize,' he admitted, 'but she was at least present.'

He'd almost forgotten that she was Eve's mother, too. She seemed so disconnected from her past. 'What if you had turned up on his doorstep every single day and he had still done this?'

Tortured eyes glistened over. 'He's my brother.'

'He's a grown man, Eve.'

'Only just. Eighteen is still a kid. And with the anxiety disorder, and depression...'

'Which he was being treated for, right? He was on it.'

'Then why did he leave?'

It was always going to come back to that question, wasn't it? And Eve was never going to be free of the big, looming question mark. 'Only Travis knows.'

She fell to an anguished kind of silence, picking at the fabric on the sofa beneath her. Marshall stacked up the rest of the dishes and put the lot outside his door on the tray left there by the staff and quietly turned back. He crossed to her and held out a hand.

'Come on.'

She peered up at him with wide, hurt eyes. 'Where are we going?'

'I'm walking you home. I think you need to be in your own place right now, surrounded by familiar things.'

She didn't argue for once. Instead, she slipped her fingers into his and let him pull her up and towards the suite's door.

'It's not really my place,' she murmured as they stepped out into the hall. 'And most of them aren't my things.'

How weird that such sorrowful words could bring him such a lurch of hope. If Eve wasn't all that attached to the Bedford or its contents maybe there was hope for him yet. Maybe he could wedge himself a place in her distracted, driven world.

He kicked off one of his shoes and left it wedged in the doorway so that he didn't lock himself out.

Down in the almost empty car park he opened the bus for her and followed her through to her bedroom. She didn't so much as glance at that presumption, and she didn't look the slightest bit anxious that he might stay. She just accepted it as though they'd been doing it for years.

He pressed his key-card into her hand. 'Breakfast on the balcony at eight?'

'Okay.'

He flipped back her bed covers and waited for her to crawl in, then he folded them back over her and tucked her so firmly in that she resembled something that had just tumbled out of a sarcophagus.

'It's not your fault, Eve.'

He was going to tell her that every day of their lives if he had to.

She nodded, but he wasn't foolish enough to think that she actually believed it. Maybe she just accepted that he didn't think so. Bending brought him dangerously close to her lips, but he veered up at the last moment and pressed his to her hot forehead instead.

'Breakfast. Eight o'clock.'

She didn't agree. She didn't even nod. But her eyes were filled with silent promise and so he killed the lights and backed out of the room and then the bus, giving the big back door a security rattle before leaving her snug and safe inside.

It went against everything in him to leave her in the car park, but Eve had been doing this a long time and she was a grown, competent woman. Just because she'd opened up a little and shown him some of her childhood vulnerability didn't mean he could treat her like the child she'd almost been when her mother killed herself and nearly her brother.

As hard as that was.

He limped along on one shoe and returned to the big, lonely suite.

A gentle kind of rocking roused Marshall out of a deep, comfortable sleep. The suite was as dark as an outback road but he knew, instantly, what was going on.

Except it wasn't eight o'clock. And this wasn't morning.

A warm, soft body slid in next to him, breathing carefully. He shunted over a bit to make room, but she only followed him, keeping their bodies close.

'Eve...?'

As if there was any question.

She snuggled up hard into his side. 'Shh. It's late.'

Or early, he suspected. But he wasn't about to argue with whatever God had sent her back to him, and he wasn't about to ruin a good thing by reading something into this. Instead, he took it—and Eve—at face value and just gathered her into him so that his sleepy heat could soak into her cold limbs.

But he wasn't so strong that he could resist pressing his lips to her hair and leaving them there.

And she wasn't of a mind to move away, apparently.

'I have no expectations,' he murmured against her scalp. 'If you tell me that going our separate ways yesterday felt okay to you then that's cool, I know where I stand. But it felt anything but okay to me and I came back so that we could just—'

'Finish things up more civilly?'

'—*not* finish things up,' he said into the dark. 'Maybe just explore this a little more. See where it goes.'

Her breathing filled his ears. His heart.

'I slept with you because you were riding off into the horizon the next day,' she whispered.

He turned a little more towards her, trying to make her out in the dark. 'And I slept with you knowing that. But then I discovered something about horizons.'

'What?' she mumbled.

'They're an awfully long way away.'

She pushed up onto one elbow, robbing him of her warmth. 'So...
you're just going to ride shotgun for the next...what—days? Weeks?'

'Until we know.'

Her voice sounded tantalisingly close to his ear. 'Know what?'

'Whether we have potential.'

'You're in the middle of an epic road trip. It's a terrible time to be
looking for potential.'

She was right. He should be aiming for fast, casual and uncomplicated. Like she had.

'That's the thing, Eve. I wasn't looking. It seems to have found me.'

She had nothing to say to that, but her steady breathing told him she
was still awake.

Listening.

Thinking.

He bundled her back in close and fell with her—lips to hairline—into
a deep slumberous heaven.

CHAPTER TEN

WAKING THE NEXT morning was like an action replay of the morning before—but without all the action. This time, he didn't catch Eve creeping out of bed. This time, she was not freaking out and sucking all the warmth out of the room. This time, she was not back-pedalling madly from what they'd shared the night before.

Even though what they'd shared overnight was more intimate and meaningful than anything they'd done with each other back at the campsite.

Two bodies, pressed together in sleep. Wrapped around each other. Talking.

No sex.

But infinitely more loaded.

'Morning,' she murmured before her eyes even opened.

'How long have you been awake?'

'Long enough to feel you staring.'

'It's the novelty.' He chuckled.

Come on. Open them...

But she just smiled and squirrelled in closer, as if she was getting ready to go back to sleep.

'It's eight o'clock,' he pointed out.

And then her eyes opened—drugged, languorous, and he'd never seen anything quite so beautiful.

'No, it's not.'

'Yeah, it really is.'

And this was a workday for both of them. Technically.

Her eyes fluttered shut and she wiggled deeper into the covers. Okay, so he was going to have to be the brave one.

'So, look at you in my bed...' he hinted.

One eye half opened and he waited for the quip to follow. Something sharp and brilliant and completely protective. But he didn't get one. Her second eye opened and locked on him, clear and steady.

'I just woke up in the middle of the night,' she murmured, 'and knew this is where I wanted to be.'

Right. What could he say to that? This was what he'd come back for, wasn't it? To see what might grow between them. Wasn't that what he'd been murmuring at midnight about? Yet, now that he was faced with it, it suddenly seemed overwhelmingly real.

He cleared his throat. 'Breakfast?'

'In town, maybe? After I get set up.'

Right. Work.

'I have to do my thing today, too.' For the people paying him.

'Where's the weather station?'

He told her and she asked a question or two. More than enough to muddle his mind. He was in bed with a living, breathing, *radiating* woman and they were talking about the weather again. Literally. But somehow it didn't feel like small talk. It felt big.

And then it hit him why.

They were having a *couple* conversation. Comfortable. Easy. And they were having it in bed. Where all conversations should happen. And that was enough to scare him upright.

'I'm going to grab a shower, then I'll get us some food while you set up.'

She pushed up onto her elbows, blinking. 'Sorry if I made things weird.'

He forced a relaxed smile onto his face.

'Not weird. Just—' *dangerously appealing* '—new.'

He padded into the bathroom and put himself under the shower Eve had enjoyed so much the night before. Images filled his head—of Eve standing with the water streaming over her slight body, head tipped back, issuing those sounds he'd heard while he leaned on the doorframe out in the hall. How badly he'd wanted to step inside and join her. Shower with her until the end of time. And now, here he was freaking out that his dreams might be coming true.

In his world, dreams didn't come true.

They shattered.

It was so hard to trust the good feelings.

He nudged the taps and cut out half of the hot water feed and then made sure to keep his shave brief.

When he emerged, Eve was gone.

For half a heartbeat the old doubts lurched to the surface but then he remembered she had no clothes up here, only what she'd crept up the stairs in, and he opened the suite door a crack and peered down through the hallway window. Like a seasoned stalker. Long enough to see Eve heading back across the car park.

Come on, man. Pull it together. This is what you wanted.

He'd just learned the hard way not to want. It only led to disappointment.

So Eve had opted for more comfortable accommodation overnight. No biggie. That was hardly a declaration of passion. She'd snuggled in and enjoyed the heat coming off him, and today she was all about Travis again.

Eve was always about Travis.

It was part of what intrigued him about her. That fathomless compassion.

But it was part of what scared him, too. Because how could there be room for him with all that emotion already going on?

He quickly shrugged something decent on and ran a quick comb through his hair so that when she swiped the suite's door he was clothed and everything that needed brushing was brushed.

He threw her a neutral smile. 'Good to go?'

The pause before she answered was full of silent query. 'Yep. Meet you in front of the Town Hall?'

Wherever that was. 'Yup.'

The question mark shifted from her eyes to her soft smile but she simply turned and let him follow her back down to where his bike was parked. She headed for the bus.

'Egg and bacon burger?' he called.

'Sounds great.'

Great.

Okay, so it was officially his turn to be off. Most guys would be stoked to wake up to a warm, willing body but, instead of converting the opportunity to a goal, he'd let it get under his skin. Weird him out. Not the best start, true, but Eve didn't look too tragic about it. Her mind was back on her brother already.

As was always the way.

The bumbling MP yesterday was pretty normal, in Eve's experience. In fact, he'd been more tactful than many of the people she'd tried to explain herself to in the past.

Herself... Her choices.

But the only people who'd understood her odyssey the way Marshall had were the other family members in her missing-persons network. Which did, in fact, make him pretty darned exceptional.

Eve smiled and passed a poster to an older lady who stopped to peruse her display. The stranger took her time and looked at every single face before wandering off, which Eve particularly appreciated. Nothing worse than the glancers. Glancing was worse than not looking at all, in some ways. Eve knew it was a big ask to hope that people might remember one face, let alone dozens, but there was no chance of people remembering them from the wall displays in post offices that were half obscured by piles of post packs or pull-down passport photo screens most of the time.

Something inside her had shifted last night when Marshall told her about his brother. As if he went from adversary to equal in her mind. He'd effectively lost a brother, too—to circumstance—so he knew what it was like to give up on a family member.

Except, in Marshall's case, he was the one who'd walked away.

And didn't that tear her up. Half of her wanted to hug him for the personal strength it must have taken to leave an intolerable family situation so young. The other half wanted to shake him and remind him he had a brother. A living, breathing brother.

And those weren't to be sneezed at.

She never would have picked him for the product of a rough neighbourhood, even with all the tattoos. He was just too *normal*. Beneath the 'keep your distance' leather smokescreen. But to find out that someone so close to him was neck-deep in criminal activity... That just made what he'd done with his life even more remarkable. Finished school, tackled university and then got himself the straightest and smartest of straight, smart jobs.

Meteorology.

A tiny smile crept, unbidden, to her lips. Who knew that she'd ever get quite so hot and bothered by a weatherman?

Yet here she was, very much bothered. And decidedly hot under the covers.

At least she had been last night.

Crawling in with him hadn't been quite the spontaneous exercise she'd confessed. The sprint across the car park had been as sobering as it was chilly and she had plenty of opportunity to think better of it. But she hadn't—because a big part of her had wanted him to roll over, see her and just keep on rolling. Up and over onto her. To make love to her like he had the first time—all breathless and uninhibited.

Another taste of lightness.

Her days were consumed by her brother—couldn't someone else have her nights? When she'd normally be asleep? Wouldn't it be okay to let go just for those few short hours? To forget?

But Marshall hadn't taken advantage. He'd just tugged her close, murmured hot, lovely words in her ear and pulled her into unconsciousness behind him. And it was only as she'd fallen asleep that she'd realised how badly she wanted *not to* do the obvious thing. The easy thing.

Sleeping with Marshall was easy.

Falling for him would be treacherous.

But morning would always come. And it dragged reality with it.

Eve's reality was that she still had a monumental task ahead of her. Marshall had chased her up the highway to see what might form between them if they gave it a chance, but how could there be any kind of something between them while she had this dismal marathon to complete?

Good sex was one thing. A *happy families* future was quite another.

She had no room for anything beyond right now.

And both of them knew that *happy families* was just a myth. They knew it firsthand.

'Thank you,' she murmured belatedly to the man who took a poster as though from an unattended pile. She'd been so lost in thought, that might as well have been true.

Nope, she hadn't promised Marshall anything more than *right now* and he hadn't asked for it.

Two people could go a long way on *right now*.

The south-western corner of Western Australia was packed with small, wine-rich country towns, each with unique personality and spaced close enough for tourists to hop from one to another on their weekend trails.

Papering the two hundred square kilometres ahead with posters was going to be a much bigger job than the two thousand before it.

But they did a good job together, she and Marshall. When he wasn't working, or they weren't curled up together in her bus or a motel room, he'd be with her, plastering Trav's face all over the towns they visited. Handing her the pins or the tape or the staple gun. Nothing she couldn't have done for herself but—boy—was it good not to have to.

Somehow, having someone to share all of this with made it more bearable. And she hadn't realised how unbearable it had become. How utterly soul-destroying. Until she felt her soul starting to scab over.

She glanced sideways at Marshall's handsome face. How fast she'd adapted to having him here by her side during her displays of *The Missing*. How willing she'd been to bring him into her journey.

A problem shared…

A man approached from the far end of the street, folded paper in his hands. He looked grim and twitchy.

'Movie tonight?'

Marshall's voice pulled her focus back to him. The two of them hadn't braved a movie since *that* night in her bus. As if the entire art form was now too loaded. The last time they'd settled in to watch a movie together they'd ended up sharing so much more.

'Maybe,' she said breathlessly. A girl couldn't live on spooning alone. And she was fairly sure neither could a man. They were well overdue for a rematch. The way Marshall's eyes locked on hers said maybe he thought so, too.

The stranger still hovered and it was only as he turned away, stuffing the paper in his pocket, that Eve's brain finally comprehended that he wanted to say something.

'I'm sorry,' she called, stretching taller in her seat. 'Can I help you?'

The man slowed. Turned.

'Do you know him?' he said, holding up the crumpled paper as he approached. It was one of her posters.

A tingle tickled between her shoulders and grew outwards until gooseflesh puckered under her shirt. 'He's my brother. Why? Do you recognise him?'

The man stepped one pace closer. 'Not sure. He looks familiar.'

Eve shot to her feet. 'What do you mean?'

'Just that I feel like I've seen him before. But I don't want to get your hopes up if I'm wrong...'

'I don't need certainty,' she was quick to reassure, 'just leads.'

She felt Marshall's heat as he stood behind her and her heart began to hammer. God, she'd been so wrapped up in the promise in his eyes she'd nearly let this guy walk off. A guy who might know something.

'Where do you think you know him from?' Marshall asked.

The guy switched focus. 'I really can't say. Just...somewhere. And recently.'

'How recent? Two months? Six?' Eve could hear the urgency in her own voice but was incapable of easing it. A big hand fell on her shoulder as if to physically suppress her.

'Where do you live?' Marshall asked, much more casually.

The guy responded to his even tone. 'Here. In Augusta. But I don't think I know him from here.'

God, the idea of that. That Travis might be right here in this little seaside town...

'Somewhere else?'

'I run trucks. Maybe I saw him on one of those. In another—'

'What other town?' Eve pressed, and Marshall squeezed harder.

Are you freaking kidding me? The first reasonable lead she'd had in nearly nine months and Marshall wanted her to relax? Every nerve in her body was firing in a soup of adrenaline.

'Where do you do your runs?' Marshall asked calmly.

'Anywhere in the South West,' the man said, visibly uncomfortable at having started the conversation at all. He immediately started retreating from his earlier thoughts. 'Look, I'm probably wrong—'

Deep panic fisted in her gut.

'*No!* Please don't start second-guessing yourself,' Eve rushed on, critically aware that her urgency was pushing him further away. She fought to breathe more evenly. God, how close she'd come to just not calling out to him.

What was happening to her?

'The subconscious is a powerful thing,' she urged. 'It probably knows something your conscious mind can't quite grasp.'

The man's eyes filled with pity and, in that moment, she saw herself as others must. As Marshall must.

Obsessed. Desperate. Pathetic.

And she didn't like his view of her one little bit.

Lines appeared on the man's time-weathered brow. 'I'm just not sure...'

'How about just jotting down the routes you usually take?' Marshall grabbed another poster, flipped it over to the blank side and handed it and a pen to the man. 'We can take it from there.'

More lines formed in his weathered skin. 'I have two-dozen routes. That'll take time...'

They were losing him. And the best lead she'd had in an age...

Eve dashed to the front of the bus and rummaged in the glove box with clammy hands for the maps she carried detailing every region she was in. One was marked up with her own routes—to make sure she never missed a town or junction—but her spare was blank, a clean slate. She thrust the spare into the man's hands.

'On this then, just highlight the routes you take. I can do the rest.'

Possibility flickered over his face. 'Can I take this with me?'

The fist squeezed harder. Not because she risked losing a four-dollar map. But she risked losing a tangible link with Travis. 'Can't you do it here...?'

'Take it,' Marshall interrupted. 'Anything you can give us will be great.'

The stranger's eyes flicked between the two of them 'Hopefully, I can be clearer somewhere...away from here.'

Eve took two steps towards the man as he retreated with the map in his hand. She spun to Marshall. 'I should go with him.'

His strong hand clamped around her wrist. 'No. You should let him go somewhere quiet and do what he has to do. He's not going to be able to concentrate with you hovering over him.'

Hovering...! As if they were talking about her chaperoning a teenage date and not possibly finding her brother. 'I just want to—'

'I know exactly what you want, Eve, and how you're feeling right now. But stalking the guy won't get you what you need. Just leave him be. He'll come back.'

'But he's the first person that's seen Travis.'

'*Possibly* seen Travis, and if you push any harder he's going to decide he never actually saw a thing. Leave him to his process, Eve.'

She glanced up the street, hunting for the man's distinctive walk. Two blocks away she spotted him, turning into the local pub. She swung baleful eyes onto Marshall.

'Leave him to his process,' he articulated.

Deep inside she knew he was right, but everything in her screamed for action. Something. Anything.

'Easy for you to say!'

He took a long breath. 'There's nothing easy about watching you suffer, Eve.'

'Try feeling it some time,' she muttered.

She turned away roughly but he caught her. 'I do feel it. In you. Every day—'

'No, I mean try *feeling* it, Marshall. From this side of the fence.'

'It's not about sides—'

'Spoken like someone who's more used to cutting people out of their life than being cut out.'

For a moment she thought he was going to let that go, but he was a man, not a saint. Words blew warmly behind her ear as Marshall murmured in this public place, 'And what's that supposed to mean, exactly?'

'What you imagine it means, I'm sure,' she gritted.

'Eve, I know this is frustrating—'

She spun on him. 'Do you, Marshall? You've been travelling with me all of ten days. Multiply that by twenty-five and then tell me how you think I should be feeling as my only lead walks away from me and into a bar.'

His lips tightened but he took several controlled breaths. 'You need an outlet and I'm convenient.'

Spare me the psychoanalysis!

'How did this become about you?' she hissed. 'This is about me and Travis.'

She glanced at the pub again and twisted her hands together.

Warm fingers brought her chin around until her eyes met his. '*Everything* is about Travis with you, Eve. Everything.'

That truly seemed to pain him.

The judgment in his gaze certainly hurt her. 'Forgive me for trying to stay focused on my entire purpose out here.'

The words sounded awful coming off her lips, doubly so because, deep down, she knew he didn't deserve her cruelty. But did he truly not get the importance of this moment? How rare it was. How it felt to go nearly nine months without a single lead and then to finally get one?

A lead she'd almost missed because she was so off mission.

She dropped back into her seat.

All week she'd been going through the motions. Putting up posters, staffing her unhappy little table, answering questions about the faces in her display. But she hadn't actively promoted. She hadn't forced posters on anyone. She hadn't made a single real impression.

All she'd done was sit here looking at Marshall. Or thinking about him when he was gone. Letting herself buy into his hopeless fantasy.

She'd failed Travis. Again.

And she'd nearly missed her only lead.

Marshall sat back and considered her in silence. And when he spoke it was careful but firm.

'I think it might be time to stop, Eve.'

She did stop. All movement, all breath. And just stared.

'Maybe it's time to go home,' he continued. 'This isn't good for you.'

When she finally spoke it was with icy precision.

'How good for me do you imagine it is sitting around the house, wondering whether Travis is alive or dead and whether anyone will give him more than the occasional cursory check twice a year?'

'It's been a year—'

'I know. I've been living it every single day. But I'm nearly done.'

'You're not nearly done. You still have one third of the country to go.'

'But only ten per cent of the population,' she gritted.

'That's assuming that you haven't missed him already.' *And assuming he is still alive.* The words practically trembled on those perfect lips.

She glared. 'What happened to "What you're doing is logical"?'

'I meant that. I completely understand why you're doing it.'

'And so...?'

'I don't like what *it's doing to you*, Eve. This search is hurting you. I hate watching it.'

'Then leave. No one's forcing you to stay.'

'It's not that easy—'

But whatever logical, persuasive thing he was about to say choked as she ran over the top of him. 'Maybe you're just unhappy that I'm putting him ahead of you. Maybe your male ego can't handle taking second place.'

She'd never seen someone's eyes bruise before, but Marshall's did. And it dulled them irreparably.

'Actually, that's the one thing I'm more than used to.'

The fist inside tightened further. How could she do this? How could she choose between two men she cared so much about? Marshall was, at least, stable and healthy and capable of looking after himself. Travis was...

Well, who knew what Travis was? Or where.

But his need was unquestionably greater.

She ripped the emotional plaster off and pushed to her feet. 'I think it's time for us to go our separate ways.'

The bruising intensified. 'Do you?'

'It's been lovely—'

'But you're done now?'

'Come on, Marshall, how long would we have been able to keep this up, anyway? Your circuit's coming to an end.' And her funds were running out.

Her casual dismissal turned the vacuum behind his lids to permafrost. 'Is that right?'

'I don't have room for you, Marshall.'

'No, you really don't, do you.'

'I need to stay focused on Travis.'

'Why?'

'Because he needs me. Who else is going to look for him?' Or look *out* for him. Like she should have all along.

'Face facts, Eve,' he said, face gentle but words brutal. 'He's either gone or he's *choosing* to stay away. You said it yourself.'

Her breaths seemed to have no impact on the oxygen levels in her body. Dark spots began to populate the edges of her vision. 'I can't believe that.'

'People walk away all the time. For all kinds of reasons.'

'Maybe *you* do.'

His voice grew as cold as her fingers. 'Excuse me?'

She started to shake all over. 'I should have thought to seek your perspective before. I have an expert on cutting loose right here with me. You tell me why a perfectly healthy young man would just walk away from his family.'

Marshall's face almost contorted with the control he was trying to exert. 'You think I didn't struggle, leaving them?'

'As far as I can see, you crossed a line through them and walked away and you seem no worse for wear. That's quite a talent.'

'Are you truly that self-absorbed,' he whispered, 'that you can't appreciate what that was like for me?'

'Yet you chose it.'

Where were these words coming from? Just pouring like toxic lava over her lips. Uncontrollable. Unstoppable.

Awful.

'Sometimes, Eve, all your choices are equally bad and you just have to make one.'

'Just go and don't look back?' she gritted. 'Who does that?'

Something flared in his eyes. Realisation. 'You're angry at Travis. For leaving.'

I'm furious *at Travis for leaving*, she screamed inside. But outwardly she simply said, 'My brother left against his will.'

How many police counsellors had she had that argument with? Or fights with her father.

'What if he didn't?' Marshall urged. 'What if he left because he couldn't imagine staying?'

Pfff... 'Someone's been reading up on the missing-persons websites.'

'Don't mock me, Eve. I wanted to understand you better—'

'Those people were desperate or scared or sick. The Travis I know wouldn't do that.'

'Maybe he wasn't your Travis, have you thought about that? Maybe he's not the kid brother you raised any more.'

The trembles were full-body shudders now.

Marshall stepped closer. Lowered his voice. 'Do you see how much of your life he's consumed, Eve? This obsessive search. It's ruining you.'

'If I don't do it, who will?' she croaked.

'But at what cost?'

'My time. My money. All mine to spend.'

He took her hand. 'And how much of life are you missing while you're out here spending it? I'm right here, Eve. Living. Breathing. But any part of you that might enjoy that is completely occupied by someone who's—'

His teeth cracked shut.

Nausea practically washed over her. 'Go on. Say it.'

'Eve—'

'Say it! You think he's dead.'

'I fear he's a memory, one way or another. And I think that memory is stopping you from living your life just as much as when your mother died.'

'Says the man who hides out behind a face full of hair and leather armour to avoid facing his demons.'

Marshall took a long silent breath.

'This has become an unhealthy obsession for you, Eve. A great idea, practically, but devastating personally. You stripped yourself away from all your support structures. Your colleagues. Your friends. Your family. The people who could have kept you healthy and sane.'

'So we're back to me being crazy?'

'Eve, you're not—'

'You need to go, Marshall,' she urged. 'I can't do what I have to do with you here. That guy nearly walked off because I was off my game. I was busy mooning after you.'

'This is my fault?'

She wrapped her arms around her torso. 'I nearly let my only lead in a year walk off because I was distracted with you.'

'I guess I should at least be happy I'm a distraction.'

Misery soaked through her. 'You are much more than a distraction, but don't you get it? I don't have room for you—for us—in my life. In my heart.'

'You don't have room for happiness? Doesn't that tell you anything?'

'I don't get to be happy, Marshall,' she yelled, heedless of the passers-by. 'Not until Travis is back home where he belongs.'

Those dreadful words echoed out into the seaside air.

'Do you hear yourself, Eve? You're punishing yourself for failing Travis.'

The muscles around her ribs began to squeeze. Hard. 'Thank you for your concern but I'm not your responsibility.'

'So, I just walk away from you, knowing that you're slowly self-destructing?'

'I will be fine.'

'You won't be fine. You'll search the rest of the country and what will you do when you get back to your start point and you've found no sign of him? Start again from the top?'

The thought of walking away from this search without her brother was unimaginable.

'I will always look for him,' she vowed.

And that wasn't fair on someone as vibrant as Marshall. Hadn't he been sidelined enough in his life? She shook her head slowly.

'Find someone else, Marshall. Please.'

Someone who could offer him what he needed. Someone who wouldn't hurt him. Someone who could prioritise him.

'I don't want someone else, Eve,' he breathed. 'I want you.'

Those three simple words stole the oxygen from her cells. The words and the incredibly earnest glitter of Marshall's flecked grey eyes that watched her warily now.

Of all the times. Of all the places. Of all the men.

The seductive rush of just letting all of this go, curling herself into Marshall's arms and letting him look after her. Letting him carry half of all this weight. Of parking the bus for good somewhere and building a new life for herself with whatever she had left. With him. Of little grey-eyed kids running amuck in the sand dunes. Learning to fish. Hanging out with their dad.

But the kids of her imagination morphed, as she watched, into Travis when he was little. Scrabbling along the riverbank at the back of their house. Getting muddy. Just being a kid. A kid she loved so completely.

Eve took several long breaths. 'If you care for me as much as you say

you do, then what I need should matter to you. And what I need is my
brother. Home. Safe. That's all I've got room for.'

'And then what?'

She lifted her eyes to his.

'After that, Eve. What's the plan then? You going to move in with him
to make sure he stays safe? Takes his medication? Stays healthy? How far
does this responsibility you feel go?'

The truth…? Just as there was nothing but black after not finding
Travis, there was nothing but an opaque, uncertain mist after bringing
him home. She'd just never let herself think about either outcome in real
terms. She'd just focused on the ten kilometres in front of her at all times.

And the ten kilometres in front of her now needed to be solo.

She twisted her fingers into his. 'You're a fantastic guy, Marshall. Find
someone to be happy with.'

'I thought I was working on that.'

It was time for some hard truths. 'You're asking me to choose between
a man I've loved my whole life and a man I've—'

She caught herself before the word fell across her lips, but only just.

—*known ten days.*

No matter how long it felt.

Or how like love.

'Would I like to be important to you?' he urged. 'Yes. Would I like,
two years from now, to live together in a timber cottage and get to make
love to you twice a day in a forest pool beside our timber cabin? Yes. I'm
not going to lie. But this is the real world. And in the real world I'm not
asking you to choose *me*, Eve. I'm begging you to choose *life*. You can-
not keep doing this to yourself.'

She stepped a foot closer to him, close enough to feel his warmth.
She slid her unsteady hand up the side of his face and curled her fingers
gently around his jaw.

'It's a beautiful image, Marshall,' she said past the ball of hurt in her
chest. 'But if I'm going to indulge fantasies, it has to be the one where
that guy with the map comes back and it leads me to finding Travis.'

The life drained right out of his face and his eyes dropped, but when
they came back up they were filled with something worse than hurt.

Resignation.

This was a man who was used to coming last.

'You deserve to be someone's priority, Marshall,' she whispered. 'I'm so sorry.'

His eyes glittered dangerously with unshed truth and he struggled visibly to master his breathing, and then his larynx.

Finally he spoke.

'I'm scared what will happen to you if I can't be there with you to hold you—to help you—when you find him, or when you don't,' he enunciated. 'Promise me you'll go home to your father and start your life over and pick up where you left off.'

'Marshall—'

'Promise me, Eve. And I'll go. I'll leave you in peace.'

Peace. The very idea of that was almost laughable. Not knowing the true nature of the world, as she did now. Blissfully ignorant Eve was long gone.

And so she looked Marshall in the eye.

And she lied.

CHAPTER ELEVEN

DID EVE HAVE any idea how bad she was at deceit?

Or maybe she just saved her best lies for the ones she told herself. There was no way on earth that this driven, strong woman was going to go back to suburbia after this was all over.

She was too far gone.

And, try as he might, she was not letting him into her life long enough for him to have any kind of influence on what happened from here. His job was to walk away. To respect her decision.

To do what his brain said was right and not what his heart screamed was so very wrong.

I'm choosing Travis.

His gut twisted in hard on itself. Wasn't that the story of his life? Had he really expected the very fabric of the universe to have changed overnight? Eve needed to finish this, even if she had no true idea of what that might mean.

He needed her to be whole.

He just hadn't understood he was part of the rending apart.

He rested his hand over Eve's on his cheek, squeezed gently and then tugged hers down and over.

'I hope you find him,' he murmured against the soft skin of her palm.

What a ridiculously lame thing to say.

But it was definitely better than begging her to change her mind. Or condemning her to search, half-crazed, forever.

He stepped back. And then back again. And the cold air between them made it easier to take a very necessary third step. Within a few more, he was turning and crossing the road without a backward glance.

Which was how he generally did things.

You crossed a line through them and walked away.

Did she truly believe that he could cauterise entire sections of his life without any ill effect? That he was that cold? His issues arose from caring too much, not too little. But maybe she was also right about it being a life skill, because experience was sure going to help him now.

This was every bit as hard as walking away from his mother and brother.

Eve was not going to be okay. He could feel it in his bones. She had no idea how much she needed him. Someone. Anyone. And if he could feel that protective of her after just a few short weeks, how much must she burn with the need to find and protect the baby brother she'd loved all his life?

He kept walking up the main street through town but then turned down a side street as soon as he was out of her view and doubled back to slide in the side door of a café fronting onto the same road he'd just walked down. From his table he could see Eve, behind her display table, rocking back and forth in the cold air.

If that guy didn't come back soon, he was going to go and drag him out of that pub and frogmarch him back up the street. If Eve wasn't going to walk away from this whole crusade, and she wasn't going to have him by her side, then he was going to do everything he could to make sure that it all came out okay.

So that *she* came out okay.

The waitress delivered his coffee and he cupped his frigid hands around it and watched the woman who'd taken up residence in the heart he'd assumed was empty. The organ he thought had long since atrophied from lack of use.

She sat, hunched, surrounded by *The Missing*, curled forwards and eyes downcast. Crying in body if not in tears. Looking for all the world as bereft and miserable as he felt.

She wasn't trying to hurt him. She hadn't turned into a monster overnight. She was just overwhelmed with the pressure of this unachievable task she'd set herself.

She just had priorities. And he couldn't be one of them. It was that simple.

At least she'd been honest.

And if he was going to be, she'd never pretended it was otherwise. She'd never promised him more than right now. No matter what he'd hoped for.

So maybe he was making progress in life after all. At this rate he might be ready for a proper relationship by the time he was in his sixties.

Out on the street, Eve's body language changed. She pushed to her feet, as alert and rigid as the kangaroos they drove past regularly, her face turned towards the sea. A moment later, the guy from the pub shuffled back into view, handed her the folded map and spoke to her briefly, pointing a couple of times to places on the map.

Marshall's eyes ignored him, staying fixed on the small face he'd come to care so much about. Eve nodded, glanced at the map and said something brief before farewelling him. Then she sank back down onto her chair and pulled the map up against her chest, hard.

And then the tears flowed.

Every cell in his body wanted to dump his coffee and jog back across the road. To be there for her. To hold her. Impossible to know whether the guy had been unable to help, after all, and the tears were heartbreak. Or maybe they were joy at finally having a lead. Or maybe they were despair at a map criss-crossed with dozens of routes which really left her no further ahead than she'd started.

He'd never know.

And the not ever knowing might just kill him.

His fingers stilled with the coffee cup halfway to his mouth. At last, he had some small hint of what hell every day was for Eve. Of why she couldn't just walk away from this, no matter how bad it was becoming for her. Of why she had no room for anything—or anyone—else in her heart. Adding to the emotional weight she carried around every day was not going to change the situation. Loving her, no matter how much, was not going to transform her. There was only one thing that would.

Someone needed to dig that brother of hers out from under whatever rock he'd found for himself. For better or worse.

A sudden buzzing in his pocket startled him enough to make him spill hot coffee over the edge of his mug and he scrambled to wipe the spillage with a napkin with one hand while fishing his phone out with the other.

He glanced at the screen and then swiped with suddenly nerveless fingers.

'Rick?'

'Hey,' his brother said. 'I've got something for you.'

Thank God for Rick's shady connections. And for health regulators. And maybe for Big Brother.

And thank God, for Eve's sake, that Travis Read was, apparently, still alive.

Rick had hammered home that the kid's name wouldn't have appeared anywhere on official records, if not for a quietly implemented piece of legislation at the start of the year. Even this was an *unofficial* record.

Accessing it certainly was—his brother had called in a number of very questionable favours getting something useful.

'The trouble with the Y-Gen is that they soon work out how to fly under the digital radar,' Rick had said over the phone. 'But he came undone by refilling his Alprazolam in his real name, even though he did it off the health scheme to stay hidden.

'As of February,' he'd continued, 'it became notifiable in order to reduce the amount of doc-shopping being done by addicts. Your guy wouldn't have known that because the GPs aren't required to advise their patients of its existence; in fact it's actively discouraged. And people call *me* dodgy...'

Marshall had ignored Rick's anti-government mutterings and scribbled the details down on the first thing at hand. The name of the drug. The town it was filled in. Ironic that prioritising his mental health had led to Travis's exposure. An obscure little register inside the Department of Health was pretty much the only official record in the entire country that had recent activity for Travis Read. Lucky for him, his brother knew someone who knew someone who knew some*thing* big about a guy in the

Health Department's IT section. Something that guy was happy to have buried in return for a little casual database scrutiny.

Marshall's muttered thanks were beyond awkward. How did you thank someone for breaking innumerable laws on your behalf? Even if they did it every day.

'Whoever you're doing this for, Marsh...' Rick had said before hanging up '... I hope they know what this cost you. I sure do.'

That was the closest he'd come to acknowledging everything that went down between them in the past. He'd added just one more thing before disconnecting.

'Don't leave it so long next time.'

And then his brother was gone. After ten years. And Marshall had a few scribbled words on half a coffee-stained napkin. The pharmacy and town where Travis Read had shown his face a few months earlier.

Northam. A district centre five hours from where he was sitting.

Marshall pulled up his map app and stared at it. If Eve's intelligence was hereditary, then chances were her brother wouldn't be dumb enough to get his medical care in the town in which he was hiding out. So, he desktopped a wobbly fifty-kilometre radius around Northam and ruled out anything in the direction of the capital city. Way too public. It was also ninety-five per cent of the state's population and so that left him with only two-dozen country towns inside his circle.

If it was *him* trying to go underground, he'd find a town that was small enough to be under-resourced with government types, uninteresting enough to be off the tourist trail, but not so small that his arrival and settling in would draw attention. That meant tiny communities were out and so were any of the popular, pretty towns.

Agricultural towns were in because they'd be perfect for a man trying to find cash work off the books.

All of that filtering left him just a couple of strong candidates inside his circle. One was the state's earthquake capital and drew occasional media attention to itself that would be way too uncontrollable for a kid intent on hiding out.

That left only some towns on the southern boundary of his circle.

One was on a main route south—too much passing traffic and risk of exposure. Another too tiny.

The third was Beverley, the unofficial weekend headquarters for a biker gang and must regularly receive police attention.

He was about to cross that one through when he reconsidered. What better place to hide out than in a town filled with people with many more secrets to keep than Travis? People and activity that kept the tourists away and the authorities well and truly occupied. And where better for a newcomer to assimilate seamlessly than a town with a transient male population?

Beverley made it onto his top three. And he made a mental note to wear as much leather as he owned.

One day's drive away and he could spend a day each hunting in all three.

Then at least he would know.

It could be him.

Hard to say under the scrappy attempt at facial hair. The best of all the options he'd seen in the past couple of days, anyway. Marshall settled in at the bar and ordered something that he couldn't remember just five seconds later. Then he pulled out his phone and pretended to check his messages while covertly grabbing an image of the man that might be Eve's brother.

Evidence that Travis was alive and well.

If that even was him. Hard to tell from this far away.

There was an easy kind of camaraderie between the young man and his companions, as if an end-of-day beer was a very common thing amongst them. How nice that Travis got to sit here enjoying a beer with mates while his sister cried herself into an ulcer every night. Well-fed, reasonably groomed, clearly not here under any kind of duress, the kid seemed to have a pretty good gig going here in the small biker town.

Just before six, he pushed back from the table and his mates let him go easily, as if skipping out early was business as usual.

Out on the footpath, Marshall followed at a careful distance. How much better would the photo be if he could give the authorities an address to go with the covertly captured picture?

Authorities.

Not Eve.

This was about giving her back her brother, not getting back into her good books. Something he could do to help. Instead of hurt.

He was no better for Eve than she was for him. He'd finally accepted that.

The guy turned down a quiet street and then turned again almost immediately. Marshall jogged to catch up. The back of these old heritage streets were rabbit warrens of open backyards and skinny laneways. A hundred places for someone to disappear into their house. The guy turned again and Marshall turned his jog into a sprint, but as he took the corner into the quiet laneway he pulled up short.

The guy stood, facing him, dirty steel caps parted, ready to run, arms braced, ready for anything.

In a heartbeat, he recognised how badly he might have blown this for Eve. How easy it would be for Travis to just disappear again, deeper into Australia, where she'd never ever find him. And he realised, on a lurch of his stomach, that this cunning plan was maybe going to come completely unstuck.

And it would have his name all over it.

'Who sent you?' the guy challenged, dark eyes blazing in the dusk light.

Marshall took a single step forward. 'Travis?'

'Who sent you?' he repeated, stepping back. As he moved and the light shifted slightly, the facet of those blazing eyes changed and looked to him more like fear and less like threat.

And he'd know those eyes anywhere...

Marshall lifted both hands, palms outward, to show he came in peace.

'I'm a friend of your sister.'

CHAPTER TWELVE

'Hey...'

Marshall's voice was startling enough out of the silence without her also being so horribly unprepared for it. Eve's stomach twisted back on itself and washed through with queasiness.

She'd only just resigned herself to him being gone—truly gone—and now he was back? What the hell was he trying to do—snap her last remaining tendrils of emotional strength?

She managed to force some words up her tight throat. 'What are you doing here, Marshall?'

It felt as if she was forever asking him that.

Compassion from him was nearly unbearable, but it rained down on her from those grey eyes she'd thought never to see again.

'Sit down, Eve.'

Instantly her muscles tensed. Muscles that had heard a lot of bad news. 'Why?'

'I need to talk to you.'

'About...?'

'Eve. Will you just sit down?'

No. No... He was looking at her like her father had the day Travis was officially declared a missing person.

'I don't think I want to.'

As if what she wanted would, in any way, delay what she feared was to come.

'Okay, we'll do this upright, then.'

His mouth opened to suck in a deep breath but then snapped shut again in surprise. 'I don't know where to start. Despite all the trial runs I've had in my mind on the way back here...'

That threw her. Was he back to make another petition for something between them? She moved to head that off before he could begin. Hurting him once had been bad enough...

'Marshall—'

'I have news.'

News. The tightness became a strangle in her throat. Somehow she knew he wouldn't use that word lightly.

'You're freaking me out, Marshall,' she squeezed out.

The words practically blurted themselves onto his lips. 'I've found Travis.'

The rush of blood vacating her face left her suddenly nauseous and her legs started to go.

'He's alive, Eve,' he rushed to add.

That extra piece of information knocked the final support from under her and her buckling legs deposited her onto the bus's sofa.

'Eve...' Marshall dropped down next to her and enveloped her frigid hand between both of his. 'He's okay. He's not hurt. Not sick.'

Eve's lips trembled open but nothing came out and it distantly occurred to her that she might be in shock. He rubbed her frigid fingers and scanned her face, so maybe he thought so, too.

'He's living and working in a small town here in Western Australia. He has a job. A roof over his head. He's okay.'

Okay. He kept saying that, but her muddled mind refused to process it. 'If he was okay he'd have been in touch...'

And then his meaning hit her. New job and new house meant new life. They meant *voluntary.* Her heart began to hammer against her ribs. Everything around her took on an other-worldly gleam and it was only then she realised how many tears wobbled right on the edges of her lashes.

'Where is he?' she whispered.

It was then Marshall's anger finally registered and confusion battled through the chaos in her mind. Anger at her? Why? But colour was unquestionably high in his jaw and his eyes were stony.

'I can't tell you, Eve.'

Okay, her brain was seriously losing it. She waited for the actual meaning to sink in but all she was left with was his refusal to tell her where her long-lost brother was.

'But you found him...?'

'He asked me not to say.'

'What? No.' Disbelief stabbed low in her gut. And betrayal. And hurt. 'But I love him.'

'I know. *He* knows,' he hurried to add, though the anger on his face wasn't diminishing. 'He told me that he would disappear again if I exposed him. So that you'd never find him. He made me give him my word.'

Pain sliced across her midsection. 'But you don't even know him. You know me.'

You love *me.*

She might as well have said it. They both knew it to be true. Not that it changed anything.

'Eve, he's alive and safe and living a life. He's on his meds and is getting healthy. Every day. He just can't do that at home.'

The thump against her eardrums intensified. 'Okay, he doesn't have to come back to Melbourne. We could move—'

'It's not about Melbourne, Eve. He doesn't want to go *home.*'

Realisation sunk in and she whispered through the devastation, 'He doesn't want to be with his family?'

God, did she look as young and fragile as her disbelief sounded? Maybe, because Marshall looked positively sick to be having this conversation.

'He wants to be healthy, Eve. And he needed to start over for that to happen.'

Start over...

'He doesn't have to come back, I can go to him. If he likes where he is—'

'I'm so sorry.' He squeezed both his hands around both of hers and held on. And, after an endless pause, he spoke, leaning forward to hold her stinging eyes with his. 'He doesn't want you to come, Eve. Particularly you.'

Particularly you.

Anguish stacked up on top of pain on top of misery. And all of it was wrapped in razor blades.

'But I love him.'

His skin blanched. 'I know. I'm so sorry.'

'I need to see him,' she whispered. 'I've been searching for so long—'

'He wants a fresh start.'

A fissure opened up in her heart and began to tug wider. Her voice, when it came, was low and croaky. 'From me?'

'From everything.'

'Is this...' The fissure stretched painfully. 'Is this about *me*?'

Pity was like a cancer in his gaze. 'He can't be with you any more. Or your dad.'

'Why?' Her cry bounced off the Bedford's timber-lined walls.

Words seemed to fail him. He studied his feet for the barest of moments and then found her gaze again.

'Because of your mother, Eve.'

She stared at him, lost. Confused. But then something surfaced in the muddle of pain and thought. 'The accident?'

His expression confirmed it.

God, she could barely breathe, let alone carry on a conversation. 'But that was years ago.'

'Not for him, Eve. He carries it every day. The trauma. The anxiety. The depression. The guilt.'

Guilt? 'But Mum wasn't his fault.'

His fingers tightened around hers again and his gaze remained steady. 'It was, Eve. I'm so sorry.'

She shook the confusion away, annoyed to have to go back over such old ground. But being angry at him helped. It gave all the pain somewhere to go.

'No. He was with her, but... She was driving drunk.'

But she could read Marshall like a book—even after just a few weeks together—and his book said something else was going on here. Something big. She blinked. Repeatedly.

'Wasn't she?'

'Didn't you say they were both thrown from the bike?'

She was almost too dizzy for words. So she just nodded.

'And the police determined that she was in control?'

'Travis was the only other person there. And he couldn't ride properly then. He was underage.'

Marshall crouched over further and peered right into her face. Lending her his strength. 'No. He couldn't.'

But it was all starting to be horribly, horribly clear.

Oh, God...

'Trav was driving?' she choked. Marshall just nodded. 'Because Mum had been drinking?'

No nod this time, just the pitying, horrible creasing of his eyes.

No... Not little Travis... 'And he never told anyone?'

'Imagine how terrified he must have been.'

A fourteen-year-old boy driving his drunk mother home to keep her safe and ending up killing her.

'He wouldn't have lied to protect himself.' Her certainty sounded fierce even to her.

'But what if he thought you'd all blame him? Hate him. That's a lot for someone to carry. Young or old. He can't face you.'

She sagged against the sofa back, this new pain having nowhere to go.

'He carried that all alone? All this time?' she whispered. 'Poor Trav. Poor baby...'

'No. Don't you take that on, too. He's getting treatment now. He's got support and he's getting stronger. He's doing pretty bloody well, all things considered.'

So why was Marshall still so very tense?

'But he knows what he wants. And needs. And he isn't going back to your world. And he doesn't want that world coming to him either.' He cursed silently. 'Ever.'

A tiny bit of heat bubbled up beneath her collar and she'd never been so grateful for anger. It cut like a hot knife through the butter of her numb disbelief and reminded her she could still feel something. And not a small something. The feelings she'd been suppressing for twelve months started to simmer and then boil up through the cracks of Marshall's revelation.

Ever.

'So...that's it?' she wheezed. 'I gave up a year of my life to find him—I broke my heart searching for him—and all this time he's been living comfortably across the country *starting over?*'

Marshall's lips pressed together. 'He's made his choice.'

'And you've made yours, apparently. You've taken his side pretty darned quick for a man you don't know.'

'Eve, I'm on your side—'

It was as if someone was puffing her with invisible bellows filled with hot air…making this worse and worse.

'Don't! How do I know you're not just making this all up to further your cause?'

'You can't be serious.'

'How would I know? The only evidence I have that any of this is true is your word. You might not have found him at all. You might just want me to think that. You might say anything to get me to stay with you.'

The words poured out uncontrollably.

'What the hell have I done to make you believe that of me?' But he rummaged in his pocket, pulled out his phone and opened his photo app. 'Believe this, then.'

Seeing Travis just about broke her heart.

Her baby brother. Alive. Healthy. Enjoying a beer. Even laughing. *Laughing!* She hadn't seen that in years.

She certainly hadn't done it in as long.

Tears tumbled.

'Eve—'

'What would happen, Marshall?' she asked desperately. 'If you told me where he is. How would he even know?'

She was flying through the stages of grief. At bargaining already.

'I know you, Eve…'

'So you're just going to take the choice away from me? Like some child?'

'You wouldn't be able to stay away. You know it.'

'I'm not about to *stalk him*, Marshall.'

'You already are, Eve! You're scouring the country systematically, hunting him down.'

Her gasp pinged around the little bus. 'Is that how you see it?'

'Why else would you want to know where he is? Unless you were going to keep tabs on him.'

'Because I *love* him. You have no right to keep this from me.'

'I'm not doing this to be a bastard, Eve. I don't want you in any more pain.'

'You think this doesn't hurt? Knowing he's alive and I can't get to him? Can't hold him? Or help him? You think that's kinder than letting me hear from his own lips that he doesn't want to come home?'

Just saying the words was horrible.

He took her chin in his fingers and forced her to look at him and, despite everything, her skin still thrilled at his simple touch. It had been days...

'Hear me, Eve,' he urged. 'If you go there he will disappear again. He knows what to do now, he'll be better at it and he might go off his meds to keep himself hidden. You will never see or hear from your brother again. Is that what you want?'

In all her wildest, worst dreams she'd never imagined she'd be sitting here, across from Marshall—of all people—fighting him for her brother's whereabouts.

But, dear Lord, fight she would.

'How is that any different to what I have now?'

'Because I know where he is and he's agreed to check in with me from time to time.'

The grief and hurt surged up right below her skin, preparing to boil over.

'So...what? You get to be some kind of gatekeeper to my family? Who the hell gave you that authority?'

'He has a legal right to go missing. He wasn't hurt, or forced, or under any kind of duress. He decided to leave.'

'He was sick!'

'And managing his condition.'

He had an answer for every single argument. 'Then he must have been desperate.'

'Maybe, but he's not now. He's doing okay, I swear.' He caught her eyes again and brought everything back to the simple truth. 'You've found him, Eve.'

'No, *you* found him. I have as little as I had before.' Less, really. 'And, whatever he's going through, he clearly needs some kind of psychological help. People don't just walk out on perfectly good families.'

'They do, Eve. For all kinds of reasons. He couldn't stay, not knowing what he'd done. Fearing you'd discover it. Knowing how much you'd sacrificed—'

The inquest. The random timing of his disappearance suddenly came into crystal focus. 'I can help him.'

'You're still protecting him from responsibility? He's an adult, Eve. He doesn't want your help.'

'He needs it.'

'Does he, Eve? Or do you just need to believe that?'

She stiffened where she sat.

'You were his big sister. You looked after him and your father after the accident. That became your role. And for the last twelve months you've been about nothing but him. You chucked in your job. You sold your house. What do you have if you don't have him?'

'I have...plenty, thanks very much. I'll go back to my career, reignite my friendships. Get a new place.'

Oh, such lies. There was no going back. She didn't even know how to be normal now.

'And then what? What are you if you're not all about your brother, Eve? You've been doing this since you were barely out of school.'

Furious heat sped up the back of her neck and she surged to her feet. 'Don't put this on me. You're choosing to protect him instead of me. How about we talk about that for a bit?'

He shot up right behind her and angry fists caught her upper arms. But he didn't shake her. It was more desperate and gentle than that.

'I would *never* protect him, Eve. I hate what he's done to you. I hate that I found him sitting in a pub having a relaxed beer with friends while your soul was haemorrhaging hope *every single day*. I hate that he's got himself a new life when he was gifted with *you* in his old one.'

He said 'you' as if that was something pretty darned special. The stress faults in her heart strained that tiny bit more.

'I hate that he ditched you and your father rather than find the strength to work through it and that he didn't believe in your strength and integrity more.' He sucked in a breath. 'I would never put him ahead of you. I'm choosing *you*. This is all about you.'

'Then tell me where—'

'I can't!' he cried. 'He will disappear, Eve. The first sign of someone else looking for him. The first poster he sees in a neighbouring town. The first time his phone makes a weird noise. The next stranger who looks at him sideways in the street. He's dead serious about this,' he urged. 'Please. Just let it go.'

'How can I possibly do that?' she snarled.

'You once told me that all you wanted was to know he was all right. To have an answer. And nothing else mattered. Well, now you know. He's fine. But you're shifting the goalposts.'

'So, knowing is not enough! Maybe I do want him home, safe, with us. What's wrong with that?'

'Nothing. Except it's not achievable. And you need to accept that. It will be easier.'

'On who?'

'While your head and heart are full of your brother, then no one and nothing else can get through.'

'Are we back to that, Marshall? You and me?'

'No. You've been painfully clear on that front. I just wanted...'

He couldn't finish, so she finished for him. 'To save the day? To be the hero? Guess you weren't expecting to have to come back and be the bad guy, huh?'

'I didn't *have* to be anything.'

'You preferred to have me despise you?'

His eyes flared as if her words hit him like an axe. But he let her go and she stumbled at the sudden loss of his strength.

'You bang on about your great enduring love for your brother,' he grated. 'But you don't recognise it when it's staring you in the face. I chose *you* here today, Eve. Not myself and certainly not Travis. I am critically aware that the end of your suffering means the end of any chance for you and me. Yet here I am. Begging you to come back to the real world. Before it's too late.'

'Reality?' she whispered. 'Life doesn't get much realer than having someone you love ripped from you and held away, just out of reach.'

His eyes bled grey streaks. 'Finally. Something we agree on.'

He pushed away and walked to the bus's back door. But he caught himself there with a clenched fist on each side of the doorframe. His head sagged forward and his back arched.

Everything about his posture screamed pain.

Well, that made two of them.

But he didn't step forward. Instead, he turned back.

'You know what? Yes. Maybe I did want to be the man who took your pain away. Who ended all your suffering. Maybe I did want to see you look at me with something more heartfelt than curiosity or amusement or plain old lust.'

Haunted eyes bled.

'You're halfway to being missing yourself, emotionally speaking. And if Travis was found, then you'd have no choice but to return to the real, functional, living world. And I wanted to be the man that helped get you there.'

'Why?'

Frustrated hands flew up. 'Why do you think, Eve? Why do any of us do anything, ultimately?'

She blinked her stinging eyes, afraid to answer.

'*Love*, Eve.' So tired. So very weary. Almost a joke on himself. He made the word sound like a terminal condition. 'I love you. And I wanted to *give* you your heart's desire if I couldn't be it.'

'You barely know me,' she breathed.

'You're wrong.' He stepped up closer to her. Towered above her. 'You spend so much time stopping yourself from feeling emotion that you've forgotten to control how much of it you show. You're an open book, Eve.

'I know you're heartbroken about Travis betraying you like this,' he went on, 'and confused about loving him yet hating this thing he's done. I know you're desperate for somewhere to send all that pain, and you don't really want to throw it at me but you can't deal with it all yourself because you've closed down, emotionally, to cope with the past year. Maybe even longer. And it's easier to hate me than him.'

Tears sprang back into her eyes.

'I know it particularly hurts you that it's *me* that's withholding Travis from you because deep down you thought we had a connection even if you didn't have the heart to pursue it. You trusted me, and I've betrayed you. Maybe that's the price I had to pay for trying to rescue you.'

She curled her trembling fingers into a fist.

'I could have told you nothing, Eve. I could have simply kept driving after letting him know that you were all looking for him. Left you thinking well of me. And maybe I could have come back into your life in the future and had a chance. But here I am instead, destroying any chance of us being together by telling you the hard truth about your brother. So you hear it from me rather than from him.'

Her voice was barely more than a croak. 'What do you mean?'

'I've seen your route maps, Eve.' He sighed. 'You would have reached his town before Christmas. And *you* would have found him drinking in that pub, and *you* would have had to stand there, struggling to be strong as he told you how he'd traded up to a better new life rather than the tough old one he'd left, and as he threw everything you've sacrificed and been through back in your face.'

She reached out for something solid to hold on to and found nothing. Because he wasn't there for her any more.

'And you would have knocked on his door the next morning with take-away coffee, only to find he'd cleared out, with not a single clue. And you would have spent the rest of your life hunting for him.

'And so, even though it hurts like death to do this to you, I would take this pain one hundred times over to spare you from it.'

She stared at him through glistening eyes—wordless—as he stepped up closer.

'I'm not fool enough to think there's a place for me here now, even if you did have some capacity in your heart. I wouldn't expect—or even want—to just slide into the emotional vacancy left by your brother. Or your mother. Or anyone else you've ever loved.

'I deserve my *own* piece of you, Eve. Just mine. I think that's all I've ever really wanted in my sorry excuse for a life. The tiniest patch of your heart to cultivate with beautiful flowering vines and tend and spoil until they can spread up your walls and through your cracks and over your trellises. Until you've forgotten what it was like to *not* have me there. In the garden of your heart.'

He leaned down and kissed her, careless of the puffy, slimy, tear-ravaged parts of her. Long, hard and deep. A farewell. Eve practically clung to the strong heat of his lips.

'But I can't do anything with the rocky, parched earth you'll have left after all this is over. Nothing will ever grow there.'

He tucked a strand of damp hair behind her ears and murmured, 'Go home, Eve. Put him behind you. Put me behind you. Just…heal.'

This time, he didn't pause at the door, he just pushed through, jumped down to the ground and strode off, leaving Eve numb, trembling and destroyed in the little bus that had become her cage.

CHAPTER THIRTEEN

Five months later

MARSHALL SPRINTED UP the valley side to the cottage, sweaty from a morning of post-hole-digging and dusting the rich dirt off his hands as he went. He snatched the phone up just before his voicemail kicked in.

Landline. Not many people called that any more.

'Hello?'

'Marshall?'

A voice familiar yet...not. Courtesy of the long-distance crackle.

'Yeah. Who's this?'

'Travis Read.'

His heart missed a beat. 'Has something happened?'

That was their agreement. Marshall would call twice a year to check in and, apart from that, Travis would only call if something was up. It had only been five months since they'd last spoken. He wasn't yet due.

'No, I'm...uh... I'm in town this afternoon and wondered if I could come and see you.'

Since Travis only had his new Victorian phone number, not his new home address, 'in town' had to mean Melbourne. That was all the area code would have told him. But what could Eve's brother possibly have to say? And why did he sound so tense? Unless it was recriminations.

It occurred to him to question why he would have caught a plane any-where since that would flag him on the Federal Police's radar and risk exposure. Unless he used a fake name. Or drove. Or maybe his family had taken him off the missing-persons register so that scarce resources weren't wasted on a man who wasn't really missing.

He'd given Travis one more go all those months ago for Eve's sake. Pointlessly tried to get him to change his mind, told him the damage it had done to his own life—in the long-term—to walk away from his family, as imperfect as they were. How it hadn't solved any of his prob-lems at all—he'd just learned to function around them.

Or not, as the case may be.

But Travis hadn't budged. He was as stubborn as his sister, it seemed. And now he wanted to meet.

Irritation bubbled just below Marshall's surface. He was already keep-ing Travis's secret at the expense of his own happiness. Hadn't he done enough?

But then he remembered how important this kid was to the woman he was still struggling to get over and he reluctantly shared his new ad-dress and gave Travis a time later in the day before trundling back down the hill to the Zen meditation of punching three-dozen fenceposts into the unsuspecting earth.

About fifteen minutes before Travis was due, Marshall threw some water on his face and washed his filthy hands. The rest... Travis would have to take him as he found him.

About six minutes after their appointed time Marshall heard a knock at his front door and spied a small hire car out of one of the windows as he reached the door.

'Trav—?'

He stopped dead. Not Travis.

Eve.

In the flesh and smiling nervously on his doorstep.

His first urge was to wrap her up in his arms and never, ever let her go again. But he fought that and let himself frown instead. His quick brain ran through the facts and decided that she was obviously here in Travis's place. Which suggested Eve and Travis were in communication.

Which meant—his sinking heart realised—that everything he'd done, everything he'd given up, counted for absolutely nothing.

'How did you find him?'

'Good to see you, too,' she joked. Pretty wanly. But he wasn't in any mood for levity. Not while he was feeling this ambushed.

'I didn't find him,' she finally offered. 'He found me.'

So Travis had finally found the personal courage to pick up the phone. Good for him.

And—yeah—he'd be a hypocrite if not for the fact that he'd since taken his own advice and done the same with Rick. His brother hadn't commented on the new mobile number but Marshall felt certain he'd tried to use the old one. That was why he'd yanked out the SIM and tossed it somewhere along the Bussell Highway the same awful night he'd last seen Eve.

The whole world could just go screw itself. Travis. Eve. Rick. Everyone.

'I was heading home,' Eve said now. 'Backtracking through Esperance. My phone rang and I thought it might be you, but...it was him.'

The flatness of her tone belied the enormity of what that moment must have meant for Eve.

'Why would you think it was me?' Hadn't they been pretty clear with each other when they'd parted?

She shrugged lightly. 'I'd tried your number several times and it was disconnected, but—you know—hope springs eternal.'

On that cryptic remark, she shuffled from left foot to right on his doorstep.

Ugh, idiot. He stepped aside. 'Sorry, come on in.'

There was something about her being here. Here, where he'd had to force himself finally to stop imagining what the cottage would be like with her in it. It felt as if he'd sprinted up the valley side and into an alternate dimension where his dreams had finally turned material.

Inside, she glanced around her and then crossed straight to the full wall window that looked out over the picturesque valley.

'Gorgeous,' she muttered almost to herself.

While she was otherwise occupied with the view, he took the opportunity to look at her. She'd changed, but he couldn't quite put his finger on how. Her hair was shorter and glossier but not that different. Her eyes at the front door had been bright but still essentially held the same wary gaze he remembered. She turned from the window and started to comment further on his view when it hit him. It was the way she carried herself; she seemed...taller. No, not taller—straighter. As if a great burden she'd been carrying around was now gone.

And maybe it was.

But having her here—in his sanctuary—wasn't good for him. It physically hurt to see her in his space, so he cut to the chase and stopped her before she offered some view-related platitude.

'What are you doing here, Eve?'

Maybe she deserved his scepticism. The way they'd left things... Certainly, Eve had known she wouldn't be walking into open arms.

'I'm sorry for the deception,' she began. 'I wasn't sure you'd see me. We didn't really leave things...open...for future contact. Your phone was dead and your infuriating Government privacy procedures meant no one in your department would give me your new one. And you moved, too.'

She caught herself before she revealed even more ways she'd tried to reach out to him. It wasn't as if she'd been short of time.

'Yet here you are.'

'I guilted Travis into hooking this up,' she confessed. 'He wasn't very happy about betraying you when you've kept his secret in good faith.'

Which explained the tension on the phone earlier. And the long-distance hum. 'To absolutely no purpose, it seems, since you two are now talking.'

'"Talking" is probably an overstatement,' she said. 'We speak. Now and again. Just him and me at this stage but maybe Dad in the future. Trav reached out a few months ago. Said you'd called him again.'

'I did.' Though it had never occurred to him that the contents of that call might some day end up in Eve's ear.

'Talking about everything that happened is pretty hard for him,' she said flatly. 'You were right about that. And you were right that he would have bolted if I'd pushed. He was very close to it.'

'That's partly why I called him again. To make sure he hadn't already done a runner.'

But not the only reason. 'Whatever you talked about, Travis got a lot out of it. It was a real turning point for him.'

Silence fell between them and Eve struggled to know how to continue. His nerves only infected her more.

'So, you went home?' Marshall nudged.

'I was paralysed for a few days,' she admitted. 'Terrified of any forward move in case I accidentally ended up in his town and triggered another disappearance. You could hardly tell me which town not to visit, could you?'

She fought the twist of her lips so that it felt more like a grimace. Great—finally tracked him down and she was grinning like the Joker.

'So I backtracked the way I'd come,' she finished. 'That seemed safe.'

'I wondered if you might still be in Western Australia,' he murmured.

So far away. 'There wasn't anything to stay for.'

Travis in lockdown. Marshall gone. Her journey suspended. She'd never felt so lonely and lost.

'So, here you are.'

'Here I am.' She glanced around. 'And here *you* are.'

All these months he'd been here, within a single day's mountain drive of her family home. God, if only she'd known. She would have come much sooner.

'Do you know where we are?' he asked.

Not exactly warm, but not quite hostile. Just very...restrained.

'The satnav says we're near MacKenzie Falls.' A place they'd both enjoyed so much on their separate trips around the country. 'That's quite a coincidence.'

'Not really. It was somewhere I wanted to come back to.'

Okay. Not giving an inch. She supposed she deserved that.

'You gave up meteorology?'

'No. I consult now. From here, mostly. The wonder of remote technology.'

She glanced out at the carnage in his bottom paddock. 'When you're not building fences?'

'Who knew I'd be so suited to farming.'

'I think you could do pretty much anything you turned your hand to.'

'Thanks for the vote of confidence. Now why are we having this conversation, Eve?'

She sighed and crossed closer to him.

'I wanted to... I *need to* thank you.'

'For what?'

Her fingers were frozen despite the warm day. She rubbed the nerves against her jeans. 'The wake-up call.'

He crossed his arms and leaned on his kitchen island. Okay, he wasn't going to make this any easier.

'When you love a missing person,' she started, 'you can't grieve, you can't move on. You can't plan or make life decisions. So it just becomes easier to...not. It hurts less if you just shut down. And when one system goes down, they all do.

'In my case,' she went on, 'I coped by having a clear, single purpose.' *Find Travis.*

'And that was all I could deal with. All I could hold in my head and my heart. I developed tunnel vision.'

Marshall studied the tips of his work boots.

'I once told you that if Travis walked in the door, healthy and alive, nothing he'd done would matter.'

He nodded. Just once.

'Me dealing with it so maturely was every bit as much a fantasy as him walking in the door unannounced. Turns out, I'm not so stoic under pressure.' She lifted her eyes. 'It matters, Marshall. It matters a lot. Even as I argued with people who warned me that he might not be alive, I secretly wanted them to be right. Rather than accept he might torture his family like this, deliberately. Leave us wondering forever. And then I hated myself for allowing those thoughts.'

Realisation dawned on his face. 'So when it turned out to be true...'

She shook her head. 'I'm very sorry for the things I said. The way I said them. I thought you were putting Travis ahead of me and that clawed at my heart. I'm sorry to say it took me days to realise that was what I did to you every single day. Put you second. The truth is, you sacrificed yourself—and any chance of us being together—for me. To help spare me pain.'

'So you came to apologise?'

Could a heart swell under pressure? Because hers felt twice its usual size. Heavy and pendulous and thumpy. And it was getting in the way of her breathing.

'You put yourself second.' After a lifetime of coming second. 'For me. Not many men would have done that.'

His voice, when it came, was not quite steady. But still a fortress wall. 'So you came to say thanks?'

She took a breath. Inside her long sleeves she twisted her fingers. Over and over. 'I came to see if I'm too late.'

Marshall didn't move. 'Too late for what?'

'For that vision you had,' she said on a sad, weak laugh. 'The timber cabin in the forest with the clear pools…and me. And you,' she finished on a rush.

And the making love twice a day part. She'd clung to that image for the many lonely nights since he'd left.

Marshall gave nothing away, simply pushed from the island bench and moved to stare out of his window.

'You stuck with me, Eve,' he admitted. 'I finished my audit and returned to Sydney, assuming that a little time was all I needed to get you out of my system. But months passed and you were still there. Under my skin like ink. I couldn't shake you. You were wedged in here.'

He tapped his chest with a closed fist.

'But it doesn't really matter what my heart thinks because my head knows better. And if my life has taught me anything, it's to listen to my head.' He turned back to her. 'I've walked away from much longer relationships than ours when they weren't good for me, Eve. Why would I set myself up to be the second most important person in your life?'

'That's not—'

'So, yes, Eve. I got the cottage in the forest surrounded by pools and, yes, I hope to be happy here. Very happy.' He expelled a long, sad breath. 'But no…there's no *you* in that plan any more.'

A rock of pain lodged in her stomach.

'At all?' she whispered.

'You don't have room for me, Eve. I'd convinced myself that you'd cast me as some kind of substitute for your brother but I no longer think that's true. I just don't think you have any emotional capacity left. And I deserve better than sorry seconds.'

She struggled to steady her breath. But it was touch and go. Every instinct she had told her to go, to flee back home. Except that when she'd come here she'd really hoped that *this* might turn out to be home.

And no home worth having came without risk. It was time to be brave.

'I wasn't out there to find Travis,' she whispered, taking the chance. 'I think I was out there trying to find a way to let him go.'

She shuddered in a breath. 'But that was terrifying. What if I had nothing but a massive, gaping hole inside where my love and worry and pain for him used to be? What if I could never fill it? Or heal it? Who was I without him? So much of *me* was gone.'

His strong arms wrapped across his chest and all she could think about was wanting them around her.

'And what little was left around the outside was just numb.' She stepped closer to him. 'But then you came in with your ridiculous orange motorbike and your hairy face and your tattoos and you were like...an icebreaker. Shoving your stubborn way through the frost. Inch by inch.'

A tragic kind of light flickered weakly behind his eyes and it sickened her that she'd been the one to extinguish it before. The memory of him standing in her bus, appealing from the heart, in visible, tangible pain. And she'd not been able to feel a thing.

But his body language was giving nothing away now.

'I'm not a plug, Eve. I'm a person. You'll have to find someone else to fill the void.'

'I don't want you to fill it. I want you to bridge it.'

His eyes came up.

Eve picked up a cushion off his sofa and hugged it close. 'When you left, it was horrible. You gone. Travis gone. Mum gone. Dad on the other side of the country. I'd never felt so alone. Which is ridiculous, I realise, given I'd been travelling solo all year.'

His brow twitched with half a frown, so quick she almost missed it. His posture shifted. Straightened. 'What changed?'

'I couldn't stay frozen.' She shrugged. 'I tried to do what I'd done before, just...deal. But all these emotions started bubbling up out of nowhere and I realised that I'd been harbouring the same feelings Travis must have had since Mum died. Despair. Anxiety. I'd been suppressing them, just like he must have.'

'So you developed some empathy for your brother. That's great.'

'I wasn't thinking about him, Marshall,' she rushed to correct. 'God knows, I should have been, and it took me a while to notice, but eventually I thought how strange it was that I should feel such despair about my brother being *alive*. Anger, sure. Resentment, maybe. But despair...?

'Travis has been absent in my life since Mum died. Even back when he was still physically present. I'd learned how to compensate for his absence and not fall apart. But there I was, trundling up the highway, completely unable to manage my feelings about the absence of someone I'd known less than a fortnight.'

His face lifted. His eyes blazed. But he didn't say a word.

'I wasn't thinking about Travis. I wasn't weeping about Travis. I was thinking about you. Missing...you.'

He had nothing to say to that.

'Nothing felt right without you there,' she whispered.

Agony blazed from his tired eyes. 'Do you understand how hard this is to hear? Now?'

It was too late.

Something grasped at her organs and fisted deep in her gut.

She gathered up her handbag. 'I don't want you thinking badly of me, Marshall. I don't want you remembering me as the outback psycho in a bus. I have years' worth of coping mechanisms that I need to unlearn. I barely know where to start. It's going to be a long work in progress.'

She stepped up to him. Determined to get one thing right in their relationship, even if that was goodbye.

'But I'm on my way. Thanks to you. I just didn't want you never knowing how much you helped me. What a difference you made. I'm just sorry I couldn't return the favour. I'm sorry I hurt you.'

She pushed up onto her toes and pressed a kiss to his face, over the corner of his mouth, and then whispered into it, 'Thank you.'

Then she dropped back onto her soles and turned for the door.

'Eve.'

His voice came just as she slid her hand onto the heritage doorknob. But she didn't turn, she only paused.

'What about that bridge?'

The one over the void where her love for Travis used to be?

'I guess I won't be needing it,' she murmured past the ache in her chest. 'It doesn't go anywhere now.'

He stepped up behind her and turned her to face him. 'Where did it go? Before?'

As she spoke, her eyes moistened and threatened to shame her. But she didn't shy away from it. She was done hiding her emotions.

'Someone once told me about a garden,' she breathed, smiling through the gathering tears. 'One which used to be barren rubble. With old stone walls and handmade trellises, and where someone had planted a beautiful, fragrant vine. That's where it went.'

He swallowed hard. 'How will you visit it with no bridge?'

'I won't,' she choked. 'But I'll imagine it. Every day. And it will grow without me—up and over the trellis, through the cracks in the wall. And eventually it will cover up all the rocky and exposed places where nothing could thrive.'

And then she'd be whole again.

Marshall glanced away, visibly composing himself. And then he spoke. 'There's something you need to see.'

He slid his fingers through hers and led her out through the front door and down the paving stones to the rear of the house where a large timber door blocked the path. He moved her in front of him and reached around her to open the door.

It swung inwards.

And Eve burst into tears.

She stepped through into the garden of her imagination. Complete with trellis, flowering vines, stone wall and even a small fishpond. All of it blurred by the tears streaming down her face.

All so much prettier than she could ever have imagined.

'Don't cry, Eve,' Marshall murmured right behind her. Closer than she'd allowed herself even to dream.

Which only escalated the sobs that racked her uncontrollably.

'It's so perfect,' she squeezed out between gasped breaths.

'I made it for you,' he confessed. 'It was the first thing I started when I came here.'

Her body jerked with weeping. 'Why?'

'Because it's yours—' he shrugged, stroking her hair '—it was always yours.'

He turned her into the circle of his arms. Warm. Hard. Sweaty from a day of work. Heartbreakingly close. One arm pulled her tighter, the other curled up behind her head so that he could press his lips there.

'You are not some outback psycho,' he soothed into her hair. 'You're passionate and warm and you feel things intensely.'

Maybe she could now that the ice inside her was starting to thaw.

'I wanted all that love you kept in reserve for your brother,' he breathed. 'I hated that Travis was hoarding it. That he'd just walked away from it as though it wasn't the most precious commodity on earth.'

She pulled back and gave him a watery smile. 'He doesn't want it.'

'Someone else does, Eve. Every single bit of it.' Grey eyes blazed down on her. 'I don't care where it comes from, or where it's been. I just care that it's here, in your garden. With me.'

She curled her hands in his shirt. 'You don't hate me?'

'I never hated you,' he soothed. 'I hated myself. I hated the world and everything in my past that stopped me from being able to just love you. And I was angry at myself for trying to be your champion and fix everything, when all I did was make things worse for you.'

'If you hadn't found Travis, I'd still be driving around the country, heartbroken.'

'If I hadn't found Travis, I'd still be driving around with you,' he avowed. 'I would never have left that easily. I would have just given you some breathing space. I was trying to protect you, not control you.'

'I couldn't face the road without you,' she admitted. 'That's why I went home.'

'I have a confession to make,' he murmured. 'This farm wasn't just about MacKenzie Falls. I picked it so that your father wouldn't have to lose you twice.'

She peered up at him and he tackled her tears with his smudged flannel shirt. 'Lose me where?'

'Lose you to here,' he said, kissing one swollen eyelid and then the other. 'To me.'

Breathless tension coiled in her belly. 'You wanted me to come here?'

'I wanted you with me.'

'Five minutes ago you said it was too late.'

'Eve...if I've learned anything from you it's that surviving is not enough. I survived by leaving my mother and brother behind but it didn't change anything—it didn't change me. I've been on emotional hold since then, just like you. And that can work to a point but it's no good forever. At some point I had to take a risk and start believing in people again. In you.'

'I let you down so badly.'

'I was expecting it. I would have found it no matter what.'

Confused joy tripped and fell over its own feet in her mind. 'You believe in me now?'

'Better, Eve. I believe in myself.'

'And you want me to stay here?'

His lips, hot and heavy, grazed hers, and it wasn't nearly enough contact after so long. She chased his touch with her own.

'I want you to *live* here,' he pledged. And then, in case her addled mind really wasn't keeping up, he added, 'With me. And the forest. Somewhere we can retreat to when our crazy all-consuming families get too much. Somewhere we can just be us.'

A joyous blooming began somewhere just behind her heart.

'I'll always worry about him,' she warned. She wasn't simply going to be able to excise Travis from her life the way he'd done to her. Once a big sister, always a big sister.

'I know. And I'll always have the family felon to help keep tabs on him.' Then, at her quizzical expression, he added, 'Long story.'

'Everything I said—'

'*Everything* is in the past, Eve. I'm asking you to choose the future. I'm asking you to choose me.'

The last time he'd asked that of her, she'd chosen her brother. And broken Marshall's soul.

She slid her arms around his gorgeous, hard middle and peered up at him from the heart of their fantasy garden.

'No,' she said breathlessly, and then squeezed him reassuringly as he flinched. 'This time *I choose us.*'

* * * * *

LET'S TALK ABOUT BOOKS!

JOIN THE CONVERSATION

MILLSANDBOON
AUSTRALIA

@MILLSANDBOONAUS

ESCAPE THE EVERY DAY AT
MILLSANDBOON.COM.AU